50 WRITERS

AN ANTHOLOGY
OF 20th CENTURY
RUSSIAN SHORT
STORIES

Cultural Syllabus

Series editor

Mark Lipovetsky (University of Colorado - Boulder)

ACADEMIC
STUDIES
PRESS

50 WRITERS

AN ANTHOLOGY OF 20th CENTURY RUSSIAN SHORT STORIES

Selected, with an Introduction,
by Mark Lipovetsky and
Valentina Brougher

Translated and Annotated
by Valentina Brougher and Frank Miller
with Mark Lipovetsky

Boston
2011

Library of Congress Cataloging-in-Publication Data

50 writers : an anthology of 20th century Russian short stories / selected, with an introduction, by Mark Lipovetsky and Valentina Brougher ; translated and annotated by Valentina Brougher and Frank Miller, with Mark Lipovetsky.
    p. cm. -- (Cultural syllabus)
    ISBN 978-1-936235-14-8 (alk. paper) -- ISBN 978-1-936235-22-3 (pbk. : alk. paper) 1. Short stories, Russian--Translations into English. 2. Russian fiction--20th century--Translations into English. I. Lipovetskii, M. N. (Mark Naumovich) II. Brougher, Valentina G. III. Miller, Frank J. (Frank Joseph), 1940- IV. Title: Fifty writers.
    PG3286.A26 2011
    891.73'010804--dc22
                            2010054411

The publication of this book is supported by the Mikhail Prokhorov Foundation. (translation program TRANSCRIPT).

Cover design by Ivan Grave
Book interior design by Adell Medovoy

Published by Academic Studies Press in 2011
28 Montfern Avenue
Brighton, MA 02135, USA
press@academicstudiespress.com
www.academicstudiespress.com

To the memory of

Walter and Anna (nee Zamorska) Golondzowski
John F. and Kathryn Brougher
and
Naum Lazarevich Leiderman

TABLE OF CONTENTS

ACKNOWLEDGMENTS

We are very grateful to Georgetown and Columbia Universities and the Kayden Research Fund at the University of Colorado at Boulder for their financial assistance. We also acknowledge our appreciation to the Georgetown Undergraduate Research Opportunities Program for providing funding for two students, Darya Bobryakova and Margarita Valkovskaya, to work with Valentina on the first drafts of many of the stories. Their love of literature, good humor, and serious interest in developing translation skills made for an enjoyable start to the project. Darya deserves special thanks for continuing to work with Valentina after the funding had ended.

We had the good fortune to have David Harris, Professor Emeritus of Georgetown University, as our sage arbiter; he was very generous with his time and linguistic expertise and helped us resolve countless questions about matters of lexicon and style. We were also very fortunate to have several colleagues who always took the time to help clarify places in the Russian texts that troubled us. We owe Professor Lynn Visson, Staff Interpreter (Retired) at the United Nations and Monterey Institute of International Studies, Professor Olga Kagan of the University of California Los Angeles, and Professor Irina Reyfman of Columbia University a huge debt of gratitude.

We express our heartfelt appreciation to our four readers. Jack Brougher, whose field of international trade may have been far removed from Russian literature, looked forward to each new story and proved to be a skillful editor, meticulous proofreader, and steadfast supporter of the whole project. Mary Giles, an experienced translator and copy editor, was a model of efficiency in returning our drafts with helpful suggestions. Tatiana Mikhailova, Instructor of Russian at the University of Colorado at Boulder, kept us in a positive frame of mind with her enthusiastic comments and judicious advice, and Jaroslava Zelinsky (Retired), Slavic History and Literature Section, the Library of Congress, dispensed reassurance and was especially helpful with the notes to the stories.

We extend a special note of thanks to Milica Banjanin, Professor Emerita, Washington University in St. Louis and eminent scholar of Elena Guro, for taking a close look at our translation of Guro's story. We also thank Michael Miller (Retired), Middle Eastern and North African

Section, the Library of Congress, for coming to our aid when we had questions about non-Russian words in several stories, and Keith Gessen, translator and writer, for supporting us in our attempts to acquire the rights to Lyudmila Petrushevskaya's story.

We are deeply grateful to Irina Chernushkina for her enormous assistance in obtaining copyright permissions in Russia and to Karen Hawley for her heroic work in managing the Kayden grant.

We especially thank Kira Nemirovsky and Sharona Vedol of Academic Studies Press for their patience and role in preparing the manuscript for publication.

We are very grateful to two publishing companies for permission to reprint the following stories:

W. W. Norton & Company, New York, for "Gedali," "The Rabbi," and "The Rabbi's Son" from *The Complete Works of Isaac Babel*, edited by Nathalie Babel and translated with notes by Peter Constantine.

Random House Inc., New York, for "Cloud, Castle, Lake" by Vladimir Nabokov from *The Stories of Vladimir Nabokov*, edited by Dmitri Nabokov.

We are eternally grateful for the generosity of the following people who provided copyrights without charge:

Sergey Sergeyevich Shilovsky: Copyright © for Mikhail Bulgakov's "Красная корона" (The Red Crown).

Viacheslav Vsevolodovich Ivanov: Copyright © for Vsevolod Ivanov's "Садовник Эмира Бухарского" (The Gardener of the Emir of Bukhara).

Mikhail Nikitich Tolstoy and family: Copyright © for Alexey Tolstoy's "Гадюка" (The Viper). Published by arrangement with FTM Agency, Ltd.

Mariya Vasilyevna Rozanova: Copyright © for Andrey Sinyavsky's "Квартиранты" (The Tenants).

Alexander Yuliyevich Daniel: Copyright © for Yuli Daniel's "Руки" (Hands).

Nataliya Konstantinovna Vorobyova and family: Copyright © for Konstantin Vorobyov's "Немец в валенках" (A German in Felt Boots).

Natalia Grigoriyevna Asmolova-Tendryakova: Copyright © 1995 for Vladimir Tendryakov's «Хлеб для собаки» (Bread for a Dog).

Natalia Dmitriyevna Solzhenitsyna and family: Copyright 1993 © for

Alexander Solzhenitsyn's "Молодняк" (The Young). Used with permission of Counterpoint Press.

Oleg Nikolayevich Ermakov: Copyright © 1995 for his "Последний рассказ о войне" (The Last War Story).

Yury Vasiliyevich Buida: Copyright © 1998 for his short stories "Все больше ангелов" and "Сон самурая" (More and More Angeles and The Samurai's Dream).

The following paid copyrights were granted either by the writers themselves, their families, or by their appointed literary agents, and we deeply appreciate their cooperation:

"Черная магия" (Black Magic) and "Рыбья самка" (The Female Fish) by Mikhail Zoshchenko: Copyright © by Tatiana and Vera Zoshchenko.

"Семейный человек" (Family Man) by Mikhail Sholokhov: Copyright © by Violetta, Maria, and Svetlana Sholokhov.

"Усомнившийся Макар" (Doubting Makar): Copyright © by Vladimir Popov, FTM Agency, Ltd., on behalf of the copyright holder.

Prose by Daniil Kharms: Copyright © 2006 by the estate of Daniil Kharms. Published by arrangement with Literary Agency Galina Dursthoff.

"Надгробное слово" (Eulogy) by Varlam Shalamov: Copyright © by Iraida Sirotinskaya.

"Дом с башенкой" (The House with a Turret) by Fridrikh Gorenshtein: Copyright © by Dan Gorenshtein.

"Победа" (Victory) by Vasily Aksyonov: Copyright © 1965 by Maya and Alexey Aksyonov.

"Мой дядя самых честных правил" (My Uncle of the Highest Principles) by Fazil Iskander: Copyright © 1966 by Fazil Iskander.

"Чудик" (Chudik) and "Верую!" (I Believe!) by Vasily Shukshin: Copyright © 1967 & 1971 by Lidiya, Ekaterina, Maria, and Olga Shukshin.

"Во сне ты горько плакал" (You Cried Bitterly in Your Sleep) by Yury Kazakov: Copyright © 1977 by Alexey Kazakov and Tamara Sudnik.

"Ручка, ножка, огуречик" (Little Arm, Leg, Cucumber) by Yury Dombrovsky: © Copyright by Klara Turumova-Dombrovskaya.

"Мой старший брат" (My Older Cousin) by Sergei Dovlatov: Copyright © 2006 by Elena Dovlatova.

"Девушка моей мечты" (Girl of My Dreams) by Bulat Okudzhava: Copyright © 1985 by Olga Artsimovich.

"Факир" (The Fakir) by Tatyana Tolstaya: Copyright © 1987 by Tatyana Tolstaya and used with permission of The Wylie Agency LLC.

"Галоши" (Galoshes) by Viktor Erofeyev: Copyright © 1988 by Viktor Erofeyev.

"Сюр в пролетарском районе" (Surrealism in a Proletarian District) by Vladimir Makanin: Copyright © 2004 by Vladimir Makanin. Published by arrangement with Synopsis Literary Agency.

"Проездом" (Passing By) by Vladimir Sorokin: Copyright © 1992 by Vladimir Sorokin. Published by arrangement with Literary Agency Galina Dursthoff.

"Бабочка. 1987" (Butterfly. 1987) by Leonid Yuzefovich: Copyright © 1994 by Leonid Yuzefovich.

"Краткая история пейнтбола в России" (A Brief History of Paintball in Russia) by Viktor Pelevin: First published in *Playboy* (Russia edition) and reprinted (in English translation) by permission of Victor Pelevin and Aragi Inc.

"Пиковая дама" (The Queen of Spades) by Lyudmila Ulitskaya: Copyright © 1998 by Lyudmila Ulitskaya. Published by arrangement with Elena Kostioukovitch International Literary Agency.

"Валюта" (Currency) by Yury Mamleyev: Copyright © 1999 by Yury Mamleyev. Published by arrangement with Literary Agency Galina Dursthoff.

"Снег идет тихо, тихо" (Snow Falls Ever So Quietly) by Irina Polyanskaya: Copyright © 2001 by Vladimir Kravchenko and family.

"Учителя без учеников, или Из-под глыб" (Teachers without Pupils, or From under the Rubble) and "В мавзолей твою" (Into the Mausoleum of Thine) by Lev Rubinshtein: Copyright © 1998 by Lev Rubinshtein.

"Степной барин" (The Lord of the Steppes) by Vladimir Tuchkov: Copyright © 1998 by Vladimir Tuchkov.

«Никогда» (Never) by Lyudmila Petrushevskaya: Copyright © 2001 by Lyudmila Petrushevskaya and used with permission of The Wylie Agency LLC.

"Опыт демонстрации траура" (Experience in Demonstrating Mourning) by Marina Vishnevetskaya: Copyright © 2001 by Marina Vishnevetskaya and published by arrangement with Elena Kostioukovitch International Literary Agency.

"Свалка" (The Dump) by Andrey Levkin: Copyright © 2000 by Andrey Levkin.

Translators' Note

With the exception of the stories by Isaac Babel and Vladimir Nabokov, all the translations are new and our own. We have tried in our translations to be faithful to the content of the original Russian texts while at the same time preserving as much as we could of the style unique to each writer. We recognize, however, that our efforts to reflect the distinguishing features and stylistic spirit of such writers as Elena Guro, Vsevolod Ivanov, and Andrei Platonov may lead some readers to wonder whether we occasionally had recourse to spirits of a more tangible sort.

We transliterated names and geographical locations in a way that would offer some indication to our students and other readers as to how these words are pronounced in Russian. To that end, we did not adhere to any specific system of transliteration. If, however, a writer favored a particular spelling of his name in English, we honored his preference.

GLOSSARY

Because acronyms were such an important part of Soviet culture and contribute to the style of a literary text, we thought it best not to translate them within the texts themselves. If an acronym appears only once or twice in the whole volume, it is explained in the Notes to the story in which it appears. If it occurs more than twice, it is marked with an asterisk (*) after its appearance in a story, alerting the reader to turn to the glossary.

Acronyms

Cheka: (ChK) - *Chrezvychainaya kommissiya po bor'be s kontrarevolyutsiyei, sabotazhem i spekulyatsiyei* - Extraordinary Commission against Counterrevolution, Sabotage, and Speculation. Created by a decree issued in December 1917 by Vladimir Lenin, and headed by Felix Dzerzhinsky from its creation until his death in 1926. As its power and responsibilities for foreign intelligence and domestic security changed and expanded during periods of restructuring, this Soviet secret police organization was renamed a number of times. Of particular relevance to the stories in this volume are the following four acronyms:

GPU (Gosudarstvennoye politicheskoye upravleniye, 1922): State Political Administration;

OGPU (Obedinyonnoye gosudarstvennoye politicheskoye upravleniye, 1923): United State Political Administration;

NKVD (Narodnyi komissariat vnutrennikh del, 1934): National Commissariat of Internal Affairs;

KGB (Komitet gosudarstvennoi bezopasnosti, 1954): Committee for State Security.

Gosplan (Gosudarstvennyi planovyi komitet): State Planning Committee.

GULAG or Gulag (Glavnoye upravleniye ispravitel'no-trudovykh lagerei): the Soviet system of forced labor camps in the Stalin era.

NEP (Novaya èkonomicheskaya politika): New Economic Policy, which from late 1923 to 1928 allowed private trade and business.

nepman: a person engaged in private trade or business under NEP.

ispolkom: (*ispolnitel'nyi komitet*): executive committee of any party organization or city council.

mestkom: (*mestnyi komitet*): local party committee.

obkom: (*oblastnoi komitet*): regional party committee.

raikom (*raionnyi komitet*): district party committee.

SR's: members of the Socialist-Revolutionary Party which was formed in 1901 and claimed to represent the Russian peasants. It may have been the most popular political party in 1917 and the chief rival of the Bolsheviks for political power.

vuz (*vyssheye uchebnoye zavedeniye*): an institution of higher learning.

zav (*zaveduyushchii*): head, person in charge.

Reference to the Following is Found in Various Stories:

bed boards (*nary*): continuous wooden shelves from one end of the room to the other, used by prisoners for sleeping.

The Decembrist uprising took place in December, 1825. A group of officers commanding about 3,000 men assembled in Senate Square, refused to swear allegiance to the new tsar, Nicholas I (Constantine, his older brother, removed himself from the succession), and proclaimed their loyalty to the idea of a constitution for Russia. For a variety of reasons the revolt collapsed and within weeks some of the leaders were executed, others exiled to Siberia. Wives of many Decembrists, as the rebels were called, followed their husbands into exile.

"*fig*": a gesture of derision or contempt, consisting of the thumb being placed between the index and middle fingers. In Russian folk belief this was the gesture used by witches and other beings to greet Satan.

The Komsomol: All-Union Leninist Communist League of Youth, a mass organization for young people aged 14-28 that served as ideological preparation for future members of the Communist Party.

makhorka: cheap, inferior tobacco.

The (Young) Pioneers: a mass youth organization for children from 10 through 14 years of age which was founded in 1922. The children participated in sports, the arts, and outdoor life and were taught Communist ideology.

wall newspaper: In the Soviet Union it was common practice to display newspapers on walls and in other prominent public places so that people did not have to buy a paper to read it.

Measurements

Today arshin, pood and verst can be found in the American Heritage dictionary and others. We include them here for the convenience of our readers.
arshin: equivalent to 28 inches
pood: approximately 37 pounds
verst: 2/3 of a mile

INTRODUCTION

Many masterpieces of the Russian short story have long ago become part of the canon of world literature. Among them are Alexander Pushkin's "The Queen of Spades" (1833), Nikolai Gogol's "The Overcoat" (1842), Fyodor Dostoevsky's "The Meek One" (1876), and Lev Tolstoy's "The Death of Ivan Ilych" (1886), to name just a few. The stories of Anton Chekhov, the great innovator of the short story form, are, of course, well known throughout the world. However, when it comes to stories written in the 20th century, perhaps only those of Isaac Babel and Vladimir Nabokov have reached a wide audience and not been limited to students of Russian literature. But the art of the short story in 20th century Russia is not poorer and, in fact, is richer, more diverse and complex than that reached at the height of Russian Romanticism and realism in the 19th century.

The texts of the fifty writers included in this anthology will expose the reader to the great variety of narrative styles and approaches to depicting reality—to the various sub-genres of the genre of the short story in the 20th century. There are stories written in a traditional, realistic style, bringing to mind the short stories of Russia's 19th century classical writers. They include works by Leonid Andreyev, Aleksandr Kuprin, Mikhail Sholokhov, Evgeny Zamyatin, Ivan Bunin, Aleksander Solzhenitsyn, Fridrich Gorenshtein, Vasily Shukshin, Konstantin Vorobyov, Yury Dombrovsky, Vladimir Tendryakov, Yury Kazakov, Lyudmila Ulitskaya, Oleg Ermakov, and others. In these stories the reader will find skillful portrayals of human psychology as well as concrete descriptions of the physical space in which the characters move. There are also short stories in a fantastic vein—those of Lev Lunts, Sigizmund Krzhizhanovsky, Andrei Sinyavsky, and Vladimir Makanin, which have a Romantic, E. T. A. Hoffman quality about them and offer striking metaphors for specific periods of Soviet life and history.

The reader will also find humorous short stories by Nadezhda Teffi and Arkady Averchenko, in which some form of the grotesque in everyday life is always present. These works have some affinity with more serious narratives about the grotesque quality and incongruities of human life in stories by Aleksei Remizov, Mikhail Bulgakov, Mikhail Zoshchenko, Isaac Babel, Andrei Platonov, Vladimir Nabokov, Varlam Shalamov, Vasily Aksyonov, Yury Mamleyev, Yury Buida, Lyudmila Petrushevskaya, Tatiana Tolstaya, and Viktor Erofeyev, as well as by new voices in post-Soviet Russian literature of the 1990s, such as Viktor Pelevin, Marina Vishnevetskaya, Vladimir Tuchkov, Irina Polianskaya and Andrei Levkin. The narrative in each of these short stories seems, at first glance, to be completely realistic; however, it is developed in such a way that the phantasms—the illusions, delusions and absurdities— that lie hidden in everyday life are exposed.

The anthology also includes works that are quite unusual and innovative: a short story by Elena Guro that intertwines poetry with prose and depicts the life of a prostitute; a story by Vsevolod Ivanov written in an "ornamental" style that is saturated with unusual imagery to capture the spirit of the revolutionary times; absurdist micro-parables by Daniil Kharms; a post-modern parody by Vladimir Sorokin; and short essayistic narratives colored with both gentle and bitter humor by Lev Rubinshtein.

Each of these sub-genres of the short story form reflects very different views of the aesthetics of the art of writing in Russian literature of the 20th century—realistic, neo-romantic, modern, avant-garde and post-modern. The short story serves as a kind of laboratory in which various artistic principles, often the most daring and innovative, are tested and applied to facets of private and public life, to themes and ideas that are in the air in a particular historical moment or period. The relative brevity of the genre makes it possible to include in one volume a wide spectrum of artistic approaches to depicting reality that Russian writers of the 20th century favored and, in some cases, introduced to the world.

Of course, the value of 20th century Russian short stories does not lie only in the richness of artistic approaches to portraying reality or the breadth of artistic experimentation. The short story was the ideal genre for a quick, sometimes even lightning-fast, reaction to the shocking events that punctuated the 20th century, and the 20th century was exceedingly "generous" in the number of historical cataclysms that came to mark Russian life. These writers lived through several revolutions and two world wars. From the 1920s they became part of an immense political and social experiment: Soviet communism. Directly or indirectly, they became victims of constant control and repression by the totalitarian regime. From this perspective, it is little wonder that the most tragic narratives about the Civil War (Babel, Ivanov, Aleksei Tolstoy, Sholokhov), the Great Terror (Kharms, Shalamov, Solzhenitsyn) and World War II (Vorobyov, Gorenshtein), the most caustic or satirical representations of Soviet life (Lunts, Zoshchenko, Sergei Dovlatov), and the most radical deconstructions of still authoritative but dying literary traditions (Sorokin) first appeared in short story form. It is only after appearing in short stories that these themes came to be explored in other genres as well.

In producing stories which resonate with the epoch and the spirit of the times, the writers were also guided to some or even to a great degree by what could be called a "sense of urgency." There were many years when a writer could not be sure of surviving another day or month, let alone a year. Given such adverse conditions, the short story permitted the writer to document the *here* and *now*, to record his/her impressions in a form that did not demand extensive time. The short story permitted him/her to put flesh on phenomena that s/he perceived as key to capturing not only the dynamics of history itself but of the lives affected and changed by that history. Given these circumstances, it is quite natural that the short story genre flourished in Russian literature of the 20th century.

There was an additional advantage to the short story form that led to its popularity with Russian writers after the revolution. The genre allowed writers to compress their thoughts and observations into concentrated form, make certain points discreetly, and portray life in society and human behavior at a certain historical time without dwelling on them at length. As such, their writing had a better chance of surviving the Soviet censorship process—the various "editors" who had to add their seal of approval—and, thus, reaching the reading public.

Last but not least, it is noteworthy that some of the best stories have an incredible "optical range": they not only capture the details of Russian life in a particular historical setting, but they also contain suggestions of how the future may unfold, although the writer could not know himself what we, today's readers, know. Thus, in reading the pre-revolutionary stories of Andreyev, Fyodor Sologub, Kuprin, Remizov, and even the humorist and satirical writer Averchenko, one cannot help but think that these authors sensed, as some of their contemporaries in the arts and politics, that some great changes, some cataclysmic events were drawing ever nearer.

In Andreyev's story, "Once Upon a Time" (1901), the dying days of a rich merchant revolve around his discovery that he has led a totally pointless life. But Andreyev expands this individual perspective by suggesting that his hero symbolizes the end of a way of life for whole segments of Russian society driven by acquisition of goods and lacking in human compassion. The merchant's impatient, intolerant attitude toward a fellow patient, a priest, who is in denial about the death that awaits him, seems to presage the treatment of the church and its members that would follow under Soviet rule.

Another story that illustrates this "optical range," a sense that a great upheaval was drawing near, is Remizov's dark portrayal of provincial life in "The Little Devil" (1906), written a year after the failure of the 1905 revolution. The central figure is a cockroach exterminator, a seemingly pious man who stands ready to do battle with the Devil, but whose secret life belongs to the Devil's evil, dark realm. The small sect of believers whom the cockroach exterminator leads in prayer and flagellation is a larger metaphor for the search for new forms of spirituality and the interest in the occult at the end of the 19th and the beginning of the 20th century. But Remizov's depiction of the search for a spiritual dimension to human life turns into a grotesque, monstrous, and even shocking hybrid of the sacred and the profane. At the end of the story, the small black devil the boy sticks on an icon of the Mother of God and the infant Jesus Christ serves as Remizov's suggestion that good and evil inhabit the same space, with evil now in the forefront.

In a different modernist key, Sologub's mythologically shaped tale, "The Invoker of the Beast (1906), embodies the gravitation of Russian life toward "symbolic suicide," toward self-destruction. And Averchenko, in his "Scenes from the Life of the Worker P. Grymzin" (1921), not only satirizes the "good life" that the revolution promised but failed to bring about, but ends with the suggestion that this may be only the beginning of a downward spiral in the quality of life ("What a big fool you've been, Pantelei").

Almost two decades later Bunin, who emigrated to France in 1920 and was the first Russian writer to win the Nobel Prize in Literature (1933), constructs a story that serves as a metaphor for loss not only on a personal but historical level as well. Set against the backdrop of provincial country life, "Tanya" (1940) is the story of a privileged man's love for a simple peasant girl whom the narrator was fated to last see in "February of that horrific year, 1917." Those words, in a story published in 1940, serve as a lament not only for a way of life lost irretrievably in the whirlwind of violent upheavals in Russian private, social and political life that followed the revolution, but evoke the tragedy and suffering that would characterize post-1917 Russian life and history even in the decades that followed Bunin's death in 1953.

The sense of urgency mentioned above undoubtedly played a role in turning many of the best short stories of the 20th century into what could be called "micro-myths." Written in a rich, dense, highly concentrated form, such a story always offers a striking and paradoxical metaphor for an epoch, people's fate, and history. Every historical detail, every description, every psychological development in such a "mythologized" short story carries more meaning than is at first apparent. Every element of the narrative serves to transform an incident or "slice of life" into a universal allegory of the history, experiences and psychology of the Russian people. The existence of a significant number of "mythologized" short stories in 20th century literature partly explains the attraction for Russian writers of imagery drawn from the world of the fantastic, the symbolic, and the folkloric, which allows them to achieve this maximum concentration. Thus we have "the red-haired man" in Kharms' "Blue Notebook No. 10" (1937) who disappears, as many did in the purges of the 1930s; and the house spirit in Sinyavsky's "The Tenants," who tries to save the writer from that "knock on the door" and arrest, but cannot. There is the magical, bottomless smoky goblet in Krzhizhanovsky's story by that name, written in 1939, right after the height of the Great Terror. The wine from this goblet, which can never be fully emptied because it constantly refills itself, promises the hero complete isolation from the reality around him. However, when it is thrown by him into the river, the magical goblet colors all of it a bloody-red color. And then there is the "mine" at a dump that is filled with books to overflowing, to which Andrei Levkin's hero in "The Dump" (2000) chooses to "emigrate" so that he can read and delve into the past and forget the present. From these and many other symbols and metaphors in which Russian short stories of the 20th century abound, it is not difficult to construct a trajectory punctuated by the significant moments and landmarks in Russian history, life, and culture in the often cruel and brutal 20th century.

Reading the stories in this volume in chronological order, it is impossible not to be struck by the continuity of certain themes. In a sense, we have before us a kind of amazing mega-novel, with different heroes, historical periods and situations which nevertheless resonate with one another and become intertwined in a multi-strand line, uniting pre-revolutionary literature with Soviet and post-Soviet, emigration with the mother country, and officially accepted writers with the underground and the dissident movement. A brief review of the key periods in Russian/Soviet history and an exploration of the major themes in these stories will illustrate this point more concretely.

Russia in the 20th century lived through a whole series of revolutions in the broad sense of the word. There was not only the Bolshevik revolution of October 1917 (after the collapse of the tsarist government in February 1917) but also the failed attempt at a peaceful revolution earlier, in 1905. There was Stalin's "revolution" (or counter-revolution) of the 1930s, which included the collectivization of the peasantry, rapid industrialization, the Great Terror, and the development of a far-flung network of labor camps, the Gulag.* The more liberal atmosphere in the early 1960s, the "thaw" under Nikita Khrushchev, began de-Stalinization but was cut short by the Communist elite, frightened that if the struggle with the cult of personality (assessing Stalin's role in Soviet life) continued, they would lose their power. The dissident movement of the 1960s, 1970s and first half of the 1980s also represented a kind of revolutionary movement, a protest by intellectuals and writers who longed for more freedom in their lives as creative voices and citizens of the Soviet Union. The glasnost and perestroika initiated by Gorbachev in the second half of the 1980s and the discrediting of communism and break-up of the Soviet Union in 1991 completed the troubled century.

Twentieth Century short stories mirror the details and facets of each major landmark in Russian/Soviet history perhaps even more strikingly and eloquently than other genres of literary writing. But the short story, with surprising consistency, also records each new revolutionary shock or convulsion in the centuries-long context of Russian—and not only Russian—history and culture. Thus Kuprin, in his "Gambrinus" (1906), written just after the revolution of 1905, depicts this historic event as an episode from the struggle between official, depressingly serious, and hypocritical culture with popular, joyful, and irreverent culture. And, of course, the ultimate victor in this struggle is popular culture. But this victory in Kuprin's view is colored with a bitter taste—after all, this struggle involves human lives and bodies, and the maimed, deformed Jew, Sashka the musician, becomes a symbol not only of the invincible nature of carnivalesque freedom but of also the heavy price a human being pays for that seemingly "natural" joy of existence.

In his cycle of stories collected under the title *The Red Cavalry* (1924), Babel offers short but superbly written narratives about the Red Army during the civil war years. But what also emerges from his writing is the suggestion that the revolution that was propelled by dreams of equality and justice may be transformed in the future into its exact opposite. This anthology includes a micro-cycle of three stories from *The Red Cavalry*: "Gedali," "The Rabbi," and "The Rabbi's Son." If a dream about an "international of good people" is featured in the first story, in the last we have the rabbi's dying son, who had tried to bring about this international and suffered a shattering defeat. The "bright future" the revolution promised becomes transformed into a dangerous phantasm which masks a return to the inequality and injustice—now perhaps even greater than before—which the revolution seemingly sought to eliminate.

The perception of the revolution as a kind of fantastic monster, born of centuries-old "social contradictions," to use a phrase favored by Marxist critics for the inequities and incongruities of Russian life, survives up to the 1990s. A story by Leonid Yuzefovich, "Butterfly. 1987" (1994), serves as an eloquent illustration. Yuzefovich's short story focuses on the recent past—the perestroika years—and the changes in political and private life that the times bring. The dialogue between the story's characters—two Russian historians and one American—is important and revealing. They discuss one thing: the different but inevitably tragic attempts to modernize Russia. It is hardly a topic that Yuzefovich selects at random, without a more contemporary purpose in mind. Although the conversation centers on the 18th century and even more distant epochs, the story is set in 1987 and the beginning of yet another attempt to bring about a radical change in Russian life and politics. The fears which sweep over the heroes in the story, including the wife of one of the Russian historians, do not come to pass at the end of the story, but they are not groundless. These fears are rooted in the long history of attempts to modernize Russia, and thus the characters' fears are not simply anecdotal but a reflection of a deeper historical intuition.

Because of the need to understand and interpret what the various revolutions in Russia have wrought, the ideals and goals that propelled them, and the human price they exacted, one of the most vital themes in Russian literature in general and in 20th century short stories in particular is illuminating and exposing the phantasms, the illusions and fantastic ideas born of a revolution that promised people a utopian existence in the near future. The continued existence of these phantasms bears witness to the fact that the inequities and injustices in the social, cultural, political and economic arenas of Russian life—the elimination of which was declared as the first goal of the 1917 revolution—not only did not disappear but intensified at times to a grotesque degree.

Lunts' satirical story, "Outgoing Paper No. 27" (1924), is an early example of this view of the revolution. It has a theme reminiscent of Franz Kafka's world: a bureaucrat, striving for a maximally rational, ordered life, dreams about transforming people into paper—and ends up becoming a piece of paper himself. It could be argued that this is satire that could be applied to any bureaucracy. But Lunts' story was written in 1924, and the dream of the Russian bureaucrat is all about achieving a utopian revolutionary order, something that was very much in the air in the post-revolutionary years in Russia.

An entirely different source of phantasms is explored by Zoshchenko. His satirical stories capture the mind-set of the masses, of the working people and peasantry who have lived through the 1917 revolution and are now both the source and the product of the most diverse illusions, based both in political and ordinary, everyday life. In "Black Magic" (1922) adherence to old folk beliefs and the abject poverty of people living in the countryside is counterpoised to the desire for the good life as well as the empowerment village men feel because the revolution has "revolutionized" traditional rules of behavior. If husbands treated their wives brutally before the revolution, they now feel free not only to beat them but to discard them at will; the revolution has brought them a perverse kind of freedom. In "Mother Fish" (1923) love is subject to new rules of morality. And more important, with the revolution, traditional spiritual values represented by the church and the priesthood are now irrelevant; the church and its property is no longer sacrosanct, and priests who speak out against these changes are subject to arrest and liquidation. In both of Zoshchenko's stories, the revolution is warping morality, destroying family life, and denying the importance of a spiritual dimension to human life; death is now even more present in Russian life than ever.

In Platonov's "Doubting Makar" (1929) Soviet bureaucratic red tape and a "scientific" transformation of reality based on various elements of communist theory is juxtaposed with the no less fantastic perceptions and responses of a hero of the traditional Russian magic tale, Ivan the Fool, who is Makar in Platonov's story. A simple village man who has "an empty head" but "clever hands," he takes the call for industrialization seriously and literally and, of course, fails miserably in his naive attempts to revolutionize Russian life. However, "scientific" and bureaucratic phantasms and those of the common people do not invalidate one another. On the contrary, they beautifully complement one another. In the final scene Makar and his buddy Pyotr become bureaucrats themselves, but of a different kind: they talk to poor people who come to see them, deciding all matters in their heads based on compassion for the poor. Soon people no longer need them because "their way of thinking was so simple that the poor themselves could think and decide things for themselves." As with all of Platonov's prose, the ending to the story is open to interpretation. He may be satirizing the "the withering away of the state," an idea first introduced by Karl Marx's collaborator, Friedrich Engels, or he may be criticizing bureaucracy and simply suggesting his own version of utopia.

Short stories of the perestroika period and post-Soviet years also very often revolve around the new phantasmagoria of life in Russia. Mamleyev in his story "Currency" (1999) bases his narrative on the economic realities of life in Russia at the end of the 1980s and at the beginning of the 1990s, when salaries were often given out not in money but in products produced at a given enterprise. In his story wooden coffins (even seemingly "used" ones) take the place of salaries and serve as objects of furniture and as barter material. But coffins belong to the world of the dead, and their presence in homes opens a kind of portal into the other world from which the dead come to claim the living. It may be that Mamleyev also intends his story to be read as a grotesque metaphor for Soviet civilization burying itself and moving to an entirely different level of existence.

Tuchkov in his "The Lord of the Steppes" (1996) raises popular stories about the "New Russians" of the 1990s to the level of the fantastic and the grotesque. Not only does a nouveau riche build his own village in which he restores serfdom and plays the role of a "stern but just landowner," he also hires "serfs" to complete his enjoyment of a way of life long past. Those "serfs," in spite of the humiliation and abuse they have to endure from their "master," readily extend their contracts with him because he pays generously in dollars. In short, they and their post-Soviet "master" are happy to escape contemporary life and retreat to the time of Russian feudalism and serfdom.

Phantasms are also revealed in quite realistic stories in terms of poetics; the grotesque is not always a device a writer employs directly, in an obvious way. The grotesque can emerge from the realistic depiction of incompatible elements, the fusion of which constituted the Soviet way of life, as for example in Solzhenitsyn's story, "The Young" (1993). In this work the scene with the professor and the student he was supposed to examine, set in the 1920s, is duplicated in a chilling, sinister way in the interrogation of the professor by that very student in an NKVD* prison in the 1930s. No matter how heinous this transformation of a university exam into an NKVD interrogation is, the central message the story embodies is that the revolution reversed Darwin's theory of the "natural selection of the fittest" and brought to the heights of the Soviet hierarchy the most mediocre and the most cynical of "the best representatives of the working class and the peasantry."

The interweaving of the pre-revolutionary past and culture with the new Soviet life and culture drives the plot lines of a variety of compelling stories in the 1920s as well as subsequent decades. In Ivanov's "The Gardener of the Emir of Bukhara" (1925), gardeners for the elite are no longer needed and greenhouses are broken up so that barracks can be built for workers. Old, noble families are now destitute and under suspicion for anti-Soviet activities, and sons and daughters are already leading a new, revolutionary way of life as they discard the values of their fathers. Pre-revolutionary ideals of beauty and spiritual harmony give way to a peculiar mixture of cynical pragmatism and utopian ideology.

The grotesque features of the new Soviet life as it was shaped in the 1930s-50s finds a reflection in "The Tenants" (1959) by Sinyavsky, a dissident writer who published his work abroad under the pen name of Abram Terts. He uses Russian folklore to illuminate communal living, the constant threat of denunciations from one's neighbors, and the intrusion of the secret police into people's daily life. The story is narrated by a kindly house spirit, and the people who live in the apartment exhibit behavior that resembles folk spirits of the dark, demonic world—

witches, forest goblins, and devils—more than people of this world.

In a much later story, Makanin's "Surrealism in a Proletarian District" (1991), a frightening huge hand (perhaps symbolizing fate), chases after the main character, an ordinary hard-working man, and eventually kills him. But that hand is integrated so artistically into everyday Soviet life in the last decades of the 20th century that its appearance does not feel like a living nightmare, although, of course, it is. This normalization of the phantasm, of the fantastic and the illusionary, can be read as a most bitter comment on the failure of all the Russian revolutions of the 20th century—all without exception, notwithstanding the fact that each new revolution invariably attempted to negate the results of the preceding one.

The theme of violence, the use of force and coercion—collective and individual, physical and emotional, political and the kind that stems from everyday, communal living—plays a pivotal role in countless stories. Violence is not only a very important social mechanism of the Soviet regime, but it also is a significant factor in Soviet day-to-day existence and psychology. In the short stories about the civil war and the first years after the revolution—be it in those of Babel, or even more clearly in a story such as Bulgakov's "The Red Crown" (1922)—violence assumes horrific forms. The narrator has been driven mad by guilt over his younger brother's violent death. As his brother was brought back from a battle, he resembled "a black display board with a colorful headdress." There was no hair and no forehead, and blood was trickling out of where his eyes had been; a "red wreath" crowned what was left of his head. Students of Russian literature will appreciate this image as an inversion of one of the most famous images of the revolution—Christ "in a wreath of white roses" leading a patrol of revolutionaries in Aleksandr Blok's poem "The Twelve" (1918).

Violence resulting in trauma to the human mind and spirit is also examined in "Hands" (1966), a short story by Juli Daniel, a dissident writer who, along with Sinyavsky, was tried and sentenced in 1966 to a hard labor camp for his "anti-Soviet" stories. Although Daniel was writing during the more liberal atmosphere of "the thaw," he could only publish his work abroad, where it appeared under the pen name of Nikolai Arzhak. In "Hands" a Cheka* executioner recalls a moment when he was overcome with absolute fear and panic: a priest he had shot several times seemed not to be affected by his bullets. Although there is a logical, realistic explanation for this seemingly supernatural occurrence, the executioner is left with permanently shaking hands, unable to be of service to the new Soviet state except in the marginalized role of a petty bureaucrat, even though the state needs executioners like him.

There is another form of violence, with no less a significant impact on society, that serves as a dominant theme in many stories. That violence is embodied in the way people communicate with one another, be they related to one another or mere acquaintances or strangers. And normalization of this kind of violence is undoubtedly connected with the normalization of the other forms of violence already discussed above.

The theme of communicative violence plays an important role in the literature of the 1920s (as evidenced in the stories by Zoshchenko or Sholokhov included in this volume). However, it finds its most creative expression in literature of the 1930s, in the absurdist miniatures and minimalist narratives of Kharms. The stories included in this anthology, taken from a cycle of stories gathered under the title *Incidents* (1933-1939), reflect quite fully the theme of communication through violence and the manifold functions of violence that lie at the basis of Kharms' world of the absurd. There is the identification of violence with creativity ("Blue Notebook No 10"); the non-separability of violence and vitality ("Old Women Tumbling Out"); the role of violence in communication with the outside world ("Kushakov the Carpenter") and as part of the inner world of an individual that appears to be indistinguishable from the external world ("A Dream"). Violence, as Kharms shows, lies at the basis of modernization projects ("The Lynching"), and the carnivalesque unity of the "great national body" ("The Start of a Very Nice Summer Day") is not possible without violence. Needless to say, these almost "abstract" short stories with their concentrated, grotesque content and form are meant to convey the cultural and social atmosphere of the Great Terror in the 1930s.

A story written in the same period as Kharms' miniatures, "Lake, Cloud, Tower" (1937) by Nabokov, who emigrated in 1919, uncovers the same kind of "normality" and, indeed, universality of violence, that leads to manifestations of diverse and not necessarily negative feelings, like collectivism and sense of purpose, etc. This type of violence appears in the cultural amusements of Berliners who take pleasure in tormenting their traveling companion for his attempts to deviate from the group's set itinerary. The historical parallelism between Kharms' miniatures and Nabokov's story is noteworthy. Kharms' stories reflect the purges of the 1930s. Nabokov's work is written in Germany in 1937, when the writer's wife and son were ordered to wear the Mogendavid; only the flight of the Nabokovs to France saved them from a concentration camp.

It would be a great simplification, however, to attribute the violence reflected in 20th century Russian short stories only to the impact of totalitarian regimes. One has only to read, for example, "Never" (2000), a story by Petrushevskaya, one of the leading representatives of women's prose in the 1980s and 1990s. The heroine comes face-to-face with the irrepressible and irrational nature of violence in the "common people," the *narod*. Some village young people threaten a city woman with physical violence simply because of vague rumors and outrageous suppositions started by the adults. This type of "communication" immediately turns a human being—even if for a short time—into the Other, towards whom no moral prohibitions apply. Perhaps more important, in Petrushevskaya's view, the experience of being the Other—even for a short period of time—leaves the soul of the potential (or actual) victim with a traumatic psychological wound for the rest of the person's life. The writer's description of the communicative (and physical) violence that people can inflict on one another is not connected with any ideology or political regime. On the contrary, it dates back to mankind's oldest instincts and plunges human life into the pre-historic "dark ages." In her prose Petrushevskaya argues convincingly that those "dark ages" have never left but can always be found somewhere nearby—in villages such as the one in her story, as well as in communal apartments and trash-filled city neighborhoods.

On the other hand, in Ulitskaya's "The Queen of Spades" (1998), violence does not come from the mob as in Petrushevskaya's story, but from a refined representative of the Soviet cultural elite. Mur, or "the queen of spades," exploits the people close to her as a matter of habit. Her cutting remarks and capricious demands poison the atmosphere in which her daughter and granddaughter live, but they are incapable of injecting Mur's forms of violence into their own daily discourse with her. Convinced of her own spiritual superiority (and sexual prowess), she uses communicative violence as a tool of control over others, mindless of the lives she is destroying. But as Rubinshtein shows in his essayistic short stories, consciousness of one's superiority, be it of a moral or more general nature, also lies at the basis of public discourse and mass communication that leads to violence of all by all. The writer argues that the need to correct and teach others, the "general didacticism" that was such a major part of Soviet public discourse, "is nothing else but a seemingly civilized form of aggression and violence which thickly impregnates the atmosphere of public and private life." He offers wonderful examples of communicative violence in the Soviet and post-Soviet period in his "Teachers Without Pupils, or From Under the Rubble" (1998).

The normalization of violence and the reproduction of terror at different levels in life in society is one of the important themes in the Russian short story of the 1960s-1990s. A number of stories from these decades focus on a child being confronted with some form or forms of violence. It is as if a child's entry into life calls immediately for being taught the "language of hatred" specific to a particular period of Russian history. For example, in Tendryakov's story, "Bread for a Dog" (written in 1969-1970 but published posthumously in 1988), a small boy is confronted with men begging for a peace of bread during the mass famine of the early 1930s brought on by collectivization and Stalin's politics of genocide, particularly of the Ukrainian peasantry. Overwhelmed not only by what he sees but by the brief exchanges he has with the starving, the boy seeks solace in feeding a frightened, starving dog. On the other hand, "My Uncle of the Highest Principles" (1966), by Iskander, an Abkhasian writer writing in Russian, takes a tragicomical look at the political paranoia of the 1930s and the communicative violence that is part of social life. The story's narrator captures many moments from his childhood in which language becomes a tool of coercion and conformity. One telling moment finds the narrator's uncle, a mentally challenged adult who, for all purposes, is a child, identifying himself with the ubiquitous portraits, busts and statues of Stalin. He is quickly hushed by the adults out of fear that, if other people overhear him, they will denounce him to the authorities for showing a lack of respect for the Great Leader.

Gorenshtein's "The House with a Turret" (1963) focuses on a small boy and the verbal dynamics between people caught in the horrifying atmosphere of mass evacuations and violence during World War II. The boy, who loses his mother to typhus, not only witnesses many acts of communicative violence by the adults who are on the train with him but becomes the object of hatred and resentment himself. As Gorenshtein shows, people who are fighting for their survival and are worn out physically and emotionally by hunger, despair, and scenes of destruction all around them become particularly adept at heaping abuse on one another. Gorenshtein's depiction belies the stereotypical depiction of the wartime "unity" of Soviet people "as one great family." "Galoshes" (1988) by Victor Erofeyev, set in the post-war years, has a number of scenes where violence in daily discourse is a fact of life for adults and particularly for one small school boy. His teacher, who has just been verbally chastised by the principal, goes on to humiliate him in front of his classmates as she questions him about some galoshes he had stuck into his pocket. Both Gorenshtein's and Erofeeyev's stories imply that communicative violence is not only a part of daily life but infectious.

If violence in its various manifestations is such a core part of life, are there ways people can resist its infectious effects? A number of stories suggest—directly or indirectly—some answers. This leads us to yet another significant theme in 20th century Russian short stories: the role the family might be able to play as a buttress and refuge against the violence outside the home, in public spaces, and, of course, particularly during historical cataclysms. But as a number of writers show, the walls of one's home and life in a family do not necessarily protect one from the many forms violence can assume.

An intriguing story that constantly shifts between violence that is part of a young woman's life as a prostitute and violence that is part of her family life is Guro's "Thus Life Passes" (1909). A whip plays the same role in her life outside the home as it does inside. For Nelka the whip takes on a symbolic significance as her source of humiliation, suffering and debasement and, paradoxically, it also possesses an erotic attraction for her which she cannot overcome.

Zamyatin's story, "The Flood" (1929), is set in Petrograd, the center of the revolution and political changes that would shape Russian life and history for decades to come. It seems that for the family unit—husband and wife—the revolution is something that is distant, that happened somewhere "out there." But the family drama that unfolds is in fact a deeply embedded metaphor for the revolution, which the motif of the flood emphasizes. The flood, a disaster of tragic proportions, can be applied both to the external world and to the heroine's own. Driven by a desire to restore her rights as a wife, and more importantly, to conceive a new life, Sofia kills the young girl her husband had begun to bed in their own home. Crucial to Zamyatin's embedded metaphor is the intertextual dialogue which Zamyatin enters into with Dostoevsky: the reasoned and calculated murder that Raskolnikov performs in *Crime and Punishment*, in the atmosphere of the revolution is now performed by an ordinary woman. The "Raskolnikov-like" murder in the family world serves as a foundation for a "new beginning": after killing her young rival, Sofia carries a new life. The family dynamics in Zamyatin's depiction parallel historical reality. Russia has been shaken and "cleansed" by the revolutionary flood, and Sofia's actions unconsciously reproduce the impetus and consequences of the revolution. Both a new human being and a new society are conceived on a foundation of blood, including human sacrifice. However, Sofia's subconscious cannot accept this configuration, bringing the reader to the story's ending that echoes Dostoevsky's in his novel.

In contrast to Zamyatin's story, in Sholokhov's "Family Man" (1924) the civil war which followed the revolution is very much a part of the family unit's life. The narrator's family is presented not as a safe haven and refuge, the antithesis of a society irreparably changed by the revolution and the civil war, but as a unit whose life parallels the horror and tragedy of that period. Caught in the struggle between the Reds and Whites, the "family man" in Sholokhov's story is forced to participate in the killing of one son and to shoot a second son. He does this in order to save the remaining children from hunger and homelessness. But these children are repelled by what he has done: a daughter tells him that it makes her sick to eat at the same table with him. Forced to participate in civil war violence and faced with communicative violence inside his own home, he poses a question to the story's narrator that encapsulates his heartbreak: "What noose should I stick my head into?"

Aleksei Tolstoi offers a different perspective on the interconnection between violence and family life in cataclysmic times, as well as on the social forms violence can assume in more peaceful times. In his "long short story" or novella (the only one included in this anthology), "The Viper" (1928), Zotova's girlish dreams of having a husband are shattered when her parents are murdered and she is left for dead. She recovers and eventually falls in love with a Red regimental commander, but his death shatters her hope for a life with him. Caught in the maelstrom of history, she goes on to fight for the Red cause in Siberia and at the end of the civil war dreams of participating in building the new society promised in the near future. But the violence she witnessed and participated in during the years of the revolution and civil war have left their mark on her personality and behavior. Communicative violence assaults her from different directions: the women who share her communal apartment criticize her behind her back; the secretaries that work in her office building ridicule her; and most important, the man she decides is the one for her rudely rejects her overtures. The revolution turns an innocent young woman, a daughter of Old Believers, into a coarse woman who smokes *makhorka* and curses as well as men, a "free spirit" whose ways ironically no longer fit in with the "Soviet family" of the NEP* years.

However, the family as a potential safe haven from the violence of history returns as a theme in many stories in the second half of the 20th century. A good example is Kazakov's story, "You Cried Bitterly in Your Sleep" (1977), written in "the period of stagnation" under Leonid Brezhnev. The hero and narrator immerses himself in remembering with great tenderness the first years of his son's life. He is also haunted with questions about the suicide of a friend who was an important part of his life at that time. At different points in the story, he falls into reflection about the spiritual dimension of human life and what happens as one ages and experiences life. He comes to feel that a child's innocence and wonder at the world are somehow connected with a spirituality which becomes more and more lost with adulthood and all the trials and disappointments that each year of life brings.

"Girl of My Dreams" (1985), an autobiographical story by Bulat Okudzhava, a Georgian-Armenian who writes in Russian, would seem at first glance to be a story about the restoration of a family. A mother who has spent many years in the Gulag* finally returns to join her student son. But family harmony will take a long time to restore, because the son cannot imagine or understand the horror that his mother went through, and the mother, numb from her ordeals in a labor camp, cannot share her son's young, shallow values in his life "in freedom." The psychological gulf between them is revealed when he takes her to see a Nazi-period German musical comedy, "Girl of My Dreams." History has passed over the family like a tank, leaving only ruins, and only a deep feeling of guilt and remorse on the part of the autobiographical narrator before his mother serves as a substitute for the family warmth that may have been lost forever.

In the post-Soviet period, in the 1990s, it is not surprising that many writers turn to stories about family life, in which historical cataclysms often play no major role, as was true of Ulitskaya's story, "The Queen of Spades" and Petrushevskaya's story, "Never." The break-up of the Soviet Union and the questioning and social chaos that followed made some writers turn inward, away from depicting public life in the context of the country's history, politics and social development to illuminating the private side of life. "More and More Angels" (1998) and "The Samurai's Dream" (1999) by Yury Buida and "Snow Falls Ever So Softly" (1999) by Polyanskaya are good illustrations of this trend. But the attraction of writing about the impact of violence rooted in history against the individual and society at large is often there. In "Experience in Demonstrating Mourning" (2000) by Vishnevetskaya, the narrator is seemingly caught up in describing in minute detail the clothing she wore to various funerals through the decades. But of course it is not the "history" of her clothing, but what she reveals about the lives of the deceased and the circumstances surrounding their death that becomes more important, with each death capturing some tragic facet of life in Soviet Russia.

If the family is not a place of comfort, a refuge from the pressures of being a member of society, are there still ways to resist violence? There is Mur's granddaughter at the end of "The Queen of Spades," who slaps her and serves her cold coffee as her first small gesture of resistance to Mur's communicative violence. But there are few examples of people resisting violence within the family unit. When it comes to ways of resisting societal violence, two writers, Shalamov and Dombrovsky, offer unique perspectives. Shalamov spent seventeen years in the Gulag and described his horrible ordeals with quasi-documentary detachment in a cycle of stories that first appeared in the 1960s in *Novy Zhurnal* in New York and then were gathered under the collective title of *Kolyma Tales*. He proposes that we look at violence from the point of view of the ultimate victim—the beaten, worn out, starving and dying forced labor camp inmate. A prisoner's path of resistance to the violence in this environment is to respond with burning hatred of the oppressors and to wage a constant war with the whole mechanism of terror that seeks to dehumanize the individual. Much of Shalamov's story included in this anthology, "Eulogy" (1960), is structured on a series of portraits of men the narrator knew in various camps, what he learned about their lives as Gulag prisoners, how some resisted the system, and how each died. These portraits taken together provide quite a comprehensive view of what life within the system of forced labor camps was like. In the last part of the story, in a bitter parody of a Christmas tale, a small group of men has gathered on Christmas Eve and each tells what he dreams of doing when (if) he leaves the Gulag. What the last man dreams of doing resonates throughout Shalamov's work. The man says he would want to be a trunk without hands or feet so that he would have the courage "to spit in their mugs for everything they're doing us."

In "Little Leg, Arm, Cucumber" (1977) by Yury Dombrovsky, who also spent years in the Gulag, the autobiographical hero struggles with the forces of terror in the post-Stalin period. He refuses to be intimidated by KGB* agents who harass him on the phone and threaten his life because of his writing. He issues a direct challenge to them—to meet them in an empty lot behind his building—and in that way confirms his freedom, regardless of the concrete consequences that such an uneven confrontation could bring.

In the post-Stalin period there are also stories that explore other ways of resisting violence. Thus one more writer who spent time in camps, Vorobyov, in his story "A German in Felt Boots" (1966), highlights the power of compassion, the pain felt in common by POWs, exhausted shadows of men, and one of their German guards. The guard shares his bread surreptitiously with a young Russian, who in turn shares it with some of his fellow prisoners. But pity for "the enemy" possesses the same explosive power as direct opposition to terror. This act of compassion is questioned and rejected by both sides because of the hold of Soviet ideology over the Russian men and fascist ideology over the German prison administration.

Almost thirty years later, a somewhat similar strategy for resisting violence is chosen by the autobiographical hero of Ermakov's work, "The Last War Story" (1995). Ermakov, a veteran of the war in Afghanistan, who succeeds in presenting a good picture of the fighting there in the limited space of a short story, clearly cannot forget this war. His act of resistance is twofold: he questions where the people are who needed this horrible war and, second and more important for him, he accept responsibility for his role in the violence, for the people he has killed as a pilot, although he himself can be considered a victim of this violence too.

The path of eccentric rebellion as yet another form of resistance to societal demands is explored in Vasily Shukshin's "Chudik" (1967) and "I Believe " (1967) and Sergei Dovlatov's "My Older Cousin" (1983). As different as the heroes of these stories are, they confront the hidden repressive forces in their daily life with their own fanciful ideas and illusions in order to break free of their nice but humdrum existence. In Shukshin's "Chudik" the hero tries to share a few days with his brother and sister-in-law, only to find himself an unwelcome guest because of his "village" mindset. In "I Believe!" Shukshin reveals much deeper reasons for his hero's eccentric behavior. The anguish in Maxim's soul stems from an existential crisis: he periodically realizes that he does not know what to believe in and what to live for. Conscious of the dull inertia of life that surrounds him and tormented by the spiritual void in his soul, he seeks the help of a priest. But the priest's discussion of good and evil, communism, life and God, and a perfect, eternal world order only leave Maxim lost and confused. Drunk on the alcohol they have consumed, the priest leads him in an energetic squatting dance to the rhythmic recitation of "buzz words" evoking Soviet ideals (scientific revolution, mechanization of agriculture, etc.), followed by suggestive phrases that put an emphasis on the personal and intimate world of a human being. Maxim's spiritual anguish should be read as being indicative of people's growing spiritual emptiness in the 1960s-1970s, given the absence of meaningful ideals and spiritual values in the dead Soviet utopia.

Dovlatov's heroes, unlike Shukshin's intuitive eccentrics, are well aware of this crisis, and they can only pretend to "fit in" with society's norms with which, in fact, they are disgusted. The protagonist in Dovlatov's story, the "older cousin," could have easily joined Soviet society's elite, but he prefers the artificial creation of difficult, crisis situations for himself. They are vital to his existence: the need to survive the various crises dictates the goals that guide his life, goals that are a far cry from the stated goals of Soviet society. Whenever his life improves again and he has achieved his objectives, he becomes bored by life's senselessness and once again rebels against the existing order of things by new acts—sometimes criminal—of eccentricity. Tellingly, Dovlatov calls his hero "a spontaneous existentialist."

The eccentric rebellion of heroes in other stories is expressed in their open attempt to escape from the social reality that surrounds them by moving into the realm of culture, game-playing, and fantasy as the equivalent of freedom. The tragicomic consequences of this strategy of opposition are explored in the post-Stalin period by Aksyonov ("Victory," 1965), under glasnost by Tolstaya ("Fakir," 1987) and in the post Soviet period by Levkin ("The Dump," 2000). The clearest example may be Tolstaya's story of a young woman who desperately wants to leave her life in a small apartment in an unfashionable part of Moscow, far from the center and its cultural life. She searches and longs for opportunities to take part in a more "refined," gentile life, and searches for the "right kind of people." But it turns out that an elderly gentleman, who befriends her and her husband and seems to exemplify the style of life she longs for, lives in his own world of fantasy, pretense, and deception.

Rebellion against the norms and policies that rule Soviet and post-Soviet society and culture reaches a new level in the writing of the two leading Russian post-modern writers, Sorokin and Pelevin. Two exemplars of this kind of rebellion are found in "Passing Through" (1992) by Sorokin and "A Short History of Paint-ball in Moscow" (1997) by Pelevin. Sorokin exposes the violence that is hidden in authoritative discourse by reproducing Socialist Realism in parody form. At the same time he adds a naturalistic dimension to what is in fact a form of symbolic repression by reducing a standard story about a visit to an enterprise by a Party functionary into a humorous and repelling ritual of the "highest fertilization." In this way Sorokin exposes the ritualistic, game-like basis of authoritative discourse (Socialist Realism) and, therefore, of society's symbolic violence. To some extent, Pelevin goes even further. He demonstrates that in post-Soviet culture a new explosion of violence, connected with criminal wars and the redistribution of "socialist" property, has transformed violence into a kind of game. Even the introduction of paint-ball as an instrument of setting scores among criminal groups becomes possible. But both in the case of Sorokin and of Pelevin the very perception of violence as a game—be it a matter of discourse or taken literally—serves as testimony of some measure of liberation from the power that violence assumed in Russian culture of the 20th century.

And thus a whole century comes to a close in the development of the short story: from the tendency toward self-destruction marked in pre-revolutionary writing to the cataclysmic revolution and civil war, and the violence and monstrous phantasms born of those upheavals—to various forms of resistance to societal mechanisms of repression and terror during the Stalin years and even more strongly in the post-Stalin period—to perestroika and the breakup of the Soviet Union, and finally an understanding of terror and repression as a kind of game which is subject to deconstruction. This is the schematic trajectory of Russian short stories of the 20th century. But of course, this is just a scheme, only the bare abstraction of the rich array of themes and styles, vivid characters, comical and frightening situations, revealing dialogues, comedies and tragedies and, more often than not, tragicomedies found in the writing of fifty writers of the 20th century. It is the specific stories of people's lives and the fate of human beings that will undoubtedly captivate the readers of this anthology and lead them to perceive that the stories capture troubling, destructive features of Russian history, life and culture, while ultimately embodying the dramas and contradictions of 20th century modernity at large.

ONCE UPON A TIME

Leonid Andreyev

The rich and unmarried merchant Lavrenty Petrovich Kosheverov came to Moscow for medical treatment and, since he had an interesting illness, he was admitted to the university teaching hospital. He left his fur coat and his suitcase with his things downstairs in the porter's room, and upstairs, where his room was located, they took off his black suit and his underwear and gave him instead a grey hospital robe, clean underwear marked in black "Ward No. 8," and slippers. The hospital gown turned out to be too small for Lavrenty Petrovich, and the nurse went to look for a new one.

"You're really big!" she exclaimed, leaving the washroom where the patients changed their clothes.

The half-naked Lavrenty Petrovich waited patiently and submissively and, with his large bald head cast down, intently examined his big chest, which sagged like an old woman's, and his somewhat swollen stomach, which lay in his lap. Every Saturday Lavrenty Petrovich would go to the bathhouse and see his body there, but now, pale-looking and covered with goose bumps, it seemed new to him and, even with its apparent overall strength, truly pitiful and sick. And from the moment they took off the clothes he was used to wearing, he no longer seemed to belong to himself and was ready to do whatever they told him. The nurse returned with a gown and, although Lavrenty Petrovich still had the strength to strike the nurse dead with one finger, he obediently allowed her to dress him and awkwardly put his head through the opening of the gown, which was gathered together at the neck and resembled a horse's collar. His head thrown back, he waited with the same submissive awkwardness while the nurse tied the collar strings, and then followed her to his ward. And with his bear-like, splayed feet he walked as indecisively and cautiously as children do when they are being taken to who knows where by adults, perhaps to be punished. The gown turned out to be still tight on him; it pulled at the shoulders when he walked and sounded as if it were ripping, but he could not bring himself to tell the nurse, although at home in Saratov,[1] one of his stern looks would force tens of people to dash about madly.

"Here's your place," the nurse pointed to a high, clean bed with a small table beside it. It was a very small space, just a corner of the ward, but it was precisely for that reason that a man worn out by life liked it. Quickly, as if escaping pursuit, Lavrenty Petrovich took off his robe and slippers and lay down. And from that moment on everything that had angered and tormented him that very morning receded, becoming alien and unimportant. Quickly, like a flash of lightning, his mind produced a picture of his whole life in the last few years—the implacable illness that consumed his strength day after day; the loneliness among countless greedy relatives in an atmosphere of lies, hate and fear; and the escape here, to Moscow— and just as suddenly his memory extinguished this picture, leaving only a dull, fading pain in his heart. And not thinking any more but enjoying the pleasant sensation of clean linen and peace, Lavrenty Petrovich sank into a deep, heavy sleep. The snow-white walls and the rays of the sun on one wall were the last things to flash before his half-closed eyes, and then there followed long hours of complete oblivion.

The next day a sign on a piece of blackboard appeared above Lavrenty Petrovich's head: "Merchant Lavrenty Kosheverov, 52 yrs. old, admitted February 25." The same kind of boards were over the beds of the two other patients who were to be found in the eighth ward. One read: "Deacon Filipp Speransky, 50 yrs. old"; the other, "Student Konstantin Torbetsky, 23 yrs. old." The chalk-white letters stood out beautifully, yet somberly, against the black background and, when the patient lay on his back with his eyes closed, the white writing continued to say something about him and took on a resemblance to grave markers indicating that right here, in this damp or frozen earth, a human being was buried. That same day Lavrenty Petrovich was weighed; it turned out that he weighed a good two-hundred forty-two pounds. After giving this figure, the medical assistant smiled slightly and joked, "You're the heaviest man in all our clinics."

The medical assistant was a young man who spoke and acted like a doctor since it was only by accident that he had not received a higher education. He expected that the patient would respond to his joke with a smile just as all the other patients, even the seriously ill, responded to the jokes of the doctors that were intended to cheer them up, but Lavrenty Petrovich did not smile or say a word. His deeply set eyes looked down, and his massive cheekbones, covered with a sparse, grayish beard, were clamped tight, as if made of iron. And the medical assistant, who was waiting for a response from him, began to feel self-conscious and awkward because, as it happened, he had been studying physiognomics[2] for a long time and, observing the large, lusterless bald spot on Lavrenty Petrovich's head, had assigned the merchant to the category of the good-hearted; now he had to move him to the category of the bad-tempered. Still not trusting his observations, the medical assistant—his name was Ivan Ivanovich—decided to ask the merchant at a later time for a note written in his own hand in order to make a more precise determination of his personality based on his handwriting.

Soon after he was weighed, doctors examined Lavrenty Petrovich for the first time; they were dressed in white garments which gave them a particularly important, serious look. And after that, they examined him once or twice daily, sometimes alone, but more often accompanied by students. Lavrenty Petrovich would take off his shirt when the doctors asked him to, and just as submissively he would lie down on the bed, with his massive, fleshy bulk extending above it. The doctors thumped his chest with a small hammer and listened with an ear trumpet, exchanging comments with each other and turning the students' attention to this or that peculiarity. They would often begin asking Lavrenty Petrovich what kind of life he had led before, and he would answer reluctantly, but obediently. It became apparent from the answers that came in bits and pieces that he ate a lot, drank a lot, worked a lot, and loved a lot of women; and with each new "a lot," Lavrenty Petrovich recognized himself less and less in the man his words were painting. It was strange to think that this was really him, the merchant Kosheverov, who had acted so badly and done such harm to himself. And all the old words—vodka, life, health—took on a new and deeper meaning.

The students listened to his heart and thumped his chest. They would often appear when the doctors were not there, and some would ask him to undress in a few direct words, others with timid indecisiveness, and his body would be examined yet again with care and much interest. Conscious of the importance of what they were doing, they kept a record of his illness, and it seemed to Lavrenty Petrovich that now all of him had been transferred to the pages of those notes. With each day he belonged to himself less and less, and in the course of almost the whole day his body was exposed and subjected to the will of all. On the nurses' orders he moved his body laboriously to the bathroom or seated it at a table where all the patients capable of moving dined and had tea. People examined him all over, devoting their attention to him as no one had in his life before, but in spite of all this attention, a vague feeling of profound loneliness stayed with him all day long. It was as though Lavrenty Petrovich were going somewhere very far away, and everything around him had a temporary quality, ill-suited for a long stay. The white walls without a single stain and the high ceilings had an air of cold alienation; the floors were always too polished and too clean; the air was too neutral. Even in the cleanest houses the air always had a distinctive smell of something that belonged only to that house and to those people. But here the air had an impersonal quality and did not have a smell. Doctors and students were always attentive and courteous; they would joke, pat him on the shoulder and comfort him, but when they stepped away from Lavrenty Petrovich, it would occur to him that the people at his side were all only employees and conductors along a mysterious road. They had already transported thousands of people and continued to transport them every day, and their conversations and inquiries were merely questions about the ticket. And the more they dealt with his body, the deeper and more terrifying the loneliness in his heart became.

"When do you have visiting hours?" Lavrenty Petrovich asked the nurse. He spoke succinctly, without looking at the person he was addressing.

"On Sundays and Thursdays. But if you ask the doctor, then on other days as well," the nurse answered readily.

"And could it be arranged so that no one at all is allowed to see me?"

The nurse was surprised, but answered that it could, and this response apparently made the sullen patient happy. And that whole day he was a bit more cheerful and, although he did not become more talkative, he now listened with a less gloomy look to everything that the sick deacon jabbered about so cheerfully, loudly and at such length.

The deacon was from the Tambov Oblast[3] and had been admitted to the clinic only the day before Lavrenty Petrovich, but he was already well acquainted with the residents of all five wards located upstairs.

He was short and so thin that, when they undressed him, all his ribs showed and his stomach was all drawn in, and his whole small, weak body—white and clean—resembled that of an underdeveloped ten-year old boy. His hair was thick, long, and grayish white, but yellow and curly at the ends. His small, dark face with correct but miniature features looked out of the hair like out of a large frame that did not match the painting. Because of his resemblance to the dark and unemotional faces of ancient icons, Ivan Ivanovich, the medical assistant, assigned him to the category of stern and intolerant people, but after their first conversation, he changed his opinion and even for a time became disenchanted with the science of physiognomics. Father Deacon, as everyone called him, talked about himself, his family and friends readily and openly and asked others about theirs with such curiosity and naiveté that no one could get angry at him and everyone would talk just as openly. Whenever anyone sneezed, Father Deacon would shout in a cheerful voice from afar: "May your wishes come true! To your heart's content!" And he would make a bow.

No one came to see him, and he was seriously ill, but he did not feel alone since he made the acquaintance not only of all the patients but also their visitors, and so he was not lonely. Several times a day he would wish the patients good health, and he would wish the healthy people joy and well-being, and he would find something kind and pleasant to say to everyone. Every morning he would greet everyone, saying on Thursday, "Happy Thursday," on Friday, "Happy Friday," and no matter what was happening outside, where he never went, he would steadfastly maintain that the weather was unusually pleasant that day. Moreover, he would laugh constantly and gaily in a drawn-out, inaudible way, press his hands to his sunken stomach, slap his knees, and sometimes even clap his hands. And he would thank everyone; sometimes it was hard to tell what for. And so, after tea, he would thank the sullen Lavrenty Petrovich for his company.

"So we've had a good time drinking our tea—just heavenly! Isn't that true, my dear man?" he would say, although Lavrenty Petrovich drank tea by himself and would not have kept anyone company.

He was very proud of his deacon's position, which he had received only three years earlier, having been a psalm-reader before. And he would ask everyone—be it a patient or a visitor—how tall that person's wife was.

"My wife is very tall," he would say proudly after this or that answer. "And the children are just like her. Grenadiers, that's for sure!"

Everything in the clinic—the cleanliness, the low price, the politeness of the doctors, the flowers in the corridor—evoked delight and tenderness in him. Now laughing, now crossing himself before an icon, he would pour out these feelings to the silent Lavrenty Petrovich and, when at a loss for words, he would exclaim, "No two ways about it! No two ways about it, as God is my witness!"

The third patient in the eighth ward was the student Torbetsky, who came from common folk. He rarely got out of bed, and a tall girl with modestly lowered eyes and light, confident movements came to see him every day. Slender and graceful in her black dress, she would walk quickly down the corridor, sit down at the head of the sick student's bed and remain there from two until exactly four o-clock when, according to the rules, visiting hours were over and the nurses would serve tea to the patients. Sometimes they had long and lively conversations, smiling and lowering their voices, but individual words, spoken loudly, would escape, precisely those that should have been uttered in a whisper: "My sunshine!" or "I love you!" Sometimes they would be silent for long periods of time and only gaze at each other with an enigmatic, misty-eyed look. Then Father Deacon would cough and leave the ward with a serious, business-like look on his face and, Lavrenty Petrovich, pretending to be asleep, his eyes not quite closed shut, would see them kissing. And he would get a burning pain in his heart, and it would begin beating unevenly and hard, and his massive cheekbones would stick out like lumps and twitch. And the white walls would watch with their usual cold alienation, and there was a strange and sad mockery in their irreproachable whiteness.

II

The day began early in the ward, when there was only a dull grayness from the first rays of morning light, and the day would be long, bright, and empty. At six o'clock the patients would be served their morning tea and drink it slowly, and then they would use thermometers to take their temperature. Many, like Father Deacon, found for the first time that they had a "temperature," and they imagined that it was something mysterious and its measurement a very important matter. A small glass wand with its small black and red lines became an indicator of life, and one-tenth of a degree higher or lower made the patient cheerful or sad. Even the eternally cheerful Father Deacon would fall into momentary depression and shake his head in bewilderment if his body temperature was lower than the one they told him was normal.

"Here's the thing, my good man! *Az* and *fert*,[4]" he said to Lavrenty Petrovich, holding the thermometer in his hand and examining it with disapproval.

"Why don't you hold it a bit longer, bargain a bit," Lavrenty Petrovich answered derisively.

And Father Deacon would bargain and, if he managed to get even one-tenth of a degree higher, he would become cheerful and ardently thank Lavrenty Petrovich for his lesson. Temperature-taking turned people's thoughts to questions of health for the whole day, and everything that the doctors recommended was done punctually and with a certain solemnity. Father Deacon brought special solemnity to whatever he did and, whether holding a thermometer, swallowing medicine or carrying out some bodily function, his face would take on the same important and serious look that it had during the discussion of his ordination. He was given, for the purposes of analysis, several small glasses, and he placed them in a certain order and asked the student to write down their numbers—one, two, three . . .—since he did not write beautifully enough himself. He would get angry at the patients who did not carry out the doctors' orders, and he constantly and strictly admonished the fat Minayev from the tenth ward, because the doctors did not want Minayev to eat meat, but Minayev would take it quietly from his neighbors at the dinner table and swallow without chewing.

From seven o'clock on, bright daylight coming through the huge windows would flood the ward and it would become as light as in a field, and the white walls, beds, polished copper basins and floors—everything would glisten and sparkle in the light. Rarely did anyone go up to the windows; the street and the whole world that existed outside the clinic walls had lost their appeal. Outside, there were people with lives; out there, a horse-drawn tram full of people was rushing, a grey detachment of soldiers was going by, shiny fire engines were passing, and store doors were opening and closing. In here, sick people lay in their beds, with barely enough strength to turn their weak heads toward the light; dressed in grey bathrobes, they wandered sluggishly, stepping on the smooth floor; in here they were sick and lay dying. The student received a newspaper, but neither he nor the others hardly ever glanced at it, and something wrong with a neighbor's bowels touched and upset them more than the war and those events that later would be called "world" events. Around eleven o'clock the doctors and students would come, and again thorough physical examinations would begin, lasting for hours. Lavrenty Petrovich always lay quietly and looked at the ceiling, answering gloomily and in monosyllables; Father Deacon would become agitated and talk so much and so unintelligibly, with such a desire to please and show respect to everyone, that it was difficult to understand him.

About himself he would say, "When I was welcomed into the clinic . . ."

About a nurse he reported, "They[5] were kind enough to give me an enema . . ."

He always knew precisely at what hour and what minute he had heartburn or nausea, at what time of night he woke up and how many times. After the doctors would leave, he would become more cheerful, express his thanks, show more emotion and be very pleased with himself if he had managed, in saying good-bye, not to make one general bow to all the doctors but to each one individually.

"It's proper this way," he would rejoice, "divine!"

And again he would demonstrate to the silent Lavrenty Petrovich and the smiling student how he had bowed first to Dr. Aleksander Ivanovich and then to Dr. Semyon Nikolayevich.

He had an incurable illness and his days were numbered, but he did not know it; he talked enthusiastically about making a trip to the Trinity-Sergiev Monastery[6] when he got well and about an apple tree in his garden called "white ripening," which he expected to bear fruit in the coming summer. And on a good day, when the walls and the parquet floors of the ward would become generously flooded with sunbeams that were without equal in their power and beauty, when the shadows on the snow-white bed linens would take on a transparent and summer-like blue hue, Father Deacon would sing loudly an affecting song: "Supreme in the heavens and the purest of the bright lights of the sun, who releases us from our vows, we honor Our Lady with song!"

His voice, a weak and delicate tenor, would begin to tremble and, in his emotional state, which he tried to conceal from those around him, Father Deacon would raise a handkerchief to his eyes and smile.

Then, after walking around the room, he would walk right up to the window and raise his eyes to the deep, cloudless sky—vast, far from earth and serenely beautiful, in itself a magnificent, divine song. And a trembling human voice, full of anxious and passionate supplication, timidly joined its solemn sounds: "My body is ailing from my many sins, my soul is ailing as well. I come to you, full of grace, the hope of those without hope, help me . . . !"

Dinner was served at the appointed time, then tea again and supper, and at nine o'clock a blue-cloth lampshade would be placed over the electric bulb, and the same long and empty night would begin all over again.

The clinics would grow quiet.

Only in the illuminated corridor, onto which the permanently open doors of the wards looked out, the nurses-in-training knitted socks and whispered quietly and squabbled with each other and, now and then, one of the attendants would pass by with loud footsteps, and the steps could all be heard distinctly and then would fade in a precise, gradual manner. By eleven o'clock even those last echoes of the day that had just ended would die away, and a ringing silence—as if made of glass— keenly preserved every faint sound and transmitted, from ward to ward, the sleepy breathing of those getting better and the coughing and light moans of the gravely ill. Those sounds in the night were light and deceptive, and a terrible mystery often lurked in them: was it a patient wheezing or was it death itself that was already roaming among the white beds and cold walls?

Except for the first night when Lavrenty Petrovich sank into a deep sleep, all the other nights he could not sleep, and they were full of new and terrifying thoughts. With his hairy hands behind his head, he would stare without moving at the bent wire which shone through the blue lampshade and think about his life. He did not believe in God, did not want to live, and was not afraid of death. Everything— whatever strength and life he had—everything had been spent and used up without any need, benefit, or joy. When he was young and had curly hair, he would steal from his master; they would catch him and beat him cruelly, without mercy, and he hated those who beat him. In middle age he squeezed the life out of the little people with his wealth and despised those who came under his power, and they repaid him with burning hatred and fear. Old age came, illness came—and people began to rob him, and he would catch those who were careless and beat them cruelly, without mercy . . . His whole life passed in this way, and it was one pervaded with feelings of bitter grievance and hatred, in which any fleeting flames of love would be quickly extinguished and leave only cold cinders and ashes in his heart. Now he wanted to leave this life, to forget, but the quiet night was cruel and pitiless, and he would now laugh at people's stupidity and his own, now clench his iron jaws spasmodically, suppressing a long moan. Distrustful of the idea that someone could love life, he would turn his head to the adjacent bed where the deacon slept. Attentively and for a long time he would scrutinize the indefinitely shaped white lump and the dark patch that was his face and beard and whisper with malicious delight, "Id-diot!"

Then he would look at the sleeping student whom the girl kissed during the day and, with even greater malicious delight, he would correct himself, "I-di-ots!"

But during the day his heart would grow still and his body would obediently do everything that they would order it to; it would take medicine and toss and turn. But with each day it grew weaker and soon it was left in almost complete peace, motionless and huge and, in this deceptively huge size, seemingly healthy and strong.

Father Deacon was also failing; he walked around the wards less and smiled less frequently, but when the sun peered into the ward, he would begin jabbering happily and at length, thanking everyone—both the sun and the doctors—and he would mention the "white ripening" apple tree even more often. Then he would sing "Supreme in Heaven," and his dark, sunken face would brighten and also take on a more important air; it was immediately apparent that it was the deacon singing and not the psalm-reader. After finishing his song, he would walk up to Lavrenty Petrovich and tell him about the document they gave him when he was ordained. "It was this big," he would show with his hands, "and there were letters and letters all over it. Some black, some shaded in gold. A rare thing, by God!"

He would cross himself before the icon and add with a sense of self-respect: "And at the bottom was the bishop's seal, huge, by God,—just like a round cheese pastry! The only way to describe it—no two ways about it! Right, my good man?"

And he would break out in rolling laughter, hiding his shining eyes in a web of thin wrinkles. But the sun would hide behind a gray snow cloud, the light in the ward would grow dim and, sighing, Father Deacon would go to bed.

III

There was still snow in the fields and the gardens, but the streets had been cleared of it long ago; they were dry and, in places with heavy traffic, they were even dusty. Thin streams of water flowed only from the courtyards and the front gardens surrounded by iron grillwork and turned into puddles along the even pavement; and from each such puddle wet footprints stretched in both directions, at first dark and close to one another but farther on more widely spaced and barely noticeable, as if the crowds of people who had passed by here had been picked up into the air all at once and brought down only at the next puddle. The light from the sun was flooding the ward and warming it so much that one had to hide from it like in the summer, and it was hard to believe that behind the thin window glass the air was cold, fresh and damp. In the light the ward itself, with its high ceilings, seemed to be a narrow, stuffy, secluded corner in which it was impossible to stretch your arms without hitting the wall. Street sounds did not penetrate the double panes of the clinic, but when in the morning one of the large ventilation panes was pushed out and opened in the ward, suddenly, without a moment's wait, the intoxicating, cheerful, and loud chirping of sparrows would burst in. All the other sounds, modest and seemingly offended, would grow quiet before it, and the chirping would spread festively through the corridors, go up along the staircases, and break insolently into the laboratory and run through it, making the small glass flasks ring. The patients, who had been moved into the corridor, smiled at the naive, boyishly-insolent chirping, and Father Deacon would close his eyes, stretch out his arms and whisper, "A sparrow! A sparrow, for sure!"

The ventilation windowpane would be closed and the ringing chirping of the sparrows would die just as suddenly as it had started, but as if they still hoped to find the hidden echoes, the patients would hurry into the ward, look around anxiously and take greedy breaths of the fresh air spreading in waves throughout the ward.

Now the patients went up to the windows more often and stood there for long periods of time, wiping the glass with their fingers, although it was clean as it was; reluctantly, grumbling, they would use the thermometers and talk only about the future. And all of them imagined this future as something bright and good, even the boy in room eleven who one morning was moved by the watchmen to a separate room and then disappeared God knows where—"checked out," as the nurses would say. Many patients saw him being moved in his bed to a private room; they carried him out head first and he did not move, only his dark sunken eyes shifted from object to object. And there was something so uncomplainingly pitiful and eerie about them that not one of the patients could stand their gaze and they all turned away. And later everyone guessed that the boy had died, but his death did not upset or frighten anyone; here, it was a simple and common matter as it probably seemed in war. Another patient, from the eleventh ward, died during this time as well. This was a rather short old man, still somewhat strong in appearance, broken by paralysis; he walked with a rolling gait, with one shoulder thrust forward, and told all the patients the same story over and over again: about the baptism of Rus[7] in St. Vladimir's time. What touched him in this story remained unknown, since he spoke very quietly and unintelligibly, rounding off his words and swallowing his endings, but he was apparently delighted with the story himself, waving his right arm and rolling his right eye—the left side of his body was paralyzed. If he was in a good mood, he would finish his story with a surprisingly loud and triumphant exclamation—"God is with us!"—after which he would leave hastily, laughing uneasily and artlessly shielding his face with his hand. But more often than not, he was sad and complained that they did not give him the warm baths that were bound to cure him. A few days before his death he was scheduled to have a warm bath in the evening, and the whole day he kept exclaiming "God is with us!" and laughing; when he was already sitting in the bathtub, patients passing by heard his hurried cooing, full of bliss; this was the little old man talking to the man looking after him and for the last time telling the story of the baptism of Rus in St. Vladimir's time. There were no noticeable changes in the condition of the patients in the eighth ward; the student Torbetsky was improving, but Lavrenty Petrovich and Father Deacon were getting weaker by the day; life and strength was leaving them with such a sinister absence of sound that they themselves almost did not suspect it, and it seemed as though they had never even walked around the room and had always lain this quietly in their beds.

And the doctors in their white gowns and the students kept coming just as regularly; they listened and thumped them and talked among themselves.

On Friday, during the fifth week of Lent, Father Deacon was taken to a lecture and returned all excited and talkative. He went into peals of laughter, as he would when he had first come here, crossed himself and gave thanks and at times brought his handkerchief to his eyes, after which his eyes would turn red.

"Why are you crying, Father Deacon?" the student asked.

"Ah, my dear man, don't even mention it," the deacon responded emotionally, "but it's so nice, that's for sure! They, Semyon Nikolayevich that is, seated me in a chair, and they stood by my side and said to the students, 'Here,' they say, 'is the deacon . . .'"

At this point Father Deacon's face assumed a self-important look and he knitted his brow, but tears welled up in his eyes again and, bashfully turning away, he explained: "Semyon Nikolayevich—they lecture very movingly! So movingly that your whole soul turns inside out. 'Once upon a time,' they say, 'there was a deacon . . .'"

Father Deacon sobbed, "'Once upon a time there was a deacon . . .'"

Father Deacon could not go on because of his tears, but after he got into bed, he whispered in a muffled voice from under the blanket: "They talked about my whole life. How I had been a psalm-reader and didn't have enough to eat. Mentioned my wife too, thanks be to them. So moving, so moving: it's as if you've died and they're saying prayers over you. 'Once upon a time,' they say . . . 'there was,' they say . . . 'a deacon . . .'"

And while Father Deacon was talking, it became apparent to everyone that this man was going to die; it became apparent with such indisputable and terrible clarity as if death itself were standing here among them. An invisible, terrible cold and darkness emanated from the cheerful deacon and, when sobbing again, he hid himself under his blanket, Torbetsky rubbed his cold hands nervously and Lavrenty Petrovich burst out laughing crudely and had a fit of coughing.

In his last days Lavrenty Petrovich was terribly agitated and continually turned his head in the direction of the blue sky beaming through the window; he violated his motionless state by wildly tossing and turning in bed, groaning and getting angry at the nurses. During the daily examinations he would greet the doctor in the same agitated state, and the doctor finally noticed it. He was a good, kind man and asked sympathetically, "What's the matter?"

"I'm bored," Lavrenty Petrovich said. And he said it in a voice used by suffering children and closed his eyes to hide his tears. But in his "journal," among the notations about the patient's pulse and breathing and the number of times he felt weak, a new note appeared: "The patient complains of boredom."

The girl whom he loved came to see the student as before, and her cheeks burned with such a lively and delicate color from the fresh air that it was nice and a bit sad, for some reason, to look at them. Bending over Torbetsky's face, she would say, "Look what hot cheeks."

And he would look, not with his eyes but with his lips, and he would look long and hard, since he was beginning to get better and had more strength. Now they did not feel shy in front of the other patients and kissed openly; the deacon would turn away tactfully in those moments, but Lavrenty Petrovich, no longer pretending to be asleep, would look at them defiantly and derisively. And they liked Father Deacon and did not like Lavrenty Petrovich.

On Saturday Father Deacon received a letter from home. He had been waiting a whole week for it, and everyone in the clinic knew that Father Deacon was waiting for a letter and worried with him. Feeling happier and more cheerful, he got out of bed and slowly wandered through the wards, showing his letter everywhere, accepting congratulations, bowing and expressing gratitude. Everyone had known for a long time that his wife was tall, but now he announced a new detail: "She really snores. When she's gone to bed, you can hit her with a stick and you won't wake her up. Snores, and that's all there's to it. Does it well, by God!"

Then Father Deacon would wink slyly and exclaim, "Have you ever seen such a thing? My good man, oh my good man!"

And he would show the fourth page of the letter on which the outline of an open child's hand was traced with clumsy wavering lines and, in the middle, exactly in the palm of the hand was written: "Tosik put his hand here." Before placing his hand there, Tosik apparently had been busy with something else, connected with the use of mud and water, since in those places where his fingers and palm left their imprint, the paper preserved clear traces of stains.

"Isn't my grandson something? Just four years old but bright, so bright that I can't even begin to tell you. Added his signature, eh?" In excitement from his witty joke Father Deacon slapped his knees and doubled over from a bout of quiet, irrepressible laughter. And his face, yellowish-pale, which had not felt fresh air for a long time, became for a moment the face of a healthy man whose days were not yet numbered. And his voice became strong and clear, and the sounds of the moving song reflected his good spirits: "Supreme in the heavens and the purest of the bright lights of the sun, who releases us from our vows, we honor Our Lady with song . . . !"

That same day they took Lavrenty Petrovich to a lecture. He returned all upset—with trembling hands and a crooked grin—and angrily pushed away the nurse who helped him get into bed and immediately closed his eyes. But Father Deacon, who had suffered through a lecture himself, waited for the moment when Lavrenty Petrovich's eyes would be half-open and began to question him about the details of his examination with sympathetic curiosity.

"How moving, don't you think, my good man? They said it about you, too, I dare say: 'Once upon a time,' they say, 'there was a merchant . . .'"

Lavrenty Petrovich's face became distorted in anger; after giving the deacon a scorching look, he turned his back to him and again shut his eyes resolutely.

"It's all right, my good man, don't you worry. You'll get better and you'll begin making wisecracks better than ever— just divinely!" Father Deacon continued. He was lying on his back and dreamily looking at the ceiling on which a sunbeam was playing, reflected from who knows where. The student had gone off to smoke, and in these moments of silence only the heavy and short breaths Lavrenty Petrovich was taking could be heard.

"Yes, my good man," Father Deacon said with quiet joy, "if you're ever in our parts, come see me. It's five versts from the station—any peasant can take you. By God, come see me, I'll show you hospitality, that's for sure. My kvass[8]—I can't even begin to tell you how sweet it is!"

Father Deacon sighed and, after a short silence, continued: "I'll go to the Trinity Monastery. And I'll take some communion bread in your name. Then I'll tour the cathedrals. I'll go to a bathhouse. What are they called, my good man—commercial bathhouses, is that it?"

Lavrenty Petrovich did not answer, but Father Deacon decided himself: "Commercial. And then, home, that's for sure!"

The deacon fell blissfully silent, and in the ensuing silence the short and irregular breathing of Lavrenty Petrovich brought to mind the angry hissing of a steam engine being held on a reserve track. And the picture of imminent happiness had not yet dissipated before the deacon's eyes when incomprehensible and terrible words reached his ear. The horror was in the rude and angry voice, dropping senseless, cruel words, one by one:

"You'll go to the Vagankov Cemetery, there's where!"

"What are you saying, my dear man?" the deacon did not understand.

"To Vagankov, to Vagankov, I say, it's time," Lavrenty Petrovich answered. He turned to face Father Deacon and even lowered his head from the pillow so that not one word would miss the one to whom it was directed. "Or else they'll drag you off to the anatomical room and there they'll cut you open—sure as anything!"

Lavrenty Petrovich burst out laughing.

"What's wrong with you, what's wrong with you, God be with you!" Father Deacon mumbled.

"There's nothing wrong with me, but how they bury the deceased here, that's real fun. At first they cut off an arm—then they bury the arm. Then they cut off a leg—they bury the leg. They drag around some luckless deceased like that for a whole year, but can't seem to finish."

The deacon kept silent and rested his gaze on Lavrenty Petrovich, but the latter continued to speak. And there was something repelling and pathetic in the shameless bluntness of what he said:

"I look at you, Father Deacon, and I think: you're an old man but, speaking bluntly, stupid to the point of saintliness. And why do you stubbornly insist on saying, 'I'll go to the Trinity, I'll go to a bathhouse.' Or also that thing about the 'white ripening' apple tree. You have a week left to live, but you . . ."

"A week?"

"Well, yes, a week. It's not me who says it—it's the doctors. I was lying in bed the other day, pretending to be asleep, but you weren't in the ward, and so the students were saying: 'Soon,' they said, 'that'll be it for our deacon. He'll last a week.'"

"La-a-st?"

"And you think *it* will spare you?" Lavrenty Petrovich articulated the word "it" with frightening expressiveness. Then he raised his huge, lumpy fist and, after sadly admiring its massive shape, continued: "Here, just take a look! If I smack anyone with it, it's *az* and *khvert*[9] and the end of him. And also . . . Well, yes, also. Oh, you empty-headed deacon: 'I'll go to the Trinity, I'll go to the bathhouse.' Better people than you have lived, but even they died."

Father Deacon's face was yellow like saffron; he could neither speak nor weep, nor even moan. Slowly and silently he brought his head down on the pillow and, trying to escape the light and Lavrenty Petrovich's words, painstakingly wrapped himself up in his blanket and grew quiet. But Lavrenty Petrovich could not refrain from speaking; each word which he hurled at the deacon brought him delight and relief. And with feigned good-nature he repeated: "So there you have it, my good man. In a week. And what is it you say: *az* and *khvert*? Here's your *az* and *khvert*. And you and your bathhouse—what an absurd fantasy! Perhaps there in the other world they'll beat us with hot brooms[10]—why not, that's very possible."

But at this point the student came in and Lavrenty Petrovich reluctantly fell silent. He tried to take cover under his blanket as Father Deacon had done, but soon he stuck his head out of the darkness and glanced derisively at the student.

"And that sister of yours, I see, they won't be coming again today?" he asked the student with the same feigned good nature and malicious smile.

"No, she's not well," the student flung out his brief, gloomy answer from where he was standing by the window.

"What a pity!" Lavrenty Petrovich shook his head. "What's wrong with them?"

But the student did not answer; he did not seem to hear the question. Three times already the girl he loved had missed visiting hours; she would not come today either. Torbetsky pretended to look out the window at the street merely from lack of something to do, but in reality he was trying to look to the left where there was an entrance he could not see, and he pressed his forehead to the glass. And so, between the window and the clock, now looking at one, now at the other, he passed the usual visiting hours, from two to four. Tired and pale, he drank a glass of tea reluctantly and got into bed without noticing either Father Deacon's strange, silent state or Lavrenty Petrovich's strange loquaciousness.

"They, your sister, didn't come!" Lavrenty Petrovich said and smiled maliciously.

IV

That night, wearisomely long and empty, the bulb burned under the blue lampshade as before, and the ringing silence shuddered and became frightened, carrying quiet moans, snoring, and the sleepy breathing of the patients through the wards. Somewhere a teaspoon fell on a stone surface, and the resulting sound was clear, like the ringing of a small bell, and it lingered for a long time in the still and quiet air. In Ward No. 8 no one slept that night, but all lay quietly and looked like people sleeping. Only Torbetsky, not concerned about the presence of strangers in the room, tossed and turned restlessly, lying now on his back, now on his stomach, groaning and fixing his sliding blanket. A couple of times he went to have a smoke and finally fell asleep, since his improved health exacted its due. His was a deep sleep, and his chest rose easily and evenly. And he must have had pleasant dreams, too; a smile appeared on his lips and did not leave for a long time, a strange and touching one, since his body was absolutely still and his eyes were closed.

Far off, in the dark and deserted auditorium, the clock struck three when a quiet, quivering and mysterious sound reached the ear of Lavrenty Petrovich, who was about to doze off. It started just after the musical striking of the clock and in the first moments it seemed delicate and beautiful like a sad song somewhere far in the distance. Lavrenty Petrovich listened; the sound became bigger and louder, and just as melodious, and now resembled the quiet crying of a child who had been locked in a dark room; the child was afraid of the dark and afraid of those who had locked it in, and it was trying to stifle the sobs and sighs struggling to break out of its chest. The next second Lavrenty Petrovich woke up completely and at once solved the mystery; an adult was crying, crying in an unbecoming way, choking back tears and gasping for breath.

"Who's that?" Lavrenty Petrovich asked fearfully, but did not get an answer.

The crying quieted down and, because of that, it became even more sad and depressing in the ward. The white walls were motionless and cold, and there was no living person to whom one could complain about being lonely and frightened and ask for protection.

"Who's crying?" Lavrenty Petrovich repeated. "Deacon, is that you?"

The sobbing seemed to be hiding somewhere right next to Lavrenty Petrovich and now, no longer held back by anything, broke free. The blanket that covered Father Deacon began to rise and fall with a wave-like motion, and the metal board banged and jingled against the iron bedpost.

"Now, now!" Lavrenty Petrovich mumbled. "Don't cry."

But Father Deacon cried, and the board kept banging more and more because it was being shaken by the sobbing and convulsing body. Lavrenty Petrovich sat up in bed, grew pensive, and then lowered his numb feet slowly to the floor. When he got to his feet, something warm and noisy rushed into his head, as if ten whole millstones had begun to turn and rumble in his brain, his breathing stopped, and the ceiling quickly floated off somewhere downward. Staying on his feet with difficulty from a bout of dizziness and, feeling his heartbeats as clearly as if someone were hitting him with a hammer inside his chest, Lavrenty Petrovich caught his breath and decisively crossed the space that separated his bed from Father Deacon's—one-and-a-half steps. Here he had to pause for breath again. Breathing hard and intermittently through his nose, he placed his hand on the quivering lump which had moved to give him room on the bed and said pleadingly, "Don't cry. Why cry?! Are you afraid of dying?"

Father Deacon pulled the blanket off his head abruptly and cried out pitifully, "Oh, my dear man!"

"Well, what? Are you afraid?"

"No, my dear man, I'm not afraid," the deacon answered in the same, plaintive singing voice and shook his head forcefully. "No, I'm not afraid," he repeated and, turning on his side again, began moaning and shaking from the sobbing.

"Don't be angry with me for saying what I did earlier," Lavrenty Petrovich asked. "It's stupid, brother, to be angry."

"Oh, I'm not angry. Why should I be angry? It wasn't you, was it, who invited death? It comes on its own . . ." And Father Deacon let out a high-pitched, ever-rising sigh.

"Why are you crying?" Lavrenty Petrovich asked in the same slow and bewildered way.

His pity for Father Deacon was beginning to disappear and to be replaced by agonizing bewilderment. With a questioning look he shifted his eyes from the deacon's dark face to his sparse grey beard, felt the weak trembling of the small, thin body beneath his hand, and did not know what to do.

"Why are you howling?" he asked insistently.

Father Deacon took his face in his hands and, rocking his head back and forth, uttered in his high singing voice, "Oh, my dear man, my dear man! I'll miss the sun. If you only knew . . . how it shines . . . in our Tambov Province. That's . . . that's for sure!"

"What sun?" Lavrenty Petrovich did not understand and got angry at the deacon. But right then and there he remembered the hot streaming light which poured through the window during the day and gilded the floor, he remembered how in Saratov Province the sun shone on the Volga River, the forest, and the dusty path in the field—and he clasped his hands and hit himself in the chest and, sobbing hoarsely, fell face down on the pillow, side by side with the deacon. And they both cried. They cried about the sun, which they would never see again, about the "white ripening" apple tree which would bear fruit without them, about the darkness that would envelop them, about dear life and cruel death. The ringing silence picked up their sighing and sobs and carried them though the wards, mixing them with the healthy snoring of the nurses-in-training worn out by the day, the moaning and coughing of the seriously ill, and the light breathing of those getting well. The student was asleep, but the smile had disappeared from his lips, and deathly blue shadows lay on his face—motionless and sad and suffering in its motionless state. The electric bulb burned with a steady, lifeless light, and the high white walls looked on with indifference and disinterest.

Lavrenty Petrovich died the next night, at five in the morning. He fell fast asleep in the evening, woke up with the realization that he was dying and that he must do something—call for help, shout, or cross himself—and lost consciousness. His chest rose high and then fell, his legs shook and spread apart, his head—which had grown heavy—slipped down from the pillow, and his massive fist rolled off his chest in a sweeping motion. Father Deacon heard the bed squeaking in his sleep and, without opening his eyes, asked, "What's going on, my good man?"

But no one answered him and he fell asleep again. During the day the doctors assured Father Deacon that he would live, and he believed them and was happy; he made a bow from the bed with only his head, expressed his gratitude and wished everyone a happy holiday.

The student was happy, too, and slept soundly like a healthy man. That day his girlfriend came to see him, kissed him passionately, and stayed exactly twenty minutes longer than the permitted time.

The sun was rising.

5-16 February 1901

NOTES

1. Saratov: a city on the Volga River, in southern Russia; it was a major trading center.
2. physiognomics: the "science" of interpreting human character and intelligence by analyzing physical characteristics. It was introduced in ancient Greece; with the growing interest in the occult in the second half of the nineteenth century, physiognomics attracted much attention again.
3. Tambov Oblast: about 288 miles southeast of Moscow.
4. "Az" is the letter A and "Fert" is the letter F in Church Slavonic. The deacon's phrase may come from the title of a light comic play, *Az i fert* (1849) by P. S. Fyodorov (1803-1879). A tyrannical patriarch has all objects in his daughter's dowry monogrammed with the initials of the groom-to-be. The groom runs away before the wedding, and the family patriarch orders that another man, with the same initials, be found immediately. What the deacon means to imply with his reference to the play is open to interpretation; one possibility is that he has the tyrannical power of illness in mind.
5. The use of the third-person plural by the deacon as he refers to the nurse (and later, as he is speaking about a doctor as well as the girl who comes to visit the student) suggests the deacon's exaggerated respect for people in authority as well as his eccentric personality.
6. Trinity Sergius Monastery: the Holy Trinity-St Sergius Monastery is located in the town of Sergiev Posad, about forty-five miles north of Moscow. Until a few years ago, it was the home of the Patriarchy of the Russian Orthodox Church.
7. Rus: a reference to the East Slavic state centered around Kiev from about

880 to the middle of the 12th century, a predecessor state of three modern nations—Ukraine, Russia and Belarus.

8. kvass: a fermented beverage made from rye or barley and water.
9. *khvert*: he means "fert."
10. Short, small brooms made of birch branches used by Russians to beat themselves in a bathhouse in order to induce perspiration.

THE INVOKER OF THE BEAST

Fyodor Sologub

It was quiet and peaceful, neither joyful nor sad. An electric lamp was burning. The walls seemed indestructible. The window was hidden behind heavy, dark-green drapes—the same color as the wallpaper, but much darker. Both doors—the large one in a side wall and the small one way back in the study opposite the window—were tightly shut. And there, behind them, it was dark and empty—both in the wide hallway and in the depressing, spacious and cold room where sorrowful plants, separated from their native country, pined away.

Gurov was lying on the sofa. A book was in his hands. He was reading. He would often stop reading. He would think and daydream—always about the same thing. Always—about them.

They were near him. He had noticed them for a long time now. They lurked. They stood close by relentlessly. They made quiet, rustling sounds. But for a long time they would not show themselves to him. Recently, however, when Gurov woke up feeling sluggish, melancholy, and pale, and lazily turned the switch on the electric lamp in order to dispel the terrible gloom of the early wintry morning—he suddenly saw one of them.

Small, grey, light, and quivering, it flitted by the head of his bed, babbled something and disappeared.

And then, sometimes in the morning, sometimes in the evening, small quivering house spirits would run past in front of Gurov.

And today he was already waiting for them, confident that they would appear.

Now and again he would get a slight headache. Now and again he would suddenly became cold or hot. Then tall, thin Likhoradka[1] with her unattractive yellow face and bony dry hands would run out of a corner, lie down next to him and embrace him, and start laughing and kissing him. And those quick kisses of sly, affectionate Likhoradka and the slow onsets of a light headache were pleasant.

Weakness would spread through his whole body. And weariness. But it too was pleasant. It seemed that all the turbulence in his life had receded. People became remote, uninteresting, and totally unnecessary. He wanted to be with these quiet beings, with the spirits of this house.

Gurov did not go out now for several days. He locked himself in the house. And he would not let anyone in. He sat alone. He thought about them. Waited for them.

II

His weary waiting was interrupted in a strange and unexpected way. A far-off door banged and in the hall outside his own door Gurov heard unhurried footsteps. Somebody was walking there with a light and confident step.

Gurov turned his head toward the door. A waft of cold air drifted by. A little boy who had a strange, otherworldy look stood before him. In a linen cloak. Half-naked. Barefoot. Very swarthy. All tanned. Black curly hair. Striking black eyes. A fantastically handsome face with regular features. So handsome that it was frightening to look at its beauty. Neither good nor evil.

Gurov was not surprised. Some sort of overpowering feeling possessed him. The house spirits could be heard hiding and concealing themselves.

And the youth said, "Aristomakh![2] Or have you forgotten your promise? Is this how valiant people act? You left me when I was in mortal danger, you made a promise you evidently did not want to keep. I've looked so long for you! And I find you living in idleness, drowning in luxury."

Gurov looked in bewilderment at the youth—half-naked and handsome—and vague memories began to awaken in his soul. Something long since buried there was taking form again in hazy outline and tormenting his memory, which could not find an explanation for the strange apparition, although the answer seemed so close and intimately familiar.

And what about the indestructible nature of the walls? Something was happening all around; some kind of change was taking place. But Gurov, lost in his futile efforts to remember something which was both close and yet slipping away from the tenacious embrace of ancient memory, had not yet managed to grasp clearly the change he was already sensing. He asked the wondrous youth: "Dear boy, tell me clearly and simply, without unnecessary reproaches, what I had promised you and when it was I left you in a time of mortal danger? I swear to you by all that is holy that my honor would never have allowed me to do such a black deed as the one for which you, for some reason, reproach me."

The youth shook his head. In a ringing voice that resembled the melodic, low rumbling of strings, he said: "Aristomakh, you were always skillful when we practiced oratory and just as skillful in matters demanding caution and courage. If I said that you left me in a time of mortal danger, I did not say this in reproach, and I do not understand why you are talking about your honor. The deed we had planned was difficult and dangerous, but who hears us today, to whom could you prove—with your craftily-woven words and feigned forgetfulness of what happened this morning before sunrise—that you did not make any promise to me?"

The light of the electric lamp grew dim. The ceiling seemed dark and high. There was a smell of some herb—it once had a delicate and delightful name, now forgotten. A coolness wafted through the air. Gurov got up. He asked, "What deed did I plan with you? My dear boy, I deny nothing—I just do not know what you are talking about. I do not remember."

It seemed to Gurov that the youth was looking at him and yet not at him. As if someone else were here, just as wondrous and mysterious as this strange newcomer, as if the wondrous body of the other one partly coincided with Gurov's body. As though someone else's ancient soul were settling into Gurov and enveloping him in the freshness of vernal perceptions long lost.

It was getting dark all around and the air was becoming fresher and cooler; the joy and lightness of primal existence was rising in his soul. Bright stars were coming out in the black sky. The youth said: "We were duty-bound to kill the Beast. I say this to you under the many-eyed gaze of the all-seeing heavens, in case you had been daunted by fear. And why should there not be fear! We undertook a grand, frightening deed so that our names would be crowned with glory by future generations."

A stream gurgled quietly, monotonously, and timidly in the stillness of the night. It was not visible, but its comforting closeness and freshness was consoling. They stood under the broad shadow of a tree and continued the conversation they had once begun. And Gurov asked,

"Why do you say that I left you in a time of mortal danger? Who am I to get frightened and run away?"

The youth laughed. His laughter sounded like music, and the sounds that formed his answer were melodic and pierced with sweet laughter.

"Aristomakh, how skillfully you pretend to have forgotten everything! I do not understand why you are doing this and doing it with such great mastery that you even level reproaches at yourself which had never occurred to me. You left me in a time of mortal danger; because that was the way it had to be, and you could not have helped me other than by leaving me at that time. Or will you persist in your denial even when I remind you of the words of the oracle?"

Gurov remembered immediately. As if a bright light had spilled into the dark realm of the forgotten. And he exclaimed in wild delight, loudly and joyfully, "One shall kill the Beast!"

The youth laughed. And Aristomakh asked, "Did you kill the Beast, Timarid?"[3]

"With what?" exclaimed Timarid. "No matter how strong my hands are, I am not the one who could have killed the Beast with a blow of my fist. We were not cautious, Aristomakh, and we were unarmed. We were playing in the sand on the shore. And the Beast suddenly attacked us, and he laid his heavy paw on me. It was incumbent on me to give my life as a sweet sacrifice to glory and our grand heroic deed, and for you to finish our task. And while the Beast would have been tearing my body, defenseless and unresisting, you could have managed, fleet-footed Aristomakh, to bring your spear and kill the Beast drunk with blood. But the Beast did not accept my sacrifice. I lay before him, calm and motionless, looking directly into his eyes filled with blood. He kept his heavy paw on my shoulder, his breath was hot and uneven, and he growled quietly. Then he licked my face with his big, hot tongue and walked away."

"Where is he?" Aristomakh asked.

Timarid answered in a strangely calm voice that resounded strangely in the quiet stillness of the humid air: "He followed me. I do not know how long I had to walk until I found you. He followed me. I lured him with the smell of my blood. I do not know why he has not touched me up to now. But I lured him to you. Get the weapon you hid so skillfully and kill the Beast and I, in turn, will go away and leave you alone in your time of mortal danger, eye to eye with the ferocious Beast. May luck be with you, Aristomakh!"

And having said that, Timarid began to run. His white cloak could be glimpsed for a few brief moments in the darkness. And then it disappeared from view. And at that moment the terrifying roar of the Beast resounded and his heavy step could be heard. Parting the bushes, the huge monstrous head of the Beast appeared in the darkness; two huge, fiery eyes flashed with crimson fire. And in the dark silence of the trees in the night, the Beast—dark and ferocious—drew closer to Aristomakh.

"Where's the spear?" a quick thought flashed through his mind.

Terror filled Aristomakh's heart. And at that moment, feeling the fresh night air rushing in his face, Aristomakh sensed that he was fleeing from the Beast. The heavy leaps of the Beast and his intermittent roaring resounded closer and closer behind Aristomakh. And when the Beast was already catching up with him, a loud cry pierced the stillness of the night. Aristomakh cried out and, remembering the frightening and ancient words, he cast a spell for walls in a loud voice.

And enchanted walls rose up all around him . . .

III

Enchanted, the walls were stable and bright. The faintly burning electric lamp cast a lifeless glow on them. Everything surrounding Gurov was ordinary and simple.

Light Likhoradka came visiting again and kissed him with her dry, yellow lips and carressed him affectionately with her dry, bony hands, sending heat and cold throughout his body. The same book—small, slender, with white pages—was on the small table by the sofa on which Gurov lay as before, enjoying the embraces of affectionate Likhoradka, who was covering him with her quick kisses. And the little spirits were laughing and rustling near him again.

Gurov said loudly and indifferently, "A spell for walls."

And he stopped. But what does the spell consist of? He had forgotten the words. Or perhaps there had never been any?

Small spirits, quivering and grey, danced around the small book with the deathly white pages and repeated in rustling voices, "Our walls are strong. We're in the walls. Tenacious fear will not come here from the outside."

One stood among them, just as small, yet not like them. He was all black. His clothing flowed in smoky-fiery folds. His eyes emitted bright flashes of lightning. Suddenly it was frightening and then, joyful again. And Gurov asked, "Who are you?"

The black guest answered: "I am the Invoker of the Beast. In a past experience, you left the body of Timarid, torn to pieces on the shore of a forest stream. The Beast sated himself on the beautiful body of your friend—he devoured the flesh which was to hold the full measure of earthly happiness; a wondrous perfection of the human form—no, more than human—perished in order to satisfy, for a moment, the hungry and always unsatiated Beast. And the blood, the wondrous blood, the divine wine of happiness and mirth, the wine of supreme blessedness which surpasses human happiness—where is this wondrous blood? Alas! The thirsting, eternally thirsting Beast got drunk on it for a moment and is thirsting again. You left the body of Timarid, torn to pieces by the Beast, on the shore of a forest stream. You forgot the promise you gave to your valiant friend, and the words of the ancient oracle did not dispel the fear in your heart. And do you think that you have saved yourself, that the Beast will not find you?"

His words sounded cruel. While he spoke, the dancing of the house spirits, little by little, came to a stop; the small, grey spirits stopped and listened to the Invoker of the Beast. And Gurov said, "What do I care about the Beast! I have cast a spell on my walls that will last forever, and the Beast will not be able to get through my barrier."

The little grey things rejoiced and made their ringing sounds and laughed and were getting ready to begin again their merry dancing and had already taken each other by the hand and formed a circle again, but the Invoker of the Beast began to speak again and the sound of his voice was harsh and stern. And he said: "But here I am. I am here because I found you. I am here because the spell on the walls has expired. I am here because Timarid is waiting for you and importuning me. Do you hear the soft laughter of the brave and trusting youth? Do you hear the threatening roar of the Beast?"

The threatening roar of the approaching Beast could be heard behind the wall.

"The Beast is roaring behind the wall, behind the indestructible wall!" Gurov exclaimed in horror. "There is a spell on my walls which will last forever and this barrier cannot be destroyed."

And the Black One spoke, expressing his words imperiously: "I say to you, man, the spell on the walls has expired. And if you want to save yourself with a spell on the walls—well, all right, say that spell for me."

A sharp chill suddenly went through Gurov's entire body. The spell! But he had forgotten the words of the ancient spell. And does it really matter? The ancient spell had expired, had expired.

And everything that was impending spoke with the irrefutable conclusiveness that the ancient spell for walls had expired—because the walls and the light and the shadows had all become lifeless and unstable. The Invoker of the Beast spoke frightening words. And Gurov's head ached and was spinning, and persistently affectionate Likhoradka wearied him with her hot kisses. The frightening words resounded almost without reaching his consciousness, and the Invoker of the Beast grew larger and larger, and intense heat wafted from him—and fear. His eyes emitted fire and, when he became so tall that he blocked the light from the lamp, suddenly the black cloak fell from his shoulders. And Gurov recognized him—it was the youth Timarid.

"Will you kill the Beast?" Timarid asked in a sonorous voice. "I have summoned him, brought him to you, and destroyed the spell on the walls. A treacherous gift from a hostile deity, the ancient spell for walls turned my sacrifice into nothing and obscured from you the heroic deed you were to perform. But the ancient spell for walls has expired. Take your sword quickly and slay the Beast. I was merely a youth. I have become the Invoker of the Beast. I sated the Beast's thirst with my blood and he thirsts again, and I sated him full with my flesh and now he is hungry again, the insatiable, merciless Beast. I have called him forth to come to you and now you, fulfill your promise and slay the Beast. Or die."

He vanished. A terrifying roar shook the walls. A cold dampness wafted by.

The wall directly opposite the place where Gurov lay opened wide, and the huge, monstrous, savage Beast emerged. With a ferocious roar he approached Gurov and laid his heavy paw upon his chest. His merciless claws pierced Gurov's heart. Terrible pain ran through his body. His bloody eyes flashing, the Beast bent over Gurov and, loudly cracking his bones with his teeth, began devouring the still palpitating heart.

1906

NOTES

1. Likhoradka: derived from the Russian *likho radet'* which means "to act or take care of someone with malicious or evil intentions." In Russian folklore there are actually twelve different *likhoradkas*, each a spirit with a specific name and role to play in human life. At the time of Sologub's story, *likhoradka* was also used as a term for various illnesses accompanied by high fever.
2. Aristomakh: variant of Greek Aristomachus. Sologub selected a name that has a mythological ring for his own myth about people's fear of death.
3. Timarid: Old Russian variant of Greek Timarides.

GAMBRINUS

Aleksander Kuprin

That was the name of a pub in a bustling port city in the south of Russia. Although it was located on one of the busiest streets, it was rather difficult to find because of its location below street level. Even a customer who was intimately acquainted with Gambrinus and well received there would often manage to walk by this remarkable establishment and turn back only after passing two or three neighboring shops.

There was no signboard of any kind. People would enter directly from the sidewalk through a narrow door which was always open. A narrow staircase, the same width as the door, led people down twenty stone steps which were uneven and worn hollow by millions of heavy boots. At the bottom of the staircase in the area over the doorway a colored depiction in high relief of the famous patron of the beer trade, King Gambrinus, approximately twice life size, attracted people's attention. It is quite likely that this sculpture was the first work of an unskilled, beginning artist, and it appeared to be crudely fashioned out of petrified pieces of touchwood, but the short red jacket, ermine robe, gold crown, and stein raised high with white foam streaming down left no doubt whatsoever in the customer's mind that this was the great patron of beer-brewing himself.[1]

The pub consisted of two long but unusually low vaulted rooms. Subterranean moisture always seeped out in quick flowing rivulets from the stone walls and glistened in the light from the gas lamps that burned day and night because there were no windows at all in the pub. Above the arches, however, it was still possible to make out reasonably clearly traces of engaging wall paintings. In one picture a large group of roguish German fellows in green hunter's jackets and hats with black grouse feathers and with rifles on their backs sat feasting. All of them, looking out into the beer hall, were greeting the public with extended tankards and, moreover, two of them had their arms around the waists of two buxom girls, maids in a small village tavern or perhaps the daughters of a kind farmer. Another wall depicted a refined society picnic in the first half of the XVIII century; countesses and viscounts in powdered wigs were gamboling with affectation in a green glade with lambs and, next to them, under spreading willows, there was a pond with swans which cavaliers and ladies were feeding gracefully as they sat in a small gold boat. The next picture depicted the inside of a *khokhol*[2] hut and a family of happy Little Russians[3] dancing the *gopak*[4] with bottles in their hands. In the background, a large barrel occupied a prominent place, and on it, entwined with grape vines and hops leaves, two outrageously fat cupids with red faces, fat lips and shamelessly sensuous eyes were toasting each other with ordinary glasses. In the second room, separated from the first by a semi-arch, there were pictures from the life of frogs: frogs drinking beer in a green swamp, frogs hunting dragonflies in thick reeds, playing in a string quartet, sword fighting, and so on. Apparently a foreign artist had decorated the walls.

Instead of tables, heavy oak barrels were arranged on the floor, which was covered with thick sawdust; instead of chairs, small barrels. To the right of the entrance, there was a raised stage with a piano on it. Here every evening, for many years now, Sashka the musician—a Jew of an indeterminate age, a meek, cheerful, drunken bald man with the appearance of a mangy ape—played his fiddle for the pleasure and entertainment of the guests. Years passed, the servers in protective leather sleeves changed, the men who supplied and delivered beer changed, and even the owners of the pub changed, but every evening by six o'clock Sashka was invariably sitting on the stage with fiddle in hand and a small white dog in his lap; and around one o'clock in the morning he would leave Gambrinus accompanied by the same little dog, Belochka,[5] barely able to stand on his feet from the beer he had consumed.

There was, however, another unchanging face in Gambrinus—a barmaid, Madam Ivanova—a plump, pale old woman who, because she was constantly in the damp beer cellar, resembled the pale, slow fish that populate the depths of sea grottoes. Like a ship's captain in a wheel-house, she gave orders wordlessly to the waiters from the raised bar counter and smoked all the time, holding a cigarette in the right corner of her mouth, her right eye squinting from the smoke. It was a rare person who heard her voice; she would always respond to anyone bowing to her with the same colorless smile.

II

The huge port, one of the world's largest trading ports, was always overflowing with ships. Huge battleships, dark rust in color, would call at the port. Yellow steamships with the big smokestacks of the Volunteer Fleet,[6] which swallowed long trains with merchandise or thousands of prisoners daily, were loaded in the port and then sent off to the Far East. In spring and fall, hundreds of flags from all corners of the globe were unfurled here, and from morning to night commands and bad language could be heard in all possible languages. Stevedores, using rickety gangplanks, scurried back and forth from vessels to countless warehouses; there were Russian tramps, in rags, almost naked, with drunken puffy faces; dark-skinned Turks in dirty turbans and in trousers wide down to the knee but tight around the calf; and stocky, muscular Persians with hair and nails stained a fiery carrot color from henna. Two- and three-masted Italian schooners, enchanting from afar, often called at the port with their precise sets of sails—clean, white, and taut like the chests of young women. Appearing from behind the lighthouse, these slender ships, particularly on bright spring mornings, looked like wondrous white apparitions, sailing not on water but in the air, above the horizon. Here tall single-masted ships from Anatolia[7] and feluccas from Trapezond[8] with their strange combinations of colors, fretwork and fanciful ornaments, rocked back and forth for months on end in the dirty-green water of the port amidst trash, egg shells, watermelon rinds, and flocks of white sea gulls. Strange narrow vessels with black, tar-spattered sails and a dirty rag instead of a flag came sailing in from time to time. Rounding the pier and coming very close to scraping it with its side, all the while listing to the side without slowing down at all, such a vessel would enter any harbor at flying speed and, to the sound of swearing, curses and threats in various languages, it would moor at the first available wharf, where its sailors—completely naked, small, bronze-skinned people, uttering guttural shouts—would take down the torn sails with incredible speed, instantly making the dirty, mysterious vessel look like a dead ship. And just as mysteriously, without putting on any lights, the vessel would disappear from the port without a sound in the dark of night. The whole bay teemed with the small light boats of these smugglers. Local fishermen and those from farther away brought their fish to town: in the spring—small Black Sea anchovies, millions of them filling their long boats to the brim; in the summer—unappealing flounder and sole; in the fall—mackerel, fatty grey mullet and oysters; and in the winter—ten- and twenty-pood white sturgeon, often caught with great danger to the lives of the fishermen many versts from shore.

All these people—sailors from different nations, fishermen, stokers, jovial ship's boys, port thieves, machinists, workers, boatmen, stevedores, divers, and smugglers—all of them were young, healthy, and saturated with the smell of the sea and the fish; they knew how difficult their work was, loved the appeal and danger of daily risk taking, and valued above all their strength, their boldness, and the provocative, trenchant nature of strong language, but on land they surrendered themselves to debauchery, drunkenness and fighting with wild abandon. In the evenings the lights of the big city, which extended up a high hill, enticed them like glowing, magical eyes which always promised them something new, joyous, and not yet experienced, and yet always deceived them.

The city was linked to the port by narrow, steep, twisting streets which respectable people avoided walking at night. At every turn there were cheap rooming houses with dirty, barred windows and inside them, the gloomy light of a solitary lamp. Even more frequently one encountered shops where one could remove and sell one's clothing down to the sailor's net underwear and then get dressed again in any navy uniform. Here there were also many pubs, taverns, eating-houses and inns with expressive signs in all languages and quite a few brothels—some blatantly obvious, others less so—from whose doorways at night crudely made-up women pressed invitations on sailors in husky voices. There were Greek coffee-houses where people played dominoes and sixty-six,[9] and Turkish coffee-houses with apparatus for smoking a hookah and with a night's lodging for a five-ruble coin; there were small Eastern taverns that sold snails, cockles, shrimps, mussels, large warty and inky cuttlefish, and other disgusting denizens of the sea. Here and there, in attics and basements, behind heavy shutters, there were gambling dens crowded together in which a game of *shtoss*[10] or baccarat often ended with a stomach being cut open or with a fractured skull; and right there around the corner, sometimes in the adjoining small room, it was possible to dispose of any stolen item, from a diamond bracelet to a silver cross, from a package with Lyon velvet to a government-issue sailor's greatcoat.

These steep, narrow streets, black from coal dust, always became sticky and foul-smelling by nightfall, as if they were sweating during a nightmare. And they resembled sewers or dirty intestines through which the large international city disgorged all its refuse, all its rot, vileness and vice into the sea, thereby infecting strong, muscular bodies and simple souls.

The rowdy inhabitants of this area rarely went up to the elegant, always festive city with its plate glass windows, proud monuments, electric lights, asphalt sidewalks, avenues lined with white acacia trees, imposing policemen, and all its ostentatious cleanliness, utilities and services. But every one of them, before throwing to the wind wads of hard-earned, dirty, torn rubles, visited Gambrinus without fail. This was a venerable, time-honored custom, even though one had to make one's way to the very center of town under the cover of evening darkness.

Many, it is true, did not even know the strange name of the famous beer king. Someone would simply propose, "Shall we go to Sashka's?"

And others would answer, "Aye-aye! Hold the course!"

And then all together they would say, "Lift!"[11]

There is nothing surprising in the fact that among the port and sea people Sashka enjoyed more respect and fame than, for example, the local bishop or governor. And without a doubt, his lively ape-like face and fiddle, if not his name, were mentioned from time to time in Sidney and Plymouth, just as they were in New York, Vladivostok, Constantinople and Ceylon, not to mention all the gulfs and bays of the Black Sea where a great many admirers of his talent could be found among the ranks of brave fishermen.

III

Sashka usually came to Gambrinus at a time when there was no one there except one or two random customers. At that hour the rooms still held the thick and sour smell of yesterday's beer, and it was somewhat dark inside because gas was used sparingly during the day. On hot July nights, when the stone city languished from the sun and grew deaf from the rumbling in the streets, one could feel the silence and coolness here with pleasure.

Sashka would go up to the bar counter, greet Madam Ivanova, and drink his first mug of beer. Sometimes the barmaid would ask, "Sasha, play something!"

"What would you have me play, Madam Ivanova?" Sashka, who was always refined and courteous to her, would inquire politely.

"Something of your own . . ."

He would sit down at his usual place to the left of the piano and play several strange, long-drawn-out, melancholy pieces. The basement would become a bit sleepy and quiet; only the muffled rumble of the city carried from the outside, with the occasional quiet rattling of dishes by the waiters behind the wall in the kitchen. Jewish sorrow, ancient like the earth itself, patterned and entwined with the mournful colors of folk melodies, flowed from Sashka's strings. At that twilight hour Sashka's face, with its tense jaw and low brow and eyes looking up sternly from under heavy eyebrows, bore no resemblance to his usual grinning, winking, dancing face, familiar to all guests of Gambrinus. The little dog Belochka sat in his lap. It had long ago learned to keep from howling to the music, but the passionately melancholy, sobbing and damning sounds unintentionally grated on its nerves; it would open its mouth wide in a spasmodic yawn, curling back its thin, pink tongue, whereupon its whole body and delicate black-eyed muzzle would shiver for a moment.

Little by little people would gather, the accompanist—who had finished some daily work that he did on the side at the tailor's or the watchmaker's—would arrive, frankfurters in hot water and cheese sandwiches would be put out on the bar counter and, finally, the rest of the gas lamps would be lighted. Sashka would drink his second mug of beer and command the accompanist, "'May Parade', ein, zwei, drei!"[12], and begin a lively march. From that moment on, he barely managed to exchange bows with all the returning customers, each of whom considered himself to be a special, intimate friend of Sashka's and would look round proudly at the other guests after making a bow. At the same time Sashka would squint now one eye, now the other, with long wrinkles collecting on his bald, sloping skull, and comically move his lips and smile in all directions.

By ten or eleven o'clock Gambrinus, with room for two-hundred people or even more, would become packed. Many, almost half, came with women in kerchiefs; no one minded the crowded conditions, his foot being stepped on, his hat being crumpled, someone else's beer spilling on his trousers; if anyone took offense, then it was only because of drunkenness and wanting to pick a fight. The basement moisture, shining dimly, would stream even more abundantly from the walls covered with oil paint, and condensation from the crowd's breathing would fall from the ceiling like sparse but heavy drops of warm rain. There was serious drinking at Gambrinus. According to the custom of this establishment, it was considered particularly fashionable to sit in twos and threes and cover the table with so many empty bottles that the person taking part in the conversation would be hidden behind them as if in a green forest of glass.

As the evening started to break down, the customers would grow flushed, hoarse, and all sweaty. The tobacco smoke irritated their eyes. People had to shout and lean across the table to hear one another in the general din. And only the tireless fiddle of Sashka, who sat at his raised place, triumphed over the stuffiness, the heat, the smell of tobacco, gas and beer, and the yelling of the insolent public.

But the customers would quickly get drunk from the beer, the presence of women, and the heat. Everyone wanted his favorite, familiar tunes. People constantly hung around Sashka, two and three at a time, with vacant eyes and unsteady legs, pulling him by the sleeve and getting in the way of his playing.

"Sash! . . . A s-suf-fering . . . Indul . . . ," the supplicant hiccuped, "indul-l-ge me!"

"In a minute, in a minute," Sashka would repeat, shaking his head quickly and dropping the silver coin in his side pocket noiselessly with the adroitness of a doctor. "In a minute, in a minute."

"Sashka, that's mean. I've given you money and I'm asking you for the twentieth time already, 'I Sailed the Sea to Odessa.'"

"In a minute, in a minute . . ."

"Sashka, 'The Nightingale!'"

"Sashka, 'Marusia!'"

"'Zets-Zets,' Sashka, 'Zets-Zets!'"[13]

"In a minute, in a minute . . ."

"'The Shep-herd!'" someone yelled from the other end of the room in a voice that did not sound human but horse-like.

And to the guffaws of everyone there, Sashka shouted to him in his squeaky voice, "In a min-u-ute!"

And he played all the requested tunes without a break. Apparently there was not a single one that he did not know by heart. Silver coins poured into his pockets from all directions and mugs of beer came his way from all the tables. Whenever he did come down from the raised stage to go to the food counter, they would pull him in a dozen different directions.

"Sashenka . . . Dear boy . . . One small mug."

"Sasha, to your health. Come here, darn it, you devil, if you're told to."

"Sashka, come dri-ink your beer!" the horse-like voice yelled.

The women, inclined like all women to admire performers, flirt and fawn on them and try to stand out from the crowd, called to him in cooing voices, with a playful, capricious giggle: "Sashechka, you just have to drink that . . . from me . . . No, no, I beg you.[14] And then play 'The Cuckoo Walk.'"[15]

Sashka would smile, make faces and bow left and right, press his hand to his heart, blow kisses, drink beer at all the tables and, after returning to the piano, on which a new mug awaited him, he would start playing some "Parting" or other. Sometimes, in order to amuse his listeners and, in keeping with the tune, he would make his fiddle whimper like a puppy, grunt like a pig, or make heart-rending, snoring bass sounds. And his listeners greeted his jokes with good-humored approval, "Ha-ha-ha-ha-a-a!"

It would become hotter. Water streamed down from the ceiling; some of the guests were already crying, pounding their chests, and others with blood-shot eyes argued over women or past wrongs and swung at each other, restrained by their more sober neighbors, most often by patrons who were sponging off them. The waiters, by some miracle, pushed their way between the full-size barrels and the small ones, between bodies and feet, as they held their hands full of mugs of beer high above the sitting people. Madam Ivanova, even more anemic, unflappable and silent than usual, directed the work of the waiters from behind the bar like the captain of a ship during a storm.

Everyone would be overcome with a desire to sing. Sashka, soothed by the beer, his own goodness, and that crude happiness which his music brought to others, was ready to play anything they wanted. And to the sounds of his fiddle the people who had already grown hoarse would yell in unison, incoherently, woodenly, and look into each other's eyes with senseless solemnity:

Why should we pa-a-rt,
Oh, why live a-pa-rt.

Isn't it better to marry,
To cherish our love?

And next to them another group, evidently ill-disposed to the first, would try to drown it out and strike up something entirely different:

I see by his gait
That his breeches are flashy.
His hair is kinda reddish,
And his boots are squeaky.

Gambrinus was often visited by Greeks from Asia Minor—*dopgolaki*—who sailed to Russian ports for the fishing trade. They, too, asked Sashka for their Eastern songs, which consisted of mournful, monotonous, nasal wailing of two or three notes, and with gloomy faces and burning eyes they were ready to sing them for hours on end. Sashka also played Italian folk ballads, and *khokhol* folk songs, and Jewish wedding dances, and much more. Once a bunch of Negro sailors dropped by Gambrinus; watching the others, they, too, wanted very much to sing. Sashka quickly picked up the bouncing Negro melody he heard them singing, immediately found the piano accompaniment and, to the great delight and amusement of the regulars of Gambrinus, the pub resounded with the strange, capricious, guttural sounds of an African song.

One reporter for a local paper, Sashka's acquaintance, somehow convinced a professor at a music school to go to Gambrinus and listen to the pub's famous musician. But Sashka suspected as much and intentionally made his fiddle meow, bleat and bellow more than usual. The Gambrinus' guests kept exploding with laughter, but the professor said contemptuously, "Clowning."

And he left without finishing his mug of beer.

IV

The delicate marquises and the feasting German hunters, the plump cupids and frogs, from their position on the walls, were witnesses quite often to large-scale debauchery such as rarely could have been seen anywhere else except at Gambrinus.

There would appear, for example, a group of thieves who had been drinking hard after a successful job, each with a girlfriend, each wearing a cap cocked at a jaunty angle and patent-leather shoes, with refined tavern manners and a contemptuous air. Sashka played special songs for them with a thieves' theme: "I've Died, Dear Boy," "Don't You Weep, Marusia," "Spring Has Passed," and others. The thieves considered dancing beneath their dignity, but their girlfriends, all not bad looking, young, and some of them practically teenagers, danced "The Shepherd," squealing and clicking their heels. Both the men and the women drank an awful lot; the one bad thing was that the thieves always ended their drinking bouts with old misunderstandings about money and liked to disappear without paying.

Large crews of fishermen, about thirty men each, would come after a good catch. In late fall there were good weeks when each plant would receive around forty thousand mackerel or grey mullet daily. During this time the smallest shareholder earned more than two hundred rubles. But a successful catch of white sturgeon enriched the fishermen even more, although on the other hand, that kind of fishing was much more difficult than most. They had to work hard, about thirty to forty versts from shore, in the middle of the night, sometimes in foul weather, when the water would pour into the long boat and immediately freeze on their clothing and oars; and this weather would last two or three days at sea until it would move about two hundred versts away, to Anapa or Trapezond. Every winter up to ten dinghies would turn up missing and only in the spring would the waves cast out upon foreign shores, now here, now there, the bodies of the brave fishermen.

However, once they returned from sea to shore, safe and sound, and with a good catch, they would be seized with a mad thirst for life. A few thousand rubles would be squandered in a matter of two or three days in the coarsest, deafeningly loud drinking bouts. The fishermen would descend on a tavern or some other place of revelry, throw out all the other customers, shut the doors and shutters tight, and for days without a break indulge in lovemaking, sing songs very loudly, smash mirrors and dishes, hit women and occasionally even each other until sleep would overtake them wherever they happened to be—at the tables, on the floor, across beds, amidst spittle, cigarette butts, broken glass, spilled wine and blood stains. The fishermen would drink hard like that for a few days in a row, sometimes changing the location, sometimes staying in the same place. After drinking away everything, even their last half-kopeck piece, they would go—with aching heads and signs of fighting on their faces, shaking from hangovers, silent, depressed and repentant—to the shore, to their dinghies, in order to take up again their beloved and accursed, difficult, and fascinating craft.

They never forgot to visit Gambrinus. They would burst in—huge, hoarse, their faces red, burned by the fierce winter northeaster, in water-proof jackets, leather pants and ox hide boots up to their thighs— the same kind of boots in which their friends went to the bottom like rocks in the middle of a stormy night.

Out of respect for Sashka they would not throw out the other customers, although they felt themselves to be the pub owners and smashed heavy mugs on the floor. Sashka played their fishermen's songs for them—drawn-out, simple, and threatening like the sound of the sea—and they all sang in unison, straining their healthy chests and strong throats to the limit. Sashka affected them like Orpheus who calmed the waves, and there were times when some forty-year-old commander of a dinghy—bearded, all weather-beaten, a beast-like man—would burst into tears, taking great care as he sung the touching words of a song in a fine voice:

> Oh, a poor, poor little boy am I,
> That was born a fisherman . . .

And sometimes they would dance, moving in place with stony faces, stomping loudly with their heavy boots that weighed a pood, and spreading throughout the pub the sharp salty smell of fish with which their bodies and clothing had become saturated through and through. They were very generous with Sashka and for long periods of time would not let him leave their tables. He knew their difficult, reckless way of life well. When he played for them, Sashka would often sense a respectful sadness in his soul.

But he particularly loved to play for the English sailors from the commercial vessels. They would come in a gang, arm in arm—all of them well-matched, broad-chested and broad-shouldered, young, their teeth white, a healthy flush on their cheeks, and bold, happy blue eyes. Their powerful muscles forced open their jackets, and straight, strong, and well-proportioned necks rose out of their deeply-cut collars. Some knew Sashka from previous moorings in this port. They would recognize him and, grinning cordially, they would greet him in Russian, "Zdraist, zdraist."[16]

Without even being asked, Sashka would play "Rule Britannia" for them. Their awareness that they were now in a country with the age-old burden of slavery must have added a particularly proud solemnity to this hymn to English freedom. And when standing, with heads bared, they sang the last splendid words:

> Never, never, never
> Will an Englishman be a slave![17]

even the most violent neighbors would take off their hats.

A thickset boatswain, with an earring in his ear and a beard fringing his neck, would approach Sashka with two mugs of beer, smile broadly, give him a friendly slap on the back, and ask him to play the English jig. At the first sounds of this rollicking sea dance the Englishmen would jump up and clear a place, pushing the barrels toward the walls. With gestures and happy smiles, they would ask the other people there to move, but if someone did not hurry, they would not stand on ceremony with that person and would simply knock the seat out from under him with a swift kick of the foot. But they rarely resorted to this, however, because at Gambrinus everybody was a lover of dance music, and they particularly loved the English jig. Even Sashka himself, without stopping to play, would get up on a chair so that he could get a better view.

The sailors would form a circle and clap their hands to the beat of the quick dance, while two would perform in the middle. The dance depicted the life of a sailor during sailing. The vessel is ready to leave, the weather is wonderful, everything's in order. The dancers have their arms crossed on their chests, their heads thrown back, their bodies still, although their feet are tapping madly. But now, a light wind has arisen, and the sailors feel the ship tossing somewhat. For a sailor it is all merriment, only the dance movements become more and more complicated and intricate. A fresh wind has begun to blow and now it is not that easy to walk on deck—the dancers are being rocked slightly from side to side. Finally a real storm comes—the sailors are tossed from side to side and the situation becomes serious. "All hands on deck! Trim the sails!" Judging by the movements of the dancers, it is clear to the point of absurdity that they are climbing up with their hands and feet to the shrouds, working the sails and strengthening the sheets while the storm is rocking the boat more and more. "Stop! Man overboard!" They lower a lifeboat. Their heads down, their powerful uncovered necks tense, the dancers row with quick strokes, now bending, now straightening their backs. The storm, however, passes, the rocking gradually subsides, the sky clears, and now the boat is running smoothly again with a fair wind and again, the dancers with their bodies rigid and hands crossed on their chests, finish dancing their merry, lively jig.

Sometimes Sashka would have to play the *lezginka*[18] for the Georgians who were engaged in wine-making on the outskirts of the city. For him there were no unfamiliar dances. As one dancer, wearing a *papakha*[19] and a Circassian coat,[20] moved lightly between the barrels, as if suspended in air, throwing first one hand, then the other behind his head, and his friends clapped in time to the beat and shouted, Sasha could not restrain himself either and would shout in an animated way, "*Khas! Khas! Khas! Khas!*"[21] There were times when he would also play the Moldavian *dzhog*,[22] and the Italian tarantella, and waltzes for the German sailors.

There were times when there were fights in Gambrinus, and pretty brutal ones at that. The old customers loved to tell of a legendary bloody fight between Russian military sailors, transferred to the reserves from some cruiser, and English sailors. They fought with fists, brass knuckles, beer mugs, and even hurled the small barrels used as chairs at each other. It must be said, not to the Russian fighters' honor, that they were first to start the brawl, first to pull out knives, and that it took them a half-hour of fighting to force the Englishmen out of the pub, although they outnumbered them three to one.

Very often Sashka's intervention stopped a quarrel that was on the verge of bloodshed. He would approach, joke, smile, make faces, and immediately glass mugs would be extended to him from all directions.

"Sashka, a small mug! . . . Sashka, with me! . . . Faith, law, troubles, the grave . . ."

Perhaps the meek and humorous goodness which radiated happily from his eyes, hidden under the sloping skull, had an effect on their simple, coarse ways. Perhaps it was a peculiar respect for talent, or something like gratitude? And perhaps this circumstance as well: the majority of the regulars of Gambrinus were in constant debt to Sashka.

In difficult moments of *dekokht*, which in sea and port slang means total lack of money, they turned freely and unfailingly to Sashka for small sums of money or for a small amount of credit at the bar.

They did not pay him back what they owed him, of course—not because of malicious intent but out of forgetfulness; but those very same debtors paid back the loan ten times over when they tipped Sashka to play tunes during their debauchery.

The barmaid would speak to him sometimes. "I'm surprised, Sasha, how you do not begrudge your money."

He objected to what she said with conviction. "But Madam Ivanova. I can't take it with me to the grave. There's enough for me and Belochka. Belinka, my sweet little doggie, come here."

V

At Gambrinus some songs would come into fashion for a period of time.

During the war between the English and the Boers, "The Boer March" enjoyed great popularity (it seems that this was just about the time of the famous fight between the Russian and English sailors). No less than twenty times per night they would force Sashka to play this heroic piece and unfailingly, at its conclusion, they would wave their caps, shout "hurrah," and look askance at those who were indifferent, which at Gambrinus was not always a good sign.

After that came the French-Russian celebrations. The town governor, with a sour expression on his face, allowed the Marseillaise to be played. It was also requested daily, but not as frequently as "The Boer March," and they shouted "hurrah" more feebly and did not wave their caps at all. This happened because, on the one hand, there was nothing in the anthem to which they could relate on an emotional level and, on the other hand, Gambrinus' customers did not sufficiently understand the political importance of the alliance; and there was a third reason—it became apparent that every night it was always the same individuals who requested the Marseillaise and shouted "hurrah."

The "cake walk" tune was fashionable for a short while, and even a small-time merchant who just happened to wander in danced it once among the barrels without taking off his raccoon coat, high galoshes, and fox hat. However, this Negro dance was very soon forgotten.

But then the Great War with Japan began. Gambrinus' customers began to live a more fast-paced life. Newspapers would appear on the small barrels, and in the evenings people would argue about the war. The most peaceful, simple people turned into politicians and strategists, but each of them trembled in the depths of his heart, if not for himself, then for his brother or, which is even more likely, for his close friend; in those days that imperceptible but strong connection which welded people together who shared labor, danger, and the daily presence of death became more clearly apparent.

In the beginning no one doubted that we would be victorious. Sashka got hold of "The Kuropatkin March"[23] somewhere and about twenty evenings in a row he played it with some success. But somehow, one evening, "The Kuropatkin March" was replaced forever by a song brought by the fishermen from Balaklava,[24] "salty Greeks" or *pindos* as they were called here:

> Oh, why were we made into soldiers
> And sent off to a Far Eastern post?
> Are we really to blame for growing,
> Just a little bit taller than most?

From that time on, they did not want to listen to anything else in Gambrinus. For whole evenings on end, only one request would be heard: "Sasha, the one about suffering! The Balaklava song! The one about the reserves!"

They sang and wept and drank twice as much as usual as, by the way, did all of Russia, to a man, at that time. Every evening someone would come to say goodbye, trying to be courageous, strutting around, flinging his cap to the ground, threatening to kill all the Japs by himself and ending up teary-eyed with the song about suffering.

One day Sashka appeared in the pub earlier than usual. The barmaid, after pouring him his first mug, said, as was her wont, "Sasha, play something of your own . . ."

Suddenly his lips twisted into a grimace and the mug started to shake in his hand.

"You know what, Madam Ivanova?" he said perplexed. "They're taking me to be a soldier. To fight in the war."

Madam Ivanova threw up her hands.

"That's impossible, Sasha! You're joking!"

"No," Sashka shook his head dolefully and submissively, "I'm not joking."

"But you're past the age, Sasha. How old are you?"

No one up to now had been interested in this question. Everyone thought that Sashka was as old as the walls, the pub, the marquises, the *khokhols*, the frogs and the colorful King Gambrinus himself who guarded the entrance.

"Forty-six." Sashka thought for a while. "And perhaps forty-nine. I'm an orphan," he answered dolefully.

"Well then, go and explain it to the right person."

"I've already been, Madam Ivanova, I already tried to explain."

"And . . . so?"

"Well, they said to me, 'You dirty Jew, you with the Jewish mug, say anything more and you'll wind up in a bug-infested slammer' . . . And they hit me here."

In the evening the news became common knowledge at Gambrinus and out of sympathy they got Sashka dead-drunk. He tried to make a wry face, to make faces and squint, but sadness and terror emanated from his meek, funny eyes. One burly worker, a boilermaker by trade, suddenly volunteered to go to war in Sashka's place. The obvious stupidity of such a proposal was clear to all, but Sashka became all emotional, teary-eyed, embraced the boilermaker, and right then and there made him a gift of his fiddle. And Belochka he left to the barmaid.

"Madam Ivanova, you look after the dog. Maybe I won't even come back, and you'll have something to remember Sashka by. My little Belinka, my little dog! Look, she's licking herself. Oh you, my poor . . . And I'll ask you another favor, Madam Ivanova. My landlord owes me money, so go get it and send it . . . I'll write the addresses for you. I have a cousin in Gomel, he has a family, and in Zhmerinka, there still lives a widow of my nephew. Every month I . . . Well, we're Jews, we're like that . . . we love our relatives. But I'm an orphan, I'm all alone. Farewell, Madam Ivanova."

"Farewell, Sasha! Let's at least kiss in farewell. So many years . . . And . . . don't be angry—I'll make the sign of the cross over you for your journey."

Sashka's eyes were deeply sad, but he could not stop himself from joking one last time.

"So, Madam Ivanova, I won't kick the bucket because of the Russian cross?"

VI

Gambrinus became dead and empty, as if it were orphaned without Sashka and his fiddle. At one point, as a way of drawing people in, the owner tried to invite a quartet of wandering mandolin players, one of whom was dressed as an Englishman in an operetta—with red sideburns and a glued-on nose, in checkered pantaloons and a collar that went up past his ears—who performed comic couplets and moved his body shamelessly. But the quartet did not have any success whatsoever; on the contrary, people whistled at the mandolin players and threw bits and pieces of frankfurters at them, and the main comic was once beaten by fishermen from Tendrovsk for making disrespectful comments about Sashka.

However, from force of habit, Gambrinus was still visited by sailors and port workers for whom the war did not entail death and suffering. At first, they remembered Sashka every evening:

"Oh, if only Sashka were here now! Without him our hearts are heavy . . ."

"Ye-es . . . Where are you now, dear, kind friend, Sashenka?"

Far away in the fields of Manchuria . . .

Someone would start the new song of the day, then he would grow quiet in embarrassment, and another would suddenly say, "A wound can go straight through you, or you can be stabbed and cut down. And there are those that tear your flesh":

Congratulations to me on the victory
And to you on losing your arm . . .

"Wait, don't whine . . . Madam Ivanova, hasn't there been any news from Sashka? A letter or postcard?"

Madam Ivanova now spent whole evenings reading the newspaper, holding it at arm's length, with her head thrown back, and moving her lips. Belochka lay in her lap and snored peacefully from time to time. The barmaid was far from the energetic captain standing at his post, and her crew wandered around the pub listless and sleepy.

To the question about Sashka's fate she would shake her head slowly.

"I don't know anything . . . There are no letters, and there's nothing in the papers either."

Then she would take off her glasses slowly, put them with the newspaper next to the warm Belochka and, turning away, sob quietly.

Sometimes, turning to the dog, she would say in a plaintive, touching small voice, "Well, Belinka? Well, sweet little dog? Where's our Sasha? Hmm? Where is our master?"

Belochka would lift her delicate face, blink her moist black eyes and howl quietly in the same tone as the barmaid.

"A-ooo . . . A-oof . . . A-oo-oo . . ."

But . . . time smoothes and washes away everything. Balalaika players replaced the mandolin players, the Russian-Little Russian choir with some girls in it replaced the balalaika players and, finally, Lyoshka, the famous accordion player and professional thief, who had decided to mend his ways because he had gotten married, established himself more firmly than the others. He was a familiar face in various taverns and for this reason they put up with him here as well and, besides, they had no choice—business was very bad at Gambrinus.

Months passed, a year passed. Now no one mentioned Sashka except Madam Ivanova, but even she did not weep any more when his name was mentioned. Another year passed. Even the little white dog must have forgotten about Sashka.

But, contrary to Sashka's fears, not only did he not kick the bucket because of the Russian cross, but he was not wounded even once, although he took part in three large battles and once took part in an attack in the front ranks of a battalion as a member of a musical detachment, where he was drafted to play the flute. Near Vafangou,[25] he was taken prisoner and, after the war ended, he was brought on a German steamship to the very same port where his friends worked and led their unruly lives.

News of his arrival traveled like an electric current through all the harbors, piers, docks and workshops . . . In the evening there were so many people in Gambrinus that most of them had to stand, the mugs of beer were passed from hand to hand over people's heads and, although many left that day without paying, Gambrinus had business as never before. The boilermaker brought Sashka his fiddle, wrapped in his wife's kerchief which he drank away right then and there. Somewhere they found Sashka's last accompanist. Lyoshka the accordion player, a vain and self-important man, took offense. "I'm paid by the day, and I have a contract!" he insisted stubbornly. But they simply threw him out the door and probably would have beaten him up if not for Sashka's intervention.

Probably not one of the fatherland's heroes from the war with Japan saw such a heartfelt and boisterous reception as was given Sashka! Strong, gnarled hands grabbed him, lifted him in the air and tossed him several times with such force that they almost banged his head on the ceiling. And their shouts were so deafening that the tongues of flame would go out, and a policeman came to the pub several times and entreated them "to quiet down, because the loud noise could be heard out in the street."

That evening Sashka played every favorite tune and dance of Gambrinus' customers. And he also played Japanese tunes which he had learned as a prisoner, but the audience did not like them. Madam Ivanova, as if she had come to life, again hovered energetically over her captain's bridge, and Belochka sat in Sashka's lap and yelped with happiness. There were times when Sashka would stop playing, and then some simpleminded fisherman, who had just now grasped the miracle of Sashka's return, would suddenly exclaim with naive and joyous amazement, "Fellows, that's really Sashka!"

The rooms at Gambrinus filled with thick, coarse laughter and jolly, ribald language, and they would grab Sashka again, throw him up to the ceiling, yell, drink, toast and pour beer on each other.

Sashka, it seemed, had not changed at all and had not grown any older in his absence; time and hardships affected his appearance just as little as they did the sculpted Gambrinus, the protector and patron king of the pub. But Madam Ivanova, with the sensitivity of a warm-hearted woman, noticed that the expression of terror and suffering, which she had seen at their parting, not only had not disappeared but had become even deeper and more pronounced. Sashka clowned as before, winked and wrinkled his forehead, but Madam Ivanova sensed that he was only pretending.

VII

Everything went back to normal as if there never had been a war or Sashka's captivity in Nagasaki. As before, the fishermen in high fishing boots celebrated a good catch of white sturgeon and gray mullet; as before, the thieves' girlfriends danced and, as before, Sashka played sailor's tunes brought from all harbors of the globe.

But strikingly different, changing, turbulent times were already approaching. One evening, the whole city began to buzz and seethe, as if some alarm had sounded, and the streets became mobbed with people at an unusual hour. Small, white leaflets passed from hand to hand together with a wonderful word, "freedom," which that evening the whole vast, trusting country repeated countless times.

Bright, festive days of elation came, and their glow illuminated even the basement rooms of Gambrinus. Students and workers came, young beautiful girls came. People with burning eyes would climb up on the barrels which had seen so much in their time and speak. Not all the words were comprehensible, but from the fiery hope and great love with which they rang, one's heart palpitated and opened to take them in.

"Sashka, the Marseillaise! H-hit it! The Marseillaise!"

No, this was totally unlike the Marseillaise which the town governor had permitted with the utmost reluctance to be played during the week of French-Russian exuberance. Endless processions with red flags and singing proceeded along the streets. Red ribbons and red flowers stood out brightly on the women. Total strangers would meet and suddenly, smiling brightly, shake each other's hand . . .

But all this joy disappeared in a flash, as if it had been washed away like children's footprints on a beach. Once, a deputy police officer—fat, small, out of breath, goggle-eyed and dark-red like a very ripe tomato—rushed into Gambrinus.

"So, who's the owner here?" he said hoarsely. "Bring me the owner!"

He saw Sashka standing with the fiddle.

"Are you the owner? Silence! What? Do you play anthems? No anthems of any kind!"

"There won't be any anthems any longer, your excellency," Sashka answered calmly.

The policeman turned blue-gray, brought his raised index finger right up to Sashka's nose and wagged it threateningly.

"Not any kind!"

"Very good, your excellency, not any kind."

"I'll teach you—revolution! I'll tea-ea-ch you!"

The deputy police officer flew out of the pub like a bomb and, after he left, everyone began to feel the crushing weight of depression.

And gloom descended upon the whole city. Dark, alarming, loathsome rumors spread. People talked guardedly, afraid of giving themselves away with even a look; they were afraid of their own shadows, they feared their own thoughts. The city, for the first time, thought with horror about the cesspool which churned silently under its feet, there below, by the sea, and into which it had thrown its poisonous waste for so many years. The city boarded up the plate-glass windows of its magnificent stores, began guarding proud monuments with patrols, and positioned artillery in the yards of beautiful homes, just in case. And God's chosen people—long abandoned by their wrathful God of the Bible, but still believing that they had not yet experienced the full measure of his difficult trials—trembled, prayed and wept from horror on the outskirts of the city in small, foul-smelling rooms and drafty attics.

Secret work was being done below, near the sea, on the streets which resembled dark, sticky intestines. The doors of taverns, tea-rooms and cheap rooming houses were wide open the whole night.

A pogrom began in the morning. The people who were once moved by the pure joy shared by all and touched by the light of future brotherhood, who walked the streets singing under the symbols of hard-won freedom, those very same people were now on their way to kill, and they were going not because they had been ordered, and not because they felt enmity against Jews, with whom they often had a close friendship, and not even because of material gain, which was unlikely, but because the dirty, cunning devil living in each man whispered in his ear, "Go. Everything will go unpunished: the forbidden curiosity about murder, and the lust for violence, and the power over another being's life."

During the days of the pogroms, Sashka walked freely about town with his funny, ape-like, completely Jewish physiognomy. He was not touched. He had that unshakable courage of the spirit, that *nonfear of fear* which protected even a weak man better than any Browning. But once, pressing against the wall of a house while trying to get away from the crowd which was pouring down the whole breadth of the street like a hurricane, a stonemason in a red shirt and a white apron swung a chisel over him and bellowed, "Yi-id! Beat the Yid! Let's see some blood!"

But somebody grabbed his hand from behind.

"Stop it, damn you, that's Sashka! You blockhead, you stupid bastard . . ."

The stonemason stopped. At this drunken, crazy, delirium-filled moment he was ready to kill just about anyone—his father, sister, priest, even the Orthodox God himself—but he was also ready like a child to obey the orders of every firm will.

He grinned like an idiot, spit, and wiped his nose on the back of his hand. But suddenly a nervous little white dog, which was shivering and rubbing against Sashka's legs, caught his attention. Quickly bending over it, he caught it by the hind legs, lifted it high, hit its head against the flagstones in the sidewalk and ran off. Sashka looked at him in silence. The man was running all bent forward, with arms outstretched, without a hat, mouth open, and eyes wide-open and white with madness.

The brains from Belochka's head spattered Saskha's boots. Sashka wiped off the spots with his handkerchief.

VIII

Then a strange time followed, resembling the dream of a paralyzed man. In the evening, not a single window in the whole town had a light in it but, on the other hand, the bright signs of the *cafés-chantants*[26] and the windows in the taverns were brightly lit. The victors were testing their power, because they had not yet had their fill of being able to act with impunity. Some lawless people in Manchurian *papakhas,* with St. George Ribbons [27] in their jacket lapels, went from restaurant to restaurant and in an insistent, rudely familiar manner demanded the playing of the national anthem and saw to it that everyone stood up. They also broke into private apartments, searched the beds and rummaged through the dressers, demanded vodka, money and the anthem, and filled the air with drunken burps.

Once ten of them came to Gambrinus and took over two tables. They conducted themselves in a most defiant manner, addressed the waiters imperiously, spit over the shoulders of the people next to them whom they did not know, put their feet up on other people's seats, and poured their beer on the floor on the pretext that it was not fresh. No one touched them. Everyone knew that this was the secret police and looked at them with the concealed horror and squeamish curiosity with which simple folk look at executioners. One of them was clearly the leader. This was a certain Motka Gundosy, red-haired, with a broken nose, who spoke in a nasal voice and, as people said, was "a man of great physical strength"; he was first a thief, then a bouncer in a brothel, then a pimp and a member of the secret police, a Jew who had converted to Christianity.

Sashka was playing "The Snowstorm." Suddenly Gundosy approached him, grabbed his right hand tight and, turning back to the audience, shouted, "The anthem! The national anthem! Brothers, in honor of our beloved monarch . . . The anthem!"

"The anthem! The anthem!" roared the creeps in the *papakhas*.

"The anthem!" a solitary, hesitant voice shouted some distance away.

But Sashka jerked his hand back and said calmly, "No anthems of any kind."

"What?" growled Gundosy. "You dare not obey? Oh you stinking Yid!"

Sashka leaned forward right up to Gundosy and, grimacing and holding his lowered fiddle by the neck, asked, "And you?"

"What about me?"

"I'm a stinking Yid. Well, fine. And you?"

"I'm Orthodox."

"Orthodox? And for how much?"

All of Gambrinus burst into uproarious laughter and Gundosy, white with rage, turned toward his comrades.

"Brothers!" he said, repeating someone else's cliched phrases in a trembling, tearful voice. "Brothers, how long are we going to put up with the outrageous attitude of the Yids towards the throne and the holy church . . . ?"

But Sashka, standing in his raised place, with one sound forced him to turn around and face him, and no customer of Gambrinus would have ever believed that this funny Sashka, who liked to clown around, could speak so powerfully and with such authority.

"You!" shouted Sashka. "You son of a bitch! Show me your face, you murderer . . . Look at me . . . ! Well . . . ?"

Everything happened quickly, in an instant. Sashka's fiddle was raised high and flashed quickly in the air and—bang!—the tall man in the *papakha* staggered from a ringing blow to his temple. The fiddle was smashed to pieces. Only the neck, which he triumphantly raised over the heads of the crowd, remained in Sashka's hands.

"Brothers-s, come he-e-lp me!" Gundosy yelled out.

But it was already too late to help him. A mighty wall of people surrounded Sashka and protected him. And the same wall carried the people in the *papakhas* out on the street.

But an hour later, when Sashka had finished his work and was walking out of the pub to the sidewalk, several men jumped him. One of them hit Sashka in the eye, whistled for help, and said to the policeman who came running, "To the Boulevard station. A political case. Here's my badge."

IX

Now Sashka was considered buried for the second and final time. Someone saw the whole thing that took place on the sidewalk by the pub and told others. At Gambrinus worldly-wise people met and talked— people who knew what kind of an establishment the Boulevard station was and what vengeance on the part of the secret police could mean.

But this time around they worried much less about Sashka's fate and forgot about him much more quickly. In two months a new fiddler (and Sashka's pupil, by the way), found by the accompanist, was sitting in Sashka's place.

And then one day, about three months later, on a quiet spring evening, just when the musicians were playing the "Anticipation" waltz, a high, frightened voice exclaimed, "Hey fellows, it's Sashka!"

Everyone turned around and got up from his small barrel. Yes, it was him, the twice-resurrected Sashka, but now he had an overgrown beard and was emaciated and pale. People rushed to him, surrounded him, squeezed him, pressed him, and thrust mugs of beer in his hands. But suddenly the same voice shouted, "Brothers, his arm . . . !"

Suddenly everyone grew silent. Sashka's left arm, which was crooked and deformed, had been twisted so that the elbow now lay against his side. The arm apparently could neither be bent nor straightened, and his fingers were permanently fixed at his chin.

"What's the matter with you, my friend?" a hairy boatswain from "The Russian Society" finally asked.

"Oh, nothing . . . just some tendon or something," Sashka answered in a casual way.

"Ah-huh . . ."

Again there was a brief silence.

"So it means no more 'The Shepherd'?" the boatswain asked sympathetically.

"'The Shepherd'?" Sashka repeated and his eyes began to sparkle. "Hey you!" he commanded the accompanist with his usual confidence. "'The Shepherd'! Ein, zwei, drei . . . !"

The piano player began to bang out the fast dance tune, looking back in disbelief. But Sashka took a small, palm-sized, longish black instrument with a protruding part, put the protruding part in his mouth, and bending to the left as much as his mangled, motionless arm would allow, suddenly began to play on the ocarina[28] the deafeningly merry "The Shepherd."

"Ha-ha-ha!" the audience rolled with happy laughter.

"Oh, hell!" the boatswain exclaimed and, much to his own surprise, deftly stepped out and launched into quick small steps. Caught up in his excitement, the customers began to dance, both the men and the women. Even the waiters, trying not to lose their dignity, moved their feet in place and smiled. Even Madam Ivanova, forgetting about her responsibilities as a captain on watch, moved her head in time to the spirited dancing and snapped her fingers lightly. And, perhaps even Gambrinus himself—old, porous, worn down by time—moved his eyebrows from time to time, looking toward the street happily; and it seemed that the simple, pathetic whistle in the hands of Sashka—whose body was maimed and twisted—sang in a language unfortunately not yet comprehensible either to the friends at Gambrinus or to Sashka himself.

No matter! You can maim a human being, but art will survive everything and overcome everything.

1906

NOTES

1. Gambrinus: The invention of hopped malt-beer is attributed by some to Jan Primus of Burgundy (13th century) or to John Sans Peur (14th century), who was also known as Gambrivius. Gambrinus is probably a corruption of the latter. In the late 19th century the image of "King" Gambrinus was a popular symbol for breweries and beer establishments.
2. *khokhol*: either a jocular or pejorative term for a Ukrainian.
3. Little Russians: a term once applied to Ukrainians.
4. *gopak*: Ukrainian folk dance, performed mainly by men, and characterized by high jumps and squat-downs.
5. Belochka means "Little Squirrel." Later in the story the dog is referred to as Belinka, which is derived from *belyi*, meaning "white." In fact, at one point in the story the dog is described as being white. Belinka can be translated as "Whitey," but it would mean eliminating the Belochka or "Little Squirrel" variant. We will keep both Russian names: Belochka and Belinka.
6. Volunteer Fleet: a merchant marine fleet that could also be used to support military operations.
7. Anatolia: also known as Asia Minor, the portion of Turkey south of the Black Sea.
8. Trapezond: a Turkish port on the Black Sea.
9. sixty-six: a two-player card game that was first recorded in 1718 under the name Mariagen-Spiel (German for "marriage game") and played with a reduced deck (24 cards).
10. *shtoss*: the most popular game of chance in the 18th and 19th centuries; called "pharaoh" in Europe and "faro" in America.
11. They are humorously using a command often heard on the docks.
12. German for "one, two, three."
13. Zets-Zets: "Sit, Sit" in German.
14. The speaker mixes Russian and Ukrainian forms and mispronounces words; it is impossible to reproduce this way of speaking in an English translation.
15. What is meant is "cake walk," a dance that was popular at the end of the 19th century which used a syncopated beat. The dance involved couples lined up in a circle and featured exaggerated imitations of traditional European dance rituals plus traditional African dance steps.
16. They mispronounce the word *zdrast* (hello) by adding a semi-vowel, i.e., *zdraist*.
17. Kuprin's version is somewhat different from the wording in the actual song, which is "Britons never shall be slaves."
18. *lezginka*: the national dance of many groups in the Caucasus, danced by men at a lively tempo.
19. *papakha*: a tall Cossack fur hat.

20. Circassian coat: a long, narrow, collarless coat worn by men in the Caucasus.

21. *Khas! Khas!*: "Good! Good!" or "Yeah! Yeah!" in Yiddish.

22. *dzhog*: a promenade dance.

23. Kuropatkin March: Aleksei Kuropatkin was the Russian Imperial Minister of War (1898-1904). He held a number of high military appointments during the Russo-Japanese war, and was held responsible for several major defeats.

24. Balaklava: a section of the city of Sevastopol in the Crimea in what is today southern Ukraine.

25. Vafangou: during the Russo-Japanese war, the site of a large battle in 1904 in which the Russian army was defeated.

26. *café-chantant*: a coffee-house where popular songs are performed.

27. St. George Ribbon: awarded for valor in Imperial Russia.

28. ocarina: a simple wind instrument typically having an oval body with finger holes and a projecting mouthpiece.

THE LITTLE DEVIL

Aleksei Remizov

First Chapter

The Divilin house by the river. Old, grey, with peeling paint. Every dog knows it.

The door of the house, with steps leading up to it, is narrow, grey and solid—there isn't a chink or crack visible—and no key hole of any kind in sight. You can knock all you want at night. And who should come knocking at night? A thief perhaps? It's of no use to a thief, we must assume; a thief can get in even without a doorway, that's why he's a thief. And if something happens, or there's some urgent need . . . Well, please don't be too hard on me—a door bell is simply not to be found.

At one time there was a note on the door: *entrance through the window.*

Perhaps this was a roguish joke, or perhaps it had to be that way because of some changes to the house; in fact, about this time some house painters were hanging about. But this doesn't make it any easier. Just you push, try! The window is way up there and, no matter how much you jump, you won't be able to reach it, you'll only strain yourself. If you could do it from a post or a street lamp . . . But the post, as luck would have it, is bent because a drayman was once going past, started gaping at something and brushed against it; the post was damaged and has been bent ever since. And when it comes to the street lamp, it's no particular joy either. If it had been just a little bit closer, but look how he banged into it: it's slanting completely toward the river. By the time you climb up and get situated . . . oh, it's not worth climbing up, it's futile! Well, it's impossible to get near the house from the street.

What if you were to jump across the fence from the embankment? Across the fence—the spikes are an obstacle; every other one will be thicker than a finger, just like this, and as for sharpness, a needle is duller. You won't be able to get the better of it, brother!

If you were to get through the gate . . . if you do get through the gate, in the yard right in front of you there'll be a huge shed; at some point the shed was used for a drayman's coach, but now only the smell of horses and manure is left, and even that is fading away. If you make your way safely to the shed, turn to the left and walk straight toward the dog's kennel; there's no dog in the kennel—there was one, its name was Belka, but it died—and so there's no dog to even do some barking. And from the kennel turn left again and you'll come upon a door. The door is covered with dirty oilcloth and has a wooden latch. When it comes to opening it, you'll open it without any difficulty, of course, it takes no particular skill, and then you'll walk down a hallway and, after stumbling to your heart's content, you'll come up against another door. Here's where you wait! Until your patience breaks, because it makes no sense; you'll spit and go.

That's how the people inside have shut themselves up!

The street is narrow and empty; in the morning the water carrier, in the evening seasonal workers—that's all the activity there is.

Yet people live in the house. But what goes on in the house, not a single soul knows.

Second Chapter

Old man Divilin was held in high regard; he appeared to be God's fool, a holy fool. Although he lived as a recluse, every so often he'd show himself. The old man went by the nickname of "drowned man." Somehow shortly after his wedding, on Epiphany, he fell into an ice-hole and drowned. They began looking for him, caught him on a boat-hook, and with this boat-hook dragged him out; then they picked him up and got the water out of him. And from that time it started: "drowned man, drowned man." And that's the whole story. And from that time it started that he began to drink a lot. If a difficult time comes, immediately all his clothing comes off and onto the floor, and in his birthday suit, right out onto the street. Be there rain or slush or hard frost or a blizzard, go on by and pay no attention. And everyone at that point looked like *crayfish* to him and he, it seemed, was the head crayfish, something like the crayfish mother. The old man would stretch out his arms, open his fingers wide like claws and try to catch someone. No matter who'd come his way, he'd catch him. He would go directly to the market and the first thing he would do is get hold of some horses. He beats the animals soundly with his fists, strikes them in the face until he has no strength left, and then he calms down, right then and there near some stall. And he lies under bast matting without moving, like a dead man, with his eyes open, big eyes without the whites showing, goggle-eyed, crayfish-like, and he himself is all red like a boiled crayfish. But after some time, he comes to, gets up, and begins muttering and carrying on. Just listen! Now the women don't give him a moment's peace. It so happened that no matter what he'd say, everything would turn out exactly as he had said it would. He never deceived. Such was his gift, it seems. The man enjoyed great respect; it's rare for a man to have such great respect from others. But he didn't give a damn, he didn't need it. The old man wanted something else.

Just like in a monastery, the old woman Agrafena won't even stick her head out the door; she never leaves the house. And anyone who saw her wouldn't say that she was an old woman: about forty, no more, and that may be too much, and being of that age doesn't mean you're old, you can still move about; another one in her place is so lithe and nimble that even a young woman would envy her. In a white scarf, she's all limpid and still as if she doesn't have any bones or is a seedless pear. She's quiet, won't smile. And she always looks the same—she neither ages nor does she get any younger. And there was a time before her marriage when she really carried on, when she did all kinds of strange, crazy things. So affectionate: she'd caress and warm everyone, and from somewhere such words would come out that she'd take possession of the person's soul, and the words would enter the soul and extinguish any kind of hell within. Any old man would love to have the knowledge she had. She'd begin questioning someone or offering that person some advice at a difficult time, and you'd listen spellbound. Her eyes were blue, her hair like flax. Not just the average man, but even a monk wouldn't be able to resist her. And so it happened that she fell head over heels in love with Ivan, the drowned man, but Ivan couldn't have cared less; what's worse, he didn't know himself why she disgusted him alone. And then it happened. She caught Ivan, got what she wanted, but not without some special help.

Here's how it happened. For a long time Agrafena had been planning something wicked—to cast a love spell. She was just waiting for Easter.

On the first day of Easter after the liturgy, when the priest came out with the holy water, she noted the *paskha*[1] on which the first drops of holy water had fallen, pinched some off, and hid it on her person. She did the same thing with the blessed Easter bread on which the holy water had fallen first. She tied the blessed Easter bread and the *paskha* in a bit of cloth, hung it around her neck, and wore it like that until the new moon. When the new moon appeared in the sky, she went to an out-of-the way place, faced the moon, took off her golden cross[2] for the moon, and began to chant an incantation—to cast a love spell.

The spell went something like this: The new moon sees everything, the new moon knows everything and sees and knows who's kissing whom. And she, Agrafena, and Ivan are kissing. And may they kiss and exchange caresses for all eternity, like a male dove with a female dove! She's riding on a young donkey, using a snake to drive the donkey, and appealing to the moon with the blessed Easter bread and the *paskha*. And now Ivan doesn't turn away, doesn't say one bad word to her. And thus for all eternity, may he not say a bad word, but always be affectionate with her.

Agrafena removed the bit of cloth from around her neck, took out the blessed Easter bread and the *paskha* and ate them, but saved a few crumbs. She ran to Ivan's house on some pretext and, without anyone noticing, threw the crumbs into his tea. She waited till he drank the tea and then went home.

Ivan lost his mind; now he couldn't live without her. And she became frightened. She sees things aren't good, she can no longer live as she had before; she's drawn somewhere, and such thoughts come to her that her blood runs cold in her veins. All this transpires so imperceptibly, so naturally, as if it's all a joke. And she senses an unusual strength in herself and feels that, were she to desire the most unbelievable thing in the world, it would immediately come true. And now she's afraid to want anything, she's afraid to think . . . She got the cross again, put it around her neck, began to fast, did absolutely everything that's called for. And calmed down. As though her life had come to a sudden end. As if the devil had crushed her. As if the devil had spit on her and left her forever, left her to live in this world in peace, in silence, without merriment, without joy, without a single smile even for an instant. And she lived serenely, never complaining. Where had everything disappeared to? She can't understand it herself. And was there really anything? She doesn't remember a thing. It's as if she had been born like that, as if she had never enjoyed herself in all her born days, never felt joy, never smiled even once. She prays and sighs, prays and sighs. What is she praying for? For her sins. But what sins?

Third Chapter

Children were born often to the Divilins. And they would die. A strong little one is born, lives about a year, even begins walking and talking, and then suddenly, without rhyme or reason, stretches out its little legs and gives up its soul to God. Out of all of them, just two lived—two boys.

The older one, Boris, had a great inclination for learning. He covered his part of the house with books. Not talkative, he'd sit and read all the time, and you couldn't distract him with anything, neither with sweets nor games. He finished the gymnasium and started the university.

The old man was passionately fond of Boris. He didn't deny him anything. He kept wishing that he'd become a doctor.

When it was quiet, when there was no hard drinking, the old man would come and sit down quietly by his son's side and ask him all kinds of questions: how did the world begin, where did the earth come from, where did man and all the beasts come from, and why did everything happen the way it did, and would there be an end to this, and would something else come to be, and what would this other be like, and why are there all the misfortunes and pain and passions on earth, and why does death come and people get born, and why is his heart shriveling . . . ?

Did the old man understand what his son was telling him from books, and did the son understand what the old man was asking him?

The old man kept pulling his thin, black beard; he'd put his claw-like fingers in it and shake his head. And just as quietly as he had walked in, he'd head back to his part of the house and there, quite often, in the dark and with only a tiny light from the icon-lamp, he'd spend whole nights walking back and forth and muttering to himself; and sticking his fingers in his thin black beard, he'd nod his head and stand absolutely still, his crayfish eyes open wide without the whites showing. He'd stand for a long time, all of him like a rock. And once again he would quietly make his way to his son's room and, if he found him with his books, he'd sit down quietly, look at him, and the deep crease between his eyebrows would look darker than any deep well.

Why does death come, and why are people born, and why is his heart shriveling?

Boris got married early. A young nun from their monastery, Glafira, kept coming to the Divilin house to visit Agrafena, the mother. And so it's Glafira he married. A daughter, Antonina, was born to them. And soon one of the darkest of stories took place in the house. One night a black carriage drove up to the house. Some people got out of the carriage. They entered the house. They took Boris. Put him in the carriage with them. The carriage drove off. Boris left in it. And never returned again. Boris never returned home again. And so he disappeared—not a word was heard of him again. Twelve years have passed since that time, and there's still no news whatsoever; and no matter how much people racked their brains, they came to no conclusion and could say nothing in answer to how, what, and why? It's been twelve years since the old man died and since Boris disappeared, and God only knows if he'll ever come back.

The old man died of grief. From the day they took Boris away, he no longer went to bed; he couldn't sleep any more. The old man would spend all his nights in Boris's room at his usual place by the desk and, with his elbows resting on the desk, look at the place where Boris used to sit with his books.

Why does death come, and why are people born, and why is his heart shriveling, the old man would mutter.

And so he died.

It was a few months later, after his death, that Agrafena gave birth to her last child. The boy was christened Denis in memory of his grandfather. Neither the death of the old man, nor what happened to her son disturbed her quiet, uneventful existence from one day to the next. Only once did her blue eyes flare up with blue fire. Only once, and then they went out. Serene, never complaining. She prays and sighs. Prays and sighs. What is she praying for? For her sins. But what sins?

Fourth Chapter

The whole house and all of the Divilin housekeeping was in the hands of the daughter-in-law, Glafira. And Glafira ran everything her own way.

Dry like a piece of kindling, thin like a match, without a drop of blood, rapacious and evil like Yaga[3] on a knotty broomstick, a real Yaga. There, in the monastery, she was quiet out of need and meek out of obedience;

here in the empty house—with its rooms, hallways, passageways, nooks and crannies, endless staircases and countless rooms of all kinds— she turned into a totally different person. Glafira married Boris . . . heaven only knows why she married him. Out of love or some other consideration, or simply because it was time . . . Now free, she was free to do everything she wanted. But what is she to do in this empty house except attend to the housekeeping? Nothing. Why nothing?

And Antonina and Deniska would catch it from her. To run around the yard or leave the house to go for a boat ride or go fishing for a while—oh no! Only on big holidays would Yaga take the children and head out on foot to the other end of town, to the monastery behind the city gate. And she would drill them the whole way and correct them at the service—what fun was that? It was worse than the punishment room where Deniska found himself often because of his laziness and pranks.

Deniska is a strapping boy and has an iron chest. During breaks and often during class, he unbuttons his jacket and shows his chest to all the boys. And they all agree, they can't help but agree that his chest is truly made of iron, and if you knock on it, it resounds splendidly. When Deniska had just started the gymnasium, he was greeted with a nickname—his father's: "drowned man." But on that first day he beat up one of the worst troublemakers in the whole gymnasium, and since then they're somewhat afraid of him. An awful lazybones, you can't make him sit with a book. He has only one passion: he loves to draw. The only thing he does is draw faces, teachers, and all kinds of things. His pockets are full of pencils, regular erasers, and *kneadable erasers*. A kneadable eraser comes in handy not only for taking out marks when shading but for pranks as well. A kneadable eraser is something that begs to be taken into the mouth. And the kneadable eraser smells of something pleasant, particularly when it's fresh and peels away easily from its backing of thin, yellow paper. Deniska loved to chew a piece of kneadable eraser; he'd chew and chew, and then even make some figure out of it, either a frog or some other silly thing, and who knows what else, thanks to which the whole class would begin screaming as one and it would become impossible to quiet them down. Then he'd blow a bubble and, when the class had quieted down, he'd take and squeeze the kneadable eraser material so that it would pop. And the bubble would burst, making a snapping sound that would travel through the whole classroom, but there would be no explanation in sight. How many times Deniska sat in the punishment room and went to the gymnasium on Sundays because of that kneadable eraser! You'd lose count if you'd try to count.

For Deniska reading books was the same as bowing during prayer. And the books which the students were issued for home use would bring on such yawning from the first few lines and produce such spasms in him that, before you know it, he'd take those very same books and tear them to pieces. But Deniska knew many different stories and they came his way in different ways; he heard his fill of them, and he also invented them in his head. An old man, the doorman Gerasim, kept an eye on the punishment room in the gymnasium. Deniska would sit and old man Gerasim would sit and check on Deniska through a little window; you can't go anywhere either, you'll be responsible for everything. And so the old man would tell stories out of boredom. And the old man talked about all kinds of things: battles, and the countryside, and sorcerers, and dead men. And once he'd begin telling a fairytale, you could sit forever in the punishment room! That's how he told stories.

Antonina was also a student at the gymnasium. But the previous winter she met with misfortune and they took her out of the gymnasium.

Somehow, when it snowed for the first time, Antonina ate some snow with Deniska. Like water off a duck's back, Deniska escaped with a tickle in his throat, but Antonina took to bed. And so seriously that all hope was lost that she'd ever get up. But nevertheless, she got better, only there was something wrong with her feet; she could step only on one foot, the left, and on tiptoe at that, but her right foot dangled like a tail. The girl had to use crutches. And where her light-colored braid used to be, now just some hairs stuck out and not a trace was left of her braid.

At first Antonina continued attending the gymnasium after her illness. The most mischievous—she was as good a prankster as Deniska— and the most irrepressible in class, she now sat like a hunchback with her head slumped down, her crutches sticking out behind her back like two damned "figs."* Her pale little face would try to make a funny expression, and her lips would become distorted, ready to produce such laughter that it would send the teacher and the blackboard flying across the classroom, but nothing would come out; instead something pitiful, frightening, and agonizing would come out, and you wanted to turn away. The teachers avoided calling on her, and when they did ask her something, she was allowed to answer sitting down. And she used to be someone who couldn't sit still for even a minute! The girl got worn out. And so they took her out of the gymnasium.

And now, from morning till evening, Antonina is in the house under the care of her mother, *Yaga*.

The children didn't like Yaga, just as Antonina didn't like the girls in her classes, just as Deniska didn't like cry-babies, whiners, the quiet ones, tattletales, the principal, and the teachers. But it was just the opposite with the old woman Agrafena. And the children often went to her part of the house. They called her *granny*. And that became the rule: granny, granny.

It's warm in the old woman's room, cozy. The walls are covered with pictures; the pictures are embroidered with silk thread and beads; there are flowers and ferocious beasts, and a monastery, and some Chinese people, and Amazon parrots—some on horses, and swans, castles, and again some Chinese. In the corner there are icons; alongside, sacred objects—small hats, shoes, gloves, ribbons, sashes, crosses, rope belts, and loin cloths—all relics of saints. On the table there are boxes—beaded, and covered with leather, and painted with designs, and crystal. Granny wears a white scarf and won't say a word, as if her mouth is full of water; she only prays and sighs. And what a *prayer rope*[4] granny has! A white prayer-rope, covered with pearls; the triangles have little pearl branches on golden velvet, and the edges and borders are also pearl; and every rung of the prayer rope is composed of a row of pearls.

The children played with the boxes, opened small chests, took out strange, wonderful things, and examined and touched everything again and again. And there was just about everything under the sun there. . . . The old woman, in the meantime, would open one of the cupboards without stopping her praying, take out a plate full of dried apples and pears and plums and grapes from the cupboard and put it on the table before the children.

"Eat the berries, the berries," her pale lips would whisper.

The children would put down the boxes and small chests and start munching away at the fruit on the plate.

"The berries, the berries," the old woman would whisper anemically.

And the plate would be emptied.

"Bye-bye, granny, thank you!" The children would kiss the old woman and go to their children's room.

Fifth Chapter

The children's room is in Boris's part of the house. After the old man's death all of Boris's books went for heat, and not one book was left lying around. Boris's disappearance was attributed to books.

"Everything's because of the books," Yaga would say, "books from the Devil, and to keep filth in the house is only to please him. And then there's the dust."

And there, in the empty room, where before there wasn't a corner that was not covered with books, Antonina would spend all her days. And she would just wait and wait for Deniska. Deniska would return from the gymnasium late; either they'd keep him, or he'd hang around with some boys.

Deniska would tell Antonina frightening and outlandish stories, and Antonina loved to listen to them. She'd ask him herself to tell them to her.

Every story, every tale of bravado, she'd accept with a kind of *suffering* pain. She knew well that her lot was to sit here, just like this, and that there was nothing more for her till her dying day. She'd get irritated and tease Deniska as she listened to his stories and imagined the escapades for which she too had once been ready. Looking up at some spot in the ceiling like a hunchback, she'd laugh as loudly as she could, choking with laughter. And her eyes would sparkle with laughter and tears, all of her would jump up a bit, and the crutches behind her would jump up too.

"Denka, dear. Denka, another one . . . !"

But Deniska had just picked up a pencil; he had just lifted his hand to draw a monster.

"Denka, the one about the woodpecker!" Antonina banged with her fist and knitted her eyebrows; she was either about to cry or hit him with a crutch.

And then the tale about the *woodpecker* would begin; Deniska would begin the tale.

The tale is well-known to everyone, how a dog fed and gave drink to a peasant and his wife, and how they drove the dog out of their house because of his old age, and how the dog found himself in such a miserable situation that he might as well lie down and die.

"And the dog got the idea of going out into the open field and feeding on field mice." Deniska sticks out his lips and squints ever so slyly, as if he's catching a mouse himself. "And the dog went into the field, and a woodpecker saw him and took him on as a friend."

And here the dog's adventures begin.

A long tale and cruel. Deniska tells it with fervor, as if the dog's fate and the woodpecker's fate were his own.

The woodpecker fed the dog until he was full and gave him all the water he could drink.

"Now that I've had my fill of food and drink, I want to laugh to my heart's content!" "Fine," answers the woodpecker. And then they saw workers threshing grain. The woodpecker sat on a worker's shoulder and began to peck on the back of his head, and another fellow grabbed a stick, wanted to hit the woodpecker but brought the worker down. And the dog rolls on the ground with laughter, rolls and laughs . . .

And the more cruel the pranks on the dog's part, the more playful Deniska's eyes became.

The dog got what he had been asking for. A peasant was traveling to town to sell pots; the dog got stuck in the spokes of a wheel and here life left it.

"The woodpecker got angry at the peasant," Deniska narrates, "got on the horse's head and began to peck out its eyes. The peasant comes running with a log, wants to kill the woodpecker; he comes running and strikes . . . the horse falls dead right then and there. But the woodpecker slipped away, flew to the wagon, and started running on the pots and beating his wings hard. The peasant goes after the woodpecker and hits the wagon with the log, again and again. He broke all the pots and went home with nothing. And the woodpecker took off for the peasant's hut and got there and flew straight through a window. The wife was building a fire in the stove at the time and a small child was sitting on a bench; the woodpecker landed on its head and started to peck. The wife leaps up and keeps trying to chase it away, but she can't; the woodpecker keeps on pecking. Then she grabbed a stick and brought it down hard; she didn't hit the woodpecker, but she hurt the child, causing its death. The peasant comes back, and he sees that all the windows are broken, all the dishes are broken, and the child is dead. He started to run after the woodpecker, got all scratched up and bruised all over, but caught him in the end. "Kill him," the wife says.

Deniska drew a nose that looked three arshins* long on paper, added little feet, and smacked his lips.

"No," says the peasant, "that's not enough punishment for it. I'll swallow it whole." And he swallowed it.

Antonina's pale face becomes covered with red splotches, a nervous tick appears under one eye, and she begins to laugh loudly.

And the light burns long after midnight in the empty children's room with its empty bookshelves and the two beds, each in its own corner, the long walls totally covered with drawings of faces, noses, and tails. But Yaga, shuffling along in her shoes, packs the children off to bed; however, even in their beds they keep on talking for a long time, bursting out in laughter and squealing like mice.

The steady light of the icon-lamp and the steady ticking of the clock that night whisper and goad them on in the empty house.

Sixth Chapter

The only guest the Divilins had was Pavel Fyodorov, the *cockroach exterminator*.

The children hid from the cockroach man, and the cockroach man disliked the children.

"Unclean,"[i] the cockroach man would say, "devil's seed. Conceived in sin, full of sin, and multiplying sin. Unclean."

Immense quantities of burdock grew in the yard and Deniska, at odd moments, when he could slip away from Yaga without being noticed, would collect the prickly *burrs* from time to time and quietly stick these burrs on the cockroach man in places he absolutely should not have.

If ever there was a striking resemblance between a human face and a dog's snout, it was Pavel Fyodorov's. There probably had never been a greater resemblance. Simply a dog, no question. All overgrown with hair, wiry, toothy, and he didn't have a voice but a muffled bark. A panting dog.

Pavel Fyodorov made the rounds of all the known merchant homes and exterminated cockroaches in them. On his shoulder he carried a black leather bag with white poison in it, and he had a stick with a leather tip in his hand.

He'd cover the tip with lard, take the jar with the white powder

---

i   unclean: belonging to the dark, demonic world, the Devil's domain.

out of his bag, open the lid carefully, and dip the stick in it. Then he'd whisper some spell for cockroaches and set to work. He'd move along a wall where there were cockroaches and slowly press the tip so that the whole wall would become covered with small white circles that looked like *fiery white tongues*. The cockroach man would press the tip slowly so that the circles would be neatly spaced and tastefully arranged. And the cockroaches, no longer afraid of the light, would crawl out for the bait and eat the small white circles; they'd crawl out of their hidden nests, from all the chinks and cracks, with their eggs and small children and eat the small white circles. After eating their fill, they'd crawl away sleepily back to their nests in the chinks and cracks, never to come out again not only in daylight but even at the very height of their whiskered cockroach life—night time.

The cockroach exterminator considered his work big and important. It's as if in the rustling of cockroaches he seemed to see the Devil himself, and to overcome the Devil, to wipe the Devil off the face of this earth, was the cockroach exterminator's first and chief mandate.

And whenever he took a break from his work, he would talk only about the topic foremost on his mind.

"The whole earth is a prisoner of the unclean spirit, everything is penetrated by his nets, and his satanic paws are everywhere. Children— the unclean seed!—are born not for glorifying God, they're born to carry out the Devil's machinations. And the end is already coming, the earth is rotting away because of unclean doings and evil deeds. And the time is already drawing near . . . The Devil and his snares will become manifest because there's no more reason for him to hide. The earth is doomed, the last of the righteous are dying, and the Devil's children are multiplying like sand in the sea. There's no reason for him to hide. He'll ascend to his throne as tsar and judge, he'll begin to rule and judge his slaves from sea to sea, and he'll turn his realm into a hell with eternal fire and worms that never leave the body.

The cockroach man had never seen the Devil face to face. But were the Devil to stand before him, the cockroach man wouldn't have been afraid to enter into a struggle with him.

After exterminating the cockroaches, Pavel Fyodorov would close his jar, put it away in his bag, hang the bag on his shoulder, and then tend to his stick; he'd wash the tip in three separate batches of boiling water, wipe it with a dry rag, put the stick in the hallway, and then, splashing and snorting, he'd wash his hands and beard and under his beard, whisper another spell to release him from his cockroach work and, after saying a prayer, he'd sit down at the table to drink tea with plum jam.

God forbid that the preserves had not been prepared the way the cockroach man liked them.

He wouldn't sit down at the table and he'd rebuke you.

"First cut the plums in half, sprinkle them with sugar, and put the frying pan in the stove for the night, and in the morning take it out of the stove and start cooking. Then one plum will stay separate from another, like one cockroach from another."

The cockroach man would then take his stick, throw on his hat, and leave. And you could beg him and beg him, but he wouldn't return for anything.

But if everything was done exactly to his liking, then the conversation would begin about the main thing.

And the owners of the house would pour out their hearts, going over all the troubles and misfortunes of family life.

"Everything is unclean," the cockroach exterminator would bark, "everything's unclean."

And no matter where he came, what he heard, whom he saw, everything smelled unclean to him, everything had a foul smell—everywhere he seemed to see the Devil.

But he never saw the Devil face to face. And if the Devil had appeared before him, the cockroach man wouldn't have been frightened of him, and he believed, truly believed, that he would be able to defeat him.

If the Devil had appeared before him!

Pavel Fyodorov's life passed in exterminating cockroaches. So, unless it had to do with work, he didn't go anywhere except to the Divilins. And then only sometimes—this happened no more than five or six times a year. He'd take off his bag with the white poison and toss his stick with the leather point to land wherever it might.

It would happen completely unexpectedly. His sternness and gloominess would suddenly reach some final limit. He'd begin to tremble all over, his eyes would cloud over, and he'd grin. A kind of dog's howling would begin to rise in his throat and, if one had chained him at that time, he'd have begun howling like a dog. He'd close all doors, pull the curtains over the windows, rummage in all the corners of the room, and look under the bed—something would be pulling him. He'd feel hollow objects, take out cups and glasses, and remove the glass chimneys of lamps; something would be pulling him, his soul would be on fire, his heart would beat hard, and his insides would feel as if they were being turned inside out.

With his teeth chattering as in a fever, the cockroach man would finally run out of the room and, shrouded in darkness, go with a numb, heavy head, feeling something pressing on his brain as if a solid layer of some kind of bark were lying on it. Blindly, the cockroach man would make his way to the menagerie. There, in the menagerie, he would wander from cage to cage, from the rabbit to the sea-cow, from the monkey to the elephant. Then, when it was getting dark, just as silently and blindly he'd leave the menagerie and make his way to the main street, where undisguised night life was already beginning. He'd walk along more and more tense and agitated, looking straight ahead, without yielding the way, without stepping aside, without making way for anyone—forcing his way through. And if the devil had prompted someone to stop him, one couldn't be certain that he wouldn't have strangled that person, or if he had a knife, that he wouldn't have killed the scoundrel. And so he'd walk more and more slowly until he'd freeze in place; then the first woman he'd meet would be doomed. He wouldn't lead but pull her and drag her to a room in a hotel or elsewhere. There he'd fall upon her— throw a bone to a hungry dog and see how it will go for it . . ! Or a fish with its bones and skin and insides . . . Breathing heavily and noisily, with its stomach growling, the dog will tear, gnaw and chew noisily, devouring the tasty, foul meat—including the bones, skin, and insides. And there was something frightening and dizzying in all of this, and it would continue whole hours on end, the whole night.

Silently, without looking, the cockroach man would leave behind not a human being, not a woman; silently, without looking, the cockroach man would leave her corpse and go home to fall sound asleep and, after getting enough sleep, to begin his usual life and work—exterminating cockroaches.

Seventh Chapter

The adventures of the cockroach exterminator remained a deep secret. Like puzzling stories, they would surface every so often, but no one would have believed that all this was his work. Everyone considered the cockroach man to be an unusual and complicated man, but for him to do such a thing . . . it wouldn't have even occurred to anyone.

The cockroach man was on everyone's tongue. Recently people became more than a bit interested in his visits to the Divilins. He won't cross anyone's threshold if there's no work there, but as for the Divilins—it's just the opposite—every Saturday without fail. But the house is in a remote location, you can't get near it, and there's no way of finding out what he does there. But everyone was very curious to find out what he really did there.

Some laughed: "Everyone has long since died in that house, there's not a single drudge left in there, and instead of people there are lots of cockroaches, and it's with these cockroaches that the cockroach man keeps company. That's the kind of clever, sneaky guy he is!"

"But Deniska?" people objected to the joker's words. "The boy goes to the gymnasium every day!"

No, this was no time for joking; you can't get rid of such questions with just jokes. And conjectures began to be made. They would remember the old man himself, the drowned man. There couldn't be any discussion without bringing in the drowned man.

They would say: "The drowned man had no intention of dying, the drowned man is alive and living in total seclusion, and he keeps company only with the cockroach man."

They would say, "The cockroach man and the Divilin women want to declare a new faith."

And others would say: "The cockroach exterminator can't make any new faith, all faiths have been already made, and he's simply living with the Divilin women: with Glafira as her lover, and with the old woman by deceiving her like a small child."

"Oh, he's not a human being at all," the cunning ones would note. "Man hasn't been given power over creatures, yet the cockroaches obey him!"

"A cockroach isn't a cow," some buttinsky would break into the conversation. "Whether it's a cow or horse or sheep or ram or some other kind of animal, all of them have been blessed by God to serve man, but the cockroaches aren't subject to man's will—nothing is said anywhere about cockroaches and mice."

There were women, women who assured people that they saw the cockroach man turning into a cockroach with their own eyes, and later heard him with their own ears grunting like a pig.

"What does a pig have to do with it?" a quick-witted man quieted the quick-witted women. "It's not a question of a pig, a pig has nothing to do with it, but where did the drowned man's older son, Boris, disappear to?"

"It's because of his books."

"Of course, because of his books. But what kind of books? You won't perish because of a simple book—he was reading the black book."[5]

"And how did he get it?"

"From the drowned man."

"And where did the drowned man get it?"

"Well, that's why a drowned man is what he is."[6]

"There isn't any black book."

"What do you mean, there isn't?!"

"Well, very simply, there just isn't."

"There isn't, you say, and so in your opinion there's no God as well?"

And if not for Fedosy, they would have given the poor man a thrashing he wouldn't have forgotten till the following spring.

Fedosy is wise; you can't get a word out of him, but if he does begin talking, he's never at a loss for words.

"There is a black book," Fedosy said clearly and distinctly, and everyone held his tongue. "The Serpent wrote the black book, from the Serpent it passed to Cain, from Cain to Ham. And when the flood came, Ham hid the book in a rock. And when the flood ended, Ham left the ark, went to the rock, pushed the rock aside, took out the book, and passed it on to his son Canaan. And the book went from son to son in the Ham line. And the sons of Ham decided to have a good laugh at God's expense, just as Ham the father had had a good laugh at his father's, Noah's, expense. The sons of Ham got the idea of building a great tower with *seven winding terraces* to unite what had been separated by God—the earth and the sky. But God got angry, confused the tongues, scattered the people over the face of the earth, and the book wound up in Sodom. And there wasn't a crime that the accursed city didn't commit. The accursed city fell, its sins and evil-doings vanished, but the accursed lake wouldn't take the book and fire wouldn't burn it. The book fell into the hands of Tsar Nebuchadnezzer. And all kinds of lawlessness went on. And all kinds of lawlessness went on for forty-two human centuries until all the kingdoms were destroyed and the book wound up at the bottom of the sea. There, under the burning Alatyr[7] rock, the book lay who knows how long. And then an Arab was taken as a prisoner for his great sins by a just tsar and confined in a copper tower. But the Devil took a liking to the Arab and taught the Arab how to get the book. The just city was burned with sorcerer's magic, the just tsar perished with his whole Christian army, and that same Arab came out of the copper tower, descended to the bottom of the sea, and got the black book from the sea bottom. And it began to travel around the whole wide world, to pass from hand to hand, until it got enclosed in the walls of the Sukharev Tower.[8] It's been there until now, and there hasn't been anyone who could get it from within the walls of the Sukharev Tower. There's an awful curse connected with it for nine thousand years plus a thousand."

"And how did he get into the wall? You can't get near that thing without some special preparation."

"But that's what a drowned man is for, oh you, big brain!"

"And he's not a drowned man at all but a cockroach man."

"Of course, a cockroach man!" they raised their voices all at the same time.

"Enough of this whole thing," a sensible man stepped in. "What puzzle are you trying to solve when everything's clear as day? The Divilins, thank God, are not *shchepotniks*.[9] They respect the law and have to have church services. You can't live like a dog, after all, and so the cockroach man goes to conduct services for them and nothing more."

"The women are very suspicious . . . ," someone expressed his doubts.

"He keeps harping, 'women, women,' but he's worse than a woman himself!"

"Old woman Agrafena, they say, had dealings with the unclean one, and the older boy who went missing was hers from the devil, and in fact that Glafira of theirs is a real Yaga."

"And what's the reason for the drowned man's granddaughter, Antonina, to sit and not use her legs? No, something's not right here."

And the guessing would begin again. Tongues would wag like crazy. And they would quarrel and engage in fistfights and then make up. Totally inappropriate things were dragged in as well. In fact, totally inappropriate.

There was one man of their mind-set who not only read books but even wrote some things having to do with the divine. People went and questioned him, but they didn't find out anything, only got more confused. That man used such words that they shook in their boots and their beards curled up to their noses.

"Maybe—but our Misha didn't start earning his living by doing cockroach work!" they decided without solving the baffling question.

There were even such sticklers for detail that they started to keep track of who came to the Divilins, but they didn't see anyone except the cockroach exterminator.

And they all agreed on one thing: something odd was going on in the house. And with the passing of time no one had any doubt anymore that the house was unclean.

But not a soul knew what was going on in the house.

Every Saturday the cockroach exterminator, Pavel Fyodorov, came to the Divilins. Everyone would gather in the icon room. Pavel Fyodorov would put on his vestments and the service would begin. The service would go on for a long time. And when the vespers ended, Glafira would take the exhausted Antonina to the children's room, almost carrying her, while Deniska would be sent off to bed with a few slaps. Sunday morning they'd celebrate the Divine Liturgy. They would have dinner after the service. And the cockroach exterminator would head home.

And that's all there was.

Thus it was in the years when the old man was alive. Thus it was even now, after his death. Then, the drowned man served as the priest and the cockroach exterminator as the deacon; now the cockroach exterminator was the priest, and Glafira-Yaga now stood in for the deacon.

And that's all there was.

The services were conducted just like they should be, according to church rules and with all the strictness laid down by the church fathers. The cockroach exterminator dragged out the service and spoke and sang through his nose so loudly that the sounds carried through the whole house; it's good that its walls were thick, otherwise he would have disturbed all the fish in the river. The cockroach man had a leather prayer-rope—scarlet leaves with blue and white branches. Yaga's prayer-rope had leaves of black velvet with a thin, blue border and they were all embroidered in gold; they shone in the candle light like little stars.

And that's all there was.

But people . . . people will say anything!

Eighth Chapter

One day after a long night service Deniska was sent to bed. Deniska lay down, but for some reason he didn't feel like sleeping. He kept lying there and lying there, and then called Antonina. Antonina didn't respond; she was breathing heavily and noisily—so worn out was she by all the standing and bowing. There was nothing Deniska could do; he got up, walked around the room a bit, and got it into his head to wander around the house in the dark and, if he got the chance, to scare Yaga. To scare Yaga so that in the future she wouldn't hit him on the back of the head. And having in mind how this could best be managed, Deniska walked out of the children's room, went down the staircase and now wanted to open the door to the hallway which went around the women's part of the house, but the only problem was that the door wouldn't give: the door turned out to be locked. How odd! He walked around. He put his ear to the key hole—couldn't hear anything. He looked in from another angle and again the same story. And so off he went, getting nowhere.

And Deniska tossed and turned for a long time, going over things in his head. Why is the door locked? The door was never locked and nothing could be heard, not even the buzzing of a mosquito. And Deniska dreamt of terrifying robbers all night; the robbers wanted either to swallow him whole or cut off his head—in a word, to do something awful to him. But Deniska was no coward; he bit the chief robber's finger and woke up.

"This matter must be looked into. It can't be left like that!" Deniska made up his mind and, after working things out with Antonina, the following Saturday he pretended to be sick. He scratched and fidgeted, and coughed to clear his throat, and rubbed his eyes, and complained that his hand had gotten numb and all his unmentionable places were getting dry, and in his head—somewhere in his very brain—there was an awful itch, and there was such ringing in his ears that it was even louder than the ringing of the bells by Ivan the Great.[10] They didn't disturb him for the vespers, of course. How could you disturb a child who had one foot in the grave?

And when the service began, Deniska leapt out of bed and ran as fast as he could into the hallway and pocketed a key from one door. He returned to the children's room, lay down, and just stayed there. The service ended and Yaga brought back Antonina, but Deniska tossed and turned in bed as if he had a raging fever, made "fig"* gestures with his fingers, and stuck out his tongue. Yaga left the door ajar, lingered a bit on the landing in front of the children's room, and then went downstairs. And everything in the house grew quiet.

Deniska bided his time and then ran out quietly into the hallway and towards the door. He thought to himself that now he'd see everything, and he rubbed his hands with glee. But no, not here—he gave a push, but the door wouldn't open; it was blocked. Deniska examined everything carefully, forced the door open somewhat by pressing his chest against it, and then he thrust himself through the small opening. And he went on. He passed the dining room, passed the room with the cupboard, and glanced into the side rooms—there was nothing, it was dark; he skirted Yaga's room, the small chapel, and the icon-room. He put his ear to the icon-room door and heard the cockroach man repeating something over and over again, but what he was repeating, you couldn't understand a word. He's repeating something again and again. And again it's quiet. And again he repeats something over and over, like a woodpecker. Deniska waited a little bit, listened, and was about to leave when a huge foot came out of nowhere, pinned him down with its boot, and stepped on him. It was a good thing Deniska had an iron chest, otherwise there would have been some fluid—the shoe would have crushed him for sure. Deniska curled up into a small ball, closed his eyes and, crawling and rolling on the floor, he made it to the door and then squeezed through the small door opening and ran into the hall and up the stairs to the children's room, collapsing on the bed. And the cockroach man is repeating something over and over, over and over in his ears.

What kind of strange things are going on? Deniska and Antonina racked their brains for a long time. Deniska tried to approach granny and pestered the old woman with this question and that, but the old woman wouldn't utter so much as a word. She just prays and sighs, prays and sighs. What is she praying for? For her sins. But what sins?

Ninth Chapter

After circulating here and there, rumors that something was not right about the Divilin house reached even the gymnasium.

The geography teacher, nicknamed *Wood-louse*, asked Deniska ostensibly by chance,

"Hey, you, Divilin, is it? What are these devils they're summoning in your house?"

Deniska stuck out his tongue at Wood-louse.

Wood-louse flew into a rage; he forced Deniska to stand a good hour without moving, and he himself stood opposite Deniska and watched him without taking his eyes off him. And Deniska, with his iron chest puffed out, stood the whole hour not only without moving but without blinking even once. Not because he was afraid of Wood-louse and obeyed him, but simply out of stubbornness and bravado.

"Like hell you'll break me . . . no way!" Every muscle froze on his delicate child's face.

But it didn't end with Wood-louse. Deniska was called to the principal's office. When a student was called to the principal's office, it meant that it had already been decided to expel him from the gymnasium. Deniska went with this in mind.

The principal wore out Deniska by keeping him a long time. Deniska stood and kept looking at the principal. The principal's shaven lip would curl up, revealing a wolf's fang, and then he'd keep biting it.

"What do your parents do?" the principal asked without looking at him.

"My father's dead," Deniska answered.

"What are your parents doing at the present time?"

"Chopping cabbage."

The principal squinted.

"I'm not asking you about cabbage . . . ," the principal said and began to tap his finger.

Deniska kept silent.

"You'll do some studying for me here, you insolent boy!" the principal's finger now threatened, and the sharp stone in his ring sparkled and poked Deniska right in the eye. "Stay after classes!"

Deniska fell into thought even more than before. He had opened the door to the hallway with the hidden key, gotten through to the icon-room, listened hard and heard the cockroach man repeating something over and over, and that was all.

At this point, to make matters worse, stories started circulating in the gymnasium, such stories, but it was now impossible for him to continue his observations. Many a Saturday Deniska had to stand in the punishment room.

And all this because of some nonsense.

Once during a long break, while running past the schoolmaster, Deniska bumped into him and shouted, "Leonid Frantsevich, which of my ears is ringing?"

"The left one," the schoolmaster answered without thinking and suddenly turned red because Deniska had stunned him with his unexpected, outrageous, and simply impossible question.

And because of this very question and, more likely, because the schoolmaster had responded to his outrageous question, he was punished severely. Deniska spent his time in the punishment room not sitting but standing. He stood straight as a pillar, as the principal had ordered, hands at his side, his head *so*. And the old man and doorkeeper Gerasim, knitting his grey soldier's eyebrows, also stood and kept an eye on him through the little window as if a shotgun were being held over him. Deniska stood and wondered himself: what was going on in their house? Everyone was asking, and everyone wanted to know, but not only didn't he know anything, he couldn't find out anything.

And returning late in the evening from the punishment room and not making it home in time for dinner, Deniska, worn out by a long night service, talked a long time with Antonina and kept trying to figure out one thing: the house, what misfortune had befallen their house?

Antonina said at one point, "Perhaps they're making babies there . . ."

"Children aren't made that way," Deniska answered seriously, "you don't understand a thing about it."

"Well, then, what else can they be doing?" Antonina corrected herself. "There aren't any cards in the house. The cockroach man took them away."

"I don't like that dog. He's such a dog!" Deniska snapped.

"And in your opinion, granny . . . ," drawing out her words and thinking of something, Antonina changed the direction of their conversation.

"Granny is crazy."

"It's a sin to talk like that—she's your mother."

"Who?"

"Granny."

"And your mother is Yaga."

Antonina didn't answer, just knitted her brows.

"Yaga says your father supposedly disappeared because of books. Of course Yaga would think that . . . Books make teachers out of people."

"I don't like the cockroach man either," Antonina said.

"You know, Antonina, I've an idea. I'll climb in the window."

"You can't see through the window," Antonina shook her head.

"Then here's what . . . I . . . dear Antoninka! I'll bore a hole in the icon-room like this, a small hole."

The girl's eyes flashed. "And you'll see everything."

"Of course, I'll see, and how!"

"And you'll tell me?"

They struck a bargain.

But in the house precautionary steps were being taken. Perhaps the rumors in town, perhaps some other suspicions, or perhaps their hearts told them something; now not only on Saturday evenings but even at ordinary times all the doors and rooms were locked so that it was impossible, or almost impossible, to get through to the hallway.

Glafira became more and more witchlike and the cockroach man became more and more devil-like. Only the old woman Agrafena kept praying and sighing, praying and sighing, never complaining and always serene.

And nevertheless, one way or another, Deniska managed to steal some minutes under various pretexts to work on boring a hole in the door. He worked on it for weeks, and by one of the Saturdays the hole was ready.

How Deniska managed to stand through the whole night service, God only knows.

And when everything grew quiet, he left the children's room and went downstairs, opened the door with the key, made his way into the small hallway and then through the dining room, the room with the cupboard, and the side room, and straight to the hole.

Antonina couldn't fall asleep as she waited. She waited for a solid hour for Deniska. Twisted thoughts went through her head, repelling ones, not the thoughts of a child but twisted ones, and they taunted and attracted her, and made her hair stand on end, and made the places that ached in her body ache even worse. Minutes dragged on; they too, it seemed, were walking on crutches.

Deniska came running at breakneck speed to the children's room.

"Do you know what they do?"

"What?" Antonina asked in fright.

"They pray."

Antonina started to cry. Her twisted thoughts and the expectation of something frightening and unusual had totally exhausted her.

But Deniska no longer knew any peace. One thought ate away at him. He kept thinking and thinking: how could he spite both the cockroach man and Yaga at the same time? What kind of trick could he invent, what prank could he somehow play on them at prayer?

Evening after evening passed in this way.

He couldn't get anything right. How much paper Deniska used up for nothing! He'd start to draw something and then tear it up.

"They pray," he kept repeating and catching himself, grasping at something, looking for a way to play a hilarious prank. "All three of them stand in a row . . . they kiss . . . that dog and Yaga . . . they pray . . ."

"What are they praying for?"

"They pray. You can only see their mouths open and then the whipping with the prayer-ropes—they whip each other."

Antonina pricked up her ears.

"And what if . . . Antoninka, you know, I've got an idea, Antoninka! This Saturday I'll sneak through to the icon-room . . ." And Deniska shook all over, laughing loudly, and burned with the idea that flashed through his poor head. "Do you understand, Antoninka? Do you understand?" And whispering directly into Antonina's ear, he said something to Antonina, cast a sidelong glance at the door, rubbed his hands in satisfaction and, grabbing a kneadable eraser from the table, began to chew it, working his facial muscles with delight.

Red spots appeared on the girl's pale face, her eyes lit up with laughter and tears, and she suddenly began to laugh loudly and, choking with laughter, laughed as loudly as she could, and she kept bouncing up and down, and the crutches behind her did the same.

"Him?" Deniska winked, taking out of his mouth the kneadable eraser and starting to form a strange figure of a devil out of the eraser.

"Him!" Antonina laughed, her face all covered in tears.

Tenth Chapter

That Saturday happened to be special—it was during Shrovetide. All week they ate far too many pancakes, their stomachs bulged out—what's a mountain in comparison! They couldn't swallow any more pancakes, they couldn't eat another bite, yet they kept eating them. That's why Shrovetide is what it is, not simple but grand.

The service dragged on so long, with such countless and difficult bows that you'd prostrate yourself, and then you couldn't get up. Yaga took Antonina to the children's room because the little girl was simply ready to collapse, but Deniska lingered for some reason and climbed up to fix the icon-lamp before the *Three Joys*. And for some reason he took so long that the cockroach man pulled him off the chair and struck him with his knee. That's how stern and gloomy the cockroach man was that Saturday. Whether it was from the pancakes or because *it* was beginning to affect him—his soul was beginning to burn, his heart to beat hard, and his insides to turn inside out—heaven only knows. And when he sang, and then repeated the prayers in his nasal voice, he grinned and all of him shook as if some evil fever, the most evil of all of Herod's daughters,[11] had taken possession of him. Deniska turned a somersault on the threshold, but the cockroach man picked him up and walloped him so hard that Deniska found himself in an instant right in his bed.

Both Antonina and Deniska pretended to be asleep.

They waited.

Their hearts were beating hard—so hard . . . !

The house is dark and quiet. All the doors are closed and locked. Yaga tries the icon-room key once more.

Praying has begun in the icon room.

He must appear today, the Devil himself must appear, and not in his mysterious form but in his incarnate form. This terrible day is to be their last. They're ready. And let Him appear to them. They'll enter into the struggle. And He'll be defeated.

There are three of them. Three faithful. The world and earth are mired in sin. Sin is growing. With each hour sin is becoming more deeply implanted in the heart, in the heart's roots. But there are three of them. Three faithful in the midst of sin and unbelief. The guardian angel is leaving the earth. With tears and sorrow the angel is flying up to the sky. His censer is empty. There's no incense of prayers and repentance. There are no human deeds pleasing to God. The Devil has triumphed over everything.

But they are ready. And let Him appear to them. They will defeat Him.

And now they make their vows. In the name of God, Christ, and the Holy Spirit. They pledge their love to Them. To God, Christ, and the Holy Spirit.

And they keep vowing that they will give up their lives, they will lose their souls, in order to preserve them.

They are ready. And let Him now appear to them. And they will overcome Him.

They will burst into flames like a bonfire. And with them the earth will burst into flame and all its creatures with it. And the earth and all its creatures will become white and bright like the Lord's raiments are white and bright.

But now they must make their confessions before each other.

Glafira and Agrafena have a grave sin on their souls; at one time they could demonstrate their faith and love of God, but the Devil confused them and shook their faith; they rejected both their faith and love of God in the name of love for man—in the name of *filth*. When the old man died, the cockroach man proposed that they sacrifice Antonina, but Glafira and Agrafena, although they took on the task, couldn't do it.

They made their confessions and repented before one another.

"You told me," Glafira confessed, "that the child I had given birth to was the most beloved thing I had and that to affirm my love of God it must die. You ordered me to give my child to Mother.[12] And I gave her the little girl. And I did as you said and stayed alone in my room. I knew what was going on behind the wall and listened. And I heard my child letting out a squeal. Then everything grew quiet. And I scratched the wall with my nails and my heart was consumed with grief. I couldn't bear it any longer. I didn't obey. I ran into Mother's room, and my little girl, my daughter, was still alive; she was in her arms, and her little mouth was laughing. Then I fell to my knees and begged Mother, 'Mother, don't kill her, let her be!' Lord! Lord! Lord! Forgive me!"

"You ordered me to choke the tiny infant," whispered the old woman Agrafena, "and I took Antonina from my daughter-in-law and carried her here to the icon-room. I put her on my knees and put a noose around her neck, but the child was smiling, the little one found it funny—the noose was tickling its little neck. I pulled the noose tighter, I pulled the rope, and at this point the little girl began to cry, it hurt—ow!—and she started crying bitterly. I loosened the noose, put it on myself as if I were just playing, and the child smiled and laughed so, and clapped her little hands, the little infant, Antoninushka. Forgive me, Lord!"

"And if you had to now?" The cockroach man's eyes froze in fear.

Glafira moved like a beast of prey, her predatory nostrils swelling like a mare's.

> It is fitting that we honor You, the Mother of God,
> The Most Upright and Most Glorious of the heavenly host,
> Virgin Most Pure, Mother of God . . .

The cockroach man began singing and, turning sharply to Glafira, hit her in the face with his leather prayer-rope.

Yaga didn't move, only a streak of bright red blood appeared on her deathly pale face.

"And if we're not worthy of seeing Him?" the cockroach man asked in a whisper. And he suddenly shouted loudly as he stared intently at the red fire in the icon lamp. "With the Living God, the Holy Trinity, and the Mother of God, I entreat You, Satan, to appear here, to appear! Appear! Appear!"

A heavy, unbearable silence tightly enveloped the icon-room. It grabbed you by the throat and choked you.

"It's cold, oh, it's cold!" Yaga screamed and fell in a dead faint; her prayer-rope on the floor sparkled like a star.

The cockroach man, clenching his fists, swept the room with a terrifying look in his eyes. Her whole body bent over, the old woman's blue eyes flared up with blue flame, and it seemed that she was going to throw herself at the cockroach man, sink her teeth into his neck, and drink his blood as the Devil himself would have drunk his blood. The cockroach man suddenly grabbed the white pearl prayer-rope out of her hands and, staggering, trembled from head to foot.

On the icon of the Three Joys, there where the pearl clothing of the Mother of God blends with the little pearl shirt of the infant, by the infant's hands raised in blessing, *a little black devil* was strikingly visible against the white—with his little legs spread wide and moving his fidgety mouse's tail.

And *it* was coming. The cockroach man's time was coming. The curtains and embroidered towels on the icons flowed in long bloody streams before him, and the light in the icon lamp was growing bigger. *It* was coming.

The old woman was smiling . . . Her blue eyes kept flaring up with blue flame.

The cockroach man's teeth were chattering; they were alien to him, cold like ice. His eyes clouded over. He couldn't breathe. *It* was coming faithfully and quickly, drawing ever nearer, rising nearer to his heart, shaking him with all its might as never before either there—at home with the locked door and the hollow objects and glasses, or there—in the menagerie, or there—on the street, or there—in the dirty hotel rooms.

And suddenly it struck and overwhelmed him.

The cockroach man ran up to the icon and, waving and twirling his pearl prayer-rope in the air, he jumped up savagely, and he jumped and jumped, trying to reach her—white, snow white, Most Pure; he ripped off her white vestments and kept lashing and lashing her.

> It is fitting that we honor You, Mother of God,
> The Most Upright and Most Glorious of the heavenly host,
> Virgin Most Pure, Mother of God . . .

And the black little devil is there, on the pearls of the infant that have been left intact, there where the pearl clothing of the Mother of God blends with the little shirt of the infant, because he hooked himself with his tail and seemed to be fidgeting and spreading his little legs wide.

The pearls rolled off like hail, showered the cockroach man, and pricked his eyes. The pearls flew around, bounced on the floor, danced on Yaga, and burned like a blue flame in the old woman's eyes.

And a dull howling of dogs pierced the night, the night and the room, as if thousands of dogs were howling and fighting, grabbing some solitary piece of sweet, *vile* meat from each other.

The old woman was smiling.

Deniska, his head buried in his pillow, was choking with laughter.

"Him!" Deniska squeaked. "I fastened him tightly to the *Three Joys*!"

"To the Three Joys," Antonina repeated with burning lips, pressing her crippled body close to Deniska's iron chest.

And the furious howling from below and some kind of maidenly, blood-wrenching cry, seemingly coming out of the ground, didn't disturb their laughter and didn't trouble the hot and happy embraces of the children.

"Him," Deniska gasped for breath, "black, with little paws and tail."

"And with a little tail," Antonina whispered with her burning lips.

And thus Deniska and Antonina fell asleep.

A deep sleep took over the children's room.

The small faces and tails on the walls slept, the empty shelves slept, the pencils and erasers and fragments of the kneadable eraser left *from the devil figure* slept, just as the impenetrable grey walls of the Divilin house were in a deep, heavy sleep.

And through sleep, it seemed one *nameless being* was guarding the sleep of those sleeping. Who is he? What's his name? Where is he from? And why did he come?

He stood on the landing, opened the door slightly and the boneless one quietly approached the beds on tiptoe.

Antonina and Deniska turned over on their other sides and opened their frightened eyes under the gaze of his huge, piercing eyes, which bored into them with fire.

Just like the Amazon parrot in granny's photo, only his head seemed to be not on a neck but on a screw, turning all the while without finding a place for itself, turning all the while like on a screw. His long, thin lips were repulsive and smiled ever so slightly.

"Him," muttered Deniska.

"Him," repeated Antonina.

And dawn was graying; a gray day was breaking there, outside the window. There, outside the window, was the river, covered with compacted, gray ice. Smoke was rising over the town from warm chimneys. Stoves were being lit very early in the morning for the last day—Forgiveness Sunday.[13]

1906

NOTES

1. *paskha*: Easter dessert. Recipes vary, but this dessert usually calls for pot cheese (farmer's cheese), sugar, butter, heavy cream, vanilla and raisins. It is spread on *kulich* or Easter bread.
2. She is practicing black magic and appealing to the dark forces with which the moon is associated; a cross would anger the devil and nullify her spell.
3. Yaga: refers to Baba Yaga, a witch in Russian folklore tales who is usually malevolent.
4. The prayer-rope or "little ladder" of the Old Believers has 109 knots or rungs. Several triangles, usually richly decorated, hang at the bottom. The rope represents the spiritual ladder one can ascend from earth to heaven through prayer. Old Believers are people who broke away from the Russian Orthodox Church in 1666-1667 because of the church reforms of Patriarch Nikon. They themselves eventually splintered into a multitude of groups, with diverse religious practices.
5. black book: Books of black magic were popular in Russia at the end of the 19th century and the beginning of the 20th as part of the general interest in all things occult.
6. According to Russian folk belief, a person who has drowned belongs to the dark world, to the world of the unclean force.
7. Alatyr: in Russian folklore a magic stone with healing properties, "the father" of all stones. It is guarded by two mythic monsters—a bird and a snake.
8. Sukharev Tower: Built at the end of the 17th century, it was one of the best known landmarks and symbols of Moscow. It was demolished in 1934 during the Stalinist reconstruction of Moscow.
9. *shchepotniks*: a derogative term Old Believers used for New Believers, who crossed themselves with three fingers.
10. According to one of the myths or legends about Ivan the Terrible (the Great), the tsar loved to ring church bells.
11. The "most evil of Herod's daughters": a reference to Salome, who asked for the head of John the Baptist on a platter and got her wish.
12. "Mother" should be read as recognition of Agrafena as the lawful head or Mother of the Divilin household. Agrafena is Glafira's mother-in-law.
13. Forgiveness Sunday: the Sunday before the beginning of the fast that Orthodox believers observe before Easter. They ask each other's forgiveness for any discourtesy and disrespect. This is because during the fast they will ask the Lord to forgive them their sins, and forgiveness will be granted only if they have first forgiven each other.

THUS LIFE PASSES

Elena Guro

Nelka is waiting. She's been told to stand here and wait for his arrival. The street rolls by. It rumbles in the distance. Gold dust was scattering the whole day in the city. Flat pavement, submissive, stretched endlessly under the downpour from the sun and the feet of pedestrians.

Nelka is all huddled up just a tiny bit boyishly under their cross-glances. She waits patiently.

The scorching air sighs by evening. The city breathes hot in the coolness. Far off the rumbling cracks and chokes passionately. The city is weary. Under her feet the pavement is hard, cruel, like pain.

She's a bit thin, like a young girl. "Hey, you, mam'selle, a gentleman will be here in two hours!" Guffawing crudely, women day laborers walked by. Gazing tenderly, she backed away from pasers-by. A gentleman tickled her cheek with the handle of a walking stick as he passed by. She moved back a bit; "it doesn't matter: men are the masters." She was used to spending the whole day out on the street.

The crowd walks by like a subjugating wave. "Hey, not bad-looking! Ha, ha!"

They walk by. Women. Men. There's someone's bicycle left by a wall; the seat seems hot, it's preserving the elasticity of the recent touch of young thighs. The burning beads of an amusement park. The strained voice of a female singer.

A handsome student in a short, double-breasted jacket passes by, moving his fresh, elastic thighs. He tossed a light walking-stick from one hand to the other. "And this one too could possess me and beat me with his elegant walking-stick." She shyly huddles up; her hands are slightly tanned, just a little awkward and defenseless. Oh, Nelka! The air takes a deeper and more velvety sigh. And it seems to her that she's stretching out her hand and asking something of the men passing by. But she's standing with her hands at her sides and not asking for anything but just looking.

The street cuddles to her importunately and breathes hot. Then it seems to her that she's a timid dog that can't bring itself to approach its master. The street is full of their will and orders.

Wet stains are spreading out on the grey window panes.

"Where are you going?" I don't know. Who knows? Austere houses with rows of clearly outlined austere windows, austere grates, black city rows of street lights, turbid ashamed mornings, and city evenings know. Every object in the city knows something about it all.

This took place once. There was still a bit of a thaw, drip - drip. She had already been walking for a long time and was overcome with spring weariness. Up ahead a gymnasium student was strolling in a smart coat that was part of his uniform. He shrugged his shoulders with contemptuous boyishness and put his hands in his pockets. She liked him. She tagged after him. So thin, pliant, like a whip. A close-cropped, thick-haired back of the head. She tagged after him wherever he went. Looked at that back with hopeless passion. He disappeared around the corner. She came to her senses. She turned back. He was still contemptuously smug. Imperious, probably, with a boyishness that valued nothing in women.

And up to that point everything was theirs by right; it seemed to her there was no one more lowly than her. It seems strange that they would sell to her if she were to walk into the store. Would a shop-assistant, squeaky clean and imposing, with the look of a foreign gentleman, really serve her? And she could walk in and ask for what she wanted. She would have asked very quietly, pushed the door very quietly—her hands and feet would have become timid so that she would have taken hesitant steps. Perhaps she would have seemed pliant to them . . .

And it was nice for her to sit down and rest on someone's front steps, intentionally on the hard edge, wiping off the dust from the pavement with her dress.

.   .   .   .

Thoughts broke off and floated away into the lonely white night, broke off and floated away.

.   .   .   .   .   .

"It's strange to think that somewhere long ago—long ago the youthful cry of a rooster could be heard and there was wet sod in city gardens in the spring, and somewhere right now, small, independent, little human beings were waiting to depart for their dacha and in the meantime were making small shapes out of damp sand, as if there were no men or women, just a child's 'papa' and 'mama' . . ."

. . . Cigar smoke covered everything . . .

. . . .

"In her boyish jacket she hung out of the window, leaning on her elbows. And it was so sweet, so sweet, because the wind tickled, making its way into her sleeves and up to her very elbows. And an impatient elasticity could be felt from her hips to her toes. Something drew her to the street, to fly out the window, into the infinite space. The windowsill was touchingly a bit dirty, with traces of an earlier, dried-out rain. And her thumbs were somewhat thin and touched the windowsill. A transparency lay suspended over the angular projections of the city. The air was moist. The sounds were turning more evening-like."

"Over there, there was a light-green city secret as big as the sky. Perhaps today it could be seen for the first time. Limpid, humid, pre-night. Moist freshness in abundance. Hitting against the walls, the grumbling of the city died away on layers of grey humidity."

"And the stepfather's prohibition, it turns out, was made of paper, invented, and the stepfather himself was made of paper, although a man, like in books, with spurs and a deep voice. It's comical . . . !"

"She walked out . . . In the grayness that descended to the window panes was the will of the city, the frightening will of the city. Palpable."

"Grey spots kept diving and spreading on the windows . . . These are someone's questions and answers. She walked . . . Something asked "Yes?" and answered barely audibly, "Perhaps." Steel pliancy of movements went running past. The air, the city spreading out before her, felt light. She wanted to run and follow the quickly moving figures."

As if somebody were teasing.

"But the apartment was left unlocked, unlocked!"

A blue expanse unfolded behind every corner. She was returning a bit tired and anxious. "Windows are like eyes in the city, windows are like eyes."

"They shouted after her, 'A slip of a girl is hanging about!' She didn't understand. She slammed the glass door. Ah, no need to ring, their place was open, the door was open . . . She began to feel uneasy in her surroundings. As if some evil spirit were lying in wait behind the door. Her stepfather had returned earlier. He advanced toward her, threatening with the evil, bloody whites of his eyes. As if he had been waiting. For some reason a whip came to be in his hands. He was unexpectedly spitting saliva. The absurd was beginning like a dream. She stopped being conscious of herself and did not understand what was happening around her. 'So, you left? Evidently you go out on dates!' Something flew around the walls, faceless, blind, and it was already too late to stop it. 'And take that, that and that'; a round pendulum glistened on the wall, rocking: 'take that, take that . . .'"

"He began to beat her with a whip. The pain bit into her. The pain flew around the walls and bit into her. The despair of merciless pain. The whip flew around twice and the ceiling came crashing down. The ecstacy of despair stunned her. A lash of the whip . . ."

"Oh! The lights in the city spread out with a crackling sound. The troika broke loose and its little bells rang furiously, carrying her off into the turbid night. Into the weak-willed night . . . "

.   .   .   .

"Satiety point. She came to. Pain was still weaving through her body. The punisher's smugness filled the room. He did not look at her out of smugness, acted indifferent. And the furniture sat around, stood around for a long time; it remained in the same place as witness. Approved by male power, it approved and looked on with satisfaction, as if just now it had received what it had been long waiting for. It always kept guard. Little by little it brought the time to this moment."

"She was ashamed to look up at it. She did not dare leave without his permission. She stood before him humiliated. Hysterics were still welling in her throat. Then, without hurrying, he lit up and intentionally blew smoke in her face, and handed her some money and sent her out on the street to get some cigarettes . . ."

The street was elegant! Ah, elegant . . . There were very many men, very many men. And the street had become somehow restlessly hot and illicit.

They looked her up and down. As if she were undressed. Pushed her rudely.

"Young people with boxes of chocolates and bonbonnierres tied with soft pink and green-colored ribbons were walking out of the confectioner's shops."

"They all knew how to issue orders. They all had an imperious span to their shoulders."

"There were lamps, windows, just as yesterday, but now they knew everything, like the furniture in her stepfather's study—they had taken it in and were examining her. They had grown heavy from curiosity. In the heat of the moment she did not notice that it was painful for her to walk. Men were looking at her as if they knew that one of them had just beaten her. Men burned her with their shoving and peered with street satisfaction into her humiliated eyes, beautiful from pain and embarrassment."

"Lights burned, glittered. As if it all descended on her at once."

"If we feel like it, we'll caress, and if we feel like it, we'll give a beating." "She had the feeling that all of them could give her orders and she would have to obey them. University students in uniforms lined in white silk walked by, glancing at her face and giving each other a shove. And they too had branded her. And this reverberated in her body as dull heaviness."

"That's the way it should be, it's all the same thing, there won't be anything else."

And suddenly it seemed that that's what she deserved: both shame and pain, and shame.

She did not dare raise her head; they were very handsome.

And there was boundlessness and there was passion in the hot stream of glances and half-kicks of the rudely familiar strollers. And there was rushing, more and more lively and quick—the lights were lashing the night.

Because of the pain, she was forced to walk even more slowly. Everything inside her sank. And they flared their drunken nostrils, and they covered her with hot, heavy glances because her humiliated eyes had become darker and more beautiful. And a hot wave surged over her head, compelling her to sink into infinite humiliation without end.

And then it seemed to her that she did not have a home to return to, or a real name . . . She thought to herself: "a woman . . ." The street was wiping clean and carrying away something. Wiping clean with a crowd of changed faces. Recklessly and wholeheartedly . . . And she began to feel unburdened, no longer ashamed, and free of bitterness. Men would shout: Nelka, Myuzetka, Zhulyetka! And something tore her away from yesterday and from home . . . No separate existence, like the grey submissive rocks on the roadway without a past, without a thought. As if she had lived permanently on the street . . .

And she seemed to find it touching to look into other people's beautiful windows, already dark and cold . . . And this was now endlessness, like the grey iridescent windows disappearing row by row into the street. Endlessness . . .

She began to feel unashamed and carefree. There was a heaviness in her body and inside something ached and rose; and she wanted the humiliations to rain down on her endlessly . . .

One tobacco shop had not closed yet because it also served the "night" person. Only the window was blocked from the street side with a piece of cardboard. Thick, worn-out door-curtains hung in swirls. In this place, where men dropped by, they looked Nelka over with hostile bewilderment. But then they grinned and gave each other a shove. And after taking her box submissively, she hurried to leave. And the men had chastely clean cuffs on their light-skinned hands and almost innocent, touchingly clean collars on their pink, washed necks.

Restaurants and snack bars glistened with pockets of light. The sound of suppressed giggles and uninhibited squeals was already moving down the street . . . Someone took her by the waist, turned her by the shoulder. They looked her over. Night secrets were burning on the walls.

And the hot glances stuck to her like hot pain and bent her down toward the ground.

A lash of lights whipped the darkness. Whipped the night. Illuminated joy without light.

"Crush me, beat me with your spurs, humiliate me . . ."

.   .   .   .

"There's a hanging street light, somewhere or other, swinging on someone's gate on a street at night. There's the street light swinging all night. The wind touches its shoulder and sighs; and the darkened street quietly asks someone with the hurried steps of its women . . ."

"There the wind touched a shoulder—it asked something and touched a shoulder. God's velvety blue eyes are looking into the city. They turn pale from the madness of the pale lights. They keep turning pale until dawn."

"Somebody in beaver-fur on the dark street imperiously helped 'his girl' into a sled, did up the traveling rug in a sprightly way, and sent the sled onward, into the night."

"On the sidewalk a student was dragging a giggling prostitute."

.　.　.　　　.　　　.　.　　　　　.　.

Trying not to raise her eyes above his feet, she offered the cigarettes to her stepfather. Trying not to see the walls. His glowing face, uneasy because of his hot, burning body, and the whip intentionally laid out in sight caught her attention. She did not want to notice his playful, scrutinizing look as well. But something bent her low and she took a long look. There lay the whip with the beautiful handle, with stamping work from the Caucasus. He beat her with the beautiful whip, so beautiful that she felt like taking and touching it, and even laying it against her cheek.

And her delicate shoulders felt as if they had been fractured, and her hands hung down by her sides.

The walls watched greedily and thirsted for humiliation. They enjoyed it. He took the whip and whipped the air. There was a whistling sound . . . She gave a start, could not help it, as if it had bitten into her body. And again. "He enjoyed the effect. She collected herself and turned to stone so as not to give her last. But he was already enjoying himself . . . He whipped the night. Silent, black-eyed night. Eh, and again! Live a while, turn a little." "As if gypsy women were singing, making their throaty sounds . . . "She became intoxicated, intoxicated . . ."

The intoxication of shame followed.

He forced her to do his bidding. And she made a point of debasing herself, and now there was boundlessness, as though by doing it she were giving herself to all those out on the street.

In the male study, all the austere furniture, with every piece of brass shining, fixed its eyes on her.

.　.　.　.　.　.　.　.　.　.　.　.　.　.　.　.

And nevertheless the next day came. The shouts of little boys carried and resounded much too loudly from the stone courtyard; they resounded even from the front and back staircases. Reverberated. Doors banged with a lashing sound, imperiously. As if there were no walls in the apartment where one could hide.

. . . .

It was terribly unpleasant to see litter and pieces of paper whirling on the road. They whirled in such a rapid, precise, ordinary way with the dust.

The days crawled on to the accompaniment of shouts. All drawn together, she walked past austere, government buildings with menacing grating, with spears and lictorian bundles crowned with a wreath. It was as if all this smelled of the tobacco in her stepfather's study. They applied seals and pressed down; this was called "a measure of strictness."

Paper litter was flying around repellingly in the road. Many details were painfully visible everywhere. Irritated men were heading for work with disgust, dusty. The days were sultry, urban, and acrid.

It wasn't always night—intoxicated night; the day shrank dimly, looking round ashamed.

Strong male hands built for themselves a beautiful city out of iron and stone. They drew it with precise calculations. They bent heavy stone. They contained the expanse with grating. In this city they had trials, punished, and forgave every day . . .

The dust whirled . . . Toward evening the Masters were strolling with their walking-sticks.

In the morning she got up in a fog. She could do nothing, neither work nor think. Opposite the windows, a house in a prescribed manner, like her whole life. Conventional, unalterable. They were striding past apathetically. Striding with shoulder straps and piping on their uniforms. There was accord and precision in all this.

But at night the street was passionate. Lights and drained faces, pale from the night, winking at each other.

They walked straight ahead so as not lose their smugness. There was a small girl among them, with timid, sensitive feet. They commanded her, looked her over smugly, pushed her, and issued orders to her the way they issued orders to their own women; whistling for their dog, they whistled to her and made her follow them. They beat her, leaving the pain of embarrassment in her body. And, moreover, graceful and elegant, they did not even notice her, simply walked past—they thought about her in passing—"a woman"—and felt they were Masters. And electricity illuminated her for them servilely.

They think: "Here's someone's woman. Well, there's a lot of such goods, let her go, of course; she's partly mine . . . Go on, go on, don't even think of pestering me . . . !"

With indifferent, bulging eyes they let the night and the glow and the women go by. Spring, pliant and pleading, glided over them like over resilient molded rubber. And they walked inviolably smug. They bathed their inviolable shoulders in the night air, and they took them for a stroll; intoxicatingly, they bore a thought that stayed with them: "Everything's mine, this is me, me, it's me walking." And the same thing was apparent in the narcissistic angle of their caps. The night clung . . . The strong backs of their heads were straight and rounded . . . They preened their covered bulging muscles. Poplar trees had sticky, greedy little twigs.

At this hour the Mashkas, Sashkas, Muzetkas were waking up, beginning life without "tomorrow." And cares, and free will, and difficult choices were not made for them, not for them—but the whip and wine, laughter and squeals, were . . .

"Whatever pleases you, nice gentleman! Whatever you want, whatever you want . . ." And no worries about a lost day and no pangs of guilt. It's simple. So simple . . . "Mister, walk me home. Walk me home, mister . . ."

The night poplars had greedy small leaves, and the warm air caressed Nelka . . .

. . . .

"There are books in the store windows—no place for her—technical—this is some significant, deep word, you most likely will never understand it. Men with wise, noble brows go in there: they can learn everything scientific and know the whole mystery of life, everything that is in those books: and that's why they have big, noble brows."

"This life—so enormous, wonderful, erudite, wise, incomprehensible in its sweep and complex turns. Enormous walls, houses, and farther on, enormous houses. This life, organized in such a civilized manner, so elegantly and beautifully by men."

"How wonderful it must be to draw the lines for blueprints, with their key importance—fine lines, serious, clear, and neat. Or to read line after line, learning something wondrous from them more and more. And the mind becomes more wonderful, more precise . . ."

Walking-sticks and cigarette holders decorated with figures of women's bodies in degrading poses, sweetened in an old man's way, were for sale in the display cases. Elegant small whips with handles made of delicate ivory, yellowish-green, and of walrus tusks, with a rosy tint of life, were for sale. Delicate, ivory-smooth, pleasant to the touch. Elegant, cruel toys for pampered, power-loving hands.

She grew weak; she immediately submitted, became meek, and right away the carefree feeling of the street embraced her . . .

.   .   .   .

In a jewelry shop a man's two large hands with hard, carefully-tended nails were re-arranging objects in the display cases with firm, precise movements. Nelka imagined that the whole city—the elegant palaces, the hustle and bustle in the streets, and the compliant riches—was being calmly and confidently crushed by a well-cared-for man's hand with angular, pink nails and a delicate blue stone on its little finger.

A crowd of students' and officers' backs, smartly cinched at the waist, was heading for a cafe and exchanging smiles.

.   .   .   .
.   .   .   .

Dim thoughts kept breaking away and falling into the selfless night. Breaking away and falling, like stars . . . Frightening shadows were moving behind lonely night cabbies. She did not care what they would do to her—whether they would hit her or insult her with repulsive caresses—there was nothing to preserve. And for her there was a frighteningly gripping beauty in the irrevocably yielding submissiveness of her steps . . .

Then the soul was taken out of the cold, frozen windows and a terrible, frightening emptiness peered out both from the walls and the dim hollows of the windowpanes.

. . . .

They spoiled her, allowed her to put her tiny, funny shoes on the tablecloth between the flower vases. The men would laugh, take her shoes from her, and hide them in their vest pockets.

They listened sweetly and patiently when she said silly things. For them she wore the most delicate lace, the glow of electricity. Violetkas.[1] She laughed . . .

A coarse mustache was kissing her small pale hand which they did not squeeze—they only held it ever so gallantly, as if afraid of breaking it.

Behind their broad shoulders windows were turning dark blue. Beyond the dark blue windows stretched the beautiful city, their city. They kept silent about the city's secret . . .

High brows shone under the street lamps; the beautifully clever knew . . .

. . . .

He had been preparing since morning for his exams—writing, reading. Even more important, more unapproachable. On the table a severe-looking writing set, truly a man's, the real thing. In dark colors of marble and brown bronze; not permitting any objections. There in his place everything was severe, orderly, and there was no room for a woman. A man's precise, dandyish thought fluttered among the severe bronze items.

The street rumbled sultrily outside the window and burst in. The absent-minded one moved the lectures aside and spilled ashes on them, since he had forgotten the cigarette in his firm fingers. She did not dare get in his way. From the street, the sound of whips lashing. There was rumbling and it was baking hot. Boring little flowers on the wallpaper of the furnished room. She was sick of them. Then he left. Then he came again . . .

He rocked her crudely on his knees. He kneaded her in a disgusting way—by force. Kept moving away his hand with the cigarette. Gallantly warned her to watch out, lest she get burned.

. . . .

She was lying with her face turned to the intrusively illuminated wall. Counting the flowers on the wall-paper. The street jingled resoundingly behind the thin wall. She was sick and tired of the wallpaper, like of delirium. She tried to think, comforting herself: all apartments, apartments around the city, the furnished rooms, have beds, and on the beds it's the same thing.

"Oh! Reveille toi, ma mignonne . . . !"[i] With despicable tenderness. Without looking back at her, he sat down at the table. Immediately satiated, with the stupid back of his head. Purified through seriousness, he was again unapproachable. She looked and saw a curl touchingly stuck to his clean brow. Touchingly. She couldn't make up her mind to approach him . . .

The street was rumbling outside the window.

. . . .

The whole day gold dust was scattering around the city. The walls and old shop signs were caressed with the immutable affection of a command, robbing them of their will.

And without a will, it was warm and as usual.

The whole day they wandered around for some reason, and she did not know why, and he kept forcing her to wait for him on the street.

As if there is nothing except cooled-down emptiness . . . Perhaps dark violets had been carried down the street this afternoon. The street sighed—and someone huge bent down from above. Nelka looks at the sky—it seems a few raindrops fell. And immediately it became even warmer. And she laughs . . .

"What are you smiling at?" "I wouldn't be able to control myself now. I should be locked up and ordered to stand for hours without moving—to the point of pain."

"And are you enjoying yourself?" "Yes, I'm enjoying myself. I'm simply enjoying myself and I feel crazy because a few raindrops have fallen. I'll follow those gentlemen right now because they have broad shoulders and beautiful, colorful chevrons on their full-dress uniforms." "No, you

---

i Oh, wake up, my sweet one! (Fr.) —Trans.

don't dare do this, you don't even dare to look at them, and you mustn't look at anyone: 'You're crazy, a woman of the streets, low-life.' How I'm enjoying myself, how I'm enjoying myself!" A few raindrops fell and the warm city lost its head, lost its head—and fell silent . . . Sometimes a wind passes down a grey, blurry street and touches someone on the shoulder. Sometimes a thing is possible that never existed before!

And she thinks, "Here he comes, all sensitive in the night . . ."

A railway engineer is passing by; he is well-built and young and stops like a very trusting man who has not made a decision yet. A smile floats directly at her. A railway engineer. Freshness exudes from the garden and sighs.

And now the air is singing loudly. Passing very close to Nelka, he drops his package, tied with a cord, and doesn't notice. She picks it up, runs up to him and says, "Sir, you lost your thing!" The student looks at her. No, she lowers her eyelashes—she doesn't want him to notice her beautiful eyes; she likes him too much.

No, it's nothing, nothing, I just wanted to hand you your package. And now he no longer looks and turns a bit red. He's already walking away, and she has a mad desire to shout after him, "Sir! My name is Nelka . . ."

But she restrains herself.

And Nelka thinks tenderly: "The city has grown younger, has touchingly gotten younger—the city has become quite the small boy! And the sky has faded from the sultriness . . . !" "Something has touched all the objects—and now everything is more uneasy and beautiful; and that is her fate . . ."

"It's hard to believe that he won't come back right now from behind the thick corner of the wall. He should walk back and forth like that until dawn . . ." ". . . What stands in the way of her running after him? She could follow him to his entrance, see where he lives and sleeps, and how his front door looks . . ."

But a sudden silence and alarm came over her . . . The house was beautiful when he had been passing by, but when the thick wall hid him from view, she stopped liking the house. And she could have gone running after him and not lost him so soon . . . And she is a bit sorry.

The city is looking younger, the city has become quite the small boy! She stayed where she was, and she was uneasy.

The street is hot. The night is deeper. Men. The air is becoming spicy from the perfumes of the women passing by. Jingling spurs are coming closer. Two officers passed with a dull, prodding gait. And one, lighting a cigarette:

"My Julie, ha, ha . . . !"

Their dull, sensual words, thrown out into the street dust at night, the presumptuous ringing of their spurs, gave her a push.

The consciousness of their crudeness, strength, and nearness.

The freshness of leafy thickets sighed after them. And again something hot and turbid pulled her.

She shuddered, pulled herself together, as if something had burned her. Her suddenly numb body, seduced by submission, longed to sink into endless humiliation.

She looks up. Immense walls, again. It's life that is so immense . . .

"They've taken control with stone and nice shining copper," she thinks quickly, descending into darkness . . . Was there something else she wanted to remember? "The houses are singing their stony song . . ." No, can't think of anything . . . And now she absolutely would not be able to collect her thoughts . . . Only her body ached. In front of her, his broad shoulders already swayed. "Time to go . . . !" He whistled softly. "Well, then. Nelka, *ici*, let's go." And without looking back, he starts walking. And she leaves and follows him mechanically, out of habit, without a will of her own, across the heady, hot wave of the boulevard.

1909

NOTES

1. Violetka: the diminutive of Violetta. This name brings to mind the main character in Giuseppe Verdi's opera, "La Traviata," who is a courtesan named Violetta. The prvileged classes in Russia were well acquainted with Verdi's opera. In Russian, *nochnaya fialka*, meaning "night violet," is one of the euphemisms for a prostitute.

FOUR PEOPLE

Arkady Averchenko

In the second class compartment of an express train there were three travelers: a government chamber functionary, Chetverorukov, his young wife Simochka, and a representative of the "Evans and Crumbell" firm, Vasily Abramovich Sandomirsky.

And at one of the stops a stranger in a ragged coat and a travel cap joined them in the compartment. He scrutinized the Chetverorukov couple and the representative of the "Evans and Crumbell" firm carefully and, taking out a newspaper, immersed himself in his reading.

A particular kind of boredom—the road kind—hung in the air over everyone. Chetverorukov was turning a cigarette case in his hands, Simochka was tapping her heels and shifting her vacant look from Sandomirsky's unremarkable face to the stranger who had joined them, and for the tenth time Sandomirsky was leafing through an awful humor magazine in which he had read everything, including the names of the typesetter and the person in charge of subscriptions.

"We still have five hours of travel left," Simochka said, yawning sweetly. "Five hours of hopeless boredom!"

"Railway travel is monotonous, which is what makes passengers weary," her husband answered didactically.

And Sandomirsky said, "Railway travel is intolerably expensive. Just imagine—a ticket costs twelve rubles."

And after leafing through his humor magazine yet another time, he added, "And I'm not even talking about a reserved seat!"

"The main thing is that it's boring!" Simochka tapped her foot.

The stranger sitting by the door folded his newspaper, looked around at the whole group again in a strange way, and burst out laughing.

And his laugh was strange, gurgling and smothered, and the words that followed surprised everyone indescribably.

"You're bored? I know why boredom arises . . . Because all of you aren't really the people you pretend to be, and that's terribly boring."

"What do you mean we 'aren't really'?" Sandomirsky objected in a hurt tone. "We're really who we are. I, as an intelligent man . . ."

The stranger smiled and said, "We're all not the people we pretend to be. Let's take you—who are you?"

"Me?" Sandomirsky raised his eyebrows. "I'm a representative of the 'Evans and Crumbell' firm—cloth, tricot, and fustian."

"Ah-ha-ha-ha!" the stranger went into peals of laughter. "I just knew you'd invent something totally ridiculous! Come now, why are you lying to yourself and to others? You're a cardinal in the Pope's Vatican and purposely hiding under the guise of some Crumbell!"

"Vatican?" a surprised and frightened Sandomirsky babbled. "Me—the Vatican?"

"Not the Vatican, but a cardinal! Don't play the fool. I know you're one of the most clever and cunning individuals alive today. I've heard a thing or two about you!"

"Excuse me," Sandomirsky said. "But I don't need these jokes!"

II

"Giuseppe!" the stranger muttered in a serious tone, placing both hands on the shoulders of the representative of the "Evans and Crumbell" firm. "You can't fool me! Instead of silly talk I would like to hear something from you about the Vatican, the customs there, and your successes with famous, religious Italian women . . ."

"Let me go!" Sandomirsky shouted in horror. "What is this?!"

"Shh!" the stranger hushed him, covering the traveling salesman's mouth with his hand. "No need to shout. There's a lady here."

He sat down in his place by the door; then he put his hand in his pocket and, taking out a revolver, aimed it at Sandomirsky.

"Giuseppe! I'm a very kind man, but if a dissembler is sitting next to me, that's something I can't bear!"

Simochka exclaimed "oh!" and settled back in the corner. Chetverorukov fidgeted a bit on the divan and attempted to stand up, but the stranger's determined gesture kept him rooted to the spot.

"Ladies and gentlemen!" the strange passenger said. "I won't do anything bad to you. Stay calm, I only ask that this man admit who he is."

"I'm Sandomirsky!" the traveling salesman whispered, his lips ashen.

"You're lying, Giuseppe! You're a cardinal."

The black eye of the revolver's barrel was looking at Sandomirsky.

Chetverorukov cast a sidelong glance at the stranger and whispered to Sandomirsky, "You can see whom you're dealing with . . . Tell him that you're a cardinal. It's easy enough to do."

"But I'm not a cardinal!" Sandomirsky whispered in despair.

"He's too shy to tell you he's a cardinal," Chetverorukov turned to the unknown gentleman ingratiatingly. "But he's probably a cardinal."

"Isn't that the truth?!" the stranger picked up. "Don't you find that there's something cardinal-like in his face?"

"There is!" Chetverorukov answered readily. "But . . . is it worth your getting upset because of it?"

"Let him say it!" the passenger demanded capriciously, playing with the revolver.

"All right, fine!" Sandomirksy shouted. "Fine! Well then, I'm a cardinal."

III

"You see!" the stranger made a triumphant gesture. "I told you . . . People aren't what they seem! Bless me, your Reverence!"

The traveling salesman shrugged his shoulders indecisively, extended both hands and waved them over the stranger's head.

Simochka snorted.

"What's so funny here?" Sandomirsky took offense. "Allow me, sir, to step out for a minute."

"No, I won't let you," the passenger said. "I want you to tell us about some entertaining love affairs with your female parishioners."

"What female parishioners? What love affairs can there . . . ?!"

Staring at the revolver, the traveling salesman lowered his voice and said dolefully, "Well, there were love affairs . . . there's no point in talking about . . ."

"Speak!!" the stranger shouted in fury.

"Put away your pistol, then I will tell you. Well, what should I tell you . . . Once an Italian lady fell in love with me . . ."

"A countess?" the passenger asked.

"Fine, a countess. 'Vasia,' she says, 'I love you so terribly much.' We kissed."

"No, in more detail . . . Where did you meet her and how did this feeling arise in you for the first time . . . ?"

The representative of the "Evans and Crumbell" firm wrinkled his forehead and, glancing with anguish at Chetverorukov, continued, "She was at a ball. A white dress with roses. An envoy introduced us. I said, 'Oh, countess, how pretty you are . . . !'"

"Why are you confusing things?" the passenger interrupted sternly. "Are you, a clergyman, really allowed to attend a ball?"

"Oh, it wasn't a ball! A small evening gathering at someone's home. She says to me, 'Giuseppe, I'm unhappy! I would like to take holy communion to [sic] you.'"

"You mean, confess!" the stranger corrected.

"Fine, to confess. All right, I say. Come see me. And she comes and says, 'Giuseppe, forgive me, but I love you.'"

"An awfully stupid romance!" the stranger declared unceremoniously. "Your neighbors listened to it without any interest. If the Pope's cardinals are all like that, I don't envy him!"

IV

He glanced benevolently at Chetverorukov and said courteously, "I don't understand how you can leave your wife feeling bored when you have such a wonderful gift . . ."

Chetverorukov turned pale and asked timidly, "Wha-at g-gift?"

"Lord! Singing, of course! You're a cunning one! Do you think that if a service cap is near you no one will guess you're a famous baritone who has been reaping laurels in the capitals . . . ?"

"You're mistaken," Chetverorukov forced a smile. "I'm the functionary Chetverorukov and this is my wife Simochka."

"Cardinal!" the stranger exclaimed, shifting the barrel of his revolver to the functionary. "What do you think, who is he—a functionary or a famous baritone?"

Sandomirsky glanced gloatingly at Chetverorukov and, shrugging his shoulders, said, "A baritone, without a doubt!"

"You see! The cardinal's lips speak the truth. Sing something, maestro . . . ! I beg you!"

"I don't know how!" Chetverorukov babbled helplessly. "I assure you my voice is unpleasant, rasping."

"Ha-ha-ha!" the stranger began to laugh. "The modesty of a true talent! I beg you—sing!"

"I assure you . . ."

"Sing! Sing, damn you!!!"

Chetverorukov glanced in embarrassment at his wife's frowning face and, hiding his hands in his pockets, began singing timidly and off key:

> On the blue waves of the ocean
> Only the stars shine in the sky . . .

Propping up his head with his hand, the stranger listened to the singing attentively, with interest. From time to time he snapped his fingers and joined in the song.

"You sing well! You get around six thousand? Undoubtedly more! You know, no matter what people say, music soothes the savage beast. Isn't that true, cardinal?"

"I'll say!" Sandomirsky said with little conviction.

"Well you see, ladies and gentlemen! You've barely stopped pretending and have become your true selves, and your mood has already improved, and boredom has disappeared as if it had never existed. You're not bored, are you?"

"What boredom can there be!" the representative of the "Evans and Crumbell" firm sighed. "It's sheer fun."

"I'm very happy. I notice, madam, that even the expression on your sweet face has changed. The worst thing in life, ladies and gentlemen, is deception, pretense. And if one tackles it boldly, energetically, everything deceitful and pretended dissipates. Earlier you probably thought this gentleman was a traveling salesman and your husband a functionary. Perhaps you believed that about your husband your whole life . . . But I unmasked them in two tries. One turned out to be a cardinal, the other a baritone. Isn't that true, cardinal?"

"You talk like a book," Sandomirsky said mournfully.

"And the most frightening thing is that falsehood is in everything. It surrounds us from the time we wear diapers, accompanies us every step of the way; we breathe it, wear it on our faces, on our bodies. Now, madam, you're wearing a light-colored dress, a corset, and high heel shoes. I hate everything that's false and deceitful. Madam! I take the liberty of asking you, most respectfully, to take off your dress! It conceals the most beautiful thing that exists in nature—the human body!"

The strange passenger gallantly directed the revolver at Simochka's husband and, staring at her directly, continued gently, "Be so good as to undress . . . Your spouse won't object . . . ?"

Simochka's husband glanced with his dull eyes at the barrel of the revolver and, his teeth chattering, answered:

"I . . . No-o. I l-love beauty myself. You can undress a bit, heh, heh . . ."

Simochka's eyes flashed lightning. She looked at the pale Chetverorukov and the silent Sandomirsky with disgust, jumped up energetically and said, laughing hysterically, "I also love beauty and despise cowardice. I'll undress for you! Only order your cardinal to turn away."

"Cardinal!" the stranger said in a severe tone. "You, as a clergyman, may not look at this scene of scenes. Cover yourself with the newspaper!"

"Simochka . . ." Chetverorukov babbled. "You . . . just a bit."

"Leave me alone! I know without your telling me!"

She undid her bodice, dropped her skirt and, without looking at anyone, continued to undress, pale and frowning.

"I'm attractive, isn't that so?" she said provocatively, a smile showing at the corners of her mouth. "If you want to kiss me, you can ask my husband's permission—he'll probably let you."

"Baritone! Permit me to touch most respectfully one of the best women I have ever known. Many consider me abnormal, but I understand people!"

Chetverorukov, silently, with his jaw trembling and with horror in his eyes, looked at the frightening passenger.

"Madam! He apparently has nothing against it. I'll kiss your hand most respectfully . . ."

The train was slowing down as it approached the station of a large town in the province.

"Why my hand?" Simochka made a pained smile. "We'll simply kiss! You do like me?"

The stranger looked at her well-proportioned legs in black stockings, her bare arms and exclaimed, "I'd be happy to!"

Without taking her passionate gaze off her husband, Simochka embraced the stranger with her bare arms and gave him a powerful kiss.

The train stopped.

The stranger kissed Simochka's hand, took his things and said, "You, cardinal, and you, baritone! The train stands here five minutes. These five minutes I will also stand on the platform with the revolver in my pocket. If one of you gets off, I'll shoot him. Understood?"

"Just go!" Sandomirsky groaned.

When the train started to move, the doors of the compartment opened slightly and a conductor's hand appeared in the opening with a note.

Chetverorukov took and read it in bewilderment.

"Admit it, we weren't bored . . . This original but truly effective method for shortening travel time has the additional advantage that everyone shows his true self. There were four of us: a fool, a coward, a brave woman and I—a convivial fellow, the life and soul of the party. Baritone! Kiss the cardinal for me . . ."

1910

SCENES FROM THE LIFE OF THE WORKER PANTELEI GRYMZIN

Arkady Averchenko

Exactly ten years ago the worker Pantelei Grymzin received from his mean, vile bloodsucker of a boss a day's wages of only two rubles and fifty kopecks for nine hours of work!!!

"Now, what can I do with this miserable amount?" Pantelei thought bitterly, examining closely the two silver rubles and a fifty-kopeck copper coin . . . "I want to have some grub and I'd like a drink, and I have to slap some new soles on my boots; the old ones, just look—one big hole . . . Oh, you, life of endless hard labor!!"

He dropped by a cobbler he knew; this cobbler charged him the exorbitant price of one-and-a-half rubles for a pair of soles.

"Do you wear a cross?" Pantelei inquired sarcastically.

The cross, to the surprise of the robbed Pantelei, turned out to be where it should be—on the cobbler's hairy chest, under his shirt.

"And now I have a one-ruble coin left," Pantelei thought, sighing. "What can you do with it? Eh . . . !"

With this ruble coin he went and bought half a pound of ham, a can of sprats, a loaf of French bread, half a bottle of vodka, a bottle of beer and ten cigarettes; he spent so much money that his remaining capital amounted to only four kopecks.

And when the poor devil Pantelei sat down to his pathetic dinner, he became so downhearted that he almost began to cry.

"What, oh what, have I done . . . ?" his trembling lips whispered. "Why do the rich and the exploiters drink champagne and liqueurs, eat hazel-grouse and pineapples, while I, except for simple grain alcohol and canned goods and ham—don't see God's world . . . Oh, if only we, the working class, could win our freedom . . . ! Then we'd live like real human beings!"

* * *

One day in the spring of 1920 the worker Pantelei Grymzin received a day's wages for Tuesday: 2700 rubles in all.

"What can I do with it?" Pantelei thought bitterly, playing with the multi-colored paper money in his hand. "I need to slap some soles on my boots, and get some grub, and drink something—I'm dying for a drink!"

Pantelei dropped by the cobbler, haggled with him and settled for two-thousand three-hundred rubles, and walked out onto the street with his four orphaned hundred-ruble notes.

He bought a pound of semi-white bread, a bottle of fruit-flavored soda, and had fourteen rubles left . . . He asked the price of ten cigarettes, spat and walked away.

At home he sliced some bread, opened the fruit-flavored soda water, and sat down at the table to have supper . . . and he began to feel so bitter that he almost began to cry.

"Why," his trembling lips whispered, "why do the rich get it all and we get nothing . . . ? Why does a rich man eat delicate pink ham, gorge himself on sprats and white bread, fill his throat with real vodka and foamy beer and smoke cigarettes, while I like some dog have to chew stale bread and sip sickening swill made with saccharin . . . ! Why do some get everything, others nothing . . . ?"

"Oh, Pantelei, Pantelei . . . What a big fool you've been, my brother."

1921

BLACK IRIS

Nadezhda Teffi
(pen name of Nadezhda A. Buchinskaya)

"Why, my dear lady, the weather isn't that bad at all. Of course . . . it's . . . a bit gusty, but still, there's no harm in taking a short drive. You, my dear lady, are simply in a bad mood!"

Doctor Katyshev was reasoning with Vekina, and Vekina was listening and thinking about the sad state of her affairs.

Her affairs were truly in a sorry state.

Three days ago Vekina's husband had left for five days in Kazan to bury an aunt, and Vekina had based all the coming joys of her life on these five days. She thought that every morning she would go for a ride with the artist Shatov, every day she would have breakfast with the artist Shatov, every evening she would have dinner with the artist Shatov, and every night she would have at least supper with the artist Shatov.

But here it was already the third of the five blissful days and they had not seen each other even once. First he phoned to say that he was finishing a painting for an exhibit, then he sent a letter saying that he had to call on a highly placed person whose portrait he was to paint, and now he sent flowers without any note and did not come himself.

"What a fool! He has to understand that such happiness may never come again because every aunt dies only once in her life. Or this is only a tactic to tease me a little? Couldn't he have picked a better time?"

"Why, my dear lady, are you depressed? What is it that you don't have?" Doctor Katyshev made an effort to talk to her.

"There he goes pestering me," Vekina thinks. "Perhaps I should start flirting with him to spite Shatov?"

"My dear lady! Truly, why? What pretty little feet you have. Come now, can one be depressed with such little feet? If I had such little feet, I don't know what . . ."

Vekina imagined fat, bald Katyshev in silver shoes and flesh-colored stockings, and she began to feel a bit nauseous.

"And so, dare I say, you like my feet?" she forced herself to say. "Would you like to kiss them?"

"It's all because of you, all because of you," she said to the artist in her thoughts.

"Well here, take that, see how you like it."

"Go ahead and kiss them, doctor."

The doctor grinned, began to wheeze, knelt down and, cradling Vekina's foot in his palms, kissed it loudly above the bow on the shoe.

"It's really not a foot but blancmange!"

"How repulsive! Just as if he's performing an operation," Vekina shivered all over. "Here's what you've reduced me to! You! You! You! Aha! Don't like it? Then take that again."

Suddenly she smiled slyly and pulled back the sleeve of her dress.

"Look what a little dimple I have on my elbow!"

The doctor puckered his lips and bent down, but Vekina pulled her hand back. "You take too many liberties!"

The doctor opened his eyes wide and was left with his lips puckered for a kiss.

Half an hour after his departure, the artist Shatov entered.

"Please, no excuses," Vekina stopped him coldly. "I don't care! Especially as I must admit something to you myself."

"...?"

"I've taken a fancy to someone else."

"...?"

"You could have seen for yourself, had you come an hour earlier. Actually, I'm happy that everything between us has ended to our mutual satisfaction."

Shatov was somewhat taken aback and his lips trembled slightly and, by the way, exactly as long as was customary for a man taken aback.

"So you find that . . . it's to our mutual . . . ?"

Vekina responded with the most ironic laughter she could manage and silently left the room.

She heard Shatov putting on his galoshes and, after he put them on, he waited a bit for some reason in the entrance hall; and when the door slammed shut, she suddenly bit her hand and began to weep.

In bed that evening she began to compose a letter.

At first as follows: "Dear Sir. I would like to get my portrait back . . ."

Then this way: "We parted friends, isn't that right? Let my portrait serve as a token of our amicable, uncomplicated relations . . ."

And finally, thus: "Evgeny! I love you. Send me your portrait . . ."

Then she fell asleep.

In the morning a messenger brought her a bouquet of black irises.

"No letter?"

"No."

She kissed every petal of the cold black flowers and smiled with trembling lips.

"People don't part like that! No! These are not flowers given in parting! They're black because he's depressed, and he's depressed because he loves me. Two more days of freedom are left and I can't waste a minute!"

"Evgeny!" she said on the phone. "Evgeny, forgive me! It's not true—I don't love someone else. I've slandered myself to get back at you. Why have I changed my mind? Because of your black flowers. The black irises told me that you're depressed and love me. I love black irises! Do you understand? Black irises! Only black irises! No! No! I'm not mad, I'm just happy!"

He promised to come; she spent the whole hour rushing between the mirror in the living room and the one in the bedroom. She tied a yellow ribbon around the irises.

"Laugh, irises!"

At three the door rang and in anticipation she closed her eyes, but when she opened them, she saw the freshly-shaved physiognomy of Doctor Katyshev.

"Well, how are you today, my dear little lady? I was worried about your health and stopped by to check."

"Not bad . . . today I'm fine. Only I'm very busy," Vekina babbled.

Katyshev glanced about the room.

"How beautifully you've tied a ribbon around the flowers. Boundless good taste!"

"Just don't touch them," Vekina said, startled. "These flowers may not be touched, they are sacred! They've brought me so much happiness that . . . in a word, it's none of your business."

Suddenly Katyshev was moved.

"My dear," he lisped. "My sweet child! Have I really pleased you so much?"

Vekina turned all cold.

"What . . . What are you saying?"

"Have I really pleased you so much with the flowers? And I didn't want to take them because they're black, but the shop assistant convinced me. 'They're the most fashionable,' he says, 'in this season.' Well, if they're fashionable, give them to me. What's the matter with you?"

Vekina stood all pale and gasping for breath.

"How dare you! You mean man! Impudent and dishonorable! How dare you send flowers without a letter and without a card!"

"Why are you like this, my dear lady, really and truly," Katyshev became frightened. "I thought you would guess yourself who sent them after yesterday's, hm . . ."

"Get out! How dare you insult a woman so! Get out, you scoundrel!"

The frightened Katyshev was going down the staircase on tip-toe— he did not dare to use his whole foot—when he met the artist Shatov coming up.

The artist was whistling cheerfully and carrying a bouquet of black irises.

"My dear friend," Katyshev grabbed him by the hand. "You're going to her? And with flowers? Forget it, I tell you as one friend to another, forget it. She's such a woman . . . ! She's a saintly woman . . . She's virtue itself . . . She's a beast. And, in my opinion, all is not well 'here.'"

And he tapped his brow with his finger.

"You think so?" The artist was put on guard. He thought it over and, accompanied by the doctor, headed down the stairs.

1921

THE RED CROWN
(*Historia Morbi*)[i]

Mikhail Bulgakov

Most of all I hate the sun, people's loud voices and the sound of rat-a-tat-tat. Rat-a-tat-tat in close succession. I'm afraid of people to such a point that if in the evening I catch the sound of someone's footsteps in the corridor and the sound of voices, I begin to cry out. For this reason, even my room is special, quiet and the best one, No. 27 at the very end of the corridor. No one can come see me. But in order to assure my safety even more, I begged Ivan Vasilyevich for a long time (even wept in front of him) to issue me a typed certificate. He agreed and wrote that I was under his protection and no one had the right to take me. But to tell the truth, I didn't believe very much in the power of his signature. Then he forced even the professor to sign it and affixed a blue round seal to the document. That's another matter. I know many cases when people stayed among the living only thanks to a piece of paper with a round seal being found in a pocket. True, that worker in Berdyansk,[1] his cheek covered in soot, was hanged on a street lamp just after a crumpled piece of paper with a seal was found in his boot. But that's entirely different. He was a Bolshevik criminal and the blue seal was a criminal seal. It brought him to the street lamp, and the street lamp was the reason for my illness (don't worry, I know perfectly well that I'm ill).

In essence something happened to me even before Kolya. I left so as not to see a man being hanged, but fear left with me in my trembling legs. Then, of course, I couldn't do anything, but now I would say boldly, "General, sir, you are an animal. You *do not* hang people."

You can already see based on this that I'm not a coward and I brought up the seal not because I fear death. Oh no, I'm not afraid of it. I'll shoot myself and this will be soon, because Kolya will reduce me to despair.

---

i   History of an Illness (Lat.)

But I'll shoot myself so as not to see and hear Kolya. The thought that other people will come . . . That is loathsome.

* * *

For whole days on end I lie on the sofa bed and look out of the window. There's an open space above our green garden; beyond it, a yellow seven-story mass with a blind, windowless wall faces toward me, and there's a huge rusty square plate right under the roof. A sign. "Dental Laboratory." In white letters. At first I hated it. Then I got used to it and, if they had taken it down, I probably would've been bored without it. It looms there the whole day; I focus my attention on it and ponder many important things. But then evening comes. The cupola becomes dark and the white letters disappear from view. I become grey and dissolve in the thick, gloomy darkness, just as my thoughts dissolve. Dusk is a frightening and critical time of day. Everything goes out, everything blends together. A ginger cat begins to wander the corridors, taking small velvety steps and, from time to time, I cry out. But I don't allow them to turn on the light because if the lamp flares up, I'll wring my hands and sob the whole evening. It's better to wait submissively for the moment when the final, most important scene begins in the undulating darkness.

* * *

My old mother said to me, "I won't be able to live like this for long. I see madness. You're the older one, and I know you love him. Bring Kolya back. Bring him back. You're the older one."

I remained silent.

Then she put all her yearning and all her pain into what she said.

"Find him. You pretend that's the way it has to be. But I know you. You're bright and you've understood for a long time now that this is all madness. Bring him to me for a day. For one day. I'll let him go again."

She was lying. Would she have really let him go again? I kept silent.

"I only want to kiss his eyes. You know he'll be killed anyway. You feel pity, don't you? He's my little boy. Who else can I ask? You're the older one. Bring him."

I couldn't take it anymore and said, averting my eyes, "Fine."

But she grabbed me by my sleeve and turned me to face her. "No, swear to me you'll bring him alive."

How can one make such a vow?

And I, a madman, swore. "I swear."

* * *

My mother is faint-hearted. With this thought, I left. But I did see the leaning street lamp in Berdyansk. General, sir, I agree that I was no less guilty than you. I accept the awful responsibility for the man covered in soot, but my brother has nothing to do with it. He's nineteen.

After Berdyansk I resolutely fulfilled my vow and found him twenty versts away, by a small stream. It was an unusually bright day. In turbid clouds of white dust, horsemen in formation were moving slowly on the road leading to the village from which the smell of burning was coming. He was riding in the first column on the outside, the brim of his cap cocked over his eyes. I remember everything: his right spur had dropped all the way down to the heel. The strap on his service cap extended down his cheek to under the chin.

"Kolya, Kolya!" I cried out and ran up to the ditch by the side of the road. He gave a start. Gloomy, sweaty soldiers in the column turned their heads.

"Ah . . . brother!" he shouted in response. For some reason he never called me by my name, but always "brother." I'm ten years older than him. And he always paid attention to what I said to him. "Stay. Stay here," he continued, "by the woods. We'll be right back. I can't leave the squadron."

At the edge of the wood, to the side of the dismounted squadron, we took greedy drags of cigarettes. I was calm and firm. Everything is madness. Mother was absolutely right.

And I whispered to him, "As soon as you return from the village, you're going to town with me. And immediately away from here, forever."

"What are you talking about, brother?"

"Be quiet," I said, "be quiet. I know."

The squadron mounted. They moved in waves and headed at a gallop for the billowing black clouds. And rat-a-tat-tat began in the distance. Rat-a-tat-tat in close succession.

What can happen in an hour? They'll come back. And I began to wait by the tent with the red cross.

* * *

An hour later I saw him. He was returning the same way, at a gallop. But there was no squadron. Only two horsemen with lances were galloping alongside him, and one of them—the one on the right— would lean over toward my brother from time to time as if he were whispering something to him. Squinting from the sun, I looked at the strange masquerade. He had left in a grey service cap, returned in a red one. And the day had come to an end. He had become a black display board, with a colorful headdress on it. There was no hair, and there was no forehead. In place of them was a red wreath with clumps of yellow teeth.

The horseman—my brother in the red, tousled crown—was sitting motionless on a horse frothing at the mouth, and if the man on the right had not been supporting him carefully, one would have thought he was going to a parade.

The horseman sat proud in the saddle, but he was blind and dumb. Two red spots with blood trickling down from where an hour ago bright eyes had been shining . . .

The horseman on the left dismounted, grabbed the reins with his left hand, and with his right pulled Kolya gently by the hand. The latter swayed.

And a voice said, "Ekh, our 'volunteer'[2]. . . hit by shrapnel. Orderly, call the doctor . . ."

Another voice sighed and answered, "S-s. . . what's the point, brother . . . a doctor? You need a priest here."

Then the black haze became thicker and covered everything, even the headdress . . .

* * *

I've gotten used to everything. To our white building, to the dusk, to the ginger cat that hangs around by the door, but I can't get used to his coming. The first time, when I was still below, in No. 63, he walked out of the wall. In a red crown. There was nothing frightening in this. I see him like that in my sleep. But I know very well that if he's wearing a crown, it means he's dead. And so he spoke, moving his lips, which were dry and caked with blood. He unstuck them, came to attention, brought his hand to the crown in salute and said, "Brother, I can't leave the squadron."

And since then, always, always the same thing. He comes in a soldier's blouse, with shoulder straps, with a curved saber and silent spurs, and says the same thing. Salutes. And then, "Brother, I can't leave the squadron."

What he did to me the first time! He frightened the whole clinic. It was all over for me. My reasoning is just common sense: if he's in a crown, he's been killed, and if he's been killed and comes and talks, it means I've gone mad.

* * *

Yes. Here's dusk. The critical hour of retribution. But there was one time when I fell asleep and saw the parlor with its old furniture upholstered in red plush. The comfortable chair with a cracked leg. The portrait on the wall in a dusty and black frame. Plants on stands. The piano lid open and the score to "Faust" lying on it. He was standing in the doorway and my heart lit up with wild joy. He wasn't a horseman. He was as he had been before those accursed days. In a black double-breasted jacket with chalk on the elbow. His bright eyes were laughing slyly, and a lock of hair had come down on his forehead. He was nodding his head.

"Brother, let's go to my room. Just wait and see what I'm going to show you . . . !"

It was bright in the living room from the stream of light emanating from his eyes, and the burden of guilt melted in me. There never had been that ill-omened day when I sent him, saying "go," there never had been any rattling or smoke or the smell of burning. He had never left and he had never been a horseman. He played the piano, the white keys resounded, a golden sheaf kept throwing out its light, and his voice was lively and he laughed.

* * *

Then I woke up. And there was nothing. Neither light, nor eyes. Never again did I have such a dream. But then that same night, in order to make my hellish torture even worse, a horseman in military gear nevertheless came, stepping quietly, and said what he had decided to say to me for all eternity.

I decided to put an end to it. I said to him forcefully, "What are you, my eternal torturer? Why do you come? I admit everything. I shift the blame from you to me, because I sent you to fighting that would prove deadly. The burden of guilt for the hanging I also take upon myself. Since I say this, forgive me and leave me in peace."

General, sir, he said nothing and left.

Then I became hardened from the torture and wished with all my heart that he'd come see you at least once and bring his hand to the crown in salute. I assure you, it would've been all over for you as it is for me. In no time at all. But perhaps you too aren't alone at nighttime? Who knows if that dirty man, covered in soot, doesn't visit you from the street lamp in Berdyansk? If so, we bear it, in all fairness. To help you with the hanging, I sent Kolya, but you did the hanging. You gave the unofficial oral command.

And so, he didn't leave. Then I frightened him away with my cry. Everyone got up. A woman medical attendant came running, and Ivan Vasilyevich was awakened. I didn't want to begin another day, but they didn't let me kill myself. They tied me with a piece of cloth, grabbed the glass out of my hands, and bandaged me. Since then I've been in room No. 27. After some medicine, I began to fall asleep and heard the medical attendant saying in the corridor, "Hopeless."

* * *

That's true. I have no hope. At dusk, in burning anguish, I wait in vain for sleep—for my old familiar room and the peaceful light from his radiant eyes. There's none of this and there never will be.

The burden doesn't get any lighter. And at night I wait submissively for my familiar horseman with the unseeing eyes to come and say to me hoarsely, "I can't leave the squadron."

Yes, there's no hope for me. He'll torture me to death.

1922

NOTES

1. Berdyansk: a Ukrainian port on the Sea of Azov, which forms the northern extension of the Black Sea.
2. The Russian term here (*vol'noopredelyayushchiisya*) refers to a person with a secondary education serving a term in the tsarist Russian army under privileged conditions.

BLACK MAGIC

Mikhail Zoshchenko

These aren't the times[1] to believe in sorcery or maybe even black magic, but it never hurts to talk about it.

Even now there are a lot of ignorant folk around. Who knows what it's like in other villages, but in the village of Laptenki,[2] that's how it is. For example, the women in the village of Laptenki use spells against sicknesses, and fire and water to tell fortunes, and they gather herbs and grasses with magical properties. As for other things, I don't know and can't say, but with sicknesses—that's very likely so. The old woman Vasilisa manages, in fact, even wonderfully.

Of course, if some smug foreigner were to come here, he'd no doubt only laugh.

"Oh," he'd say, "Russia, Russia, what a backward country!"

So what does he care? Give him a doctor in a top hat and jacket, but he won't even look at old Vasilisa. And maybe he won't even look at the doctor's assistant, Fyodor Ivanych Vasilchenko. That's the way it is! That's how smug he is!

But I won't even waste my time arguing with such a person. They've a different life over there, not like ours, and maybe they don't have our kinds of sicknesses over there either.

For example, they say hot-water bottles have been put in their trams so that their feet won't be exposed to the slightest draft, if you please . . .

What is this? That really takes the cake! Perfect European enlightenment and culture . . .

Well, but our life here is different and our folk aren't like they are either. For example, we lost a woman because of black magic. Dimitry Naumych's wife.

2

And it turned out to be all in vain at that. Bear in mind, Dimitri Naumych threw her out of the house. And everything happened because of that. Well no, not because of that.

There was a different incident earlier in the village. That son of a bitch, Vanyushka, got mixed up in that business. That's what happened.

Once upon a time there lived this Vanyushka, a sick and penniless fellow . . . And it's because of him that everything happened. Of course, all kinds of things happened here in the village even before that. For example, some villagers took to drowning each spring—first Vasily Vasilych, a rather rich peasant, drowned, then a village elder dove in accidentally, and then Vanyushka . . . But all this was just the result of merrymaking, but such a thing as, for example, throwing your wife out—no one even had the habit of doing such a thing here.

So then, sick and penniless Vanyushka . . . As soon as I got settled in Laptenki, I turned my full attention to Vanyushka right away. Just imagine, he struts around, happy as a lark, rubbing his little hands, the bastard. I took note of him, stopped him then in the village, and took him aside.

"What's this all about," I ask, "you walking around like a smart aleck, rubbing your little hands, you snake?"

And he, as I recall now, looked at me with such venom.

"And why," he says, "should I grieve and sorrow? I'm in clover now, you know. I may be sick and penniless, but now I'm going to live like a real man. I have really great prospects when it comes to a rich bride and dowry."

"Come on now," I say, "why are you lying?"

"Nope," he says, "I'm not lying. Take it any way you like. A guy goes for a high price now, but bear in mind, only a guy who's single, unmarried . . . But take a look yourself at what's going on around here," he says.

I took a look around and, well, I do see all kinds of goings-on: there are swarms of women in the village, young girls dance like fools with each other at evening get-togethers, and their suitors have vanished into thin air. None of their suitors are around. None of the young fellows, mind you, returned home from the German war.

"Well," I think, "Yup . . ."

And Vanyushka walks around the village and boasts.

"My time has finally come," he says. "I can do as I please. I've got my hands on a splendid life. I may be sick and penniless, but I'm a guy. You have to tell it the way it is."

Well, Vanyushka walked around the village for about a week, that son of a bitch began gulping down moonshine in his joy, and got in the habit of going across the river . . . On the other side of the river there lived this broad, Nyushka, a cheerful soldier's wife. And, just imagine, Vanyushka drowned. He was returning drunk from the soldier's wife and drowned, the fool. Couldn't hold on to his happiness.

Whereupon the village men made a lot of fun of him.

3

Well, fine. He drowned, let's say, around midnight. In the morning some fellow villagers walked along the shore, had a good laugh, and then began looking for him in the water.

They set out in their boats, pushed on with their boat-hooks, and dragged their grapnels along the bottom—no Vanyushka.

And the small river isn't much of a river—it's just called that.

The villagers got upset.

"Good Lord! What in the world is this?" they say. "We found Vasily Vasilych right away, we also found the village elder right away, but now, just imagine, we can't find such a small bug, such a nothing!"

They sent pots down the river . . . Well, yes. Ordinary pots. Clay . . . This isn't some ignorant belief or perhaps even an old custom—it's a wonderful way of finding a drowned body. And it can actually be proven with scientific facts. Let's say there's a corpse and maybe his foot got caught on something. There you have it. The water will whirl for sure above the corpse and form a funnel . . . The pot goes there and, just imagine, there it spins.

And that's the way it was here too . . . The pots were let go. One pot floated to the center of the river, and we look—it's spinning there. We poked around a bit with a boat-hook—it's deep there. A hole. We did some dragging and the grapnel got left there.

What the hell?!

The fellow villagers decided someone had to dive in.

This one, that one, the fifth one—they all say "no."

"Dimitri Naumych . . ."

He didn't argue for long, took off his miserable clothing, made a sign of the cross over his mug, and dove in.

And here, note, is where it all began.

4

Dimitri Naumych told me the story later.

"I dove in," he says. "It's fine. And as soon as I dove in, it suddenly dawned on me:

Well now, I think, there was this Vanyushka, a bachelor, unmarried, who used to go courting, but then he choked on water. Why should I pass up, I think, such a great opportunity? I'll drive my wife out, for instance, and marry a nice, little rich one."

He thought that and almost choked on the water himself, the fellow almost died. He was in the water more than the time allowed. Even the villagers began to worry, because a large bubble appeared on the water.

But only a minute later Dimitri Naumych floated up to the earthly world above, lay down on the sand, and lay there looking terribly doleful and even shivering.

"Well," thought the fellow villagers, "there's gotta be a monster on the bottom."

But on the bottom, bear in mind, everything's calm; Vanyushka is lying on the bottom, his pants caught on a snag.

The fellow villagers began questioning him—what, what was there?—and Dimitri Naumych says, "Start dragging with the grapnel, everything's calm."

The guys began dragging . . . only there's no point in going on, we don't need Vanyushka any more for this, because things took a different turn. Well, as for Vanyushka, yes, they did pull him out. Dimitri Naumych went running home.

"So," he runs and thinks, "a single man brings a high price in all the villages around here. I'll wipe her off the face of the earth," he thinks, "or maybe drive her away."

And so he thought about it some more and saw these were the very words he needed. He came home and began to strut around.

He doesn't like the way his wife walks, and the view from the window, by the way, is bad too.

His wife sees her husband is sad, but why he's sad, who knows. She then approaches him with words, and all her words are gentle.

"Why do you, Dimitri Naumych," she said, "seem so sad?"

"Yes," he answers rudely, "I'm sad. I want," he says, "to be rich, and you, bear in mind, are in my way."

His wife didn't say anything.

And it must be said that Dimitri Naumych's wife was actually a truly remarkable woman. The one misfortune was that she wasn't rich but poor. But in all other respects she was fine: her voice was gentle and pleasing, and she didn't waddle like a duck—from side to side, for instance. She had a wonderful gait and walked as if she were floating.

Her sister, her very own sister, was in fact killed by some fop because of her beauty. She didn't want to live with him.

That happened in Kiev . . .

Well, and this one, too, was really very beautiful. Everybody thought so. But Dimitri Naumych paid no heed to this opinion now and had his own ideas.

And so they had their talk, the wife kept quiet, and Dimitri Naumych, mind you, looked for a reason to throw her out.

He walked around a bit in the hut.

"Come on woman," he yells, "give me something to eat, will you!"

But it was a long time to dinner. His wife, with good reason, answers. "My dear Dimitri Naumych," she says, "I hadn't even thought of lighting the stove yet."

"Ah," he says, "you thought, thought," he says, "maybe you thought of starving me to death? Gather your junk," he says, "your kvass and bread rolls. You," he says, "are no longer my lawful wife."

At this point the wife got terribly scared and began to think.

She sees he's throwing her out. And why he's throwing her out, who knows. She's clean in all her dealings, like a mirror. She thought she'd solve the matter peacefully. She bowed at his feet.

"Why don't you beat me, you Pilate and torturer, because I've no place to go."

But Dimitri Naumych, even though he fulfilled her request and beat her, still threw her out of the house.

5

And so the wife gathered her junk—some pathetic skirt full of holes—and walked out into the yard.

But where does a wife go if she's no place to go?

She hung about the yard, howled and cried a bit, and thought about it some more.

"I'll go," she thinks, "and see my neighbor, perhaps she can give me some advice."

She went to her neighbor. The neighbor sighed and moaned a bit, and spread some cards on the table.

"Yes," she says, "things are pretty bad for you. Frankly," she says, "things are really terrible. Just take a look yourself. Here's the king of spades, here's the eight of spades, and the queen of spades is about to leave. The cards don't lie. Your husband has something against you. Only it's all your fault. That's for sure."

Note what a fool that neighbor was. Just when she should have comforted the woman who was beside herself, she began to chant as follows: "Yes," she chanted, "it's all your fault. If you see your husband's sad, put up with it, don't jabber. For example, he throws hard-to-take words at you, but you say, 'Allow me to take off your boots and wipe them with the driest rag I can find'—a husband likes that . . ."

Ugh, you old fool! Such words . . .

She should have comforted the wife, but instead she upset her to no end.

The wife jumped to her feet, trembling.

"Oh, what in the world have I done? Oh, for God's sake," she says, "give me some advice! I'll agree to anything now. I've no place to go, you know."

But the old fool, ugh, it's disgusting even to say her name, just threw up her hands.

"I don't know," she says, "my dear young woman. Frankly, I can't tell you anything. Nowadays a guy is worth a lot. And you won't entice him with your beauty and charms alone. Don't even think about it."

Then the wife rushed out of the hut, ran out to the backyard, took the back street and headed along the outskirts of the village. The poor thing was ashamed to go into the village itself.

And lo! The wife sees a little old woman, no one she knows, coming toward her. The old woman is walking—swaying lightly from side to side—and whispering something to herself.

Our wife bowed to her and began to weep.

"Hello, dear old woman, granny, whoever you are," she says. "Just look," she says, "at the goings-on in this world."

The old woman glanced at her and maybe nodded her little head.

"Yes," she says, "all kinds of things are going on . . . Oh, my young woman, my young one, I know everything that goes on in this world. All people have to be killed—that's what's going on. But just don't cry, I beg you, don't ruin your eyes. In a case like this, tears are of no use. But here's what: I know various ways—there are herbs and grasses with magical properties. There are also spells that can be said, but they're not worth very much when it comes to such a big undertaking. And there's only one remedy for such a thing—for keeping your man at your side. It's a frightening way, and it involves a special, magnificent black cat. You can always recognize this kind of cat. Oh, this kind of cat likes to look into your eyes, and when it looks into your eyes, it deliberately moves its tail slowly and arches its back . . ."

The wife listens to the old woman's frightening words and her heart is overcome with fear.

Of course, no one heard what the old woman said except our wife, but all this is absolutely true. Yulia Karlovna also spoke of it. Later on, this became quite clear. And later on, it also became clear that you had to take this black cat, heat up the bathhouse at midnight, and throw the cat live into a kettle.

"I beg you," the old woman said, "make sure you throw in a live cat and not a dead one. And when everything's over, take out a small bone, the round one and, I beg you, always keep it with you."

When the wife heard this, she was overcome with terror and bowed low to the old woman.

"I'll go," she thinks, "bow once more to Dimitri Naumych, and if he doesn't change his mind, then I have a frightful remedy, a magnificent one."

6

The wife went back to the village to bow to Dimitri Naumych, but she went, bear in mind, in vain.

How could Dimitry Naumych have changed his mind if he was dying to go to town and had even tried to put an end to the matter?

I had dropped in on him at that point. He was already harnessing his horse. He told me a lot of things at the time.

"I would never have thrown such a wife out, honest to God! It would've been better to tear me to pieces and scatter the pieces in the field," he says, "but I never would've agreed to such a thing. She, my wife, suited me very well. But listen, I'm dying to be rich and live a nice life. Take a look yourself. What kind of a man am I really? I have only one joy and that's my horse, but otherwise everything's going to rack and ruin. Well listen here, my friend, tell me for God's sake, do I have, for example, a cow?"

"No," I say, "you don't have a cow, Dimitri Naumych. That I can confirm. You," I say, "don't even have a lousy sheep."

"Well now," he says, "you see! What kind of a man am I after that?"

"Well," I say, "for you not to have a cow is like for a tailor not to have hands."

"And you," he says, "you keep saying 'wife'! What's a wife? Only that's she's pretty, but listen, there aren't any other benefits when it comes to her . . . . Well, her sister, for instance, was killed for her beauty. That was in Kiev. So what's it to me now? I can't even get a miserable coat out of it. And, I'll say it frankly, I don't really care now."

He speaks like that, explaining things to me, but his wife, mind you, is standing right next to him.

He saw her and started shouting.

"What do you need?" he shouted "Leave! Do me the favor!"

And the wife got frightened by his shouting and didn't say what she should have.

"I'm leaving," she says, "Dimitri Naumych, I don't know where to yet, most likely the Kiev Cave Monastery,[3] so allow me, in parting, to steam myself in your bathhouse."

The husband looked at her to see if she was trying to trick him. No, she wasn't.

Dimitri Naumych became kinder.

"Fine," he says, "go steam yourself a while. I'm not going to gripe about it," he says. "I'm not, you know, some animal. Why did I throw you out? You're a very good woman and all that, but excuse me, you're nothing but dirty old rags. You don't have anything and, admit it, you never did. And listen, those relatives of yours, if only someone could have done some little thing for me in all those years. Someone at least could've given me a gift just for the fun of it. If only someone had treated me, for example, to a shirt for the holidays, for Easter. 'Wear it,' so to say, 'Dimitri Naumych, and enjoy it . . .' But there was nothing of the kind." The woman didn't listen to him long, turned around and left, and Dimitri Naumych climbed into the wagon, let out a whistle and a whoop and off he went.

And so, just imagine, he's going to town, but his wife in the meantime has heated up the bathhouse, lured the priest's black cat into the bathhouse and locked it in, and waited for night to fall.

I met her, the poor woman, that night. She was running through the village. She had the cat pressed to her bosom ever so tightly and was running, running bareheaded and looking sort of frightening.

"Oh," I thought, "that woman is done for. But just keep in mind, it's none of my business."

7

Toward midnight the man did what he had to do, had the tiniest bit to drink with his brother in town, and headed back happy, even singing some tunes. And he has no sense, no idea, of what's about to befall him. But something completely surprising is about to befall him—a twig, well, a dry branch, let's say, will catch in a wheel, and his horse will die . . .

Only more about that later. The time isn't right for that yet. But I must just say: if the horse hadn't fallen at that point, then maybe nothing would've happened to the wife. Dimitri Naumych would've made it in time, but instead, can you imagine, the horse fell.

All right . . . So, stretched out in the wagon with his hands flung out, the fellow is riding through the forest. He's riding.

And the horse is moving at a trot; he doesn't even have to drive it. But then, Dimitri isn't driving it. Bear in mind, he had even let go of the reins.

And he did the right thing because a horse will always find its way home, both day and night. I know this perfectly well. I was actually a coachman myself for more than a year.

And so, Dimitri Naumych's horse is trotting along, and Dimitri Naumych has let go of the reins and is singing tunes to himself. And the night, bear in mind, is as dark as can be.

All right. He's nicely drunk and humming "Brown Eyes," except he looks and sees he's approaching a churchyard.

And the fellow began to feel uneasy.

"Good heavens! How many poor people are buried here," he thinks, "and I can't escape such a place either. But I'm occupied, just think, with such things as, for example, throwing my wife out for the sake of some riches and luxury . . . ."

He drove up to the churchyard feeling gloomy and forgot all about his tunes. He lies in the wagon and feels bored.

Only he senses that someone seems to be staring at him.

"Who's there?" the fellow shouted.

"Oo!" shouts came from the churchyard.

The fellow wanted to urge his horse on, but he sensed that he was too scared to even move his hand.

"Well," he thinks, "better pass such a haunt of vice quickly." The very moment he expressed that wish to himself, someone smacked him in the mug.

Dimitri Naumych froze and grew cold.

And just imagine, the branch turned once more in the wheel, and smack!—right in his face again! Dimitri Naumych let out a deathly cry. And the horse is stupid. The horse hears the peasant shouting and thinks he's shouting at it. It took off.

The fellow shouts in a voice not his own, and the horse is really rushing on, speeding toward home. After they had covered in all likelihood about five versts, Dimitri Naumych saw that no one was hitting him in the face anymore. He stopped screaming and came to his senses.

He came to his senses; whoa and whoa—he couldn't stop his horse.

The fool should have said "sh-sh," but he pulled on the reins. He pulls on the reins and the horse evidently heads to the side. The horse evidently heads to the side, and on the side, bear in mind, is a tree.

The horse ran into the tree. Smacked its head against the tree and dropped dead.

The fellow fell out of the wagon and took off his cap.

Yes, he sees the horse is dead. "Oh," he thinks, "this is a real misfortune. I haven't had such a disaster in my whole life! Well," he thinks, "I've been sent this misfortunate for no other reason than because of my wife."

The fellow stands there and can't believe his eyes.

And he feels sorry both for himself and for his horse—it's something so valuable, so much a part of his peasant life, and he's so sad about his wife that it's unbearable even to say anything. He just stands there, just stands.

"Well," he thinks, "what's happened has happened. I'll head for the

village as quickly as I can, maybe nothing's happened to my wife yet."
Those were his thoughts as he began to hurry, tied the horse to the tree
for some reason, lifted the shaft-bow and harness onto his back, and set
out with a quick step.

Only he was rushing in vain. It was already too late. Something that
the fellow never would have dreamed of happened.

8

The wife had begun doing it—the black magic, when Dimitri Naumych
was approaching the churchyard.

The wife had come to the bathhouse at that hour, left her cross[4] and
pathetic clothing in the changing room, and went into the bathhouse
with nothing on. She went into the bathhouse, took the lid off the kettle,
and started looking for the cat.

"Where's the cat?" she wonders. No sign of it for some reason." She
looks and sees the cat hiding under the bench.

The wife calls it, "Here, kitty, kitty," but just imagine, it bares its teeth
and looks her straight in the eye.

The wife reached for it; it tried to bite her. Somehow the wife managed
to grab it by its fur, plunked it in the kettle, and quickly put the lid on.

She puts the lid on and hears the cat putting up such a terrible struggle
in the kettle that even the cast iron lid is lifting up. The wife presses down
hard on the kettle and becomes weak all over from fear, and any second
now, she sees, she won't have the strength to hold on. And something is
moving around and around in the kettle and then it stops.

The wife added some more wood, stepped away from the stove, and
sat down on the bench. She waited. And then it sounded to her like the
water was boiling. She took a look: yes, the lid was rising and shaking
violently.

"Well," the wife thinks, "now it'll be over."

She rushed up to the kettle and had barely lifted the lid when the cat
or something else leapt out at her face. The wife threw up her hands and
collapsed on the floor.

9

Of course, no one knows exactly how this happened. More likely than not, the wife opened the kettle and got burned by the steam. And in her fright the wife thought the cat had leapt out at her. She went and died from fright. And that's how the whole thing ended.

I came to the village in the morning and saw the fellow, Dimitri Naumych, running as quickly as he could, and just imagine, fittingly enough, there was a shaft-bow and harness on him.

I was very surprised and he turned to me.

"Have you seen my wife?" he shouts.

"No, I haven't seen your wife," I answer. "Now yesterday," I say, "yes, I did see her. She was heating the bathhouse last night."

He grabbed my hand and we started running.

We burst into the bathhouse, crossed the threshold, and were presented with the following unbearable scene.

Just imagine, the wife was lying on the floor, dead as dead can be. Dimitri Naumych moaned, grabbed his head and said, "Now," he said, "because of my greed, I've lost such a faithful spouse!"

And, of course, he shed bitter tears.

1922

NOTES

1. After the revolution of 1917 emphasis was placed on structuring life along rational lines. Folk beliefs and superstitions came under increasing attack as being part of the "dark," unenlightened past.
2. Laptenki: the diminutive form of *lapti*, the bast shoes worn by peasants.
3. The Kiev Cave Monastery: famous for its catacombs in which the bodies of monks and various church leaders have been preserved for centuries.
4. She removes her cross in order not to anger the unclean force or devil as she attempts to perform black magic.

THE FEMALE FISH
(*Deacon Vasily's Story*)

Mikhail Zoshchenko

It's not right—this shame, feeling awkward at the sight of priestly attire—but out on the street you feel uncomfortable anyway and sense your chest tightening.

Of course, these past three years[1] priests have been really disgraced. These past three years, one could say, some have been even driven to the point of rejecting their vows and renouncing God publically. That's what they've been driven to.

And as for the attacks and torments the priest Triodin had to endure, there's no counting them. And he endured them not only from the government authorities, but even from his own wife.[2] But he didn't reject his vows and didn't renounce God. On the contrary, he was proud in his heart—persecution, so to say, of pastors.

The priest would get up in the morning and say sternly, "My wife, I believe."

And only then would he do everything else.

And who could imagine that such strength would be found in such an unimposing man? It's ridiculous. The priest had no presence whatsoever. Absolutely no presence at all. To look at him, he was completely red-haired and short—he came up only to his wife's shoulders.

Oh, and more than once his wife would reproach him for his unimposing appearance. And that's right. It's surprising how really small today's men are. All the women in the district are pretty big, but the men don't look like that. All the women, for example, do men's work easily, and the men, it's come to pass, have even gone and taken up women's work.

Of course, such men should really be shot. But it's also true that many men have been wiped out by state executions and war. And if anyone has survived, life has reduced them to almost nothing.

Is there now, for instance, a thinking Russian man who would gain weight and get fat? There's no such man.

Of course, that's little comfort to the priest, and the priest would say: "You reproach me, wife, you reproach me with the way I look, but in the life of fish according to Darwin, the female fish is always larger than the male fish and even eats him when angered."

And in response to such words by the priest, the wife would slam down a plate, for example, or let's say a cup, and her feelings would be hurt, although she wouldn't know why.

2

And now it's the third year that the priest and his wife are leading separate lives.

And just when the wife could have approached her husband with heartfelt affection and said, "It's truly difficult for you, husband, because of the persecution, and so please accept my affection," such was not the case. The wife wasn't like that. It's true, the wife wasn't in her declining years, but she should have been ashamed to powder her nose day in and day out and wag her tail in the evening.

And what consolation is there in life for a priest if family foundations have been shaken?

The priest's consolation lay in playing a bit of preference[3] a little at a time on non-church holidays and, before a game of preference, in having a conversation about state and even European issues and the impossibility of the Christian era coming to an end.

Words sounded very sweet to the priest's ears. And he felt that he always found the right words. At first something insignificant, let's say the price of bread has gone up, so our life is not that great. And if our life is not so great, what's the reason for it? As they got to talking, the priest played with various ideas in his mind: state policies, Soviet power, the foundations of life have been shaken.

And when a word like "Soviet" is said . . . then he really gets started. The priest has old scores to settle with the Soviets. Too many hurt feelings and attacks. There was even a time when they came to his house at night, grabbed him by the beard, and threatened him with a piece of wood.

"Come on, tell us," they say, "are there any relics in the church? People have to see the deception for themselves."

And what relics can there be in a church, if the church is the poorest in the whole Bygriansk district?

"There aren't any," says the priest, "no holy relics of any kind, and be so kind as to let go of my beard."

But they keep on threatening him and wielding the piece of wood to frighten him.

And they didn't believe the priest.

"Take us anyway," they say, "show us what the church has."

And the priest started to lead them to the church.

But it was already late at night. And it turned out somehow strangely. The priest kept leading them and leading them through the town, but there's wasn't any church. His mind, perhaps, was overcome by fear; the priest had taken the wrong streets. But suddenly an unusually pleasant feeling spread through his veins.

"A matter," the priest thought, "like that of Susanin."[4]

And he led them to the very edge of town, beyond the flea market. And they flew into a rage, grabbed him by the beard again, and pointed out the way themselves.

During the night they wreaked havoc with the church property, fouled the air with tobacco and left footprints all over, but didn't find any relics.

"Well," they said, "you priest's cassock, there aren't any relics, so you know what? We'll establish a movie theater in your church."

And with that they left.

"How can that be—a movie theater?" the priest said to his wife. "Can you establish a movie theater in a church? It's just said to frighten me, wife. The parish won't let it come to that, although their religious belief has been terribly shaken. The parish won't let it come to that."

Here's where the wife should have approached her husband with heartfelt affection, but no—the wife had her own things to do. And just what are those things the wife had to do, tell me? Here she is, all dressed, if you please, and here she's gone and left, and don't you say a word. No great liking for family life.

But such behavior goes on not only in the priest's house and everyone says, "A woman," they say, "looks elsewhere." What's happened to Russian women?

3

And so, what's happened to Russian women? There's nothing funny about a Russian woman doing a man's work, or the fact that, let's say, she's cut off her braid.[5]

The Chinese had a critical year like that; the Chinese began cutting off their braids in public. And so what? It means the braid has gone out of fashion historically. There's nothing funny here.

But that's not the point. The point is this: great shamelessness and lechery have taken hold of our women. And the priest, time and time again, appeared in his vestments before the people and harangued them with these bitter words: "Citizens and parishioners and my beloved flock. Family and marital foundations have been shaken. The fire is going out in the family hearth. Come to your senses in your disbelief and satanic shamelessness."

And the priest kept selecting such beautiful words that they struck one's heart and evoked tears. But the lechery didn't abate.

And there never has been such shamelessness and such easy relationships among the people as there are this year. Of course, there's always a sharp rise in lechery in the spring, but go, please, to a military club and listen to what intolerable talk there is around women as a class. It's just terrible!

And what can you do? If the priest's wife powders her nose and the priest doesn't say a word, then can anything be done? And though the priest understood this very well, nevertheless he stuck to his bitter sermons.

And it was in such a lecherous spring that a railroad worker was assigned to live with them. This was in the wife's not so declining years.

The priest was steadfast and patient, but from this blow he lost no less than ten years of life. The railroad worker was really very handsome and robust.

And his good looks notwithstanding, the worker was unusually polite and could even discuss various subjects. And discussing various subjects, he was interested in the fine points, for example, how and why it has become the custom among people that, upon meeting a priest, a passer-by makes a "fig"* with his fingers.

But in discussing various subjects and showing an interest in the fine points, the worker inevitably turned to the question of women as a class and talked about love.

And even if the worker could have conversed on European topics, the priest wouldn't have treated him nicely. This worker was really very dangerous.

"Arguing in a limited way," the priest would say, "not on a European scale, why is there such persecution of priests? Why move in, for instance, a railroad worker? Our poor apartment is not huge, as you know yourself. Either a carambole[6] will come of it, or constraint of the individual."

And people would shake their heads in response to such words from the priest, saying, "Exactly, it's hard for people of your station; there are constraints on the priesthood."

But the priest's wife would shrug her shoulders insolently.

4

That's precisely what happened; the priest had a *carambole* with the railroad worker.

And it happened that the priest's partners and friends in life— Venyamin, the deacon, and Ivan Mikhailovich Gulka, a city teacher in what used to be a four-year school for boys—came to visit the priest.

A conversation started about insignificant matters, of course, and then about the persecution of priests. But Venyamin, the deacon, a zealous deacon, is not the least bit interested in abstract politics.

The priest is talking about the Christian era, and Venyamin the deacon is admiring his cards—placing one queen next to his other queen . . . And as soon as there's a break in the conversation, he's already saying, "Well," he says, "without losing any precious time . . ."

They broke off their conversation, sat down at the table, and dealt the cards. And at this point the priest announced, "Eight cards. Who's going to bid?"

And right away the priest got such a worthless hand. Venyamin the deacon trumps his diamond, and the teacher Gulka beats his club, but it doesn't matter.

At this point the priest got very agitated and, using the evening tea as an excuse, went out for a drink of water.

He drank a ladleful of water and on his way back went up to his wife's door.

"Wife," the priest said, "wife, don't get upset. What about evening tea?"

But his wife wasn't in the room. The priest went to the kitchen—no wife. The priest looked here and there and everywhere—no wife.

And then the priest checked the worker's room. His wife was sitting in a depraved pose with the railroad worker.

"Oh," said the priest and quietly closed the door. And tip-toeing back, he went to finish the game with his guests.

He came and sat down, as if nothing had happened.

The priest keeps playing—only his face is white. He throws down his cards, shakes his head, taps the table with his fingers, and says, "The female fish has devoured us."

And what sort of female fish, tell us?

And suddenly the priest got lucky. The teacher Gulka, let's say he discards the ace of diamonds, and the priest trumps it; the teacher Gulka tries to win back the cards of the same suit using a spade, and the priest uses his trump card. And the most valuable card is moving and moving in the priest's direction.

And the priest won handsomely that evening. He folded the new banknotes and smiled with a heavy heart.

"Yes, everything's fine," he said, "but why such persecution? Why move in railroad workers?"

Venyamin the deacon and Gulka the teacher took offense.

"He won," they say, "the priest robbed us, but he's pretending to be unhappy. And he didn't even treat us to tea, that priest's cassock."

The offended guests left and the priest put away the cards, went into the bedroom and, without waiting for his wife, lay down quietly on the bed.

5

There's great sadness in the world. It has accumulated and settled in various places and you can't see it right away.

Let's say the priest's sadness is funny; it's funny that the priest's wife promised the worker some money, but she can't get it. And what the railroad worker said about the priest's wife—"a real old woman"— is funny too. And gather all this and put it all together, and you have great sadness.

The priest woke up in the morning and touched the cross on his chest.

"Wife, I believe," he said.

And having said "wife," he remembered the day before.

Oh, the female fish! His wife had devoured him. And what's bad is not that she had sinned, but what's bad is that now everything has gotten worse for the priest; everything has come together against him, and he has no way out.

The priest got dressed, didn't look at his wife, and left the house without having tea.

Oh, and how sadly weep the bells, and how sad is human life! The priest should lie on the ground like an inanimate object or do something heroic, like accept execution and save humanity.

The priest got up and with heavy step went to the church.

After he finished celebrating the liturgy, the priest, according to his habit, gave a sermon. "Citizens," he said, "and parishioners, and my beloved parish. Family foundations have been shaken and destroyed. The fire has gone out in the family hearth. It has come to pass. And looking at this, I can't reconcile myself to it and recognize the authority of the state."

That evening some thugs came to the priest's, went through all his church things and property, and took the priest away.

1923

NOTES

1. After the revolution of 1917 many churches were pillaged and all but destroyed; countless priests were killed or exiled to Siberia.
2. In the Orthodox tradition, a priest's wife is referred to as *matushka* (derived from *mat'*, meaning "mother"). We are translating *matushka* as "priest's wife" or "wife," depending on what best suits the English text.
3. preference: a three-player card game from Europe, similar to bridge, euchre and five-hundred.
4. Susanin: a reference to the legend about Ivan Susanin, a logger who was said to have saved the life of Mikhail Romanov in 1612, when the latter had just been elected to the Russian throne. A Polish detachment, loyal to Sigizmund III Vasa who still laid claim to the Russian throne, tried to find and kill the new tsar. Susanin promised to take them via a shortcut through a forest to the monastery where the tsar could be found. They were never seen again, presumably because the forest was so deep and the February weather so cruel.
5. It was traditional for an unmarried village woman to wear a long braid down her back. After the revolution young women, particularly in the cities, began to cut their hair short as a mark of their liberation and the new mores.
6. *carambole* (Fr.): a move in billiards when one ball hits another and then ricochets to hit a third.

Three Stories from RED CAVALRY

Isaac Babel

(Notes at the end of the third story —Eds.)

GEDALI

On the eve of the Sabbath I am always tormented by the dense sorrow of memory. In the past on these evenings, my grandfather's yellow beard caressed the volumes of Ibn Ezra. My old grandmother, in her lace bonnet, waved spells over the Sabbath candle with her gnarled fingers, and sobbed sweetly. On those evenings my child's heart was gently rocked, like a little boat on enchanted waves.

I wander through Zhitomir looking for the timid star.[1] Beside the ancient synagogue, beside its indifferent yellow walls, old Jews, Jews with the beards of prophets, passionate rags hanging from their sunken chests, are selling chalk, bluing, and candle wicks.

Here before me lies the bazaar, and the death of the bazaar. Slaughtered is the fat soul of abundance. Mute padlocks hang on the stores, and the granite of the streets is as clean as a corpse's bald head. The timid star blinks and expires.

Success came to me later, I found the star just before the setting of the sun. Gedali's store lay hidden among the tightly shut market stalls. Dickens, where was your shadow that evening?[2] In this old junk store you would have found gilded slippers and ship's ropes, an antique compass and a stuffed eagle, a Winchester hunting rifle with the date "1810" engraved on it, and a broken stewpot.

Old Gedali is circling around his treasures in the rosy emptiness of the evening, a small shopkeeper with smoky spectacles and a green coat that reaches all the way to the ground. He rubs his small white hands, tugs at his gray beard, lowers his head, and listens to invisible voices that come wafting to him.

This store is like the box of an intent and inquisitive little boy who will one day become a professor of botany. This store has everything from buttons to dead butterflies, and its little owner is called Gedali. Everyone has left the bazaar, but Gedali has remained. He roams through his labyrinth of globes, skulls, and dead flowers, waving his cockerel-feather duster, swishing away the dust from the dead flowers.

We sit down on some empty beer barrels. Gedali winds and unwinds his narrow beard. His top hat rocks above us like a little black tower. Warm air flows past us. The sky changes color—tender blood pouring from an overturned bottle—and a gentle aroma of decay envelops me.

"So let's say we say 'yes' to the Revolution. But does that mean that we're supposed to say 'no' to the Sabbath?" Gedali begins, enmeshing me in the silken cords of his smoky eyes. "Yes to the Revolution! Yes! But the Revolution keeps hiding from Gedali and sending gunfire ahead of itself."

"The sun cannot enter eyes that are squeezed shut," I say to the old man, "but we shall rip open those closed eyes!"

"The Pole has closed my eyes," the old man whispers almost inaudibly. "The Pole, that evil dog! He grabs the Jew and rips out his beard, *oy*, the hound! But now they are beating him, the evil dog! This is marvelous, this is the Revolution! But then the same man who beat the Pole says to me, 'Gedali, we are requisitioning your gramophone!' 'But gentlemen,' I tell the Revolution, 'I love music!' And what does the Revolution answer me? 'You don't know what you love, Gedali! I am going to shoot you, and then you'll know, and I cannot *not* shoot, because I am the Revolution!'"

"The Revolution cannot *not* shoot, Gedali," I tell the old man, "because it is the Revolution."

"But my dear *Pan!* The Pole did shoot, because he is the counterrevolution. And you shoot because you are the Revolution. But Revolution is happiness. And happiness does not like orphans in its house. A good man does good deeds. The Revolution is the good deed done by good men. But good men do not kill. Hence the Revolution is done by bad men. But the Poles are also bad men. Who is going to tell Gedali which is the Revolution and which the counterrevolution? I have studied the Talmud. I love the commentaries of Rashi and the books of Maimonides. And there are also other people in Zhitomir who understand. And so all of us learned men fall to the floor and shout with a single voice, 'Woe unto us, where is the sweet Revolution?'"

The old man fell silent. And we saw the first star breaking through and meandering along the Milky Way.

"The Sabbath is beginning," Gedali pronounced solemnly. "Jews must go to the synagogue."

"*Pan* Comrade," he said, getting up, his top hat swaying on his head like a little black tower. "Bring a few good men to Zhitomir. *Oy,* they are lacking in our town, *oy,* how they are lacking! Bring good men and we shall give them all our gramophones. We are not simpletons. The International,[3] we know what the International is. And I want the International of good people, I want every soul to be accounted for and given first-class rations. Here, soul, eat, go ahead, go and find happiness in your life. The International, *Pan* Comrade, you have no idea how to swallow it!"

"With gunpowder," I tell the old man, "and seasoned with the best blood." And then from the blue darkness young Sabbath climbed onto her throne.

"Gedali," I say to him, "today is Friday, and night has already fallen. Where can I find some Jewish biscuits, a Jewish glass of tea, and a piece of that retired God in the glass of tea?"

"You can't," Gedali answers, hanging a lock on his box, "you can't find any. There's a tavern next door, and good people used to run it, but people don't eat there anymore, they weep."

He fastened the three bone buttons of his green coat. He dusted himself with the cockerel feathers, sprinkled a little water on the soft palms of his hands, and walked off, tiny, lonely, dreamy, with his black top hat, and a large prayer book under his arm.

The Sabbath begins. Gedali, the founder of an unattainable International, went to the synagogue to pray.

THE RABBI

"All things are mortal. Only a mother is accorded eternal life. And when a mother is not among the living, she leaves behind a memory that no one has yet dared to defile. The memory of a mother nourishes compassion within us, just as the ocean, the boundless ocean, nourishes the rivers that cut through the universe."

These were Gedali's words. He uttered them gravely. The dying evening wrapped him in the rosy haze of its sadness.

"In the ardent house of Hasidism," the old man said, "the windows and doors have been torn out, but it is as immortal as a mother's soul. Even with blinded eyes, Hasidism still stands at the crossroads of the winds of history."

That is what Gedali said, and, after having prayed in the synagogue, he took me to Rabbi Motale, the last rabbi of the Chernobyl dynasty.

Gedali and I walked up the main street. White churches glittered in the distance like fields of buckwheat. A gun cart moaned around the corner. Two pregnant Ukrainian women came out through the gates of a house, their coin necklaces jingling, and sat down on a bench. A timid star flashed in the orange battles of the sunset, and peace, a Sabbath peace, descended on the slanted roofs of the Zhitomir ghetto.

"Here," Gedali whispered, pointing at a long house with a shattered facade.

We went into a room, a stone room, empty as a morgue. Rabbi Motale sat at a table surrounded by liars and men possessed. He was wearing a sable hat and a white robe, with a rope for a belt. The rabbi was sitting, his eyes closed, his thin fingers digging through the yellow fluff of his beard.

"Where have you come from, Jew?" he asked me, lifting his eyelids.

"From Odessa," I answered.

"A devout town," the rabbi said. "The star of our exile, the reluctant well of our afflictions! What is the Jew's trade?"

"I am putting the adventures of Hershele of Ostropol[4] into verse."

"A great task," the rabbi whispered, and closed his eyelids. "The jackal moans when it is hungry, every fool has foolishness enough for despondency, and only the sage shreds the veil of existence with laughter . . . What did the Jew study?"

"The Bible."

"What is the Jew looking for?"

"Merriment."

"Reb Mordkhe," the rabbi said, and shook his beard. "Let the young man seat himself at the table, let him eat on the Sabbath evening with other Jews, let him rejoice that he is alive and not dead, let him clap his hands as his neighbors dance, let him drink wine if he is given wine!"

And Reb Mordkhe came bouncing toward me, an ancient fool with inflamed eyelids, a hunchbacked little old man, no bigger than a ten-year-old boy.

"*Oy,* my dear and so very young man!" ragged Reb Mordkhe said, winking at me. "*Oy,* how many rich fools have I known in Odessa, how many wise paupers have I known in Odessa! Sit down at the table, young man, and drink the wine that you will not be given!"

We all sat down, one next to the other-the possessed, the liars, the unhinged. In the corner, broad-shouldered Jews who looked like fishermen and apostles were moaning over prayer books. Gedali in his green coat dozed by the wall like a bright bird. And suddenly I saw a youth behind Gedali, a youth with the face of Spinoza, with the powerful forehead of Spinoza, with the sickly face of a nun. He was smoking and twitching like an escaped convict who has been tracked down and brought back to his jail. Ragged Reb Mordkhe sneaked up on him from behind, snatched the cigarette from his mouth, and came running over to me.

"That is Ilya, the rabbi's son," Mordkhe wheezed, turning the bloody flesh of his inflamed eyelids to me, "the damned son, the worst son, the disobedient son!"

And Mordkhe threatened the youth with his little fist and spat in his face.

"Blessed is the Lord," the voice of Rabbi Motale Bratslavsky rang out, and he broke the bread with his monastic fingers. "Blessed is the God of Israel, who has chosen us among all the peoples of the world."

The rabbi blessed the food, and we sat down at the table. Outside the window horses neighed and Cossacks shouted. The wasteland of war yawned outside. The rabbi's son smoked one cigarette after another during the silent prayer. When the dinner was over, I was the first to rise.

"My dear and so very young man," Mordkhe muttered behind me, tugging at my belt. "If there was no one in the world except for evil rich men and destitute tramps, how would holy men live?"

I gave the old man some money and went out into the street. Gedali and I parted, and I went back to the railroad station. There at the station, on the propaganda train of the First Cavalry, I was greeted by the sparkle of hundreds of lights, the enchanted glitter of the radio transmitter, the stubborn rolling of the printing presses, and my unfinished article for the *Krasny Kavalerist*.[5]

THE RABBI'S SON

Do you remember Zhitomir, Vasily? Do you remember the River Teterev, Vasily, and that night in which the Sabbath, the young Sabbath, crept along the sunset crushing the stars with the heel of her red slipper?

The thin horn of the moon dipped its arrows in the black waters of the Teterev. Little, funny Gedali, the founder of the Fourth International,[6] who took us to Rabbi Motale Bratslavsky for evening prayer. Little, funny Gedali, shaking the cockerel feathers of his top hat in the red smoke of the evening. The candles' predatory pupils twinkled in the rabbi's room. Broad-shouldered Jews crouched moaning over prayer books, and the old jester of the Chernobyl line of *tsaddiks* jingled copper coins in his frayed pocket.

You remember that night, Vasily? Outside the window horses neighed and Cossacks shouted. The wasteland of war yawned outside and Rabbi Motale Bratslavsky, clutching his tallith with his withered fingers, prayed at the eastern wall. Then the curtains of the cabinet fell open, and in the funerary shine of the candles we saw the Torah scrolls, wrapped in coverings of purple velvet and blue silk, and above the Torah scrolls hovered the humble, beautiful, lifeless face of llya, the rabbi's son, the last prince of the dynasty.

And then, Vasily, two days ago the regiments of the Twelfth Army opened the front at Kovel. The victors' haughty cannonade thundered through the town. Our troops were shaken and thrown into disarray. The Polit-otdel train[7] crept along the dead spine of the fields. The typhoid-ridden muzhik horde rolled the gigantic ball of rampant soldier death before it. The horde scampered onto the steps of our train and fell off again, beaten back by rifle butts. It panted, scrambled, ran, was silent. And after twelve versts, when I no longer had any potatoes to throw to them, I threw a bundle of Trotsky leaflets at them. But only one of them stretched out a dirty, dead hand to grab a leaflet. And I recognized Ilya, the son of the Zhitomir rabbi. I recognized him straightaway, Vasily! It was so painful to see the prince, who had lost his trousers, his back snapped in two by the weight of his soldier's rucksack, that we broke the rules and dragged him up into the railroad car. His naked knees, clumsy like the knees of an old woman, knocked against the rusty iron of the steps. Two fat-breasted typists in sailor blouses dragged the dying man's timid, lanky body along the floor. We laid him out in the corner of the train's editorial compartment. Cossacks in red Tatar trousers fixed his slipped clothing. The girls, their bandy bovine legs firmly planted on the floor, stared coolly at his sexual organs, the withered, curly manhood of the emaciated Semite. And I, who had met him during one of my nights of wandering, packed the scattered belongings of Red Army soldier Ilya Bratslavsky into my suitcase.

I threw everything together in a jumble, the mandates of the political agitator and the mementos of a Jewish poet. Portraits of Lenin and Maimonides lay side by side—the gnarled steel of Lenin's skull and the listless silk of the Maimonides portrait. A lock of woman's hair lay in a book of the resolutions of the Sixth Party Congress, and crooked lines of Ancient Hebrew verse huddled in the margins of *Communist* pamphlets. Pages of *The Song of Songs* and revolver cartridges drizzled on me in a sad, sparse rain. The sad rain of the sunset washed the dust from my hair, and I said to the young man, who was dying on a ripped mattress in the corner, "Four months ago, on a Friday evening, Gedali the junk dealer took me to your father, Rabbi Motale, but back then, Bratslavsky, you were not in the Party."

"I was in the Party back then," the young man answered, scratching his chest and twisting in his fever. "But I couldn't leave my mother behind."

"What about now, Ilya?"

"My mother is just an episode of the Revolution," he whispered, his voice becoming fainter. "Then my letter came up, the letter 'B,' and the organization sent me off to the front...."

"So you ended up in Kovel?"

"I ended up in Kovel!" he shouted in despair. "The damn kulaks opened the front. I took over a mixed regiment, but it was too late. I didn't have enough artillery."

He died before we reached Rovno. He died, the last prince, amid poems, phylacteries, and foot bindings. We buried him at a desolate train station. And I, who can barely harness the storms of fantasy raging through my ancient body, I received my brother's last breath.

NOTES

1. The Star of David.
2. A reference to Charles Dickens's novel *The Old Curiosity Shop*.
3. The Third Communist International, 1919-1943, an organization founded in Moscow by the delegates of twelve countries to promote Communism worldwide.
4. In Yiddish folklore, a trickster. See Babel's story "Shabos-Nakhamu."
5. The newspaper *The Red Cavalryman*.
6. See the story "Gedali," in which Gedali envisions an ideal International that would supplant the Third Communist International founded in Moscow in 1919 to promote Communism world-wide.
7. The train sent out by the Polit-otdel, the political organ of the new Soviet government charged with the ideological education of the military.

Edited by Nathalie Babel

Translated with Notes by Peter Constantine

FAMILY MAN

Mikhail Sholokhov

The sun is sinking into the faint-green stubble of the undergrowth beyond the outskirts of a *stanitsa*.[1] I'm walking from the *stanitsa* to the Don, to the river crossing. The damp sand under my feet smells of decay like a tree that's rotten and swollen with water. The road zig-zags like a rabbit's path and slips along the undergrowth.

Straining and turning crimson, the sun drops behind the village graveyard, and dusk wreathes the undergrowth behind me in blue.

The ferryboat is tied to a mooring line, and the violet water cackles under the boat's bottom; bobbing up and down and turning side-to-side, oars groan in their oarlocks.

As he bails out water, the ferryman scrapes a bucket along the moss-covered bottom. Raising his head, he gives me a side-long glance with his yellowish, slit-like eyes and says gruffly, half-heartedly, "Going to the other side? We'll go right now—untie the mooring line."

"Are we both going to row?"

"We've got to. It's getting to be night and other people might show up or might not."

Rolling up his wide Cossack trousers, he looked at me again and said, "I can see you're not one of our folk, not from around here . . . Where in the world are you coming from?"

"I'm on my way home from the army."

The ferryman threw off his cap, with a nod of his head tossed back his hair which looked like blackened filigree silver from the Caucasus, then winking at me, he grinned, revealing worn-down teeth.

"How're you going—got a pass, or on the sly?"

"Demobilized. They released my year."

"Well, then, nothing to worry about . . ."

We sit down at the oars. The Don playfully pulls us towards the submerged young growth of the riverside forest. The water makes a dull sound as it beats against the rough bottom of the boat. The ferryman's bare legs, streaked with blue veins, swell with knots of muscle; the blue soles of his feet stick to the slippery cross plank as they press against it. His hands are long and bony, his fingers are gnarled. He's tall, narrow-shouldered; he rows awkwardly, all hunched over, but the oar comes down obediently on the crest of a wave and plunges deep in the water.

I hear his even, uninterrupted breathing; his knitted wool shirt smells strongly of sweat, tobacco, and fresh water. He let go of the oar and turned to face me.

"Looks like it's gonna send us crashing into the forest. A bad joke, but there's nothing we can do about it, my boy!"

The current is stronger in the middle. The boat rushed on, restively lurching in the rear and listing to one side, headed for the forest. In half an hour we were tossed against some flooded willows. The oars snapped. A splintered piece flapped about in the oarlock, as if offended. Water came sloshing in through a hole. We climbed a tree to spend the night. The ferryman, his legs wrapped around a branch, sat next to me, puffing away on his clay pipe, talking and listening to the whirring of the wings of geese cutting through the thick darkness above our heads.

"You're going home, to your family . . . Your mother's probably waiting for you. Her sonny boy the breadwinner is gonna come back and take care of her in her old age, but you probably don't take it to heart that she, your mother, pines for you during the day and weeps her eyes out at night . . . All you sonny boys are like that . . . Until you've got kids of your own, you don't really care about your parents' suffering. And how much each of them has to bear!"

"A woman cuts open a fish and crushes its spleen. You eat the fish soup, but it's unbelievably bitter. And so here I am: I keep on living, but my lot in life is only to swallow bitterness... Sometimes you put up with it and put up with it, and then you say, 'Life, oh life, when are you gonna get even worse?'"

"You're not one of us, you're an outsider—go on, use your head. Which noose should I stick my head into?"

"I've got a daughter, Natashka, this year she'll see her seventeenth spring. And she says to me, 'It makes me sick, father, to eat at the same table with you. When I look at your hands, I remember right away that you killed my brothers with those hands—and it makes me want to throw up.'

"But the little bitch doesn't understand why it turned out that way! It was all because of them, because of the children!"

"I married young. I got a fertile woman, she foaled me eight mouths to clothe and feed, and kicked the bucket with the ninth. She gave birth, but on the fifth day she ended up in a coffin because of a fever . . . I was left alone, like a woodcock in a marsh, but not one of the children did God take away, no matter how much I begged . . . The oldest was Ivan . . . He looked like me, dark-haired and good-looking. He was a handsome Cossack and an honest worker. I had another son, four years younger than Ivan. That one had his mother's looks from birth: short, plump, so fair-haired that he was almost white, brown eyes, and he was dearest to my heart, my most beloved. His name was Danila . . . The other seven mouths were little boys and girls. I married off Ivan to someone in our hamlet and soon they had a child. I was also about to try marrying off Danila, but then a time of troubles arrived. We had an uprising against Soviet power in our *stanitsa*! The next day Ivan comes running to me."

"Father," he says "let's go over to the Reds. I beg you in the name of Christ the Lord! We have to support their side 'cause their government is extremely just."

"Danila also dug in his heels. They tried for a long time to lure me, but I said to them: I won't keep you against your will, you go ahead, but I'm not going anywhere. Besides you, I have seven more mouths to feed, with every mouth asking for some food!"

"With that they disappeared from the hamlet, and our whole *stanitsa* armed itself with whatever it could, and me they packed off under White command to the front."

"I said at the gathering: Dear village elders, you all know I'm a family man. I have seven little ones. So, if they knock me off, who's gonna watch out for my family then?"

"I say this and that, but no . . . ! Showing no regard whatsoever, they grabbed me and sent me to the front."

"The front-line positions ran right below our hamlet. And so, it happened right before Easter, nine prisoners were herded into our hamlet and Danilushka—my favorite—was among them . . . They led them through the square to the regimental captain. The Cossacks poured into the street and raised a din."

"Kill them, the bastards! As soon as they bring them out from interrogating them, leave them to us!"

"I'm standing among them, my knees are shaking, but I don't show I feel sorry for my son, for my Danilushka . . . I turn my eyes like this, to one side and the other, and see the Cossacks whispering and nodding their heads in my direction . . . The cavalry sergeant-major, Arkashka, comes up to me and asks, 'Well, Mikishara, are you going to kill the commies?'"

"I am, those so-and-so scoundrels . . . !"

"'Here, take this bayonet and go stand on the porch.' He gives me the bayonet and, grinning, says, 'We're keeping an eye on you, Mikishara... Watch out—or you'll be sorry!'"

"I stood on the porch steps, thinking: Most Holy Mother, am I really going to kill my own son?"

"I hear the captain shouting. The prisoners were brought out, and my Danila was out in front . . . I looked at him and my blood ran cold . . . His head was swollen like a bucket, as though the skin had been ripped off . . . It was caked with dry blood, and wool mittens were on his head so that they wouldn't beat him on the bare spots . . . The gloves were soaked with blood and stuck to his hair . . . That's from the beating they got on the way to the hamlet . . . He's walking down the steps and staggering. He looks at me and reaches out his hands toward me . . . He wants to smile, but his eyes are bruised black and blue, and one is filled with blood."

"At this point I realized that if I didn't strike him, my fellow villagers would kill me, and my small children would be left poor orphans . . . He came alongside me."

"Father dear," he says, "goodbye . . . !"

"Tears are washing the blood down his cheeks, and I . . . forced myself to raise my hand. It seemed to have become all numb . . . I've got the bayonet gripped in my fist. I struck him with the end that fits on the rifle. I struck him right here, above the ear . . . He cries out 'oh!' and covers his face with his hands and falls down the steps . . . The Cossacks roar with laughter."

"Make them soak in their own blood, Mikishara! It's obvious you're taking pity on him, on your Danilka! . . . Strike him again, or we'll make your blood flow!"

"The captain came out on the porch; he was swearing, but his eyes were laughing . . . When they began to slash them with their bayonets, my heart couldn't bear it. I started running down a small street, looked to the side, and saw them rolling my Danilushka on the ground. The sergeant stuck his bayonet in his throat, but only 'khrrr' came out of him."

Down below, the boards of the boat made cracking sounds from the pressure of the water; you could hear the water gushing in, and the willow quivered and made a drawn-out, creaking sound. With his foot Mikishara touched the back part of the boat sticking up and, knocking out a yellow snowstorm of sparks from his pipe, said, "Our boat is sinking. Tomorrow we'll have to be on duty till noon on this willow. What a thing to happen!"

He was silent for a long time and then, lowering his voice, he said in a quiet, flat tone, "For that there business they made me a senior non-commissioned officer . . ."

"A lot of water has flowed down the Don since then, but even now at night I sometimes think I hear someone wheezing, choking . . . At that time, when I was running, I heard Danilushka wheezing . . . It's my conscience, and it's killing me . . ."

"We held the front against the Reds till spring, then General Sekretyov joined forces with us and we drove the Reds beyond the Don, to the Saratov Province. I'm a family man, but they wouldn't give me a break, because my sons went over to the Bolsheviks. We reached the town of Balashov. There's neither hide nor hair of Ivan, my oldest son. Hell only knows how the Cossacks found out that Ivan had left the Reds and was now serving in the thirty-sixth Cossack battery. The villagers threatened, 'If we come across Vanka, we'll beat him to death.'"

"We took this one village, and the thirty-sixth was there . . ."

"They found my Ivan, tied his hands, and brought him to our company. Here the Cossacks gave him a brutal beating and said to me, 'Take him to regimental headquarters!'"

"The headquarters was about twenty versts from the village. The captain gives me a document and, without looking at me, says, 'Here's a document for you, Mikishara. Get your son to headquarters. It's better if you do it—he won't run away from his father!"

"And at this point the Lord brought me to my senses. I figured they're making me the escort because they think I'll set him free, and then they'll catch him and kill me . . ."

"I come to the hut where Ivan was being held under arrest and say to the guard, 'Let me have the prisoner. I'm going to take him to headquarters.'"

"Go on, take him, we don't care!"

"Ivan threw his greatcoat over his shoulders, but he twisted and twisted his cap in his hands and then threw it on a bench. He and I walked out of the village and up the knoll. He doesn't say anything, and I don't say anything. I look back from time to time—I want to see if they're keeping an eye on us. We went only half-way, passed a small chapel, and I couldn't see anyone in back of us. At this point Ivan turned to me and said pitifully, 'Father, they'll kill me at headquarters anyway. You're taking me to my death! Is your conscience really still asleep?'"

"No, Vanya," I say, "my conscience isn't asleep!"

"And don't you feel sorry for me?"

"Yes, I do, my son, I'm so sick at heart I could die . . ."

"And if you feel sorry for me, let me go . . . I haven't lived long enough in this world!"

"He fell to his knees in the middle of the road and bowed down to the ground three times before me. I say to him in response: When we reach the ravines, start running, and for appearance' sake I'll fire a couple of times after you . . ."

"And just imagine, when he was a little boy, you couldn't get an affectionate word out of him at times, but now he threw himself at me and began kissing my hands . . . We walked about two versts. He doesn't say anything, and I don't say anything. We drew near the ravines and he stopped."

"Well, dad, let's say goodbye! If I happen to stay alive, I'll take care of you for the rest of your life. You'll never hear a harsh word from me . . ."

"He embraces me, but my heart bleeds for him."

"'Run, my dear son!' I say to him."

"He started running toward the ravines, looking back and waving at me."

"I let him go about one hundred fifty feet, then took the rifle from my shoulder, got down on one knee so that my hand wouldn't falter, and I got him . . . in the back . . ."

Mikishara took a long time getting his tobacco pouch, a long time striking the flint to get a spark, and then he began puffing on his pipe and smacking his lips. The tinder glowed in his cupped hand, the muscles on the ferryman's face twitched, and his squinting eyes looked out from under his swollen eyelids with a hard and unrepentant gaze.

"Well, there you are . . . Ivan jumped up, covered another sixty feet or so, running madly, grasped his stomach with both hands, and turned to me, "Father, why?" He fell down and his legs began to jerk.

"I run to him, bend down, and his eyes have rolled back, and there are bubbles of blood on his lips. I thought he was dying, but right away he rose slightly and, touching my hand, said, 'Father, I've got a wife and child . . .'"

"His head dropped to the side and fell down again. He's pressing down on the wound with his fingers, but what's the use . . . Blood spurts out through his fingers . . . He begins groaning, lies flat on his back and looks at me very seriously, but his tongue is already stiffening . . . He wants to say something, but only "Fa-ther . . . fa . . . fa . . . ther" comes out. Tears came pouring down from my eyes and I said to him, 'Vaniushka, accept a martyr's crown for me. You have a wife and child, but I've seven mouths to feed. If I had let you go, the Cossacks would kill me, and the children would go out in the world begging for their bread . . .'"

"He lay there a bit longer and then died, but he held my hand in his . . . I took off his greatcoat and boots, covered his face with a piece of rag, and went back to the village."

"Well, now you be the judge, my good man! How much grief I've carried because of them, those children, how much grey hair I've gotten. I keep bread on the table, I don't have any peace day or night, but they . . . take my daughter, Natasha, for example. She says, "It makes me sick, father, to eat at the same table with you.""

"How can I possibly bear all this now?"

His head hanging down, Mikishara the ferryman looks at me with a heavy, fixed stare. A foggy dawn is curling behind him. On the right bank, in a black mass of shaggy poplars, the quacking of ducks blends with a hoarse and sleepy shout: "Mi-ki-sha-ra-a! You dhe-e-vil! Hur-ry up, bring the fer-ry back!"

1925

NOTES

1. *stanitsa*: a constellation of two or three Cossack villages, with 700 to 10,000 people, headed by a local military commander called an *ataman*.

OUTGOING PAPER NUMBER 27
Diary of an Office Manager

Lev Lunts

January 3, 1922. Nighttime.

. . . I consider today a great day, because today it dawned on me what would make my name famous and earn eternal gratitude for me from my grateful descendants.

I got up at eight o'clock in the morning. But here I must make a small digression and point out that I slept badly last night, because since yesterday I have been under the influence of a passionate speech by my director, and all night I thought about the new basis. Returning to the thread of my narration, I hasten to note that since getting up this morning, I have continued to think about the new basis.

I came to work exactly at ten o'clock. To my great indignation I discovered that none of the office workers were in their places. In order to ascertain the correctness of my indignation, I read the September 7 order from the Director of the *Politprosvet*,[1] in which it is stated that work in the *Politprosvet* is structured on a new basis (this is not the new basis which was spoken of yesterday, but the old one), and that every employee must get to work at exactly ten o'clock. Those who arrive late are to be sent to the Palace of Labor as deserters from their designated jobs. As Office Manager, I considered it my duty to read this order to everyone who was late, to which everyone replied that they already knew it by heart. If they know it by heart, then why are they late?

My whole day was filled with annoying things. Thus in the periodical press department I discovered an irregularity, consisting of the fact that it had distributed papers not to 43, but to 42 offices of records. But the most distressing thing awaited me at twenty-five minutes past three, namely, Barinov, the club instructor, appeared in the office for no special reason, in spite of the fact that there is a sign on the door that reads: "No Entry without a Special Reason." And after appearing without a special reason, he began to converse with the typist, which kept her from working. And when I began to argue that such behavior was unworthy of a Communist, he told me to go to hell and that he knew his Communist duty better than me, because I was a paper-pusher. In response I answered that I was an honest proletarian worker. In response he said like hell I was a proletarian worker if I served for twenty years as a record keeper in the Senate. Then I withdrew to my desk and began to write a report to the Director of the *Politprosvet*.

And it is at this point that a great idea suddenly struck me. Namely, we are proposing to conduct a radical restructuring of our *Politprosvet*. But how can we reorganize, if the entire institution consists of an irresponsible element? Therefore, it is impossible to reorganize, but we have to reorganize, because such is the logic of revolutionary life. Therefore, it is necessary to reorganize the workers themselves, in other words, the citizens, on a new basis. Such is the remarkable conclusion which my line of reasoning reached. I immediately understood the total profundity of the discovery I had made. Greatly excited, I laid aside my report and tried to do the work at hand but could not.

January 4. Morning

Slept badly last night. Decided to submit a memorandum to the *Sovnarkom*,[2] for I feel that the make-over of citizens on a new basis must be carried out on a broad government scale.

January 5. Morning

Slept badly last night. Decided that the reorganization of citizens must be carried out on a world, in other words, cosmic scale.

The same day. Evening.

After coming home, I immediately sat down at my desk and began to compose a memorandum. But reaching the practical part, I was forced to stop, because my line of reasoning had stopped as well. Namely, I did not know what kind of matter to turn the citizens into and how.

My line of reasoning had just reached that point when my wife, greatly excited, suddenly burst in. Her cheeks were glowing red, and her chest was heaving. She informed me that a hypnotist had moved into our building, who was now demonstrating wondrous things on the premises of the *Domkombed*.[3] I objected to this and said to her that, according to the applicable decrees, no wondrous things were possible. On entering the *Domkombed* premises I witnessed the following scene. The room was filled with people. In the corner stood a suspicious-looking man and, as he moved his hands above the head of a sleeping person, he ordered him to do this and that. Then I stepped forward and gave a speech pertinent to the current moment. Then those present began to curse me with words that should not be repeated in written form; the hypnotist began to stare at me intently and I began to feel sleepy, after which I ceased remembering anything. On coming to, I saw that people were laughing and the hypnotist was smiling triumphantly. It turns out that he had put me to sleep and turned me into a donkey, and I hee-hawed like a donkey, and when I was given hay, I enjoyed it greatly. Made indignant by such an insult, I announced that I would dispatch the hypnotist to the Cheka,* to which he answered that he was not afraid of me, because he had a document from the Commissariat of Public Health. Then I departed, accompanied by my weeping wife.

The same day. Night.

This evening is a great evening, for today I have found the missing link in my line of reasoning. A donkey, I thought, is a useless animal, but it *is* possible to transform a citizen into a cow and thereby solve the dairy crisis. Or transform a person sentenced to forced labor into a horse and give him to the *Avto-guzh.*[4]

But all this is for the unreliable element—for the bourgeoisie and their stooges—for a cow, donkey, and horse are not higher matter. What can one transform honest workers into?

But here my line of reasoning was interrupted by a thought: do I have the right to seek the aid of a hypnotist, and does seeking such aid not contradict the established world view? But here I remembered that the use of a hypnotist was sanctioned by the *Komzdrav,*[5] and I calmed down. New possibilities opened before my eyes. The Commissariat of Public Health has registries of all hypnotists, organizes short-term hypnotism studios, and produces a cadre of shock-worker hypnotists who act on the orders of a higher authority.

January 6. After work.

At two in the afternoon the Director of the *Politprosvet* summoned us executives into his office in order to acquaint us with his project for restructuring the *Politprosvet* on a new basis.

Its essence can be summarized as follows. The initiative of the masses is placed at the base and, in order to raise the masses, the institution of managers is eliminated; namely, the Director of the *Politprosvet* remains as the head of the institution, and all the remaining directors of sub-departments, sections, and subsections are renamed senior instructors. This way, the *Politprosvet* will draw closer to the masses, for the masses do not trust directors. The project was met by those at the meeting enthusiastically. Then the system of registries and files is reworked and their number increases by 40%; similarly the number of forms which every worker is required to complete increases from 10 to 16. Furthermore, oral explanations between directors and subordinates are abolished, and all dealings between them take place in the form of written reports kept in special registries with a special numbering system.

All of these suggestions were also met by the people at the meeting enthusiastically, but Barinov, the club instructor, declared that this whole new basis would not lead to anything and only increase the amount of red tape and paper. Then I, in spite of the indignation that constricted my chest and would not allow me to speak, took the floor and in short but strong phrases accused Barinov, the club instructor, of having a bourgeois world view, because proper record-keeping, based on proper records management, is the basis of structuring something and, consequently, paper is . . . but here my voice broke off, and I lost my ability to speak, for at that moment a great idea suddenly struck me.

The higher matter into which citizens are to be transformed is paper. I immediately expounded this thought in a memorandum arguing in the following manner: first, paper is thin matter, in other words a higher matter; second, paper is matter that lends itself easily to record keeping; third, paper is matter and in this respect is now highly valued by Soviet Russia, which is experiencing a severe material crisis. Having set forth my main ideas, I moved to the practical part. While doing so, my enthusiasm grew and grew, words sang under my pen and made for wondrous harmony. I was becoming a poet. The numerous advantages of a cosmic scale appeared before my enraptured eyes.

First and foremost, in other words in the first place, the struggle on all fronts becomes easier. For example, the commander of a division or even of an entire army can turn his Red Army men into bits of paper and, having packed them into a suitcase, he can make his way into the rear of the White bandits and then, by transforming the papers back into human form, he can attack the enemy from the rear. In the second place, food, fuel and economic crises are solved, because paper has none of the needs peculiar to man. Under this point go the related questions of the struggle with criminals and women not accustomed to labor.

Finally, in other words in the third place, thereby the paper crisis is solved, because citizens can be used as paper, in the true meaning of the word.

In general outline, such was my line of reasoning. After finishing, I stood up and, excited, set out for home. My wife asked me why I was so pale, but I did not say anything to her, for although I also support the platform of equal rights for women, I believe that women are of more inferior matter than men and feel they should be turned into paper of lesser quality.

January 7.
I suspect that Barinov, the club instructor, suspects something. Have got to be careful.

January 8.
Slept badly last night. Tried to figure out what to do. Could not think of anything.

January 9. Evening
Today at work it dawned on me: Could I not hypnotize myself, in other words turn myself into a piece of paper? After work, in a most agitated state of mind, I dashed off to the hypnotist for the purpose of receiving the appropriate instructions, which he gave me readily. It turns out that in order to turn yourself into some kind of matter, you have to think for a long time that you are that needed matter. Moreover, this experiment demands long practice and a long period of silence and solitude. You have to think for three or four hours.

January 10. Morning.
An unexpected, fundamental obstacle appeared on my path. Namely, three or four hours of absolute silence are essential for the transformation, but my wife, being of inferior matter, cannot remain

silent for more than three or four minutes. I thought I would try my first experiment at night, when she fell asleep, but when she was in sleep's embrace, my wife prevented me from doing it because she snored. I waited until four o'clock in the morning in the hope that she would calm down, but under the influence of the excitement of the previous day, I fell asleep without ever noticing.

The same day. Evening.

On arriving home I sent my wife to her mother's in order to take advantage of her absence. After she left, I began to think I was a piece of paper. But paper is an indefinite concept that includes various images, including some indecent ones, and it is uncomfortable, in general, to think about paper. In view of this, I decided to concentrate on some one product of paper production. After mature reflection, I settled on incoming or outgoing papers, which are the most delicate, in other words the most ethereal, phenomenon. Some time passed and suddenly, oh happiness! I felt my left foot rustle. This occurrence produced such a strong impression on me that I jumped up, thereby ruining the entire experiment. But the beginning had been made. More self-control is crucial.

January 11. Evening

Today I achieved even greater results. Both my legs and the left side of my abdomen rustled. But as soon as the rustling started moving into my fingers, my wife suddenly returned and ruined everything. I do not know what to do.

January 12. Morning.

I slept badly, for the whole time I tried to figure out what to do. And then a brilliant idea suddenly struck me. Namely, tomorrow night I am on duty in the *Politprosvet*, where I will transform myself into a piece of paper, because transformation at home is connected with inconveniences. In the first place, my wife does not leave the house for more than three hours. In the second place, even if I transform myself into a piece of paper at home, I do not know what I am going to do next, for the appearance of an outgoing paper in the marital bed can arouse suspicion in my wife. Both of these inconveniences are eliminated if the experiment is conducted in the *Politprosvet*.

12 January. Politprosvet. Night.

My hand is trembling as I write these lines, for now I will set to work on my critical experiment. I am alone in the entire *Politprosvet*. Only the wind is howling behind the walls and a fire is crackling in the fireplace. My soul is full of heavenly visions, my heart is beating like a clock, and my chest is contracting.

I decided to lie down on the desk, so that after turning into an outgoing paper, I could lie in the place assigned to the above-mentioned papers because I do not like disorder.

I decided to transform myself not into an actual outgoing paper but into one for internal distribution, because an outgoing paper would go through all the channels, in other words, it would leave the premises of the *Politprosvet*, which is undesirable for me.

13 January. Dawn

And so, the great event has taken place, for I am writing these lines in a state of paper existence. The rays of the rising sun are flooding the room, birds are chirping outside the window, and in my soul, enveloped in a paper membrane, there is exaltation. A great thing has taken place.

I feel that something has been written on me. After several attempts, I succeed in overcoming the obstacles on my path and read myself, thereby solving the most difficult task posed by one foreign philosopher: "Read yourself and you will learn who you are."

For distribution.
R.S.F.S.R. *Politprosvet*—13 January 1921, No. 37.
    To: Petrocommune
    To: Distribution Center.
The *Politprosvet* . . . . informs you that the potatoes sent by you in the amount of 63 poods,* 12 lbs. for satisfying the allowance of home-front rations for workers of the *Politprosvet* turned out to be in a most inedible state.
Manager of the *Politprosvet*: (signature)
(M. P.) Secretary (signature):
After reading the aforementioned contents of the outgoing paper, I turned cold for the following reason. I wondered, if I was an outgoing paper for internal distribution, why was I lying on the Director's desk?

Papers for distribution are supposed to be in special registries. It goes without saying that if I were in my human form, in other words, in the form of Office Manager, I would quickly restore order. Now I am afraid that the distribution of the outgoing paper will get lost. The cleaning women in the next room are making noise. Now the day that is here will begin.

The same day. Evening.

I am writing the lines which follow, lying on the floor, due to the reason set forth below.

At three o'clock a general meeting of the workers of the *Politprosvet* took place in the Director's office to discuss the topic of professional unions.

Then my comrades began to disperse, and at this point I had an unfortunate thing happen to me because Barinov, the club instructor, brushed me with his service jacket and, after I fell on the floor, he stepped on me with his foot, which caused me sharp pain. But this pain was deadened by an even more acute concern for the fate of outgoing paper No. 37, for lying on the floor put it in danger of being thrown into the wastebasket. Then I remembered that tonight Barinov, the club instructor, would be on duty. What if he suspects that outgoing paper No. 37 for internal distribution is the Office Manager? Since he hates me, he can cause me serious problems.

In view of the aforementioned reasons, I decided to transform myself back to my human form and began concentrating on the fact that I am human. But half an hour had not even passed when a thought suddenly struck me that made me turn cold. Namely, if I turned into a human being, then paper No. 37 for distribution would disappear. As Office Manager I could not permit such an irregularity. Therefore I decided to delay my transformation for the time being.

The same day. Night.

It's dark. Quiet. The clock on the wall is ticking. Barinov, the club instructor, has disappeared somewhere. He has probably left his post. I will have to submit a report to the Director about this.

My heart feels light and joyous. Now there cannot be any discussions, in other words, debates concerning my invention. I have been in a state of paper existence for almost an entire day and have not experienced either hunger or thirst or any other needs without which not one person in human form can survive.

And an orderly line of reasoning unfolded before my shining eyes.

All people are equal, in other words, all people are bits of paper. The ideal of mankind has been achieved.

My chain of reasoning had just achieved this lofty and hallowed link when all of a sudden someone bent over me. It was Barinov, the club instructor. He was looking for something.

"Ah, here we go!"

He grabbed me by my head, in other words by the edge of the paper, and ran his fingers over me.

"Soft paper. It'll do just fine."

With these words he picked me up and . . .

The diary of the Office Manager breaks off here for unknown reasons. He disappeared without a trace. All efforts to find him came to naught.

1924

NOTES

1. *Politprosvet*: acronym for *Politiko-prosvetitel'nyi otdel* (Department of Political Enlightenment).
2. *Sovnarkom*: acronym for *Sovet narodnykh komissarov* (Council of People's Commissars.
3. *Domkombed*: acronym for *Domashnii komitet bednoty* (Housing Office for the Poor).
4. *Avto-guzh*: abbreviation for *Avto-guzhevoi transport* (Department of Motor and Horse-Drawn Transportation)
5. *Komzdrav*: acronym for *Komissariat zdravookhraneniya* (Commissariat of Public Health).

THE GARDENER OF THE EMIR OF BUKHARA

Vsevolod Ivanov

1. The Gardener is in an Elegiac Mood

The war ended.

And the sea immediately became slate red, the color of dried blood. The cypresses stood deathly still by the bloody puddle. Their foliage resembled greatcoats; they were soldiers turned dark green.

And in the second half of the day the gardener has the same contented smile.

In the first half of the day he tries to wake up; his sleep is post-war, long, and ridiculous, like the Crimean parks where right next to the palm trees the *mestkoms** have planted cucumbers. In the first half of the day the cares of his life are great and faintly scented, like the flowers of a magnolia tree.

In the first half of the day, more often than not, a woman who sells *Izvestiya*[1] to the vacationers and the communists who are repairing the electrical lines comes to see him. She's the only one in town who remembers that she's a descendant of a most illustrious merchant family, the Galitsyns, who owned countless mines in the Urals and vast vineyards in the Crimea. As if continuing the gardener's dream, she talks about her husband, that he's alive and living in Tula. She'd like to amass a bit of money; she'd like to borrow some and, strangely enough, she finds the money, like in a dream, and goes to Tula for a short while. She's taller and more wearisome than her dreams; she's forty-seven, and a lot, a whole lot, of her life and clothing has been lost.

She's the one person whom the gardener Kara-Dmitreyev is able to see in the first half of his day. Other things—flowers, greenhouses, and the palace—are also part of his day.

Before moving to the second half of his day (all the action will take place there), we find out that now in the palace of the Emir of Bukhara[2] there is a museum of the East, and on the first floor, where an Extraordinary Troika[3] met during the war, the director of symphonic concerts trains fox terriers. The director's name is Korshunov, and he's big and light like a wave; he loves olives, and even his boots smell very strange.

When he leaves for concerts in the evening, he looks at the palace with regret and says, "This emir lived like a European and survived, but the other emir was executed by a firing squad in Turkistan, and the latter had eighty wives, and all of them are now typists in the Cheka*."

But the gardener can't understand how Korshunov could divide one emir into two and, therefore, he doesn't talk to him.

Why speak about emirs when the earth is in bloom?

Once he had a dream and, when he woke up and went to the sea for a swim, for a long time it seemed to him that he was still dreaming.

It seemed to him that right after the end of the war, when people had paid for their evil with hunger and death, coral-red ash had spread over the gardens. The sea had taken in blood, the trees had taken in the action of wars, and the flowers, the color of battles.

And indeed, in the harbor he saw a tree of ships, schooners, and feluccas (the sails above the ships, like ripened fruit, were taut and ready to sail off on a raid). The tree was carrying toward the granite embankments apples that resembled roses as well as yellow-bodied pears, yellow *mushmala* pears which ripen fully only on the Japanese islands, but which suddenly and without precedent had ripened here. Dust-covered Tatars are hauling watermelons, and snub-nosed *rabfak*[4] students are examining the imperial palaces.

The dreadnoughts in Sevastopol have been sunk; the British have removed the bolts from the countless fort armaments and tossed them into the sea. No one is searching for the bolts, but by force of habit watchmen stand guard over the useless armaments.

Kara-Dmitriyev believes his eyes; he likes his eyes.

A tranquil, flowery, olive-green feeling of delight comes over him completely unexpectedly, and even in the second half of the day the gardener can't understand what he's waiting for and what he needs.

Complete, measured silence, like that of ancient tulips, enters the greenhouses, gardens and parks. The chain of human days can be measured by his tired soul. The chain starts out light and elusive, like the morning half of all his days.

2. The Eastern Measure of Existence Is Not Created by Architecture

The Emir liked the gardener for his dull-bronze shoulders. When the Emir was strolling in the park, leaning against the gardener's bare torso, he liked to accept roses from him. As for wines, the Emir preferred cognac, and as for women, Warsaw prostitutes, but, even more vividly than when he read the verses of Saadi,[5] his gardener's long curly beard made him think of tightly coiled Persian bas reliefs.

But just as the flowerbeds of the palace have become overgrown with tall weeds as well as potatoes planted by the *mestkom*,* so has the face of Pavel, the gardener's son, taken on a confusing, peasant look. In the winter he walks around with a briefcase made of oilcloth. His body suddenly remembers winter: it's in a greatcoat and soldier's boots, even though it's winter here for only two days a year. In the summer he's almost naked. His women are women of war; the time he spends taking them is short, like their short hair. They come and go, as if he's darting from village to village. He doesn't understand his father's words— "You're in a city here"—and why he shouldn't wear a greatcoat. He rarely brings his father money and, relentlessly bragging about the revolution, advises his father to look for work in the port. Soon the greenhouses won't be needed and now, he says confidently, flowers will be cultivated according to a new system.

His father smiles and says, "We'll see."

The son becomes excited and shouts about fruit-bearing flowers invented in America. All technology now comes from there and our ideas, united by the International,[6] go there. For people of the old regime, even those in the flower business, there's nothing left but manual labor. The father smiles again, sincerely, in his curly-headed way. "What kind of an old-regime man am I? I, too, am glad the Emir's gone."

"You still smell like your flowers. Go to the port."

A warm wind from the mountains lifts the gardener's beard. The blooming wisteria makes him raise his eyes. "Both flowers and love are the same everywhere," he thinks. He's seen his son several times with the daughter of the newspaper seller who comes to him in the first half of the day to tell him her dreams. Almost no one in the town remembers the Galitsyns; almost the whole town, like any hospital, changes every summer; he knows what Maria Galitsyn's love will cost and what flowers his son will still ask him for.

One day the gardener receives a letter with foreign stamps. The letter makes him think of 1919. A lot happened back then, even in the simple life of a gardener. Nowadays, why would he bother to bury a dilapidated box in a cemetery? Now it would stand on an icon shelf, for example, the one in his room. The earth was damp, and he felt as if he were sinking into it with his whole body; the rotten smell of seaweed was coming from the sea. The evening was like an abandoned tavern. It's true, a lot of the taverns in the town had been abandoned, and ships carried refugees across the sea. Old man Galitsyn cried over the box, but for some reason didn't take it with him. Those tears were probably the reason why Kara-Dmitriyev hadn't dug up the box later and forced himself to think that papers of little importance were now rotting in it.

The gardener goes to the port to meet a steamship. The papers have rotted, he tells himself, and perhaps old man Galitsyn won't ask. The gangplanks smell of fish and the sea. "How old must he be now?" thinks the gardener. "Most likely very old." The sister of the newspaper seller disembarks with old man Galitsyn; her name is Ksenia Konstantinovna. "The old woman must have died," the gardener thinks and crosses himself inconspicuously. The cemetery and the box come to mind again. He should have reburied it in another place; by now it has rotted. The soil is vicious now and, like the past years, rapaciously eager to decay things.

There's an orphanage on the former Galitsyn estate; they're also thinking of opening a cafeteria in town. With the skill of an old merchant, Galitsyn asks in a pleasant voice, "Do rich people come here now or is everything free?"

During the night the gardener takes Galitsyn to the cemetery . . . Now there are big, wooden five-pointed stars on neighboring graves instead of crosses. Galitsyn asks in a whisper, "Do they bury Communists without a funeral service, or is it allowed?" He's old and thoughts of the box make him happy, even though he doesn't believe in a lot of things. It seems to him that the gardener is holding an ax behind his back, that he'll get the box and kill him . . .

The dry earth flies up against the gardener's yellow overcoat, the color of horns; he continues to break it up. "You can't hold a shovel in one hand," Galitsyn thinks, "but a gardener can hold a shovel in one hand and a knife in the other."

The same thought occurs to the gardener, only from a different perspective. People are killed for treasures like this. And the faster he digs, the bigger the treasure seems to him; he becomes hot and he pants. He hears the same sighing from Galitsyn as well.

It's dangerous and difficult for the old man to carry the box, but he won't hand it over; he quickly turns down an offer to stop at the gardener's place for a rest. Ksenia Konstantinovna will be waiting, waiting anxiously for him, and she's very worried. The gardener doesn't want to insist, but nonetheless he does.

"No, I'll just go home, my dear man, home," the old man mumbles.

When he gets home, the gardener is frightened for some unknown reason. In 1919 it was more terrifying to bury things, but then your arms and legs didn't tremble like this and your head wasn't covered with sweat.

"Well, to hell with them . . . ," he mutters and goes to bed.

The room is creaky, and the windows have been knocked out—the year 1919 still clings to the window frames.

Who needs papers from 1919 now?

He just needs to test his honesty and not worry about the price.

3. Nature Brings Tranquility Only in Idleness

A ring with a ruby from the Urals appeared on the gardener's hand. And while he was examining it or, more accurately, joyfully feeling the red drop on his finger (crimson and honest, like his blood), the newspaper seller came running toward him down a tree-lined path. Four o'clock in the afternoon. "What's this, does she really sleep during the day?" the gardener thought. An acrid drop of sweat hangs above her eyebrow. The sun is drying and bleaching her already worn-out body. Her lips are all chapped and, from afar, her voice resembles the shrill droning of cicadas.

"Let's go."

The gardener jokes good-heartedly, "What dreams will you tell me, Elena Konstantinovna?"

But for some reason she is furiously cursing her daughter. With a smile the gardener thinks about his son and flowers.

The scorching street rushes to the scorching mountain.

The newspaper seller brings the gardener into a small garden which is awakening purposely in the soapy-white heat of the hill. The dry masonry walls have partially collapsed and, beyond them, one can see local people walking down a narrow lane, carrying heavy bundles of firewood from the mountains. Roosters are crowing in exhausted, steamy tones.

Galitsyn looks at the gardener disapprovingly and asks his older daughter, the newspaper seller Elena, "What did you let come between us, my dear? I'll be blunt—it's a bad thing." His younger daughter Ksenia sits down on the rocks and rubs her thin, long arms.

"Nothing papa, just *Izvestiya*."

"Ksenia, I'm proud of my honest work," Elena says. "The whole town knows about me, what I do, but just where were you abroad, and where did you learn to wag your rear end like that?"

"Stop it, Elena! Are you a little girl or something?" Galitsyn says. "People are stopping, and you've brought in an outsider for some reason. That's not good, Elena, that's not good. How old are you? Ksenia and I have come back for peace and quiet."

Two swarthy passers-by grin; Ksenia is crying quietly; she didn't write anything in any of her letters about what she was doing in Constantinople.

Elena the newspaper seller is covered in acrid sweat; she wants to touch her sister, but instead jumps back, crosses herself, and thanks someone.

"Thank God, thank God! You're wailing, aha! I can understand everything, everything. I dreamed of my husband today. He's been exiled to a village in the Vologda[7] region. Now, I'll . . ."

She searches in her dirty bag for the address she wrote down when she woke up. Her father's the only one who doesn't believe she's mad; he approaches the swarthy men and in a whisper suggests they move on. "Move on yourself," one of them answers angrily.

Elena says: "I've come to ask them for money for the trip; they've left gold icon frames and gems from the Urals, just in case . . . I'm asking them to give me some. But she, that slut, that slut, won't give me anything for the trip."

At the word "gems" everyone perks up. The silent men exchange glances with Eastern craftiness, as if they're already examining the gems in the palms of their hands. Now the petty bourgeois in the south talk not about politics but about the treasures of the aristocrats. The swarthy ones exchange whispers. "The counts must have returned. Maybe they'll sell some of their stuff?"

The gardener's beard, black like black currants, crumples up.

"You have no shame, Elena," her father says wearily. "Just think what you're saying."

"I should be ashamed in front of thieves, me? You spent everything there. What's left here is mine. I have to save my husband. I have to go to him!"

With a shriek the newspaper seller spreads her fingers and throws herself at her sister.

"I'll rip it from her throat. Are you looking for a husband for her . . . ? Do you think you're going to buy a husband with what's left?"

The old man pulls back his older daughter and looks at the gardener reproachfully—he thinks the latter has told the newspaper seller everything. His lips are surprisingly straight, and they are used to saying a lot of things. Slowly he tells Elena: "Semyon Nikolayevich was executed a long time ago, my dear, shot. Now we have to find his grave, but here you are, looking for some gems. There's nothing for you to do in the Vologda region, and I'm telling you in all honesty, if you don't want to go looking for me there, too, don't shout. Let's go and have some tea instead."

"You're not going to give me anything?"

"You're mad Elena; you were and are mad. Well, tell me, where have I gone lately?"

The newspaper seller points to the gardener. "I've brought him so that before him—he's a pure and holy person—you'll swear to God that you don't have anything and don't have any money for my trip."

"Half the town has come to see what all this shouting's about. Are you going to come and have some tea or not? I'll swear to you, if you like; I'll swear by all that's holy."

He frowns and waves his hand wearily.

Then the gardener pulls off his ring and thrusts it at the newspaper seller. His fingers are sweaty, and the ring is slow to come off. Galitsyn watches him closely and, at the same time, wearily. Elena tries to kiss the gardener's hand; then Galitsyn walks quickly toward the cottage.

The roosters continue to make their worn-out cries.

The gardener meets Marusia by the gate. She's wearing a Tatar dress and, in a dress like that, I'd compare her to a captive woman. By the way, the gardener doesn't know anything about the Scythians, the Tatars, or the Genoese.[8]

"Is mama here?" she asks the gardener.

"Yes, and have you seen my Pashka around here?"

"No."

The gardener takes a big step and asks, "Do you believe in *razryv-trava*,[9] young lady?"

"Is that on the eve of Ivan Kupala,[10] with the fern?" For a moment she stops and thinks, perhaps about her mother. "I'd like to believe."

The gardener takes an even bigger step. "But my Pashka doesn't want to at all."

4. The Gardener Gets His Conclusions Confused

If it doesn't harm anyone, let people live out their lives the way they know how. Instead of working, Galitsyn started searching for his treasure; let him live off his treasure. The newspaper seller can live off her newspapers, and let the old man's younger daughter look for a husband. Life is short, and if the gardener is able to make it easier, that's great. A hard life is like an unripened orange. Its juice is bitter and makes your fingers sticky, and even flies landing on it die like on a toadstool. The gardener Kara-Dmitriyev goes to the sea and waits for Galitsyn to walk out on the embankment in his new clothing and for his thick cane to ring nicely against the sandstone, and for him to approach a table in the restaurant calmly and confidently and order a bottle of wine. The gardener looks around—what kind of silks are the women wearing now? Their bright striped dresses look like Hindu cupolas or large petals, and their curls, like bunches of grapes.

Both father and daughter will feel good in their new clothing.

Umph, push the swing, devil;[11] it must be nice for you to think that you had almost given the world to a very distinguished merchant, Galitsyn. The Galitsyns are unknown in Russia now, but abroad they're hardly forgotten. Weren't a lot of goods and Ural gemstones shipped there, and a lot of valuables brought from there? Quite a lot.

It'll happen that, in a letter or to an acquaintance he meets, Galitsyn will let something slip about the gardener's honesty. The gardener could have known that there were gems and gold there—he could have known and yet he didn't dig up the box. It had lain there for four years, and so as not to disturb his peace of mind, he believed that it held all sorts of papers and monarchical letters.

Fame will pass . . . Nonsense, what is fame worth when nothing is left of the true fame of the Galitsyns? One woman trades in newspapers, and God knows what the other trades in . . .

Turning things over in his mind, the gardener walked to the seashore, to the embankment.

Yes, it's nice and warm even for your clothing to take a walk by the sea.

And then one evening the gardener met Galitsyn.

He looked older and walked hunched over, with a dirty, torn sack under his arm. He reeked of the cheapest and most disgusting fish, which looks as if it's all scales and no meat—a fish called *khamsa*.[12]

He passed by and didn't say hello.

His long, strong chin was covered with hair, and his foreign suit was mended crudely at the elbows.

"Eh, dear man," thought the gardener, "you're frugal, and you have your own particular thoughts."

He turned and followed him and, since he had a difficult time acquiring human craftiness, never mind a flowery way with words, asked softly, "Konstantin Konstantinovich, is that you?"

And suddenly Galitsyn stopped unexpectedly under the chestnut trees, and it was such an awkward spot—in a small area next to a public toilet. One hell of a smell—it's awkward, there's no way you can ask that question here again.

Galitsyn leaned over and hissed right in the gardener's face, "Leave me alone, you lackey, you hypocrite and louse!"

The gardener walked over to a clean place.

The sea continues to toss up its pebbles.

The waves still smell like slightly rotten eggs.

"It's impossible to understand how people live out their lives," the gardener said.

5. A Political Meeting with Visiting Propagandists

His son had a soldier's habit of swinging his arms energetically as if he were holding dumbbells in his fists. He walked down cypress-lined lanes with a total lack of respect for this kind of tree. When he felt happy, he liked to imitate salespeople, and in the Crimea there are the most dishonorable salespeople—they sell heaven and earth.

"Pop, do you have any desire to go to an anti-religion meeting? Moscow and Stavropol propagandists will be there. That's where the

Galitsyns have headed too."

The gardener stroked his beard and answered sullenly, "I saw them yesterday, no, not them, but I almost saw him, the old man."

"Can you explain why they've come back to Russia, pop?"

"To live."

"Then why did they leave?"

"Also to live. You would've shot them."

"If it had come to that, pop, I would've."

"Do they have in mind to train their sights on the sister, the newspaper seller?"

"I think so."

"But the newspaper seller has a daughter."

The cypresses still resemble soldiers, but what flowers do soldiers like? Russian soldiers aren't used to flowers.

"You have to go, pop. They're going to speak about the living church and the dead church and then bring death to both of them. They won't pass any resolutions, and people can approve as well as criticize. I'm registered there as a speaker. I'm also worth listening to."

"What church are you for?"

"I'm for the one without a cross and with a red flag." He slaps himself on the thighs, turns a somersault on the grass, and shouts, "And what church did the Emir belong to?"

The gardener strokes his beard. His son doesn't upset him—he himself had become unaccustomed to thinking about God long ago; long ago, with the death of his wife, the colors on the icon faded, and then in 1919 the icon somehow disappeared altogether. Now there are spider webs instead of icons in the corners. Now he tends to feel sorry for the web-covered corners, sorry for the emptiness in his life and for his old age, which is why he says sternly, "Stop being such a wise-guy."

"So, will you go?"

"I suppose I could."

When a narrow-shouldered man in yellow glasses appeared on the stage, Pavel nudged his father. "Nothing will be left of your god," he whispered. The man took slow steps and seemed to take a whole hour to reach the table. He spoke slowly, too, and was evidently used to speaking to peasants, because he frequently included jokes and short, light stories.

The Galitsyns sat solidly in their seats; the old man leaned against the back of the bench as if settled in for life. The newspaper seller had evidently made her peace with them; she was wearing a clean woolen sweater. Pavel tried to make his way over to Marusia, but it was very crowded and he wanted to see how his father was doing.

"Or there was this kind of incident, fellow citizens," droned the man from the stage. "Let's say one comrade is on his way to a park to attend to something. The lad is young, his steps are light, he walks quietly. And completely out of the blue he sees two people in front of him, that is, they're heading straight for the cemetery. Naturally, that's suspicious. The lad follows them and sees them digging. Naturally, the lad waits. They dig and dig and then start back, and one of them has a heavy object under his arm that looks like a small chest of different proportions. If he demands it right away, the two will kill him; the cemetery's outside of town and, for the time being, the lad follows them. In town the one who's empty-handed lags behind; the one weighted down keeps on walking, and as soon as he turns into one of the streets where it's possible to suspect the existence of a policeman, our comrade, the lad, quite deliberately says to him, "Stop for a moment, mister citizen. The nights here are such that one of my galoshes fell off yesterday and I looked for it for an hour and couldn't find it." The citizen is the suspicious type and the box crashes to the ground, of course, and off he runs into a side street! Where can you run to with such a weight to carry? Citizens and comrades, the church has left the political and economic arena; all its reasons and arguments are the old ones. And what do you think was found in that box? In that box, comrades, were found gold icon frames hidden by priests and precious stones from icon settings. Out of what was hidden from confiscation a total of 15,000 pre-revolutionary rubles has been given for the benefit of the starving. At present we have eliminated the most acute features of hunger, but comrades, how this small trunk would have come in handy at an earlier period! But better late than never, and after my speech, the comrade who found the trunk and the suspicious characters will tell you about his religious beliefs in connection with this . . ."

The gardener shook his head; some kind of darkness was spreading from behind him. He wanted to ask what the small chest looked like and whether it had happened long ago, but he saw Galitsyn's eyes staring at him from the bench in front of him. There was reproach, empathy, and anger in them. Growing slightly weak all over, the gardener thought, "I know he's speaking about me."

But the worst possible thing happened next. Pavel walked out on stage and, waving his arms, started to speak. His face was sweaty and the collar of his shirt was unbuttoned the way seamen wear them.

"Through the strength of our iron solidarity we have succeeded in such a short period . . . antireligious propaganda and the like . . . I'm walking along, comrades, and in front of me I see what look like two priests. One taller, more portly—he resembles our archpriest—and the other one smaller and evidently of lower rank, because he was lugging a small chest the whole time, and the portly one was walking in front. After this, how can you trust them when it's been absolutely established that these valuables were brought from Russia and no such things were registered in our parts? Perhaps they intended to take this gold abroad for the support of plots against the Union Republic, solidarity . . ."

The gardener got up and, lightly tapping his fingers in the area of his heart, began to push his way to the exit. The Komsomol members were shouting, "To hell with them, the cheaters! Into the sea with them and all their belongings!" A pungent and heavy smell, like that of rotting fish, wafted from the crowd. And by the exit he said into the face of some girl with a red armband, "Lies, all lies, you know, and nothing but shame."

To which the girl, displaying her ample breasts, answered, "Then you get on the stage, citizen, and object. We have freedom of speech in religious matters."

Her red calico scarf was sliding off to the side; her upper lip was sweaty. The gardener went out onto the porch.

The day was hot and bright, like always.

From the sea, as always, a hot and light wind.

A lone felucca heads out to sea slowly, as if for the last time.

It's difficult to understand even the felucca and the wind.

And it's even more difficult to understand a human being.

A day out on the sea is like a lone felucca with a lone man who doesn't understand anything.

And a day is dear to the body, like a son.

6. What Occurred on the Seashore Most Often Occurs on the Riverbanks of Russia.

Next to the palace of the Emir of Bukhara, in a garden overgrown with scrub oak, are wrought iron gates which stand by themselves without any fence. Written in white on black tin is "Sleep, battle eagles." The same thing is written in Tatar, and below that, "Cemetery for Commune Members."

A black banner, "To the Victims of the Sea," blows in the wind; the musicians are eating pears. The gardener stopped and asked, "Who's drowned?"

"A Petersburg Komsomol member. He was swimming and got a cramp."

The gardener never read newspapers, so the speech of the Communist speaker didn't remind him of them. By the way, what's so bad if newspapers define why a man lives?

The speaker shook himself as if he'd just come out of the sea. His hair was faded and disheveled.

The funeral reminded the gardener of yesterday's girl with the red calico scarf. Then he remembered Marusia and then, Pavel. The newspaper seller with the family name that was hard to remember—Galitsyn—has only one daughter. It's too bad that generations of merchant families are disappearing; for them and priests the most important thing was family, and love of family.

The thought of returning home, especially along the cypress-lined lane, made his heart really ache. The gardener had never planted cypresses, but grew up to be a soldier himself—coarse, pitiless, and cheerful.

The gardener headed through the streets made worse by the heat toward the bare rocks on the seashore. From afar the music had a despairing sound, as if the musicians didn't give a damn about life or death. And he didn't like the funeral either; the mourners couldn't keep still, like in an office without any management.

For eight years he's been wearing a small straw hat and the same light-blue morning coat that used to cover the Emir's shoulders. In the morning, when he was putting on the coat, he noticed it had become all worn out in the underarms. A person often breaks out in a sweat from unaccustomed thoughts.

The cicadas behind the rocks try to out-drone the pebbles rolling into the blue shadows of the rocks.

The shore is coming to an end and soon the imperial parks will begin. A jackass, given to the young emperor by the Italian king, now delivers the collective farm milk. And there was a time when the jackass was met at the ship by a Cossack honor guard and taken with music to the estate.

Suddenly the steady, rhythmical sound of the pebbles breaks off.

He looks out to the sea.

What should he care why the rhythmical sound of the pebbles has stopped?

Of course it doesn't matter—he pretends he's looking out to the sea. He has no thoughts of his own, and he would have been glad to see some passers-by. He would have given some thought to their clothing, shoes, and their way of walking.

Of course, the sea frequently smells different. But he has flowers, and it would be nice to find a person who could tell him what flowers smell like at midday and in the evening, and when they should be picked.

Some people are emerging from behind the boulders of the yellowish-red precipice. He doesn't look at them, but from the sound of the pebbles he can recognize the free and easy, lively and simple gait of a man and a woman, a woman who doesn't feel the heat and is totally lost in herself, wiggling her shoulders and body.

"Hello," says the gardener.

If they answer, he'll turn around completely and speak to them. Now, of course, they want to talk.

The woman, not noticing him, wrinkles the smooth skin on her face and says to her companion with irritation, "You should straighten out your clothing."

"Oh, well . . ."

Here the gardener turns around.

It's his son Pavel and Marusia, the daughter of the newspaper seller Galitsyna.

Pavel laughs loudly, slapping his thighs.

He has unusually large nostrils, with thick cartilage.

"What are you doing here, pop? Looking for a place to fish? You need to use a line and tackle here. Look over there—the grey mullet are running."

He strokes the woman's sloping shoulders and sniffs the pungent air.

"Grey mullet," he repeats, searching for something with his lips.

The woman looks at the mullet and blushes, turning blood red. She has her own thoughts, and it's doubtful she sees the fish jumping out of the waves. The gardener feels sorry for her.

But Pavel, his eyebrow twitching, says: "I've been given a good job at the collective farm and in general, besides that, I intend to marry and love Marusia. Apart from the ideological destruction on all fronts, she's leaving her mother. Let's get moving home, Marusia."

"Hold on, Pavel."

"What?" Pavel scratched his ribs and said with cheerful weariness: "We're boiling hot. Better talk later. Here the sea affects you better than alcohol. If you're going to drag things out as regards your fatherly rights, I warn you ahead of time: you'd better not. Her old lady also gave up and went back to her own people."

The gardener said repentantly, "I'm talking about something else."

The son walked over to the precipice and sat down. "And there's nothing for us to talk about, pop. If you like, I'll get you a job in the port or at the collective farm. You'll have to earn your bread. Your life has become overgrown with trivial things, and that's why you wander around. You'll leave the palace, and that'll be the end of it. To put it to you like that, in spiritual terms, you have shadows wandering around in you. We forgive many prejudices and you, too, will be forgiven."

The gardener looks askance at the woman.

She has yellowish eyes with a stubborn look and brooding curly eyelashes. She leans her shoulder against Pavel in encouragement, who blurts out, "It's all over for your greenhouse existence."

Shattered, the gardener gratingly repeats the unnecessary words. "All over?"

"That's it, amen."

Pavel swings his arms and slaps the woman hard on her hips.

"Does the old man Galitsyn know about the small chest?" the gardener asks.

"What's the point of asking ridiculous questions when I've spoken publicly about it at the political meeting? He's lucky I didn't say anything and didn't denounce him, otherwise they'd have put on a show trial with you, and if they'd really gotten into a cross-examination, they wouldn't have just made snide remarks."

Embracing roughly, like soldiers, Pavel and Marusia start climbing the hill.

The gardener throws a pebble into a wave, green and dense like fatback.

The sea washes more and more pebbles up to his feet. The tiny crabs also look like pebbles. Like pebbles, you can't count your thoughts and you can't wash them away with tears.

Perhaps he should go and say the most important thing. The war isn't over.

But what will this explain and what will it lead to? Events move at their own pace, like those two going uphill.

7. Elegiac Moods Are Again Introduced into the Tale

Old man Galitsyn goes around town in patched clothes that make his body look even older. His daughter Ksenia gives the vacationers plenty to eat, but there are less of them and they look for both board and women that are coarser and cheaper. At night, when the sisters go to sleep in crude beds made out of planks, they reproach one another.

"You can get plenty of women here for nothing and no one, Elena, wants to read your newspapers."

"Don't interfere with my dreams. Maybe I'll still get some indication of my husband's whereabouts, and then he could rescue us from all of this."

"Your father thought all that Constantinople stuff would end in Russia. We have an estate close by and everyone knows us, but we keep on living with these consumptives, these consumptives . . . I want to go to Moscow, Elena."

"It's the same everywhere, let me sleep; I have the same dreams everywhere."

And, in a teeny-tiny whisper, so as not to wake up their father, using long words heard in Constantinople and in ports, she curses the gardener, his son, and Marusia, who's fallen for his strong coachman's body. Love should be clingy and rare, but this, a coachman's love, is fast and hot, like flaming birch bark.

The town is hot and with its burning hot, stone terraces tries to overcome the heat and become like the Yaila Mountains.[13] Its terraces are like staircases into the mountains. Slaves stand on the staircases, exercising dominion over them. The castles, estates, and dachas of the masters have been seized by people weary from the war. There are many of them, the weary—the whole country in fact. And only this weariness prevents them from turning the mountains into one continuous staircase so that all can rest.

Thus far they've produced one type of flower.

There's a huge red canvas above the white slabs of flat houses.

The slaves have created just this one flower. And they've crowned themselves with these roses.

That's what the gardener could have thought wandering around the town which was flat like a tortoise. But his thoughts were impersonal and eyeless, like Arabic weaving. His ring with the ruby from the Urals is for sale in a second-hand shop, and the vacationing women in their silks try it on their fat fingers. The gardener's flowerbeds are in good order. The wild horses are tethered. Nevertheless, his old heart feels the glow of battles. That's why only the scents of his thoughts remain, like piles of fallen leaves. The sea is a greenish ash-grey color, the mountains, chestnut brown. The rocks smell of pitch and sulfur. And the sky above them is like a green petal.

I can't help exclaiming here, "The horses neigh at midnight. Check your saddles, mankind!"

Because the war isn't over—war is approaching.

A marble slab by the gates of the palace and etched in gold: "The Emir of Bukhara Seid Saad Shifi." Tourists write their names on it in pencil, and the gardener erases one of them—"Fyodor Radish." Actors in ridiculous make-up are making a propaganda film, "The Collapse of the Old World," inside the fenced-in area of the palace. A fat director in a grey suit shouts, "Get ready, comrades . . . ! But run, run! Action!"

The cameraman hurriedly cranks human passions onto the reel.

"Are you the gardener?" an actress asks him.

"Yes."

"Could I have a tea rose?"

By the greenhouse she starts complaining that she's paid less than a laundry woman and that, for example, they make them walk more than five versts along a dusty highway to Livadia[14] to get filmed in this heat. Suddenly rubbing off her lipstick, she asks out of curiosity, "Is it true that they can't find five bricked-up rooms in the palace?"

"Nonsense, madam."

"You know, it's very boring right now."

However, she later tells everyone in confidence that the gardener had admitted to her that it was a very boring time, but that he knew there were bricked-up rooms and that there were Korans in them (in the springtime the Tatars here valued the Koran very much).

And the experienced old man Galitsyn helps them stage the scene of a court reception. And so that they'll pay him more, he lies that he's related to their Highnesses the Golitsyns and says he spells his name with an "a" instead of an "o" for the Bolsheviks. He has a totally expressionless face, the color of Russian leather, and the director, encouraging him with his future prospects, reluctantly gives him the role of the butler.

"Not everything at once, not everything. Motion pictures have great possibilities in the republic, and you and I do too."

On noticing the gardener, Galitsyn asks that outsiders be removed.

The director, wiping his sweaty cheekbones with a towel, shouts pompously, "All outsiders kindly disperse! Citizens, show respect for labor!"

The hand is withered, with prominent veins, and the pencil in the hand of the person who comes up looks like a green pod that has suddenly grown out of it. Shaking his face, shielded by glasses, he jabbers: "Put moss between the panes of glass, but be careful! Put the nails in the boxes. Don't break up the thin planks—I'll mark them with chalk or pencil! Leave that part which the gardener . . . and in general, there's the committee."

"May I note," Kara-Dmitriyev the gardener says from the doorway, "all the greenhouses are valuable and not just some of them . . . I can't do anything in this regard. Look here, I have a Russian rose."

The pencil whirled in front of his face as if he were seeing not with his eyes but with this green pod. "Wachu say? C'mrad gar'nr, we've seen to everything, everything. Recom' you refer to the Sector for the Protection of Old Monuments and Forests with such questio . . ."

"The old days. Flowers are the old days."

"Whachu think, c'mrad gar'nr? Without a doubt, the old days— economic, real old days. Now the ord'r of the day—you're building econo'mic'ly, for the time being with history . . . The greenhouses are for build'g barracks for the renovation of labor, it's very clear. We leave the greenhou' its benefits, like bison or sales to nepmen.* Yes, flowers are needed; when an infirmary is taken down, barracks turn into greenhouses too, very simply econom . . ."

He bowed and ordered with the green bean, "Pl'se, dismantle immea'ly, except for what the gardener indica . . ."

And he disappeared, cutting his steps short just as quickly as his words.

The carpenters squatted down slowly next to the porch.

"How much pay do you get?" one of the carpenters asked the gardener.

"I make do."

"So why should you worry?"

The youngest one remarked wearily, "A lot of panes will get broken."

"Yeah, we'll have enough glass," they all agreed.

Glass crashing down; they all spat, one after another. Then they talked some more about glass panes and the Emir ("they say he was shot, but maybe he got away. He was a robust guy, ruined a lot of girls all over the Crimea") and, after each one of them picked a bouquet of roses, they left, promising to start work the next day after lunch.

And in the evening the panes of the greenhouse took on a dark blue color and the window frames suddenly looked like black veins. A breeze passed by, rippling the flowers, and the air became like sea water.

The gardener was walking among some shrubs.

A lot of flowers had withered. The spider webs on them resembled jellyfish. His legs grew heavy and he was short of breath, although the flowers had almost no scent. His lips sensed a salty after-taste. "It's like an aquarium," he thought.

And really, the flowering plants looked like seaweed. Their long stalks, which had turned blue, and their soft, huge, thick leaves which didn't look Russian, lightly touched his shoulders and seemed to be floating away. The falling, scent-free petals were carried upwards toward the absent sun, to the water's surface. The broken wrought iron benches without backs or seats looked like reefs.

He stumbles on them and rips his clothing and cuts his hands.

"I have to report it to the Sector for Old Monuments," he jokes despondently about his cuts. He walks along, swinging his arms wide as if he's rowing. And he's like a big, sick fish here.

He wanders about until he starts feeling hungry. The Emir's park is full of oak, magnolia, cypress, and oleander. In the whole park, as if intentionally, there's not a single fruit-bearing tree. It's as if the Emir didn't want to eat. It's hard to live off flowers; there's not much of a market for them. And when they break up the greenhouses, then what? And only now does he see with fright that almost all the greenhouses are empty and everything has wilted or dried up.

The scent of flowers, which he took more pride in than the scent of the sea—the scent of flowers is long gone.

How long? It's difficult for him to remember. Is it worth thinking about what happened before or after Galitsyn's arrival?

His son will feed him at the collective farm. "H'm . . ." the gardener smiles. Feebly and almost vacantly.

The Emir is gone; he's a dead gardener. His thoughts, which he had here until recently, are dead thoughts, like the smell of the flowers that had seemed to fill him. The dead flowers and smells have run away to follow their master.

His son is gone, but had he come at all? His son doesn't have a house but lives in the barracks, and you can visit the barracks only on Sundays.

By digging up the box, he had buried his soul. Or it may turn out differently. It doesn't turn out differently. He'll have to make up stories about the Emir and the Emir's palace and explain what neither the Emir, nor the builders of the palace, nor his servants knew.

Did the palaces create emptiness?

8. The Concluding Verdure of Lines but Not of Thoughts

Along with his shirt he puts into his bag what's left of the bread, three cucumbers, and a tattered old book (in his childhood and later he read a lot of books, but in the springtime he talked with the Emir not about books but about flowers). His things don't fit into his knapsack neatly, just like kindling.

Next he writes a statement for the housing committee and glues it to the lock to his room. There's nothing explanatory in the statement. And finally he replaces his eight-year-old straw hat with the cap his son had forgotten. His neck is short and sinewy, his head with the curly beard is planted boldly and firmly, his gait is confident; his steps are big, loud, and quick.

And here he is in the vineyard.

Four cornelian cherry poles securely hold the boughs that have been thrown over them. Towards evening the shadows grow darker underneath a shelter of branches, and the earth smells of saltpeter. The shelter's tenant, the renter of the vineyard, a Greek with thick lips, leans importantly against the hut and says calmly and rhythmically, "I like having only one watchman living with me. And it's to his advantage to be the only one—he gets more money, and the advantage for me—one mouth will eat less. So, ten pounds of grapes today, ten tomorrow, and then it'll be hard to eat even two pounds. Just don't try it with bread."

And now the watchman Kara-Dmitriyev is walking past the vines that are joined in pairs (these are the first vineyards after the war and there aren't enough poles to tie the vines to). Below, on the slope, the rows of vines of the vineyard have breaks between them, and the ground shows through amidst the green.

The ground is inviting, pleasant, and resembles spilled wine. The grapes still have the smell of vine leaves. A nut tree grows next to the hut of the guard. Its fruit is unknowingly rough-looking, yet for some reason it's pleasant for the eyes to rest on this fruit.

Kara-Dmitriyev smiles anxiously and sadly and looks below without understanding anything. He has purple circles around his eyes, and his face is strangely non-shiny.

He looks down the slope. The first halves of his days have ended; his dreams have disappeared.

The road through the vineyards is deserted.

Why isn't anyone walking?

Which and whose soldiers will drink the wine from these fields? Will they transport arms or icons, or will they beat up their fathers on the thresholds of their houses, or will they appeal to them without getting an answer? Or, drunk on wine, will they create new palaces and summon their new gardeners here? Beyond the vineyards is the languid sea filled with hidden passion. In the sea are the same kind of flowerbeds as here on the slopes; dolphins are leaping, guarding the fruits of the sea from children and birds. But the road is deserted; it awaits pedestrians in vain, and the trees bend down in vain, in a vain attempt to sweep it clean.

There is emptiness and barrenness in the heart of the earth—in wine and in man.

1925

NOTES

1. *Izvestiya*: one of the leading newspapers in the Soviet Union.
2. The Emir of Bukhara had a number of residences before the revolution, including a palace on the Black Sea. The Emirate of Bukhara existed from 1785 to 1920, when the state was conquered by the Bolsheviks and replaced with the Bukharan People's Soviet Republic (most of it in what is today Uzbekistan).
3. Extraordinary Troika: Special Board established for extrajudicial prosecution.
4. *rabochii fakul'tet* : "workers' faculty." A division of courses for workers that prepares them for entrance to institutions of higher learning.
5. Saadi (Muslikhidden Abu Mukhammed Abdallakh ibn Mushrifaddin): a 13ᵗʰ century classical Persian poet.
6. The Third [Communist] International: an organization founded in 1919 for the support of Communist parties around the world.
7. Vologda Oblast: about 275 miles north of Moscow.
8. During its 3000-year history, the Crimea has been settled, and sometimes controlled, by many different peoples and ethnic groups, including the Scythians, the Tatars, and the Genoese.
9. *razryv-trava*: In Russian folk belief, at midnight on St. John's Eve this grass produces a bloom that looks like a flame. No one knows where it grows and devils threaten the life of any human who seeks to find it and use its powerful magic (it can open any lock, all weapons are powerless against it, etc.).
10. Ivan Kupala or St. John's Eve: a folk holiday celebrating the summer solstice. People believed that a wondrous fern would flower that night and reveal buried treasure.
11. This phrase may be a reference to "The Devil's Swing"(*Chertovy kacheli*), a poem by Fyodor Sologub, in which the devil pushes a man sitting on a swing, an image suggesting that the devil is in charge of human life.
12. *khamsa*: a small fish of the anchovy family.
13. The Karabi-Yaila mountain range in the Crimea; much of it is pasture land.
14. Livadia: a resort town in the Crimea, where the last Russian tsar, Nicholas II, and his family vacationed.

THE VIPER
(A Long Story about One Girl)

Aleksei Tolstoy

Whenever Olga Vyacheslavovna would appear in a cotton-print bathrobe, her hair uncombed, a glum look on her face—everyone in the kitchen would stop talking; only the Primus stoves[1]—carefully cleaned and full of kerosene and hidden fury—would emit a hissing sound. Some kind of danger emanated from Olga Vyacheslavovna. One of the tenants said of her: "There are bitches like that with a cocked gun . . . Stay away from them, my dear friends . . ."

With a cup and a toothbrush in her hand and a Turkish towel around her waist, Olga Vyacheslavovna would go up to the sink and wash, letting the water from the tap pour over her dark, close-cropped hair. When there were only women in the kitchen, she would drop her bathrobe to the waist and wash her shoulders and breasts with brown nipples, breasts that were barely developed, like a teenager's. Standing on a small stool, she would wash her strong and beautiful legs. Then you could see a long scar across her thigh, and on her back—above the shoulder-blade—a shiny, pink depression, the exit point of a bullet, and on her upper right arm, a small bluish tattoo. Her body was well-proportioned, dark-skinned, with a golden hue.

All these details were carefully studied by the women who populated one of the many apartments in a large building in Zaryadiye.[2] The dressmaker Marya Afanasyevna, who hated Olga Vyacheslavovna with a passion, called her a "branded woman." Roza Abramovna Bezikovich, unemployed—her husband lived in the Siberian tundra—literally felt ill at the sight of Olga Vyacheslavovna. The third woman, Sonia Varentsova, or Lialechka[3] as everyone called her, a very sweet girl who worked in the *Makhorka** Trust, would abandon her humming Primus and leave the kitchen whenever she caught the sound of Olga Vyacheslavovna's footsteps. And it was a good thing that both Marya Afanasyevna and Roza Abramovna were so nice to her, otherwise

Lialechka would have had to eat burnt kasha almost every day.

After washing herself, Olga Vyacheslavovna would look at the women with her dark, "wild" eyes and go back to her own room at the end of the corridor. She did not have a Primus stove, and the people in the apartment could not imagine what she ate in the morning. Vladimir Lvovich Ponizovsky, a former officer and now a middleman for the sale and purchase of antiques, tried to convince people that Olga Vyacheslavovna drank 60 proof cognac in the morning. Anything was possible. Actually, she did have a Primus stove once, but out of misanthropy she used it in her room since doing so had not been forbidden by any order of the building association. Zhuravlyov, the building manager, after threatening to take Olga Vyacheslavovna to court and evict her if this "scandalous anti-fire behavior"[4] were ever to be repeated, was almost killed. Olga Vyacheslavovna threw a burning Primus at him—it's a good thing he ducked—and showered him with such obscene language as he had never heard in all his born days even on the street on a holiday. Of course, the kerosene stove disappeared.

At half-past nine Olga Vyacheslavovna would leave. Along the way she would probably buy a sandwich with some sausage fit only for dogs and have it with tea at work. She never returned at a fixed time. She never had male visitors.

Examining her room through a keyhole never satisfied anyone's curiosity: bare walls—no photographs, no postcards, only a small revolver above the bed. As for furniture, five pieces: two chairs, a chest of drawers, an iron bedstead, and a table by the window. Sometimes the room would be tidy, the window curtain raised, a small mirror, comb, and two or three small vials all lined up on the peeling chest of drawers, a pile of books on the table, and even a flower in a small bottle that had contained heavy cream. Sometimes everything would be in nightmarish disorder until late in the evening; it would look as if people had struggled and thrashed about on the bed, the whole floor would be covered with cigarette butts, and there would be a chamber pot in the middle of the room.

Roza Abramovna would moan in a weak voice, "This is a demobilized soldier, not a woman . . ."

In one way or another, Olga Vyacheslavovna's life was the object of daily gossip and the tenants' petty passions would begin to seethe; if it were not for Olga, it probably would have become terribly dull in the communal apartment. Nevertheless, not a single curious eye could penetrate into the inner reaches of her life. It even remained a mystery why the most inoffensive Sonechka Varentsova constantly trembled in Olga Vyacheslavovna's presence.

They would question Lialechka, she'd shake her curls, say something that made no sense and talk instead about trifling matters. Lialechka, if not for her nose, would have been a screen star long ago. "In Paris they'd make the sweetest-looking thing," Roza Abramovna would say to her, "out of your nose in Paris . . . So, you'll go to Paris, oh, my Lord . . . !" But Sonia Varentsova would just grin at this, her cheeks would turn pink and her little blue eyes would blink, betraying some ardent dream . . . Pyotr Semyonovich Morsh said of her: "Not a bad-looking girl, but a fool . . ." That's not true! Lialechka's strength lay in appearing to be a fool, but the fact that at nineteen she had so unerringly found her style pointed to her practical mind and hidden intelligence. Elderly men, exhausted by work, the executives and economic planners, liked her very much. She produced tender smiles from within the forgotten depths of their souls. They wanted to put her on their laps and, rocking to and fro, forget the rumble and foul smell of the city, the columns of numbers, and the rustle of office papers. When after wiping her little nose with a handkerchief she would sit down at the typewriter nice and straight, spring would burst into bloom on the dirty wallpaper in the gloomy quarters of the *Makhorka* Trust. She knew all this very well. She was harmless and, really, if Olga Vyacheslavovna hated her, it meant that there was something mysterious behind it.

On Sunday, at half past eight, the door at the end of the corridor squeaked as usual. Sonia Varentsova dropped her saucer, gasped softly, and rushed out of the kitchen. She could be heard locking her door with a key and letting out a sob. Olga Vyacheslavovna walked into the kitchen. There were two small wrinkles at the corners of her tightly closed mouth, her high eyebrows were knitted, and her thin gypsy face looked ill; a towel was pulled as tightly as possible around her small, wasp waist. Without raising her eyes, she turned on the faucet and began to wash, splashing and making a puddle on the floor, "like a dog . . ." "And who's going to wipe it up? A fine thing," Marya Afanasyevna whispered.

After drying her wet hair with the towel, Olga Vyacheslavovna, her eyes gloomy, took in at a glance the kitchen, the women, and short Pyotr Semyonovich Morsh, who had come in at that point through the back door with a chunk of bread in his hand, a bottle of milk, and his repulsive, constantly trembling little dog. His dry lips smirked maliciously. . . .

Then a strange sound came from Olga Vyacheslavovna's throat as if everything brimming to overflowing in her had burst forth in what sounded like a squawk or perhaps a snatch of rueful laughter.

"What in the hell!" she said in a low voice, threw the towel over her shoulder, and left.

A satisfied little smirk appeared on Pyotr Semyonovich's parchment-like face.

At that point at the end of the corridor "Oh, what in the hell!" could be heard again and a door slamming shut. The women in the kitchen exchanged glances. Pyotr Semyonovich went to drink tea and to change from his at-home trousers into his Sunday ones. The wall clock in the kitchen showed nine.

At nine in the evening a woman walked swiftly into the local police station. A brown helmet-shaped hat was pulled down over her eyes, the high collar of her coat covered her neck and chin, and the part of her face that was visible seemed to be covered with a white powder. The station chief took a good look at her and discovered that this was not powder but pallor—there was not a drop of blood in her face. Pressing her chest to the edge of the ink-stained counter, the woman said quietly, with heart-rending despair, "Go to Pskov Lane . . . I've done something there, but I don't know what myself . . . I have to die now . . ."

Only then did the station chief notice the small revolver clutched in her fist, which had turned blue. The station chief threw himself across the table, grabbed the woman by the hand, and wrested the dangerous toy from her.

"And do you have a permit to carry a weapon?" he shouted for some reason.

The woman threw her head back because the hat was in her way and continued to look at him vacantly. "Your first name, last name, address?" he asked her more calmly.

"Olga Vyacheslavovna Zotova . . ."

2

Ten years ago in Kazan,[5] on Prolomnaya Street, in the middle of the day a fire started in the house of a merchant of the second guild, Old Believer[6] Vyacheslav Illarionovich Zotov. The firemen discovered two bodies on the first floor, tied with electrical wire—Zotov himself and his wife—and on the floor above, the unconscious body of their daughter, Olga Vyacheslavovna, a seventeen-year-old girl and gymnasium student. Her nightgown was in shreds, her hands and neck covered in scratches; everything all around pointed to a desperate struggle. But the bandits apparently could not get the better of her, or in their rush to leave had simply hit her with the weight on a small leather strap that lay on the floor near her.

The house could not be saved, and all of Zotov's property burned to the ground. Olga Vyacheslavovna was taken to a hospital; her shoulder had to be set and the skin on her head stitched. For several days she lay unconscious. Her first sensation was that of pain when her bandages were being changed. She saw a military doctor with kindly looking glasses sitting on her cot. Touched by her beauty, the doctor shushed her to stop her from moving. She stretched out her hand to him. "Doctor, what beasts!" and burst into tears.

A few days later she said to him: "I don't know two of them—whoever they were, they wore greatcoats . . . The third I do know. I danced with him . . . Valka, from my seventh grade. I heard them killing my mom and dad . . . Their bones crunched . . . Doctor, why did this happen? What beasts!"

"Shh-shh," the doctor hushed her in a frightened whisper and his eyes behind the glasses were moist with tears.

No one visited Olechka Zotova in the hospital; this was not the time to do so, and other things were on people's minds. A civil war was tearing Russia apart, stable life was breaking up and falling to pieces, and the words in the decrees—posted white notices that assaulted the eye no matter where the passerby cast a sidelong glance—were full of raging fury. The only thing Olechka could do was to cry all day long from unbearable pity (in her ears rang her father's terrible cry "Don't!" and the inhuman shriek of her mother who had never screamed like that in her whole life), and from fear (how was she to live now?), and from despair before the unknown which thundered and shouted and fired at night under the hospital windows.

During those days she must have shed every last tear allotted to her for her whole lifetime. Her carefree, feckless youth had come to an abrupt end. Her heart became covered with scars like a wound that had healed over. She did not know yet how much dark and passionate strength smoldered in her.

One day a man with his arm in a sling sat down next to her on the bench in the corridor. He wore a hospital robe, drawers, and slippers, and yet a fiery, cheery health emanated from him like from an iron stove. Barely audibly, he was whistling "Little Apple"[7] and tapping his bare feet. His grey hawk's eyes more than once turned in the direction of the beautiful girl. His broad, tanned face, its muscles covered with a small beard that was never shaved, conveyed a devil-may-care attitude and even laziness; only his hawk's eyes were cruel and hard.

"From the venereal?" he asked indifferently.

Olechka did not understand, but then she became filled with indignation. "They tried to kill me but didn't, that's why I'm here." She moved away from him and began to breathe hard, her nostrils flaring.

"Oh my goodness, that's a real adventure! There must have been a good reason. Or simply bandits? Eh?"

Olechka stared at him. How could he question her as if he were asking her about the most ordinary thing out of sheer boredom . . .

"Have you really not heard about us? The Zotovs, on Prolomnaya Street?"

"Ah, so that's it! I remember . . . You're a real fighter of a girl, you know—you didn't give in . . . (He wrinkled his brow). Those people should be burned alive, boiled in cauldrons, perhaps then we'd get somewhere with them . . . So much of this vile element has crawled out—more than we ever imagined—that we just throw up our hands. It's a disaster." (His cold eyes looked Olechka over.) "You, of course, perceive the revolution only through this violence . . . And it's a pity. Are you yourself one of those Old Believers? You believe in God. Never mind, it will be all right (he rapped his knuckles on the arm of the divan). Here's what you should believe in—the struggle."

Olechka wanted to reply to him with something malicious and absolutely justified on behalf of the whole state of ruin of the Zotovs, but under his derisively expectant look all her thoughts appeared and disappeared without reaching her tongue.

He said, "There now . . . But the horse is hot! Good Russian blood with a bit of gypsy blood added . . . Otherwise you would've lived out your life as everyone else, watching life through a window from behind a rubber tree plant . . . Boredom."

"And this, what's going on now, is it more fun?"

"Well, isn't it? You have to go and have a bit of fun sometimes, not just move and click the abacus beads . . ."

Olechka grew indignant again, and again no words came, only her shoulders twitched; he was so very confident . . . She only grumbled, "You've destroyed the whole town, and you'll destroy all of Russia, you shameless people . . ."

"Big deal—Russia . . . We're getting ready to cover the whole world on our horses . . . The horses have broken loose from their chains, perhaps we'll stop only at the ocean . . . So, like it or not, join us in the fun."

Bending toward her, he grinned and his teeth flashed in wild merriment. Olechka's head began to spin as if she had already heard those words, and she remembered that grin and white teeth as if memories were rising from the darkness of her blood and generations of voices from long ago were shouting, "To horses! Have fun, my soul . . . !" Her head began to spin, and again the man with his arm in a sling was sitting there in a hospital robe . . . But her heart filled with passion and anxiety—in some way this grey-eyed man had become dear to her . . . She frowned, moved to the end of the bench . . . And he, whistling, began to tap his foot again . . .

The conversation was brief—out of sheer boredom in the hospital corridor. The man whistled a bit and left. Olga Vyacheslavovna did not even find out his name. But when the next day she sat down again on the same bench and turned to peer into the depths of the stuffy corridor and earnestly mulled over the thought that she should say something convincing and very wise to deflate his self-confidence, but he did not come—instead of him some people came hobbling along on crutches—it suddenly became clear to her that she was terribly upset by yesterday's meeting.

After this she waited perhaps a minute more in all; tears welled up in her eyes from hurt feelings that here she was waiting for him and little did he care. She left, lay down on her cot, and began to think the most unjustified things about him that would enter her head. But how, how had he upset her?

Curiosity tormented her more than hurt feelings—if at least she could catch a glimpse of him! What's he like? Oh, there's nothing special about him . . . There are millions of fools like that . . . A Bolshevik, of course . . . A bandit . . . And his eyes, his brazen eyes . . . And her young woman's pride tormented her: to think about someone like that all day! To wring your hands because of someone like that!

At night the whole hospital was roused from sleep. Doctors and hospital orderlies rushed about, dragging bundles. Frightened patients sat on their cots. Wheels rumbled outside the windows; furious cursing began to spread through the whole place. The Czechs were entering Kazan. The Reds were evacuating. Everyone who was able to leave left the hospital. Olga Vyacheslavovna was left behind; they forgot about her.

At dawn some broad-chested Czechs, cleanly dressed in foreign style, banged their rifle butts in the hospital corridor. They were dragging someone—the breaking voice of the deputy director yelled, "I've been here against my will, I'm not a Bolshevik . . . Let me go, where are you taking me?"

Two paralytics crawled over to the window which looked out on the courtyard and announced in a whisper, "They've taken him to the shed, to hang the poor fellow . . ."

Olga Vyacheslavovna got dressed; she wore a government-issue grey dress and concealed the bandage on her head with a white scarf. The festive ringing of bells floated above the city. Dawn was breaking. Military music of the entering regiments could be heard—now louder, now dying away. The thunder of heavy guns moving off into the distance rumbled beyond the Volga.

Olga Vyacheslavovna walked out of the ward. A patrol stopped her around a bend in the corridor—two mustached Czechs, who had been walking slowly, hushed her and hissed, and ordered her to turn back.

"I'm not a prisoner, I'm a Russian," Olga Vyacheslavovna shouted to them, her eyes glistening,

They laughed and reached out to pinch her cheek, her chin . . . But she was not about to thrust her chest against two bayonet points. She turned back, her nostrils flaring, and sat down on her cot, her teeth lightly chattering.

In the morning the patients did not receive their tea and began to grumble. At dinner time the Czechs took five men—amputees, Red Guards. The paralytics at the window announced that the poor souls were being led to the shed. Then a Russian officer, with a belt cinched high around his waist and wearing wide riding-breeches that looked like the wings of a bat, walked into the ward. The patients pulled their blankets up over themselves. He looked round at the beds and his squinting eyes settled on Olga Vyacheslavovna. "Zotova?" he asked. "Follow me . . ." He seemed to be flying on the batwings of his riding-breeches, and his ringing spurs filled the empty corridor with their loud jangling.

They had to go through the courtyard. At that point, a curly-haired youth in an embroidered Russian shirt walked out of the doorway to which she was being led and glanced at her fleetingly as he pulled on his peaked cap and hurried to the gate . . . Olga Vyacheslavovna stumbled . . . She thought she saw . . . No, it couldn't be . . .

She walked into the receiving room and sat down at the table, looking at the military man whose face was long and distorted like in a crooked mirror. He looked at her, too, with eyes that were of different colors.

"And you're not ashamed, the daughter of a respected man in town and an educated girl, to get mixed up with this rabble?" she heard his reproachful voice, contemptuously emphasizing every vowel.

She tried to understand what he was saying . . . Some persistent thought prevented her from concentrating. Sighing, she clenched her fists on her lap and began telling him everything that had happened to her. The officer smoked slowly, leaning on his elbow. She finished. He turned over a sheet of paper—under it was a short note written in pencil.

"Our information doesn't quite agree," he said, wrinkling his forehead pensively. "I'd like to hear something from you about your connections with the local Bolshevik organization. What do you have to say?" One corner of his mouth curled up and his eyebrows contorted.

Olga Vyacheslavovna observed the terrible asymmetry of his cleanly shaven face with horror.

"But you . . . I don't understand . . . You're mad . . ."

"Unfortunately, we have irrefutable information, strange as it may seem." (He held a cigarette in his outstretched hand, as he rocked back and forth, and let out a puff of smoke—one could not imagine anyone more high society than this man.) "Your sincerity is winning me over . . ." (A ringlet of smoke.) "Be candid to the end, dear . . . By the way, your Red Guard friends died heroes." (One of his skewbald eyes became fixed on something outside the window, from where the gates of the shed were visible.) "So, we continue to be silent? Well, then . . ."

Placing his hands on the arms of the chair, he turned to the Czechs, "*Bitte*, please . . ."

The Czechs ran up, lifted Olga Vyacheslavovna from the chair, felt her sides and bosom and, moving their mustaches in satisfaction, pawed her and looked for pockets under her skirt. He rose up a little from his chair and looked on, his eyes of different colors open wide. Olga Vyacheslavovna began to gasp for breath. She was blushing and her cheeks were on fire. She broke away and cried out . . .

"To the prison!" the officer ordered.

For two months Olga Vyacheslavovna sat in prison, first in a common cell, then in solitary. During those first days she almost went mad from constant thoughts of the gate to the shed against which a board had been placed. She could not sleep; in sleep her neck would become entangled in rope.

She was not interrogated, no one summoned her; it was as though they had forgotten about her. Little by little she began to ruminate. And suddenly it was as if a book had been opened before her—everything became clear. The curly-haired fellow in the embroidered shirt was Valka, of course, the murderer; she was not mistaken. Afraid that she would inform on him, he rushed to slander her; the note written in pencil was his denunciation of her.

Olga Vyacheslavovna could pace like a puma in her solitary cell as much as she wanted to; when she pleaded passionately (into the peep-hole in the door) to see the prison warden, an investigator, or a public prosecutor, the grim prison guards simply turned away. In her frenzied state she still believed in justice and kept devising fantastic plans: to get hold of pencil and paper and write the whole truth to some higher authorities who were just, like God.

One night she was awakened by rough, barking voices and the banging of a door being opened. Someone was going into the neighboring cell. A sallow-faced man with glasses was confined in there—all she knew about him was that he coughed convulsively at night. Jumping up, she listened intently. The voices behind the wall rose till they turned into shouts—hurried, unbearable. Then they became strained and died down. Moaning was heard in the silence, as if someone was being hurt and was trying to restrain himself, like in a dentist's chair.

Olga Vyacheslavovna huddled in a corner under a window, frantically staring with her wide-open eyes into the darkness. She remembered the stories (from when she had been in the common cell) about torture . . . She seemed to see a man's sallow face with glasses lying on the floor, his flabby cheeks trembling from the torture . . . They were binding his wrists and ankles with wire so tightly that the wire cut through the flesh to the bone . . . "You'll talk, you'll talk," she seemed to make out . . . The sound of blows resounded, as if they were beating a rug, not a man . . . He did not say anything . . . One blow, then another . . . And suddenly something began to bellow . . . "Aha! You'll talk . . . !" And now it was not bellowing but a pain-filled howling that filled the whole prison . . . As if the dust from that awful rug had covered Olga Vyacheslavovna, she felt nausea rising in her throat, her legs gave out, and the stone floor began to sway under her—she hit the back of her head on it.

That night, when man was torturing man, shrouded all of her timid hope for justice in darkness. But Olga Vyacheslavovna's passionate soul could not be silent and idle. And after some dark days, when she had almost lost her mind as she paced across her cell from corner to corner, she found her salvation in hatred, vengeance . . . Hatred, vengeance! Oh, if only she could get out of here!

Raising her head, she looked at the small, narrow window. Dusty windowpanes made a faint ringing sound and dried up spiders swayed in a cobweb. Heavy guns were letting out rumbling thunder somewhere. It was the Fifth Red Army moving on Kazan.

The guard brought dinner and, sighing loudly, cast a sidelong glance at the little window. "I've brought you some nice bread, miss . . . If you need something, just knock . . . We always support the political ones . . ."

Around midnight a commotion started in the prison corridors: doors banged, threatening shouts resounded. Several officers and civilians, making threatening gestures with their weapons, were driving a crowd of about thirty prisoners downstairs. They dragged Olga Vyacheslavovna out of her cell and then hurriedly down some stairs. She wriggled like a cat and tried to bite their hands. For a moment, she caught a glimpse of the windy sky in the inner courtyard, and the cold air of a fall night filled her chest. Then, a low door, some stone steps, and the putrid dampness of a basement filled with people; cones of light from flashlights darted about on the brick walls, over pale faces and wide-open eyes . . . Frenzied obscene language and cursing . . . Gun shots rang out and the basement arches seemed to topple . . . Olga Vyacheslavovna flung herself into the darkness . . . For a second Valka's face popped up in a beam of light from a flashlight . . . Something hot hit her in the shoulder, a fiery spindle pierced her chest; something tore at her back . . . Stumbling, she fell into mold on the floor which smelled of mushrooms . . .

The Fifth Red Army took Kazan, the Czechs left on ships for the south, and the Russian detachments dispersed—each going its own way. Half of the inhabitants fled to the ends of the earth out of fear of Red terror. For several weeks along both banks of the Volga—swollen from the fall rains—refugees who did not behave like people any more, with bundles and walking sticks, roamed and suffered unheard-of deprivations. Valka left Kazan too.

Olga Vyacheslavovna, counter to what common sense would lead one to expect, remained among the living. When the bodies of the executed were carried out of the prison basement and placed side by side in the courtyard under the overcast sky and in the drizzling rain, a cavalryman in a sheepskin coat crouched by her and gently turned her head.

"This girl is breathing," he said. "Someone should get a doctor, brothers . . ."

This was the same toothy one, with the eyes of a hawk. He carried the girl himself to the prison hospital, in the chaos of the conquered city ran trying to find "a professor from the old regime without fail," burst into the apartment of one professor, arrested him in the heat of the moment, thereby frightening him to death, delivered him to the field hospital on his motorcycle and, pointing to the unconscious Olga Vyacheslavovna who did not seem to have a drop of blood in her face, said, "Make sure she lives . . ."

She lived. After they dressed her wound and gave her some camphor, she half-opened her bluish eyelids and apparently recognized the hawk's eyes bent over her. "Closer," she muttered barely audibly and, after he had moved quite close to her and waited for a long time, she said for whatever reason, "Kiss me . . ."

There were people by her cot, it was wartime; the man with the eyes of a hawk sniffed, turned around, and shrugged his shoulders. "I'll be damned . . ." However, he did not bring himself to do it, just fixed her pillow.

The cavalryman's name was Emelyanov, Comrade Emelyanov. She asked his name and patronymic—his name and patronymic was Dmitry Vasilyevich. After finding this out, she closed her eyes and moved her lips, repeating, "Dmitry Vasilyevich." Emelyanov's regiment was being formed in Kazan, and he visited the girl every day. "I must tell you," he repeated to her, trying to encourage her, "you're tenacious of life, Olga Vyacheslavovna, like a viper . . . When you get better, I'll enroll you in the squadron as my personal orderly . . ."

He said this to her every day, and he never tired of saying it, nor she of hearing it. He would laugh, his teeth gleaming, and a gentle smile would form on her weak lips. "We'll cut your hair, I'll get you a pair of light boots—I've put some aside from a gymnasium student who was killed. At first, of course, we'll strap you to the saddle with a belt so you don't fall off. Ha-ha-ha."

Olga Vyacheslavovna was truly tenacious of life, like a viper. After all that had happened to her, it seemed there was nothing left of her but her eyes, but they burned with a sleepless passion and an avid, impatient desire for something. Her past life was left behind on a distant shore: her father's strict, prosperous house, the gymnasium, her sentimental girl friends, the snow on the streets, girlish enthusiasm for visiting artists, and infatuation, as was usually the case, with the Russian language teacher—

the stout, handsome Voronov; the gymnasium's "Herzen[8] Club" and the rapturous enthusiasm of her friends in the club; the reading of novels in translation. . . . The dacha, the pine trees and meadows, the glistening Volga. . . . All this was remembered perhaps only in her dreams, in the warmth of her hospital pillow wet with tears.

Into these dreams—so she imagined—Valka himself, in the flesh, would burst in, raging with fury, with a five-pound weight on a leather strap. This Valka Brykin had been thrown out of the gymnasium for hooliganism; he left as a volunteer for the front and a year later reappeared in Kazan, flaunting his lancer's uniform and his soldier's St. George Cross. People said that his father, the police officer Brykin. . . . had sent a request to the commander of the forces in the district, begging him to send his son Valka to the front-lines where he was sure to be killed, since it was better for a parent's heart to see this scoundrel dead rather than alive . . . Valka was always hungry and greedy for pleasure, and daring like a devil. The war taught him a few tricks, and he found out that blood smells sour and nothing more. And the revolution untied his hands.

His five-pound weight shattered the rosy, light ice around Olechka's dreams to pieces. The ice turned out to be frightfully thin, but she had dreamed of building her well-being on it: marriage, love, a family, a solid happy home . . . Under the thin ice an abyss lay hidden . . . The ice cracked and life—crude and passionate—swamped her in its turbid waves.

Olga Vyacheslavovna took life for what it was: a mad struggle (two times they had tried to kill her but did not, and now she was absolutely not afraid of anything), hatred to the full extent that her heart would allow, a crust of bread for each day, and passionate anxiety about love not yet experienced—this was life . . . Emelyanov would sit by her cot, she would put her pillow behind her back and squeeze the edge of the blanket with her thin fingers, and talk and look in his eyes with innocent trust. "This is how I imagined it: my husband is a respectable, fair-haired fellow, I'm in my pink peignoir, we're sitting and we're both reflected in a nickel-plated coffee pot. And this is happiness. I hate myself for having been happy . . . I invented a pink peignoir . . . How idiotic . . ." Emelyanov laughed at her stories. . . .

In November Olga Vyacheslavovna was released from the hospital. She had no relatives or acquaintances in the city. Northern clouds floated above the deserted streets and boarded-up stores and lashed

the town with rain and snow. Emelyanov waded spryly through mud
from one side-street to another in search of living quarters. Olechka
trudged along, a step behind him in her sheepskin coat—soaked and
weighing a ton—and in the boots of the dead gymnasium student; her
knees wobbled, but she would have rather died than lag behind Dmitry
Vasilyevich. He had received an authorization from the *ispolkom**
for living space for Comrade Zotova, who had suffered greatly at the
hands of the White Guards, and he tried to find something out of the
ordinary. Finally he decided on a huge mansion that had belonged
to the Starobogatov merchants that had columns and plate-glass
windows and had been abandoned by its owners, and requisitioned it.
In the uninhabited house the wind came in freely through the broken
windows and moved through the suite of rooms with decorated ceilings
and tattered, gilded furniture. The crystals in the chandeliers kept up a
doleful clinking. In the garden the bare lindens rustled mournfully. With
a kick of his foot, Emelyanov threw open the folding doors.

In the front room he broke up the oak organ—the size of a whole
wall—and took the wood to a corner room with divans, where he made
a hot fire in the fireplace.

"Here you can also put on a tea kettle to boil, and it's warm and light
in here—the bourgeois knew how to live . . ."

He produced for her a tin kettle, dried carrots for making a kind of
tea, groats, fatback, and potatoes—rations for about two weeks—and
Olga Vyacheslavovna was left alone in the dark and empty house, where
the stove pipes howled frightfully, as if the ghosts of the Starobogatov
merchants were sobbing their hearts out from grief and sitting on the
roof in the falling rain.

She had all the time she wanted for reflection. She would sit down on
a small stool, look at the fire where the tea kettle was beginning to sing,
and think about Dmitry Vasilyevich, wondering if he would come that
day. It would be nice if he came; the potatoes had just finished cooking.
She could hear his footsteps resounding on the parquet floor from afar;
he would enter—cheerful, with those awful eyes of his—and her life
would enter with him. . . .

After having his tea and rolling a cigarette out of *makhorka*, he would
tell her about military matters and describe cavalry battles vividly,
sometimes getting so excited that it was frightening to look into his
hawk's eyes.

". . . The revolution created the cavalry . . . Do you understand? The horse is an elemental force . . . A cavalry battle is a burst of revolutionary passion . . . Here I have just my sword in my hand, but I cut into an infantry formation, I fly at the machine-gun nest . . . Can the enemy bear my look? He can't. And so he runs in panic and I strike him down—I have wings behind my back. . . . "

His eyes glistened like steel; a steel sword whistled through the air . . . Olga Vyacheslavovna, a chill of excitement running down her spine, looked at him, her sharp elbows resting on her knees and her chin pressed against her clenched fists . . . It seemed that were the whistling blade to cut her heart, she would have cried out in joy: she loved that man so . . .

Why did he take mercy on her? Could it be only out of pity for her? Did he feel pity for an orphan like for a dog picked up on a street? Sometimes she seemed to catch his sidelong glance—fleeting and clouded over with more than brotherly feelings . . . Her cheeks would grow hot, she would not know where to look, and her excited heart would fall into a dizzying abyss. But no—he would pull out a Moscow newspaper from his pocket and sit in front of the fire, reading satirical sketches out loud to her in which the world bourgeoisie was being constantly ridiculed for all it was worth in the crudest language imaginable. . . .

Winter came. Olga Vyacheslavovna's health was improving. One day Emelyanov came to see her early, before it was light, told her to get dressed, and took her to the drill ground where he taught her the basic rules for mounting a horse and taking care of one. At dawn a soft snow fell. Olga Vyacheslavovna galloped across the white drill ground, leaving sandy prints in the snow from her horse's hooves. Emelyanov yelled, "Damn you, you sit like a dog on a fence! Sit up straight, don't bend down so much."

She thought it was funny, and the wind whistled happily in her ears, exhilarated her, and snowflakes melted on her eyelashes.

3

Iron strength lay hidden in the fragile young woman; it was not clear where it all came from. After a month of training on the drill ground, in mounted and unmounted formation, she learned to carry herself straight like a stretched musical string; the frosty wind gave her face a rosy color. "To look at her," Emelyanov would say, "you could knock her over with one good sneeze, but you know—she's a little devil . . ." And she was devilishly beautiful. The young cavalrymen would turn their heads and the experienced men would become pensive when Zotova— tall and slim, with a head of dark hair cut in a nice bob and in a short sheepskin coat tightly belted at the waist, her spurs jangling—would pass through the *makhorka* smoke in the barracks.

Her thin hands learned how to handle a horse adroitly and with sensitivity. Her legs, which had seemed to be good only for bourgeois dances and silk skirts, developed and grew strong, and Emelyanov was particularly surprised at the way her legs gripped a horse: steel, sensitivity, she sat like a tick in the saddle, and the horse underneath her behaved like a lamb. She even learned to wield a blade; she would cut down a stack of things or a twig in a spirited way but, of course, it was not a real blow because all the strength for a blow comes from the shoulder, but her small shoulders were those of a young girl.

She was not stupid either when it came to political education. Emelyanov was afraid of "bourgeois survivals of thinking" in her—the times were harsh then.

"Comrade Zotova, what goal is the Red Army of peasant workers pursuing?"

Without hesitation, Olga Vyacheslavovna would answer, "The struggle with bloody capitalism, landowners, priests, and interventionists for the happiness of all workers in the world."

Zotova was enlisted as one of the fighters in the squadron that Emelyanov commanded. In February the regiment was loaded into heated box cars and dispatched to the Denikin[9] front.

As Olga Vyacheslavovna stood and held the reins of her horse in the dirty, manure-covered snow of the station where the special trains had been unloaded, looking at the gloomy, wind-swept clouds and the spring sunset with the red and blue glow of burning coals and listening to the distant rumbling of heavy guns, her whole recent past rose up in her with never-to-be-forgotten pain and hatred filled with vengeance.

"Sto-op smoking . . . ! Mount your horses . . . !" Emelyanov's voice resounded.

With a light movement she leapt in the saddle and her sword hit her hip . . . Now you won't try to rip my nightgown off, threaten me with a five-pound weight, or drag me under my arms to the basement!

"At a trot, march . . . !"

Her saddle crunched, the raw wind whistled, and her eyes looked at the dark crimson color of the sunset. "The horses have broken loose from their chains and perhaps we'll stop only at the ocean," the words of her dear friend came into her head like a wild, intoxicating song . . . Thus began her military life.

In the squadron everyone called Olga Vyacheslavovna Emelyanov's wife. But she was not his wife. No one would have believed it; had they found out that Zotova was still a virgin they would have died laughing. But both she and Emelyanov kept this a secret. It was easier and simpler to be considered his wife; no one tried to paw her—everyone knew that Emelyanov had a heavy fist. Several times he had already proven it, and so Zotova was just everyone's kid brother.

Because of her duties as an orderly, Zotova was constantly by the side of the squadron commander. On the march she spent the night with him in the same hut and often in the same bed—he with his head turned to one side, and she, to the other, each covered with a sheepskin coat. After an exhausting day's march of around fifty versts, after taking care of her horse and gulping down some food from the communal kettle, Olga Vyacheslavovna would pull off her boots, undo the collar of her cotton shirt and fall asleep, barely managing to put her head down on a bench, a stove,[10] or the edge of a bed . . . She would not hear Emelyanov going to bed, or getting up. He slept like an animal, not much, as if listening for sounds in the night.

Emelyanov treated her with sternness, did not single her out for praise among the fighters, and picked on her probably more than on the rest. It was only now that she understood the power of his hawk's eyes: this was the look of battle readiness. . . .

Zotova was taking a small package of letters to the division headquarters. . . . The road went past a pond half-overgrown with sedge; a chalky cliff, all in folds, was reflected in it. The horse broke step and pulled toward the water. Zotova dismounted and unbridled it, and the horse, going knee-deep into the water, started to drink, but it had just taken a sip when it raised its bald muzzle and, shaking all over, began to neigh loudly and uneasily. Immediately it was answered with neighing from the willow bushes at the end of the pond. Zotova quickly bridled her horse and jumped into the saddle; staring intently, she pulled out the stock of her carbine from behind her back. Two heads dove down into the willow bushes and riders came galloping out on the shore—two of them. They stopped. This was a mounted patrol, but whose? Ours or White?

The horse of one rider lowered its head, driving a horsefly off its leg; the rider stretched to reach the reins and a gold stripe flashed on his shoulder . . . "Giddyup!" Olga Vyacheslavovna prodded her horse with her legs, leaned forward, and wormwood bushes and dry burdock came flying toward her. The heavy clatter of horse hooves could be heard behind her back, catching up with her . . . A shot . . . She squinted—one of the riders was moving in from the right to cut her off. His chestnut horse, from the Don Cossack area, was galloping like a borzoi hound. Again a shot from behind . . . She ripped the carbine from her back and let go of the reins. The rider on the Don horse was galloping about fifty steps away from her. "Stop, stop!" he shouted in a spine-chilling voice, brandishing his sword . . . It was Valka Brykin. She recognized him, urged on her horse with her legs; galloping towards him, she raised her rifle and fired, and a shot flashed with burning hatred . . . The Don stallion, jerking its head, reared up on its hind legs and immediately came tumbling down, crushing its rider . . . "Valka! Valka!" she screamed wildly with glee, and at that moment the second horseman came riding at her from behind . . . She saw only his long moustache and his big eyes bulging in astonishment. "A woman!" he cried out, and his raised sword made a feeble, jingling sound against the barrel of Olga Vyacheslavovna's carbine. The horse carried him forward. She no longer had the carbine in her hands—she must have thrown it away or dropped it (later, in telling the story, she could not remember); her hand felt the heavy, beckoning weight of her unsheathed sword, her constricted throat let out a shrill scream, her horse gave chase at full gallop, caught up with the man, and she struck a swinging blow. The man with the mustache fell forward on the horse's mane and grasped the back of his head with both hands.

Breathing hard, the horse carried Olga Vyacheslavovna across the wormwood-covered steppe. She saw that she was still gripping the handle of her sword. She struggled to put it back in its sheath. Then she reined in her horse; the chalky cliff and the pond lay to the left, far behind her. The steppe was empty, no one was chasing her, and the shooting had stopped. Larks were singing in the radiant blue of the sky; they sang nicely and sweetly, as in her childhood. Olga Vyacheslavovna gripped the shirt on her chest and squeezed her throat with her fingers, trying to get hold of herself in her fright, but nothing came of her efforts: tears gushed from her eyes and, as she wept, her whole body began to shake in the saddle.

Then, on the way to the division headquarters, she kept wiping her eyes angrily for a long time, first with one fist, then with the other.

Zotova was forced to tell this story hundreds of times to the men in the squadron. The fighters would guffaw, shake their heads in disbelief, and nearly collapse on the floor laughing.

"Oh, I can't take it, brothers, what a riot! A woman sends two men to the grave . . . !"

"Wait, tell us. So he comes flying at you from behind and suddenly cries out, 'A woman!?'"

"And did he have a big mustache?"

"His eyes bulged—he was surprised."

"And he never got to raise his hand?"

"Well, of course not."

"And at that point you give him a whack on the back of his head . . . Oh, brothers, I'm going to die laughing . . . That's a cavalier for you—smashed to pieces."

"Well, and then what did you do?"

"What do you mean 'then'?" Olga Vyacheslavovna would answer. "I wiped my blade as usual and rode to the division headquarters with the package of letters."

There was one real drawback to this life on the march: Olga Vyacheslavovna could not overcome her shyness. It was particularly irksome for her when the squadron would suddenly come across a river or pond on a hot day. The fighters—stark naked, in rainbows of splashing water—would ride into the water on their unsaddled horses, laughing loudly and whooping. Zotova had to find a place apart from them, somewhere behind a bush, behind some reeds. . . .

Washing herself at a well also had its difficulties for her; she had to get up before the others and run on the cold dew when dawn was just breaking like a crimson fissure in the layers of clouds and fog. One day she used the well sweep, which creaked pitifully, pulled up a bucket of pleasantly smelling ice-cold water, placed the bucket on the well's edge and undressed, huddling from the dampness, and something seemed to silently touch her back. She turned around. Dmitry Vasilyevich was standing on the porch and staring at her in a strange way. Then she slowly stepped behind the well and crouched down so that only her unblinking eyes could be seen. Had this been one of her comrades, she would have simply shouted, "Why are you staring, you devil, turn away!" But her throat turned dry from shame and emotion. Emelyanov shrugged his shoulders, grinned and left.

The incident was insignificant, but everything changed from then on. Everything suddenly became complicated, even the simplest thing. The squadron stopped for the night in some burned down homesteads. As was often the case, there was only one bed for her and Emelyanov. That night Olga Vyacheslavovna lay down on the very edge, on a smelly horse blanket, and for a long time she could not fall asleep, although she closed her eyes as tight as she could. However, she did not hear Emelyanov come in. When the cries of the roosters woke her up, he, as it turned out, had slept right on the floor, by the door . . . Simplicity disappeared . . . In conversations Dmitry Vasilyevich knitted his brow and looked away; she sensed the same forced, feigned mask on his face as well as on her own. And nevertheless all this time she lived like someone drunk with happiness.

Up to this point Zotova had not been in a real battle. Their regiment continued to retreat to the north with the rest of the division. During minor skirmishes she inevitably found herself by the side of the squadron commander. But then there was some serious trouble somewhere at the front; they began to talk about it with alarm and in hushed tones. The regiment received an order: to break through the enemy lines, move along the enemy's rear lines, and then break through to their army's outside flank. This was the first time that Olga Vyacheslavovna heard the word "raid." They set out at once. Emelyanov's squadron left first. By nightfall they stopped in a forest without unbridling their horses or lighting a fire. A warm rain fell noisily on the leaves; you could not see your outstretched hand in front of you. Olga Vyacheslavovna was sitting on a stump when a gentle hand came to rest on her shoulder; she guessed who, sighed, and threw back her head.

Dmitry Vasilievich bent over her and asked, "You won't get scared, will you? Well, just watch out . . . Stay close to me . . ."

Then a quiet command was given; the fighters got on their horses in silence. As she turned, Olga Vyacheslavovna happened to touch Dmitry Vasilyevich with her stirrup. They rode at a slow pace for a long time. The ground made a smacking sound under the horses' hooves, and from somewhere came the smell of mushrooms. Then dull shafts of light appeared in the pitch-black darkness—the deciduous forest was beginning to thin out. On the right, very close by, fiery needles came flashing by, and loud shots tore through the forest. Emelyanov gave a drawn-out shout, "Draw your swords, forward march . . . !" Wet branches whipped their faces; the horses crowded together, snorted, their forelegs brushing against tree trunks. And all of a sudden a grey, smoky meadow that sloped downward spread out before their eyes, and shadows of horsemen were already racing across it. The slope ended abruptly. Olga Vyacheslavovna dug in her spurs, and the horse, rearing up on its hind legs, jumped into the river.

The regiment broke through to the enemy's rear. They galloped in the darkness under low clouds; the steppe hummed under the hooves of five hundred horses. As they galloped at full speed, buglers' trumpets strained as they sounded. An order was given to dismount. Epaulettes and cockades were given out to the squadrons. Emelyanov gathered some fighters in a circle.

"With the goal of disguising ourselves, we are now the combined regiment of the North-Caucasus Army of Lieutenant-General Baron Wrangel.[11] Have you memorized it, you chicken heads? (The fighters roared with laughter.) "Whoever is laughing there—cut it out, or you'll get a punch in the mouth! From now on I'm no longer 'comrade commander' but 'Your Honor, captain, sir.'" (He struck a match and a gold shoulder strap with one stripe glistened on his shoulder.) "You're now no longer 'comrades' but 'the lower ranks.' Stand at attention, salute, use the formal 'you.' Si-lence, stand at attention! Got it?" (The whole squadron roared with laughter; they stood at attention, saluted, and to "Your Honor" added all kinds of simple little words.) "Sew on your epaulettes, hide your Red star in a pocket and put the cockade on your cap . . ."

For three days the disguised regiment galloped along Wrangel's rear flank. Columns of black smoke rose in its wake—railroad stations, trains, and military warehouses were set on fire, water pump stations and gunpowder cellars were blown up. On the fourth full day the horses slowed down, began to stumble, and the regiment halted for a day in an out-of-the-way village. Olga Vyacheslavovna took care of her horse and right there, without stepping over a pile of hay, dropped down in it and fell asleep. A woman's loud laughter woke her up; an apple-cheeked young woman in a black skirt tucked up above her bare calves said to someone, pointing at Zotova. "What a nice-looking boy . . ." The young woman was hanging laundered foot cloths out to dry in the yard.

When Olga Vyacheslavovna walked into the hut, Emelyanov was sitting at the table, sleepy-eyed, happy, with bits of down in his hair, barefoot. So that meant it was his foot cloths that had been washed.

"Sit down, they'll bring borscht any minute now. Want some vodka?" he asked Olga Vyacheslavovna.

The same apple-cheeked young woman walked in with a pot of borshcht, turning her rosy cheek away from the fragrant steam. She put the pot down loudly right in front of Emelyanov, her plump shoulder thrusting forward toward him.

"It's like we'd been waiting for you, here's the borshcht already . . ." She had a high, sing-song voice—and she was lively, brazen . . . "I've washed your footcloths and, before you know it, they'll be dry . . ." And she stroked Dmitry Vasilievich with her bitch's eyes. He grunted approvingly, gulping down the soup. He was all gentleness, sitting there.

Olga Vyacheslavovna put down her spoon; a ferocious snake bit her heart—she turned numb, lowered her eyes. When the young woman disappeared behind the door, she caught up with her in the entryway, grabbed her by the arm and, gasping for breath, said in a whisper, "What's with you, have you got a death wish?"

The young woman exclaimed "ah!" as she wrenched her arm free and ran away. Dmitry Vasilievich glanced dumbfounded a few times at Olga Vyacheslavovna: what had gotten into her? And when he was getting on his horse, he saw her fierce, sullen eyes and flared nostrils, and the bare-headed wench peeping out fearfully like a rat from behind a corner of the shed. And he understood everything, burst out laughing the way he used to laugh long ago, grinning and baring his white teeth. Leaving through the gate, his knee touched Olechka's, and he said with unexpected affection, "Oh, you little fool . . ."

She almost burst into tears.

On the fifth day it was discovered that a whole Cossack division was hot on the trail of the disguised Red regiment. Now they moved at full speed and abandoned exhausted horses. When night fell, a rear-guard battle began. The regimental banner was handed over to the first squadron. Without stopping, they rushed into a dark village without any lights. They banged on the shuttered windows with their sword handles. Dogs howled, everything seemed dead all around, and only the bell in the belfry clanged once and fell silent.

At last two peasants were brought in—they found them in the straw, tousled like forest goblins. Looking round at the cavalrymen, they only kept repeating, "Brothers, dear friends, don't kill us . . ."

"Is your village for White or for Soviet power?" Emelyanov shouted, leaning towards them in the saddle.

"Brothers, dear friends, we don't know ourselves . . . They've taken everything from us, robbed us, destroyed everything . . ."

Nevertheless, they managed to find out from them that for the time being the village was not occupied by anyone, that they were in fact waiting for Wrangel's Cossacks, and that on the other side of the river, beyond the railroad bridge, there were some Bolsheviks in trenches. The men in the regiment took off their shoulder straps, put on the Red stars and crossed the bridge to their own side. Here it came to light that the Whites were attacking like madmen along the whole front, and an order was given to defend the bridge to the death. But there was nothing to fight with: the machine-gun rounds did not fit the machine guns, there were lice on the men in the trenches, there was no bread, and the Red Army men had become terribly bloated from eating cooked grain. As soon as it would be night, they would run away; there had been a political agitator, but he died from dysentery.

The commander of the regiment got in touch on a direct line with the *glavkoverkh*;[12] it was true—they were ordered to defend the bridge to the last drop of blood until the army broke out of the encirclement.

"Olya, we won't get out of here alive," Emelyanov said. He scooped up some river water into two mess-tins and handed one to Olga Vyacheslavovna and, squatting down next to her, stared at the vague outline of the distant shore. A dim, yellow star hung over the river. All day Wrangel's batteries kept destroying the Bolshevik trenches with rapid fire. And in the evening an order came: charge the bridge, drive the Whites away from the river, and take the village.

Olga Vyacheslavovna looked at the dim, motionless remnant of the star reflected on the surface of the river—there was sadness in it.

"Well, let's go, Olya," Dmitry Vasilievich said, "we must get an hour's sleep." (For the first time he was using her first name.)

Figures of fighters with mess-tins crawled stealthily out of the bushes to the steep shore; all day there was no way to get near the river, and no one had a drop of water. Everyone already knew about the terrible order. For many it seemed that this night would be their last.

"Kiss me," Olga Vyacheslavovna said with gentle sadness.

He put down the mess-tin carefully, pulled her by the shoulders toward him—her cap fell off, her eyes closed—and began to kiss her eyes, mouth, and cheeks.

"I'd make you my wife, Olya, but now's not the time, you understand . . ."

Their night attacks were repelled. The Whites fortified their end of the bridge by winding barbed wire across it and fired their machine guns along it. A grey morning set in over the steaming river, over the damp meadows. The ground on both banks of the river would constantly fly up as if black bushes were sprouting up and then coming down. The air howled and screamed, and shrapnel exploded in small dense clouds. People were going crazy from the noise. A great many bodies lay sprawled face down, scattered near the bridge. It was all in vain. The men could no longer mount attacks against the machine-gun fire.

Then beyond the railroad embankment eight riders gathered under the regimental banner, torn and shot through; it seemed a bloody color at dawn. Two squadrons mounted their horses. The regimental commander said, "It's time to die, comrades," and rode at a slow pace to take his place under the banner. The eighth was Dmitry Vasilyevich. They drew their swords, spurred on their horses, rode out from behind the embankment, and broke into a full gallop over the booming boards of the bridge.

Olga Vyacheslavovna saw one man's horse tumble against the railing, and both the horse and rider went flying into the river from a height of some twenty-one meters. The other seven made it to the middle of the bridge. One more, as if sleepy, fell from his saddle. The ones in front, when they reached the end of the bridge, started hacking the wire with their swords. The strapping standard-bearer began to sway, the banner dropped, Emelyanov grabbed it, and at that moment his horse fell down dead.

The bullets sang all about. Olga Vyacheslavovna rushed along the boards full of cracks over a dizzying height. Right behind Zotova the iron bridge supports began to hum and shake; one hundred fifty throats let out a roar. Dmitry Vasilyevich stood with his feet wide apart and held the pole in front of him—his face was deathly still and blood was coming out of his open mouth. Galloping past, Olga Vyacheslavovna grabbed the banner out of his hands. He swayed toward the railing and sat down. The squadrons galloped quickly past—horses' manes, bent backs, and glistening blades.

They all broke through to the other side; the enemy was on the run, the heavy guns fell silent. The banner, torn to shreds, waved for a long time above the wall of horsemen galloping across a field and disappeared behind the white willows of the village. Now a broad-faced Red Army fellow was galloping with it, urging the horse on with his bare heels and waving the pole with the torn banner and shouting, "Strike them down, strike them down, kill them!"

Olga Vyacheslavovna was picked up in the field; she was stunned by a fall and badly wounded in the hip. Her squadron comrades felt terribly sorry for her; they did not know how to tell her that Emelyanov had been killed. They sent a delegation to the regimental commander so that Zotova would get an award for her act of heroism. They thought for a long time about what to give her. A cigarette case? She didn't smoke. A watch? Women didn't wear watches. Then in one cavalryman's knapsack they found a broach of pure gold—a heart with an arrow through it. The regimental commander agreed to this award without any objections, but in his written order added a proviso: Zotova to be awarded the gold broach for her heroic deed; the arrow was fine, but the heart, as a bourgeois emblem, had to be removed . . ."

4

Like a bird that streaks across a windy, crazy sky and suddenly falls like a ball with broken wings to the ground, so all of Olga Vyacheslavovna's life, her passionate, innocent love, came to an abrupt end and broke apart, and difficult and troubled days that she did not need stretched before her. For a long time she lay in various field hospitals, underwent evacuation in putrid, heated freight cars, froze under her pathetic greatcoat, and went hungry. People were strangers, angry; for everyone she was number so-and-so on a hospital list. She had no one close in the whole world. Life was tiresome and grim, and yet death did not take her.

When she was released from the hospital, her hair all cut off, her body so thin that her greatcoat and the tops of her boots hung loosely on her like on a skeleton, she went to the train station where people who no longer looked like people lived and died on the floor in the waiting rooms. Where was she to go? The whole world was like an uncultivated field. She returned to town, to the assembly point of the *voenkom*,[13] produced her documents and the arrow broach that had been awarded to her, and soon left on a special train for Siberia—to fight there.

The sound of train car wheels, iron heat from a small stove in the grey smoky air, thousands and thousands of versts, songs long like the road, stench and filthy snow of the barracks, screaming letters on military posters, scraps of posters, and devil knows what other notices. . . . and again snow, pines trees, smoke of camp fires, freezing cold, burned-down villages, bloody prints in the snow, and thousands and thousands of corpses like scattered wood, covered by the snow of blizzards. All this became muddled in her memories and fused into one scroll of never-ending miseries.

Olga Vyacheslavovna was thin and gloomy; she could drink motor alcohol fuel, smoked *makhorka* and, when necessary, swore no worse than anybody else. Very few people deemed her a woman; she was very skinny and vicious, like a viper. . . .

Then the war ended. At a market, Olga Vyacheslavovna bought a skirt made from a green plush curtain and went to work in various establishments: as a typist in the *ispolkom*,* as a secretary in *Glavles*,[14] and as a young copyist, moving with her writing table from one floor to another.

She did not stay long in any one place; she kept moving from town to town—closer to central Russia. She thought it would be nice to cross the bridge above the riverbank where Dmitry Vasilyevich, after scooping up some river water in his mess tin, sat with her for the last time. She would also find that brittle willow bush and the trampled spot where they had sat . . .

The past was not forgotten. She lived alone, bleakly. But military hardness left her little by little—Olga Vyacheslavovna was becoming a woman again . . .

5

At twenty-two she had to start a third life. What was happening now she imagined as an effort to harness a battle horse in a working horse's collar. The shaken country was still bristling, eyes that were still bloodshot were searching for things to destroy, but already everywhere, screening off the present from the very recent past, white leaflets with decrees began to appear in great numbers, calling on people to repair, reconstruct, and build. . . .

The decree leaflets called on people to restore and create. With whose hands? With your own hands, with these here—still bent like the claws of a bird of prey . . . ? Olga Vyacheslavovna loved to wander through the town in the sunset hours, peering into the mistrustful, gloomy faces of people with wrinkles from rage, horror, and hatred that had never smoothed out; she knew very well that trembling of the mouth, those holes and stumps instead of teeth, worn down by the war. Everyone had spent time there—from boy to old man . . . And now they wander through the dirty town in sour-smelling clothing made out of sacks or bourgeois curtains, in worn-out bast shoes, disheveled, and ready to weep or kill at any moment . . .

The decree leaflets insistently demanded creativity, creativity, creativity . . . Yes, this was more difficult than to blow up a bridge with a pyroxylin charge, hack a battery crew to pieces with a cavalry charge, or shell a factory building where the enemy was entrenched. Olga Vyacheslavovna stopped in front of a bright poster near a rickety fence. Someone had already put an "x" on it with a piece of plaster and scratched an obscene word on it. She scrutinized the happy faces, the unfurled banners, the hundred-storied buildings, the smokestacks and lines of smoke rising to the dancing letters that spelled "industrialization" . . . She was impressionable like a young innocent girl and daydreamed before the well-designed poster; the grandeur of this new struggle excited her. . . .

She managed to get a work assignment in Moscow; she arrived there in her green skirt made from a plush curtain, filled with determination and dedication.

Olga Vyacheslavovna treated life's deprivations calmly: she had seen even worse. The first weeks in Moscow she took shelter wherever she found it, then she received a room in a communal apartment in Zaryadiye. After filling out a great number of forms and submitting numerous applications, she immediately became subdued because of the great complexity involved in processing all her documents and the noise in the multi-storied establishments humming like beehives; she went to work in the control department of the Non-Ferrous Metals Trust. She felt like a sparrow that had flown into the thousand-wheel mechanism of the chimes in a clock tower. She pulled in her claws. She came to work on time, not a minute late. She familiarized herself with things and grew timid because, no matter how much she put her mind to it, she could not determine what benefit she brought by copying pieces of paper. Here her agility, her reckless courage, her viper's anger were of no use to anyone. Here only the Underwood typewriters made clicking sounds like little hammers in the ears of someone in a delirium from typhus; papers rustled and commanding voices mumbled something into telephone receivers. It was not like that in the war; there, it was clear, straightforward, to the accompaniment of bullets whistling by— always towards a visible goal . . .

Then, it goes without saying, she got used to it little by little, made do somehow, and "smoothed out her ruffled feathers." Work days—

monotonous, quiet—began to pass by quickly. . . .

She received the first blow from the deputy director who sat to the side of her outside the door that led to the director's. This happened on account of her smoking *makhorka*. The deputy director said, "I'm surprised at you, Comrade Zotova. You're such an interesting woman in general, but you've stunk up the whole premises with your *makhorka*. Don't you have any sense of femininity? You should smoke 'Yava.'"[15]

This trivial comment must have come at a timely moment. Olga Vyacheslavovna began to feel bad and felt hurt to the point of tears. Leaving work, she stopped on a landing before a mirror, and for the first time in many years took a good look at herself as a woman. "Hell knows what this is—a garden scarecrow," she thought to herself. Her worn-out plush skirt had ridden up in front, the back hem was frayed from the heels of her man's half-boots, and she had on a gray, cotton jacket . . . How had this happened?

Two typists in seductive skirts and pink stockings turned around as they ran past and looked at Zotova standing and looking bizarre in front of the mirror—and on the landing below they snickered. She could only make out, ". . . horses would get frightened . . ." Blood rushed to Olga Vyacheslavovna's attractive gypsy face. One of those typists lived in the same apartment in Zaryadiye as she did—her name was Sonechka Varentsova.

A few days later the women who lived in the apartment on Pskov Lane (that's in Zaryadiye) were surprised by Olga Vyacheslavovna's strange behavior. In the morning, when she came to the kitchen to wash, she fixed her eyes, shining like those of a viper, on Sonechka Varentsova, who was heating some milk. She walked up to her and, pointing to her stockings, asked, "Where did you buy those?" She lifted up her skirt and pointing to her underwear, asked, "And where did you buy that?" And she posed her questions with malice, as if she were cutting with a blade.

Sonechka, a gentle creature by nature, became frightened by her brusque behavior. Roza Abramova came to her aid. In a soft voice she explained in detail to Olga Vyacheslavovna that she would be able to obtain all those things on Kuznetsky Most,[16] that women in Paris were now wearing the "chemise" and flesh-colored stockings, and so on and so on.

As she listened, Olga Vyacheslavovna nodded her head and repeated, "I get it. Yes . . . I understand." Then she grasped one of Sonechka's blonde curls, although this was not a horses's mane but a most delicate lock. "And this—how do you comb it?"

"Cut it, my precious one, no question," Roza Abramova sang, "à la garçon,[i] wavy . . ."

Pyotr Semyonovich Morsh came into the kitchen, listened and, his bald head shining smugly, made a ludicrous comment, as always. "You're making the transition from war communism a bit late, Olga Vyacheslavovna . . ."

She turned around swiftly toward him (subsequently he would say that he even heard her grate her teeth) and uttered quietly but distinctly, "You bastard, you should have been eliminated long ago. Had I come across you in the field . . ."

In the administration of the Non-Ferrous Metals Trust everyone looked perplexed initially when Zotova appeared at work in a black silk dress with short sleeves, flesh-colored stockings, and nice patent-leather shoes; her chestnut-colored hair had been cut à la garçon and shone like dark brown fur. She sat down at her desk and bent her head over her papers; her ears were burning.

The deputy director, a young and naive fellow, stared at her goggle-eyed as he sat before a madly ringing phone. "Well, I'll be!" he exclaimed. "Where did this come from?"

Truly, Zotova was devastatingly good-looking: a thin, refined face with dark down on her cheeks, eyes like the night, long eyelashes. She had washed the ink stains off her hands—in a word, roll the cameras. Even the director himself, by the way, stuck his head out of his office, and gave Zotova a piercing stare. "What a striking girl!" he later said of her.

People came from other rooms to look at her. All talk was about Zotova's surprising transformation. Her new skin felt light and free as

i   à la garçon: cut in a boyish way.—Trans.

in the old days when she wore her gymnasium dress or a cavalryman's helmet, a tightly cinched sheepskin coat, and spurs. But if the men stared too much, she would lower her eyelashes walking by as if she were shielding her soul from view.

. . . On the third day, at five-o-clock, when Zotova broke off a piece of blotting-paper and, after moistening it with her saliva, used it to clean off an ink stain on her elbow, the young deputy director, Ivan Fyodorovich Pedotti, walked up to her and said they "had to have a very serious talk." Olga Vyacheslavovna slightly raised the beautiful bands that were her eyebrows and put on her hat. They walked out. Pedotti said, "It's simplest to go to my place—it's just around the corner." Zotova shrugged her shoulder slightly. They went. . . . They climbed up to the fourth floor. Olga Vyacheslavovna walked into his room first and sat down on a chair.

"Well?" she asked. "What did you want to talk to me about?"

He flung his briefcase on the bed and tousled his hair. . . . and began beating the stale air in his room with his fists.

"Comrade Zotova, we always approach a matter head-on, directly . . . With great dispatch . . . Sexual attraction is a fact of life, and a natural need . . . All that romantic stuff should have been thrown overboard long ago . . . Well, there you are . . . I've explained everything in advance . . . Do you understand everything?"

He seized Olga Vyacheslavovna under her arms and started to pull her off the chair toward his chest in which his ignorant heart was beating furiously and shamelessly as if he were standing on the edge of an indescribable abyss. But he immediately felt resistance: it was not that easy to pull Zotova off the chair—she was slim and resilient, as if made of steel. Without showing embarrassment, almost calmly, Olga Vyacheslavovna gripped both of his hands by the wrist and twisted them in such a way that he moaned loudly, jerked and, since she continued inflicting pain, shouted, "That hurts, let me go! To hell with you!"

"In the future keep your hands off if you haven't asked for permission, fool," she said.

She let Pedotti go, took a "Yava" cigarette out of its box, lit up, and left . . .

... After the incident with Pedotti, who came to hate her with the full force of wounded male pride, a silent hostility formed around Zotova on the part of women, and a derisive attitude on the part of men. They were afraid of quarreling with her. But she could feel the unkind looks which followed her behind her back. Nicknames like viper, branded woman, and squadron pelt became more and more firmly attached to her name—she made them out in their little whispers and read them on the blotting paper. And what was strangest of all, she accepted this nonsense painfully . . . She felt like shouting to them all, "I'm not like that!"

It's not without reason that Dmitry Vasilyevich had once called her a little gypsy . . . With a dark melancholy she began to notice that desires were awakening in her again, but now with full force . . . Her virginity was indignant . . . But what was she to do? Wash with ice-cold water under the faucet from head to toe? She had been burned much too painfully; it was frightening to throw herself into the fire yet another time . . . This was unnecessary, this was terrible . . .

Olga Vyacheslavovna looked at the man for only a minute, and her whole being told her: it's *him* . . . It was inexplicable and just as catastrophic as colliding with a bus that had come rumbling around a corner.

The man, in a loosely fitting shirt made of sailcloth, tall and apparently beginning to put on some weight, was standing on a staircase landing and reading a wall newspaper.* Workers kept running past—in and out of doors, up and down the staircase. There was a smell of dust and tobacco. Everything was as usual. With a languid smile, the man was examining a caricature of the business director of the *Makhorka* Trust (who had his office on the floor above) in the center of the wall newspaper. Since Olga Vyacheslavovna also lingered by the paper, he turned to her and pointed to the caricature (his hand was big, heavy, and beautiful).

"You're in the editorial office, I believe, Comrade Zotova? (His voice was strong and low.) "Portray me with everything you've got, I've nothing against it . . . But no one needs this . . . this is trivial, without talent!"

In the caricature he was depicted with a glass of tea between two ringing phones. The witticism consisted of his liking for sipping tea just when the phones were calling him to work.

"They were afraid to take a painful bite and made a feeble yelp, lackey style . . . So what if it's tea? In 1919 I drank alcohol with cocaine to keep from falling asleep."

Olga Vyacheslavovna looked into his eyes: grey, somewhat cold, the color of dull steel; they reminded her in some way of those—those beloved ones, extinguished forever . . . A cleanly-shaven face—correct, large, with a languid and intelligent grin . . . She remembered: in 1919 he was in Siberia as a provisions dictator, supplied the army; his name evoked terror in people for tens of thousands of versts . . . She imagined such people walking with their heads in the clouds . . . He shuffled events and lives like a pack of cards . . . And now, here he was, with his briefcase, a weary smile on his face—and the life he had given birth to was running past, pushing him aside with its elbows . . .

"If you trivialize everything so clumsily," he said again, "you can reduce the whole revolution to cheap little caricatures . . . The old men have done their part, so to say, and off to the dump heap with them . . . You've gotten your pay, now go have some beer . . . The young generation is good, but it's dangerous to lose touch with the past. Only ephemeridae, one-day creatures, live in the present . . . So . . ."

He left. Olga Vyacheslavovna looked at the strong back of his head and his broad back as he slowly walked up the stone steps, and it seemed to her that he was making a great effort not to bend under the weight of the times. She began to feel excruciatingly sorry for him. And pity, as we know . . .

At the first opportunity, with a document from the *mestkom*,* Olga Vyacheslavovna went up to the gloomy rooms of the *Makhorka* Trust and walked into the office of the business director. He was stirring a glass of tea with a teaspoon; a yeast-dough roll lay on his briefcase. A typist was pounding the typewriter keys very loudly and quickly. Olga Vyacheslavovna was so nervous that she paid no attention to her; all she saw was his steely eyes. He read the document she handed to him and signed it. She continued to stand. He said, "That's all, comrade . . . You can go."

That was in fact all. When Olga Vyacheslavovna was closing the door behind her, she thought she heard the typist let out a giggle. Now all that was left for her was to go mad . . . Because she won't be hit a second time with a weight, won't be shot in a basement, he won't carry her out in his arms, won't sit by her cot, won't promise her the boots of a dead gymnasium student . . .

That night she spent in a way that's best not to remember. In the morning the tenants scrutinized her room though the key hole. . . . "Our viper is going mad," they said in the kitchen.

Sonechka Varentsova flashed an enigmatic smile; unshakeable confidence slumbered serenely in her blue eyes.

Shyness is more difficult to overcome than the fear of death, but it was not for nothing that Olga Vyacheslavovna went through the school of battle: if it has to be done, it has to be done. To wait for an opportunity, for happiness, to resort to trivial things—here to reveal flesh-colored stockings for a second, there to expose a bare shoulder—was not in her character. She decided to go to him directly and tell him everything. Let him do whatever he wanted with her . . . But this—this was not life . . .

Several times she rushed behind him on the staircase so that there, on the street, she could grab him by his sleeve and say, "I love you, I'm dying . . ." But every time he would get in his car without noticing Zotova among the other working women . . . It was exactly during those days that she sent a burning Primus stove flying at Zhuravlyov. The communal apartment was becoming saturated with an electrical charge. Sonechka Varentsova was nervous and would leave the kitchen the minute she heard Zotova's steps. . . .

At last he left work on foot (his car was in the repair shop). Olga Vyacheslavovna caught up with him and called to him sharply and somewhat rudely—her mouth, her throat were dry. She walked beside him, unable to raise her eyes, stepping awkwardly, with her elbows stuck out. A second turned into an eternity; she felt hot and cold, tender and angry. But he continued to walk on—indifferent, unsmiling, and stern.

"The thing is . . ."

"The thing is," he immediately interrupted her at once with disgust, "I hear about you from everywhere . . . I'm surprised, yes, yes . . . You're pursuing me . . . Your intentions are clear—please don't lie, I don't need any explanations . . . You've simply forgotten that I'm not a nepman,* I don't start salivating at every pretty face I see. You showed your good side doing work for the community. My advice to you—throw away dreams of silk stockings, face powder and the like . . . You can still develop into a good comrade . . ."

Without saying goodbye, he crossed the street where, on the sidewalk near the confectionary shop, Sonechka Varentsova took his arm. Shrugging her shoulders, indignant, she began to tell him something. He continued to frown, freed his arm, and went on with his heavy head lowered. A cloud of gas exhaust from a bus hid them from Olga Vyacheslavovna's view.

And so, Sonechka Varentsova turned out to be a heroine. It was she who informed the business director of the *Makhorka* Trust about the past and present life of Zotova, the "squadron pelt." Sonechka was victorious, but she was terribly frightened . . .

Sunday morning, as already described by us above, when Olga Vyacheslavovna's door squeaked, Sonechka ran into her room and began to weep loudly, because living in constant fear had become unbearably painful for her. After washing up, Olga Vyacheslavovna said, "Oh, what in the hell" twice, who knows for what reason—once in the kitchen and another time as she was going back to her room—after which she left the house and courtyard.

The tenants gathered again in the kitchen: Pyotr Semyonovich was in his Sunday trousers and a new peaked cap with a white top, and Vladimir Lvovich looked unshaven and happy from having had too much to drink; Roza Abramovna was making mirabelle plum preserves, and Marya Afanasyevna was ironing a blouse. They chatted and cracked jokes. Sonechka Varentsova appeared with puffy little eyes.

"I can't take it anymore," she said as she stood in the doorway, "there has to be some end to this . . . She'll pour acid over me . . ."

. . . Only Marya Afanasievna said what had to be said.

"Although you're uncommonly secretive, Lialechka, tell the truth. Have you registered your union with the director formally?"

"Yes," Lialechka answered, "the day before yesterday we were in *zags*[17] . . . I was even insisting on a church wedding, since that's more lasting . . .

But he didn't want to hear of it . . ."

"So why don't you," Marya Afanasyevna said, shaking her iron, "throw your *zags* certificate in her face? You must talk to her . . ."

"Oh, no . . . Not for anything in the world . . . I'm so afraid—I have such heavy forebodings . . ."

"We'll all stand by the door while you talk. . . ."

They talked Lialechka into it.

Olga Vyacheslavovna returned at eight in the evening, bent over from exhaustion, her face sallow. She locked herself in her room, sat down on the bed, letting her hands fall on her lap . . . Alone, alone, in this savage, hostile life, lonely, as at the moment of death, not needed by anyone . . . Ever since yesterday a strange absent-mindedness was taking possession of her more and more. And so now, for example, she saw the revolver in her hands and did not remember when she had taken it down from the wall. She sat, thinking and looking at the deadly steel toy . . . And suddenly she grinned . . .

At that point there was a knock on the door. Olga Vyacheslavovna got up without saying anything and opened the door wide. The tenants, pushing and shoving each other, were rushing behind Sonechka in the darkness of the hallway—it seems they had brushes and pokers in their hands . . . Sonechka Varentsova walked into the room, pale, with pursed lips . . . Right away she began to speak in a tone that turned into shrill screaming.

"It's utter shamelessness—to throw yourself at a man who's married . . . Here's our *zags* certificate . . . Everyone knows that you have venereal diseases . . . And that you intend to make a career with them . . . ! And through my lawful husband at that! Here's our certificate . . ."

Olga Vyacheslavovna looked at the screeching Sonechka as if she were blind . . . And a wave of familiar, savage hatred welled up, constricting her throat, and her whole body hardened like steel . . . A cry escaped from her throat . . . Olga Vyacheslavovna fired and continued to fire at the white face rushing about frantically in front of her . . .

1928

NOTES

1. Primus: a portable oil-burning stove for cooking.

2. Zaryadiye: in central Moscow, a slum district that was inhabited mainly by craftsmen and petty merchants.

3. Lialechka: literally, Little Doll or Dolly.

4. Tolstoi is suggesting the low educational level of many who, in trying to sound official, misused words to an absurd point.

5. Kazan: a city that lies at the confluence of the Volga and Kazanka Rivers in Russia.

6. Old Believers: people who refused to recognize the church reforms carried out by Patriarch Nikon in the 17th century and separated themselves from the Orthodox Church.

7. "Little Apple": a song and dance popular among revolutionary soldiers and seamen.

8. Herzen, Aleksandr (1812-1870): one of the more influential social-political thinkers in Russian intellectual history.

9. General Anton Denikin led white anti-Bolshevik forces in southern Russia. In 1920 he left the Crimea for Constantinople, lived in exile in Europe and America, and wrote several books about the Russian civil war.

10. The Russian stove is a large mass made of clay and brick, with an oven for cooking and baking, that heats the whole hut. It has an area on top where a person can sleep and keep warm.

11. Baron Pyotr Wrangel was elected in 1920 Commander-in-Chief of the White forces in the Crimea. After losing half of his Russian Army, he organized a mass evacuation for anyone who wanted to leave Russia.

12. *glavkoverkh*: acronym for *verkhovnyi glavnokomanduyushchii*—commander-in-chief.

13. *voenkom*: acronym for *voyennyi komitet*— military committee.

14. *Glavles*: acronym for *Glavnaya lesnaya promyshlennost'*—Chief Department of the Timber Industry.

15. The "Yava" brand would have better tobacco and she would not have to roll her own cigarettes.

16. Kuznetsky Most (Bridge): a street in central Moscow where fashionable shops were located.

17. *zags*: acronym for *zapis' aktov grazhdanskogo sostoyaniya*— registry office.

THE FLOOD

Evgeny Zamyatin

The world around Vasilevsky Island[1] lay like a distant sea: a war had taken place somewhere out there, then a revolution. But in Trofim Ivanych's boiler room, the boiler hummed as usual and the pressure gauge indicated the same nine atmospheres. Only the coal was different: it used to come from Cardiff, now it was from the Donetsk Basin.[2] It crumbled, black dust got in everywhere, and nothing would wash it off. And it was just as if this same black dust had imperceptibly coated everything at home as well. Outwardly, nothing had changed. They lived together as before, without children. Sofya, although she was now close to forty, was still light and firm of body, like a bird; her lips, seemingly pressed together forever for everyone, would open to Trofim Ivanych at night as before—and yet something was not right. What was "not right" was still unclear—it had not yet taken on the permanence of words. It was said in words for the first time only later, in the fall, and Sofya remembered that it was Saturday night, there was a wind, and the water in the Neva was rising.

The water gauge on the boiler in Trofim Ivanych's boiler room had burst during the day, and he had to go and get a spare one in the machine shop storehouse. Trofim Ivanych had not been in the shop for a long time. When he walked in, he thought he had come to the wrong place. Before, everything here would be moving, ringing, buzzing, and singing—as though the wind were playing with steel leaves in a steel forest. Now it was fall in this forest, the transmission belts flapped idly, just three or four machines turned sleepily, and somewhere a washer squeaked monotonously. Trofim Ivanych began to feel unwell, the way it feels if you're standing over an empty hole dug for who knows what. He quickly went back to his boiler room.

He returned home toward evening—and he still did not feel quite right. He had his dinner and lay down to rest. When he got up, everything had already passed and was forgotten—just that he was left with the feeling that he had had a dream, or lost a key, but what dream, what key—he simply could not remember. It was only at night that he remembered.

All night a wind from the sea beat right against their window, the windowpanes rang, and the water in the Neva rose. And the blood in his veins also rose as though connected with the Neva through underground veins. Sofya could not sleep. Trofim Ivanych's hands found her knees in the dark; he was with her for a long time. And again it was not right; there was some kind of void in his heart.

He lay there and the windowpanes kept jingling monotonously. Suddenly he remembered the washer, the machine shop, and the belt flapping idly . . . "That's it," Trofim Ivancyh said aloud. "What?" Sofya asked. "You're not bearing any children, that's what." And Sofya realized it too: yes, that was precisely it. And she realized that if there were no child, Trofim Ivanych would leave her; he would imperceptibly trickle out of her drop by drop, like water from a dried-out barrel. Such a barrel stood in the hallway behind the door. Trofim Ivanych had long intended to put new hoops on it, but there was never any time.

At night—it must have been toward morning—the door opened wide and, as it swung open, it crashed against the barrel, and Sofya ran out into the street. She knew that it was the end, that there was no turning back. Sobbing hard and loud, she ran to Smolensk Field[3]; someone was lighting matches there in the darkness. She tripped and fell—her hands went right into something wet. It became light and she saw that her hands were covered with blood.

"Why are you screaming?" Trofim Ivanych asked her. Sofya woke up. There really was blood, but this was her usual, female blood.

Before, those were simply days when it was uncomfortable to walk, when her legs were cold and not clean. Now it was as if each month she were on trial and waiting for the sentence. When the time approached, she could not sleep, she was afraid, and yet wanted it to come quickly: what if this time there is none—if suddenly it turns out that she . . . But nothing would happen—there was a hole, an empty feeling inside her. Several times she noticed that when she called shyly in a whisper to Trofim Ivanych to turn toward her, he would pretend to be asleep. And then Sofya would dream again that she was running alone in the darkness to Smolensk Field; she would cry out, and in the morning her lips would be pressed together even more tightly.

During the day the sun continually floated above the land in circles like those a bird makes. The land was bare. At dusk all of Smolensk Field steamed like an overheated horse. One April day the walls became very thin—children could be clearly heard shouting in the courtyard, "Catch her! Catch!" Sofya knew that "her" meant the carpenter's daughter, Ganka. The carpenter lived above them, and he was sick in bed, probably with typhus.

Sofya went down into the yard. Ganka, with her head thrown back, rushed straight at her, with four of the neighborhood boys in pursuit. When Ganka saw Sofya, she said something over her shoulder to the boys as she ran and approached Sofya alone, with measured steps. Ganka exuded heat, she was breathing hard, and her upper lip with its small black mole was visibly quivering. "How old is she? Twelve, thirteen . . . ," Sofya thought. This was exactly how long Sofya had been married; Ganka could have been her daughter. But she was someone else's; she had been stolen from her, from Sofya . . .

Suddenly something contracted in her stomach and rose up to her heart; Sofya began to hate Ganka's smell and that barely quivering lip of hers with its black mole. "A lady doctor has come to see Dad, he's unconscious," Ganka said. Sofya saw Ganka's lips trembling; she was bending down and must have been choking back her tears. And immediately Sofya ached with shame and pity for her. She took Ganka's head and pressed it close to her. Ganka let out a sob, broke away, and ran to a dark corner of the yard; the boys dashed there after her.

With a pain that had lodged somewhere inside her like the broken end of a needle, Sofya entered the carpenter's place. To the right of the door, a lady doctor was washing her hands at the washstand. She was bosomy, snub-nosed, and wore a pince-nez. "Well, how is he?" Sofya asked. "He'll last till tomorrow," the woman doctor said cheerfully. "And then you and I will have more work." "Work . . . what kind?" "What kind? There will be one man less, and we'll have to give birth to extra children. How many do you have?" A button on the doctor's chest was undone; she tried to button it, but she could not—she laughed. "I . . . don't have any," said Sofya, but not immediately; it was hard for her to open her lips.

The carpenter died the following day. He was a widower, he did not have anyone. Some neighboring women came, stood in the doorway and whispered, and then one of them, wrapped in a warm shawl, said, "Well, my dears, are we going to just stand around?" and began to take off her shawl, holding the pin in her teeth. Ganka sat on her bed, hunched over in silence, her legs thin, pitiful, and bare. A piece of untouched black bread lay in her lap.

Sofya went down to her apartment; she had to make something for dinner—Trofim Ivanych would be coming home soon. When she had prepared everything and began setting the table, the sky—unstable, pierced by a solitary, cheerless star—was already turning dark. Upstairs the door kept banging: the women neighbors must have finished everything already and were heading home, but Ganka continued sitting on her bed the same way as before, with a piece of bread in her lap.

Trofim Ivanych came home. Broad and short-legged, he stood by the table as though his feet had become rooted in the earth up to his ankles. "You know, the carpenter has died," Sofya said. "Oh-h, he died?" Trofim Ivanych asked absent-mindedly, without really paying attention; he was taking bread out of a sack, and bread was more rare and unusual than death. Bending down, he began to slice it carefully, and at this point, as if for the first time in all these years, Sofya saw his burnt, ravaged face, and his gypsy head, sprinkled thickly with grey as if with salt. "No, there won't be, won't be any children!" Sofya's heart quickly cried out in despair. And when Trofim Ivanych had taken a piece of bread in his hands, Sofya instantly found herself upstairs. Ganka was there alone, sitting on her bed, she had bread in her lap, and a spring star—sharp like the point of a needle—was looking in the window. And the grey hair, Ganka, the bread, the solitary star in the empty sky—all this fused into a single whole that was incomprehensibly interconnected and, much to her own surprise, Sofya said, "Trofim Ivanych, let's take the carpenter's Ganka, let her take the place of . . ." She could not go on.

Trofim Ivanych looked at her in surprise, then her words penetrated inside him through the coal dust and he began to smile—slowly, as slowly as when he was loosening the sack with the bread in it. When he had loosened his smile completely, his teeth gleamed, his face looked new, and he said, "You're a fine woman, Sofya! Bring her here, there's enough bread for three."

That same night Ganka already spent in their kitchen. Lying in bed, Sofya heard her moving around on the bench, then breathing evenly. Sofya thought "Now everything will be all right" and fell asleep.

2

The children in the yard were playing an entirely new game, "kolchak."[4] One—the "kolchak"—would hide and the others would go looking for him; then to the beating of a drum and singing, they would shoot him with their sticks. The real Kolchak had also been shot, now no one ate horsemeat any more, and sugar, galoshes and flour were sold in the stores. The boiler at the factory was heated with the same coal from Donetsk, but Trofim Ivanych now shaved his beard, and the coal dust washed off easily. He did not have a beard for many years before his marriage, and now it seemed he had returned to those years; he even smiled sometimes as in the old days, and his teeth would flash white like keys on an accordion.

This would usually happen on Sundays when he was at home and Ganka was at home. She was now finishing school. Trofim Ivanych would make her read the newspaper out loud. Ganka read quickly and briskly, but she garbled all the new words in her own way: "molbization," "*glavnuka*."[5] "What, what?" Trofim Ivanych asked, trying to contain his laughter. "*Glavnuka*," Ganka repeated calmly. Then she told him that a new man had come to her school the day before and explained that there were bodies on earth and also bodies in the sky. "What bodies?" Trofim Ivanych asked, now barely able to keep himself from laughing. "What kind? Why, like this!" and Ganka poked her breast, which stood out sharply under her dress. Trofim Ivanych could contain himself no longer and laughter broke out through his nose and mouth like steam from the safety valves on a boiler bursting from pressure.

Sofya sat alone, by herself. *Glavnauka*, heavenly bodies, Ganka with the newspaper—to Sofya all this was equally incomprehensible and remote. Ganka talked and laughed only with Trofim Ivanych and, if she was left alone with Sofya, she would remain quiet, heat the stove, wash the dishes, and talk to the cat. However, at times her green eyes would slowly come to rest intently on Sofya, clearly thinking something about her, but what? Cats look that way, staring at someone's face and thinking their own thoughts—and one suddenly gets an eerie feeling from those green eyes, from the strange, incomprehensible thoughts in them. Sofya would slip on her jacket, throw a warm shawl around her, and go out somewhere—to the store, to church, or simply into the darkness of Maly Boulevard—just to avoid staying alone with Ganka. She would walk past black ditches that had not yet frozen over, past fences made of metal roofing; she felt wintry, empty. On Maly across from the church, there was a house just as empty, with corroded windows. Sofya knew that no one would ever live in it again and happy voices of children would never be heard in it.

One evening in December she happened to find herself near the house. As always, she rushed to pass it quickly without looking at it. As she hurried past and looked out of the corner of her eye the way birds do, she saw a light in an empty window. She stopped: it couldn't be! She retraced her steps and glanced through a hole in the window. Inside, amid pieces of brick, a fire was burning and around it sat four boys in rags. One, facing Sofya, a black-eyed boy, must have been a gypsy; he was dancing, a silver cross kept bouncing on his chest, and his teeth gleamed.

The empty house had become alive. The small gypsy boy in some way resembled Trofim Ivanych. Sofya suddenly felt that she too was still alive, that everything could still change.

Excited, she entered the church across the street. She had not been there since 1918, when Trofim and other men from the factory were leaving for the front. The same small, gray, moss-grown priest was conducting the service. The singing made Sofya feel warm, the ice was melting, the winter within was passing, and in front of her, in the darkness, candles were being lit.

When Sofya returned home, she wanted to tell Trofim Ivanych everything, but what—what everything? She no longer knew what it was herself and just said that she had been to church. Trofim Ivanych started laughing: "You're going to the old church. At least you could go to the Living Church,[6] their god seems to have a party card." He winked at Ganka. With that squinting eye, without a beard, his face had a mischievous look like that of the gypsy boy—with a lot of teeth, bright and greedy. Ganka sat looking flushed; she hid her eyes and frowned, casting a greenish, sidelong glance at Sofya.

From that day on Sofya went to church often, until one day a new priest from the Living Church came with a crowd of his own people for the liturgy. The priest was a big, red-haired fellow in a short cassock, like a soldier in disguise. The old grey priest shouted, "I won't let you, I won't let you!" and grasped him firmly; both went rolling out onto the church porch, and fists flashed like banners over the crowd. Sofya left and never went back there. She began going to Okhta; there the shoemaker Fyodor—with a yellow bald spot on his head—preached the "Third Testament."

Spring came late that year; the trees were just beginning to break into leaf on Whit Monday; their buds would tremble imperceptibly to the eye and burst open. In the evening the weather was unstable and bright and swallows flew about. The cobbler Fyodor was preaching about Judgment Day coming soon. Large drops of sweat rolled around on his yellow bald spot, and his blue, wild-looking eyes shone so that you could not tear your eyes away from them. "Not from the heavens, no! But from here, right from here, right from here!" His whole body trembling, the cobbler hit himself in the chest and ripped open the white shirt he was wearing, exposing a yellow, sagging body. He put his hands on his chest and wanted to tear it open like the shirt—he could not breathe; he shouted, taking a desperate last gasp and dropped to the floor in an epileptic seizure. Two women stayed with him, but everyone else left quickly without finishing the meeting.

All tense—like the buds on the trees—from the cobbler's crazed eyes, Sofya returned home. There was no key in the door; the door was locked. Sofya realized that Trofim Ivanych and Ganka must have gone off for a stroll somewhere and would probably come home only around eleven— she had told them herself not to expect her before eleven. Should she perhaps go upstairs and sit there until they return?

Pelageya and her husband, a coachman, now lived upstairs. She could be heard through an open window saying to her child, "Goo-goo, goo-goo, googlee-goo. . . Like this, like this!" Sofya could not— she had no strength left—to go there and look at her and her child. Sofya sat down on the wooden steps. The sun was still high, and the sky was glistening like the cobbler's eyes. The smell of hot black bread came from somewhere. Sofya remembered that the latch on the kitchen window was broken, and Ganka had probably forgotten to tie the window closed—she always forgot. So, you could open it from the outside and climb in.

Sofya walked around to the back. And in fact the window had not been tied closed. Sofya opened it easily and climbed into the kitchen. She thought: anyone could get in this way—and perhaps someone already had? There seemed to be some kind of rustling sounds in the adjoining room. Sofya stopped. It was quiet, only the clock was ticking on the wall and inside Sofya, and everywhere. Without knowing why, Sofya began to walk on tip-toe. She caught her dress on the ironing board that was leaning against the wall, and the board came crashing down to the floor. Immediately the shuffling of bare feet started in the room. Sofya gasped quietly and staggered back toward the window—to jump out—to call for help . . .

But she did not have time to do anything because Ganka, barefoot, wearing only a rumpled pink shift, appeared in the doorway. She looked dumbfounded—she opened her mouth and eyes wide when she saw Sofya. Then all of her shrank the way a cat does when someone has raised his hand threateningly at it, and she shouted "Trofim Ivanych!" and dashed back into the room.

Sofya picked up the ironing board, put it back in its place, and sat down. She had lost all feeling in her hands and legs—she could feel only her heart, which was doing somersaults like a bird and falling, falling, falling.

Almost immediately Trofim Ivanych walked in. He was dressed— apparently he had not taken off his clothes. Broad, with his large head and short legs, he stood in the middle of the kitchen as if sunk in earth up to his knees. "You . . . how come you came back so early today?" Trofim Ivanych asked and was surprised at himself for asking that—how could he have asked that? Sofya did not hear him. Her lips were quivering— that's the way the skin on milk quivers when it's already cooling. "What's this, what's this, what's this?" Sofya uttered quietly with some difficulty, without looking at Trofim Ivanych. Trofim Ivanych knitted his brow; he shrank into some corner inside himself and stood silently like that for about a minute. Then he ripped his legs with their roots out of the earth and went back into the room. There Ganka was already stomping in her ankle boots, all dressed.

Everything in the world went on as before and life continued. Sofya got supper ready. Ganka brought the plates, as always. When she brought the bread, Trofim Ivanych turned around, his head hit it, and the bread fell in his lap. Ganka burst out laughing. Sofya looked at her, their eyes collided, and they stared at one another for an instant in a totally new way. Sofya felt something rising slowly within her—roundly, from her stomach, from below, then faster, hotter, and higher; she started breathing fast. She could no longer look at Ganka's dark-blond bangs, the black mole on her lip—she felt she must start shouting right now, like the cobbler Fyodor, or do something else.

Sofya lowered her eyes; Ganka grinned.

After supper Sofya washed the plates. Ganka stood with a towel and dried them. It took forever—this was perhaps the most difficult thing that whole evening. Then Ganka went to sleep in her place in the kitchen. Sofya started making their bed, everything inside her was burning, and she was shaking. Turning away, Trofim Ivanych said to her, "Make my bed on the bench by the window." Sofya made it. At night, when she had stopped tossing in bed, she heard Trofim Ivanych get up and go to the kitchen to Ganka.

3

A glass jar stood turned upside down on Sofya's window sill and, who knows how, a fly had gotten into the jar. It could not go anywhere, yet it still crawled about all day. There was an indifferent, slow, stifling heat in the jar from the sun, and the same kind of heat hung over all of Vasilevsky Island. Nevertheless, Sofya moved about all day, forever doing something. Clouds would often gather during the day, grow heavy, and any minute now the green glass above would crack, and a downpour would finally burst through and continue falling. But the clouds silently floated off, and by nightfall the glass became thicker, more stifling, and more impenetrable. No one heard the distinct breathing of the three of them at night: one—her head buried in her pillow so as not to hear anything, and two of them—through clenched teeth, greedily, hotly, like a nozzle burner in a boiler.

In the morning Trofim Ivanych would leave for the factory. Ganka had already finished her studies; she stayed home with Sofya. To Sofya she was very far away, because Sofya now saw and heard both Ganka and Trofim Ivanych and everything around her from afar. From there she would say to Ganka, without parting her lips: sweep up the kitchen, wash the millet, chop some firewood. Ganka swept, washed, and chopped. Sofya heard the blows of the ax, she knew that this was Ganka, that same Ganka, but all this was very far away—she could not see anything.

Ganka always chopped kindling squatting down, with her round knees spread wide apart. One time, who knows why, it happened that Sofya saw—saw those knees and the slightly curly bangs on her forehead. A hammering started in her temples, and she quickly turned away and said to Ganka without looking at her, "I'll . . . myself . . . Go outside." Ganka shook her bangs gaily and returned home only toward dinner time, right before Trofim Ivanych came home.

She began leaving every day in the morning. Pelageya, the woman who lived upstairs, once said to Sofya, "Your Ganka keeps running to the empty house with some boys. You should keep an eye on her before the girl gets into trouble." Sofya thought, "I have to tell Trofim Ivanych about it . . ." But when he came home, she felt that she could not utter the name—Ganka—out loud. She said nothing to Trofim Ivanych.

The whole summer passed in this way—glassy, tearless, with dry oppressive clouds, and the fall was starting out just as dry. One blue and unseasonably warm day a wind began to blow from the sea. Through the closed window Sofya heard a dull, cottony boom, then soon a second and a third—the water must have been rising in the Neva.[7] Sofya was alone—neither Ganka nor Trofim Ivanych was at home. Again cannon fire resounded softly against the window, and the window panes began ringing in the wind. Pelageya came running from upstairs—loud-voiced, ample-bodied, all of her wide open. She shouted to Sofya, "Have you lost your mind—why are you sitting? The Neva has overflowed its banks, and now it will flood everything!"

Sofya ran out after her into the yard. Immediately the whistling wind wrapped itself tightly around her like a piece of linen. She heard doors banging somewhere, and a woman's voice yelling, "The chicks, the chicks, gather them up quickly!" The wind was carrying a large bird quickly, at an angle, overhead—its wings were spread wide. Suddenly Sofya began to feel better as though this was just what she needed, this kind of wind, so that everything would get covered with water, washed away, and flooded . . . She turned to face it, her lips parted wide, and the wind burst in and started singing in her mouth; her teeth felt cold, good.

Sofya and Pelageya quickly carried the bedding, clothing, food, and chairs upstairs. The kitchen was already empty, only a chest decorated with flowers stood in a corner. "And that?" Pelageya asked. "It's . . . hers," Sofya answered. "Whose—hers? Ganka's, is that it? Why are you leaving it?" Pelageya picked up the chest and, supporting it with her protruding stomach, carried it upstairs.

Around two o'clock the wind broke a windowpane upstairs. Pelageya ran up to stuff the opening with a pillow and suddenly wailed aloud, "We're done for . . . Oh Lord, we're done for!", and grabbed her child in her arms. Sofya looked out the window and saw that where there had been a street, green water now flowed, pitted by the wind; somebody's table floated by, turning slowly, and a white and ginger cat was sitting on it with its mouth open—it must have been meowing. Without calling Ganka by name, Sofya thought of her and her heart started pounding.

Pelageya was heating the stove. She kept running from the stove to her child and to the window where Sofya was standing. In the house across the street, on the first floor, the little ventilation window was open and water could now be seen rocking it. The water kept rising; it carried logs, boards, and hay, and then something round appeared for a second—it looked like a head. "Perhaps my Andrei and your Trofim Ivanych . . . ," Pelageya did not finish and tears rolled down her face— lots of big tears, which flowed freely and simply. Sofya was surprised at herself: how could she have forgotten about Trofim Ivanych and all the time been thinking only about one thing, about that Ganka.

All at once—both Sofya and Pelageya—heard voices somewhere in the yard. They ran to the kitchen, to the windows. Pushing through some wood, a boat was moving across the yard and in it stood two strangers and Trofim Ivanych without his hat. He wore a dark blue shirt over his quilted vest, the wind pressed it close to his body on one side and made it billow out on the other so that he seemed broken in the middle. The two men asked him something, the boat swung around the corner of the house, and some split firewood collided with it and was left behind.

Wet to his waist, Trofim Ivanych ran into the kitchen; water poured off him, but he seemed not to notice. "Where . . . where is she?" he asked Sofya. "She went out in the morning," Sofya said. Pelageya also understood whom he was asking about. "I told Sofya long ago . . . And now she's gotten what she was asking for, she's floating somewhere . . ." Trofim Ivanych turned to the wall and began tracing something with his finger on it. He stood like that for a long time; water kept dripping off him, but he did not feel it.

Toward evening, when the water had already receded, Pelageya's husband came home. His substantial, well-developed bald spot shone under the hanging lamp; he told them about a gentleman with a briefcase swimming to his entrance using a paddling stroke, and about ladies running and lifting their skirts ever higher. "Did a lot of people drown?" Sofya asked without looking at him. "It's horrible! Thousands!!" the coachman screwed up his eyes. Trofim Ivanych got up. "I'm going," he said.

But he did not go anywhere because the door opened and Ganka stood in the doorway. Her dress clung to her chest and knees, she was all dirty and wet, but her eyes were shining. Trofim Ivanych smiled but not in a good way—slowly, just showing his teeth. He walked up to Ganka, grabbed her by the hand and led her off to the kitchen, closing the door tightly behind him. You could hear him saying something through his teeth and then beating her. Ganka kept sobbing. Then she took a long time splashing and washing, and walked into the room cheerful again, shaking the bangs on her forehead.

Pelageya made a bed for her in the pantry behind the partition, and she made a bed on the bench in the kitchen for Trofim and Sofya. They were left alone. Trofim Ivanych put out the lamp. The window turned pale, the moon trembled in a thin shift of clouds. Looking white, Sofya undressed and lay down, then—Trofim Ivanych.

Lying in bed, Sofya thought now about one thing only: he must not notice how much she was trembling. She lay all stretched out, as if covered with a crust of the thinnest ice; such fragile layers of ice cover tree branches early in the morning in the fall, and if a wind just barely stirs the branches, the layers crumble into powder.

Trofim Ivanych did not move; Sofya could not hear him. But Sofya knew he was not sleeping because he always smacked his lips in his sleep like children when they are breastfeeding. And she knew why he was not sleeping: here he could not go to Ganka. Sofya closed her eyes, pressed her lips together, and retreated into herself so that she would not have to think about anything.

Suddenly Trofim Ivanych, as if he had decided something, quickly turned to Sofya. All of her blood suddenly stopped flowing, her legs went numb, and she waited. The moon, wrapping itself in a blanket of clouds, trembled outside the window for a minute or two. Trofim Ivanych raised his head, looked out the window, trying not to touch Sofya, and turned his back to her again.

When he finally began breathing evenly and was smacking his lips in his sleep like infants when they are breastfeeding, Sofya opened her eyes. She quietly bent over Trofim Ivanych, so close to him that she could see a long black hair coming down from his eyebrow right into his eye. He moved his lips. Sofya looked and she no longer remembered anything about him; she just felt pity for him. She reached out her hand—and pulled it back right away; she wanted to stroke him like a child, but she could not, she did not dare . . .

It was like that every night the whole three weeks while the apartment downstairs was drying out. Every morning before going to the factory, Trofim Ivanych would go down there for half an hour and fix one thing or another. One day he came back happy from there and joked with Pelageya, but Sofya saw his eyes following Ganka; Ganka, bent over, was sweeping the room. As he was leaving, Trofim Ivanych said to Sofya, "Go on, move downstairs, it's time—everything's ready." And then to Ganka, "Heat the stove real well and don't spare the wood, so that it's warm by evening."

Sofya thought: not by evening, by nightfall. She did not say anything, did not raise her eyes, only her lips quivered slightly, like the skin on milk when it's almost cooled down.

4

The coachman, Pelageya's husband, was leaving only in the afternoon that day; before that he quickly moved everything downstairs with Sofya's and Ganka's help. "Well now, what do I wish you—a happy house-warming in the old place?" he said to Sofya.

Quickly, like a large bird flapping its wings a few times, Sofya let her eyes take in the room. Everything was as before: the chairs, the dim mirror, the clock on the wall, and the bed where Sofya would sleep alone once more at night. What had been upstairs seemed like happiness to her because there at night she could hear his breathing, he was not with that one, the other one—he was no one's. But now—today, today . . .

Ganka was not there, she had gone for some firewood. Sofya stood pressing her forehead against the window. The windowpanes made a ringing sound, the wind beat against them, and grey, city, stony, low clouds floated by quickly—as if those stifling clouds that did not burst open and produce heavy rain the whole summer had returned again. Sofya felt that those clouds were not outside the window but in her, inside; they had been piling up like stones on top of one another for whole months on end and, so that they would not suffocate her now, she had to smash something to pieces, or run away from here, or scream in the same voice as the shoemaker had that time about Judgment Day.

Sofya heard Ganka coming in, dropping the wood on the floor, and then feeding it into the stove. The window shook as though a heart had knocked against it from the outside. It was the cannon; the wind was driving the water again, and the water was swelling the blue veins of the Neva. Sofya continued to stand as before, without turning around, so as not to see Ganka.

Suddenly Ganka began to sing quietly to herself—that had never happened before. Sofya turned around. She saw that Ganka had put down the ax and was making some kindling with a knife. Her round knees, spread wide apart, were shaking under her dress and the bangs on her forehead were shaking too. Sofya wanted to take her eyes off her and could not. Slowly, with difficulty, like a barge being pulled by rope to shore against the current—the rope was quivering and could break at any second—Sofya approached Ganka. Ganka was all flushed from her work, and the hot, sweetish smell of her sweat overwhelmed Sofya— she must smell like that at night.

And as soon as Sofya took a whiff of that smell, something rose up in her from below, from her stomach, poured over her heart, and flooded all of her. She wanted to grab something, but she was being swept along just as the wood and the cat on the table had been swept along by the torrents of water that day in the street. Seized by a wave, she picked up the ax from the floor without thinking—she did not know why herself. The huge heart of the cannon thumped against the window once more. Sofya saw with her eyes that she was holding the ax. "Lord, Oh Lord, what am I doing?" one Sofya shouted in despair inside, but that very second the other one struck Ganka in the temple and the bangs with the butt of the ax.

Ganka did not cry out; her head just dropped to her lap, then from a squatting position she softly rolled over on her side. Sofya hit her head quickly, greedily, several more times with the sharp end of the ax; blood gushed out onto the iron sheet in front of the stove. And it was as though this blood were from within her, from Sofya, as though an abscess had finally burst inside her and blood was flowing from there and dripping, and with each drop she felt better and better. She threw down the ax, took a big, deep breath as though she had never breathed before and was taking her first huge gulp of air for the first time. There was nothing—neither fear nor shame—only some new feeling in her body—a lightness—like after a long fever.

And then it was as if Sofya's hands thought completely independently of her and did everything that had to be done, but she herself was somewhere to the side, blissfully resting, and only from time to time would her eyes open—she was beginning to see, she looked at everything in astonishment.

Ganka's shoes, her brown dress and her shift, all doused with kerosene, were already burning in the stove, and Ganka herself—all naked, pink, steamy—lay face down on the floor, and a fly was crawling on her slowly and confidently. Sofya saw the fly and chased it away. Sofya's alien hands easily, calmly cut the body in half—otherwise it would have been impossible to take it away. At that point Sofya remembered that the potatoes Ganka had not finished peeling were lying in the kitchen on the bench and should be cooked for dinner. She went into the kitchen, closed the door and latched it, and heated the stove in there.

When she returned to the room, she saw that the new, grey oilcloth with the marble pattern had been taken out of the chest of drawers and was lying on the floor, torn into two pieces. Sofya wondered who had torn it and why. But then she remembered, spread the oilcloth on the bottom of a sack and put half of the pink body in it. The same fly kept settling on her hands and sticking to them. Sofya kept chasing it away, but it kept coming back. Once Sofya saw it really up close; its legs were thin, as though made of black thread from a spool. Then both the fly and everything else disappeared, and there was only one thing: somebody was knocking on the kitchen door.

Sofya went to the threshold on tip-toe and waited. Again there was a knocking on the door, louder and louder. Sofya watched the hook jump from the rapping on the door—and she did not really watch but felt it: the hook was now part of her—like her eyes, her heart, and her legs which had instantly turned cold. A seemingly familiar voice shouted from behind the door, "Sofya!" She kept quiet and could hear somebody's footsteps stamping noisily down the stairs. Then Sofya began to breathe and looked out the window. It was Pelageya; the wind was whipping her dress tightly around her, and she seemed to be walking with her knees bent.

Again, for a long time, there were only Sofya's hands, but she herself was absent. Suddenly she saw that she was standing at the edge of a ditch, the water in the ditch was violet and glassy from the sunset, and the whole world, the sky, and the insanely quick, violet clouds had been thrown in there, into the ditch, but on Sofya's back there was a heavy sack and her right hand was holding something under her coat—Sofya could not understand what. But the hand remembered that this was a shovel and again everything became simple. A separate part of her crossed the ditch and only her eyes looked around: no one was in sight, she was alone on Smolensk Field, and it was turning dark quickly. She dug a hole and dumped everything in the sack into it.

When it was quite dark, she brought another full sack, filled up the hole, and headed home. Black, uneven, swollen earth was under her feet, and the wind was whipping her legs with cold, tight towels. Sofya stumbled. She fell, her hand touched something wet, and she walked on like that with her hand wet, afraid of wiping it. Far away, it must have been on the seashore, a light would come on and go out, and perhaps it was quite near—perhaps someone was lighting a cigarette in the wind.

At home Sofya quickly scrubbed the floor, washed herself in the basin in the kitchen, and put on everything fresh, like after confession before a holiday. The wood Ganka had lit had burned down long ago, but the last blue flames still flickered over the coals. Sofya threw the sack, the oil cloth, and all the remaining trash in there. The fire flamed up brightly, everything burned, and now it was quite clean in the room. And all the trash in Sofya had burned as well; it was clean and quiet within her too.

She sat down on the bench. All the knots in her loosened and immediately became undone; she suddenly felt more tired than she had ever been in her whole life. She put her head down on her hands, on the table, and instantly fell asleep—completely, happily, with all of her being.

5

The pendulum on the wall was swinging like a bird in a cage sensing a cat's eyes staring at it. Sofya was asleep. This continued for perhaps an hour, or perhaps from one swing of the pendulum to the next. When she raised her head, Trofim Ivanych, his feet rooted in the earth, stood before her.

His shirt felt tight and he unbuttoned the collar. "Where is she?" he asked, bending over Sofya. He smelled of wine, and a taut, intense heat was coming from him. "Where's Ganka?" he asked again. "Yes, where is she now?" Sofya thought and answered aloud, "I don't know." "Ah-h . . . You don't know?" Trofim Ivanych said slowly and wryly. Sofya saw his eyes close up—they resembled bared teeth. He had never beaten her, but now it seemed that he just might hit her. But he only looked at Sofya and turned away—had he hit her, perhaps it would have been easier.

They sat down to dinner. Sofya was alone; she sensed that Trofim Ivanych did not see her—he saw someone, but it was not her. He swallowed a mouthful of cabbage soup and stopped, gripping the spoon tightly in his fist. Suddenly he took a loud breath and hit the table with his fist, and some cabbage flew out of his spoon onto his lap. He picked it up and did not know where to put it. The tablecloth was clean and he held the cabbage in a funny, distracted way, like a little boy—like that gypsy boy whom Sofya had seen that time in the empty house. She got a warm feeling inside from pity for him and placed her own, now empty, plate in front of him. Without looking, he threw the cabbage there and got up.

When he returned, he had a bottle of Madeira in his hand. Sofya realized that it had been bought for the other one, and her heart immediately froze—she was alone again. Trofim Ivanych kept pouring and drinking.

After dinner he moved the lamp silently toward himself and picked up the newspaper, but Sofya saw that he was reading the same line over and over again. She saw the newspaper suddenly shake in his hands: the floor boards creaked in the hallway . . . No, it wasn't anyone coming to see them; it was for the people upstairs. It became quiet again, and only the pendulum swung on the wall like a bird. You could hear something heavy being moved upstairs—they were probably already going to bed there.

There was still no Ganka. Trofim Ivanych walked past Sofya to the clothes rack, put on his hat, stood a while, then tore it off as if he wanted to tear off his head along with the hat so that he would not have to think any more, and then he lay down on the bench, his face to the wall. "Wait, let me make your bed," Sofya said. He got up, looked at her, and his eyes passed through Sofya like a draft.

She made his bed, went up to the door, stretched out her hand to hook it shut—and stopped: and what if Trofim Ivanych suddenly asks why she knows that Ganka won't return? She knew she should not do it, but Sofya turned around. She saw Trofim Ivanych watching her, watching her hand, which was reaching for the hook but did not dare touch it. "What? Why are you standing there?" he sneered, twisting one side of his mouth. "He knows everything . . . ," Sofya thought; the pendulum swung once in front of her and froze. Trofim Ivanych turned red slowly, silently; he pushed the table away and something fell— it was in Sofya, inside her. Right now, right this minute, he will say everything . . .

Pulling his feet out of the earth with great effort, he moved toward Sofya; a blue vein on his forehead swelled up like the Neva. "Well? Why aren't you doing it?" he shouted; everything in the room came to a stop. "Lock it! Let her spend the night with whoever she wants—on the street, under a fence, with the dogs! Lock it, do you hear?" "What . . . what?" Sofya said, still not believing. "Just like that!" Trofim Ivanych snapped at her and turned away. Sofya latched the door.

She shivered for a long time under her blanket until she finally warmed up, believing that Trofim Ivanych could not, did not know. The clock above her pecked the wall loudly with its beak. Trofim Ivanych began tossing and turning on the bench, breathing greedily through his clenched teeth. Sofya heard it all as if he were saying everything in words, loudly, aloud. She saw the hateful white curls on the forehead— and that very second the curls disappeared because Sofya remembered that they were gone and would never return. "Thank God . . . ," she said to herself and caught herself right away. "Thank God for what? Oh Lord!"

Trofim Ivanych began tossing and turning again; Sofya thought that he was not there either and never would be, that now she would always have to live alone, in a draft, and then what was the need for all that had happened today? With difficulty, in stages, she began to take breaths of air as if she were lifting a rock from somewhere at the bottom with her breathing. Just as it came to the surface, this rope broke, and Sofya sensed that she could not breathe. She sighed and silently began to sink into sleep, like into warm, deep water.

When she was almost at the bottom, she heard bare feet plop down on the floor. She shuddered and immediately floated up to the surface. The floor was now creaking there. Trofim Ivanych was gingerly going somewhere. At night he used to go like that to Ganka in the kitchen; Sofya would always roll up in a ball so as not to breathe or cry out, and she did so now. She realized that he was being pulled there, that he would perhaps grab and squeeze her pillow or simply stand there, before Ganka's empty bed . . .

The floor boards creaked, then ceased creaking. Trofim Ivanych stopped. Sofya half-opened her eyes: Trofim Ivanych, his figure looking white, was standing halfway between his bench and the bed where she was lying. And suddenly it struck Sofya that he was not heading to the kitchen but to her—to her! A wave of heat enveloped her, her teeth began to chatter, and she closed her eyes. "Sofya . . . ," Trofim Ivanych said quietly, and then even more quietly, "Sofya." She recognized that same, special, night voice of his; her heart broke off from its branch and, turning over unsteadily, fell downward like a bird. Without any conscious thought but in some other way—with her knees squeezed together until they hurt and with the folds of her body—Sofya decided that it would be simpler and easier if she did not push him away, and she lay trying not to breathe and be quiet.

Trofim Ivanych bent over her; she heard his breathing near her—he must have been looking at her. It was only for a second, but Sofya was afraid that she would not be able to stand it and she cried out inaudibly, "Oh Lord! Oh Lord!" Up above, a thousand versts from here where clouds were madly rushing, Pelageya started laughing barely audibly. A hot, dry hand touched Sofya's legs, she slowly opened her mouth and all of her opened to her husband completely—for the first time in her life. He squeezed her as if he wanted to inflict all the malicious anger he felt at that one, the other one, on her. Sofya heard his teeth gnashing and Pelageya laughing quietly upstairs—and remembered nothing more.

6

In the morning there was a frost, the windows looked like rock candy, and a yellow-grey rabbit was crawling on the white wall. Sofya went into the yard. Everything had quieted down during the night, the morning was calm and clear; smoke—straight and pink—was rising into the sky.

Pelageya was in the yard. She said to Sofya, "So your Ganka has run away, hm? That's what you get for feeding the likes of her!" Sofya looked at her with eyes made light and direct by the morning and tried to remember what had happened yesterday—and could not. It was all very far away; most probably none of it had happened. Pelageya told her that Trofim Ivanych, before going to the factory, had dropped by their place, asking if they had seen Ganka. Sofya laughed to herself. "What is it?" Pelageya was surprised. "Nothing . . . ," Sofya said. She looked at the straight, pink smoke—the same kind of smoke was in the village from which Trofim Ivanych had brought her. They must be chopping cabbage there, cabbage cores—cold, white, and crunchy. It seemed to her that it had been only yesterday, and that she was the same as she had been when she was eating the cabbage cores.

When he returned from the factory, Trofim Ivanych just asked, "Well? Not here?" Sofya knew what he was asking and calmly said, "No." Trofim Ivanych had his dinner and went somewhere right away. He returned late in a dark mood—he must have been searching everywhere, asking everybody. At night he went to Sofya again—just as silently, angrily, and greedily as the night before.

The next day Trofim Ivanych notified the police about Ganka. Sofya, Pelageya and her husband, and the neighbors were called in. A young rookie in a cap sat at a desk; a serious-looking, frameless pince-nez rested on his nose, and his face was scrawny and pockmarked; crusts of black bread lay under some papers on his desk. Everyone told him the same thing: that they saw Ganka running around with some boys, and boys not from the harbor area but outsiders, from the Petersburg side. Pelageya recalled that Ganka had said once that she was tired of this place and was going to leave. The rookie in the cap kept writing things down; Sofya looked at his pock-marked face, the pince-nez and the crusts of bread, and began feeling sorry for him.

When they were walking home from there, Sofya asked Trofim Ivanych to buy her a new ax because the old one must have been stolen, or perhaps it had fallen somewhere—she could not find it anywhere. Sofya did not think anymore about Ganka, and Trofim Ivanych did not say one word more about her either. But at times he would sit staring at one and the same line in the newspaper, and Sofya knew what he was being silent about. Just as silently he would raise his coal-black, gypsy eyes at her and, heavily, silently, he would follow her with his eyes. It would unnerve her: What if he suddenly said something? But he didn't say anything.

The days continued clear and crisp, but they were getting shorter as if at any moment, today or tomorrow, they would flare up for a last time like a burnt-down candle wick—and it would be dark, the end of everything. But the next day would come and still there would be no end. Nevertheless something began to be wrong with Sofya. She did not sleep one night, then a second and a third; there were dark circles under her eyes, and they had a sunken look. In the same way in the spring snow darkens, settles and disappears, and suddenly the earth underneath it becomes exposed. But spring was still far away.

In the evening Sofya was pouring kerosene into the lamp through a tin funnel. Trofim Ivanych yelled to her, "Watch out, watch out— what are you doing, it's running over the brim!" Only then did Sofya see that the lamp was already full and that the kerosene must have been spilling out on the table for a long time. "Over the brim . . . ," she repeated absentmindedly. Her lips, always pressed together, were now parted, like at night; she was looking at Trofim Ivanych, and he thought she wanted to say something to him. "Well, what?" he asked her. Sofya turned away. "Is it . . . something about her . . . about Ganka?" she heard his voice coming through his clenched, white, gypsy teeth. She did not answer.

When she was serving dinner, she dropped a plate of kasha on the floor. Trofim Ivanych raised his head and saw her eyes that now somehow looked new to him and had a sunken look, like the snow; and he began to feel bad looking at her: it was not her. "What's wrong with you, Sofya?" And again she said nothing.

At night he came to her; he had not been with her even once since those two nights. When she heard that same, night voice of his, "Sofya, tell me, I know—you have to tell me," she could not bear it, it was too much, and she burst into tears. They were warm—Trofim Ivanych felt them with his cheek and became frightened. "What, what is it? It doesn't matter—tell me!" Then Sofya said, "I'm . . . going to have a baby . . ." This was in the dark, he could not see. Trofim Ivanych passed his hot, dry hand over her face in order to see; his fingers trembled, he felt Sofya's lips and found them parted wide and smiling. He only said, "So-o-fka!" He had not called her that for a long time, for about ten years. She laughed blissfully, heartily. "When did it . . . ?" Trofim Ivanych asked. It happened during one of those two nights, right after Ganka disappeared. "Do you still remember . . . Pelageya upstairs . . . and I thought even then I would have one like Pelageya . . . No, I'm lying. I didn't think anything then, just now I . . . I don't believe it even now . . . no, I do believe it!" She got all confused and tears flowed easily like streams of melted snow along the ground. Trofim Ivanych put his hand on her stomach and carefully, timidly passed his hand over it, from below up. Her stomach was round—it was the earth. Ganka lay deep in the earth, not visible to anyone, and seeds not visible to anyone burrowed in the earth with their tiny white roots. This was at night;

then day and evening came again.

In the evening, for dinner, Trofim Ivanych brought a bottle of Madeira. Sofya had already seen precisely such a bottle once before; it would have been better if he had brought something else. Sofya did not even think this—she merely made a note of it with her eyes, but it did not penetrate inside. Her whole body was smiling, it was full to the brim, and there was no more room for anything else there. She was just afraid that the days were getting shorter and shorter; that any time now they would burn out altogether and then that would be the end, and she must hurry, she must say or do something before the end.

One day Trofim Ivanych returned home later than usual. He stopped on the threshold, broad, his feet firmly planted in the earth; there was coal dust on his face. He said to Sofya, "Well, they summoned me again." Sofya immediately understood where and why; inside her the pendulum stopped and missed—one, two, three beats. She sat down. "And?" she asked Trofim Ivanych. "Well, they said the case was closed, they didn't find her. She went off somewhere with that guy of hers—to hell with her! Just so she doesn't turn up now . . ." Sofya's heart revived: it was not the end yet.

And that very moment a second heart seemed to start breathing and come to life inside her. She gasped aloud and grabbed her stomach with her hands. "What's wrong?" Trofim Ivanych ran up to her. "It's . . . moving," Sofya was barely able to say. Trofim Ivanych shook his head, grabbed Sofya and picked her up; she was light as a bird. "Let go," she said. He put her down, his teeth gleaming white like the keys on an accordion, and he began laughing with all the keys at once. He said to Sofya, "Well, here's what, Sofka: remember—if she turns up now, I'll . . ."

There was a knock on the door and they both turned quickly; Sofya heard Trofim Ivanych thinking almost aloud, "Ganka," and the same thought occurred to Sofya. She knew that it could not be—and yet there it was. "Open it?" Trofim Ivanych asked. "Go ahead," Sofya answered in a completely colorless voice.

Trofim Ivanych opened it, and Pelageya walked in—loud-voiced, voluminous body, all of her wide open. "Why are you . . . so pale?" she asked Sofya. "You have to eat more now, dear woman." Pelageya had given birth twice already; she began talking about it with Sofya, and Sofya's whole body started smiling again—she forgot about Ganka.

At night, when she was already sinking way to the bottom and falling asleep—Ganka suddenly flashed before her for a second, who knows why, as if she were lying on this nocturnal bottom. Sofya shuddered and opened her eyes: bright spots were splashing around on the ceiling. She heard a driving wind outside the window and the windowpanes were ringing faintly—it had been the same that day too. She tried to remember how it had all happened, but she could not remember anything and lay awake like that for a long time. Then, seemingly for no reason and apart from everything else, she saw a piece of marble-patterned oilcloth on the floor and a fly crawling on a pink back. The fly's legs could be seen clearly—thin, of black thread from a spool. "Who, who did that? It's her—that one—I . . . Trofim Ivanych is lying next to me, and I'm going to have a child—and that's me?" All the hair on her head became alive, she grabbed Trofim Ivanych by his shoulder and began shaking him; he must say right now that this hadn't happened, that she wasn't the one who did it. "Who . . . who? Is that you, Sofka?" Trofim Ivanych barely unstuck his eyes. "It wasn't me, not me, not me!" Sofya screamed and stopped because she realized that she couldn't, mustn't, say anything more, and that she never would because . . . "Oh Lord . . . If only I could give birth soon!" she said aloud. Trofim Ivanych laughed. "You silly woman! There's still time!" and soon started smacking his lips again in his sleep.

Sofya could not sleep. She had stopped sleeping at night. And there were almost no nights anymore; bright, heavy water kept swaying outside the window all the time, and summer flies kept buzzing non-stop.

7

In the morning, as he was leaving for the factory, Trofim Ivanych said that an oiler got caught on a flywheel and spun on it for a long time, and when they got him down, he felt his head and asked "Where's my hat?" and died.

The window had already been taken out; Sofya was wiping the windowpanes with a rag and thinking about the oiler, about death, and it seemed to her that it would be quite simple—like when the sun sets and it's dark, and then it's day again. She climbed up on a bench to wipe the top—and here the flywheel caught her, she dropped the rag and cried out. In response to her cry, Pelageya came running, that part Sofya still remembered, but that was all—everything was spinning, everything was flying past, and she was screaming. Once, for some reason, she heard very clearly the distant ringing of a streetcar and children's voices in the yard. Then everything suddenly stopped moving and there was stillness, like that of a pond. Sofya felt blood pouring and pouring out of her. The same thing must have happened to the oiler, when he was taken down from the flywheel.

"Well, this is the end," Pelageya said. This was not the end, but Sofya knew that there were only minutes to the end, and that she had to do everything quickly, quickly. "Quickly!" she said. "What—quickly?" Pelageya's voice asked. "My little girl . . . show her to me." "And how do you know it's a girl?" Pelageya wondered and showed Sofya the red, living piece torn out of her: tiny toes were moving on feet raised up towards the little belly. Sofya looked and looked. "Here, here, go on, take her," Pelageya said and placed the child in bed next to Sofya, and then went off to the kitchen.

Sofya undid her buttons and placed the child at her breast. She knew that this was supposed to be done only the next day, but she could not wait, she had to do it quickly, quickly. The child began sucking blindly, awkwardly, choking on the milk. Sofya felt warm tears, warm milk, warm blood flowing out of her; she opened up completely, her lifeblood was pouring out of her. She lay warm, blissful, damp, resting, like the earth—she had lived her whole life for the sake of this one moment, and everything had been for this. "I'm going to run upstairs—don't need anything else?" Pelageya asked. Sofya only moved her lips, but Pelageya understood that she did not need anything more now.

Then Sofya seemed to be dozing; it was very hot under the blanket. She heard the clanging of the streetcars and children in the yard shouting, "Catch her!" All this was very far away, through the thick blanket. "Which her?" Sofya wondered and opened her eyes. Far away, as if on a distant shore, Trofim Ivanych was lighting a lamp. A heavy rain was falling and it was dark because of it; the lamp was tiny, like a pin. Sofya saw white teeth like accordion keys—Trofim Ivanych must have been smiling and saying something to her, but she could not understand what he was saying—she was being pulled to the bottom.

In her sleep, Sofya was constantly aware of the lamp: tiny, like a pin, it was now somewhere inside her, in her stomach. Trofim Ivanych said in his night voice, "Oh, you . . . my Sofka!" The lamp began to burn her so badly that Sofya called Pelageya. Pelageya sat dozing by Sofya's bed; her head jerked up, like a horse's. "The la-a-mp . . . ," Sofya got out with difficulty—her tongue felt like a mitten. "Put it out?" Pelageya dashed to the lamp. Then Sofya really woke up and said to Pelageya that her stomach was on fire, in the lowest part.

At dawn Trofim Ivanych ran for the doctor. Sofya recognized her: the same one, bosomy, wearing a pince-nez; she had been with the carpenter before he died. The doctor examined Sofya. "Yes . . . good . . . very good . . . Does it hurt here? Yes, yes, yes . . ." Then she cheerfully turned her snub-nose to Trofim Ivanych and said, "We've got to get her to the hospital quickly." Trofim Ivanych's teeth lost their brightness, and he grabbed the foot of Sofya's bed with his hand covered in coal-black veins. "What's wrong with her?" "I don't know yet. It looks like childbirth fever," the doctor said cheerfully and went to the kitchen to wash her hands.

They put Sofya on a stretcher and began turning it toward the door. Everything that she had lived with went past her—the window, the wall clock, the stove—as though a ship were casting off and everything familiar on the shore was floating away. The pendulum on the wall swung to one side, then to the other—and then out of sight altogether. Sofya felt that she still had to do something here, in this room, for the last time. When the door of the carriage was already opening, Sofya remembered what it was—she quickly undid her clothing and took out her breast, but no one understood what she wanted. The orderlies started laughing.

For some time there was nothing. Then the lamp appeared again—it was now overhead, under a white ceiling. Sofya saw white walls and white women in their beds. Very close to her a fly was crawling on something white; it had thin legs of black thread from a spool. Sofya cried out and, waving it away, began sliding down from the bed onto the floor. "Where are you going? Where? Lie still!" the nurse said and grabbed Sofya. The fly was gone, and Sofya closed her eyes peacefully.

Ganka came in—with a sack full of wood. She squatted down, spreading her knees wide apart, turned to look at Sofya and, smirking, shook the white bangs on her forehead. Sofya's heart started beating hard, she hit her with the ax, and opened her eyes. A face with a snub-nose and a pince-nez was bending over her, its thick lips were saying quickly, "Yes, yes, yes," the pince-nez glistened, and Sofya closed her eyes. Immediately Ganka came in with the wood and squatted down. Sofya hit her again with the ax, and again the woman doctor, shaking her head, said, "Yes, yes, yes . . ." Ganka's head dropped in her lap and Sofya hit her once more.

"Yes, yes, yes . . . Good," the doctor said. "Is her husband here? Call him quickly." "Quickly, quickly," Sofya cried out; she understood that this was the end, that she was dying, and that she must hurry with all her strength. The nurse ran out, slamming the door. Somewhere very close by, the cannon let out a boom, and the wind was beating madly against the window. "A flood?" Sofya asked, opening her eyes wide. "Just a moment, just a moment . . . Lie still," said the doctor.

The cannon kept booming, the wind howled in her ears, the water kept rising higher and higher—any moment now it would pour out and sweep everything away—she must quickly, quickly . . . Yesterday's familiar pain tore her in half and Sofya opened her legs. "I have to give birth—give birth quickly!" she grabbed the doctor by the sleeve. "Quiet, quiet. You've already given birth—who else can you give birth to?" Sofya knew to whom, but she could not utter her name; the water kept rising higher, she must quickly . . .

Ganka, with her head tucked in her lap, was squatting down by the stove; Trofim Ivanych walked up to her and shielded her. "Not me—not me—not me!" Sofya wanted to say—it had happened like that once before already. She remembered that night and now realized what she had to do—her head was completely lucid, clear. She sprang up, got on her knees on the bed, and cried out to Trofim Ivanych, "It was me, me! She was heating the stove—I hit her with the ax . . ." "She's out of her mind . . . she doesn't know what she's saying . . ," Trofim Ivanych began saying. "Keep quiet!" Sofya shouted, and he fell silent. Huge waves were rushing out of her and drowning him, drowning everyone; everything quieted down instantly, and only the eyes were left. "I—killed her," Sofya said firmly, with a heavy heart. "I hit her with the ax. She lived with us, she lived with him, and I killed her, and I wanted for you to . . ." "She's t-t-te-li-rious . . . te-lirious," Trofim Ivanych's lips trembled, and he could not get anything out.

Sofya became afraid that they would not believe her. She gathered all the strength that was left in her, she did her best to remember and said, "No, I know. Then I threw the ax behind the stove, it's still there . . ."

All around everything was white, and it was very quiet, like in winter. Trofim Ivanych was silent. Sofya realized that he believed her. She sank back in bed slowly, like a bird. Now everything was good, blissful; she was finished, all of her had poured out.

Trofim Ivanych recovered his senses first. He threw himself at Sofya and gripped the headboard so as to hold her, not let her go. "She's died!" he cried out. Women started jumping out of bed, running up and craning their necks. "Go away, go away! Get back in bed!" the nurse waved at them, but they would not leave. The doctor picked up Sofya's hand, held it for a moment, and then said cheerfully, "She's asleep."

In the evening the whiteness in the room turned slightly greenish, like calm water, and the sky outside the windows was the same color. The bosomy doctor was standing by Sofya's bed again, and next to her stood Trofim Ivanych and yet another young, cleanly shaven fellow with a scar on his cheek—the scar gave the impression that he was in pain all the time but was still smiling in spite of it.

`The doctor took out her stethoscope and listened to Sofya's heart. Sofya's heart was beating evenly, calmly, and her breathing was the same. "Yes, yes, yes . . . ," the doctor became pensive for a moment. "She'll survive, by God, she'll survive!" She took off her pince-nez, and her eyes became like those of children when they're looking at fire.

"Well, let's begin!" the clean-shaven young man said and took out a piece of paper; he was still in pain, but with a smile on his scarred face. "No, let her sleep, you can't," the doctor said. "You'll have to come tomorrow, my dear comrade." "That's fine. It's all the same to me." "And it's been all the same to her for a long time—now do whatever you want to with her!" The doctor's pince-nez glistened, and the young man, smiling through his pain, walked out.

The doctor kept standing and looking at the woman. She was sleeping, breathing evenly, quietly, blissfully; her lips were parted wide open.

1929

NOTES

1. Vasilevsky Island: one of the largest islands of St. Petersburg.
2. Donetsk Basin: also known as Donbas, this area in present-day Ukraine is famous for its rich coal fields,which were discovered in the early 18th century.
3. Smolensk Field: in the middle of Vasilevsky Island a large open space where in the 18th and 19th centuries people used to be executed.
4. Kolchak, Admiral Aleksandr V. (1874-1920): in 1917 supported Kerensky's Provisional Government. Appointed Minister of War and Navy in the anti-Bolshevik government established in Omsk, Siberia; led the White forces in Siberia during the civil war and was executed by the Bolsheviks.
5. *glavnuka*: she means *Glavnauka* (Chief Directorate for Research, Science, Art and Museums, which existed from 1922 to 1933).
6. The Living Church: a group of Russian Orthodox clergy formed in 1922 who called for "the revision and change of all facets of church life which are required by the demands of current life." Their reforms included the right of bishops to marry and the right of priests to marry and remarry. The Living Church found itself in great conflict with the patriarchal Russian Orthodox Church.
7. Cannon shots were fired to warn people of impending floods from the Neva River.

DOUBTING MAKAR

Andrei Platonov

Among all the other laboring masses, there lived two members of the State: a typical peasant, Makar Ganushkin, and a more prominent one—Comrade Lev Chumovoi, who was by far the most clever man in the village, and because of his intellect supervised the people's progress forward along a straight line towards the common good. And for this reason, anytime he passed by on his way somewhere, the whole population of the village would say about Lev Chumovoi: "There goes our leader, marching off somewhere—just you wait, tomorrow some measures will be taken . . . A clever head, only his hands are idle. He lives by his bare intellect . . ."

But Makar, as any peasant, liked various trades more than plowing, and worried not about grain but about spectacles because, as Comrade Chumovoi concluded, he had an empty head.

Without getting permission from Comrade Chumovoi, Makar once organized a spectacle—a people's carousel that was driven by wind power. People gathered around Makar's carousel like a thick storm cloud and waited for the storm that would be able to get the carousel moving. But for some reason the storm was delayed; people stood around with nothing to do, and in the meantime Chumovoi's foal ran off into the meadows and got lost there in the wetlands. Had the people been at leisure, they would have caught Chumovoi's foal right away and wouldn't have allowed Chumovoi to suffer a loss, but Makar had diverted the people from their rest and thereby helped Chumovoi to suffer a loss.

Chumovoi didn't go chasing after the foal himself, but approached Makar, who was longing silently for the storm, and said, "You're distracting the people here, and I don't have anybody to chase after my foal . . ."

Makar came out of his reverie because something dawned on him. He couldn't think, because he had an empty head above his clever hands, but on the other hand, he could suddenly get a hunch about something.

"Don't lament," Makar said to Comrade Chumovoi, "I'll make you something that goes by itself."

"How?" Chumovoi asked, since he didn't know how to make something with his idle hands that goes by itself.

"From hoops and ropes," Makar said without thinking but feeling the pulling power and rotation of those future ropes and hoops.

"Then go ahead and do it quickly," Chumovoi said, "or else I'll make you answer in court for your illegal spectacles."

But Makar wasn't thinking about the fine—he wasn't able to think— he was trying to remember where he had seen some iron and couldn't, because the whole village was made of materials that were found above ground: clay, straw, wood, and hemp.

No storm came, the carousel didn't move, and Makar returned to his home.

At home Makar drank some water out of sorrow and tasted the pungent quality of the water.

"That must be why there's no iron," Makar figured, "because we drink it up with the water."

At night Makar climbed down into a dry, dead well and spent the whole day there, looking for iron under the damp sand. On the second day some men pulled Makar out under the supervision of Chumovoi, who was afraid that a citizen might die outside the front line of socialist construction. Makar was awfully heavy to lift—there turned out to be brown chunks of iron ore in his hands. The men pulled him out and cursed him for his heaviness, and Comrade Chumovoi promised to slap an additional fine on Makar for causing a public disturbance.

However, Makar didn't heed him and in a week made iron from the ore in the stove, after his wife had baked bread in it. How he smelted the ore in the stove—nobody knows, because Makar worked with his clever hands and silent head. And a day later Makar made an iron wheel, and then another, but neither wheel went by itself: they had to be rolled using one's hands.

Chumovoi came to Makar and asked, "Did you make something that goes by itself to replace the foal?"

"No," Makar said, "I was figuring they'd roll by themselves, but they don't."

"Why did you deceive me, you spontaneous head!" Chumovoi exclaimed in an official tone. "Then make me a foal!"

"There's no meat, or else I'd make one," Makar declined.

"But how did you make iron out of clay?" Chumovoi asked, remembering the iron.

"I don't know," Makar replied, "I have no memory."

Here Chumovoi became offended.

"Oh, so you're hiding a discovery of national economic significance, you individualist-devil! You're not a man, you're a lone wolf! I'll slap every possible fine on you—that'll teach you to think!"

Makar became submissive. "But I don't think, Comrade Chumovoi. I'm an empty man."

"Then reduce your reach. Don't make what you can't understand," Comrade Chumovoi rebuked Makar.

"If I had your head, Comrade Chumovoi, then I'd think too," Makar admitted.

"Exactly right!" Chumovoi confirmed. "But there's only one such head in the whole village, and you must obey me."

And here Chumovoi fined him so thoroughly that Makar had to set out for Moscow to find work in order to pay off the fine, leaving the carousel and his farm under the zealous care of Comrade Chumovoi.

* * *

Makar had ridden trains nine years ago, in 1919. Back then he rode for free, because Makar looked right away like a farm laborer for hire, and they didn't even ask him for any documents. "Travel on," the proletarian guard would say to him, "we like you, because you don't have a thing."

Now Makar, just like nine years ago, got on the train without asking anyone, surprised by how few people there were and the open doors. But nonetheless, Makar sat down not inside a train car but on the couplings, so as to watch how the wheels work in motion. The wheels began to turn, and the train went to the center of the country—Moscow.

The train went faster than any half-breed horse. The steppes rushed towards the train and never seemed to end.

"They'll tire out the machine," Makar said, feeling sorry for the wheels. "Really, there are all kinds of things in this world, since it's vast and empty."

Makar's hands were idle and their clever power was free to go into his empty, spacious head, and he began to think. Makar was sitting on the couplings and thinking about whatever he could. However, Makar didn't sit for long. An unarmed guard walked by and asked to see his ticket. Makar didn't have a ticket on him since he assumed there was a strong Soviet government which now let all needy people ride completely free. The guard and ticket-taker told Makar to get off from sinning at the first whistle-stop, where there was a snack bar so that Makar wouldn't die of hunger in a god-forsaken section of the railroad between stations. Makar saw that the government cared about him, since it didn't simply force him off but offered him a snack bar, and he thanked the train master.

All the same, Makar didn't get off at the next whistle-stop, although the train stopped to unload envelopes and post-cards from the mail car. Makar remembered one technological concept and stayed on the train to help it go farther.

"The heavier a thing is," Makar imagined, comparing a stone and a feather, "the farther it flies when you throw it; and so I, too, am traveling on the train like an extra brick, so that the train reaches Moscow."

Not wanting to offend the train guard, Makar climbed deep into the machinery under the train car and lay down there to rest, listening to the surging speed of the wheels. The tranquility and the sight of the railway sand made Makar fall into a deep sleep, and he dreamed that he broke free of the ground and was flying with the cold wind. This luxurious feeling made him feel sorry for the people who remained on earth.

"Seryozhka, why are you leaving the axle pins hot?"

These words woke Makar up and he touched his neck to make sure his body and all of his inner life were safe and sound.

"It's no big deal!" Serezhka yelled from far off. "It's not far to Moscow; it won't burn up!"

The train was standing at a station. The workers were checking the cars' axles and swearing under their breath.

Makar climbed out from under the car and saw in the distance the center of the whole country—its main city, Moscow.

"Now I'll even make it on foot!" Makar realized. "I reckon the train will make it even without the additional weight!"

And Makar set off in the direction of towers, churches, and forbidding buildings—to the city of scientific and technological wonders to earn a living for himself.

Having unloaded himself from the train, Makar headed towards the

Moscow that was in sight, since he was interested in that central city. So as not to lose his way, Makar walked along the railroad tracks and was surprised at the frequent station platforms. Not far from the platforms there were pine and fir woods, and in the woods, small wooden houses. The trees were sparse and candy wrappers, wine bottles, sausage skins, and other spoiled goods lay scattered under them. The grass, oppressed by man, didn't grow here, and the trees also suffered more and didn't grow much. Makar understood such nature only vaguely.

"A special breed of crooks must live here that even the plants die from having them around! Why, it's very sad that man should live and create a desert close to him! Where's science and technology around here?"

Makar stroked his chest with regret and walked on. On a station platform empty milk cans were being unloaded from a train car, and the ones filled with milk were being loaded into the car. Makar stopped because he had a thought.

"Again, no technology!" Makar evaluated the situation out loud. "They transport the containers with milk—that's the right thing to do: in the city there are children, too, and they're waiting for milk. But why transport the empty cans on a machine? Why, it's just a needless waste of technology, and the containers take up a lot of room."

Makar approached the milk supervisor who was in charge of the cans and advised him to build a milk pipe from here right up to Moscow, so as not to run train cars with empty milk containers.

The milk supervisor heard Makar out—he respected people from the masses; however, he advised Makar to turn to Moscow because the cleverest people were there, and they were in charge of all repairs.

Makar got angry. "But it's you who's transporting the milk, not them! They only drink it, they don't see the needless waste of technology!"

The supervisor explained, "My job is to allocate the loads. I'm an executor, not an inventor of pipes."

Makar then left him alone and, full of doubt, headed on foot all the way to Moscow.

It was late morning in Moscow. Tens of thousands of people were rushing along the streets, like peasants rushing to harvest their crops.

"What are they going to do?" Makar stood and thought in the thick of a crowd of people. "There are probably mighty factories here that clothe and shoe all the far-off village folk."

Makar looked at his boots and said "Thank you!" to the running people—without them, he would have lived without shoes or clothes. Almost all the people had leather bags under their arms, which probably contained shoemaker's nails and cobbler's thread.

"But why are they running and wasting their energy?" Makar puzzled. "It'd be better if they worked at home, and their food could be brought around to their houses by cart!"

But the people kept running, climbing into streetcars until the springs were completely compressed, and didn't spare their bodies for the sake and benefit of labor. Makar was completely satisfied. "Good people," he thought, "it's hard for them to get to their workshops quickly, but they really want to!"

Makar liked the streetcars, because they moved on their own and the driver simply sat in the front car, as if he weren't driving anything. Makar also got into the car without any effort, since he was pushed by the people hurrying behind him. The car began to move smoothly; the invisible power of the machine roared under the floor, and Makar listened and sympathized with it.

"Poor worker!" Makar thought about the machine. "It's transporting people and straining. But then, it's bringing useful people to one place— saving living feet!"

A woman—the woman in charge of the streetcar—was passing out receipts to people, but Makar, so as not to bother her, declined a receipt.

"I'll go without!" Makar said and walked past.

People were shouting at the woman in charge of the streetcar so that she would give them something on demand, and she'd agree. In order to check on what was being given out here, Makar also said, "Woman in charge of the streetcar, give me something on demand too!"

The woman in charge pulled on a rope, and the streetcar quickly stopped where it was.

"Get off—on demand we say to you," the citizens said to Makar and pressed and pushed him out.

Makar came out into the open air.

The air was that of a capital city: it smelled of stirred-up gasoline from cars and cast-iron dust from streetcar brakes.

"And where here is the very center of the country?" Makar asked a random person.

The man pointed with his hand and threw a cigarette into a trash can on the street. Makar walked up to the can and also spit in there, in order to have the right to use everything in the city.

The buildings were so massive and tall that Makar felt sorry for the Soviet government, because it must be difficult for it to maintain such a collection of houses in good condition.

A policeman at an intersection raised a red stick, the butt end up, and made a fist with his left hand at the driver of a cart carrying rye flour.

"They have no respect for rye flour around here," Makar concluded to himself. "Here they live on gingerbread cookies made with white flour."

"Where's the center here?" Makar asked a policeman.

The policeman directed Makar down the hill and informed him, "By the Bolshoi Theater, in the ravine."

Makar went down the hill and found himself between two flower beds. On one side of the square there was a wall, and on the other, a building with columns. Those columns supported a foursome of cast-iron horses, but the columns could have been made a bit thinner because the foursome wasn't that heavy.

Makar began to look for some pole with a red flag on the square that would signify the middle of the central city and the center of the whole country, but there was no such pole anywhere; instead there was a stone with an inscription. Makar leaned against the stone in order to stand in the very center and be filled with respect for himself and for his country. Makar sighed happily and began to feel hungry. Then he headed for the river and saw a huge building under construction.

"What are they building here?" he asked a passerby.

"An eternal building of iron, concrete, steel and bright glass!" the passerby replied.

Makar decided to pay a visit there, so that he might work for a while on the construction and get something to eat.

There were guards at the gate. A guard asked, "What d'you want, jerk?"

"I'd like to get some kind of work—because I've gotten awfully thin," Makar stated.

"And how would you work here when you've come without any coupon?" the guard uttered sadly.

At this point a mason came up and got caught up in listening to Makar.

"Go to our barracks, to the communal pot, the guys there will feed you," the mason said, helping Makar. "But you can't join us right away;

you're living out in the open air, so you're nobody. First you must enroll in a workers' trade union and make it through the class observation."

And so Makar went to the barracks to eat from the pot in order to sustain life in him for further better fortune.

Makar got on well at the construction of that building in Moscow, which the man Makar had met called eternal. At first he ate his fill of dark, nourishing kasha in the workers' barracks, and then he went to look at the construction work. Indeed, the ground was pitted with holes everywhere, people were bustling about, and machines he didn't know what to call were driving piles into the ground. Cement kasha was flowing by itself through troughs, and other work was also going on right before his eyes. He could see that a building was being built, although who knows for whom. Makar wasn't even interested in who would get what—he was interested in technology as the future good for all people. Makar's superior from his native village, Comrade Lev Chumovoi, he, on the contrary, of course would've gotten interested in the distribution of living space in the future building and not in the cast-iron pile driver, but only Makar's hands had learning, his head didn't; and so he just kept thinking about how to make something.

Makar walked around the whole construction site and saw that the work was going quickly and without any problems. However, there was a mournful longing in Makar—for the moment, who knows for what. He walked out to the middle of the work site and took in at a glance the general picture of the work: clearly something was missing at the site, something had been lost, but who knows what. But some kind of conscientious worker's melancholy was growing in Makar's heart. From sadness, and because he had eaten a filling meal, Makar found a quiet place and dozed off there. In his sleep Makar saw a lake, birds, and a forgotten village grove, but what was needed, what was missing at the construction site, Makar didn't see. Then Makar woke up and suddenly discovered the shortcoming at the construction site: the workers were packing cement into iron frames to make a wall. But this wasn't technology, but manual labor! In order to have technology, you have to send the cement up through pipes, and the worker will simply hold the pipe and not get tired, thereby not allowing the beautiful power of the mind to go into a laborer's hands.

Makar immediately went to find the main Moscow office of science and technology. Such an office was located in a solid, fireproof building in a city ravine. Makar found a young fellow there at the door and told him he had invented a construction hose. The fellow heard him out and even asked him about things Makar didn't know himself, and then sent Makar up the stairs to the chief clerk. The clerk was a learned engineer; however, for some reason he had decided to write on paper and not to touch construction work with his hands. Makar told him about the hose too.

"Buildings shouldn't be built but cast," Makar said to the learned clerk.

The clerk heard him out and said in conclusion, "But how will you prove, comrade inventor, that your hose is cheaper than the usual way of pouring concrete?"

"By the fact that I feel it very clearly," Makar said as proof.

The clerk thought something to himself in secret and sent Makar to the end of the hallway. "There they give poor inventors a ruble for food and a return train ticket."

Makar took the ruble, but declined the train ticket, since he had decided to live forward and without going back.

In another room Makar was given a trade union document so that he could receive increased support there as a man from the masses and inventor of a hose. Makar thought that at the trade union they would give him money today to put together the hose and he went there happily.

The trade union was located in an even bigger building than the technological office. Makar wandered through the canyons of that trade union building for about two hours in search of the director of people from the masses whose name was written on the document, but the director happened not to be at his work place—he was somewhere else worrying about other workers. The director came at dusk, ate some fried eggs, and read Makar's document with the aid of his assistant—a rather nice-looking and progressive young woman with a big braid. The young woman went to the cashier's office and brought Makar a new ruble, and Makar signed for it as an unemployed farm laborer. The document was returned to Makar. On it, among other letters, was now written: "Comrade Lopin, help this member of our union put together his invention of a hose along the industrial line."

Makar was satisfied, and the next day went to look for the industrial line in order to see Comrade Lopin on it. Neither the policeman nor the passers-by knew of such a line, and Makar decided to find it on his own. In the streets there were posters and red sateen with an inscription of the very institution that Makar needed. The posters clearly stated that the whole proletariat must stand firmly on the line of industrial development. That convinced Makar right away: first he must find the proletariat, and underneath it would be the line, and somewhere nearby would be Comrade Lopin.

"Comrade policeman," Makar addressed him, "show me the way to the proletariat."

The policeman got out a book, found the address of the proletariat, and gave that address to a grateful Makar.

Makar walked across Moscow toward the proletariat and was in wonder of the power of the city flowing in buses, streetcars, and the living feet of the crowd.

"It takes a lot of food to feed such bodily movement!" Makar reasoned in his head, which knew how to think when his hands weren't occupied.

A worried and troubled Makar finally reached the building whose location had been pointed out to him by the officer. The building turned out to be a shelter for the night, where the poor class laid down its head at night. Before, in pre-revolutionary days, the poor class simply laid its head down on the ground, and over that head rain came down, the moon shone, the stars wandered and the winds blew, and the head lay, got cold and slept because it was tired. But today the head of the poor class rested on a pillow under a ceiling and the metal cover of a roof, and nature's night wind no longer disturbed the hair on the head of a poor man, who once used to lie right on the surface of the earth.

Makar saw several clean, new buildings and remained pleased with the Soviet government.

"Boy, that's some government!" Makar made his evaluation. "Only it mustn't get spoiled, because it's ours!"

In the building with lodging for the night there was an office, as in all residential buildings in Moscow. It turns out that without an office, chaos would begin everywhere at once, but the clerks put all life on a perhaps slow but correct track. And so Makar respected the clerks.

"Let them be!" Makar concluded about them. "They must be thinking of something, since they're collecting a salary, and if their position makes them think, then they'll probably become smart people, and that's exactly what we need!"

"What d'you want?" the supervisor of the lodging for the night asked Makar.

"I'd like to find the proletariat," Makar informed him.

"Which layer?" the supervisor inquired.

Makar didn't have to think—he knew ahead of time what he needed.

"The lowest," Makar said. "It's a bit thicker. There are more people there, and that's where the masses are."

"Aha!" the supervisor understood. "Then you need to wait for evening. Whichever has the most people, that's the one you'll go and spend the night with—either with the poor or with the seasonal workers . . ."

"I'd like to be with those who are building socialism itself," Makar requested.

"Aha!" the supervisor again understood. "Then you need those who build new buildings?"

Here Makar grew doubtful.

"But they built buildings even before, when there was no Lenin. What kind of socialism can you have in an empty building?"

The supervisor also fell to thinking, especially since he didn't know himself exactly in what form socialism should appear—would there be incredible happiness in socialism, and what kind?

"They did build buildings before," the supervisor agreed. "Only then scoundrels lived in them, but now I'm giving you a coupon for a night's stay in a new building."

"That's true," Makar was very pleased. "That means you're the right helper for the Soviet government."

Makar took the coupon and sat down on a pile of bricks from the construction that had been left unattended.

"Then, too . . . ," Makar reasoned, "there are bricks under me, but the proletariat made those bricks and suffered. The Soviet government is too small—it doesn't see its own property!"

Makar sat on the bricks until evening and watched as one after another, the sun went out, the lights came on, and the sparrows disappeared from the manure for rest.

At last the proletarians began to appear: some with bread, some without, some sick, some tired but all nice-looking from long labor and kind with the kindness that comes from total exhaustion.

Makar waited until the proletariat lay down on government cots and caught their breath from the day's construction work. Then Makar confidently entered the large sleeping room and, standing in the middle of the floor, declared, "Comrade laboring workers! You live in your native city of Moscow, in the central power of the country, but there's disorder and loss of valuable things in it . . ."

The proletariat stirred in their cots.

"Mitry!" someone's booming voice said indistinctly. "Let him have it, but not too hard, to make him normal . . ."

Makar didn't get offended because before him lay the proletariat and not a hostile force.

"You haven't thought of everything," Makar said. "Milk containers are being transported on valuable machines, but they're empty—people have already drunk the milk. Here you'd only need a pipe and a piston pump . . . The same thing's true in the construction of houses and sheds—they should be cast entirely using a hose, but you build them out of small pieces . . . I've already come up with that hose, and I'm giving it to you free so that socialism and other improvements may come sooner . . ."

"What hose?" the same indistinct voice of the invisible proletarian said.

"My hose," Makar confirmed.

The proletariat was silent at first, but then someone's clear voice shouted some words or other from a distant corner, and Makar heard them like the wind: "Power isn't dear to us, we'll build buildings even out of small pieces of material—it's the soul that's dear to us. If you're a human being, then buildings don't matter, but the heart does. We all work here for wages, we live to preserve labor, belong to trade unions, take a great interest in clubs, but we pay no attention to one another— we've entrusted one another to the law . . . Give us a soul, since you're an inventor!"

Makar immediately became downhearted. He had invented all kinds of things, but he hadn't dealt with the soul, and for the people here this turned out to be the most important invention. Makar lay down on a government cot and grew quiet from doubt: he might have been doing non-proletarian work his whole life.

Makar didn't sleep for long because he began to suffer in his sleep.

And his suffering turned into a dream: he dreamed he saw a hill or an elevated area, and a scientific man was standing on the hill. And Makar lay at the foot of the hill, like a sleepy fool, and looked at the scientific man, waiting for word or deed from him. But the man stood and kept silent, not seeing the sorrowful Makar and thinking only about the whole scope of things but not about Makar the individual. The face of the most learned man was illuminated with the glow of the life of the masses in the distant future, which spread out below him far in the distance, but his eyes were frightening and dead from being up high and gazing too far ahead. The scientific man was silent, and Makar lay in his dream and anguished.

"What can I do in life to be useful to myself and others?" Makar asked and grew quiet from horror.

The scientific man was silent as before and didn't answer, and millions of lives being lived were reflected in his dead eyes.

Then Makar, in wonder, began to crawl to the top along dead, stony soil. Three times he was overcome by fear of the motionless scientific man, and three times his fear was driven away by curiosity. If Makar had been a smart man, he wouldn't have climbed up to that height, but he was a backward man, with only curious hands beneath his unconscious head. And because of his curious stupidity Makar reached the most educated man and lightly touched his fat, enormous body. The unknown body moved from the touch as if alive and immediately came crashing down on top of Makar because it was dead.

Makar awoke from a blow and saw the night shelter supervisor standing over him, who had touched Makar's head with a teakettle to wake him up.

Makar sat up on his cot and saw a pockmarked proletarian who had washed himself with water from a saucer without losing a drop. Makar was surprised at this way of washing yourself clean with a handful of water, and asked the pock-marked fellow, "Everyone's left for work. Why are you the only one standing here and washing up?"

The pockmarked guy patted his wet face with a pillow, dried himself, and answered, "There are plenty of working proletarians, but few thinking ones—I decided to do the thinking for everybody. Do you understand me, or are you silent from stupidity and oppression?"

"From grief and doubt," answered Makar.

"Aha, well then come with me and we'll do the thinking for everybody," the pockmarked fellow said, getting an idea.

And Makar got up to leave with the pockmarked man, whose name was Pyotr, to find his calling in life.

A great diversity of women, dressed in tight clothes, which indicated that the women wanted to be nude, came toward Makar and Pyotr; there were also many men, but they covered their bodies more loosely. A great many thousands of other men and women, trying to spare their bodies, rode in cars and carriages as well as in barely moving streetcars that screeched under the people's live weight but put up with it. The riders and pedestrians pressed ahead with a scientific expression on their faces, which at the core resembled that great and mighty man whom Makar had contemplated inviolately in his dream. From observing nothing but scientifically literate individuals, Makar began to feel terrified in his gut. He looked to Pyotr for help: couldn't even he be simply a scientific man looking into the distance?

"You probably know all the sciences and see too far ahead?" Makar asked timidly.

Pyotr concentrated.

"Me? I assume an important look to exist like Ilich, Lenin; I look far, and near, and wide, and deep, and upwards."

"Yeah, that's it!" Makar calmed down. "Because the other day I saw a huge scientific man: he only looks into the distance and near him—two sazhens away—lies a separate person and suffers without any help."

"I'll say!" Piotr said wisely. "He stands on an incline, and so it seems to him that everything's in the distance and there's not a devil nearby! And the other only looks at his feet, scared of tripping on some clump and killing himself, and considers himself right, but it's boring for the masses to live at a slow pace. We, brother, aren't afraid of clumps of soil!"

"Our people have shoes now!" Makar confirmed.

But Pyotr kept his thinking moving forward, not taking a break for anything.

"Have you ever seen the communist party?"

"No, Comrade Pyotr, they didn't show it to me! In the village I saw Comrade Chumovoi!"

"There's a whole collection of Chumovoi's comrades here too. But I'm talking about the pure party, which has a clear vision of the exact target. When I find myself at a meeting among party people, I always feel like a fool."

"Why is that, Comrade Pyotr? You're almost a scientific man in appearance."

"Because my mind is eating up my body. I'd like some food, but the party says: first we'll build the factories—grain doesn't grow well without iron. Do you understand what I'm saying, what action is being taken just at the right time?!"

"I understand," Makar responded.

Those who build machines and factories he understood right away, as if he were a scientific man. From the day he was born Makar observed clay-and-straw villages and didn't have any faith in their fate without fiery machines.

"There you are," Pyotr said. "And you say you didn't like the man the other day! Both the party and I don't like him either: he's the product of stupid capitalism, and we push people the likes of him gradually down the slope!"

"I also feel something, only I don't know what!" Makar declared.

"And if you don't know what, then follow my lead in life; otherwise you'll inevitably fall off the fine line and hurt yourself."

Makar got distracted looking at the people of Moscow and thought: "People here have enough to eat, they all have clean faces and live a life of plenty—they should be multiplying, but there aren't any children in sight."

Makar communicated this to Pyotr.

"Here you have not nature, but culture," Pyotr explained. "Here people live in families without multiplying, here they eat without producing labor . . ."

"How's that?" Makar was surprised.

"Well, it's like this," the knowledgeable Pyotr informed him. "Someone will put down one thought on a certificate and, for that, he and his family are fed for a whole year and a half . . . But another doesn't even write anything—he simply exists for the edification of others."

Makar and Pyotr walked around until evening; they saw the Moscow River, streets, and shops where textiles were for sale, and got hungry.

"Let's go to the police station for dinner," Pyotr said.

Makar went; he figured that they feed people at police stations.

"I'll do the talking, and you stay quiet and be sort of tormented," Pyotr warned Makar ahead of time.

At the police station there were robbers, homeless people, people who were like animals, and other nameless unfortunates. And across from everyone an overseer sat on duty and received people lined up behind one another. Some he sent to jail, others to the hospital, and still others he got rid of, sending them back to where they came from.

When it got to be Pyotr's and Makar's turn, Pyotr said, "Comrade chief, I've caught a crazy guy on the street for you and brought him here by the hand."

"What sort of crazy man?" asked the overseer on duty at the station. "What law did he break in a public place?"

"Oh, nothing," Pyotr said openly. "He walks around all agitated, and then he'll up and kill someone—put him on trial then. The best fight against crime is prevention. And so I've prevented a crime."

"Makes sense," the chief agreed. "I'll send him to the institute for madmen right away—for a general examination . . ."

The policeman wrote up a piece of paper and began to lament, "There's no one to dispatch with you, all the people are tied up elsewhere . . ."

"Let me take him," Pyotr offered. "I'm a normal man—he's the one who's crazy."

"Go ahead!" the policeman was overjoyed and gave Pyotr the piece of paper.

An hour later Pyotr and Makar got to the institute for the mentally ill. Pyotr said that the police assigned him to a dangerous fool and he couldn't leave him even for a minute, but the fool hadn't eaten anything and would fly into a rage any minute now.

"Go to the kitchen, they'll give you something to eat there," a kind caretaker-nurse directed them.

"He eats a lot," Pyotr declined. "He needs a big pot of cabbage soup and two big pots of porridge. Let them bring it here, otherwise he might spit into the common pot."

The nurse issued instructions in an official manner. They brought three portions of tasty food for Makar, and Pyotr ate his fill along with Makar.

In no time at all, a doctor received Makar and began to ask him about such weighty ideas that Makar, owing to his ignorant life, answered the doctor's questions like a madman. Here the doctor examined Makar and found that there was extra blood gurgling in his heart.

"We have to keep him for tests," the doctor concluded about Makar.

And Makar and Pyotr stayed to spend the night at the mental hospital. In the evening they went to the reading room, and Pyotr began to read

Lenin's books aloud to Makar: "Our institutions are crap," Pyotr read Lenin, and Makar listened and was surprised at the accuracy of Lenin's mind. "Our laws are crap. We're good at issuing instructions but bad in carrying them out. There are people sitting in our institutions who are hostile to us, and some of our comrades have become high officials and work like the idiots they are . . ."

The other mentally ill patients also got caught up in Lenin's words— they hadn't known before that Lenin knew everything.

"That's right!" both the mentally ill workers and the peasants agreed.

"We need more workers and peasants in our institutions," the pockmarked Pyotr read on. "Socialism must be built with the hands of a man from the masses and not with bureaucratic pieces of paper from our institutions. And I don't lose hope that one day they'll hang us for this, and it will serve us right . . ."

"You see?" Pyotr asked Makar. "Institutions could tire out even Lenin, and we're just walking around and lying about. That's the whole revolution for you, written in the flesh . . . I'll steal this book from here because this is an institution, and tomorrow we'll go to one office or another and say we're workers and peasants. You and I will sit down in the institution and think for the government."

After the reading, Makar and Pyotr went to sleep in order to rest after the day's cares at the madhouse. Especially since the next day they both had to go fight for Lenin's and the poor people's common cause.

Pyotr knew where to go—to the RKI:[1] they love complainers and all kinds of oppressed people there. Half opening the first door in the hallway on the top floor of the RKI, they noticed the absence of people there. Above the second door was a poster with a short message: "Who'll prevail over whom?"[2] and Pyotr and Makar went in there. There was no one in the room except Comrade Lev Chumovoi, who was sitting and managing something, having left his village at the mercy of the poor folk.

Makar wasn't afraid of Chumovoi and said to Pyotr, "Since it says, 'Who'll prevail over whom?' then let's . . . him . . ."

"No," the experienced Pyotr rejected the idea. "We have a government, not noodles. Let's go higher."

They were received higher up because there they missed people and real rank-and-file minds.

"We're members of the working class," Pyotr said to the high official. "We've accumulated a lot of sense. Give us power over the oppressive paper-pushing bastards . . ."

"Take it. It's yours," the high official said and handed them power.

From then on, Makar and Pyotr sat at their desks across from Lev Chumovoi and began to talk to the poor people who came there, deciding all matters in their heads, based on compassion for the poor. Soon people stopped coming to Makar's and Pyotr's institution because their way of thinking was so simple that the poor themselves could think and decide things that way too, and the working people began to think for themselves in their apartments.

Lev Chumovoi was left alone at the institution, since no one had recalled him from there in writing. And he was present there until a commission was appointed to handle the liquidation of the State. Comrade Chumovoi worked for that commission for forty-four years and died amidst the oblivion and bureaucratic matters in which his golden gov-mind had been invested.

1929

NOTES

1. RKI: acronym for *Raboche-krestiyanskaya inspektsiya*—Worker-Peasant Inspectorate, which existed in 1920-1934. It was created to exercise control over labor, production and output, social organizations, bureaucracy and red tape, etc.
2. During NEP there was serious competition between the private sector and the State. "Who'll prevail over whom?" (*Kto kogo?*)—was often used to question who would get the upper hand, the owners of private businesses or the State.

Six Stories from INCIDENTS

Daniil Kharms

BLUE NOTEBOOK NO. 10

There was a certain red-haired man who didn't have eyes or ears. He didn't even have hair, so they called him red-haired theoretically.

As for speaking, he couldn't, since he didn't have a mouth. As for a nose, he didn't have one either.

He didn't even have arms or legs. And he didn't have a stomach, and he didn't have a back, and he didn't have a spine, and he didn't have any innards. He didn't have anything! So it's not clear who is being discussed.

Well, in that case it's better for us not to talk about him anymore.

January 6, 1937

OLD WOMEN TUMBLING OUT

An old woman tumbled out of a window because of excessive curiosity, fell and was killed.

Another old woman leaned out of a window and began to look down at the one who had gotten killed, but she too tumbled out of the window because of excessive curiosity, fell and was killed.

Then a third old woman tumbled out of a window, then a fourth, then a fifth.

When a sixth old woman tumbled out, I got tired of watching them and I went to the Maltsevsky Market where, they say, a blind man was given a knitted shawl as a gift.

1936-1937

KUSHAKOV THE CARPENTER

Once upon a time there lived a carpenter. His name was Kushakov.

Once he walked out of the house and went to the store to buy some carpenter's glue.

There was a thaw and it was very slippery outside.

The carpenter took a few steps, slipped, fell and hurt his forehead.

"Good grief!" the carpenter said, got up, went to the pharmacy, bought a band-aid and applied it to his forehead.

But when he went outside and took a few steps, he slipped again, fell and hurt his nose.

"Phooey!" said the carpenter, went to the pharmacy, bought a band-aid and applied the band-aid to his nose.

Then he went outside again, slipped again, fell and hurt his cheek.

He had to go to the pharmacy again and apply a band-aid to his cheek.

"I tell you what," the pharmacist said to the carpenter, "you fall and hurt yourself so often, I advise you to buy several band-aids."

"No," said the carpenter, "I won't fall anymore!"

But when he went out, he slipped again, fell and hurt his chin.

"Lousy ice!" the carpenter shouted and again ran to the pharmacy.

"Well, you see," said the pharmacist, "you've fallen again."

"No!" the carpenter shouted. "I don't want to hear anything! Quick, give me a band-aid."

The pharmacist gave him the band-aid; the carpenter applied it to his chin and ran home.

But at home they didn't recognize him and wouldn't let him into the apartment.

"I'm Kushakov the carpenter!" shouted the carpenter.

"You don't say!" they answered him from the apartment and locked the door and put on the chain.

Kushakov the carpenter stood a bit on the staircase, spat and went outside.

1935

A DREAM

Kalugin fell asleep and dreamed that he was sitting in some bushes and a policeman was walking past the bushes.

Kalugin woke up, scratched his mouth and fell asleep again and dreamed that he was walking past the bushes and a policeman was sitting in the bushes and hiding.

Kalugin woke up, put a newspaper under his head so as not to wet the pillow with his drool and fell asleep again, and again he dreamed that he was sitting in the bushes and a policeman was walking past the bushes.

Kalugin woke up, changed the newspaper, lay down and fell asleep again. Fell asleep and dreamed again that he was walking past some bushes and a policeman was sitting in the bushes.

At this point Kalugin woke up and decided not to sleep anymore, but fell asleep that instant and dreamed that he was sitting behind the policeman and the bushes were walking past.

Kalugin screamed and tossed in bed, but now he couldn't wake up.

Kalugin slept for four days and four nights in a row and on the fifth day he woke up so thin that his boots had to be tied with string to his feet so they wouldn't fall off. At the bakery where Kalugin always bought his whole-wheat bread they didn't recognize him and slipped him half-rye. And a sanitary commission, walking through the apartments and seeing Kalugin, found him unsanitary and fit for nothing and ordered the *zhakt*[i] to throw Kalugin out with the trash.

They folded Kalugin in half and threw him out as trash.

1935

---

i *ZhAKT (Zhilishchno-arendnoe kooperativnoe tovarishchestvo)*: Rental Housing Cooperative Association, which existed in Moscow in 1931-1937.

THE START OF A VERY NICE SUMMER DAY
A Symphony

The rooster had barely crowed when Timofey jumped out of the window onto the roof and frightened everyone walking down the street at that time. The peasant Khariton stopped, picked up a rock and threw it at Timofey. Timofey disappeared somewhere. "That's a dodger for you!" the human herd shouted, and a certain Zubov got a running start and with all his might rammed his head into the wall. "Oh!" a woman with an abscessed tooth exclaimed. But Komarov gave that woman a good whacking, and the woman ran howling into a back street. Fetelyushin was walking by and chuckling. Komarov walked up to him and said, "Hey you, piece of lard!" and hit Fetelyushin in the stomach. Fetelyushin leaned against the wall and started hiccuping. Romashkin was spitting from a window above, trying to hit Fetelyushin. At that very point not far from there, a woman with a big nose was beating her child with a trough. And a plump young mother was rubbing her pretty little girl's face against a brick wall. A little dog with a thin, broken leg was lying on the pavement. A little boy was eating something disgusting from a spittoon. There was a long line for sugar at the grocery store. Women were cursing loudly and pushing each other with their bags. The peasant Khariton, drunk on methyl alcohol, was standing in front of the women with his trousers unbuttoned and saying bad words.

This was how a nice summer day was starting.

1939

THE LYNCHING

Petrov gets on a horse and, turning to the crowd, delivers a speech about what will happen if an American skyscraper is built on the spot where the public garden is located. The crowd listens and apparently agrees. Petrov writes something in his small notebook. A man of average height emerges from the crowd and asks Petrov what he wrote in his small notebook. Petrov answers that it concerns only him. The man of average height persists. One word leads to another and a quarrel begins. The crowd takes the side of the man of average height, and Petrov, to save his life, urges on his horse and disappears beyond a bend in the road. The crowd is restless and, lacking another victim, grabs the man of average height and tears off his head. The torn-off head rolls along the paved street and gets stuck on the manhole cover of a drainage sewer. The crowd, its passions satisfied, disperses.

(undated)

CLOUD, CASTLE, LAKE

Vladimir Nabokov

One of my representatives—a modest, mild bachelor, very efficient—happened to win a pleasure trip at a charity ball given by Russian refugees. That was in 1936 or 1937. The Berlin summer was in full flood (it was the second week of damp and cold, so that it was a pity to look at everything which had turned green in vain, and only the sparrows kept cheerful); he did not care to go anywhere, but when he tried to sell his ticket at the office of the Bureau of Pleasantrips he was told that to do so he would have to have special permission from the Ministry of Transportation; when he tried them, it turned out that first he would have to draw up a complicated petition at a notary's on stamped paper; and besides, a so-called "certificate of nonabsence from the city for the summertime" had to be obtained from the police.

So he sighed a little, and decided to go. He borrowed an aluminum flask from friends, repaired his soles, bought a belt and a fancy-style flannel shirt—one of those cowardly things which shrink in the first wash. Incidentally, it was too large for that likable little man, his hair always neatly trimmed, his eyes so intelligent and kind. I cannot remember his name at the moment. I think it was Vasiliy Ivanovich.

He slept badly the night before the departure. And why? Because he had to get up unusually early, and hence took along into his dreams the delicate face of the watch ticking on his night table; but mainly because that very night, for no reason at all, he began to imagine that this trip, thrust upon him by a feminine fate in a low-cut gown, this trip which he had accepted so reluctantly, would bring him some wonderful, tremulous happiness. This happiness would have something in common with his childhood, and with the excitement aroused in him by Russian lyrical poetry, and with some evening skyline once seen in a dream, and with that lady, another man's wife, whom he had hopelessly loved for seven years—but it would be even fuller and more significant than all that.

And besides, he felt that the really good life must be oriented toward something or someone.

The morning was dull, but steam-warm and close, with an inner sun, and it was quite pleasant to rattle in a streetcar to the distant railway station where the gathering place was: several people, alas, were taking part in the excursion. Who would they be, these drowsy beings, drowsy as seem all creatures still unknown to us? By Window Number 6, at seven a.m., as was indicated in the directions appended to the ticket, he saw them (they were already waiting; he had managed to be late by about three minutes).

A lanky blond young man in Tyrolese garb stood out at once. He was burned the color of a cockscomb, had huge brick-red knees with golden hairs, and his nose looked lacquered. He was the leader furnished by the Bureau, and as soon as the newcomer had joined the group (which consisted of four women and as many men) he led it off toward a train lurking behind other trains, carrying his monstrous knapsack with terrifying ease, and firmly clanking with his hobnailed boots.

Everyone found a place in an empty car, unmistakably third-class, and Vasiliy Ivanovich, having sat down by himself and put a peppermint into his mouth, opened a little volume of Tyutchev, whom he had long intended to reread; but he was requested to put the book aside and join the group. An elderly bespectacled post-office clerk, with skull, chin, and upper lip a bristly blue as if he had shaved off some extraordinarily luxuriant and tough growth especially for this trip, immediately announced that he had been to Russia and knew some Russian—for instance, *patzlui*[i]—and, recalling philanderings in Tsaritsyn, winked in such a manner that his fat wife sketched out in the air the outline of a backhand box on the ear. The company was getting noisy. Four employees of the same building firm were tossing each other heavy-weight jokes: a middle-aged man, Schultz; a younger man, Schultz also, and two fidgety young women with big mouths and big rumps. The redheaded, rather burlesque widow in a sport skirt knew something too about Russia (the Riga beaches). There was also a dark young man by the name of Schramm, with lusterless eyes and a vague velvety vileness about his person and manners, who constantly switched the conversation to this or that attractive aspect of the excursion, and who gave the first

---

i *patzlui* is a phonetic approximation of *potselui*, meaning "a kiss" (eds.).

signal for rapturous appreciation; he was, as it turned out later, a special stimulator from the Bureau of Pleasantrips.

The locomotive, working rapidly with its elbows, hurried through a pine forest, then—with relief—among fields. Only dimly realizing as yet all the absurdity and horror of the situation, and perhaps attempting to persuade himself that everything was very nice, Vasiliy Ivanovich contrived to enjoy the fleeting gifts of the road. And indeed, how enticing it all is, what charm the world acquires when it is wound up and moving like a merry-go-round! The sun crept toward a corner of the window and suddenly spilled over the yellow bench. The badly pressed shadow of the car sped madly along the grassy bank, where flowers blended into colored streaks. A crossing: a cyclist was waiting, one foot resting on the ground. Trees appeared in groups and singly, revolving coolly and blandly, displaying the latest fashions. The blue dampness of a ravine. A memory of love, disguised as a meadow. Wispy clouds—greyhounds of heaven.

We both, Vasiliy Ivanovich and I, have always been impressed by the anonymity of all the parts of a landscape, so dangerous for the soul, the impossibility of ever finding out where that path you see leads—and look, what a tempting thicket! It happened that on a distant slope or in a gap in the trees there would appear and, as it were, stop for an instant, like air retained in the lungs, a spot so enchanting—a lawn, a terrace—such perfect expression of tender well-meaning beauty—that it seemed that if one could stop the train and go thither, forever, to you, my love... But a thousand beech trunks were already madly leaping by, whirling in a sizzling sun pool, and again the chance for happiness was gone.

At the stations, Vasiliy Ivanovich would look at the configuration of some entirely insignificant objects—a smear on the platform, a cherry stone, a cigarette butt—and would say to himself that never, never would he remember these three little things here in that particular interrelation, this pattern, which he now could see with such deathless precision; or again, looking at a group of children waiting for a train, he would try with all his might to single out at least one remarkable destiny—in the form of a violin or a crown, a propeller or a lyre—and would gaze until the whole party of village schoolboys appeared as in an old photograph, now reproduced with a little white cross above the face of the last boy on the right: the hero's childhood.

But one could look out of the window only by snatches. All had been given sheet music with verses from the Bureau:

> *Stop that worrying and moping,*
> *Take a knotted stick and rise,*
> *Come a-tramping in the open*
> *With the good, the hearty guys!*
>
> *Tramp your country's grass and stubble,*
> *With the good, the hearty guys,*
> *Kill the hermit and his trouble*
> *And to hell with doubts and sighs!*
>
> *In a paradise of heather*
> *Where the field mouse screams and dies,*
> *Let us march and sweat together*
> *With the steel-and-leather guys!*

This was to be sung in chorus: Vasiliy Ivanovich, who not only could not sing but could not even pronounce German words clearly, look advantage of the drowning roar of mingling voices and merely opened his mouth while swaying slightly, as if he were really singing—but the leader, at a sign from the subtle Schramm, suddenly stopped the general singing and, squinting askance at Vasiliy Ivanovich, demanded that he sing solo. Vasiliy Ivanovich cleared his throat, timidly began, and after a minute of solitary torment all joined in; but he did not dare thereafter to drop out.

He had with him his favorite cucumber from the Russian store, a loaf of bread, and three eggs. When evening came, and the low crimson sun entered wholly the soiled seasick car, stunned by its own din, all were invited to hand over their provisions, in order to divide them evenly—this was particularly easy, as all except Vasiliy Ivanovich had the same things. The cucumber amused everybody, was pronounced inedible, and was thrown out of the window. In view of the insufficiency of his contribution, Vasiliy Ivanovich got a smaller portion of sausage.

He was made to play cards. They pulled him about, questioned him, verified whether he could show the route of the trip on a map—in a word, all busied themselves with him, at first good-naturedly, then with malevolence, which grew with the approach of night. Both girls were called Greta; the red-headed widow somehow resembled the rooster-leader; Schramm, Schultz, and the other Schultz, the post-office clerk and his wife, all gradually melted together, merged together, forming one collective, wobbly, many-handed being, from which one could not escape. It pressed upon him from all sides. But suddenly at some station all climbed out, and it was already dark, although in the west there still hung a very long, very pink cloud, and farther along the track, with a soul-piercing light, the star of a lamp trembled through the slow smoke of the engine, and crickets chirped in the dark, and from somewhere there came the odor of jasmine and hay, my love.

They spent the night in a tumble-down inn. A mature bedbug is awful, but there is a certain grace in the motions of silky silverfish. The post-office clerk was separated from his wife, who was put with the widow; he was given to Vasiliy Ivanovich for the night. The two beds took up the whole room. Quilt on top, chamber pot below. The clerk said that somehow he did not feel sleepy, and began to talk of his Russian adventures, rather more circumstantially than in the train. He was a great bully of a man, thorough and obstinate, clad in long cotton drawers, with mother-of-pearl claws on his dirty toes, and bear's fur between fat breasts. A moth dashed about the ceiling, hobnobbing with its shadow. "In Tsaritsyn," the clerk was saying, "there are now three schools, a German, a Czech, and a Chinese one. At any rate, that is what my brother-in-law says; he went there to build tractors."

Next day, from early morning to five o'clock in the afternoon, they raised dust along a highway, which undulated from hill to hill; then they took a green road through a dense fir wood. Vasiliy Ivanovich, as the least burdened, was given an enormous round loaf of bread to carry under his arm. How I hate you, our daily! But still his precious, experienced eyes noted what was necessary. Against the background of fir-tree gloom a dry needle was hanging vertically on an invisible thread.

Again they piled into a train, and again the small partitionless car was empty. The other Schultz began to teach Vasiliy Ivanovich how to play the mandolin. There was much laughter. When they got tired of that, they thought up a capital game, which was supervised by Schramm. It consisted of the following: the women would lie down on the benches they chose, under which the men were already hidden, and when from under one of the benches there would emerge a ruddy face with ears, or a big outspread hand, with a skirt-lifting curve of the fingers (which would provoke much squealing), then it would be revealed who was paired off with whom. Three times Vasiliy Ivanovich lay down in filthy darkness, and three times it turned out that there was no one on the bench when he crawled out from under. He was acknowledged the loser and was forced to eat a cigarette butt.

They spent the night on straw mattresses in a barn, and early in the morning set out again on foot. Firs, ravines, foamy streams. From the heat, from the songs which one had constantly to bawl, Vasiliy Ivanovich became so exhausted that during the midday halt he fell asleep at once, and awoke only when they began to slap at imaginary horseflies on him. But after another hour of marching, that very happiness of which he had once half dreamt was suddenly discovered.

It was a pure, blue lake, with an unusual expression of its water. In the middle, a large cloud was reflected in its entirety. On the other side, on a hill thickly covered with verdure (and the darker the verdure, the more poetic it is), towered, arising from dactyl to dactyl, an ancient black castle. Of course, there are plenty of such views in Central Europe, but just this one—in the inexpressible and unique harmoniousness of its three principal parts, in its smile, in some mysterious innocence it had, my love! my obedient one!—was something so unique, and so familiar, and so long-promised, and it so understood the beholder that Vasiliy Ivanovich even pressed his hand to his heart, as if to see whether his heart was there in order to give it away.

At some distance, Schramm, poking into the air with the leader's alpenstock, was calling the attention of the excursionists to something or other; they had settled themselves around on the grass in poses seen in amateur snapshots, while the leader sat on a stump, his behind to the lake, and was having a snack. Quietly, concealing himself in his own shadow, Vasiliy Ivanovich followed the shore, and came to a kind of inn. A dog still quite young greeted him; it crept on its belly, its jaws laughing, its tail fervently beating the ground. Vasiliy Ivanovich accompanied the dog into the house, a piebald two-storied dwelling with a winking window beneath a convex tiled eyelid; and he found the owner, a tall old man vaguely resembling a Russian war veteran, who spoke German so poorly and with such a soft drawl that Vasiliy Ivanovich changed to his own tongue, but the man understood as in a dream and continued in the language of his environment, his family.

Upstairs was a room for travelers. "You know, I shall take it for the rest of my life," Vasiliy Ivanovich is reported to have said as soon as he had entered it. The room itself had nothing remarkable about it. On the contrary, it was a most ordinary room, with a red floor, daisies daubed on the white walls, and a small mirror half filled with the yellow infusion of the reflected flowers—but from the window one could clearly see the lake with its cloud and its castle, in a motionless and perfect correlation of happiness. Without reasoning, without considering, only entirely surrendering to an attraction the truth of which consisted in its own strength, a strength which he had never experienced before, Vasiliy Ivanovich in one radiant second realized that here in this little room with that view, beautiful to the verge of tears, life would at last be what he had always wished it to be. What exactly it would be like, what would take place here, that of course he did not know, but all around him were help, promise, and consolation—so that there could not be any doubt that he must live here. In a moment he figured out how he would manage it so as not to have to return to Berlin again, how to get the few possessions that he had—books, the blue suit, her photograph. How simple it was turning out! As my representative, he was earning enough for the modest life of a refugee Russian.

"My friends," he cried, having run down again to the meadow by the shore, "my friends, good-bye. I shall remain for good in that house over there. We can't travel together any longer. I shall go no farther. I am not going anywhere. Good-bye!"

"How is that?" said the leader in a queer voice, after a short pause, during which the smile on the lips of Vasiliy Ivanovich slowly faded, while the people who had been sitting on the grass half rose and stared at him with stony eyes.

"But why?" he faltered. "It is here that..."

"Silence!" the post-office clerk suddenly bellowed with extraordinary force. "Come to your senses, you drunken swine!"

"Wait a moment, gentlemen," said the leader, and, having passed his tongue over his lips, he turned to Vasiliy Ivanovich.

"You probably have been drinking," he said quietly. "Or have gone out of your mind. You are taking a pleasure trip with us. Tomorrow, according to the appointed itinerary—look at your ticket—we are all returning to Berlin. There can be no question of anyone—in this case you—refusing to continue this communal journey. We were singing today a certain song—try and remember what it said. That's enough now! Come, children, we are going on."

"There will be beer at Ewald," said Schramm in a caressing voice. "Five hours by train. Hikes. A hunting lodge. Coal mines. Lots of interesting things."

"I shall complain," wailed Vasiliy Ivanovich. "Give me back my bag. I have the right to remain where I want. Oh, but this is nothing less than an invitation to a beheading"—he told me he cried when they seized him by the arms.

"If necessary we shall carry you," said the leader grimly, "but that is not likely to be pleasant. I am responsible for each of you, and shall bring back each of you, alive or dead."

Swept along a forest road as in a hideous fairy tale, squeezed, twisted, Vasiliy Ivanovich could not even turn around, and only felt how the radiance behind his back receded, fractured by trees, and then it was no longer there, and all around the dark firs fretted but could not interfere. As soon as everyone had got into the car and the train had pulled off, they began to beat him—they beat him a long time, and with a good deal of inventiveness. It occurred to them, among other things, to use a corkscrew on his palms; then on his feet. The post-office clerk, who had been to Russia, fashioned a knout out of a stick and a belt, and began to use it with devilish dexterity. Atta boy! The other men relied more on their iron heels, whereas the women were satisfied to pinch and slap. All had a wonderful time.

After returning to Berlin, he called on me, was much changed, sat down quietly, putting his hands on his knees, told his story; kept on repeating that he must resign his position, begged me to let him go, insisted that he could not continue, that he had not the strength to belong to mankind any longer. Of course, I let him go.

1937

Edited by Dmitri Nabokov

THE SMOKY GLASS GOBLET

Sigizmund Krzhizhanovsky

"Perhaps you would like to take a look at a collection of old coins? Numismatists have praised it. Or . . . "

"You want me to buy money that lost its purchasing power long ago? I'd rather see . . . "

"Then take a look at my collection of miniatures. If you take a magnifying glass . . . "

"Tell me, what's that goblet over there, on the left, on the shelf?"

"Would you like to see it? Just a minute."

The antique dealer, shifting his small black hat from his bald spot to his forehead, placed a step ladder next to a shelf—and there was the goblet on its straight, round little foot on top of the counter, its smoky glass twinkling.

"Strange—it doesn't seem to be empty. What's in it?"

"Wine. As befits a goblet. Aged a thousand years. I recommend it. We'll remove the dust with this teaspoon made in Venetian Murano."[1]

The customer in the antique shop picked up the goblet by its thin stem and held it up to the window to take a look; inside the smoky glass there was a smoky liquid with a light ruby glow.

The buyer brought the goblet to his lips and tasted a few drops. The smoky surface of the wine stayed sleepy and motionless. In his mouth it had a tart taste, like the pricking of hundreds of needles.

"Like a snake bite," the buyer said and pushed the goblet away. "By the way, I was told you have a selection of Jain[2] statuettes. I would like . . . but it's strange—my sip of wine didn't lower the level in that goblet of yours."

The antique dealer's lips moved apart guiltily, revealing gold fillings:

"You see, there are, if only in fairy tales, not only magic *chervontsy*[3] but also goblets that can never be emptied."

"Strange."

"Oh, the word 'strange' is not threatened with unemployment in our world."

"And you're selling this goblet?"

"If into good hands—perhaps."

"How much do you want?"

The antique dealer pulled out a pencil from behind his ear and wrote on the counter.

"That's beyond my means."

"All right. I'll cross out the zero on the right. The important thing— into good hands. May I wrap it up?"

"Please."

The buyer walked out of the store. In his right hand he held the goblet, wrapped in paper. A man with eyes covered with round patches of smoky glass in metal frames walked past him. Someone's elbow brushed against his elbow; dark-red spots appeared on the paper by the goblet's base. "Spilled," the man thought and walked on, hugging the walls of the buildings and guarding his purchase from any bumps.

However, when he came home and unwrapped the crystal, the goblet was full to the brim as before, although the spilled drops were still running down the round stem.

The man who had become the owner of the goblet that could never be emptied did not immediately set about testing his purchase. The day was waning. The sun was beginning to set. Soon the air at twilight took on the color of the thin-stemmed glass. The man took the silent goblet with the fingers of his right hand and brought it to his lips. The tart wine stung his lips. And the goblet, which he had put aside, stood full to the brim again, the ruby liquid pressing against the gold border at the top of the glass.

During the first few days the one-legged goblet guest that had stepped with its round glass foot into the life of the lover of rarities conducted itself modestly and almost good-naturedly. Giving up mouthfuls, it would immediately fill up with the wine liquid exactly to the gold rim of the glass. It knew how to vary the effect: one sip would produce a sensation of zesty delight, another would pierce the tongue with poisonous needles, and a third would enmesh the brain in a smoky-scarlet cobweb. For the man who had acquired it, the goblet soon became something like a gustatory lamp. In the light of its blood-red drops, the man would read and reread his books and write in his notebooks. Almost emptied, the goblet would immediately fill up to the gold rim and again offer itself to his lips. The man began to drink . . . Time after time he would raise the transparent heel and drink. Scarlet drops danced in his brain. Thoughts collided with one another, dissipating in a fiery dust of sparks. The emptied liquid would rise just like the sun that rises after it has set and has been seemingly killed outright and buried by the night. The man drank in daylight, in moonlight, and in moonless darkness. The glass clinked against his teeth, "Have more, more!"

Once, as he was falling asleep, the man tipped over the goblet. The next morning, when he woke up, he saw his room flooded with a dark-red liquid. The liquid, giving off a sharp wine smell, was beginning to reach the dangling edge of his blanket. A night slipper was floating in the middle of the room, knocking against a table leg. People came from downstairs, from a neighboring apartment, to find out what was going on; some strange red spots were coming through the ceiling. The man thrust his arm up to the elbow in the liquid and found the wine-dispensing goblet with difficulty. He placed the goblet, sticky with wine essence, on the table and immediately dark-red liquid rose to the gold band. The man gulped it down and began to put his room in order.

Sometimes the smoky cut crystal, particularly after being touched by his lips some ten-twenty times, seemed to their owner to be a glassy smoke rising from a camp-fire. At times he thought he saw in the inward curve of the goblet's golden rim a mean smile mocking him with its gold fillings.

Once—this was on a bright sunny day, when scarlet sparks were diving into the red drops—the man, as he threw back his head and drank from the goblet, noticed by chance that there was some kind of a zig-zag on the bottom, a combination of symbols, perhaps letters. But immediately the symbols that had just appeared became obscured by a new influx of wine reaching to the very top of the goblet. The man again emptied the goblet, trying to catch a glimpse of the run-away letters. But the dark-red liquid obscured them again before he had a chance to make out the inscription. He could remember only the first symbol that looked like an alphabet letter, and he had only a dim sense of the ten or eleven symbols that followed it.

"Once more," the man thought and again quickly drank another glassful. Somewhere from the middle—like a thin mast with a cross-beam—a word floated up and in an instant drowned in the wine, like a ship with a hole in it. The man brought the goblet to his lips once more.

He made an effort to drink slowly. The word, moving its eleven letters, was swimming up to his eyes, but his eyes clouded over and the man could not understand what he saw.

From that day on a game with the goblet began. The odds were clearly unequal. After two or three jolts of alcohol, a smoky fog would envelop his brain. The man who had become the proprietor of the undeciphered inscription now rarely crossed the threshold of his home. Dust to the thickness of a finger accumulated on the windowsills. The curtains did not open their yellow eyelids. The owner of the smoky goblet rarely parted with his glass guest. Only once or twice was he seen walking along the embankment: his coat buttons were done up all wrong—they were not in the right buttonholes, and he walked on without noticing people greeting him or hearing their comments.

* * *

A stooping man with a grey stubble on his face walked into the antique shop. A chair was courteously moved toward him, but the man who had entered continued to stand.

"How may I help you?"

"Do you have a duplicate of that, of that smoky thing?"

"Could you be a bit clearer?"

"That smoky goblet. I'm closer to destitution than poverty. But you, remember, crossed out a zero then. And if . . ."

"Sorry, I'm seeing you for the first time. There, across the square, is another antique store. Probably . . ."

"No. The same little cap and . . . Smile!"

"That's to say?"

"Without 'that's to say.' Well, look: the same gold fillings, the same crafty grin. There's no mistake. Moreover, when I threw it—the goblet that can't be emptied—into the river from St. Stephen's Bridge, the river itself . . . but that's for our four ears only, otherwise . . . So, that's it."

The customer thrust his hand in his coat and took out a small bottle. He turned the tightly inserted cork.

"So, that's it. The next day I went down to the river and took a sample. This one. It turns out that it, the smoky thing, had enough strength to color the water in the Danube, the whole Danube, a bloody-reddish color. By the way, it's got a slightly tart taste. You don't believe me? Take a swallow. Don't want to? Then I'll make you do it . . . !"

Only the counter separated the two. But the bell over the door rang and a third person walked into the store. He was wearing a well-fitted policeman's uniform.

Ah-h," the antique dealer drawled out joyfully, opening his gold mouth wide, "you've come here apropos the taxes? Gladly, gladly . . . Well, and you," he turned to the customer, who was still holding the sample in his hands, "you need to go across the square! 'Antiquité'[i]— black on yellow. You've confused the doors."

The customer, knitting his eyebrows, put the bottle away after carefully forcing the cork in, and then asked, "And are there many of them, those . . . doors?"

The antique dealer shrugged his shoulders. The policeman only raised his eyebrows.

The customer stepped over the threshold.

* * *

About two days later the owner of the antique shop—whom we've met—was looking through the news items in the newspaper and came across the line: "Yesterday a man threw himself from St. Stephen's Bridge into . . ."

The bell over the door broke off his reading . . .

1939

NOTES

1. Isle of Murano, off the coast of Venice, famous for its glassworks.
2. Jain statuettes: connected with Jainism, an ancient religion and philosophy in India.
3. In fairy tales magic coins stay with the owner no matter what he has purchased with them; *chervontsy* are gold coins in 3-, 5- or 10-ruble denominations.

---

i   "Antiques" (French). Author.

TANYA

Ivan Bunin

She was a maid for his relative, the small landowner Mme. Kazakova, and had already turned seventeen; she was not very tall, and this was particularly noticeable when she would walk around barefoot or in felt boots during the winter, with her skirt gently swishing and her breasts showing slightly under her blouse. Her plain face was merely pretty, and her grey peasant eyes were appealing only because of her youth. At that distant time he wasted himself recklessly, led a life of wandering, and had numerous, chance romantic encounters and liaisons—and he regarded this liaison as one of them.

She quickly came to terms with that fateful, wonderful thing that had suddenly happened to her somehow that autumn night; she wept for several days, but with each passing day she became more and more convinced that it was not bad but good fortune that had come her way. He was becoming more dear and precious to her in moments of intimacy, which soon began to occur more and more frequently, and she already called him Petrusha and spoke about that night as their shared and cherished past.

At first he did and did not believe her. "Is it really true you weren't pretending to be asleep?"

But she would just open her eyes wide. "Couldn't you[1] tell I was asleep? Don't you know how boys and girls sleep?"

"Had I known for sure you were really sleeping, I wouldn't have touched you for anything in the world."

"Well, I felt nothing, nothing. Nothing, almost to the last minute! But what made you think of coming to my room? You arrived here and didn't even look at me; it was evening before you asked, 'You must have been hired recently. Your name, I think, is Tanya?' And then for some time you didn't seem to pay any attention to me. So, were you pretending?"

He told her that of course he'd been pretending, but he lied. Everything had turned out unexpectedly for him as well.

He had spent the first part of autumn in the Crimea, and on his way back to Moscow he stopped off to see Mme. Kazakova, spent about two weeks leading a peaceful, simple life on her estate during the bleak days of early November, and now he was about to leave. That day, in order to bid farewell to the countryside, he spent the whole day on horseback, a rifle over his shoulder, and rode about the empty fields and barren copses with a foxhound. He did not find anything and, tired and hungry, returned to the manor house and for supper ate a pan of meatballs in sour cream and drank a carafe of vodka and several glasses of tea while Mme. Kazakova, as always, talked about her late husband and her two sons who were working in Orlov. Around 10 o'clock the house, as always, was already dark; only a candle was burning in the study behind the parlor where he stayed whenever he visited. When he entered the study, she was kneeling on the bedding on the divan with a candle in her hand, moving the burning candle back and forth along the log wall. Catching sight of him, she put the candle down on the nightstand and, jumping off, started to dash away.

"What's going on?" he said, perplexed. "Wait, what were you doing here?"

"I was burning a bedbug," she whispered quickly. "I began to make your bed and noticed a bedbug on the wall."

And she ran away laughing.

He followed her with his eyes and, with his coat still on, removed only his boots and lay down on the quilt on the divan, still hoping to have a smoke and think a bit—he was not used to falling asleep at 10 o'clock, but he fell asleep right away. He woke up for a second because in his sleep he worried about the flickering flame of the candle, blew it out, and fell asleep again. When he opened his eyes again, outside the two windows facing the courtyard and the side window facing the garden and filled with light was an autumn moonlit night—tranquil and beautiful in its solitude. He found his slippers in the darkness beside the divan and went into the hall next to the study so that he could walk out onto the back porch—they had forgotten to give him what he needed for the night. But the hallway door turned out to be locked from the outside, and he made his way through the house, mysteriously illuminated by the light streaming from the yard, to the front porch. People would go out there through the main entrance hall and the large outer entrance hall made of logs. In this entrance hall, opposite a large window above an old wooden chest, there was a partition, and behind it a windowless room where the maids always stayed. The door in the partition was slightly open; it was dark behind it. He struck a match and saw her sleeping. She was lying on her back on a wooden bed wearing only a blouse and a flannel skirt—her breasts were round under the blouse, her bare legs were exposed to the knees, her right arm rested against the wall, and her face seemed lifeless on the pillow. The match went out. He stood for a moment and then carefully approached the bed.

As he was going to the porch through the dark outer entrance hall, he thought feverishly, "How strange, how unexpected! And was she really sleeping?"

He stood for a while on the porch and then set out across the court-yard . . . And the night was somewhat strange. The wide, empty courtyard was brightly illuminated by the high moon. Opposite the barn were the cattle yard, the carriage shed, and the stables with their thatched roofs of old, compacted straw. Beyond these roofs, on the northern horizon, mysterious night clouds—snowy, lifeless mountains—were dispersing. There were only light, white clouds above his head, and the moon— high in the sky—shone through like an uncut diamond and now and then appeared in the dark-blue gaps in the starry depths of the sky; it seemed to light up the roofs and the courtyard even more brightly. And everything around him was somehow strange in its nocturnal existence, estranged from everything mortal, and shining aimlessly. And strange also because it was if he were seeing this entire nocturnal, lunar, autumnal world for the first time . . .

He sat down next to the carriage shed on the footboard of a tarantass spattered with dried mud. As it is sometimes in autumn, it was warm and there was the smell of an autumn garden . . . The night was solemn, passionless, and mellow, and in some surprising way it harmonized with the feelings he carried away from the unexpected union with the innocent, semi-childish, female creature.

She began to weep quietly, when she had regained her senses, as if it was only at that moment that she realized what had taken place. But perhaps not "as if" but "really?" Her whole body had surrendered to him as if it were lifeless. At first he tried to wake her with a whisper, "Listen to me, don't be afraid . . ." She did not hear, or pretended not to hear. He kissed her burning cheek carefully; she did not react to the kiss at all, and he thought that she had tacitly consented to everything that might follow after that. He parted her legs, their soft, burning warmth; she only sighed in her sleep, stretched languidly, and tossed her arm over her head.

"What if she wasn't pretending?" he thought as he got up from the footboard and gazed anxiously into the night.

When she started to weep, sweetly and pitifully, he—not only with feelings of animal gratitude for what she had given him but also of rapture and love—began to kiss her neck and bosom which smelled intoxicatingly of something rural, virginal. And weeping, she suddenly answered him with an unconscious feminine reflex—firmly and, it seemed, also gratefully, she grasped his head and pulled it to herself. In her semi-awake state she did not realize who he was but, nevertheless, he was the one with whom she, at a certain time, was destined to unite in the most mysterious and blissfully mortal intimacy. This shared intimacy had taken place and nothing in the world could undo it, it would be forever with him; and now this unusual night was admitting him into its unfathomable, bright kingdom together with it, this intimacy.

How could he leave and think of her only on occasion? How could he forget her sweet, guileless voice, her sometimes joyful, sometimes sad but always loving, devoted eyes? How could he love others and let some of them be much more significant in his life than she was?

———

The next day she went about her work with downcast eyes. "Why are you like that today, Tanya?" Mme. Kazakova asked.

She answered obediently, "I have lots of sorrows, ma'am . . ."

After she had left the room, Mme. Kazakova said to him, "Of course, she's an orphan, no mother, and her father is a destitute, dissolute muzhik."

As evening approached, when she was setting up the samovar on the porch, he walked by and said to her, "No need to think . . . I fell in love with you long ago. Stop crying and upsetting yourself! It won't help . . ."

She answered quietly, blinking away her tears and putting hot kindling into the samovar: "If you've really fallen in love with me, everything would be easier . . ."

Then she started to glance at him from time to time as if she were asking timidly with each look, "Really?"

Once in the evening, when she came in to make his bed, he approached and put his arms around her shoulders. She looked at him in fright and, turning all red, whispered, "Leave me alone, for God's sake. The old woman could come in at any moment . . ."

"What old woman?"

"The old maidservant, as if you didn't know."

"I'll come see you tonight . . ."

She looked as if she'd been burnt; for the first time the old maidservant terrified her.

"What are you saying, what are you saying! I'll go mad with fright!"

"Well, don't, don't be afraid. I won't come," he said quickly.

She now did her work as before, quickly and in a caring way; once again she would run like a whirlwind across the courtyard to the kitchen as she used to do before and, finding a convenient moment, she would secretly cast embarrassed, joyful glances at him. And so, once in the morning, when it had just turned light and he was still sleeping, she was sent to town to do some shopping. At dinner Mme. Kazakova said, "What am I going to do? I sent my foreman and his worker to the mill, and I don't have anyone to send to the station for Tanya. Perhaps you could go and pick her up?"

Restraining his joy, he answered with feigned nonchalance, "Why not, I'm happy to take a drive."

The old maidservant, who was serving, frowned. "Why, ma'am, do you wish to ruin the girl's reputation forever? What are they going to say about her in the whole village after that?"

"Well, then, you go get her," Kazakova said. "What's she to do, walk from the station?"

Around four in the afternoon he set out in a carriage drawn by a tall, old black mare and, afraid of being late for the train, he drove her hard once he passed the village, forcing her to gallop along the oily, bumpy road which had frozen over and then partially thawed; the last few days had been damp and foggy, and that day the fog was especially thick. Even when he was driving through the village, it seemed that night was falling, and smoky-red lights that looked somewhat strange in the blue-grey color of the fog were already visible in the huts. Further on in the field it grew almost totally dark and, because of the fog, pitch-black. A cold wind and damp haze blew toward him. But the wind did not drive away the fog; on the contrary, it made its dark-grey smokiness even thicker and scented it with its fragrant dampness. And there seemed to be nothing beyond its impenetrable darkness—just the end of the world and everything living. His cap, caftan, eyelashes, and moustache—everything became covered with the tiniest beads of moisture. The black mare rushed on boldly and the carriage, bouncing on the slippery bumps in the road, was hitting him in the chest. He found a comfortable position and lit a cigarette—the sweet, aromatic, warm cigarette smoke coming from a man blended with the primordial scent of the fog, the late autumn, and the wet barren field. And it was growing dark and gloomy all around him, up above and down below; the dimly darkening, long neck of the horse and its alert ears were barely visible. And his feeling of closeness with the horse kept growing—the only living creature in this wilderness, in the lifeless hostility of everything to the right and to the left, in front of and behind, of all that unknown which was so ominously hidden in the thickening and blackening smoky darkness that was descending on him.

When he drove into the village where the station was, he was filled with joy at seeing the dwellings, the pitiful small lights in the shabby small windows, their endearing coziness; and at the station everything about the building seemed like another world—alive, energetic, and urban. And he did not even have enough time to hitch up his horse when the train came rumbling in, its bright windows glowing as it approached the station and covered it with the sulfurous smell of coal. He ran into the station with the emotions of a man who had been waiting for his young wife, and he immediately saw her—dressed like a town woman—entering through the opposite doors right behind the station guard who was dragging her two bundles of purchases. The station building was filthy, it smelled of the kerosene lamps that dimly illuminated it, but she was glowing—her eyes were filled with excitement, the youthfulness of her face was colored by the anxiety which this unusual journey had produced, and the guard was using the formal "you" as he said something to her. And suddenly her glance met his and she even stopped in confusion: "What's going on, why is he here?"

"Tanya," he said hurriedly, "hello, I've come to pick you up. There was no one else to send . . ."

Had she ever had such a blissful evening in all her life? "He's come for me himself, and I've just come from town. I'm all dressed up and so pretty as he could never have imagined me, since he's seen me only in an old skirt and a plain cotton blouse. My face is like a modiste's under this white silk scarf, I'm wearing a new brown worsted dress under my cloth jacket, I have on white cotton stockings and new ankle boots with copper tips." Trembling on the inside, she started speaking to him in a tone people use when they're guests in someone's home and, lifting the hem of her skirt, she followed him with small feminine steps, expressing her astonishment in a condescending way. "Oh, Lord, it's so slippery here! How much dirt the muzhiks have tracked in!" Standing completely still from joyous trepidation, she lifted her skirt above her calico petticoat so as to sit down on the petticoat and not on her dress, climbed into the carriage and sat down next to him as if she were his equal, and settled in awkwardly, trying to avoid the bundles at her feet.

He prodded the horse silently and drove it into the icy darkness of the night and fog, past the lights flickering here and there in the huts, over the holes and bumps of the tortuous country road in November. Dismayed by his silence, she did not dare utter a single word. Was he angry about something? He understood this and remained silent deliberately. And suddenly, when they had left the village behind and already plunged into complete darkness, he slowed down the horse, took the reins in his left hand and with his right he squeezed her shoulders and jacket sprinkled with cold, wet beads of moisture and, mumbling and laughing, he said, "Tanya, Tanyechka."

And she threw herself at him and pressed his cheek with her silk scarf, with her delicate face aglow, her eyelashes wet with hot tears. He found her lips, wet with tears of happiness and, stopping the horse, could not tear himself away from them for a long time. Then, like a blind man unable to see anything in the fog and darkness, he got out of the carriage, threw his caftan on the ground, and pulled her toward him by the sleeve. She understood everything and jumped down to him instantly and, raising her new dress and petticoat—her precious attire—quickly and carefully and, feeling her way, lay down on the caftan, surrendering to him forever not only her entire body, now fully his property, but also her entire soul.

He delayed his departure again.

She knew that it was because of her, she saw how affectionate he was with her, how he already spoke with her as he would with a close, secret friend in the house, and she stopped being afraid and trembling as she did in the beginning when he would come near her. He became more calm and direct during their intimate moments—she quickly began to feel comfortable with him. She changed totally with the quickness that the young are capable of, became his equal, blissfully happy, already called him Petrusha with ease, and at times even pretended that he was pestering her with his kisses: "Lord, you don't give me a moment's peace! The moment he sees me alone, he heads straight for me." And this gave her special joy: "It means he loves me, it means he's all mine, if I can talk to him like that." And there was another happy thing: expressing her jealousy to him, her right to him.

"Thank God there's no work going on in the threshing barn, otherwise there'd be girls there and I'd show you how to go and watch them," she would say.

And she would add, suddenly embarrassed, with a touching attempt at a smile, "Am I not enough for you?"

Winter arrived early. After some periods of fog, a freezing northern wind came in and froze the oily bumps on the roads, turned the earth to stone, and killed the last bits of grass in the garden and courtyard. Whitish, leaden clouds appeared, and the completely bare garden rustled hurriedly and uneasily as if running away somewhere; at night a white half-moon bobbed up and down in puffs of clouds. The estate and village seemed hopelessly poor and crude. Then a light snow began to fall, whitening the frozen mud as if with powdered sugar, and the estate, and the fields visible from it, turned into a bluish-white expanse. In the village they were winding up their work—tossing potatoes into cellars for the winter, sorting them, and discarding the rotten ones. One day he happened to put on a fur hat and a coat lined with fox fur and go for a walk in the village. The northern wind ruffled his moustache and burned his cheeks. A gloomy sky hung above everything, and the bluish-white sloping field beyond the river seemed very close. In the village by the doorways lay pieces of burlap with piles of potatoes on them. Old women and young girls bundled up in hemp shawls and tattered jackets and wearing worn-out felt boots, their faces and hands blue from the cold, sat working on the burlap. "Their legs are totally bare under their skirts!" he thought, horrified.

When he got home, she was standing in the entrance hall, wiping the steaming samovar with a piece of cloth to bring it to the table, and immediately she said in a low voice, "I suppose you've been to the village; the girls there are sorting potatoes . . . Well, go on, go on and have fun, find the prettiest one for yourself!"

And holding back her tears, she dashed into the main entrance hall.

Toward evening it started to snow really heavily and, rushing past him in the parlor, she glanced at him and whispered teasingly, with irrepressible child-like mirth: "Well, are you going to get your fill of fun now? It's going to get even worse—the dogs are rolling about in the yard—there's going to be such a storm you won't be able to even stick your nose out of the house!"

"Lord," he thought, "where will I find the courage to tell her that I'm about to leave?"

And he got a terrible longing to be in Moscow as soon as possible. Freezing cold weather, snowstorms, a pair of grey horses with bells lightly resounding on the square opposite the Iversksy Chapel, the electric lights high up on the lampposts on Tverskaya in the whirling snowstorm . . . In the Bolshoi Theater the chandeliers are sparkling, the music of string instruments is flowing, and here he is, tossing his snow-covered fur coat to the doormen and wiping his moustache, wet with snow, with a handkerchief, walking briskly, as was his habit, on the red carpet into the warm, crowded hall, into the din of voices, into the smell of food and cigarettes, to the fussing footmen and the now dissolutely languishing, now rollickingly stormy music of the string instruments which drowned out everything.

All during supper he could not lift his eyes and look at her tranquil face, her carefree bustling.

Late in the evening he put on felt boots and the late Mr. Kazakov's raccoon coat, pulled his hat down over his ears and went out through the back porch into the blizzard—to get a breath of fresh air and watch the storm. But a big snowdrift had already piled up to the overhang of the porch; he fell down and got his sleeves full of snow, and then it was really hell—white rushing madness. Sinking into the snow, he made his way around the house to the front porch with difficulty and, stomping his feet and shaking off the snow, he ran into the dark outer entrance hall, which was humming from the storm, and then into the warm entrance hall, where the candle was burning on the wooden chest. She jumped out from behind the partition barefoot, in the same cotton skirt, and threw up her hands. "Lord! Where did you come from?!"

He threw his cap and the fur coat on the trunk, sprinkling snow all over it and, in a mad moment of rapture and tenderness, grasped her hands. Overcome with the same rapture, she freed herself, grabbed a broom and began to brush off his felt boots, white with snow, and pull them off. "Lord, they're full of snow too! You'll catch your death of cold."

At night in his sleep he sometimes heard a monotonous sound and a monotonous pressure on the house; then it would blow violently and strike the shutters with a rattling sound, shaking them and making the snow fall off, and lull you to sleep . . . The night seemed endless and sweet—the warmth of the bed, the warmth of the old house, alone in the white mass of the rushing sea of snow.

In the morning it seemed to him that the night wind was blowing the shutters open with a bang and pounding them into the walls; he opened his eyes—no, it was already light, and whiteness, whiteness, piled up to the very windowsills, was peering from everywhere into the windows covered in snow, and its white reflection was on the ceiling. The storm was still raging, the snow was swirling, but now more quietly, as it had during the day. From his position on the divan he could see opposite him two windows with small, square double frames that had darkened and cracked with time; the third, to the left of the head of the bed, was the whitest and brightest of all. Its white reflection was playing on the ceiling, and in a corner of the room the damper in the stove droned and made tapping sounds as the growing fire was drawn up into it. How nice, he slept and did not hear anything, and Tanya, his faithful and beloved Tanyechka, had opened the shutters, quietly entered the room in her felt boots, feeling cold all over, her shoulders and head bundled up in a hemp shawl and covered with snow and, kneeling down, had stoked the fire. And before he had time to think, she entered, this time without her shawl, carrying a tray with tea. Placing the tray on the nightstand by the head of the divan, with a barely perceptible smile she glanced at his clear, sleepy morning eyes that had the surprised look of someone just half awake.

"Why are you sleeping so late?"

"What time is it?"

She looked at the clock on the nightstand and didn't answer right away—she still couldn't tell time easily. "Ten, ten minutes to nine . . ."

He looked at the door and pulled her toward him by her skirt. She moved aside and pushed back his hand. "There's no way we can—everyone's awake."

"Oh, just for a minute!"

"The old lady will come in . . ."

"No one will come in—just for one minute!"

"Oh, what a pest you are!"

Quickly removing her boots, one after the other, from her feet in wool stockings, she lay down and looked back at the door . . . Oh, that peasant smell of her hair, her breathing, the apple-like coolness of her cheeks! He whispered angrily, "You're kissing again with your lips pressed together. When will I break you of this habit?!"

"I'm no lady . . . Wait, I'll get a bit lower . . . Well, hurry up, I'm scared to death."

And they gazed into each other's eyes—intently and vacantly, expectantly.

"Petrusha . . ."

"Quiet. Why do you always talk at times like this!"

"Well, when am I supposed to talk to you if not at times like this! I won't press my lips together any more . . . Swear that you don't have anyone in Moscow . . ."

"Don't squeeze my neck like that."

"No one will ever love you like I do. Here you've gone and fallen in love with me, and it's like I've fallen in love with myself—I couldn't be happier . . . But if you leave me . . ."

Her face flushed, she ran out into the snowstorm and under the overhang of the back porch and, sheltered there, crouched down for a moment and then rushed headlong through the white whirling snow onto the front porch, sinking into the snow to above her bare knees.

The entrance hall smelled of the samovar. The old maidservant was sitting on the trunk under the high window covered with snow and sipping tea from a saucer and, without stopping, looked at her askance. "Where in the dickens have you been? You're all covered with snow."

"I was serving Pyotr Nikolayevich his tea."

"And did you serve him tea in the servants' quarters? We know what your 'tea' means!"

"Well, so you know, and you're welcome. Has the mistress gotten up?"

"Now you've thought of her! She was up before you."

"Oh, you're always angry!"

And sighing happily, she went behind the partition to get her cup, and there she began to sing barely audibly:

> When I go out to the garden,
> To the green garden,
> To the green garden for a stroll,
> To meet my beloved . . .

In the afternoon, while sitting with a book in the study and listening to the same noise—now weakening, now intensifying menacingly—around the house which was sinking deeper and deeper into the snow amidst the milky whiteness flying at it from all sides, he thought, "As soon as it subsides, I'll leave."

In the evening he seized a moment to tell her to come to his room a bit later that night, when everyone would be sound asleep, and stay the night until morning. She shook her head, thought for a moment, and said, "Fine." This was terribly frightening, but all the sweeter.

He felt the same way too. And his pity for her also troubled him; and she did not even know that this was their last night!

During the night he would fall asleep, then wake up feeling anxious: would she decide to come? The darkness of the house, the noise surrounding this darkness, the rattling shutters, the howling in the stove every now and then . . . Suddenly he awoke in fright: he did not hear—it was impossible to hear her because of the way she moved, with the caution of a criminal, through the house in the deep darkness; it was impossible, he did not hear her but sensed that she was already there, invisible, standing by the divan. He reached out for her. Silently, she dove under the blanket and joined him. He heard her heart beating, felt her frozen bare feet, and whispered the most passionate words that he could find and say.

For a long time they lay like that, face to face, kissing so hard that their teeth ached. She remembered that he did not want her to keep her lips pressed together and, trying to please him, she would open them like a baby jackdaw.

"You probably haven't slept at all?"

She answered in a happy whisper, "Not for a minute, I kept waiting . . ."

He groped for some matches on the night table and lit a candle. Terrified, she gasped, "Petrusha, what are you doing? And what if the old lady wakes up and sees the light . . . ?"

"To hell with her," he said looking at her flushed face. "To hell with her, I want to see you . . ."

He held her in his arms and did not take his eyes off her. She whispered, "I'm afraid—why are you looking at me like that?"

"Because there's no one more beautiful in the world than you. This sweet head of yours with the small braid wound around it like that of a young Venus."

Her eyes began to sparkle with laughter and happiness. "Who's this Venus?"

"Well, she's. . . . And this simple shift . . ."

"Why don't you buy me a calico one . . . I guess you really love me a lot?"

"I don't love you at all. And again, you smell either like a quail or dried hemp . . ."

"And why do you like that? And you said I always talk at times like this . . . and now . . . you're talking yourself."

She started to press him even closer to herself; she wanted to tell him something more, but no longer could.

Then he blew out the candle and lay quietly for a long time, smoking and thinking: "All the same, I have to tell her, it's terrible, but I have to!" And he began speaking, his voice barely audible, "Tanyechka . . ."

"What?" she asked him just as mysteriously.

"I have to leave, you know . . ."

She even sat up. "When?"

"Actually soon . . . very soon . . . I have some things to do that can't be put off . . ."

She collapsed on the pillow. "Oh, Lord!"

Those things of his, somewhere there in some kind of Moscow, filled her with something like awe. But nevertheless, how could she part with him because of those things? And she fell silent and quickly and helplessly searched her mind for a way out of this insoluble horror. There was no way out. She felt like shouting, "Take me with you!" But she did not dare—was it really possible?

"I can't stay here forever . . ."

She listened and agreed, "Yes, yes."

"I can't take you with me . . ."

Suddenly she uttered in despair, "Why not?"

He quickly thought, "Yes, why not, why not?" And he quickly responded, "I don't have a home, Tanya. I've traveled from place to place my whole life. In Moscow I live in hotel rooms . . . And I'll never marry anyone."

"Why not?"

"Because I was born that way."

"And you'll never marry anyone?"

"No one, never. And I give you my word, I have to go, honest to God, I have very important, urgent business. I'll return by Christmas without fail!"

She pressed her head against him, lay a while, her warm tears falling on him, and whispered, "Well, I'll go . . . It's going to start getting light soon . . ."

And getting up, she began to make the sign of the cross over him in the darkness: "May the Heavenly Tsaritsa, the Mother of God, protect you!"

After running back to her room behind the partition, she sat down on her bed and, pressing her arms to her breasts and licking the tears from her lips, she began to whisper to the din of the storm in the outer entrance hall: "God our Father! Heavenly Tsaritsa! O Lord, grant that it not quiet down for at least another two days."

Two days later he left—the subsiding whirlwinds were still blowing about the yard, but he could no longer prolong his and her secret torment and did not succumb to Mme. Kazakova's attempts to persuade him to wait until at least the next day.

Both the house and the whole estate became deserted, dead. And it was impossible to imagine Moscow and him in it, his life there, and those things he had to do there.

He did not come for Christmas. What days those were! In what anguish of unsettled expectations, in what self-delusion that she was not waiting for anything did the time pass from morning till night! And during the whole Yuletide season she wore her best outfit—the dress and ankle boots she was wearing when he met her in the fall at the train station on that unforgettable evening

On Epiphany she was convinced for some reason that at any moment a peasant's sleigh, which he would hire at the station, would appear from behind the hills, since he had not sent a letter asking them to send horses for him; all day she did not get up from the trunk in the entrance hall and watched the yard until her eyes hurt. The house was empty—Mme. Kazakova had left to visit some neighbors, and the old maidservant had dinner in the servants' quarters and stayed there after dinner, delighting in passing malicious gossip to the cook. But she did not even go to dinner, said she had a stomach ache . . .

And then evening began to fall. She looked again at the empty yard covered with shiny, encrusted snow and, getting up, said to herself resolutely, "That's it, I don't need anyone else, I don't want to wait for anything!" And all dressed up, she strolled down the hall and through the parlor bathed in the light of the yellow, winter twilight coming through the windows, and began to sing loudly and lightheartedly— relieved that life was over and done with.

> When I go out to the garden,
> To the green garden,
> To the green garden for a stroll,
> To meet my beloved . . .

And precisely at the words about her beloved she walked into the study, saw his empty divan, the empty armchair beside the desk where he used to sit with a book in his hands, and fell into the chair and put her head on the desk, sobbing and wailing, "Heavenly Tsaritsa, send me death!"

He came in February—when she had already buried all hope of seeing him just one more time in her life.

And it was as if everything that had been before had come back.

He was shocked when he saw her—she had become so thin and pale; her eyes were so timid and sad. She, too, was taken aback initially because he seemed different to her: older, unfamiliar, and even unpleasant—his mustache seemed to have grown bigger, his voice coarser, his laughter and talking in the entrance hall while he was taking off his coat overly loud and unnatural; she found it awkward to look into his eyes . . . But both tried to conceal all this from one another, and soon everything seemed to go on as before.

Then that terrible time began to draw near again—the time of his new departure. He swore to her on an icon that he would return by Holy Week and then, for the whole summer. She believed him but thought: "And what's going to happen in the summer? The same thing as now?" This "now" was not enough for her—she absolutely needed either all that was before and not just a repetition, or a shared life with him, without separations, without new torments, without the shame of futile expectations. But she tried to drive away these thoughts, tried to imagine all the happiness in the summer when they would have so much freedom everywhere . . . at night and during the day, in the garden, in the field, in the barn; and he would be beside her for a long, long time . . .

On the eve of his new departure the night was already spring-like, bright and breezy. Beyond the house, the garden was rustling, and from there, carried by the wind, came the fierce, helpless, intermittent barking of the dogs at the edge of the pit in the fir grove. There was a fox there that Mme. Kazakova's forester had caught in a trap and brought to the master's yard.

He lay on the divan with his eyes closed. She lay on her side next to him, her hand under her sad, little head. Both were silent. Finally she whispered, "Petrusha, are you asleep?"

"No, why?"

"Well, you don't love me anymore, you've ruined me for nothing," she said calmly.

"Why for nothing? Don't talk nonsense."

"You'll have a sin on your conscience. Where can I go now?"

"Why do you have to go anywhere?"

"Well, you'll go to that Moscow of yours yet again, but what am I going to do here by myself?"

"The same as you've done before. And then—I've already given you my word: During Holy Week I'll come back for the whole summer."

"Yes, maybe you'll come back . . . Only before you didn't say words to me like, 'And why do you have to go anywhere?' You truly loved me and said you'd never seen anyone prettier than me. Was I really like that?"

"Yes, not like this," he thought. "You've changed terribly. You've gotten thinner—I can hear your bones rattling . . ."

"My time has passed," she said. "I used to slip in to see you—and be deathly afraid and joyful at the same time: well, thank God, the old woman has fallen asleep. And now I'm not even afraid of her."

He shrugged his shoulders. "I don't understand you. Give me my cigarettes on the night table . . ."

She handed them to him. He lit up. "I don't understand what's wrong with you. You're simply not well . . ."

"That's probably why you don't think I'm pretty any more. What am I sick with?"

"You don't understand me. I'm saying that you're not well emotionally. Because just look at what's happened: why do you think I don't love you anymore? And why do you have to keep repeating, 'it used to be, it used to be' . . ."

She did not answer. The window was shining, the garden was rustling, and the intermittent barking could be heard—angry, hopeless, whining . . . She slid off the divan without a sound and, pressing her sleeve to her eyes and her head shaking, she walked quietly in her grey wool stockings toward the door leading to the parlor. He called her softly and sternly, "Tanya."

She turned around and answered, barely audibly, "What do you want?"

"Come here."

"What for?"

"I told you, come here."

She approached him obediently, her head down so that he would not see that her whole face was covered with tears.

"Well, what do you want?"

"Sit down and stop crying. Kiss me. Well?"

He sat down, she sat next to him and embraced him, weeping quietly. "My God, what am I going to do!" he thought in despair. "Again those warm, childish tears on this hot, childish face . . . She doesn't even suspect the full extent of my love for her! But what can I do? Take her with me? Where to? For what kind of life? And what would come of it? To tie myself down, ruin myself forever?" And he began to whisper rapidly, feeling his own tears tickling his nose and lips. "Tanyechka, my joy, don't cry, listen: I'll return in the spring for the whole summer, and then we'll really go into 'the green garden'—I heard your song and I'll never forget it. We'll ride into the forest in the carriage—remember how we rode in the carriage from the station?"

"No one will let me go with you!" she whispered bitterly, shaking her head lying on his chest, using the familiar form of "you" to him for the first time. "And you won't go anywhere with me . . ."

But he already heard timid joy and hope in her voice.

"I will, I will, Tanyechka. And don't you dare to use the formal "you" with me anymore. And don't you dare cry . . ."

He placed his hands under her legs in wool stockings and lifted her light body up onto his lap. "Now say, 'Petrusha, I love you very much'!"

Hiccupping from crying, she repeated dully, "I love you very much . . ."

This was in February of the horrific year 1917. He was then in the countryside for the last time in his life.

22 October 1940

NOTES

1. When he addresses her here and during most of the story, he uses the familiar singular form of "you" (*ty*); she uses the formal plural form (*vy*). This is in keeping with the master-servant relationship.

THE TENANTS

Andrei Sinyavsky (pseud. Abram Terts)

Oh my, Sergei Sergeyevich, Sergei Sergeyevich! Do you really think you're Nikolai Nikolayevich's equal? That's even funny. You're nothing special when it comes to looks, and your biceps have grown flabby just like—please forgive the comparison—nipples on a small emaciated dog. And you start guzzling cognac in the morning—only, where does the money come from? But Kolya, that is, Nikolai Nikolayevich, was a young looking man, an engineer—a builder of electric engines, twenty-nine years old, in the prime of his life. And even he couldn't cope. One day he calls me into the kitchen. "What's," he asks, "what's happening, Nikodim Petrovich?" he asks. And he's totally white. Like the ceiling.

There's no comparison between you, Sergei Sergeyevich, and him! He was a songster! An athlete! He'd wake up early in the morning, do all his calisthenics to the radio, brush his teeth, and start singing:

> Ever higher, and higher, and higher,
> We direct the flight of our birds,
> In each propeller there breathes
> The tranquility of our frontiers.[1]

It's a pleasure to listen to him. Even though he's a tenor and I prefer a bass voice. Believe an old man, get away from here. While you're still in one piece. A small suitcase in your hand and God be with you. If you like, I'll write a note for you, using my personal connections. To the city housing department, to Shestopalov himself. You really haven't heard of him? Shestopalov. He decides housing questions. I reported to him for thirteen years. I was in charge of a student dormitory and two apartment houses. A superintendent or house manager—call me what you will. Until I retired. On Ordynka Street. Five and six stories. He can find any amount of floor space in five minutes. Of course, of course! Through my intercession . . . !

You'll feel at home in your new place. We'll leave your library here temporarily. I'll keep an eye on it. I'll do some reading, with your permission. You wouldn't happen to have *A Boer Boy of the Transvaal?*[2] I was reading it before the war. Don't remember the author. Some foreigner, a Frenchman.

It's a pity, a real pity. The nights are long and my legs ache. Rheumatoid arthritis. A basic chronic illness. What's that? Pour it, pour it; it won't do any harm.

To your health!

Hmm, yes-s . . . Your cognac is truly of the most select grade, just what the doctor ordered. It caresses the throat going down. I'll become a drunk like you. No, no, don't trouble yourself, I don't like to eat anything when I drink. The whole aftertaste is lost. Really, Sergei Sergeyevich, move to another apartment. Here, speaking confidentially . . . You'll moan and groan when you find out, but it'll be too late. Why do you keep saying, "I won't go, I just won't go." That's just laziness on your part and nothing else. And then, before you know it, I'll be right there behind you. We'll get a place together. If you don't want to get in touch with Shestopalov, we can arrange an exchange. Let's place an ad. My room plus yours comes to thirty-one meters. And there you are, a separate apartment! OK?

I'll create the right living conditions for you as a writer. So there's quiet, order. I, too, need peace. Perhaps you'll still be able to marry, and we'll raise some grandkids and kittens. I'd stay with them. As a grandfather. We'll wipe the thought of cognac totally out of our heads. Perhaps just on major holidays: New Year's, the First of May.[3] We'll set up our household. *Der tisch, das shrank,*[4] and we'll buy me some new felt boots. Oh, and we'll really start to live! Let's have a drink, what do you say?

To your health, Sergei Sergeyevich.

Frankly speaking, do you know why I became friends with him, with Kolya, that is? He's a good guy, thrifty, handy around the house. As soon as he comes from work, he starts doing something. He made a bookcase with a coping saw and assembled a radio receiver out of almost nothing. With his own hands. And I also liked his Ninochka at first. She bustles about like a bird. She brings everything home, everything. Half a year hadn't passed—would you believe it?—and they already bought a new wardrobe. With a full length mirror on the door. They hung lace curtains. And on twenty-five, thirty rubles a pay period, a kopeck at a time you could say, they created their family hearth. And everything came to naught. Oh, Kolya! Kolya! Where are you now, who's kissing your fingers . . . ? Ye-es! In a home for the mentally ill. In a madhouse, to use an expression from the old days. But is that really a home? It's just the semblance of a home—it's nothing but a dormitory for madmen.

What's that? How did it start? It started with something trivial. He's eating a bowl of pea soup one evening and suddenly fishes out—can you imagine?—some woman's hair. An ordinary tuft of a woman's hair and nothing more. To put it in village terms, "combings." He turns to his Ninochka, of course, and asks her rather calmly what one is to make of that. She gets all red and says, also rather calmly, "That's Krovatkina, Kolya dear," she says, "putting her hair in our pot instead of meat."

And the hair, incidentally, is grey. Grey . . .

Sh! And so I ask you, Sergei Sergeyevich, would you happen to have that interesting book, Fenimore Cooper, *The Last of the Mohicans*? Yes! *The Last of the Mohicans*! About the Indians of South America! Yes, yes, yes! So you don't have it! You don't! What rainy weather! The weather, I say, is rainy. . . !"

She's left . . . That's her all right, Krovatkina herself. A real witch. She puts her ear to the door and checks on what we're talking about. I sense her, I know her. If I say so, that means I do know! I have my own feel for this. I wasn't born yesterday. I can guess their intrigues with my back turned. From ten meters away.

What do you mean? What kind of tricks can there be here? If you don't believe me, I can prove it. Right now, at this moment, I'll turn my back to you and won't be able to see anything, but I'll guess everything. Every movement or gesture.

Aha-ha-ha! My legs don't feel like my own. All right! Begin.

Tsk-tsk. At this very moment you're picking your nose. With your little finger. Now you've stopped. You've grabbed your left ear. You're sticking out your lower lip. So, have I guessed? Hee-hee. Oh, you're a joker. What a pantomime you've put on behind me! He thinks I won't find out. Stuck out his tongue, wrinkled his brow . . . And your eyes, Sergei Sergeyevich, are really squinting. You're tipsy. This potion has overpowered you.

Well, that's enough for today. That's not all I can do. But now—let's have one last drink—and off to bed. It's late already. What will the neighbors think?

No, no. And don't even ask. I'll tell the rest some other time. That Krovatkina interrupted me. The whole mood was spoiled. Better yet, why don't I do something in parting? This very moment—if you like—I'll disappear without leaving this place. I'll up and vanish into thin air. One, two, three! I was here and now I'm go-o-ne!

Good night, Sergei Sergeyevich!

2

. . . In this way soon only the *rusalkas*[5] were left. And even they . . . You know yourself: industrialization of natural resources. Make way for technology! Streams, rivers, and lakes became permeated with the smell of all kinds of chemicals. Methylhydrate, toluene. Fish—they'd simply die and go belly up. And they, the *rusalkas,* would pop out of the water, clear their nostrils as best they could, and you wouldn't believe the tears of grief and disappointment that poured from their eyes. I saw it myself. Everywhere on their voluptuous bosoms there is ringworm, eczema and even—forgive my lack of delicacy—signs of recurrent venereal diseases.

Where can you hide?

Without much thought, they followed the wood spirits and witches to the city, to the capital. Along the Moscow-Volga Canal, through those very sluices to the water supply network, where it's a bit cleaner and there's more to eat. Farewell, native land, primordial conditions!

How many of them perished here! Countless numbers. Of course, not forever. They're immortal beings, after all. Nothing can be done about it. But some of them have more flesh on them—they would get stuck in the water pipes. But you've probably heard them yourself. You turn on the kitchen faucet—suddenly sobbing resounds from there, all kinds of floundering about, swearing. You wonder—whose antics are they? It's their voices—the *rusalkas'*. One gets stuck in the wash-basin and starts being capricious and sneezing!

Incidentally, one former *rusalka* lives quite easily and freely in our apartment. According to her passport, she's Sofya Frantsevna Vinter. You know her, of course. Runs around in her flannel bathrobe and does her water treatments from morning to night. First she bathes for three hours on end in the bathroom (other inhabitants don't have a place to wash their hands), then she perches on the wash basin and sings verses about a Lorelei. In German:

> Ich weiss nicht was soll es bedeuten,
> Das ich so traurig bin . . .[6]

Heinrikh Heine composed that. I said to her yesterday: "Sofa! You should at least have some shame in front of the new tenant. He's a writer, after all. But you run around the hallway wearing only a bathrobe—unbuttoned, untied—and every time you move, you throw it open half a meter."

But she, that shameless girl, only grins. "Your writer," she says, "gave me 'White Lilac.' That's a perfume. I've had an understanding with him, grandpa, from the moment we laid eyes on each other."

Watch out, Sergei Sergeyevich. God forbid you start courting her. She'll tickle you to death. And as for anything more fundamental, I'll put it this way: she has fish blood in her and the rest of her is fish. Only her appearance is womanly, to tempt men . . .

Here you go laughing again and not believing anything. And although you're a writer, you have no powers of observation whatsoever. Well, what can you say, for example, about Anchutker? Your neighbor. Anchutker. Right here, behind this wall. Nothing special. A citizen like any other. Except perhaps that he's a Jew. Moisei Iyekhelevich. So what! Karl Marx must have descended from Jews too.

But if you take a closer look, a more careful one . . . ? What a head of hair he has! Have you ever seen such animal hair on a man in your life? And the color of his face? Where will you find a man with skin so blue? And he doesn't have a happy look, his shoes are size twelve and, what's more, they're always mixed up: the right shoe is on the left foot, and the left on the right.[7] He walks around like that, an uncivil bear, both at home and at the ministry.

Furthermore, note what literature he's reading. Korolenko's[8] "The Rustling Forest," Leonid Leonov's new novel, *The Russian Forest*.[9] I don't deny it—the novel is remarkable. But why, I ask you, does it always have to be on that subject? And why does he, that damn Anchutker, work in the forestry department? He counts birches and fir trees with his slide rule and changes them to cubic meters . . . And he's not Anchutker at all, but correctly, in scholarly terms, Anchutka.[10] Now you're getting it! Exactly!

No, Sergei Sergeyevich, you won't find a single living person among our tenants. Even though they're my kinfolk. From one village, so to say. Oh, what's the use! My reputation is worth more. It's ignoramuses and semi-literate women lacking in culture who say a house spirit is the same as a wood spirit. You're wrong! It's an entirely different profession. It's impossible not to see principal differences when it comes to this question. A house spirit—he's gotten used to a home, to warmth, to human smells. From time immemorial. He isn't the same as devils and witches. Perhaps you think they have a common nature? I wouldn't say so! What does nature matter? Man, for example, is also descended from an ape. However, he subsequently emerged as a separate species. He deals with apes only in Africa and in zoos. How can I—I!—an elderly man, so to say, live in communal conditions?!

As soon as they moved into our apartment—Nikolai Nikolayevich and Ninochka—I said to them right away, "Kolya!" I said. "Ninochka! Be on your guard. Don't give in to provocation. Keep your distance. And I'll warm myself by your side in my old age."

"No!" Ninochka answers. "He who lives with wolves learns to howl like a wolf.[11] I won't forget that story with Krovatkina and the pea soup. She steals our meat and I'm supposed to chew her hair? What's more, it's grey and dirty. You can catch an infection from it."

And she orders her Nikolasha to put steel padlocks on all their pots. To lock the food, in effect, while it's cooking on the communal stove and no one's watching it. There were times when she'd steal up to the stove on tip-toe, open the pot as quickly as possible, add some salt and butter, and lock it up again.

Only that didn't help. Perverse things continued to happen. For example, she starts cooking a chicken and attaches the locks. Opens it—a dead cat has cooked in the chicken broth. Not even skinned—fur, tail, and all.

Ninochka took offense. In the meantime another neighbor, Avdotiya Vasiutkina, had enticed Ninochka to her side. An alliance was formed. Avdotiya and Krovatkina have their own personal accounts to settle: they can't work out how to share Anchutker. Both have children by Anchutker. Little wood goblins, I mean. And so they fight, the female enemies, over their witch's love for Anchutker.

Can you picture the scene? The kitchen. There's a fearful commotion. In the smoke these witches are swaying back and forth and gripping each other's disheveled locks. They spit at each other at close range. They say bad words very clearly, "Witch! Trollop!"

"You're the witch! Where did you go for a ride in the toilet bowl last night?"[12]

Small blue-bellied children are scrambling about underfoot. Trying to bite the calves of the opposing side. They're still small but have claws and rather large teeth.

And, just imagine, Ninochka is there too. Her nice hair is tousled. Her little eyes are blazing like the bulbs in a flashlight. There's a rolling pin in her hands, and her little chicken ribs are shaking and heaving under her torn blouse.

I saw this picture and for the first time started to cry. Can I, an old man, control three raging women? I run around and beg. "Shoo!" I scream, "To your corners! Otherwise I'll call the police." They don't even want to listen. There's groaning in the whole dwelling, stomping, and the thundering of pans. And what's more, in the bathroom the *rusalka* Sofa can't stop laughing hysterically . . .

In the evening I say to Nikolai, "Here's what. Quiet down your Ninochka. It won't end well. You'll see. Take off her woolen knickers and give her a few light strokes with some birch twigs like a good husband so that she doesn't meddle in other people's fights."

How can you say that? He even got offended. "I'll," he says, "appeal to the Supreme Soviet, but I won't leave it like that. Krovatkina should be taken to court. She's a fascist. She insults my wife both in word and deed. And Ninochka has never laid a finger on anyone in her young life . . ."

Kolya, the simple soul, loved her, loved her madly. And so it all began for them . . .

Sergei Sergeyevich, sit still. Don't move. Do you see a rat running around under the bed? Take off your shoe quietly and hit it. Just don't miss. Otherwise it'll get away. Come on! Any second now it'll show itself again. So throw it! At its head. Kill it on the spot. G-go! . . .

Oh, you've missed! Hit it, Seryozha! Grab it! Get it with the bottle! The bottle . . .

Boy, you're an inept man . . . I told you, the bottle. Gosh! Even your legs are trembling. Your nerves are totally shattered . . .

And do you know, Sergei Sergeyevich, who that was? That was

Ninochka, you know, who came to see us . . . She misses her Nikolasha. And so she comes to her old place, our Ninochka.

3

Don't be scared—I didn't knock. It's something that can't wait. There's trouble. Sergei Sergeyevich! Trouble! That Krovatkina sniffed it all out and told Anchutka. What's going to happen to us now? What's going to happen?!

Listen, I can't be found in your room. Especially looking like this. The tenants might notice. As it is, I came in through a crack. Squeezed under the door. At my age . . .

Just a minute! I'll disguise myself a bit right now, and then we'll talk.

What do you have around here that would work? Aha! Let me be a drinking glass. And you sit at the table as if you're drinking. If someone looks in, talk to yourself. Let them think you're drunk. It's less dangerous that way.

Come, come here! I'm already on the table. You see, you had three glasses and now you have four. No, not that one! How unobservant you are, truly! Here I am, here! Near the plate.

Ow! Don't touch me with your hands! You could drop and break me. My bones ache as it is.

Sergei Sergeyevich, concentrate and hear me out in all seriousness. Our situation couldn't be worse. We've been discovered. An investigation is being conducted. Anchutker has stopped saying hello to me as of yesterday. I know they want to put me on trial. For disclosing their secrets. Tomorrow at twelve midnight a Council will be called in the kitchen. Everything would seem to be all right, but Shestopalov is unhappy with me. He's issued an order. "We," he says, "trusted him, but he meets with alien elements from time to time. We forgave him the incident with the newlyweds," he says, "so now he's forming a friendship again with someone he's not supposed to. And his new friend, a writer, writes down everything he says. That could lead to all kinds of unpleasantness. Punish the chatterbox so as to teach others not to try it. We'll take care of the writer separately. It's a good thing that he's an alcoholic—soon he'll think he's seeing real devils."

Do you understand, Sergei Sergeyevich, what this means?! They'll separate us. Take the last human away from me. Deprive me of a roof over my head. Send me under the floor. Into the dampness, into the cold, among the microorganisms. Or they'll send me head first through the sewer system. And I'll be forced to circulate there until the end of the world. Like the Eternal Jew called Agasfer.[13] Have you read the novel of the same name by Eugene Sue?[14] Exactly. The same way. From bathroom to bathroom.

And you're in for it too. They'll surround you with ugly mugs, frightful old hags, and vampires. It'll be terrifying. You'll drink more than ever. And the more you drink, the more terrifying it'll get. Until you go out of your mind like poor Nikolai Nikolayevich!

We need to escape. Everything's been seen to. Tomorrow at half past eleven I'll show up and get you. Right before the holiday begins, right before the Great Kitchen Council. Be ready. They'll be waiting for guests, getting all dressed up. They'll start preparing appetizers. Made of carrion and rotten eggs. Maybe in the commotion their control will weaken. At that moment put me in your pocket (I'll try to fit in there somehow), put a coat over you so that I don't catch a chill from the wind, and with a quick step go outside. As if you've had a bit to drink and decided to take a walk, to get some fresh air.

In the beginning we'll live in a hotel. And later, we'll arrange for a house or an apartment. Without tenants or neighbors. We'll be our own masters. "Neither God, nor Tsar, nor hero is needed!"[15]

An icon can be hung, as a preventive measure, just in case. Don't let it make you uncomfortable—I've gotten used to it, I was raised in a village. Those superstitions are widespread among the common people.

You don't want an icon, your convictions won't allow it? We'll make do with a simple reproduction. We'll cut out a Raphael painting of a child from *General History* and stick it in a prominent place. It also works well against the unclean force and the evil eye. And it's totally appropriate, progressive. It's art, after all. You can't find fault with it.

The main thing, Sergei Sergeyevich, is to stick together. I'll never ever be able to get out of here without your, without your human help. I can walk about the premises as much as I like. If I feel like it—on the walls, if I feel like it—on the ceiling. But not a step beyond the threshold. Laws of physiology don't permit it.

And you—I'm not going to be modest—will perish without me. But with me—God willing—you'll have world fame. Charles Dickens. Mayne Reid.[16] I know—I know everything, you're such a cunning one.

I—walk in the door and you—pick up your pen. Even when you're not quite yourself and can't speak well . . .

So what are they, our chats! A meager fraction. I have a whole *Decameron*[17] of these fables. And everything's based on my personal experience. It could be published in five volumes. With illustrations. You and I, Sergei Sergeyevich, we'll outdo the Brothers Grimm.[18]

Ow-w! What are you doing? Why are you pouring cognac into me? I'll choke, choke! Rinse out my mouth, immediately . . .

You sure have given me a fright, Sergei Sergeyevich. Bear in mind, not even a tiny bit tomorrow. Not one little drop! Be careful, vigilant. Both in word and deed. Refrain from cutting phrases with allusions, please. Because you know what happens. Did you see Ninochka yesterday? Well, yes, Ninochka in her rat form. Now she'll stay that way . . . Can't change her back.

Kolya put up with it and put up with it, and then one day he said all of a sudden, "Go to hell, Ninochka! I'm sick of these scandals."

And as soon as he pronounced those fateful words, Anchutker walked into their room. Seemingly to get something, a cigarette. And he looks intently at Ninochka, and Ninochka looks at Anchutker, and at that very moment they take a real liking to each other.

By that time Ninochka was not what she had been. Her hair had gotten thin, her eyes had become sunken, and her stomach was just the opposite—it now bulged out. From inner malice. And her behind, you know, also grew noticeably. In a word, she suited his taste, and meetings, pinching, gentle grabbing, and the rest began between them. She turned into a total witch. Made peace with Krovatkina. Even began learning how to fly in the toilet bowl at night. Like a rocket engine. With the help of intestinal gas.

And when Nikolai Nikolayevich was taken away to the insane asylum, her cohabitant abandoned her. Abandoned her in her pregnant state. And so as not to pay alimony and stop Avdotiya's jealousy, she was turned into a silent creature of appropriate substance. She later gave birth to a bunch of little rats in her rat hole. She bore seven of them.

Perhaps she should be pitied. But personally I see a real allegory in these facts. She undermined moral principles—it serves her right! And it's a great pity really that you didn't hit her in the head with your shoe. There would've been a direct benefit and just retribution. For Nikolasha. Like in *Anna Karenina*.[19] He was a good man.

I've gotten carried away talking to you. It seems Shestopalov was right in calling me a chatterbox. You know, it's easy for him to say that! You're cut off from human habitation. Have no one to say a word to. You're silent, silent, for whole days on end. And whole nights on end. Shuffling in your felt boots on the parquet floor.

Enough already. If only we could just get away from here. I know such stories about that Shestopalov! You'll die laughing.

So, it's decided! Until tomorrow then. You give your word? Come on!

I'll leave now the same way I came, without being noticed. Don't be nervous, please. No one saw us, no one heard. It's all hush-hush.

4

Hey!

Sergei Sergeyevich!

It's time!

This is it!

Where are you? Where did you go?

Left? Left without me! Left an old man to be torn to pieces. A homeless old man . . .

What's this? What's this? Lying on the floor? Can he really be dead? Sergei Sergeyevich, my dear man . . . His heart is beating. His eyes are blinking. Wake up! Let's get out of here. Time is running out. They've just phoned. Shestopalov is expected for the festive occasion. Any minute now. They don't care about us right now. The fuss, the preparations.

What have you been doing, Sergei Sergeyevich . . . ? But I thought . . . You should be ashamed of yourself! Even gave your word . . . Found a fine time to do it . . . Couldn't restrain yourself . . .

How can you go down the street looking like that? They'll take you to the police station.

In any case, on your feet! We have four minutes at our disposal. Get up, I'm telling you!

What do you mean you don't have the strength? Your legs won't obey you? Don't fool around!

My dear fellow, let's try together. Make an effort. Grab my neck. Come on! Once more. You sure are heavy, brother. Stop, stop, don't fall down . . . !

Sh-sh-sh-sh! You've gone mad! Making a racket in the whole

apartment. They'll figure it out and come for us. And where will I go? Don't you hear me asking you—what would you have me do?

Well, why are you mumbling? I could care less about your apologies. Do you hear me? Do you . . . ? Krovatkina is putting her ear to the door. We're lost. Now she'll call Anchutker, Shestopalov . . .

Sergei Sergeyevich! My dear son! Save me . . . ! Get up at least on your knees. Here, let me help you. That's it. That's it. Now start praying. I'll support you from behind. I'll hold you up by the shoulders. Start praying! Pray, I tell you, you drunken mug!

What do you mean—you've forgotten? How do I know? It's you who should know. You're the human, not me. And so this is right up your alley. I can't, I'm not supposed to.

How is it, Sergei Sergeyevich, that you live with devils, write stories about devils, but haven't learned how to pray?!

Fine. Do it lying down. Turn on your back. It's high time you realized—this is the last resort. Would I do this at another time?! Put your fingers together. At first to your forehead. Now here . . . Why are you pretending? You're lying! You can snore all you want, but I'm not going to believe it. You're perfectly aware of everything, you understand everything . . . Are you really the devil or something . . . ?

And who else is this? Ah-ah! Ninochka. Hello, Ninochka . . . Don't be afraid, don't be afraid. I won't touch you. I don't care now . . .

Here! Admire this handsome man. Your future husband. The third, if you keep count. You'll settle down in a hole . . . Smell his eyes, smell them. Lick them. He's letting you . . . He can't deal with you now. He feels sick, the room is spinning. And devils are already leaping before his eyes. And rats.

Well, we've been expecting them and here they are. A whole gang of them is coming. They're stomping down the hallway. They'll break in at any moment. They've come for me. And for you too, Sergei Sergeyevich. And for you too. And for you too.

1959

First published in France under the pseudonym of Abram Terts; circulated in the USSR in samizdat in 1960-1965. Published in the Russia in 2003.

NOTES

1. This is the refrain from the "March of the Soviet Air Force," "Vsyo vyshe"; words by P. German, music by Yu. Khait. The first stanza includes the lines, "Reason has given us steel arms-wings, and a fiery engine instead of a heart."
2. *The Boer Boy of the Transvaal: Pieter Maritz, der Buersohn von Transvaal* (1885), a novel by the German author August Niemann (1839-1919), available in an English translation by Kate M. Rabb in 1900.
3. The First of May: International Day of Workers' Solidarity.
4. *Der tisch, das shrank*: "table, mirror." Both *tisch* and *shrank* should be capitalized, but Sinyavsky does not observe this rule of German grammar.
5. *rusalka*: the Russian version of a water nymph. A female demonic being, she represents the spirit of an unbaptized child or, more frequently, a young woman who has died an unnatural death, usually because of unrequited love. In Russia proper her image is that of an evil, malicious, vengeful spirit with a pale face and green hair and eyes. In the south of Russia and Ukraine she is beautiful, with long flowing hair, happy to weave garlands of flowers, sing and dance. *Rusalkas* enjoy luring men into their waters and tickling them to death.
6. German. Literally, "I don't know what it means, that I am so sad." According to German folk legend, Lorelei was a beautiful young maiden who threw herself into the Rhine because of an unfaithful lover. She became one of the many sirens, luring sailors to their death with her singing.
7. This description fits one of the popular folk spirits of the demonic world: the *leshii* or spirit that inhabits woods and forests.
8. Vladimir G. Korolenko (1853-1921): Russian short story writer, known for his descriptions of desolate nature.
9. *The Russian Forest*: a novel about World War II, published in 1953, and highly praised by the authorities. Leonov (1899-1994) received the Lenin Prize for it.
10. Anchutka: this is one of the folk names for the devil, derived from the word "Antichrist."
11. We've kept the literal Russian here because the reader will have no trouble understanding this Russian saying. Dictionaries of Russian idioms give, "When in Rome, do as the Romans do," as the equivalent.
12. The witch Baba Yaga of Russian folklore usually rides in a mortar which she steers with the pestle.
13. Agasfer: Russian name for Ahasuerus, the name given to the "Wandering Jew" from the early 17th century. The Wandering Jew is a figure from medieval Christian folklore. He was portrayed as a man who had taunted Jesus on the way to the cross and was cursed to walk the earth until the Second Coming.
14. Eugene Sue's novel, published in 1844, is really called *Juif Errant* or *The Wandering Jew*.
15. This is the second line of "The Internationale" translated from the French into

Russian by Arkady Yakovlevich Kots (1872-1943): *Nikto ne dast nam izbavleniya* (No one will rescue us) *Ni Bog, ni tsar i ne geroi* (Neither God, nor Tsar, nor hero). "The Internationale" was the Soviet national anthem until 1944.

16. Thomas Mayne Reid: a 19th-century Irish-American writer (1818-1883) of adventure tales and hunting romances.

17. *The Decameron*: a collection of 100 tales written in the 14th century by Giovanni Boccaccio.

18. The Brothers Grimm: Jacob and Wilhelm Grimm, two German professors best known for collecting and publishing folk tales and fairy tales in the first decades of the 19th century.

19. *Anna Karenina*: a novel by Leo Tolstoy in which the heroine, ostracized by society for leaving her husband for her lover, commits suicide by throwing herself under the wheels of a train.

EULOGY

Varlam Shalamov

They all died . . .

Nikolai Kazimirovich Barbe, one of the organizers of the Russian Komsomol, a comrade who had helped me drag a large rock out of a narrow pit, a work brigade boss, was shot because the camp section where Barbe's brigade worked didn't fulfill the plan—according to the report of the young camp section commandant, the young communist Arm. He received a medal for his work in 1938 and later was director of a gold mine, the head of the administration; Arm made a great career for himself. Nikolai Kazimirovich Barbe had one thing which he took special care of: a camel hair scarf, a long, warm, light-blue scarf, real camel wool. Thieves stole it in the bathhouse when Barbe turned away—they simply took it, and that was that. And the next day Barbe got frostbite on his cheeks, bad frostbite—the blisters never healed to the day he died.

Ioska Ryutin died. He was my work partner; the hard workers didn't want to work with me. But Ioska worked with me. He was much stronger and more agile than me. But he understood why they had brought us here. And he didn't resent me for working badly. In the end a senior overseer—the mining ranks used in 1937 were the same as those used in tsarist times—ordered them to give me a "single measure"[1]. . . . And Ioska was paired with somebody else. But our places in the barracks were next to each other, and someone in leather, who smelled of sheep, was moving clumsily and woke me up suddenly. This someone, with his back turned to me in the narrow passageway between the bed boards, was trying to wake up my neighbor: "Ryutin? Get dressed."

And Ioska started to hurry and get dressed, and the man who smelled of sheep began searching through his few things. A chess set was found among his few belongings, and the man in leather put it aside.

"That's mine," Ryutin said quickly. "My property. I paid money for it."

"So what?" the sheepskin said.

"Leave it."

The sheepskin burst out laughing. And when it got tired of laughing and wiped its face with a leather sleeve, it said, "You won't be needing it any more . . ."

Dmitry Nikolayevich Orlov, the former assistant to Kirov, died.[2] He and I sawed wood on the night shift in the mine and, as possessors of a saw, worked during the day in the bakery. I remember well what a critical look the toolsmith and stock keeper gave us when he was issuing the saw, an ordinary crosscut saw.

"Here's what, old man," the toolsmith said. We were all called old men even back then, and not only twenty years later. "Can you sharpen a saw?"

"Of course," Orlov said hurriedly. "Is there a setting block?"

"You can separate the teeth with an ax," said the stock keeper, who realized that we were people who knew what to do, not like those intellectuals.

Orlov walked down the path hunched over, his hands in his sleeves. He held the saw under his arm.

"Listen, Dmitry Nikolayevich," I said, skipping along to catch up with him. "I don't know how. I've never sharpened a saw."

Orlov turned to me, stuck the saw in the snow, and put on his gloves.

"I think," he said in an instructive tone, "that every man with a higher education is obliged to know how to set and sharpen a saw."

I agreed with him.

The economist Semyon Alekseyevich Sheinin, my work partner, a good man, died. For a long time he didn't understand what was being done to us, but finally he understood and waited calmly for death. He had more than enough courage. One day I got a package—the fact that the package reached me was a great rarity—and in it was a pair of felt aviator boots and nothing more. How little did our relatives know about the conditions in which we lived! I knew perfectly well that the boots would be stolen, taken away from me that first night. And I sold them without walking out of the commandant's office for one hundred rubles to Andrei Boyko, a foreman. The boots cost seven-hundred, but I sold them for a good price. I could buy a hundred kilograms of bread, and if not a hundred, then some butter and sugar. The last time I had butter and sugar was in prison. And I bought a whole kilo of butter. I remembered how good it was for you. The butter cost forty-one rubles. I bought it during the day (we worked at night) and ran to Sheinin—we lived in different barracks—to celebrate receiving the package. I bought some bread too . . .

Semyon Alekseyevich became emotional and happy.

"But why me? What right do I have?" he mumbled, utterly overcome by emotion. "No, no, I can't . . ."

But I persuaded him and he ran joyfully to get some boiling water.

And that very moment I fell to the ground from a terrible blow to my head.

When I jumped up, the bag with the butter and the bread was gone. The one-meter long log used to hit me was lying next to the cot. And all around everyone was laughing. Sheinin came running with the boiling water. For many years afterward I couldn't recall the theft without getting terribly, overwhelmingly emotional. And Semyon Alekseyevich—died.

Ivan Yakovlevich Fedyakhin died. He and I were on the same train, the same steamboat. We wound up in the same gold mine, in the same work brigade. He was a philosopher, a peasant from Volokolamsk,[3] the organizer of the first collective farm in Russia. Collective farms, as is well known, were organized by the SRs* in the twenties, and the Chayanov-Kondratiev group represented their interests "above" . . . Ivan Yakovlevich was also an SR, from a village, one of the million who voted for that party in 1917. And for organizing the first collective farm, he got to do time—five years in prison.

One day at the very beginning, during the first fall in Kolyma,[4] in 1937, he and I were working on unloading a cart—we stood in the infamous mine production line. There were only two carts, the kind that could be detached. While the man handling the horse was taking one to the washing apparatus, two workers would barely manage to fill the other. There wasn't enough time to smoke and, what's more, the overseers didn't allow it. Our horse handler, on the other hand, did smoke—he'd smoke a huge cigar, rolled out of almost half a pack of *makhorka** (there was still *makhorka* back then), and leave it on an edge of the coal seam so that we could have a drag.

Mishka Vavilov, the former deputy chairman of the "Industrial Imports Trust," was the horse handler, and Fedyakhin and I were face workers.

Without hurrying to throw the ore into the cart, we talked with one another. I told Fediakhin about the lesson they gave to the Decembrists in Nerchinsk—according to *The Memoirs of Maria Volkonskaya*[5]—three poods* of ore per man.

"And how much does our quota weigh, Vasily Petrovich?" Fedyakhin asked.

I counted: about 800 poods.

"Just look, Vasily Petrovich, how the quotas have increased . . ."

Later, during the hungry winter, I'd get tobacco—I'd beg, save up, and buy some—and trade it for bread. Fedyakhin didn't approve of my "commerce."

"It doesn't become you, Vasily Petrovich, you shouldn't do that . . ."

I saw him for the last time in the winter in the mess hall. I gave him six dinner meal tickets that I had received that day for making copies by hand of some materials in the office. My good penmanship sometimes helped me. The meal tickets were good only for so long—they had dates stamped on them. Fedyakhin got the dinners. He sat at the table and poured the portions of the watery soup into one bowl—the soup was terribly thin and not one drop of grease floated in it . . . The pearl barley kasha he received for all six meal tickets didn't even fill a half-liter bowl . . . Fedyakhin didn't have a spoon, and he licked up the kasha with his tongue. And wept.

Derfel died. He was a French communist who had even been in the stone quarries of Cayenne.[6] Besides being hungry and cold, his morale had plummeted—he didn't want to believe that he, a member of the Comintern,[7] could find himself here, doing Soviet hard labor. His horror would have lessened had he noticed that he wasn't the only one. Everyone he came with, lived with, and was dying with, was like that. He was a small, weak man and beatings were now becoming popular . . . One time the work brigade boss hit him, hit him simply with his fist, to maintain order, so to say, but Derfel fell and didn't get up. He was one of the first to die, one of the more fortunate. In Moscow he worked for TASS[8] as an editor. He had a good command of Russian.

"In Cayenne it was bad too," he said to me once. "But here it's really bad."

Fritz David died. He was a Dutch communist, a Comintern worker, who was accused of espionage. He had beautiful wavy hair, deep blue eyes, and a child-like shape to his mouth. He knew very little Russian. I met him in a barracks packed with so many people that you could sleep standing up. We stood side by side; Fritz smiled at me and closed his eyes.

The space under the bed boards* was packed with people to overflowing; you had to wait to sit down, to squat down, and then lean against some bed boards, a post, or someone's body—and fall asleep. I waited with my eyes closed. Suddenly something next to me fell down. My neighbor Fritz David had fallen. He got up embarrassed.

"I fell asleep," he said, startled.

Fritz David was the first man in our transport of prisoners who received a package. His wife sent him the package from Moscow. In the package there was a velvet suit, a nightshirt, and a large photograph of a beautiful woman. It was in this velvet suit that he squatted next to me.

"I want to eat," he said, smiling and turning red. "I really want to eat. Bring me something to eat."

Fritz David went insane and he was taken away somewhere.

The nightshirt and the photograph were stolen from him the first night. When I was telling people about him later, I always felt perplexed and indignant: why did anyone need someone else's photograph?

"Even you don't know everything," some clever fellow said one day when I was talking to him. "It's easy to guess. This photograph was stolen by the professional criminals and, as these criminals say, for a "seance." For masturbation, my naive friend . . ."

Seryozha Klivansky died, my friend from my first year at the university, whom I met in Butyrka Prison[9] ten years later in a cell of prisoners bound for transport. He was expelled from the Komsomol in 1927 for a report on the Chinese revolution in a current politics club. He managed to finish the university, and he worked as an economist with Gosplan* until the atmosphere changed there and Seryozha was forced to leave. He won a competition for a position in the Stanislavsky Theater Orchestra and was its second violinist—until his arrest in 1937. He was a cheerful man, a wit, and always full of irony. He showed an interest in life, in its events too.

In the cell for prisoners bound for transport, everybody walked around almost naked, poured water on himself, and slept on the floor. Only a hero could endure sleeping on the bed boards. And Klivansky would joke, "This is torture by steaming. After this, we will be subjected to torture by freezing in the North."

This was an accurate prediction, but it was not the whining of a coward. At the mine Seryozha was cheerful and sociable. He tried to master thieves' vocabulary with enthusiasm and was as happy as a child when he could repeat thieves' expressions with the appropriate intonation.

"Right now, I think I'll go rest a bit," Seryozha would say, as he crawled onto the upper bed boards.

He loved poetry and often recited it from memory in the prison. In the camp he didn't recite poetry.

He would share his last piece of bread, that is to say, he still shared . . . It means that he never lived to see the time when no one had a last piece, when no one had anything to share with anyone.

The work brigade boss Dyukov died. I don't know and didn't ever know his first name. He was one of the "non-political prisoners" and his sentence had nothing to do with Article 58.[10] In the camps on the mainland he was a so-called chairman of a collective; he wasn't exactly disposed toward revolutionary romanticism, but he was ready "to play a role." He arrived in the winter and gave a remarkable speech at the first meeting. The non-political prisoners had meetings because, you see, those who had committed "non counter-revolutionary" or work-related crimes as well as the recidivist thieves were considered "friends of the people," subject to being reformed and not subject to punitive measures. Unlike the "enemies of the people"—sentenced under Article 58. Later, when the recidivists began to be sentenced under Point Fourteen of Article 58— for sabotage (refusing to work)—the whole fourteenth paragraph was eliminated from Article 58, which removed various punitive measures that could go on for many years. The recidivists were always considered "friends of the people"—up to and including Beria's[11] famous amnesty of 1953. Hundreds of thousands of unfortunate people were sacrificed to theory and Krylenko's[12] "elasticity" and notorious "reeducation."

At that first meeting Dyukov proposed taking a brigade of men sentenced under Article 58 under his leadership; usually the work brigade boss of the "political prisoners" was a political himself. Dyukov wasn't a bad fellow. He knew that peasants work very well in camps, best of all prisoners, and he remembered that there were a lot of Article 58 men among the peasants. Ezhov's[13] and Beria's special wisdom should be seen in this, for they realized that the labor value of the intelligentsia was not high and consequently the camps might not be able to fulfill the production goals, unlike the political goals. But Dyukov didn't go into such lofty considerations; it's doubtful anything came into his head except the men's capacity for work. He selected a brigade for himself—

exclusively of peasants—and began working. This was in the spring of 1938. Dyukov's peasants had already stayed there the whole hungry winter of 1937-38. He didn't go to the bathhouse with his brigade, otherwise he would've realized long before what the problem was.

They didn't work badly and just needed to be given more food than they were getting. But the administration refused Dyukov's request in the harshest way. The hungry brigade kept reaching its quota by working with tremendous effort. Then Dyukov began to be shortchanged: by the men who measured the output, the bookkeepers, the overseers, and the work bosses. He began to complain, to protest more and more sharply, the brigade's production output kept falling and falling, and the food kept getting worse. Dyukov tried turning to the higher-ups, but the higher-ups advised the relevant workers to add Dyukov's brigade, including the work brigade boss himself, to the infamous lists. This was done and all were executed at the infamous Serpentine Mine.

Pavel Mikhailovich Khvostov died. The most frightening thing in hungry people is their behavior. Everything's like in healthy people, and yet they're half-insane. The hungry always fiercely defend the cause of justice—if they're not terribly hungry, not terribly emaciated. They're eternal squabblers, desperate fighters. Usually only one out of a thousand people who have quarreled with someone, their voices strained to the limit, will go on to fight. Hungry people always fight. Arguments flare up for the wildest, the most unexpected of reasons: "What are you doing with my mining pick . . . why did you take my place?" The one who is shorter, not as tall, tries to trip his opponent and bring him down. The one who is taller—to fall upon his enemy and bring him down with his weight, and then scratch, hit, and bite him . . . All of this is done weakly—it's not painful and not fatal—and all too often, just to arouse the interest of those around. Fights are not broken up.

Khvostov was just like that. He fought with someone every day— in the barracks and in the deep drainage trench that our brigade was digging. He was my *winter* friend—I didn't see his hair. He had a hat with earflaps, with torn white fur. And his eyes were dark—hungry, shining eyes. I sometimes recited poetry, and he looked at me like I was half-crazy.

Suddenly he began to hit the rock in the trench desperately with his pick. The pick was heavy; Khvostov kept making swinging blows and hitting the rock almost non-stop. I marveled at such strength. We'd been together for a long time, had been hungry for a long time. Then the pick fell and made a ringing sound. I glanced back. Khvostov was standing with his legs spread apart and swaying. His knees were buckling. He swayed and fell face down. He stretched his hands out in front of him in the same mittens that he mended every evening. His arms became exposed—there were tattoos on both forearms. Pavel Mikhailovich had been a sea captain.

Roman Romanovich Romanov died before my very eyes. At one time he had been something like our company commander. He distributed packages and kept an eye on cleanliness in the camp compound, in a word, he was in such a privileged position as not one of us could dream of—we of Article 58 and *lityorki*, as the professional criminals called us, or *literniki*, as the higher administrators of the camp said.[14] The best we could dream of was laundry work in the bathhouse or mending clothes on the night shift. Except for rocks, everything was forbidden to us by Moscow's "special instructions." Such a document was included in each of our files. And so, Roman Romanovich occupied such a position, beyond our reach. And he even quickly grasped all its secrets: how to open a box with a parcel in it so that the sugar would spill onto the floor; how to break a jar with preserves; and how to throw dried bread crusts and dried fruit under the trestle-bed. Roman Romanovich learned all this very quickly and didn't maintain any contact with us. He was rigidly official and conducted himself as a polite representative of those higher authorities with whom we couldn't have personal contact. He never gave us any advice. He only explained: one letter may be sent per month, packages are given out from 8 to 10 in the evening in the camp commandant's office, and so on. We didn't envy Roman Romanovich, we were just amazed by him. Evidently, some personal chance acquaintance of Roman's played a role here. However, he wasn't the company commander for long, just two months in all. Either there was the next scheduled staff review (such reviews took place from time to time and without fail by New Year's), or someone "ratted" on him, to use the colorful camp expression. And Roman Romanovich disappeared. He had served in the military and was a colonel, it seems.

And so four years later I found myself on a "temporary vitamin assignment"—gathering the needles from trailing shrubs, the only year-round green plants there. These needles were brought from many hundreds of versts to a vitamin plant. There they were cooked and the needles turned into a gooey, brown mixture with an unbearable smell and taste. It was poured into barrels and sent to various camps. In terms of the local medicine at that time, it was considered the main remedy—available to all and obligatory—against scurvy. Scurvy was rife and rampant and, what's more, appeared in combination with pellagra and other vitamin deficiency diseases. But everybody who had to swallow even a drop of the horrible potion agreed it was better to die than to be treated with such a hellish brew. But there were orders, and orders are orders, and you wouldn't get any food in camp until a dose of this medicine was swallowed. The man on duty stood right there with a special tiny scoop. You couldn't enter the mess hall and bypass the dispenser of the needle brew, and so the very thing that a prisoner values—dinner, food—was irreparably spoiled by this preliminary, obligatory exercise. And so it continued for more than ten years . . . Doctors who were a bit more competent were bewildered—how could vitamin C, which is unusually sensitive to all temperature changes, be preserved in such a sticky "ointment"? The treatment made no sense at all, but the extract continued to be handed out. Right there, next to all the settlements, were a lot of wild rose bushes. But no one even dared to gather the rose hips—nothing was said about them in the orders. And only much later after the war, in 1952 I think, a letter was received—again, however, from the local medicine folk— in which giving out the extract of needles from trailing shrubbery was categorically forbidden since it had a destructive effect on the kidneys. The vitamin plant was closed. But at the time I met Roman, the needles from the trailing shrubs were being collected with a vengeance. They were collected by the "goners"—the mine slag and refuse of gold mine work—semi-invalids, hungry and chronically sick. The gold mines made invalids out of healthy people in just three weeks: hunger, lack of sleep, heavy work for many hours on end, and beatings . . . New people would join the brigade and Molokh[15] would chew them up . . . By the end of the season there was no one in Ivanov's work brigade except the work brigade boss Ivanov. The rest went to the hospital, to "boot hill," and on "vitamin" assignments, where they were fed once a day and where it was impossible to receive more than 600 grams of bread daily. That fall Roman and I did not work collecting needles. We worked in "construction." We were building a dwelling for ourselves for the winter; in the summer we lived in torn tents.

An area was measured off in footsteps, stakes were driven in, and then we put in a widely-spaced fence consisting of two rows. The space between them was filled with pieces of frozen moss and peat. Inside was a sleeping platform made of poles, just one level. In the middle stood an iron stove. We were given a ration of wood, figured out empirically, for every night. However, we had neither a saw nor an ax—those sharp objects were kept by the guards who lived in a separate, heated tent covered with plywood. Saws and axes were handed out only in the morning when we were marched off to work. The problem was that in a neighboring brigade on temporary "vitamin" duty some criminals had attacked the work brigade boss. Professional criminals are unusually disposed to theatrics, and introduce it into their lives in a way that even Evreinov[16] would envy. A decision was made to kill the work brigade boss, and the proposal of one of the professional criminals—to saw off the boss's head—was met with excitement. His head was sawed off with an ordinary crosscut saw. That's why there was an order forbidding axes and saws to be left with prisoners for the night. Why only for the night? But no one ever tried to find logic in the orders.

How do you cut wood so that the logs fit in the stove? The thinner ones were broken with our feet, and all the thick ones were put in the opening of the burning stove, the thinner end first, and gradually burned away. Someone would push them deeper into the stove with his foot—there was always someone to look after this. The light from the open stove door was the only light in our dwelling. Until snowfall, the wind went through our small house, but then we piled up snow around the walls and poured water on it—and our winter hut was ready. A piece of tarpaulin was hung over the door opening.

It's here, in this very shed, that I met Roman Romanovich again. He didn't recognize me. He was dressed like a "flame,"[17] as the hardened criminals say and, as always, appropriately—clumps of cotton stuck out of his padded jacket, pants, and hat. Quite a few times, it's true, Roman Romanovich had to run "behind a corner" to light the cigarette of some criminal . . . His eyes had a hungry shine, and his cheeks were red like before, only they didn't bring to mind balloons but were stretched rather tightly over his cheekbones. Roman Romanovich was lying in a corner and loudly breathing in and out. His chin rose and fell.

"He's dying," Denisov, his neighbor, said. "He has good footcloths . . ." And after nimbly pulling off the felt boots from the dying man's feet, he unwrapped his footcloths of green blanket material that was still holding together . . . "That's the way," he said, looking at me threateningly. But I didn't care.

Roman's corpse was carried out when we were lined up before being marched off to work. He didn't have a hat either. The flaps of his open jacket dragged along the ground.

Did Volodya Dobrovoltsev, the *pointist* die? *Pointist*—is that a job or a nationality? This was a job which evoked jealousy in the barracks of Article 58 prisoners. Separate barracks for the political prisoners in the general camp, where there were also barracks behind barbed wire for the "non-political prisoners" and the recidivist criminals, were a mockery of the legal system, of course. This didn't protect anyone from attacks and bloody settling of scores by the professional criminals.

A *point*—that's an iron pipe with hot steam. This hot steam warms the rock layer, the frozen pebble bed; from time to time a worker scoops out the warmed rock with a metal spoon, the size of a human hand, which has a three-meter handle.

This work is considered skilled labor, since the *pointist* must open and close the valves that control the hot steam moving through the pipes from a boiler in a shed—a primitive steam contraption. To be a boiler man is even better than to be a *pointist*. Not every Article 58 engineer-mechanic could dream of work like that. And not because this was skilled labor. It was pure chance that out of thousands of people Volodya was sent to do this work. But this changed him. He didn't have to think how to get warm—the eternal thing on your mind . . . The freezing cold didn't go through his whole being, didn't stop his mind from working. The hot pipe was his salvation. That's why everybody envied Dobrovoltsev.

There was talk that it was no accident that he was a *pointist*—it was reliable proof that he was an informer, a spy . . . Of course, the professional criminals always said that if you worked as a medical orderly in camp, it meant you drank working men's blood, and people knew the price of judgments like that; envy is a poor advisor. Volodya somehow grew immeasurably in our eyes, as if a remarkable violinist had been found among us. The fact that Dobrovoltsev would leave alone (he had to because of the conditions of his work) and, as he was walking out of camp past the guard shack, would open the guard window and shout out his number "twenty five" in such a cheerful, loud voice—that was something we had gotten unused to a long time ago.

Sometimes he worked near our coal seam. And since we knew him, we ran and took turns warming ourselves by his pipe. The pipe was about one and half inches in diameter; you could put your hand around it, hold it tightly in your fist, and feel the warmth passing from your hands to your body, and then you couldn't bear to break away and return to the coal seam, into the freezing air . . .

Volodya didn't chase us away like other *pointists*. He never said a word to us, although I know the *pointists* were forbidden to allow our kind to warm themselves by the pipes. He'd stand, surrounded by clouds of thick white steam. His clothing would be stiff from the cold. Every fiber on his jacket glistened like a crystal needle. He never talked with us—this work was evidently worth too much.

On Christmas Eve of that year we were sitting by the stove. Its iron sides were redder than usual on account of the holiday. A human being senses the difference in temperature instantly. Sitting by the stove, we were getting sleepy and longed for some lyric poetry.

"It would be nice to return home, brothers. There are miracles, you know . . . ," said Glebov the horse handler and former professor of philosophy, famous in our barracks because a month before he had forgotten his wife's name. "Only mind you, the truth."

"Home?"

"Yes."

"I'll tell the truth," I answered. "It would be better to return to prison. I'm not joking. I wouldn't want to return to my family now. They would never understand me, they wouldn't be able to understand me. What seems important to them I know is a mere nothing. What's important to me—the little that I have left—isn't given for them either to understand or feel. I'd bring them a new fear, one more fear added to the thousands of fears that their lives are more than full of. What I've seen—a human being shouldn't have to see or even know about. A prison—that's another matter. A prison—that's freedom. It's the only place I know where people weren't afraid and said everything that was on their mind. Where they rested spiritually. Where they rested physically, because they didn't work. There every hour of existence had meaning."

"Oh, come on! You're talking nonsense," said the former professor of philosophy. "It's because they didn't beat you during the investigation.

But anyone who passed through method number three has a different opinion . . ."

"Well, and you, Pyotr Ivanych, what will you tell us?"

Pyotr Ivanovich Timofeyev, the former director of the Ural Trust, smiled and winked at Glebov.

"I'd return home to my wife, to Agniya Mikhailovna. I'd buy rye bread—a whole loaf! Cook some millet kasha—a bucketful! Soup with little dumplings—also a bucketful! And I'd eat it all. For the first time in my life I would have my fill, eating this good stuff, and what would be left, I'd force Agniya Mikhailovna to eat."

"And you?" Glebov turned to Zvonkov, the coal miner in our brigade, and in his first life a peasant—from either the Yaroslavl or Kostroma area.

"Home," Zvonkov answered seriously, without smiling. "I think I'd go home now and not take a step away from my wife. Wherever she goes, I go too—wherever she goes, I go too. Only they have broken me of the habit of working—I've lost my love for the land. Well, I'll find something somewhere . . ."

"And you?" Glebov's hand touched the knee of our barracks orderly.

"First thing I would go to the district committee of the party. There, I remember, they had cigarette butts on the floor—an endless amount . . ."

"Don't joke . . ."

"But I'm not joking."

Suddenly I saw that only one man was left who hadn't answered. And this man was Volodya Dobrovoltsev. He raised his head without waiting for the question. The light from the glowing coals in the open door of the stove fell on his eyes—his eyes were lively and sparkled.

"And I," and his voice was calm and deliberate, "would want to be a trunk. A human trunk, you understand, without hands or feet. Then I would find the strength in myself to spit in their ugly mugs for everything that they're doing to us."

1960

NOTES

1. single measure: As the story "A Single Measure" in *Kolyma Tales* illustrates, a prisoner whom the authorities feel is not able to do his share of the work in a brigade is assigned a quota he must fulfil by working by himself. If he cannot meet that quota, he is executed.

2. Sergei Kirov (1886-1934): a rising star in the Communist Party when he was assassinated in 1934. His death was used by Stalin as a reason to initiate purges and show trials.

3. Volokolamsk: about 80 miles north-west of Moscow.

4. Kolyma: remote region in the Russian Far East, where a large number of Gulag camps was located.

5. Princess Maria Volkonskaya (1805-1863): wife of Prince S. G. Volkonsky. When her husband was exiled to Siberia after the Decembrist revolt (1825), she joined her husband and shared his exile.

6. Cayenne: capital of French Guiana, where the notorious French penal colony, Devil's Island, was located.

7. Cominterm: Communist International, also known as the Third International; founded in 1919 to coordinate the efforts of the communist parties around the world in order to bring about an international communist revolution.

8. TASS: The Telegraph Agency of the Soviet Union (established in 1925), which was responsible for gathering and disseminating all news, domestic and international.

9. Butyrka Prison: located in Moscow, built in 1879; during the Great Purge of the 1930s, thousands of prisoners were shot there and hundreds of thousands passed through it to various labor camps.

10. Article 58: part of the Soviet Penal Code put in force in 1922, it authorized the arrest of people suspected of counter-revolutionary activities. It was revised, expanded and "updated" a number of times, and used with increasing frequency against millions of prisoners during the purges of the 1930s. Those sentenced under Article 58-1, were "traitors"; those under 58-14, "saboteurs."

11. Krylenko, Nikolai (1885-1938): served in a variety of posts in the Soviet legal system; rose to the position of Commissar of Justice and Prosecutor General of the RSFSR. He believed that political considerations more than anything else should guide the application of punishment. Perished during the Great Purge himself.

12. Beria, Lavrenty (1899-1953): head of the NKVD* from 1940 to 1953. One of the most cruel and amoral men of the Soviet regime. Executed in 1953.

13. Ezhov, Nikolai (1895-1940): People's Commissar and "Stalin's loyal executioner," NKVD (secret police) chief. Succeeded by Beria after his execution.

14. *lityorki*: the diminutive and pejorative form of *literniki*. Literniki, or literally "the letter ones," were prisoners who had been sentenced according to one of the categories listed in Article 58. The categories were reduced to a letter or two; for example, anti-Soviet elements would be AS, S would be a member of a sect, etc.

15. Molokh: in the Old Testament represented as an old man with ram's horns, holding a scythe, to whom small children were sacrificed.

16. Evreinov, Nikolai (1879-1953): theater director, dramatist, and author. He believed in the theatricalization of life and developed his theories in a number of books, including the three-volume *The Theater for Oneself* (1915-1917). In his early and most famous essay, "Apology for Theatricality" (1908), he wrote that "the stage must not borrow so much from life as life must borrow from the stage."

17. "flame": a very resourceful, restless young thief.

THE HOUSE WITH A TURRET

Fridrikh Gorenshtein

The boy had trouble distinguishing faces; they were all the same and they inspired fear in him. He found a spot for himself in a corner of the train car, by the head of his mother who, in her fluffy beret and coat buttoned all the way up, was lying on some bundles. Someone said in the dark, "We'll suffocate here, like in a mobile gas chamber. She's always soiling herself . . . After all, there are children here . . ."

The boy quickly took out his mitten and began to wipe up the puddle on the train car floor.

"Why are you so stubborn?" a man asked. "Your mother's sick. They'll take her to a hospital and make her well. But on this special train[1] she can die."

"We've got to get there," the boy said in a despairing voice. "Granddad will meet us there."

But he understood that they would make them get off the train at the next station for sure.

His mother said something and smiled.

"What is it?" the boy asked.

But his mother did not answer; she looked past him and hummed quietly.

"A terrible voice," people sighed in the darkness.

"Not terrible at all," the boy snapped back. "You yourselves have terrible ones . . ."

It became light. The small windows of the freight car turned blue, and the tops of telegraph poles began to rush by in them. The boy didn't sleep the whole night and now, when the voices had died down, he took his mother's hot hand in his two hands and closed his eyes. Rocking gently, he fell asleep right away with his back hitting against the wooden side of the car. He woke up right away as well from someone touching his cheek.

The train had stopped. The door of the car was open and the boy saw that four men were carrying his mother on a stretcher across the train tracks. He jumped down on the gravel of the railroad embankment and ran after them.

The men carried the stretcher holding it high and supporting it on their shoulders, and his mother swayed indifferently to the rhythm of their steps.

It was early in the morning and cold, with the usual frost but no snow in this steppe area, and the boy tripped a few times on rocks frozen to the ground.

People were walking on the platform; some turned around and looked, and a lad, about five years older than the boy, asked him with curiosity, "Is she dead?"

"She got sick," the boy answered. "It's my mother."

The lad looked at him fearfully and walked away.

They carried the stretcher through the station door, and the boy wanted to go in there too, but a nurse in a padded jacket thrown over her medical gown took him by the shoulder and asked, "Where are you going?"

"That's her son," said one of the men and added, "And where are your things? The special train will leave and you'll be without your things . . ."

The boy ran back towards the special train but got lost and found himself on a city square on the opposite side of the train station. He noticed the line for the bus, an old one-story house with a turret, and an old woman in wool stockings and rain boots selling fish.

Then he ran back, but the railroad tracks by the platform were empty—the train had already left. The boy didn't even have time to get scared before he saw his things piled up on the platform. Everything was there, except the bag with the flat cakes and dried apricots.

"Your things?" asked a woman in a railroad greatcoat.

"Mine," the boy answered.

"And what's in that bundle?" she asked as she pushed the dirty, crushed bundle with her foot.

"Mom's felt boots," the boy said, "and two quilted blankets . . . And a length of brown cloth . . ."

Without checking, the woman took the bundle and the suitcase, the boy took the other bundle and suitcase, and they went into the train station. They brought the things to a warm hall, where there were a lot of people sitting on wooden benches as well as directly on the floor.

"I'm going to the first-aid station," the boy said. "My mom's sick."

"I'm not going to watch your things."

"Oh, just a little longer. I'll pay."

"Dummy," the woman made a wry face. "I've my work to do."

But the boy had already run out onto the platform. He found the doors of the first-aid station with difficulty. Someone was lying all stretched out on a bench covered with oilcloth; the boy swallowed hard a few times and, as he came closer, he saw a hand with blue fingernails. Only then did he notice that this was an old man he didn't know. His face was covered with a handkerchief and two women were sitting next to him, bent over. One, a bit younger, was crying, and the other, a bit older, was silent.

The boy quickly stepped back.

"Where's my mom?" he asked and looked around.

The nurse in the padded jacket walked out of a side door.

"Your mother's been sent to the hospital," she said.

"What hospital?" the boy asked.

"We have only one hospital in town . . . If you take the bus, you'll make it there . . ."

Then he remembered the square, and the line, and the house with the turret, and the old woman in wool stockings selling fish. He ran again to the other side of the train station and saw all those things. He got in line behind a fur jacket with fur buttons on the back strap. But there was no bus and he ran across the square. He found himself on a narrow street among old wooden houses, and at this point remembered that he didn't know where the hospital was.

The street was empty; only two little girls were playing with a small dog near an ice-covered water hydrant.

"Where's the hospital?" he asked. But the little girls looked at him, burst out laughing, and ran through a gate, and the dog nipped at his heels and, baring its teeth, began to bark. The boy picked up a piece of ice and threw it at the dog. The dog began to howl. A woman in a hat with ear-flaps and the two little girls walked out of the gate, the latter making faces at him without being seen. The woman began to shout something, but the boy didn't understand why and what she was shouting.

"Where's the hospital?" he asked quietly.

The woman stopped shouting.

"You're going the wrong way," she said. "Cross the square and take the bus."

The boy turned around and headed back, and again saw the house with the turret, the line, and the old woman selling fish.

He got in line behind a greatcoat with a pinned-up sleeve that had lost its lining, and again he waited for a long time, but no bus came. Then he asked the greatcoat where the hospital was.

"It's far," the greatcoat said. "Do you see the smokestack? It's a kilometer more beyond the smokestack. You've got to take the bus."

But there still was no bus, and the boy headed in the direction of the smokestack. Immediately, at the beginning of the street, the bus passed him.

The boy walked for a very long time, and during this period of time he got used to the fact that his mother was in the hospital and he was alone among strangers. The important thing now was to make it to the smokestack and find the hospital. As he was heading there, the bus passed him several more times. Up close, the smokestack turned out to be huge and rusty, with a brick foundation. The boy stood a while and rested, and with his mitten-covered hand held onto the wire that extended from the smokestack to the ground. The wire was cold and slippery. Then he went on and a passer-by pointed out the hospital. The boy went up the steps, walked into the corridor, and ran into a woman in a gauze kerchief.

"Where are you going?" the woman asked and spread her arms wide. "Where are you going in a coat . . . ? What do you want?"

The boy dove under her arms, pushed the glass door, and immediately saw his mother. She was lying on a bed in the middle of the ward.

"Here," he said. "Here, here . . ."

"What do you mean 'here'?" the woman asked. "What do you mean—'here'?" But the boy held onto the door handle and repeated, "Here, well, here . . ."

His mother's hair was completely shaved off, and her eyes—very dark against her yellow face—were looking at the boy. She was conscious.

"Son," she said in a whisper. And then the boy began to cry.

"Oh, be quiet!" the woman in the kerchief said. "Give me your coat and go to your mother."

"I was looking for you," the boy said, continuing to cry.

"I feel better already," the mother said. "How do you feel?"

"Good," the boy said. "And you'll get well soon?"

"Soon," the mother said. "Have some gruel. Nurse, give him a spoon."

"That's not allowed," the nurse said.

"Take the little teaspoon," the mother said, "and sit down on the stool."

"That's not allowed," the nurse repeated. "I'll be forced to remove the boy."

"Eat, eat, my son," the mother said, "don't be afraid."

"I'll hang up your coat in the corridor," the nurse said angrily and walked out of the ward.

"I've got to send a telegram to granddad," said the boy. "I have money ... And I left our things at the station ... The important thing is for you to get well."

"I'll get well," the mother said. "How thin you've gotten ..."

"When we get there, I'll put on some weight," the boy said. "The war will end soon."

The nurse reappeared. "Hey, boy, leave the ward. The rounds are going to begin now ..."

"I'll send the telegram and come back," the boy said. "I'll come right back to you."

"Bend down," his mother said.

The boy bent down and she kissed him on the cheek. Her lips were chapped and hot.

He walked out on the street and the bus came very quickly; the stop was directly opposite the hospital.

"Everything's fine," the boy thought. "This is much better than half an hour ago when I was walking and didn't know anything."

It was hot in the bus and the boy took off his mittens and undid the hook on his coat collar. Then he got cold and fastened the hook again, and stuck his hands in his pockets.

He got off at the square where the old woman was selling fish as before, suddenly felt hungry, bought a baked brown fish and sniffed it—it smelled of something unfamiliar—and, walking across the square toward the house with the turret, where there was a post office, he tried to remember how he had walked up to the old woman, what he had said, and how much he had paid for the fish.

He pulled the heavy post office door toward himself, and behind it there was a short winding staircase that led to another door. And behind that door there was a room divided with a wooden partition.

Other people's backs hid the post office windows from view; wherever the boy tried to go, everywhere he ran against backs.

"What do you want?" a man asked. "What are you hanging around here for?"

"I've got to send a telegram," the boy said and, remembering that he had never sent a telegram in his life, added, "You write the telegram for me."

"Wait," the man said. "Sit down, don't get underfoot."

The boy sat down on a chair and broke off a small piece of the fish. Under the brown skin it was very white and not salty. Then he looked out the window and began to feel uneasy; it was already beginning to get dark.

"Auntie," he said to a woman in a kerchief, "Write a telegram for me."

"What an impatient boy!" the man said. "Well, what do you need? What kind of a telegram?" And he took a telegram blank.

"Mom is sick, in the hospital," the boy dictated, "granddad, come."

The man and woman looked at the boy.

"Oh my, people are having a hard time," the woman sighed. "Oh my, how people are suffering . . ."

The boy paid for the telegram, hid the receipt in his mitten, and began to feel calmer. He walked out on the square and ran to the bus that had just arrived. In the middle of the square he remembered that he had forgotten the fish at the post office, but he didn't bother going back and ran on.

While he was running, something wet and cold touched his face a few times out of the darkness, and when the bus stopped at the hospital, there were already white stripes on the road and snow was flying around the street lamps.

The boy quickly climbed the snow-covered steps, went into the familiar corridor, and from there into the dimly-lit ward.

"Mom," he said, "I've sent a telegram to granddad . . ."

"Quiet," an angry nurse with a syringe in her hands appeared from somewhere, "your mother's sleeping, can't you see . . . ?"

His mother was lying on her side, her mouth was half open, and the boy suddenly thought that she wasn't breathing.

"Is she alive?" he quietly asked the nurse.

"Alive, alive," the nurse answered, "she needs to sleep . . . And what are we going to do with you? Do you have a place for the night?"

"I'll sit here," the boy said.

"It's not allowed here," the nurse said. "Again right into the ward in a coat!" And she took him by the collar of his coat.

Then the boy jerked and broke free, but the nurse moved the syringe from her right hand to the left and again took the boy by the collar, but now more firmly.

"I'll call a policeman," she said.

Then someone took the boy by the hand and turned him around so that the boy was facing him.

And the boy saw a hospital gown all covered in yellow spots; directly in front of the boy's eyes there was a spot that looked like a beetle, and a bit to the left, by the bone buttons, there was a spot that looked like a turtle with a long neck.

"He's that one's son, from the special train," the nurse said to the gown.

"All right, you, unbutton your coat," the gown said, and he put his hard hand on the boy's forehead, and when he did this, the beetle jerked and began to crawl, and the turtle moved its neck.

The boy wanted to break free, but the nurse stood and held him firmly from behind.

"All right, you," the gown repeated and took the boy by the wrist with his other hand. The other hand was soft, with nails trimmed short and dark little hairs on the fingers, and the boy calmed down a bit.

"Get undressed," the gown said.

"Can I stay?" the boy asked.

"Yes . . . We'll get both of you well and you'll be able to travel on."

"Am I really sick too?" the boy asked.

"Yes," the gown answered impatiently; he was being called to another ward. "Nurse, put him on this cot." He pointed to a free cot at the other end of the ward and left . . .

"Let's go," the nurse called to him and walked out into the corridor.

She brought him to a very small room without windows and clicked on the light switch, but the room stayed dark; apparently the light bulb had burned out. Then the nurse lit a candle, and in the light of the candle the boy began to shiver for some reason.

He got undressed and threw everything on the floor, and the nurse grumbled as she picked up his clothing and shoved it into a sack. Then he put a foot into one leg of the grey hospital pajamas and lay down to rest.

The nurse lifted him up, pulled the second pant leg on, put a shirt on him, and took him to the ward, holding him by the shoulders.

Face down on the bed, the boy pressed his head against the pillow, but the nurse disturbed him again and gave him half of some tablet.

"Swallow," the nurse said. "Let saliva collect in your mouth and then swallow."

The boy's mouth was dry and the bitter tablet melted on his tongue . . .

"Give me something to drink," the boy said. "And when do you serve food?"

"So that's why you've come here," the nurse said angrily. "Supper's already over . . ."

She went far into the ward and brought a glass of cold tea and a few crackers.

"Here . . . Your mother didn't eat . . ."

The boy drank the tea and ate the crackers, and then lay down. There were three cots between him and his mother, and to see his mother he had to lean on his elbows, because either an old man's head or an old woman's with a pointy nose and protruding chin was in his way.

His mother was now lying on her back; the blanket on her chest rose and fell often.

The boy fell asleep for a short time and didn't dream of anything, but when he woke up, it was night as before, and his mother was lying on her back as before. He raised himself on his elbows, then sat up, sensing that his whole body was trembling; stepping barefoot on the cold floor, he walked up to her bed and stood like that and waited for a long time for his mother to move. And she did move; she raised her knees and took a deep and quiet breath.

Then he returned to his cot and, peering into the darkness at the ceiling, imagined how they would come home to their own town and remember all this. The old man next to him began to move around and moan, and so that these moans wouldn't get in the way of his thoughts, the boy covered his head with his blanket. During the night he got up a few more times, walked over to his mother, and waited for her to move. And then he'd lie down and fall asleep and then wake up. When he woke up for the last time, the ceiling was already grey and the falling snow could be seen through the windows. And he was happy that the night was over. He leaned on his elbows, looked at his mother, and was happy again because she was moving, even raising herself and saying something.

The boy smiled, and he wanted to tell his mother about the telegram and about being afraid at night when she was lying without moving.

But suddenly the old man next to him shouted, "Nurse, the woman is dying!"

The boy got off the cot and saw that his mother was gurgling and her neck was straining while her head was resting deep in the pillow.

The nurse approached, took the mother's chin in her fingers, and then pulled the blanket over her face with a practiced motion. The blanket lifted a bit and for a second the boy saw a yellow foot and a bare stomach.

He looked at the now motionless lump covered with the blanket, and a strange indifference overcame him. "That's it," he thought, and went out of the ward into the corridor.

The nurse caught up with him.

"Lie down," she said, "you're ill."

"Where's my clothing?" the boy asked. "I must travel on now."

The nurse said something to him, but he didn't hear what she said.

There were women with bags in the corridor, probably women simply passing through; no one knew how they had gotten there. They were looking at the boy and one of them asked, "What's going on?"

And one of them said, "The boy's mother has died."

And one of them dabbed her eyes with a handkerchief. And the boy sat on the wooden bench in the corridor, shivering from the cold, and didn't look at all those people. He suddenly had the thought that when he'd arrive in his own town, his mother would meet him at the train station.

He wasn't a little boy anymore and he understood that his mother had died, yet he had that thought.

"I want to go home," he said to the doctor.

"Don't be foolish," said the doctor, "you'll get better and then you'll go."

"I'm already well," the boy said. "Where's my clothing?"

At that point they brought in someone on a stretcher from the outside. A robust man was walking behind, weeping loudly and blowing his nose. The doctor waved his hand and followed the stretcher. And the nurse said to the boy, "Wait here." And she left too.

She returned in about twenty minutes and led the boy to a storeroom.

She took his wrinkled clothing out of the bag, and he began to get dressed. Then she took out a coat, his mother's fluffy beret, and shoes from another bag and rolled them all into a bundle. For a long time she wrote something on a piece of paper with a violet stamp and asked the boy his name and where he was going.

"We'll bury her in her dress," she said. "Sign for the things and count the money."

He did not bother counting it, signed and headed for the door. The nurse called out after him and thrust the paper with the violet stamp into his pocket.

A lot of snow had piled up at night; the smokestack was now standing not on a brick foundation but on a huge mound of snow. The boy walked past and remembered stopping here for a rest yesterday and holding onto the wire. Then he noticed that he was walking on the snow next to a beaten path and that was probably why he was so tired. His back and neck were wet with sweat, and his right hand, with which he held the bundle close to him, had become completely numb.

He walked out onto the square near the train station; it was totally unfamiliar to him, quiet and white. The house with the turret looked different—low—and the waiting line looked different, and there was no more old woman selling fish.

He walked into the train station and began to be pushed from all sides. There were a lot of people, and all of them were scrambling towards the ticket windows; the boy understood right away that there was no way for him to get through to the ticket windows. His face got pressed against someone's leather coat in the crowd and, while they were being pushed this way and that way together, the boy got used to this yellow coat, and he had always loved the smell of leather.

"Uncle,"[2] he said, when they were pushed out to an open area, "punch my ticket."

The uncle didn't say anything, only cast a cursory glance at the boy and wrinkled his brow and rubbed his elbow, which he had bumped against a corner.

"I'll pay," the boy said.

"Wipe your snot, rich guy," the uncle said.

The boy threw himself into the crowd again, but he remembered that his things had remained with the woman in the railroad greatcoat and went to look for her.

He walked around the platform for a long time, got terribly cold, and went to warm up in the waiting room. All the benches were taken; he sat down on the windowsill and saw the uncle in the leather coat. The latter was busy with a huge suitcase—he was pressing it with his knee, putting a belt around it and tightening it—and next to him, on a bench, slept a woman in exactly the same kind of leather coat with a chubby little child who bore a surprising resemblance to the uncle; the boy immediately named him "small uncle" in his mind.

The uncle probably sensed that someone was looking at him and turned around.

"Here I am!" he said. "What do you want?"

"I'm waiting for a train too," the boy said and showed his ticket. Along with the ticket the boy pulled out a few more pieces of paper, and two of them fell to the floor.

The boy picked up one, the uncle the other.

"What's this meaningless scrap of paper?" the uncle asked, squinting because he was near-sighted.

"It's a document from the hospital," the boy said.

The uncle put on his glasses, read it, and immediately started to hurry.

"What do you say, let's go," the uncle said, gave a shove to the sleeping woman and put the boy's bundle near her, and took the boy by the shoulder.

He led him through the waiting room into the corridor where a lot of people were crowded at the door, but the uncle showed the document and they were let through. In the room behind the door there were also a lot of people, and a railroad worker sitting at the table began to shout, but the uncle showed the document and the railroad worker stopped shouting.

"And where's the lad?" he asked, and the uncle quickly produced the boy from behind some people's backs.

"Was it you who were taken off the special train?" asked the railroad worker.

"Yes, us," the boy answered.

"Go to the luggage storage room and get your things." And he wrote something on the piece of paper.

"We're from the same region," the uncle said. "I'll get him home like my own son."

"Fine," said the railroad worker and wrote something on another piece of paper.

"The only thing is—I have a family," the uncle said after reading the piece of paper, "a wife and son . . . I'll have two sons."

"Fine," said the railroad worker and changed the number on the piece of paper.

"Let's go, let's go, my little friend," the uncle said and gave him a big hug.

He took him to the platform and then the luggage storage room, and the boy received his things: two bundles and two suitcases.

The uncle took one bundle and suitcase, and the boy took the other bundle and suitcase, and they headed for the waiting room.

Here he sat the boy down on the bench, exchanged some whispered phrases with the woman in the leather coat, and left.

The woman had curly hair; she was short and fat. She rocked the little uncle on her knees, put her hand under his collar, patted him on the neck and said, "You see, that boy didn't listen to his mother and she died. If you don't listen, I'll die too."

"And how did she die?" the little uncle asked.

"Closed her little eyes, and that was all," the curly-haired woman said.

"Like Uncle Vasya?" the little uncle asked.

"No, Uncle Vasya was killed at the front," the woman said.

"And can they make them alive again?" the little uncle asked.

"Of course not, silly," the curly-haired woman said.

"And if they could," the little uncle said, "I'd rather bring back our Uncle Vasya than his mother . . ."

"Oh, my silly little boy," the curly-haired woman burst out laughing and began to pat the little uncle lightly on the neck. "Oh, my silly, silly, silly little boy. . . !" She looked at the boy, moved further away from him, moved his things and asked, "Did your mother die from spotted fever?"

"No," the boy answered. He was sitting and imagining arriving in his home town and his mother meeting him who, as it turns out, had stayed behind in the town with the partisans. And during the evacuation he was with another woman, and this other woman died in a hospital. It was nice for him to think this way, and he kept thinking constantly about one and the same thing, but each time in greater and greater detail.

"Why are you smiling?" the curly-haired woman asked. "Your mother died and you're smiling . . . Shame on you . . ."

Then the uncle appeared and, with him, an invalid. The invalid was wearing a navy pea-jacket and a black navy cap with ear-flaps. He had an empty, flattened sleeve where his arm should have been, and an artificial limb was making tapping sounds where his leg should have been.

The uncle said something and smiled, and the invalid also said something to the uncle, and then he suddenly thrust a huge "fig"* right in front of his nose.

The uncle backed away and again began to say something, nodding his head in a friendly way, and then the invalid spit in his face.

The curly-haired woman cried out and ran to the uncle, and the uncle quickly wiped himself with his hand and again smiled for some reason. A soldier on patrol walked up and dragged the invalid off somewhere by his only arm.

"He wouldn't stop pestering me, the drunken swine!" the uncle said and stopped smiling. "I'm walking and he's pestering me. I'm not bothering him—I'm walking and he's pestering me . . ." The uncle had an angry face and looked upset, and he half-shouted at the boy, "Why are you just sitting there? Get ready . . . ! I've gotten the tickets punched . . ."

The boy quickly jumped off the bench and took the bundle in one hand and the suitcase in the other.

The uncle took a rope out of his pocket, tied the two bundles together, and hung them over the boy's shoulder.

"And take the suitcases," the uncle said.

Boarding began and the boy immediately fell behind the uncle, and he was pushed to the very edge of a huge crowd from where he could see only the tops of the green train cars. The boy tried to squeeze through closer and managed to do so, even began to make out windows and faces in the windows, and then he saw the uncle in a window. Then he began to push forward with all his strength and sensed that the rope which held the bundles together had broken. He managed to grab the bundle in front with his teeth, but the bundle on his back fell, and the boy stepped on it. But at this point the boy was shoved hard in the back and found himself right at the train car.

The uncle in the car noticed him, disappeared from the window and appeared on the steps.

"Give it here," the uncle shouted, stretched out his hand and took the bundle from the boy's teeth, and with his other hand pulled him along with the suitcases onto the steps. "And now everything's fine," the uncle said and led him through the jammed corridor.

"And now up," the uncle said and helped the boy to the upper berth. "Put the bundle under your head and sleep well."

The curly-haired woman sat under the berth on a bench, the little uncle on another, and the uncle himself stood and said to people carrying suitcases, "Move on, it's free up ahead . . . Move on, there are three families traveling here, it's taken here . . ."

Then the train car lurched and the boy realized that they were moving.

He saw a snow-covered platform and a fence, and behind the fence a square and people waiting in line, and he saw the old woman who sold fish; she was walking across the square in felt boots with a net bag in her hand. At the end of the square there was the house with the turret where there was a spiral staircase. And if you went to the left, you could reach the smokestack and from there, the hospital.

And suddenly something twisted in his chest and began aching, and the boy was surprised because he had never had such an ache before.

In the window there was now a field, the same white one all the while; poles that were all the same seemed to use the wires to pull each other past the window, and as the boy looked at the wires, the aching inside him grew weaker. The boy lay all curled up, because the uncle's large suitcases were at his feet, and he tried not to look down where someone was walking, dishes were rattling, and heads were flashing by. He was here alone, in his berth, and the berth was shaking and taking him home.

The boy fell asleep and he dreamt of something, but when he woke up, he looked out the cold window, forgot his dream, and remembered that his mother had died. A choking feeling started in his throat and an ache in his face, above his eyebrows, and he let out a sob and then began to sob more loudly, with the sobs coming more frequently, and he was surprised himself that he couldn't stop but just kept on sobbing.

Someone's head appeared above the edge of the berth right next to his face, and the boy recognized the uncle from yesterday.

"What's the matter?" the uncle asked. "You shouldn't do that, you're a big boy . . ."

The uncle disappeared and appeared again with a piece of pie. The pie was spread with a slightly sour plum jam, and thin, crunchy tubes of dough lay on top of the jam.

The boy at first bit off the little tubes and sucked them like candy, then he licked off the jam, and then he ate the rest.

"Nice uncle," the boy thought and looked down.

It was morning. The little uncle was sleeping on a huge, red pillow, and the curly-haired woman and the uncle were speaking about something in a whisper.

The boy got down from the berth and the curly-haired woman glanced at him, and the uncle said, "Go and stand in line for the toilet."

The boy went down the narrow corridor, knocking against the berths and the corners of suitcases, and got in line behind an old man. The old man was in a coat torn to shreds but with a beautiful pince-nez of thick glass on his nose and with a little snatch of grey beard under his lower lip. A row began up front; some woman wanted to get through without waiting her turn.

"I have diarrhea!" she shouted.

"I don't give a damn about your diarrhea!" a male voice answered her. "I've been at this post since seven in the morning!"

"Mores," the old man in the pince-nez said and made a wry smile, and the patch of beard shifted to the left, "the mores of the third year of the war . . ." He looked at the boy and, probably because he was bored, asked, "Traveling with your mother?"

"No," the boy answered, "my mother is in a partisan detachment." He said this unexpectedly for himself and was immediately sorry, but it was too late.

"Is that right?" the old man displayed some interest. "And what about you?"

"I'm here," the boy said, feeling his heart beginning to beat joyfully. "I'm with my uncle," the boy said and suddenly saw the uncle's curly-haired wife walking down the corridor.

He turned red and quickly turned away from the old man, who was getting ready to ask another question.

"Who's in front of you?" the curly-haired woman asked. "I see, but who's behind you?"

A fat woman was standing behind the boy, to be more precise, at one time she had been fat, but now her skin hung on her like an empty sack.

"That won't do," she said. "He can let a whole half-car go in front of him."

"Don't get upset," the curly-haired woman said. "The boy will leave and I'll take his place."

But the fat woman apparently was incensed that they didn't let her go out of turn. She blocked the corridor with her arm and said, "Not a bad exchange. The boy needs five minutes in there, and you two hours . . ."

"You should be ashamed of yourself," the old man said. "There's a war, people are sacrificing themselves . . . This boy's mother, for example, is in a partisan detachment . . ."

"Which one's?" the curly-haired lady asked. "This one's? Why are you lying?" she said to the boy. "Your mother died the day before yesterday in a hospital . . ."

The boy began to feel very hot, and there was a strong ringing in his ears.

"He's ashamed of his grief," the fat woman said.

The boy quickly went back and climbed into his berth. He again felt a choking sensation in his throat and a pain above his eyebrows and, so as not to sob, he closed his eyes tight and clenched his teeth. He lay this way for a long time, and the berth squeaked, and a hum came from below, and something knocked above his head. Then everything died down all at once; the boy opened his eyes and saw a platform through the window along which a lot of people were running. The uncle wasn't in the compartment, but the curly-haired woman was feeding the little uncle condensed milk with a little spoon. It seemed to the boy that you could eat and eat this sweet condensed milk, that you could eat it the whole day if you wouldn't put it in a teaspoon but dip the teaspoon in it and lick it.

The curly-haired woman looked at the boy, and the boy suddenly became frightened; without the uncle she'd put him out on the platform and he'd be alone again.

"Have you got any money?" the curly-haired woman asked.

"I do," the boy answered hastily, reached into his pocket and took out his money.

The curly-haired woman took the money, counted it, and said, "What are people thinking when they set out on such a journey? What was your mother thinking . . . ? There isn't enough here even for you."

"We also had a bag of dried apricots and flat-cakes," the boy said, "but it got lost. And there's still a length of cloth," the boy said. "It can be sold."

He wanted to open the dirty, crushed bundle, but his mother had sewn it with strong, coarse thread and the boy cut his finger. He looked at the torn skin, at the growing drop of blood, and let out a sob.

"What's the matter with you?" the curly-haired woman asked.

"I've cut my finger," the boy answered.

"You're bawling," the curly-haired woman said. "Aren't you ashamed, such a big bruiser like you?"

"I'm not bawling," the boy said, "and when uncle comes, I'm going to tell him what untrue things you're saying about me."

Then the curly-haired woman began to laugh and said, "Why don't you button up your fly, hero . . . ?"

At that point the train lurched and the curly-haired woman began to shout, "Oh, he's being left behind, he's being left behind!"

And the little uncle began to cry. The boy began to feel sorry for the little uncle and said, "Don't you cry, daddy will catch up with the train in a plane . . ."

Then the woman shouted, "Keep quiet, stupid . . . You're a stray that's latched on to us." And she began to wring her hands.

But at this point the uncle appeared with a full bag that he was holding against his chest, and right away the curly-haired woman began to lash out at him as he silently took some bread, steaming whole potatoes, cucumbers, and a large oily herring out of the bag and put them on the small table.

The boy turned his face to the wall and closed his eyes, but nevertheless he didn't forget the oily herring with the potatoes and cucumbers. He would have eaten all this food separately, so that it would last longer. At first the cucumbers, in small bites, then the herring with the bread and, to top it all off, the potatoes. He even moved his lips, turned his face toward the appetizing smell, and suddenly saw directly in front of him a large warm potato and half a cucumber and a crust of bread with some of the soft part.

"Eat, boy," the uncle said, "have your dinner . . ."

The boy ate the potato with its skin; under the skin it was soft and yellow like butter. As for the cucumber, he first bit it all around and left the inside part for last. Then he looked down carefully to see if anyone was looking and, with the piece of greasy newspaper on which the uncle had given him the food, he rubbed the crust and the soft part of the bread. As a result he got bread with herring, and the boy ate it slowly, taking small bites.

After the food the boy felt warm and happy, and he wanted to do something nice for the uncle.

He ripped the bundle open by biting through the strong thread with his teeth, pulled out the length of brown cloth that smelled of naphthalene and said, "Uncle, make yourself a suit."

The uncle raised his eyebrows in surprise, but the curly-haired woman quickly jumped up and stretched out her hand.

"That's not for you, it's for the uncle," the boy said and gave the length of cloth to the uncle.

The old man in the pince-nez walked up to the berth; now he was not wearing a torn coat but a woman's short cardigan.

"In such a tragic time," he said, "it's hard to be a grown man . . . It's hard, in general, to be a human being . . ."

The little uncle looked at the old man and began to cry, and the curly-haired woman said, "Move on, granddad, you've frightened the child."

But the old man continued to stand, rocking back and forth and blinking frequently, his eyelids all red; then the uncle jumped up, took him by the collar of the cardigan, and pushed him well into the corridor.

The boy burst out laughing because the old man made a funny waving motion with his hands and his pince-nez flew off and came to hang on a piece of cord, and he thought, "Good uncle, he got rid of the old man."

The train traveled on and on, the berth squeaked, a humming came from below and a knocking from above, and soon outside the window the boy saw black, burnt-out houses in the middle of the snow. And a tank with a lowered barrel. And a truck with its wheels turned up in the air. And one more tank, and one more truck . . .

The train was moving very quickly, and all this flew by and was left behind; the boy could not make out anything clearly. Then someone approached again and stopped by the berth, and the boy became frightened because he recognized the invalid with the flattened sleeve.

The invalid held a military man by the hand who was wearing a greatcoat without epaulets and a hat with ear-flaps and had a concertina over his shoulder. The face of the military man was covered in dark-green spots and he was wearing dark glasses.

And the uncle became frightened too; the boy saw the uncle choking on a herring tail—the tail was now sticking out of the uncle's mouth.

The uncle coughed, and the invalid and the military man stood silently and looked on.

Finally, the uncle put his fingers in his mouth, pulled out the herring tail, and said to the invalid, "Hello," as if the invalid had never given him the "fig"* and had never spit in his face.

"Hello," the invalid answered politely, "we've seen each other before somewhere."

"Of course, of course," the uncle said. "Perhaps you'd like to have a bite. Take a seat and join us."

"Thank you," the invalid said, "we have our own." And he put an aluminum flask and a package wrapped in newspaper on the small table.

"Kitten," the uncle said to the curly-haired woman, "go take a walk with the child while people eat."

The curly-haired woman looked angrily at the uncle, took the little uncle in her arms, and walked out into the corridor, and the uncle quickly rummaged through a basket and placed two small, nickel-coated, metal tumblers on the table.

The invalid unscrewed the top of the flask and filled the small tumblers, and the military man began to grope around the table with his fingers, first coming upon the flask and then upon the package until he knocked over one tumbler.

"Oh-h," the invalid said, "it's pure alcohol, you know." He poured again and put the tumbler in the military man's hand.

The uncle quickly got a rag and began to wipe up the small puddle on the table.

"Why?" the invalid asked, making a wry face.

"Why not, why not," the uncle said, "the blind comrade here will get his sleeve wet."

The invalid and the military man drank, grunted in approval, and the invalid began to unwrap his package with one hand. In the package there was exactly the kind of pie which the boy had eaten in the morning, only not a small but huge piece; it would have been enough for the boy for a whole day and perhaps even two.

"This pie is awful," the invalid said, "and they sold it at market price . . ."

He took a heavy, gilded cigarette case out of his pocket and opened it. The cigarette case was tightly packed with sauerkraut. The invalid took a pinch of sauerkraut, then grabbed the military man's hand and also stuck it into the cigarette case. They had a drink and right away, without catching their breath, they poured some more and drank again.

At that point the train began to make a thumping sound crossing a bridge, and the invalid said to the military man, "Here it is, the Volga!"

They had another drink and the military man's face became red, but the invalid's cheeks, in contrast, turned white. Their heads swayed low over the table, and past their heads in the window, extending to the very horizon, there were tanks dusted with snow, vehicles, and simply shapeless pieces that could not be identified.

"A graveyard," the invalid said, "an awful lot of metal has been broken up."

They had another drink and the invalid said, "Let's have a front-line song . . ."

The military man often lost his concertina fingering; he'd give up on the melody in the middle and begin all over again.

Soon a lot of people gathered in the compartment. The fat woman said, "Hey, friend, perhaps you'll play 'Cornflowers—Sweet Cornflowers'?"

But the military man continued to play the same melody, breaking it off in the middle and beginning all over again.

He had turned his head to the window and his glasses were looking at the snow-covered, iron graveyard where crows—very black above the white snow—were flying.

The military man's greatcoat was smeared at the elbow with jam from the pie, and the invalid took the pie, got up unsteadily on his legs, and said to the boy, "Eat, kid."

The boy saw before him a poorly-shaven face, with hot breath and a sharp, unpleasant smell coming out of its mouth through yellow teeth, and he withdrew a bit more into the corner.

"If the boy doesn't want it," the old man in the pince-nez said, "I can take it."

"No," the invalid said, "let the kid eat it." And he placed the pie near the boy.

The train began to thump less; it hissed, lurched, and stopped by a burned-out house.

"Your stop," the invalid said to the military man.

He got up and together they walked down the corridor.

"So it's off with them?" the curly-haired woman asked, looking into the compartment. "They've left a pigsty, the alcoholics!"

"Quiet," the uncle said, "he'll come back . . ."

The train started again, this time without lurching, and while it slowly gathered speed, snow-covered ruins and a snowy road—on which people were walking among the ruins—crawled past the window.

The train was already rumbling at full speed when the invalid returned to the compartment and sat down, leaning over the unfinished tumbler and propping up his head with his hand.

He sat this way for a long time and didn't say anything, and the uncle sat on the very edge of the bench and didn't say anything, and the curly-haired woman would look into the compartment and then leave again.

Finally the uncle asked very quietly and very politely, "Maybe you want to sleep? Maybe you want someone to take you back?"

But the invalid continued to sit, and his head kept shaking over the unfinished tumbler.

Then the uncle walked up to the invalid and carefully touched him on the shoulder, and the latter said in a tired voice without raising his head, "Get away from me, you louse, who never served at the front!"

At this moment the curly-haired woman appeared and started to scream. "You don't have the right . . . ! We had something like this happen: an invalid cursed out a man, and the man turned out to be in the organs,[3] and the invalid was put in prison."

"Citizen," the uncle said in a more severe tone, "vacate the seat. My wife and child are sitting here."

The invalid got up slowly, looked at the uncle, and suddenly grabbed the uncle's nose and squeezed it with his fingers.

"Give his things back to the boy," the invalid said. "Give back what you've taken . . ."

The uncle's nose at first turned green, then white, and a thin red stream went running down his paramilitary service jacket all the way down to his riding breeches, and then down his boot.

The curly-haired woman let out a loud scream and the little uncle began to cry, and the boy, although he was frightened, also yelled, "Don't touch the uncle, let go of him . . . !"

At this point the curly-haired woman bent over a suitcase and threw the length of cloth that was a gift for the uncle right into the boy's face, and the conductor and the fat woman pulled the invalid away from the uncle, and the uncle immediately ran off somewhere.

The invalid, bracing himself wearily against the berth with his hand, licked his lips and asked the conductor, "Hey pop, do you have the head open . . . ? I feel sick . . ."

"Like you really needed that alcohol," the conductor with the mustache shook his head and led the invalid off, propping him up in the back with his hand.

The uncle appeared and began to grab his suitcases. He said to the curly-haired woman, "Get your stuff together. I've worked things out in the third car."

"Uncle, wait!" the boy yelled.

But the uncle didn't even look in his direction—he was in a great hurry.

The boy had a choking sensation in his throat again. However, he didn't shut his eyes tight and he didn't clench his teeth so as not to cry because he wanted to cry; and tears flowed down his cheeks and chin and onto the collar of his sweater and his fingers. Everything became wet with tears.

"Is he really his uncle?" the fat woman asked.

"I don't know," the old man in the pince-nez answered. "They were traveling together."

The invalid appeared; his face, neck, and hair were wet, and he kept snorting as if he were still under the faucet.

"Citizens," he said, "fathers and mothers, we need to get the kid home . . . The kid, citizens, is afraid of me . . ." The invalid undid his watchband with his teeth and put the watch on the small table. "Will you get him home, conductor, pop? I have no money . . . I've drunk it all away, pop." He took the cigarette case from his pocket, shook out what was left of the sauerkraut right onto the floor, and put the cigarette case on the table, next to the watch. "Now this is something . . . ! I was offered a whole liter for it." Next he took a cigarette lighter, a pocket knife, and a flashlight out of his pocket, then thought a bit, unbuttoned his pea jacket, and began to unwind his warm, fleecy scarf.

"Wool," he said.

"What are you doing?" the conductor asked and pushed everything that was on the table back toward the invalid. "Stop unwinding your scarf . . . We'll get him back home, it's no big deal . . ."

But the fat woman took the cigarette case and said, "He'll drink it up anyway . . . better to exchange it for food for the boy, there's a junction coming up . . ."

The invalid looked at her, swayed, and suddenly grabbed her around the waist with his only hand and kissed her drooping cheek.

"Just like from a wine barrel," the fat woman said and pushed him away, but she didn't get angry; on the contrary, she smiled and straightened her hair in a coquettish way.

The invalid wiped his eyes on his sleeve, turned around, and winked at the boy.

"Don't worry," he said, "Don't worry, my boy. Courage." And he headed down the corridor.

The boy saw his hunched back, the shaven back of his head, and his big, fat fingers as he adjusted and cocked his sailor's cap with the ear-flaps.

It got darker in the car and the conductor lit the candle in the lamp that hung from the ceiling.

The boy lay on his back on the gutted bundle and looked at the burning candle. The fat woman had given him some bread with white animal fat and a glass of sweetened boiled water, and now he was lying and not thinking about anything.

Gradually the footsteps and voices died down, and only the usual hum of the train and the squeaking of the berth remained. The boy's eyelids closed over his eyes and he saw bright pink circles before him.

He realized this was the candle and turned on his side, and the circles became black. Then he remembered that the uncle's suitcases were no longer there; he stretched out his legs and was just about to fall asleep when some kind of rustling awakened him. The old man in the pince-nez was walking about the compartment. He was walking on tiptoe, with his arms half-bent, and peering into the faces of the sleeping. Then he stretched his hands out in front of him very slowly, like a blind man, and took a step toward the window.

He turned his head jerkily, first to one side, then to the other; his lips were moving. The boy lay quietly; he saw part of the fat woman's sleeping face and her open mouth, and he saw the candle flame in the dark window and the old man's fingers extended toward the flame. His fingers stretched even more and the flame appeared first in the old man's hair, then in his small beard. Suddenly his fingers quickly touched the net bag with the bread that was hanging on a hook by the window and, just as quickly, as if this bread were red-hot, they drew back.

The fat woman made a strange sound with her lips that resembled a kiss and pulled her hand out from under her head. Her eyelashes twitched.

When the boy raised his head, there was no old man in the compartment.

The boy lay a while longer with his eyes open, and his heart began to beat more quietly and more calmly. Then he closed his eyes and wanted to turn toward the wall, but instead he again opened one eye.

The old man was standing right by the berth. Dirty white skin was visible under his thin grey hair.

He had taken off his cardigan and was now in a rumpled silk shirt; its frayed cuffs were secured with wire instead of cuff-links.

He moved hunched over—that's how spies walked in movies, and this was very funny—but the boy didn't find it funny and became frightened like in the morning when he woke up and remembered that his mother had died.

The old man's fingers slid along the crust and broke off a little piece of the brown crust along with the soft grey part, and at that moment he glanced back and met the boy's gaze. The train was moving in darkness, illuminated just the tiniest bit by the snow; it seemed that outside the windows there was no longer any life, only some kind of indefinable objects going past the windows from time to time.

The fat woman was sleeping again with her mouth open, and a metal tooth glistened now and then deep inside her mouth.

The old man straightened himself up carefully, his head swaying, and he transferred the bread from his hand to the back pocket of his trousers.

He kept looking at the boy without blinking, and the boy raised himself on his elbows, broke off a corner of the pie left by the invalid, and offered it to the old man. The old man took it and immediately swallowed it. The boy again broke off a piece from the bottom of the pie where there was no jam, and the old man took it just as quickly and swallowed it. The boy gave the old man the whole bottom part of the pie, piece by piece; and the upper part, with the jam and the baked, crunchy little tubes, he left for himself.

The conductor came and wrapped the lamp in a dark rag to mask the light; now only a foggy spot contracted and expanded on the ceiling. The old man stood wrinkling his brow and remembering something, and then he went down the car past the snoring berths, past the sleeping people who were sitting up and half lying down, all the way up to the exit area of the car, where some people were also lying on bundles.

"Can it be that this will never end?" the old man said quietly and went back.

He stood at the boy's berth and looked at the boy sleeping.

The boy was asleep on the gutted bundle, and his cheek rested on the top part of a woman's felt boots.

The sleeves of his sweater were rolled up and his shoes were unlaced.

The boy dreamed of the house with the turret, the uncle, the old woman selling fish, the invalid with the strong, fat fingers, and of other, different faces and objects which he immediately forgot in his sleep. Then right before dawn, when the burned-out candle went out and the old man covered the boy's feet with a warm cardigan, the boy saw his mother, sighed in relief and smiled.

In early morning, someone opened the door to the exit area of the car, cold air woke the boy up, and he lay there smiling a while longer . . .

1963

NOTES

1. special train (*èshelon*): in wartime a train for transporting large numbers of people—soldiers as well as civilians.
2. Russian children use "uncle" to address a male stranger. An American child would use "mister" in such situations, but "mister" does not fit a number of exchanges and descriptions in the story, and thus a decision was made to use "uncle" throughout the text.
3. organs: a reference to the secret police, the NKVD at the time.

"VICTORY"

A Short Story with Doses of Hyperbole

Vasily Aksyonov

In a compartment of an express train a grandmaster was playing chess with a fellow passenger.

That man had immediately recognized the grandmaster when the latter entered the compartment, and immediately developed an inconceivable burning desire for an inconceivable victory over the grandmaster. "So what," he thought, casting sly, inquiring glances at the grandmaster, "so what. Big deal—he's just some wimp."

The grandmaster realized right away that he had been recognized and gloomily accepted the fact that at least two games would be unavoidable. He also recognized immediately what kind of man this was. At times he would see the pink, high foreheads of people like this through the windows of the Chess Club on Gogolevsky Boulevard.[1]

Once the train started moving, the grandmaster's fellow passenger stretched with a look of unsophisticated slyness and asked indifferently, "How about playing a small game of chess, friend?"

"I suppose we could," mumbled the grandmaster.

The fellow passenger stuck his head out of the compartment, called the train car attendant, and a chess set appeared; given his indifference, he grabbed it much too quickly, spilled the chess pieces out on the table, took two pawns, clenched them in his fists, and held his fists out in front of the grandmaster. A tattoo in the fleshy part between his thumb and index finger read "G.O."

"The left one," the grandmaster said and frowned slightly, imagining the punches those fists could deliver, both the left and the right one.

He drew white.

"We have to kill some time, right? Chess is just the thing when you're traveling," G.O. said in a good-natured way as he arranged the chess pieces.

They quickly played the Northern gambit and then everything got confused. The grandmaster kept an attentive eye on the board, making small, insignificant moves. Several times possible ways to a checkmate with the queen appeared in lightning flashes before his eyes, but he extinguished those flashes by lowering his eyelids and submitting to the wearisome note of compassion, resembling the buzzing of a mosquito, that droned within him.

"Khas Bulat the Brave,[2] your *saklya*[3] is poor . . ," G.O. sang in a monotone.

The grandmaster was the embodiment of meticulousness, the embodiment of fastidious dress and manners that is so typical of people who lack confidence and are easily wounded. He was young, wore a grey suit, a light-colored shirt, and a simple tie. No one except the grandmaster himself knew that his simple ties had the "House of Dior" label. This little secret somehow always warmed and comforted the young and quiet grandmaster. His glasses saved him quite frequently as well by concealing his timid gaze and lack of confidence from others. He regretted his lips, which had a tendency to break out in a pathetic smile or tremble. He would have readily shielded his lips from the eyes of others but, unfortunately, it was not yet socially acceptable.

G.O.'s playing amazed and distressed the grandmaster. On the left flank the pieces crowded together to form a tangle of fraudulent, cabalistic signs. The whole left flank became permeated with the smell of bathroom and chlorine, the sour smell of barracks and wet kitchen rags, and there was also the lingering smell of castor oil and diarrhea from the grandmaster's early childhood.

"You are grandmaster so-and-so, aren't you?" G.O asked.

"Yes," the grandmaster acknowledged.

"Ha-ha-ha, what a coincidence!" G. O. exclaimed.

"What a coincidence? What coincidence is he talking about? This is something inconceivable! Could something like this happen? I refuse, please accept my refusal," the grandmaster quickly thought in his panic and then guessed what was going on and smiled. "Yes, of course, of course."

"So you're a grandmaster, but I'm pinning your queen and rook," G.O. said. He raised his hand. The knight-provocateur hung poised over the board.

"A pin in the rear," the grandmaster thought to himself. "That's some *vilochka!*[4] Grandfather had his own fork and he never let anyone use it. His property. His personal fork, spoon and knife, his personal plates and his small spittoon. The 'lyre'[5] fur coat also comes to mind. A heavy coat of "lyre" fur used to hang in the entrance; grandfather almost never went outside. A pin on my grandfather and grandmother. It's sad to lose the elderly."

While the knight hung poised over the board, glowing lines and points of possible pre-checkmate attacks and victims flashed again before the grandmaster's eyes. Alas, the horse's rump with the dirty purple, thick flannelette that was coming off was so persuasive that the grandmaster shrugged his shoulders.

"Are you giving away your rook?" G.O. asked

"What can I do?"

"Sacrificing your rook for an attack? Did I guess right?" G.O. asked, still not able to bring himself to place his knight on the desired square.

"I'm simply saving the queen," the grandmaster mumbled.

"You're not trying to trick me?" G.O. asked.

"No, what do you mean? You're a strong player."

G.O executed his cherished pin. The grandmaster hid his queen in a secluded corner behind a terrace, behind the half-collapsed stone terrace with carved, slightly rotting posts, where there was the pungent smell of rotting maple leaves in the fall. Here you sit it out comfortably—squatting. It's nice here; in any case, your self-esteem does not suffer. Rising in his seat for a second and looking out from behind the terrace, he saw that G.O. had removed his rook.

The intrusion of the black knight into the pointless crowd on the left flank, his occupation of square B4, at any rate, now made the grandmaster think.

The grandmaster realized that in this case, on this green spring evening, youthful myths alone would not suffice. It's all true, there are nice fools wandering around in the world—sea cadets named Billy, cowboys named Harry, beauties named Mary and Nelly—and a brigantine is raising its sails, but there comes a moment when you feel the dangerous and real proximity of the black knight on square B4. A struggle was coming—difficult, subtle, captivating, tactical. Ahead was life.

The grandmaster won a pawn, took out a handkerchief, and blew his nose. The few moments of complete solitude, when his lips and nose were covered by the handkerchief, brought on a banally philosophical mood in him. "That's the way you try to attain something," he thought to himself, "but then what? All your life you're trying to attain something, then victory is yours, but there's no joy in it. Take for example the city of Hong Kong—distant and very mysterious—but I've already been there, I've already been everywhere."

The loss of a pawn did not distress G.O too much, since he had just taken a rook. He responded to the grandmaster's move by moving his queen, which brought on heartburn and a fleeting headache.

The grandmaster knew that there were still a few joys left in store for him. For example, the joy of prolonged moves of his bishop along the entire length of the diagonal. If you drag the bishop along the board a little bit, then it can substitute to some extent for rapidly gliding in a skiff on the sunny and lightly stagnant water of a pond near Moscow— out of the light, into the shade, out of the shade, into the light. The grandmaster felt an irresistible, fervent desire to take square H8, since this was the square of love, a small knoll of love, over which transparent dragonflies hovered.

"Very clever how you took my rook, but I just blew it," G.O. said in a deep voice, with only his last words betraying his annoyance.

"Sorry," the grandmaster said softly. "Maybe you'd like to take back a few moves?"

"No, no," G.O. said "no favors, I beg you."

"I'll give my sword, give my steed, give that rifle of mine . . . ," he started to sing, absorbed in contemplating his strategy.

The tempestuous summer holiday of love on the field did not bring the grandmaster joy and, moreover, disturbed him. He sensed that soon in the center there would be a build-up of externally logical but internally absurd forces. The cacophony would be heard again and there would be the smell of chlorine, like in those distant corridors of his damned memory on the left flank.

"So, I wonder, why are all the chess players Jewish?" G.O. asked.

"Why all of them?" the grandmaster said. "Take me, for example. I'm not Jewish."

"Is that so?" G.O. said in surprise and added, "Don't get me wrong, I don't mean it like that. I'm not at all prejudiced in that respect. Just curious."

"Well, take yourself, for example," the grandmaster said, "you're not Jewish."

"How could I be!" G.O. mumbled and again became absorbed in his secret plans.

"If I do this, then he'll do that," G.O. thought to himself. "If I take his piece here, he'll take one there, then I move here, he responds by . . . I'll still finish him off, I'll still break him. Big deal—grandmaster, cheatmaster. You still don't have the strength to beat me. I know your championship games; you all strike a deal ahead of time. I'll still crush you, or at least bloody your nose!"

"Ye-es, the quality of my playing has gone down," he said to the grandmaster, "but never mind, there's still time."

G. O. launched an attack in the center, but of course, just as expected, the center was immediately transformed into a field of pointless and terrible actions. It was non-love, non-reunion, non-hope, non-hello, non-life. A flu-like chill and yellow snow again, post-war discomfort, the whole body itching. The black queen in the center cawed like a love-struck crow, crow love; moreover, at the neighbors' they were scraping a tin bowl with a knife. Nothing proved as definitively the pointless and illusory nature of life as that position in the center. It was time to end the game.

"No," the grandmaster thought, "you know, there's something else besides this." He put on a long tape of Bach's piano pieces, calmed his heart with sounds that were clear and measured, like the lapping of waves, then walked out of the dacha and headed down to the sea. The pine trees rustled above him and slippery and springy pine needles were under his feet.

Remembering and imitating the sea, he began to examine his position and harmonize it. His soul suddenly felt pure and light. Logically, like the Bach coda, checkmate to the black was at hand. The checkmate situation began to glow dimly and beautifully, complete like an egg. The grandmaster looked at G.O. He was silent, scowling at the furthest positions of the grandmaster. He did not notice that he was in danger of putting his own king in checkmate. The grandmaster was silent, afraid of breaking the spell of the moment.

"Check," G.O. said softly and carefully, moving his knight. He could barely contain the roar within him.

. . . The grandmaster screamed and broke into a run. The owner of the dacha, Evripid the stableman, and Nina Kuzminichna ran after him, stamping and whistling. The dog Nochka, which had been let off its chain, was running ahead of them and catching up to the grandmaster.

"Check," G.O. said one more time, moving his knight and taking a breath of air with painful pleasure.

. . . The grandmaster was being led through a hushed crowd that made way for him. The person walking behind him was touching his back lightly with a hard object. A man in a black coat with SS insignia on his lapels was waiting for him up ahead. One step—half a second, another step—one second, another—one and a half, another step—two . . . Stairs going up. Why up? Such things should be done in a ditch. Must be brave. Is that obligatory? How much time does it take to put a foul-smelling burlap sack over a person's head? Then it became completely dark and difficult to breathe, and only somewhere very far off an orchestra was playing with bravura "Khas Bulat the Mighty."

"Checkmate!" G.O. shouted like a copper trumpet.

"There you are," the grandmaster mumbled, "congratulations!"

"Gosh," said G.O . "Gosh, I've really worn myself out. I'll be damned! Just think of it, it's unbelievable! Unbelievable, but I've slapped a checkmate on the grandmaster. Unbelievable, but a fact!" he burst out laughing. "Good for me!" He jokingly patted himself on the head. "Oh grandmaster of mine, grandmaster," he began to drone, putting his hands on the grandmaster's shoulders and squeezing them in a friendly way, "you're a good fellow, young man . . . Your poor nerves gave out, is that it? Admit it!"

"Yes, yes, I broke down," the grandmaster acknowledged hastily.

G.O. cleared the pieces off the board with a broad, sweeping movement. The board was old, chipped, the polished top layer had come off in places, exposing worn-out, yellow wood; here and there partial round stains were left from glasses of railroad tea placed there in times past.

The grandmaster looked at the empty board, at the sixty-four absolutely dispassionate squares which were able to contain not only his own life, but an endless number of lives, and that endless alternation of light and dark squares filled him with awe and quiet joy. "It seems," he thought, "I haven't committed any major base deeds in my life."

"And you can tell someone, but no one will believe you," G.O. sighed bitterly.

"Why wouldn't they believe you? What is so unbelievable about it? You're a strong player with will power," the grandmaster said.

"No one will believe me," G.O. repeated, "they'll say I'm lying. What proof have I got?"

"Allow me," the grandmaster said, slightly offended, looking at G.O.'s pink, high forehead. "I'll give you convincing proof. I knew I'd meet you."

He opened his briefcase and took out a large gold medal, the size of his hand, on which was beautifully engraved: "The bearer of this medal won a chess match against me. Grandmaster so-and-so."

"All that's left is to fill in the date," he said, took out an engraving kit from his briefcase, and beautifully engraved the date in a corner of the medal. "This is pure gold," he said, handing him the medal.

"For real?" G.O. asked.

"Absolutely pure gold," the grandmaster said. "I've already ordered a lot of these medals and I'll be constantly replenishing my supplies."

1965

NOTES

1. Gogolevsky Boulevard, House #14 was, in fact, where the Central House of Chess and the Chess Museum were located in the 1960s.
2. "Khas-Bulat the Brave": a popular folk song dating to tsarist times, which was part of the repertoire of many choral groups in Soviet times.
3. *saklya*: a mountain hut in the Caucasus.
4. *vilochka*, the diminutive form of *vilka*. *Vilka* means both "fork" (as in spoon, knife and fork) and "pin" (in chess, a situation brought on by an attacking piece in which a defending piece cannot move without exposing a more valuable defending piece on its other side to capture by the attacking piece. The player must decide which piece to sacrifice). The grandmaster's mind moves between the two meanings of the same word in Russian, but in English a choice has to be made between two words, "fork" and "pin."
5. lyre: Skunk fur coats were called "lyre" (*lirnye*) because the skins were cut and sewn in a shape resembling a lyre.

HANDS

Yuli Daniel (pseud. "Nikolai Arzhak")

You're an educated man, Sergei, polite. That's why you're silent, why you don't ask any questions. But our guys at the plant, they say straight out, "So Vaska, it's your drinking that has messed you up like this?!" They're talking about my hands. Think I didn't notice you looking at my hands and turning away? And right now you keep trying to look past my hands. I understand everything, brother—you're doing this out of tact so as not to embarrass me. But go ahead, look, look, it's all right. I won't be offended. You're not likely to see something like this every day. It's not from heavy drinking, my friend. I don't drink often—more in the company of other people or on special occasions, like with you now. We've just got to drink to us meeting again. I remember everything, brother. How you and I stood hiding, how you talked in French to the White[1] soldier, how we captured Yaroslavl . . . Remember how you spoke at the political meeting and took me by the hand—I happened to be next to you—and you said, "With these here hands . . . " Ye-e-s. Go on and pour, Seryoga, or I'll start sniveling. I forget what it's called, this shaking, in medical terms. It's all right, I have it written down. I'll show it to you later . . . So—what made me this way? An incident. If I take it in the order things happened, then I'll tell you that when we were demobilized in that victorious year of 1921, I immediately returned to my old plant. Well, as a revolutionary hero, it was clear that I had the esteem and respect of others and, then again, I was a member of the party, a conscientious worker. Of course, I did have to set some people straight. All kinds of talk had started at that time: "Here's what our fighting has brought us," they'd say, "here's what being in charge has led us to. No bread, not a damn thing . . ." Well, I stopped that kind of talk. I was always firm. You can't fool me with that Menshevik[2] gibberish of theirs. Yeah. Go ahead and pour, don't wait for me. I worked for only about a year, no more, then wham!—they call me to the *raikom*. "Here are travel orders for you, Malinin," they say. "The party," they say, "is mobilizing you, Malinin, Vasily Semyonovich, into the ranks of the heroic Extraordinary Commission,[3] to fight against the counter-revolution. We wish you success," they say, "in your struggle with the world bourgeoisie, and if you see comrade Dzerzhinsky,[4] give him our best regards." And me—what can I say? I'm a party man. "Yes sir!" I say, "I'll fulfill the party's command." I took my travel orders, dropped by the plant, said good-bye to the guys there and left. I'm walking and daydreaming about how I'm going to hunt down all those counter-revolutionaries mercilessly so they don't defile our young Soviet power. Well, I go there. I did, in fact, see Dzerzhinsky, Felix Edmunovich, passed on greetings from the *raikom* guys to him as I was told. He shook my hand, thanked me, and then all of us—there were about thirty of us, mobilized by the party—he lined us all up and said that you can't build a house in a swamp, at first you have to drain the swamp, and he said all kinds of toads and snakes would have to be destroyed in doing that, and he said there was an iron necessity to do that. And all of us, he says, have to give it the attention it deserves . . . That's to say, he told a sort of fable or anecdote, but everything was clear, of course. He's stern, doesn't smile. And afterwards they began assigning us jobs. Who, what, where—they questioned us. "How much schooling?" they ask. My schooling, you know yourself, was the German war and the civil war, and I drudged at the lathe—and that was all my schooling . . . Finished two years of parochial school . . . Well, they assigned me to a special service team—to put it simply, to carry out death sentences . . . The work wasn't exactly difficult, but you couldn't call it easy either. It affects your heart. It was one thing at the front, you remember yourself: either you get him, or he gets you. But here . . . Well, I got used to it, of course. You walk behind him through the courtyard, and think, and say to yourself: "You have to, Vasily, H-A-V-E T-O. If you don't kill him now, the bastard will destroy the whole Soviet Republic. I got used to it. I'd drink, of course, couldn't do without it. They'd give us alcohol. As for some special rations—that the men of the Cheka* were fed chocolate and white bread—those are all bourgeois inventions. The rations were just rations, the usual ones, a soldier's—bread, millet, and roach. But they really did give us grain alcohol. You can't do without, you know yourself. Well, so there you are. I worked like that for about seven months, and here's where the incident took place. We were ordered to liquidate a group of priests. For counterrevolutionary agitation. For slander. They were stirring up the parishioners there. Maybe it was because of Tikhon.[5] Or against socialism in general—I don't know. In a word—enemies. There were twelve of them. Our commander gave us orders: "You, Malinin, will take three, and you, Vlasenko, and you, Golovchiner, and you . . ." I forgot the fourth one's name. He was a Latvian—he had a strange name, not one of ours. He and Golovchiner went first. And this is how things were set up: the guard room—it was exactly in the middle. On one side was the room where the condemned were held, and on the other side, the exit to the yard. We took them one at a time. You finish one off in the yard, drag him with the guys to the side, and go back for another. You had to drag them away, otherwise it would be that you'd walk out behind another one, but when he'd see the dead man and begin fighting and struggling to get free, you'd have no end of troubles, and it's clear why. It's better when they're quiet. Well then, Golovchiner and the Latvian finished off theirs, and it was my turn. And I'd drunk some alcohol before that. It wasn't that I was afraid or attached to religion. No, I'm a party man, firm, and I don't believe in that stupidity—all kinds of gods, angels, and archangels, but all the same, I began to feel kind of strange. It's easy for Golovchiner, he's a Jew, they don't even have icons, people say, but I don't know if that's true, and I sit and drink, and all kinds of nonsense keeps coming into my head: how my dead mother used to take us to the church in the village and how I'd kiss the hand of our priest, Father Vasily, and he—he was an old man—would call me his namesake. . . Yea-ah. So then, I went for the first one, led him out. Returned, had a smoke, led out the second. Went back, had a drink—and I began to feel sick to my stomach. "Wait, guys," I say. "I'll be back in a minute." I put the Mauser on the table and walked out. Drank too much, I think to myself. I'll stick my fingers down my throat right now, throw up, wash up, and everything will be fine. So I went and did everything I had to—but no, I wasn't better. Fine, I think, to hell with him, I'll finish everything now and go to sleep. I took my Mauser, went for the third. The third was still young, a fine figure of a man—such a big priest, handsome. I lead him down the hallway, look at how he picks up his long cassock over the threshold, and I get sick to my stomach—I don't understand myself what that's all about. We walked out into the courtyard. And he lifts his beard and looks at the sky. "Move, father," I say, "don't look back. You've earned paradise for yourself with all your prayers." I made a joke to bolster myself. Why— I don't know. Nothing like that had ever happened to me—to talk with a condemned man. Well, I let him get three steps ahead of me, as required, placed the Mauser between his shoulder blades and fired. A Mauser—you know yourself—is like a cannon when it fires! And the recoil is such that it almost pulls your arm out of the shoulder socket. But I look, and my executed priest is turning and heading for me. Of course, it's never the same twice: some fall flat on their faces right away, some turn round and round, and there are times when some start walking and staggering like drunk. But this one is heading for me with small steps, seemingly floating in his cassock as though I hadn't fired into him. "What's this, father? Stop!" And I put my gun once more—this time to his chest. But he opened his cassock wide and ripped it open. His chest is hairy and curly, and he's walking and shouting at the top of his voice, "Go on, shoot me, you Antichrist! Go ahead and kill me—your Christ!" I lost my head at this point, fired again and again. But he keeps on walking! There's no wound and no blood, and he's walking and praying: "Oh Lord, you stopped the bullet from the evil hands! I accept the suffering for You . . . ! A living soul can't be killed!" And something more . . . I don't remember emptying the cartridge clip, I only know for sure I couldn't have missed—I fired point-blank. He's standing before me, his eyes afire like a wolf's, his chest bare, and a glow seems to be coming from his head. It's only later I figured out he had blocked the sun for me—it was setting. "Your hands," he shouts, "are covered with blood! Take a look at your hands!" At this point I threw my Mauser to the ground, headed for the guard room, knocked someone over in the doorway and ran inside, and the guys looked at me like at a madman and laughed their heads off. I grabbed a rifle from the stack and shouted, "Take me," I shouted, "to Dzerzhinsky this very minute, or I'll bayonet every one of you right now!" Well, they took the rifle away from me and led me off in a quick march. I walked into his office, broke free from my comrades, and said to him trembling all over and stuttering, "Shoot me, Felix Edmundovich, I can't kill a priest!" I said this and fell down, I don't remember anything else. I came to in a hospital. The doctors say, "An attack of nerves." To tell the truth, they gave me good medical treatment, they were very caring. And there was care and cleanliness, and the meals—given the times—were simple. They cured me of everything, but my hands, as you can see for yourself, keep shaking. The attack of nerves must have gone into them. I was discharged from the Cheka, of course. They need different hands there. You can't return to work at the lathe either, that's obvious. They assigned me to the plant warehouse. Well, and so what, I do my job there too. True, I don't fill out all sorts of papers and way bills myself—because of my hands. I have an assistant for that, a bright young girl. And so that's how I live, brother. And as for that priest, I found out later what went on. And there's nothing divine here. It's just that when I'd gone to relieve myself, our guys took out the cartridge clip in my Mauser and put in another—with blanks. They played a trick. Well, I'm not angry at them—they were young, they didn't have it easy either, and so they dreamed it up. No, I'm not angry with them. Only now my hands . . . aren't good for any kind of work at all . . .

1966

NOTES

1. The Whites fought against the Reds during the revolution and civil war.
2. The All Russian Social Democratic Workers Party, founded to overthrow the tsarist regime, split into two groupings in 1903. At a party meeting those who recieved a minority of the votes came to be known as the Mensheviks. In subsequent years they clashed with the Bolsheviks on basic issues of Russia's development and were outlawed by Lenin in 1922.
3. Exraordinary Commission: the Cheka*.
4. Dzerzhinsky, Felix (1877-1926): He headed the Cheka*.
5. Patriarch Tikhon: 1863-1925: in 1921, during the famine that affected vast regions of Russia in the last year of the civil war, he instructed churches to use their articles of value to raise money for the starving.

A GERMAN IN FELT BOOTS

Konstantin Vorobyov

At the time it was already the beginning of spring in the Baltics. Buds were now starting to swell on the poplar tree in our camp, and along the forbidden line—near the wire fences—grass was breaking through and some dandelions could be spotted. It was already warm, but that German guard appeared wearing our Russian felt boots with the tops cut off and a fur jacket under his uniform. He appeared in the morning and crossed the barracks twice from the door to the blind wall; first he surveyed the bed boards* on the left, then on the right, looking for someone among us. He was stocky, broad-faced, and red-haired like a sunflower and walked softly with the lumbering gait of a village tomcat.

We—forty-six prisoners who had broken camp rules—were sitting in the bottom row of the bed boards and looking at the German's feet— his Siberian felt boots with the tops cut off did not bode well for us. Clearly, the German had fought in the winter near Moscow. And who knows what crazy ideas had occurred to him with the arrival of warm weather, and whom he was looking for here and why! He sat down in an empty place on the bed boards, threw one leg over the other, and frowned. I knew from my own experience that frostbitten toes always hurt in warm weather. Especially the little toes . . . And so it was with the German. And you never know what he has in mind now! I was sitting way in the back on the bed boards, and a weapons mechanic, Ivan Voronov, had his back pressed against me—he was a goner and living out his last few days. There, where Voronov and I had our places, the darkness never dissipated—the window was above the third row of bed boards—but the German still spotted us, just me to be exact. He extended his hand towards me and bent and straightened his index finger several times.

I laid Ivan down and climbed down from the bed boards. You only needed four normal-sized steps to cover the distance, but it took me a while. The German was leaning back, holding his feet up and looking

— 417 —

at me with a grimace expressing pained disgust, while I had to balance myself and make sort of rowing motions now with my right hand, now with my left, in order to stay on course and approach him in a straight line. I miscalculated and stopped too close to the bed boards, grazing the German's raised feet with my bony knees. He growled something—cursed, probably—and moved away, staring at my bare feet with frostbitten toes. I stood still, keeping my balance, and waited, and it was quiet and cold in the barracks. He asked me something curtly and angrily as he looked at his feet, and I shook my head "no." We knew that the guards and convoy escorts beat with particular zeal the sick, the goners, and those who tried to shield themselves from punches and groaned.

"*Schmerz nicht?*"[i] the German asked and looked at me strangely; there was disbelief, surprise, and bewilderment in his blue eyes edged in pale lashes. "*Du lügst,Mensch!*"[ii] he said. I understood what he meant and repeated that my feet didn't hurt. He could've hit me now— I was prepared not to shield myself and not to moan, and to answer questions in the same way that I had started. The wait for the inevitable, if you're a prisoner and twenty-two years old, is worse than the event itself, because a person doesn't know how it'll begin, how long it'll last, and how it'll end, and I was beginning to grow tired of waiting, but the German was in no hurry. He was sitting, thinking about something, glancing at me strangely from time to time, and holding his feet in the felt boots with the tops cut off up in the air. It was quiet and cold in the barracks. Finally the German thought of something and stuck his hand in the right pocket of his pants. I moved my feet apart, leaned slightly forward, and closed my eyes—I now knew the inevitable was about to begin. It took a long time to start and, when the German said something, I fell on top of him because my eyes were closed and I took the sound of his voice to be the fading echo of the event's end. The German pushed me aside silently and easily, and I swayed a bit and sat down on the edge of the bed boards. It was very quiet and cold in the barracks. Voronov had probably seen me going up to the German, and now he was moving towards us, using

---

i   "No pain?" This phrase and others in subsequent footnotes are translations into English of German phrases Vorobyov gives in Cyrillic letters within his text and translates into Russian for his readers in footnotes. We have restored the German in the text.
ii   "You're lying, man!"

the same technique I had used—he seemed to be swimming. He was looking straight at my forehead—maybe he had picked a reference point so that he wouldn't lose his way, and his eyes looked round and shone insanely. The German didn't notice Voronov since he was trying to seal the cigarette he had rolled—I had broken it when I fell on him—and Ivan kept walking and walking, rowing now with his right arm, now with his left. I didn't know what my goner friend was thinking. Having taken care of his cigarette, the German saw Voronov and at first waved at him like a cat moves his paw—in front of his nose—and then shouted, *"Zurück!"*[iii]

"Go back!" I said to Ivan. "And . . . you . . ?" he said, pausing for breath after each word and still looking straight at my forehead with his insane eyes.

"I'll go too," I said.

"And him? What's with him?"

"Fort!"[iv] the German yelled and waved his hand right in front of his nose.

"Go to your place! Quickly!" I said and Voronov slowly turned around; something drew him away from our place in the corner of the bed boards. The German's lighter didn't work—the flint had probably worn out, or there was no more lighter fluid, and he kept flicking and flicking it without letting Ivan out of his sight; maybe he was scared that Ivan would turn and come this way again. Voronov made it to his place and lay down on his stomach, placing his head on his outstretched arms like a dog. He was looking at my forehead. In the gloom of the bed boards his eyes shone like burning coals among ashes, and the German waved his hand at them again with a catlike gesture from afar, and Ivan said in a thin, dying voice, "To hell . . . with you!"

"Was wünscht dieser Verrüchter?"[v] the German asked. It's possible that he didn't use those words—I didn't know German well then, but he was asking about Voronov and I replied, touching my Adam's apple, "He's asking for a drink."

The German wrinkled his forehead as he looked at my mouth and understood. *"Wasser?"*[vi]

---

iii "Go back!"
iv "Quickly!"
v "What does that madman want?"
vi "Water?"

"Yes," I said.

"*Bekommt ihr denn kein wasser?*"[vii]

"No," I understood what he said.

"*Scheisse!*"[viii] the German swore quietly and gloomily, and Ivan asked me in a small, breaking voice, "Sash, tell him . . . to go to hell!"

He wasn't wishing him hell but something else entirely that in Ivan's mind seemed no better than the cold around Moscow. I nodded, promising to do that, and Voronov quieted down and his eyes stopped shining. The German lit his cigarette, but it didn't burn well because it was broken, and he offered it to me. I squeezed the torn part together and inhaled as long as I could. The cigarette shrank in half, and I thought that thirty seconds would be enough for Ivan and took a second drag. I saw the German waiting for me to exhale the smoke, but there was none—it had settled down there, inside me. The barracks, the bed boards, and the waiting German began to float away from me without actually moving, and at that moment Ivan called out as if from beyond the horizon, "Sash, twenty . . . all right?"

"*Jetzt will er rauchen?*"[ix] the German asked, pointing at Ivan and the cigarette. I nodded "yes" and the German swore in surprise. I decided that I had to overcome the distance—just four normal-size steps long—by falling forward, then my legs would pick up a running pace on their own and not lead me to the side. Voronov was waiting for me in the same position, only he had spread out the index and middle fingers of his right hand—he was ready. I placed the cigarette butt between them and waited. Ivan took a drag and closed his eyes—probably floated off with the barracks, and then I looked back at the German. He looked at my forearm, then at my feet for a while, and then summoned me not with his finger as before, but aloud.

"*Alle sind da Flüchtlinge? Komm-Komm!*"[x] he asked and imitated mincing steps with his short fingers covered with copper-colored hair.

"All of us," I said and sat back down in my place. "Only not at the same time, and from different camps."

The German lifted his feet off the floor, and his face became stone-

---

vii "Didn't he get any water?"
viii "Shit!"
ix "Does he want to smoke now?"
x "Is everyone here a runaway? Come here, come!"

like and tense; his toes had probably begun to ache. I wanted to lie down in my place next to Voronov, lift my knees to my chin, and squeeze the soles of my feet with my hands to stop the pain in my little toes. Without realizing it, I lifted my feet to the same level as the German's and accidentally let out a groan. "*Schmertzen?*"[xi] the German asked.

"Yes, they hurt, they hurt!" I said angrily. "That makes you feel better, does it?"

Our eyes met and I saw an interest in the German's eyes that could turn out to be dangerous for me, a hope that even he wasn't aware of. "Now you feel better, do you?" I asked. Evidently he didn't understand what I was talking about because he turned toward me, leaning on his hands without lowering his feet, and said hurriedly, "*Ich bin Bauer, verstehst? Ba-u-er. Und du?*"[xii]

From a military dictionary I knew what a *bauer* was. Of course! He had to be that *bauer* and nothing else. They guzzle beer—"*noch ein mal*"[xiii]—eat old yellow sausage, grow red hair, and then go to war with the whole world and get frostbite on their feet near Moscow . . . ! I didn't know what he had gotten into his head in the warm weather, what he wanted from me, and didn't answer his question.

"*Ich bin Bauer, verstehst? Ba-u-er!*" the German said it as if he had just remembered something joyous. "*Und du?*"

Maybe because the pain in my little toes didn't go away that whole time and I was thinking about shoes, I chose a cobbler's trade. The German didn't realize right away what that meant, so I pointed at my bare feet and waved an imaginary hammer.

"*Schumacher?*" the German asked, figuring it out.

I nodded. He looked at his worn-out Siberian shoes and grumbled something; he didn't like my profession. As before, a painful silence remained in the barracks; the prisoners were waiting for the episode to end, and the German was holding up his feet and remaining silent. I kept watching the expression on his face. It was grave and strained.

"*Na, alles,*" he said. "*Zeit zu gehen!*"[xiv]

A prisoner was supposed to walk about six steps ahead of his escort.

---

xi   "Do they hurt?"
xii   "I'm a farmer. Do you understand? A far-mer. And you?"
xiii   "One more."
xiv   "Well, that's all . . . Time to go."

Such a distance is very dangerous if you've made up your mind to run away—not from the barracks, of course, but once you're outside the camp, when it's clear where both of you are headed. The one who tried it always fell down dead ten steps from the escort if he rushed straight ahead, fifteen if he ran to the left, and about twenty if he dashed to the right. The prisoners knew this inexplicable principle well, and the one destined to take a walk outside the camp invariably ran to the right. Of course, you didn't have to run, but the number twenty is fourteen more than six, and it's clear why a runaway would chose the right, if you take into account that in this case his heart would be shielded from the escort by his right side.

And so I walked to the exit in front of the German, but he said, "*Moment,*" and I lingered but didn't look back so as not to see Ivan's eyes. The German caught up with me and we walked side by side—I, rowing now with my right arm, now with my left—and he with a lumbering gait, frowning and looking at my feet. In the cement floor near the door there was a deep pit filled with the piss of the goners, an amber-yellow color of the rainbow. We tripped there at the same time, and the German let out a few short, harsh curses, and I swore at length, probably letting out a whole stream of curses, because he grew quiet and listened to my words closely. I had to rub my stubbed toes to straighten them out, and I sat down and swore again, invoking the souls of both the living and the dead.

"What are you mumbling over there?" the German asked suspiciously and quietly. "After that they don't hurt, right?"[1]

It's possible that he used different words, but that was the general sense of his question; I couldn't have been wrong. There was no point in my trying to convince him otherwise, and I confirmed his supposition with words and gestures. One of ours started to laugh thinly and in pain, and the German probably understood the malicious intent of the laughter because he looked me over from head to toe appraisingly. I had already taken care of my feet and was ready to go, and then the German asked me something twice that I didn't understand.

"*Ich heisse* Willy Brode," he said and poked himself in the chest with his thumb. "*Und wie ist deine Name?*"[xv]

I said my name. The German sounded it out carefully and incorrectly

---

xv   "My name is Willy Brode . . . And what's yours?"

and walked away slowly, taking big steps. I stood by the door for a while and wandered back to my place. Ivan stirred and, without opening his eyes and sobbing, asked, "What did he want?"

"Don't know. . . ," I said. "Maybe he'll come back."

"To hell . . . with him."

I lay down as I'd been wanting to, bringing my knees to my chin and squeezing my toes with my fingers. It was cold and quiet in the barracks all day and all night, and in the morning the German appeared again. He didn't want to step over the pit and stood by the door. Voronov and I sat the way all goners had learned to do—back to back—and I leaned back just a little bit so that the post of the bed boards would shield me from the German. It did hide me, but then the German called out "Alekshandr," breaking my name into two parts, and I laid Ivan down and climbed down from the bed boards. The German stood by the door—thickset, unkempt, and reddish-haired, like a dandelion in our camp's forbidden zone. For some reason he probably wanted me to trip in the same place as yesterday; he was looking at me the way you look at a man when you're expecting something from him, but I stopped in front of the pit and began to wait as well.

"*Moen*,"[xvi] the German said unintelligibly and gloomily. I didn't understand what that meant and kept quiet. He glanced back at the door—sneakily and warily—and stuck his right hand into the pocket of his service jacket. Now it's difficult to say what would have happened if I had done what I was thinking about at that moment because the German couldn't see me or use his right arm; he'd fall straight into the pit, and I'd fall too, only on top of him . . .

But that didn't happen.

He said "*Nimm*"[xvii] twice, holding his hand out in front of him; he seemed to want me to climb over the pit like yesterday. I had a hard time seeing what was in his hand, and I didn't move or sway.

"*Hast du gut gefrühstückt, ja?*"[xviii]

He said it angrily, looking back at the door and extending his hand to me, and I made out a small, square package wrapped in gray paper. The

---

xvi   The German is mumbling and "Morgen" (Morning) is heard as "Moen" by the first person narrator.—Trans.

xvii   "Take."

xviii   "You've had a good breakfast, yes?"

ends were carefully folded under, like in a parcel, and I took the package and immediately felt the almost imperceptible weight of some bread and its vital, hidden, bodily warmth. The German should have left then so that I could carry the bread to the bed boards and sit there for a bit and manage somehow to gather my thoughts about myself, our whole imprisoned, accursed world, and him—the guard-*bauer* in our felt boots without the tops. He should have left, but he kept looking at me with an offended, expectant air, and I stayed silent and tried to put the package into the chest pocket of my soldier's blouse without taking my eyes off the barracks door. There was a good reason why he kept looking back at it himself.

"*Ah, Mensch!*"[xix]

He waved his hand towards the door like a cat, stepped over the pit and pushed me lightly towards the empty bed boards; the prisoners were all huddling in the back of the barracks, away from the door. We sat down and immediately lifted up our legs. I could smell the tempting aroma of the bread; the edge of the package was sticking out of the pocket of my soldier's blouse, and my head was leaning towards it against my will.

"*Nun, vas wartest du noch? Iss dein Frühstück!*"[xx] the German said. He was pointing at the package, and I understood that for some reason he needed the bread to be eaten in his presence. He took the wrapper away from me and put it in his pocket. The evenly trimmed square of bread was smeared either with margarine or some other crude substitute. I turned the bread so that the smeared side was facing down so as not to drop any crumbs, and the German grumbled something and motioned with his hand towards the door.

I could have eaten about five dozen of those sandwiches. The German kept looking at my face relentlessly and intently, and I had to take microscopic bites, chew slowly for a long time, and then swallow dispassionately so that my neck wouldn't stretch out and my Adam's apple wouldn't move.

"*Schmeckt es?*"[xxi]

He didn't have to ask that; I couldn't agree slavishly since I was eating so slowly and impassively.

---

xix   "Oh, man!"
xx   " Well, what are you waiting for? Eat your breakfast!"
xxi   "Is that good?"

"*Gut?*" the German wasn't giving up.

"Well, *gut, gut!*" I said. The silence in the barracks felt hostile to me. Ivan was lying prone silently in his place, and his eyes smoldered like hot coals in ashes.

"Don't go nuts over there! I remember!" I said. By that time exactly half the bread was left, but I evened out the corners a bit more and, when the sandwich became rounded like a biscuit, I stuck it jerkily in my chest pocket.

"*Zu Mittag?*"[xxii] the German asked suspiciously and looked at the bed boards where Ivan was lying.

"Yes. For *abend.*[xxiii] For me!" I confirmed, poking myself in the chest. The German said "*Zehr gut,*" took out the wrapper and carefully tore off half. I wrapped the rest of the sandwich in it.

It was time for us to go—for the German to go back to his place and for me to go back to Ivan. He was doomed as it was, even without this wait. But the German wouldn't leave. He sat silently, looking up at me every once in a while, and I at him. Everything about him seemed to suit him well: the scratchily cat-like wave of his hand and the yellowness of his hair, which was the color of straw, and the felt boots without the tops. The thought ran through my mind that he was a bad shot; with him, if you dashed to the right, you could stay alive . . .

He left after we found out how old we were—the German was a whole childhood older than me. It was difficult for me to make my way back to my place because people had half-risen on the bed boards and were looking at me with alienation and vengeance in their eyes. I didn't feel any guilt before them, and they didn't accuse me either. They just kept looking, and you can't reason with twenty-two pairs of large, frenzied, wrathful eyes, like those of saints in church paintings.

"What did he want again?" Voronov asked me.

"I don't know. He gave me this bread," I said. We spoke in a whisper, and Ivan finished eating the sandwich quietly, his forehead pressed against the bed boards as if he were praying. From that moment on I began to wait for the day to end and for the night to be over. The next sandwich would have to be divided not into two, but into four parts, the next one into four again, then again and again . . .

---

xxii   "For dinner?"
xxiii   "For evening."

Willy Brode came at his usual hour. He called me from the door and grumbled, "*Moen.*" We sat down on the bed boards and he gave me a sandwich—no bigger and no smaller than before. I turned the bread so that the smeared side was facing down, broke off one quarter and ate more lazily than yesterday. Willy's face was wrinkled and sullen; he kept frowning and constantly raising and lowering his legs.

"Put them here," I pointed at the bed boards. He understood and sat down like me; he brought the bottoms of his feet together, bent his knees, and leaned with his elbows on them. "You feel better now, right?"

Willy shook his head, removed the beat-up shoe from his left foot, then he pulled off a gray wool sock the color of his service jacket, and I could make out something white scattered in there and crawling about.

"*Läuse,*"[xxiv] Willy explained and looked at me helplessly and pitifully.

"That's all right," I said, "I've got them too."

"*Viel?*"[xxv] he livened up.

"Enough," I said.

He took a long time to unwrap the bandage carefully. All five of his toes seemed to be the same size, and they were the color of reddish prunes.

"They'll cut them off," I said because there was nothing to be done in a case like his. Willy nodded, apparently having decided that I had simply tried to comfort him. I looked at my own toes and said that they'd cut them off too, if there were someone to do it. Willy nodded in agreement again, and there was hope in his rust-colored eyes. He was clearly waiting for something; maybe he wanted me to say the same words over his frostbitten toes that I had said over mine yesterday, and so I said, "They'll chop them the hell off! And they'll chop mine off too, damn it, while I'm a prisoner in this war, in the severe cold, and during a blizzard!"

He probably understood my lament in his own way, understood it the way he wanted to, because his fat, chapped lips broke out in a smile and he pawed and shook my shoulder. He left more upbeat than yesterday; maybe his toes stopped aching? I walked him to the pit by the door, and he nodded to me and said something, possibly promising to come back tomorrow.

Ivan was now sitting instead of lying down. I gave him his share—half

---

xxiv   "Lice."
xxv   "Many?"

as much as yesterday—and the rest I carried to the back of the barracks. Here it was not a question of "the sacred feeling of friendship," and not of my "self-denial," because for prisoners who had tried to escape, these were nothing but mere words. Here things were much more to the point; I simply knew that after only one bite of bread, a goner was able to get up and walk a few steps. That's all. I knew it and carried the bread—one bite apiece—to my first two goners. It could be that it should have been done right away, yesterday, but . . . everyone had seen how it all happened with the German, me and Voronov—my partner in running away and sharing the bed boards. There's no point in thinking about yesterday. Today doesn't count either. And tomorrow four "fresh" goners will get bread, the day after tomorrow four more, then four more and four more—you never know how many times that man will get it in his head to come here!

I didn't feel that wobbly anymore, and for some reason I was carrying the bread in the palms of both hands. The prisoners were lying on the bed boards facing the aisle, and only Turin, a military engineer, was sitting up. He was around forty. We knew his army rank—you didn't last long in the camp if one of the SS men[2] found out your officer rank—and for that reason Turin was our secret barracks leader. He was referred to as a military engineer and huddled in relative isolation in a corner; we wanted it that way. He sat on his hands, leaning towards the edge of the bed boards and following me with his insane, saintly eyes. It's towards him that I headed, after nodding from afar to let him know, so to say, that everything would be all right, and he shouted to the prisoners, without changing his pose, in a strained voice that became imprinted in everyone's memory, "Comrades! Remember what I said . . . He who accepts the enemy's bait will have to pay dearly! Be strong, comrades!"

He lay down right away and I tripped, dropped the bread, and picked it up.

"You're sucking up to the guards . . . You swine!"

It was not the senior leader who said that but someone else, and I reached my place by falling forward. Ivan was sitting and looking straight at me in shock.

"What's the matter with you?" I asked and broke the bread in half. "Here! Eat! Are you in a stupor or something?!"

He shut his eyes and took the bread.

The whole day and night it was quiet, cold, and bleak in the barracks.

Since morning Turin was preparing for something with a lot of show and fuss. He even said goodbye to everyone except me and Ivan, but Ivan was sleeping the sleep of the righteous and didn't hear anything. Shortly before the time Willy Brode usually appeared, Turin wrapped his feet in foot cloths, which he tied with strings, and got down from the bed boards. In a hoarse and anguished voice he sang the opening lines of the song "You Fell as Martyrs"[3] and looked around at the barracks and the prisoners in farewell. For some reason I woke up Ivan and climbed down from the bed boards. I headed for Turin with my arms pressed to my sides, and he stood at attention too.

"Are you planning to be an unintentional martyr, comrade military engineer? Or a posthumous hero?" I asked. "Nothing will come of it . . . You'll stay here! With us! You won't rise higher than senior leader!"

"Go and do your dirty deed!" Turin whispered, looking past me at the door of the barracks. I turned around and saw Corporal Benk and Sergeant Klein from the commandant's office—who among us didn't know them? Willy Brode was walking between them, in the middle. His uniform jacket was open and his field cap sat askew, high on top of his head. I was standing in front of Turin. They came closer and Klein, without looking at me, asked Willy in an indifferent voice, "*Diesem?*"[xxvi]

Willy said quickly and loudly "*Nein*" and jerked his head, and pressed his open hands to his sides.

"*Diesem?*" Klein pointed at Turin. I didn't hear what Willy said; Benk stepped past me and with a swinging blow hit Turin in the mouth with his open hand. Turin fell down onto the bottom row of bed boards and slid close to the wall because of inertia.

"It was me who took the *brot*! *Ich*!" I said to Corporal Benk and my heart rose to my throat. "That man didn't eat it! Only me! *Ich*!"

Klein hit Willy in disgust—also in the mouth, with the back of his hand—and Benk struck me in the back of the head with something heavy, rounded, and blunt like a club. I fell on the floor, facing the door, and so for that reason remembered how Benk, Klein, and Willy left the barracks. He was walking in the middle, and they flanked him, and Willy stumbled near the pit with our piss, but his hands stayed pressed to his sides . . .

That's all.

---

xxvi "This one?"

By the way, Ivan Voronov survived.

Sometimes I wonder if Willy Brode is alive. And how are his feet? It's not good when frostbitten toes start bothering you in the springtime. Especially when your little toes start aching and pain is your escort on the left and on the right . . .

1966

NOTES

1. The German speaks in Russian here; perhaps this is meant to emphasize that the narrator remembers what was said but not how it was phrased in German.
2. SS: a reference to Waffen-SS, a second German army within the German armed forces which operated in tandem with the regular German army. The SS was responsible for operating concentration and extermination camps.
3. "You Fell as Martyrs": a funeral march of the Russian revolutionary movement, dating to the 1870s; words by A. Archangelsky, the melody taken from a popular song. It mourns and celebrates men who died—many in tsarist prisons—fighting for the honor and freedom of the common people.

MY UNCLE OF THE HIGHEST PRINCIPLES[1]

Fazil Iskander

When the kids on our street would start bragging about their famous relatives, I'd keep quiet, and I'd let them have their say.

The military belonged to the top category. But even the military had its own special chain of command invented by the imagination of little boys. Border guards were in first place, pilots in second, tank drivers in third, and then all the rest. Firefighters were in a class by themselves.

Back then there was no war yet and, as ill luck would have it, I didn't have a single relative in the army. But I had my own trump card that I'd use rather successfully.

"I have a crazy uncle," I'd say in a calm voice, pushing aside my friends' all too real heroes for a while. To be crazy—that's unusual and, most important, it's an almost unattainable thing. You could become a pilot or a border guard if you studied hard, at least that's what the adults claimed. And they, of course, knew what was what. But you couldn't become crazy, no matter what kind of a high achiever you were. Unless, of course, you studied too much. But we were in no danger of that.

In short, you have to be born crazy, or have a lucky fall as a child, or catch meningitis.

"Is he really crazy?" one of the kids would ask warily.

"Of course," I'd say, expecting the question, "he's got written proof he's nuts; he was examined by professors."

There really were papers to that effect; they were in my aunt's Singer sewing machine.

"And why doesn't he live in an insane asylum?"

"Grandma won't let him go there."

"And you're not afraid of him at night?"

"No, we're used to him," I'd say calmly, like a tour guide, waiting for the next question. Sometimes they'd ask stupid questions, like whether he bites, but I wouldn't bother answering them.

"And you're not crazy?" someone would think to ask and look at me with piercing eyes.

"I can be a little," I'd say with a modest dose of pride.

"I wonder who would win: Fran Goot or the insane guy?" someone would wonder out loud, and dozens of interesting suggestions would be offered immediately. Fran Goot was a famous wrestler from a big top traveling circus. He was a Negro and that's why we all rooted for him.

My uncle lived on the second floor of our house with my aunt, my grandmother, and the rest of the family. There were two family versions of the story that explained his not entirely ordinary condition. The first one claimed that it happened to him in his childhood after an illness. This was an uninteresting and therefore implausible version. According to the second version, which was spread by my aunt and finally replaced grandma's recollections, it seemed that he fell off an Arabian race horse in his early youth.

For some reason my aunt didn't like it when people called him crazy.

"He's not crazy," she'd say, "he's mentally ill."

That had a nice ring to it, but it was impossible to understand. My aunt liked to color the truth, and she was successful at it to some extent. But nevertheless he was crazy, although almost normal too.

Usually he didn't bother anybody. He'd sit on a bench on the balcony and sing songs he had made up. For the most part they were love songs without words.

True, sometimes something would come over him. He'd remember some old grudges and begin slamming doors and running down the long, second-floor hallway. At times like that, it was better to stay out of his sight. Not that he'd necessarily do something bad, but still, it was better to stay out of sight. If grandma was at home at the time, she'd bring him to his senses pretty quickly. Grandma would turn down his shirt collar and unceremoniously stick his head under the faucet. After a good dose of cold water, he'd calm down and sit down to have some tea.

His vocabulary, like that of contemporary poets and songwriters, was extremely limited. Shake out the contents of a second-grader's notebook on the table and there you'll find all the words that my uncle used to get by in life. True, he had a few expressions that you clearly wouldn't find in a second-grader's notebook or even in a book. He'd use them like normal people in moments of extreme emotional agitation. Only one of them can be repeated: "Motherfucker."

He spoke mainly in Abkhazian,[2] but cursed in two languages: Russian and Turkish. Apparently, combinations of words would become engraved in his memory depending on how tense he felt. Thus you can conclude that in moments of anger, Russians and Turks produce expressions of roughly the same emotional richness.

Like all insane people (and some sane ones), he was very strong. At home he'd perform any work that didn't require much intelligence. He'd pour out the slops, bring in fresh water before there was indoor plumbing, carry bags from the market, and chop firewood. He worked conscientiously and even with inspiration. When a powerful stream of slop, tracing a sharp trajectory from the second floor, would plop into the refuse pit with a hollow sound, the stray cats rummaging around in there would fly up in the air as if tossed up by a shock wave.

My grandma felt sorry for him; she thought he might strain himself working. Sometimes, on the days she'd be doing general house cleaning, she'd force him to go to bed and declare that he was sick. She'd bandage his head or cheek and he'd lie there, confused and somewhat bewildered by the deception. Finally he'd get tired of lying in bed and try to get up, but grandma would push him back into bed. It was impossible to get him to do anything during those times. He'd shrug his shoulders and say, "Grandma doesn't let me." He called my grandma "grandma," even though she was his mother. That's how he was—he had his eccentricities.

My uncle was surprisingly clean. He was always held up as an example for us children. Ever since then, whenever I see too clean a person, I can't get rid of the thought that there must be something wrong with his mind. Of course I don't say that to him, but I do think it to myself.

In short, my uncle was terribly clean. Sometimes you had better not come near him when he was carrying fresh water, or a bag of groceries, or was sitting down to eat. And he washed his hands every ten or fifteen minutes. He was scolded for that because he'd wear out the towel, but they couldn't break him of the habit. Sometimes someone would shake his hand and he'd run to the sink right away. The adults often made fun of him and said hello to him on purpose many times in a single day. Out of some sense of tact Uncle Kolya couldn't decline to offer his hand, even though he understood that they were playing games.

More than anything in the world he loved sweets, and of all the sweets, water with syrup. If we were sent to the market and were passing by a stand with fruit-flavored water, he—who was not usually prone to sentimentality—would touch me with his hand and, pointing to the cylinders with syrups of various colors, say timidly, "Kolya wants a drink."

It was nice to treat a grown, grey-haired man to some sweetened water and to feel next to him like an experienced man who was kind and indulged his childish weaknesses.

And he also loved to get a shave. True, he was not given that pleasure all that often. About once a month. Sometimes they'd send him to the barber shop, but more often than not, my aunt would shave him herself.

He took the process of shaving seriously. He'd sit without grimacing or moving while my aunt mercilessly scraped his soaped-up, haughtily raised head. At times like that I could stick out my tongue at him from behind my aunt's back or shake my fist at him, and he wouldn't pay any attention, so absorbed was he in the bliss that being shaved brought him. And this was so, despite the fact that his beard—and even more, the hair on his head—was thick and curly as if it had sprouted in virgin soil; it desperately resisted the razor. Sometimes my aunt would ask me to hold his ear still or to pull the skin tight on his neck. I would readily agree, of course, fully aware of the unattainable nature of this pleasure under normal circumstances. With a somewhat exaggerated diligence, I'd hold his big, swarthy ear, turning it in the required direction and examining the bumps of wisdom on his head.

Usually resembling a good-hearted bee-keeper with a curly beard, he'd change dramatically after his shave because his face would take on the offensively arrogant expression of a Roman senator in an ancient history textbook. In the days right after his shave, he'd become aloof and contemptuous, then the Roman senator would gradually disappear into the depths of the beard, and the good-hearted, democratic disposition of a village bee-keeper would emerge.

I wouldn't say that he suffered from delusions of grandeur, but passing by the statue in the town square, he'd become rather excited and, motioning with his head toward the statue, he'd say, "That's me." He'd say the same thing whenever he saw a large-size portrait of a man in a newspaper or magazine. To be fair, you have to say that he took any large-size depiction of a man to be him. But since it was the same man[3] who was almost always depicted like that, it could be taken as a hostile allusion, a dangerous train of thought, and defamation in general. Grandma tried to break him of this habit, but she didn't get anywhere.

"Don't, don't, the commission," grandma would say sternly, pointing with her finger at the portrait and pulling my uncle away from it like from the unclean force.[4]

"Me, me, me," my uncle would say to her joyfully, tapping the same picture with his hard fingernail. He didn't understand anything.

I didn't understand anything either, and the adults' apprehensions seemed simply stupid to me.

My uncle was truly afraid of the commission. The fact of the matter was that from time to time the neighbors, purely out of love of fellow man, would write anonymous denunciations. Some would state that my uncle resided illegally in our house and that he should live in an insane asylum like all regular, insane people. Others would write that he worked all day and they should check to see if there wasn't a secret exploitation of one human being by another.

The commission would show up about once a year. While its members warily made their way up the stairs, my aunt would manage to dress him in a new holiday shirt, hand him grandma's prayer beads, and in a stern whisper order him to sit still and not move. The members of the commission, somewhat perplexed by their unusual task, would apologize and ask my aunt the obligatory questions, glancing at my uncle from time to time with moderate curiosity. My aunt would produce my uncle's documents from the Singer sewing machine.

"He's got a golden personality," she'd say. "And physical labor is good for him. Doctor Zhdanov said so himself. And what does he actually do? He brings in a couple of buckets of water out of boredom, and that's all."

While she talked, my uncle would sit at the table, squeezing the prayer beads with a wooden expression on his face and looking with the direct, unblinking gaze typically seen in village photographs.

Before leaving, one of the members of the commission would begin to feel more bold and comfortable and ask my uncle, "Do you have any complaints?"

My uncle would look questioningly at grandma, and grandma at my aunt.

"He's hard of hearing," my aunt would say with an expression that seemed to imply that this was his only shortcoming.

"I said, do you have any complaints?" the man would ask louder.

"Batum, Batum . . . ,"[5] my uncle would mutter pensively through his teeth. He was beginning to get angry at this whole comedy, because he'd bring up Batum only during times of extreme irritation.

"But what complaints could he have? He's joking," my aunt would say with a charming smile and walk the commission members to the door. "He lives like a count with me," she'd add in a voice growing stronger as she looked at the backs of the departing commission. "If certain brazen women looked after their husbands the way I look after my invalid, they wouldn't have time to make up Armenian fairytales."

That was a challenge to the courtyard neighbors, but they would hide and keep a cowardly silence.

After the commission would leave, they'd take the holiday shirt off my uncle, and my aunt would send him to fetch water to spite her neighbors. Rattling the buckets, he'd set out happily on his way, clearly preferring the ancient work of a water carrier to communal tricks.

More than anything in the world, my uncle didn't like cats, dogs, children, or drunks. I don't know about the rest, but I'm partially responsible for his dislike of children.

Over the many years together I got to know all his propensities, likes, and weaknesses. My favorite pastime was to tease him. My jokes were cruel at times, and I regret them now, but you can't take back what's been done. The only thing that comforts me to some extent is that I got my fair share of punches from him as well.

There were times when we'd be sitting in the warm kitchen on a wet winter day. Grandma's busy at the stove, my uncle is sitting on a bench nearby, and I'm sitting on the couch and reading a book. The fire is crackling, the kettle whistling, the cat purring. Finally this quiet, crazy coziness begins to get to me. More and more often I put my book aside and look at my uncle. My uncle looks at me with his green Persian eyes. He looks at me because he knows that sooner or later I'll play some sort of trick on him. And since he knows it and is waiting for it, I can't restrain myself.

The easiest way to make him lose his composure is to stare him in the face for a long time. He begins to squirm in his chair, then he lowers his eyes and examines his large hands, but I know very well what he's thinking. Then he quickly looks up to see if I'm looking at him or not. I continue looking. I even settle into a calm, comfortable pose. That should make him think that I intend to keep looking at him for a long time, and that it doesn't require much effort on my part. He begins to get upset and says under his breath, "That little fool is teasing me."

He doesn't want to raise a fuss before it's necessary; he says it for my benefit. It's as though he's rehearsing his future complaint in front of me.

I stubbornly continue looking at him. The poor guy turns away, but not for long. He wants to see if I'm still looking. I am, of course. Then he covers his eyes with his hand. But that doesn't help either. He wants to see if I've finally left him alone. Thinking I don't notice, he spreads his fingers somewhat and looks at me through them. I look as if nothing has happened. Then he loses his temper and makes a scene.

"He's looking at me! I'm going to kill him!" my uncle screams and his eyes blaze with anger. Instantly I turn my gaze to the book and then raise my head with the air of a man who has been unexpectedly distracted from his peaceful pursuits.

"What do you want, for his eyes to be put out or something?" grandma says and, hitting him lightly on the back of the head, advises him not to look in my direction if my look upsets him so much.

But sometimes, infuriated by my more mean-spirited jokes, he hits me on the back of the head, grabs a piece of firewood or a poker, and then the frightening moment comes. Especially if grandma or strong adult men aren't around. "Dear God," I whisper to myself, "save me this one time and I'll never tease him again in my whole life. And I'll always love you and even pray to you with grandma. You'll see, just save me." But apparently I don't count on the deity that much, especially since I always let him down. Despite my fear, my mind is working quickly and clearly. I run, if my uncle hasn't yet cut off the way to the door. But if it's now impossible to run, the only salvation lies in coming up to him unexpectedly and, bowing low, offering my head—go ahead, hit me. It's a rather terrifying moment because there's an armed madman in front of you, and he's furious at that.

But evidently this pathetic pose, this complete submission to fate, disarms him. Some innate sense of nobility prevents him from hitting me. He weakens instantly. Sometimes he just pushes me away in disgust and walks away, shrugging his shoulders in bewilderment at the fact that people can be so insolent and so pathetic at the same time.

Once I read a wonderful book in which a spy pretended to be a deaf-mute, but then he was unmasked because he began to speak German in his sleep. One of our counterspies intentionally fired a shot over his head, but he didn't even flinch. He was a strong individual. But as he dreamed, he stopped being a strong individual because he was asleep.

And so he began to speak German, and a boy unmasked him. Another boy had also heard the spy speaking in his sleep, but he couldn't unmask him because he was a poor student of German and didn't understand what language the man was speaking. But that's not the important thing. The important thing is that the spy pretended to be a deaf-mute.

My thoughts made a brilliant leap. I realized that my uncle was not insane at all but a real, genuine spy. The only thing that troubled me a bit was that grandma remembered him as a child. But I quickly overcame even that obstacle. I figured out that they had switched him. There had been a crazy uncle, but the spies studied his habits and words, and one fine day they kidnapped my uncle and slipped a spy in his place. And he pretended to be fastidious on purpose so that no one would poison him.

I recalled that much in his behavior was suspicious. At times he'd write something on pieces of paper with colored pencils. He'd carefully hide those pieces of paper. I would take a peek at them, of course, but at that time they looked like the scribbling of an illiterate man. He was fooling us in a big way! And the fishing pole!

My uncle would sometimes go fishing in the sea. There wouldn't have been anything strange about that, since normal people take a great interest in fishing too. But the fact of the matter was that there were no hooks on his fishing line. And we even laughed at him. Maybe there was a secret radio inside the fishing pole and he was sending information to an enemy submarine?

My brain was on fire. In my mind I was already reading a big headline in "Pioneer Pravda"[6]: A pioneer has unmasked a spy. Children, be vigilant!

There followed my picture and the story, which began with the following words:

"Some time ago pioneer so-and-so (that is, me) became quiet and sad. His shortsighted parents (that is, my parents) thought that he was ill. But in fact he was trying to figure out how to unmask a sophisticated spy who for a long time had been posing as his insane uncle. It was not easy to take such a step. But the pioneer didn't lose his head. It was a battle of nerves." And so on, in the same spirit, and even better.

The first thing to do was to steal his fishing pole and inspect it. It was under my uncle's bed. He wouldn't let me come near his bed, supposedly because of his fastidiousness. But I seized an opportune moment when they sent him for water, pulled the fishing pole out from under his bed, took a file and secretly, in the vegetable patch, began filing through the bamboo stick full of ringed joints. I cut each section in half, but the fishing pole turned out to be empty. I didn't become downhearted and noticed that the very first section at the base of the fishing pole didn't have the usual natural joint; the joint was broken and you could stick a finger in there. Everything was clear! He sticks his radio in there and then he takes it out and hides it. What a cunning guy! I buried the fishing pole in the vegetable garden and began considering what to do next.

I had to hurry before he discovered that his fishing pole was missing. But then my aunt left the house to attend to some things, my grandma went out in the yard to sit where it was cool, and I went upstairs. My uncle was sitting in the kitchen as usual and looking out the window at the entryway—watching to see that no strangers got into the building. I walked into the kitchen and sat down at the table across from him. The most important thing, I decided, was pressure and surprise. He thinks I'm going to start teasing him, but actually I . . .

"Your career is over, Lieutenant Colonel Shtauberg," I said distinctly and felt goose bumps rising on my back like bubbles on the surface of carbonated water.

I don't know where I got the idea that he was Lieutenant Colonel Shtauberg; evidently I trusted my intuition, just like many counterspies of genius whom I had read about, including Major Pronin himself.[7]

"Leave me alone," my uncle replied in that melancholy voice he used when he thought I was beginning to tease him and he had no desire to get involved with me.

Not a single muscle on his face twitched. "A man of iron," I thought, shaking with excitement, and went on to do what had to be done at that moment.

"You played your part well, but we weren't sleeping either," I said, generously acknowledging the enemy's cunning. The words that came to me were strong and precise; they made me believe I was doing the right thing.

"Crazy boy," my uncle said with a certain tinge of annoyance. He always called me a boy, as if I didn't have a name.

"He's trying to get out of it, the scoundrel," I thought, breathless from the inspiration I was feeling, and decided it was time to hint at a few things to him.

"Aren't the fish biting?" I asked, smiling shrewdly and looking into his eyes. "Is the sea stormy, or the fishing pole no good?"

"The fishing pole?" he repeated, and a semblance of a thought flashed in his dull eyes.

"Exactly, the fishing pole," I said, realizing that I had seized the link that would help me pull out the whole chain as well without making too much noise.

"My fishing pole?" he repeated, beginning to realize something.

"You've fallen for the bait, Lieutenant Colonel," I remarked, trying to be witty, and leaned back in my chair, as I waited for what would come next.

"The fishing pole, the fishing pole, motherfucker!" he mumbled, very upset and, finally realizing something, dashed for the door.

"Don't move!" I shouted. "The house is surrounded!"

"Batum!" he shouted and ran to his room.

I was taken aback somewhat. Instead of giving himself up with dignity and saying, "You outsmarted me this time, lieutenant," he ran to find the fishing pole as if that meant something.

A few minutes later he came running back into the kitchen and everything got all confused.

"My fishing pole's been stolen!" he shouted, enraged, trying to grab me.

"A voluntary confession will lighten your fate!" I shouted back, running around the table and pushing chairs in his way in a maneuver tested by the English[8] intelligence service.

"Thief! My fishing pole! Motherfucker!" he shouted, getting excited by the scuffle.

"Name your accomplices!" I yelled back, turning sharply at one corner of the table. That was my salvation, because he didn't know how to slow down and he'd miss hitting me and run past. However, sometimes he still managed to smack me from across the table, or hit me with his fist from behind as he pursued me.

I knew that the battle of nerves could be terrible, but when one is striking and the other is merely ducking, sooner or later the one who is striking will win.

Finally I jumped up on the couch and, fending him off with my foot, shouted as loud as I could, "Grandma!"

She was already coming up the stairs anyway. Evidently the noise made by our scuffle could be heard in the yard. Seeing her, the poor man rushed to her and began trying to justify himself. By the way, he almost never succeeded in doing that. It's difficult enough for a normal person to justify his actions, but no one wants to even listen to someone like that.

"My fishing pole, my fishing pole," he babbled in his agitation, forgetting the few words he knew.

And suddenly I felt pity for him. I somehow understood that in his whole life he never would be able to vindicate himself in a way that would make any sense. And I had in fact ruined his fishing pole. But I didn't have enough courage to admit that I was entirely to blame—I didn't have enough courage. I knew that the adults were used to thinking him guilty in situations like this, and I guessed that it would be unpleasant for them to change a habit they were comfortable with and take into account more complex reasons.

I said he had attacked me, but that he nevertheless didn't have time to hit me. It was a compromise way out of the situation, unfortunately the one most commonly used by people.

I no longer suspected him of being connected to a foreign intelligence service.

No matter how long I've put it off, I now have to tell you about his great love which he, unfortunately, couldn't hide from the people around him. He was in love with Auntie Faina. Everyone knew about it, and the adults discussed his passion with relish without being very concerned that children who were not fully prepared for it were listening to them.

To this day I still don't understand why he chose her in particular— the dirtiest, most heavily freckled, and stupidest woman of all the women in our whole courtyard. I'm far from saying that a Sulamith[9] or a Sofia Kovalevskaya[10] could be found among them. But still, he chose the most unattractive woman and the stupidest one. Perhaps he felt that the path between their inner worlds was the least tiring.

Auntie Faina was a seamstress. She sewed for our whole courtyard. In general she was entrusted with the job of altering old clothes, children's shirts and briefs, and all kinds of small articles.

"Ruffles, cuffs," she'd say, fussily measuring a client with a tape measure and trying to seem professional.

Apparently she sewed badly, and she was paid very little for her work, and sometimes she wouldn't receive anything in advance for orders that were placed.

"Thank you, Fainochka, we'll settle later," they'd say, placing their order.

"You can't buy bread with a thank you," she'd respond, smiling sadly with a certain amount of abstract hurt in her voice, as if she were offended not by her clients, but by those who wouldn't sell bread for a thank you.

In her free time, or sometimes while she was working, Auntie Faina would quarrel with her closest neighbor, an unmarried young woman without a specific occupation. Her name was Auntie Tamara. Sometimes sailors would visit her in the evenings. They'd sing wonderful, long-drawn-out songs and Auntie Tamara would sing along with them. The effect was very beautiful, but for some reason we weren't allowed in there. The neighborhood women didn't like Auntie Tamara, but they were afraid of her.

"She fights like a man," they'd say.

Auntie Faina and Auntie Tamara were always quarreling. The fact of the matter was that they were both redheads. And redheads never get along, especially as neighbors. They can't stand each other.

"Red-headed gang!" Auntie Tamara shouts—as it would happen at times—as she stands at the clothes line, clothes pins hanging on her like machine gun belts.

"You're a redhead yourself!" Auntie Faina responds quite fairly.

"I'm not a redhead. I'm a lemon blonde," Auntie Tamara smirks.

"Sailors visit you," Auntie Faina says nervously.

"I wonder who'd come to visit you?" Auntie Tamara says snidely.

"I've got a husband," Auntie Faina argues. "Everyone knows my husband—he's an honest man."

"I don't give a damn about your husband!" Auntie Tamara says in a somewhat insulting tone and, after hanging up her laundry, withdraws to her room.

My poor uncle was in love with that very same Auntie Faina. As I now realize, it was the most selfless and long-lasting love I've ever encountered in my whole life. That saintly blindness that gives a man wings, or makes him crazy, was given to him at birth.

He didn't need anything from his beloved except to be near her, to see her Crimean freckles, which were the color of fresh red mullet, and to hear her voice, which was that of a professional mourner.

When she'd come over to my aunt's house to sew something, he'd sit down next to her and look at her with his languid eyes.

"Why does he love me so much?" she'd say if she was in a good mood.

My uncle couldn't live even a day without her. Near Auntie Faina's room there was a kitchen extension, actually a little market stall that her husband had bought cheaply. For whole days she'd busy herself in that little kitchen and look out into the courtyard from time to time to see who was walking where and trying to guess from the expression on the faces of her women neighbors if products in short supply weren't being sold somewhere. When she'd look out from there, she'd have a rather frightened expression on her face, as if she were afraid that while she was busily fixing dinner, she'd miss something important in life, or someone would simply do away with her. Sometimes a bird has that kind of look when it's absorbed in pecking something, but then, suddenly remembering danger, quickly lifts its head and cautiously looks around.

So then, my uncle would usually approach that little kitchen from the back and, leaning against the plywood wall, observe her through a small hole. He couldn't see anything except her cooking, but it apparently was enough for him. He could stand like that for hours and watch her until she'd lose her temper and shout to my aunt across the whole courtyard, "Tell him I've got a husband, because he's courting me again."

My aunt would send him packing home and scold him, true, more for show. Caught at the scene of the crime, the poor man felt the shamefulness of his passion and, passing by my aunt, he'd vaguely shrug his shoulders, showing that it was stronger than him.

"Buy him some water with a double portion of syrup, and let him calm down," Auntie Faina would advise.

But it seems that water with a double portion of syrup was too poor a consolation. An hour or two later my uncle would escape grandma's watchful eye and again make his way to his cherished corner.

In the evening, when Auntie Faina's husband would come home from work, she'd tell him about the day's cares without forgetting my uncle too. Her husband was a cross-eyed cobbler, a peaceful and kind man.

"I like everything to be calm. My wife isn't bothering anyone," he'd say semi-loudly so that no one would get offended, but it would be clear that he was defending his wife. With that, he'd plug up or caulk another small hole my uncle had made in the kitchen wall.

The adults often talked about this unusual love. Apparently for many of them it was enough of an abnormal symptom in itself.

They would talk right in front of him, thinking that he didn't understand anything. But I'm sure that he guessed what they were talking about. At such moments I'd notice his eyes filled with sadness and shame; I'd notice his lips quivering slightly and his hand sometimes making an involuntary gesture of protest, as if he wanted to say, "Leave me alone, you should be ashamed of yourselves!"

He loved her until the end of his days, and never once was he honored with any attention from his cruel beloved.

My uncle died soon after my grandma. He missed her very much and would always ask where she had gone, even though he was there when she died. He quickly forgot about her death, but he remembered her life because that life had surrounded his insanity with human warmth and love. Mothers love their foolish children more—they are more in need of their protective love.

My aunt would say later that my uncle became lucid right before his death, as if fate decided to show him for a moment what it's like to be of sound mind. And that was doubly cruel, because that brief burst of reason would've been just enough for him to feel the inhumanity of passing from one emptiness to another.

But I think my aunt just imagined it. She liked everything to be beautiful, and so she had to exaggerate a lot.

Now I regret that I didn't have time to do anything nice for him while he was alive. With the exception perhaps of treating him to some sweetened water and going to the public bath with him. He loved to wash. At the bathhouse he was no different than the other bathers and was only more shy than the others, trying to cover up his nakedness with a sort of biblical gesture.

I remember a wonderful, sunny day. A road above the sea. We're walking to the village. It's about twelve kilometers from town. Me, grandma, and him. My uncle is in front and we can barely keep up with him. He's covered with bundles, and there are suitcases in his hands and a samovar on his back. It's the beginning of summer. The greenery isn't covered with dust yet, and the sun isn't sultry yet, and an invigorating sea breeze is blowing on us, cooling our chests with that sweet feeling of newness that comes with being on the road. Grandma is puffing on a home-rolled cigarette and tapping her cane, and my uncle is walking in front of us with the samovar, golden like the sun, on his back. And he's singing his endless songs because he feels good and feels the brisk freshness of the summer day, the allure of this small journey.

No, life didn't deprive even him of happy moments. He sang and his singing was simple and joyful like the singing of birds.

1966

NOTES

1. The title is taken from the first line of Aleksandr Pushkin's novel in verse, *Eugene Onegin*, written in 1823-1830.
2. Abkhazian: one of the languages spoken in the Caucasus. In the Soviet Union Abkhazia was an autonomous republic in the republic of Georgia.
3. Busts, portraits, and statues of Stalin were everywhere.
4. "unclean force": i.e., the devil and the demonic.
5. Batum (or Batumi): a seaside city on the Black Sea and the capital of Ajaria, an autonomous republic in southwest Georgia.
6. *Pionerskaya Pravda*: the official newspaper of the Young Pioneers.*
7. Major Pronin was the fictional creation of the writer Lev Ovalov. A masterful counter spy, Pronin's adventures first appeared in print in 1939, with the last tale in 1962.
8. Although the author writes "English" intelligence service, correctly it is the British intelligence service.
9. In the opera "Regina di Saba" (Queen of Sheba) Sulamith is the beautiful daughter of the high priest in King Solomon's court. She is betrothed to Assad, but he falls in love with a mysterious woman who turns out to be the Queen of Sheba, who is paying a visit to King Solomon.
10. Sophia Kovalevskaya (1850-1891): a brilliant mathematician.

CHUDIK[i]

Vasily Shukshin

His wife called him "Chudik." Sometimes affectionately.

Chudik had one peculiarity: something was always happening to him. He didn't want it to, he'd suffer when it did, but he always got himself into some sort of trouble—minor, but still annoying.

Here are some episodes from one of his trips.

He got a vacation and decided to go visit his brother in the Urals; they hadn't seen each other for about twelve years.

"And where's that fishing lure . . . that's like chub?" Chudik yelled from the storeroom.

"How should I know?"

"But they were all right here!" Chudik tried to give her a stern look with his round bluish-white eyes. "All of them are here, but that one, you see, isn't."

"Looks like chub?"

"Yup. For pike."

"I must've fried it by mistake."

Chudik was silent for a while.

"Well, and how was it?"

"What?"

"Taste good? Ha-ha-ha . . . !" He wasn't any good at all at making jokes, but he wanted to badly. "No broken teeth? It's made of duralumin, you know . . . !"

. . . They spent a lot of time packing—until midnight.

And early in the morning Chudik strode through the village, suitcase in hand.

"To the Urals! To the Urals!" he'd say whenever asked where he was

---

i   Chudik: "weirdo, oddball, kook, screwball; a quirky, strange or odd person." —Trans.

headed. And saying that, his round fleshy face and round eyes would express a totally couldn't-care-less attitude toward long trips; they didn't scare him. "To the Urals! I need to stretch my legs."

But it was still a long way to the Urals.

For the time being he had arrived safely in the district capital, where he still had to buy a ticket and get on a train.

There was a lot of time left yet. In the meantime Chudik decided to buy a bunch of presents for his little nephews—candy, gingerbread cookies . . . He went into a grocery store and got in line. A man wearing a hat was in front of him, and in front of the hat, a plump woman wearing lipstick. The woman was saying softly, quickly, and heatedly to the hat:

"Can you imagine how rude and tactless you'd have to be? He has sclerosis, fine. He's had sclerosis for seven years now, however, and no one suggested he retire. And that man has been in charge only a short time—and already he's saying, 'Maybe you should retire, Alexander Semyonych?' What arrogance!"

The hat nodded in agreement.

"Yes, yes . . . They're like that now. So what if he has sclerosis? And Sumbatych? Lately he's been unable to keep up a conversation as well. And that one, what's her name . . . ?

Chudik respected city folk. Not all of them though. He didn't respect hooligans and salespeople. He was a bit afraid of them.

His turn came. He bought some candy, gingerbread cookies, and three chocolate bars. And stepped aside to put everything in his suitcase. He opened his suitcase on the floor and started to put everything away . . . He looked down at the floor and, by the counter where the line was, a fifty-ruble bill was lying at people's feet. That silly little green thing was just lying there and no one saw it. Chudik even began to tremble in his excitement; his eyes lit up. Hurrying, so that no one would beat him to the punch, he began thinking quickly how to tell the people in line about the bill in the most amusing and witty way possible.

"You must be living pretty well, citizens!" he said loudly and cheerfully.

Everybody turned to look at him.

"Where I come from, for instance, they don't throw bills like that around."

At this point everyone got a bit agitated. After all, this wasn't a three-ruble bill or a five-ruble one—this was fifty rubles, half a month's wages. And the bill didn't have an owner.

"Probably that guy in the hat," Chudik figured.

They decided to put the bill in a prominent place on the counter.

"Someone will come running soon," the saleswoman said.

Chudik left the store in the most pleasant of moods. He kept thinking about how easily he had come up with his amusing comment, "Where I come from, for instance, they don't throw bills like that around!" Suddenly he went hot and cold all over: he remembered that he had gotten a bill just like that and also a twenty-five ruble one at the savings bank back home. He had just broken the twenty-five ruble one, but the fifty-ruble bill should still be in his pocket . . . He put his hand in his pocket—not there. He looked here and there—nothing.

"That bill was mine!" Chudik said loudly. "Damn it . . . ! My bill!"

His heart even started to throb with grief. His first instinct was to go and say, "Citizens, that was my bill. I got two of them at the savings bank: a twenty-five ruble one and a fifty ruble. One, the twenty-five rubles, I just broke, but the other I don't have." But he just imagined how everyone would be taken aback by his announcement, how many would think, "Of course, since no owner could be found, he's decided to pocket it." No, he couldn't make himself do it, couldn't reach for the damn bill. They might not even give it to him . . .

"Why am I like that?" Chudik asked himself bitterly out loud. "What should I do now?"

He had to return home.

He went back to the store and wanted to look at the bill, even if from afar, and stood by the entrance for a while . . . but didn't go in. It would be too painful. His heart might not be able to take it.

He rode the bus and swore softly—he was building up his courage. He still faced giving his wife an explanation.

They took fifty more rubles from their savings account.

Chudik was riding on a train, crushed by his worthlessness, which his wife described to him in great detail yet again (she even hit him on the head a few times with a slotted spoon). But his bitterness was gradually leaving him. Forests, copses, and small villages flashed by outside the window . . . Various people were going in and out of the compartment and telling all kinds of stories . . . Chudik also told one to an intelligent-looking comrade when they were standing in the open entrance area of the train car and smoking.

"We also have a fool in a neighboring village . . . He grabbed a smoldering piece of wood and took off after his mother. Drunk. She's running away from him and screaming: 'Your hands'—she screams— 'don't burn your hands, son!' It's him she's worried about. But he presses on, the drunken ugly mug. Runs after his mother. Imagine how rude and tactless you'd have to be . . ."

"Did you make that up yourself?" the intelligent-looking comrade asked sternly, looking at Chudik over the rims of his glasses.

"Why?" he didn't understand. "Across the river from us there's a village called Ramenskoye . . ."

The intelligent-looking comrade turned away toward the window and didn't say anything more.

After the train, Chudik still had to fly for an hour and a half on a local plane. He had flown once before. A long time ago. He got on the plane with some apprehension. "Can it really be that not a single screw on the plane will come loose in the hour and a half?" he wondered. Later on it was all right, he felt bolder. He even tried to start a conversation with his neighbor, but the man was reading a newspaper and was so interested in what was in the paper that he didn't want to listen to a living person. And here's what Chudik was trying to find out: he had heard they give you something to eat on the plane. But for some reason they weren't bringing anything. He wanted very much to eat on the plane—out of curiosity.

"They've swiped it," he decided.

He began to look out the window. There were mountains of clouds below. For some reason Chudik couldn't say for sure if it was beautiful or not. And all around him people were saying, "Oh, how beautiful!" He just had the stupidest desire to fall into them, into the clouds, like into a pile of cotton. And he also thought, "Why am I not amazed? After all, it's almost five kilometers from me to the ground." He mentally measured out those five kilometers on the ground and then stacked them upright so that he could feel amazed, but he felt no amazement.

"That's man for you . . . ! Look at what he's come up with," he said to his neighbor.

The neighbor looked at him without saying anything and began to rustle his newspaper again.

"Fasten your seatbelts!" a pleasant-looking young woman said.

"We're about to land."

Chudik obediently fastened his seatbelt. But his neighbor paid zero attention. Chudik cautiously nudged him, saying, "They've told us to fasten our seatbelts."

"It's all right," the neighbor said, put aside his newspaper, leaned back in his seat and, as if remembering something, said, "Children are the flowers of life, they should be planted head first."

"What do you mean?" Chudik didn't understand.

The newspaper reader burst into loud laughter and didn't say anything else.

They began to descend quickly. Here's land already—just a stone's throw away, swiftly flying backwards. But still no landing jolt. As knowledgeable people explained later, the pilot had "missed." Finally, the landing jolt, and everyone began to be thrown around so much that you could hear teeth gnashing and chattering. The newspaper reader was jerked out of his seat, butted Chudik with his bald head, got thrown against the window, and then ended up on the floor. During the whole time he didn't make a sound. And everyone around him was also silent; that amazed Chudik. He, too, was silent. They came to a stop. The first ones to regain their wits looked out the windows and discovered that the plane was in a potato field. The gloomy pilot came out of the cockpit and headed for the exit. Someone asked him cautiously, "It seems we landed among potatoes?"

"What, can't you see for yourself?" the pilot said.

Their fear subsided and the most spirited among them were already hesitantly trying to joke.

The bald newspaper reader was looking for his dentures. Chudik unfastened his seatbelt and began to look as well.

"Are these them?" he exclaimed joyfully and handed them to the reader. Even the reader's bald patch turned dark-red.

"Why must you grab them with your hands?" he yelled, lisping.

Chudik was taken aback.

"With what then?"

"Where am I going to boil them? Where?!"

Chudik didn't know either.

"Would you like to come with me?" he asked. "I have a brother who lives here . . . You're afraid I got germs on them? I don't have any."

The reader looked at Chudik in surprise and stopped yelling.

At the airport Chudik wrote his wife a telegram.

"Landed. A bough of lilac fell upon my breast, my darling Grusha, don't forget me. Vasyatka."

The telegraph clerk—a stern, dry woman—read the telegram and suggested, "Write it differently. You're a grown man, not a kindergartner."

"Why?" Chudik asked. "I always write like that in letters to her. It's my wife after all! You probably thought . . ."

"You can write whatever you like in letters, but a telegram is a form of communication. It's an open text."

Chudik rewrote it: "Landed. Everything's fine. Vasyatka."

The telegrapher changed two words herself, "landed" and "Vasyatka." It became "arrived" and "Vasily."

"'Landed' . . . What are you, a cosmonaut or something?"

"Well, all right," Chudik said, "let's leave it like that."

. . . Chudik knew that he had a brother named Dmitry and three nephews . . . Somehow it never entered his mind there must also be a sister-in-law. He had never seen her. And it was she, the sister-in-law, who ruined everything, the entire vacation. For some reason she disliked Chudik from the start.

He and his brother had a few drinks that evening, and Chudik began to sing in a quavering voice:

> The pop-la-ars . . .
> The pop-la-ars . . .

Sophia Ivanovna, the sister-in-law, peeked out from the other room and asked angrily, "Do you have to shout? You're not in a train station, are you?" And she slammed the door.

His brother Dmitry became uncomfortable.

"That's . . . the kids are sleeping over there. She's a good person on the whole."

They drank some more. They began to reminisce about their youth, their mother and father . . .

"Do you remember . . . ?" his brother Dmitry asked happily. "Although how could you remember anyone? You were still breast feeding. They'd leave you with me and I'd cover you with kisses. One time you even turned blue. I got in trouble for that. Then they stopped leaving you with me. But no matter, as soon as they looked away, I'd be with you, kissing you again. Hell knows what kind of a habit that was. I was still a snot-nosed kid and this . . . with the kisses . . ."

"Do you remember?!" Chudik also recalled. "How you . . . me . . ."

"Will you stop yelling?" Sophia Ivanovna asked again, very angrily and irritably. "Who needs to listen to your stories about all your snot and kisses? They keep on talking as if they've got something to say."

"Let's go outside," Chudik said.

They went outside and sat on the front steps.

"Do you remember . . . ?" Chudik continued.

But at that point something happened to his brother Dmitry; he began to cry and pound his fist on his knee.

"There it is, my life! Did you see? How much anger there is in a person . . . ! How much anger!"

Chudik comforted his brother.

"Stop it, don't get upset. No need. They're not angry, they're crazy. Mine's like that too."

"Why does she dislike you so?! Why? She dislikes you, you know . . . But why?"

It was only then that Chudik realized that his sister-in-law did in fact dislike him. And why, exactly?

"Here's why—it's because you don't have an important job, you're not a boss. I know her, that foolish woman. She's crazy about those important people of hers. And who's she?! Works in a snack bar in some administration building, a small fry who thinks she's a big fish. Gets all sorts of ideas there and starts in . . . She hates me too, because I come from a village and don't have an important job."

"In what office?"

"That one . . . the mining something or other . . . I can't pronounce it right now. But why did she have to marry me? Didn't she know where I came from?"

This cut Chudik to the heart.

"What's the problem anyway?" he loudly asked not his brother, but someone else. "And if you want to know, almost all famous people came from a village. Like when you see someone's picture with a black border, it's someone born in a village. You have to read the newspapers . . . ! No matter what kind of a bigwig, it's someone born there, you know, who left early on to work elsewhere."

"And how many times I tried to prove to her that village people are better—they don't put on airs."

"And do you remember Stepan Vorobyov? You knew him . . ."

"Sure I knew him."

"Talk about coming from a village . . . But there you are, he's a holder of the Order of Glory of Three Degrees.[1] Destroyed nine tanks. He rammed them. His mother will now get a sixty-ruble pension for the rest of her life. But they found out only recently—they considered him missing in action . . ."

"And Maximov, Ilya . . . ! We left together. There you are, a third-class Cavalier of the Order of Glory! But don't tell her about Stepan . . . Don't bother."

"All right. And that one . . . !"

The excited brothers continued on noisily for a long time. Chudik even paced near the front steps and waved his arms.

"The village, you see . . . ! The air alone is priceless there. You open the window in the morning and, hey, it just washes over you. You could almost drink it—it's so fresh and fragrant and smells of different grasses, herbs, and flowers . . ."

Then they got tired.

"Did you put on a new roof?" the older brother asked quietly.

"I did." And Chudik sighed quietly. "Added on a veranda—it's a joy to look at. You walk out on the veranda at night . . . and begin daydreaming. If only mother and father were still alive, you'd come with the kids—we'd all sit on the veranda drinking tea with raspberry preserves. There's a ton of raspberries this year. Dmitry, don't fight with her, or she'll dislike me even more. And I'll try to be nicer to her. She'll probably come around."

"But she's from a village herself!" Dmitry marveled in a somewhat quiet and sad voice. "And here . . . She's worn the kids out, the foolish woman: one boy she's worn out on the piano, the girl she's signed up for figure skating. My heart bleeds for them, but I don't say anything, or there'd be a fight right away."

"Hrrmph!" Chudik became agitated again for some reason. "I just don't understand these newspapers: here's a woman, they report, who works in a store—she's rude. Oh, you . . . ! And when she comes home, she's the same. That's where the trouble is! And I don't understand!" Chudik exclaimed, pounding his fist on his knee. "I don't understand. Why have they gotten so angry?"

When Chudik woke up in the morning, there was no one in the

apartment; his brother Dmitry had left for work, his sister-in-law had too, the older kids were playing in the yard, and the little one was at daycare.

Chudik made the bed, washed up, and began thinking about what nice thing he could do for his sister-in-law. Just then a baby carriage caught his eye. "Aha," Chudik thought, "I'll paint some pictures on it." He had painted the stove at home so well that everyone was in total awe. He found the kids' paints, a brush, and got to work. An hour later it was finished: the baby carriage was unrecognizable. At the top of the carriage he drew some cranes—a V-shaped flock, and at the bottom— different kinds of flowers, some young grass, a couple of roosters and baby chicks . . . He looked at the carriage from all sides—a feast for the eyes! Not a carriage but a plaything. He imagined how pleasantly surprised his sister-in-law would be and grinned.

"And you say—country bumpkins. What an odd woman." He wanted to live in peace with his sister-in-law. "It'll be like the baby is in a basket."

The whole day Chudik walked around town and gawked at shop windows. He bought a toy boat for his nephew—such a nice little boat, white, with a light. "I'll decorate it too," he thought.

Around six o'clock Chudik went to his brother's house. He walked up the steps to the entrance and heard his brother, Dmitry, arguing with his wife. To be more exact, the wife was arguing and his brother, Dmitry, was only repeating, "Well, what does it matter . . . ! Enough . . . ! Sonya . . . Enough already . . . !"

"That fool better not be here tomorrow!" Sophia Ivanovna yelled. "He has to leave tomorrow!"

"All right, that's enough . . . ! Sonya . . ."

"It's not all right! It's not all right! He doesn't even have to wait—I'll throw his suitcase the hell out of here and that's it!"

Chudik hurried down the steps . . . And he didn't know what to do next. He felt hurt again. When someone hated him, he felt very hurt and afraid. It seemed like, well, it's all over now, why go on living? And he wanted to go somewhere far away from people who hated or laughed at him.

"Why am I like that?" he whispered bitterly, sitting in a small shed. "I should've guessed she wouldn't appreciate, wouldn't appreciate folk art."

He sat in the shed until dark. And his heart kept aching. Then his brother Dmitry came. He wasn't surprised, as if he knew that his brother Vasily had been sitting in the shed for a long time.

"Well . . . ," he said. "That's . . . she's throwing another fit. The baby carriage, you know . . . maybe you shouldn't have."

"I thought it'd catch her fancy. I'll go, brother."

His brother Dmitry sighed . . . And didn't say anything.

When Chudik arrived home, rain was falling in big, steamy drops. Chudik got off the bus, took off his new shoes and ran on the warm, wet ground, a suitcase in one hand and his shoes in the other. He skipped along and sang loudly:

The pop-la-ars . . .

One edge of the sky was already clear and blue, and the sun was somewhere close. And the rain was becoming lighter, big drops plopping into puddles; bubbles formed and burst in them.

In one place Chudik slipped and almost fell.

. . . His name was Vasily Yegorych Knyazev. He was thirty-nine years old. He worked as a cinema operator in his village. He was crazy about detectives and dogs. As a child he dreamed of being a spy.

1967

NOTES

1. Order of Glory of Three Classes: the speaker mixes things up. The recipient is awarded the decoration in one of three classes: 1st, 2nd, or 3rd. Established at the end of 1943, it was awarded to the rank-and-file of the armed forces as well as to some officers for bravery on the field of battle.

I BELIEVE!

Vasily Shukshin

On Sundays a particular kind of anguish would suddenly attack. The kind that eats away at you, somewhere deep inside . . . Maxim felt it physically, that vile thing, as if a slovenly, not quite healthy peasant woman—shameless, with a strong smell coming from her mouth—were groping him all over with her hands, caressing and trying to kiss him.

"Again . . . ! It's here again."

"Oh . . . ! Lord . . . You cry-baby. You just want to follow the crowd . . . anguish! Maxim's wife Liuda taunted him. She was an unaffectionate, working woman, and she didn't know what anguish was. "What's this anguish from?"

Maxim Yarikov looked at his wife with his black eyes that had a feverish shine to them . . . He clenched his teeth.

"Go ahead, cuss and swear—you'll see, it'll pass, that anguish of yours. You're a master at swearing."

Sometimes Maxim would get hold of himself and not swear. He wanted to be understood.

"You can't understand it."

"Why can't I understand? Explain it, I'll understand."

"Look, you've got everything here—arms, legs . . . and other organs. How big they are—that's another question, but everything's in its place, so to say. If your leg starts hurting—you feel it, if you get hungry—you fix dinner . . . Right?"

"And so?"

Maxim sprang lightly to his feet (he was a forty-year-old man of slight build, ill-tempered and impetuous; he could never wear himself out at work, even though he worked a lot), walked around the room, and his eyes shone fiercely.

"But a person also has . . . a soul! Here it is, right here—it aches!" Maxim pointed to his chest. "I'm not making it up! I simply feel it—it aches!"

"It doesn't ache anywhere else?"

"Listen!" Maxim yelped. "Since you want to understand, listen! Even though you were born a blockhead, at least try to understand that some people do have a soul. I'm not asking you for three rubles for vodka, I just want . . . Oh, you fool!" Maxim totally lost his temper, because all of a sudden he understood clearly that he'd never be able to explain what was going on with him—his wife Liuda would never be able to understand him. Never! If he ripped his chest open, took out his soul and showed it to her in his hands, she'd say, "That's just nothing but your insides." And even he didn't believe in it like that—as some piece of meat. Then all of this must just be empty words. Why get worked up about it? "In the end, if you asked me who I hate the most in the world, I'd answer: people who don't have a soul. Or who have a rotten one. Talking to you is the same as bashing my head against the wall."

"Oh, you wind bag!"

"Get out of my sight!"

"And so why are you so angry if you have a soul?"

"And what do you think a soul is—a gingerbread cookie? In fact, it doesn't understand why I'm dragging it around, that soul of mine, and it aches. And that's why I get worked up. I get upset."

"Go ahead and be upset, to hell with you! People wait for Sunday and then relax in a civilized way . . . They go to the movies. But this one—he's upset, you see. The cry-baby."

Maxim stopped by the window, stood still for a long time and looked out.

Winter. It's freezing. The village is blackening the cold, clear sky with its gray smoke—people are keeping warm. An old woman walks by with buckets on a yoke; even behind the double-pane windows you can hear the firm, packed snow crunching under her felt boots. A dog foolishly begins barking and quiets down—it's freezing outside. People are in their homes, where it's warm. They're talking, fixing dinner, discussing their loved ones . . . Some are drinking, but even there, there's little joy.

When Maxim feels anguish, he doesn't philosophize, he doesn't think about asking anyone for anything—he just aches and feels angry. And he doesn't direct this malice of his at anyone, he doesn't want to punch anyone in the face, and he doesn't want to hang himself. He doesn't want anything—that damned anguish! And he doesn't want to lie flat on his back and not move. And he doesn't want to drink vodka, and he doesn't want to be a laughingstock—that's offensive. There were times he'd drink . . . Drunk, he'd suddenly begin confessing such hideous sins that they'd make him and others feel sick later. One time at a police station he was beating his head drunkenly against a wall with all sorts of posters on it and bellowing. It turns out that he and some other guy, the two of them together, invented a powerful engine the size of a matchbox and handed the plans over to the Americans. Maxim acknowledged that this was abominable treason and that he was a "scientific Vlasov."[1] He asked to be taken to Magadan[2] under escort. And moreover, he wanted to walk there, and it had to be barefoot.

"Why did you hand over the plans?" the sergeant probed. "And to whom?!!"

Maxim didn't know; he only knew that he was "worse than Vlasov." And he wept bitterly.

On one such agonizing Sunday, Maxim was standing by a window and looking at the road. The weather was clear and freezing again, and smoke was coming out of the chimneys.

"And so what?" Maxim thought angrily. "It was like that a hundred years ago. What's new here? And it'll always be like that. There goes a little kid, Vanka Malofeyev's son . . . And I remember when Vanka himself was like that, walking around, and I was that age too. Then they'll have their own kids just like that. And the kids will have their kids . . . Is that all there is? But why?"

Maxim got a really sickening feeling . . . He remembered that a relative of Ilya Lapshin's wife had come for a visit, and that the relative was a priest. An honest-to-goodness priest, with long hair. The priest had something wrong with his lungs—he was sick. He'd come for treatment. And the treatment was badger fat; Ilya would get the badgers for him. The priest had a lot of money, and he and Ilya would often drink pure grain alcohol. The priest would drink only pure grain alcohol.

Maxim went to the Lapshins.

Ilyukha and the priest happened to be at the table, drinking alcohol and talking. Ilyukha was already in his cups—he was nodding off and droning on about how next Sunday, not this Sunday but next Sunday, he'd bring him twelve badgers at once.

"I don't need that many. I just need three good ones—fat ones."

"I'll bring you twelve, and you can choose which ones yourself. My job is to bring them. And you can choose which ones are better yourself. The important thing is for you to get well . . . and I'll get the twelve badgers here for you . . ."

The priest was bored with Ilyukha and he was happy when Maxim came.

"What's the matter?" he asked.

"My soul is aching," Maxim said. "I came to find out if the souls of believers ever ache."

"Do you want some grain alcohol?"

"Just don't you think the only reason I came over was to have a drink. I could, of course, have a drink, but I didn't come for that. I'm interested in finding out: does your soul ever ache?"

The priest poured some alcohol into glasses and pushed one over to Maxim along with a carafe of water. "Dilute it to your taste."

The priest was a large sixty-year old man, broad shouldered, with big hands. In fact, it was hard to believe that there was something wrong with his lungs. And the priest's eyes were clear, intelligent. And he was staring intently, even arrogantly. Such a man should be hiding from alimony, not waving a censer. He was hardly saintly or pious—he didn't seem to be the kind, with that mug of his, to be untangling the living, quivering threads of human grief and sorrow. However, Maxim sensed right away—things would be interesting with the priest.

"Your soul aches?"

"It does."

"I see." The priest downed his drink and wiped his lips on the starched tablecloth, on one of its corners. "Let's approach this from a distance. Listen carefully and don't interrupt." The priest leaned back in his chair, stroked his beard, and began speaking with delight:

"As soon as the human race appeared, evil appeared. When evil appeared, the desire to fight it appeared, the evil, that is. Good appeared. It means good appeared only when evil appeared. In other words, if there's evil—there's good, and if there's no evil—there's no good. Do you understand me?"

"Go on."

"Don't tell a horse to go on, for you haven't put on the harness yet." Evidently the priest loved to argue that if you have this, then you have that, and he did it in a strange, remote, and irresponsible way. "What is

Christ? He is good incarnate, called forth to destroy evil on earth. For two thousand years he has existed among men as an idea fighting evil."

Ilyukha fell asleep at the table.

The priest poured some more for himself and Maxim. With a nod of his head he invited him to drink.

"For two thousand years evil on earth has been destroyed in Christ's name, but there's no end in sight to this war. Don't smoke, please. Or go over there by the vent and fume away."

Maxim put out his home-rolled cigarette on the sole of his shoe and continued listening with interest.

"What's wrong with your lungs?" he asked out of politeness.

"They hurt," the priest explained curtly and reluctantly.

"Does the badger meat help?"

"It helps. Let's keep going, my poor slob . . ."

"What did you say?" Maxim said in surprise.

"I asked you not to interrupt me."

"I asked you about your lungs . . ."

"You asked what makes a soul ache. I'm painting you a picture of the universe in a way you can understand so that your soul finds peace. Listen carefully and try to understand. And so, the idea of Christ arose from a desire to defeat evil. Otherwise, why would it arise? Imagine good has triumphed. Christ has triumphed . . . But then, why do you need him? He's no longer necessary. That means he's not something eternal, everlasting, but rather a temporary instrument, like the dictatorship of the proletariat. But I'd like to believe in eternity, in an eternal, great power and an eternal order that will come to be."

"In communism, is that it?"

"What about communism?"

"Do you believe in communism?"

"I'm not supposed to. You're interrupting again!"

"That's it. I won't anymore. Just you . . . try to speak a bit more clearly. And don't rush."

"I am speaking clearly—I want to believe in eternal good, in eternal justice, in an eternal Higher Power that started all this on earth. I want to get to know this power and want to hold on to the hope that this power will triumph. Otherwise—what's all this for? Hmm? Where's such a power?" The priest gave Maxim a questioning look. "Does it exist?"

Maxim shrugged his shoulders. "I don't know."

"I don't know either."

"You don't? That's a good one!"

"Here's another good one for you. I don't know of such a power. It's possible that it's not for me, a human being, to even know what it is and to grasp it, to fully understand it. If that's the case, I refuse to comprehend my existence here on earth. That's exactly what I'm feeling, and you've come to the right place with your aching soul—my soul aches too. Only you came for a nice ready-made answer, but I'm still trying to get to the bottom of it myself, but . . . it's an ocean. And we can't scoop it all out using glasses. And when we're gulping down this vile liquid . . ." The priest downed the alcohol and wiped his lips on the tablecloth. "When we're drinking this, we're scooping water from the ocean in the hope of reaching the bottom. But using glasses, glasses, my son! It's a closed circle—we're doomed."

"Forgive me . . . may I make one comment?"

"Let's have it!"

"You're . . . an interesting priest. Are there really such priests?"

"I'm a human being, and nothing human is alien to me. So said one famous godless man, and he said it very well. Somewhat presumptuously, it's true, for no one took him for God while he was alive."

"So if I understood you correctly, there's no God?"

"I said—no. Now I'll say—yes, there is. Pour me some more alcohol, my son, dilute it so that it's twenty-five-percent water, and give it to me. And pour some for yourself as well. Pour some, my simpleminded son, and we'll see the bottom yet!" The priest downed it. "Now I'll tell you there is a god. His name is Life. I believe in this god. But what kind of god do we picture for ourselves? Kind, indefinable, without horns, a milquetoast, a calf. Just look at us! . . . There's no such god. There is a stern, powerful one—Life. That one offers good and evil together—that, as a matter of fact, is God. Why did we decide that good should triumph over evil? Whatever for? I find it interesting, for instance, to realize that you came to see me not to find the truth but to drink alcohol. And you're sitting here, straining to keep your eyes open, pretending you're interested in listening . . ."

Maxim stirred in his chair.

"I find it no less interesting to realize that after all it's not the alcohol you need but the truth. And it's most interesting, finally, to establish which is correct. Did your soul bring you here or the alcohol? You see,

I'm using my head, instead of simply feeling sorry for you, you poor little waif. Therefore, in accordance with this God of mine, I say: Your soul aches? Good. Good! You've at least begun to stir, damn it. Or we wouldn't be able to pull you off the stove[3] if you were in a state of spiritual equilibrium. Live, my son, weep and dance. Don't be afraid that you'll be licking frying pans in the other world, because already here, in this life, you'll get both heaven and hell aplenty." The priest spoke loudly, his face was burning red, and he got all sweaty. "You came to find out what to believe in. You guessed correctly: believers don't have aching souls. But what to believe in? Believe in Life. How it will all end, I don't know. Where it's all heading, I don't know either. But it's extremely interesting for me to run along with everyone else, and if possible, even to overtake the others . . . Evil? So there's evil. If someone does a nasty thing and trips me in this marvelous competition, I'll get up and punch him in the mug. None of this 'turn the other cheek.' I'll punch him in the mug and that'll do."

"And if he's got a bigger fist?"

"That means it's my lot in life—to run behind him."

"And where are we running to?"

"To Whereto Mountain. Why do you care? What difference does it make to you—where? All of us are heading in the same direction—both the good and the evil ones."

"For some reason I don't feel I'm heading anywhere," Maxim said.

"Well then, you're weak-kneed. Paralyzed. Well then, it's your lot in life—to sit and whine in one place."

Maxim clenched his teeth . . . He bored into the priest with a burning, angry look.

"Why did I get such an unhappy lot in life?"

"Weak. Weak . . . a weakling, like a boiled rooster. Don't roll your eyes."

"Hey, you big, fat priest! . . . And what if I, for example, let you have it on the forehead right now, then what?"

The priest broke out in a fit of loud, hearty laughter despite his sick lungs. "You see?" He held up his big, strong hand. "It's dependable. This is where natural selection would take place."

"And I'll bring a rifle."

"And they'll execute you. You know that, so you won't bring a rifle because you're weak."

"So, I'll stab you with a knife. I can."

"You'll get five years. I'll be in pain for about a month and then it'll heal. You'll be serving five long years."

"Fine. Then why does your own soul ache?"

"I'm sick, my friend. I ran only half the distance and started limping. Pour me some more."

Maxim poured.

"Have you flown on a plane?" the priest asked.

"I have. Many times."

"And I flew here for the first time. It's great! When I was boarding, I thought: if this flying barrack comes tumbling down, then that's how it's supposed to be. I won't regret it or be a coward. I felt wonderful the whole way! And when it tore me away from the ground and carried me off, I even stroked its side—well done. I believe in the plane. Overall, there's a lot of fairness in life. For example, people regret that Esenin[4] didn't live long. He lived the length of a song. Had the song been longer, it wouldn't have been as heart rending. There are no long songs."

"But at your church . . . once they get started . . ."

"We don't have songs, we have moans. No, Esenin . . . In this case the life lived was exactly the length of a song. Do you like Esenin?"

"I do."

"Shall we sing?"

"I can't."

"Try to sing along, just don't interfere."

And the priest began to drone on about an ice-covered maple tree, and somehow he did it so sorrowfully and cleverly that it really was heart rending. At the words, "Oh, I've become unsteady now for some reason," the priest hit the tabletop with his fist and began crying and shaking his mane.

"Dear, dear fellow . . ! You loved the peasants . . . Pitied them! Dear fellow . . ! And I love you. Fair enough? Yes. Is it too late? Too late . . ."

Maxim felt that he, too, was beginning to love the priest.

"Father! Father . . . Listen here!"

"I don't want to," the priest wept.

"Listen here, you blockhead!"

"I don't want to! You're weak-kneed. . ."

"I'll overtake people like you in the first kilometer! Weak in the knees . . . You're the TB case!"

"Pray!" the priest stood up. "Repeat after me . . ."

"Go to hell . . . !"

With one hand the priest easily picked up Maxim by the scruff of his neck and put him down beside himself.

"Repeat after me: I believe!"

"I believe!" Maxim said. He liked this phrase very much.

"Louder! Solemnly: I-be-lieve! Together: I belie-e-eve!"

"I belie-e-eve!" they cried out in their frenzy. Then the priest began to chant in his usual rapid singsong:

"In aviation, in the mechanization of agriculture, in the scientific revolu-ution! In space and weightlessness! For that's objecti-ive! Together! After me . . . !"

Together they started yelling, "I be-lie-eve!"

"I believe that soon everyone will gather in big, stinking cities. I believe they'll gasp for breath there and run back to the open fields. I believe!"

"I be-lieve."

"In badger fat, the horn of bull, the erect sha-aft! In the flesh and bodily softness! "

. . . When Ilyukha Lapshin forced his eyes open, he saw the massive priest vigorously throwing his mighty body around the room, launching into a squatting dance at full speed and yelling and repeatedly slapping his sides and his chest:

> Oh, I believe I believe!
> Ta-da, ta-da, ta-da—one!
> I believe, I believe!
> Oompah, oompah, oompah—two
> I believe, I believe . . . !

And Maxim Yarikov was circling the priest, taking small steps, his hands on his hips and repeating loudly in a woman's voice:

> You've got, you've got, you've got three!
> I believe, I believe!
> Hey-ya, hey-ya four in all!

"After me!" the priest exclaimed.

I believe! I believe!

Maxim got behind the priest; they danced and circled the room in silence, then the priest launched into the squatting movements again, dropping down to the floor as if into a hole in the ice, with his arms flung out . . . The floorboards sagged.

> Oh, I believe, I believe!
> You take, you take, you take five!
> All the shafts—to a T!
> I believe! I believe!
> And where there are sticks, there are six!
> I believe! I believe!

Both the priest and Maxim were dancing with such anger, with such frenzy, that it didn't even seem strange that they were dancing. At this point they could either dance, or tear the shirts off their chests and cry and gnash their teeth.

Ilyukha looked and looked at them and finally joined in the dancing too. But he could only shout, "Yee-ha! Yee-ha!" in a thin voice from time to time. He didn't know the words.

The priest's shirt—on his back—became soaked, and his bulging muscles rippled powerfully under his shirt; evidently he had never known any fatigue before, and the illness hadn't yet bitten through his taut sinews. They're probably not that easy to bite through; before that happens, he'll gobble up all the badgers. And if need be, if they recommend it, he'll ask to have a fatty wolf brought to him—he won't leave that easily.

"After me!" the priest commanded again.

And the three of them, with the fierce, burning hot priest at the head, danced in circles round and round. Then the priest, like a big, heavy animal, jumped into the middle of the circle again, making the floorboards sag . . . Plates and glasses began to jingle on the table.

"Oh, I believe! I believe . . . !"

1971

NOTES

1. Vlasov, Andrei (1900-1946): Soviet general, a hero of the battle of Moscow in World War II. After capture (1942) by the Germans, he was allowed to form the "Russian Liberation Army" in 1944 to oppose Stalin and his regime. He was forcibly repatriated and, after a show trial in Moscow, hanged in August of 1946.
2. Magadan: a port town in the Russian Far East. During the Stalin era, it was a major transit center for prisoners being sent to labor camps in Kolyma and elsewhere.
3. Russian stove: See Aleksei Tolstoi's "The Viper," note 10.
4. Esenin, Sergei: (1895-1925). The most popular of the "peasant poets," who wrote romantic lyrics about village life, some pervaded with melancholy. He committed suicide in 1925.

BREAD FOR A DOG

Vladimir Tendryakov

Summer of 1933.

There was a small public garden with birch trees that one could walk through; it was behind a fence with its paint peeled off, next to a soot-covered train station building painted in government ochre. In it, right on its beaten paths, on the tree roots, on the surviving dusty grass, lay those who were no longer considered people.

True, each one had to keep somewhere deep in his lice-covered rags a well-thumbed document—if it had not been lost—proving that its bearer had such-and-such family name, first name and patronymic, was born there and there and, based on such and such a decision, exiled with the deprivation of his civil rights and the confiscation of his property. But no one cared any more that he, so-and-so, deprived of his civil rights, exiled by the administration,[1] hadn't reached his destination; no one was interested that he, so-and-so, deprived of his rights, wasn't living anywhere, wasn't working, and didn't have anything to eat. He was no longer a member of the human race.

For the most part, these were dispossessed[2] peasants from around Tula, Voronezh, Kursk, Oryol, and from all over Ukraine. The southern word *kurkul*[3] came with them to our northern parts as well.

Even in their outward appearance the *kurkuls* didn't resemble people.

Some of them were skeletons, with dark, wrinkled, seemingly rustling skin drawn tight around them—skeletons with huge, timidly burning eyes.

Others, on the contrary, were tautly bloated—any minute their skin, blue from being stretched, could split open; their bodies swayed, their feet looked like pillows, and their dirty fingers seemed sewn on and were covered with cankerous white flesh.

And they also didn't behave like people.

Someone would be pensively gnawing the bark on the trunk of a birch tree and peering into space with inhumanly big, smoldering eyes.

Someone, lying in the dust and emitting a bad, sour smell from his half-rotten rags, would be wiping his fingers in disgust with such energy and persistence that it seemed he was ready to clean the skin off them.

Someone would be spread out on the ground like jellied meat, not moving and only screeching like a large bird, and his insides would make gurgling sounds like a huge, boiling tea urn.

And someone would be dolefully stuffing into his mouth a small piece of station garbage picked up from the ground . . .

Those who had already managed to die had the most resemblance to people. They were lying peacefully—sleeping.

But before dying, one of the meek who had been gnawing bark quietest of all, who had been eating garbage, would suddenly rebel. He'd stand up straight, clasp a smooth, strong birch trunk with his stick-like, fragile hands, press his bony cheek against it, and open his black, blindingly toothy mouth wide, undoubtedly getting ready to shout a curse to reduce things to ashes, but only a rattle would come out and foam would bubble up around his mouth. Tearing off the skin on his bony cheek, the "rebel" would slide down the trunk and . . . grow silent forever.

Ones like this, even in death, didn't resemble people; they squeezed the trees like monkeys.

The adults avoided the public garden. Only the stationmaster in his new uniform cap with a bright red top strolled out of duty along the platform and the low fencing. He had a swollen, leaden-colored face; he looked down at his feet and didn't say anything.

From time to time Vania Dushnoi the policeman would show up, a staid fellow with a frozen expression—"just you watch out!"

"No one's crawled out?" he'd ask the stationmaster.

But the latter wouldn't answer; he'd just walk past without raising his head.

Vania Dushnoy watched to make sure that the *kurkuls* didn't crawl away from the public garden—either onto the platform or onto the tracks.

We, the small boys, also didn't go into the public garden itself but watched from behind the small fence. No horrors could stifle our beastly curiosity. Petrified with fear, overcome with squeamishness, breaking down from hidden pity, we watched the bark-eaters and the outbursts of the "rebels" which ended in a rattle, foam, and sliding down a tree trunk.

The stationmaster—"the red cap"—once turned his reddened, dark face in our direction, looked for a long time and finally said either to us or to himself or to the indifferent sky in general, "What will such children grow up to become? They enjoy looking at death. What kind of a world will there be after us? What kind of a world . . . ?"

We couldn't stand the garden for long. We'd tear away from there, breathing deeply—as if we were airing all the nooks in our poisoned souls—and run to the settlement.

There, where there was a normal life, where you could often hear the song:

> Don't sleep, arise, my curly-headed one!
> Its workshops filled with ringing,
> The country rises in glory
> To greet the day . . .

When I was already an adult, I wondered in amazement for a long time why I, a generally impressionable, vulnerable small boy, didn't fall ill and didn't go mad right after I saw a *kurkul* for the first time, dying with foam and a rattle right before my eyes.

Probably because the horrors of the public garden didn't appear right away, and I had a chance to get used to them somewhat, to become callous.

I experienced my first shock, by far stronger than the death of a *kurkul*, during a quiet street incident.

A woman in a worn-out coat of a simple, nice design with a velvet collar, and her face just as nice and worn-out, slipped right in front of my eyes and broke a glass jar with milk in it which she had bought on the station platform. The milk spilled into a dirty, ice-encrusted horse's hoofprint. The woman dropped down before it like before a daughter's grave, let out a stifled sob, and suddenly took a simple, chewed-up wooden spoon out of her pocket. She cried and scooped up the milk with her spoon from the small hole left in the road by the horse's hoof; she cried and ate, cried and ate—carefully, not greedily, in a refined way.

But I stood to the side and—no, I didn't wail with her—I was afraid that passers-by would start laughing at me.

My mother would give me lunch to be eaten at school: two pieces of black bread heavily smeared with cranberry jam. And so there came a day when during a noisy break I took out my bread and with my whole being sensed the silence that had set in around me. I got flustered and didn't dare offer any of the bread to the kids at the time. However, the next day I took now not two but four pieces . . .

During the long recess, I took them out and, afraid of the unpleasant silence which is so hard to break, I cried out much too hastily and awkwardly, "Who wants some?!"

"Me a tiny piece," Pashka Bykov, a kid from our street, answered.

"Me too . . . ! Me too . . . ! Me too . . . !"

Hands stretched out from all directions, eyes glistened.

"There won't be enough for all!" Pashka tried to push away the kids pressing against each other, but no one backed off.

"Me! Me! A small piece of crust . . . !"

I broke off a little piece for everybody.

Somebody pushed my hand, probably out of impatience without any evil intent, the bread fell, the kids in the back who wanted to see what had happened to the bread pressed against the ones in the front, and several feet stepped on the pieces and crushed them.

"You butterfingers!" Pashka scolded me.

And he walked away. All the others followed him and then crept off in different directions.

The bread lay in pieces on the floor now colored with the jam. We felt as if we had accidentally killed an animal in the heat of the moment.

Olga Stanislavna, the teacher, walked into the classroom. Judging by the way she averted her eyes, by the way she didn't ask any questions right away but only after some barely noticeable hesitation, I realized—she was hungry too.

"Who is so full here?"

And all those whom I had wanted to treat to some bread announced willingly, triumphantly, perhaps even with malicious joy, "Volodka Tenkov is full! He's the one . . . !"

I lived in a proletarian country and knew full well how shameful it was to be full. But unfortunately I truly was full; my father, a high-ranking official, received a high-ranking man's rations. My mother even baked cabbage pies with chopped eggs and used white flour!

Olga Stanislavna began the lesson.

"Last time we covered spelling . . ." And she fell silent. "Last time we . . ." She tried not to look at the crushed bread. "Volodya Tenkov, get up and pick up after yourself!"

I got up obediently without arguing, picked up the bread, and wiped the cranberry jam off the floor with a sheet of paper torn from my notebook. The whole class was silent; the whole class was breathing over my head.

After that, I flatly refused to take any lunch food to school.

Soon after that I saw the emaciated people with the huge, meekly sad eyes of Eastern beauties . . .

And those sick with dropsy, with swollen, smooth, featureless faces, with light-blue elephant legs . . .

The emaciated ones—just skin and bones—people in our area started calling them "shkeletons" and those sick with dropsy, "elephants."

And so the public garden with the birches near the train station . . .

I managed to get used to some things and not go mad.

I also didn't go mad because I knew that those who were dying in our birch grove by the train station in broad daylight were our enemies. It was about them that the great writer Gorky[4] had recently said, "If the enemy doesn't surrender, he's annihilated." They wouldn't surrender. So . . . they found themselves in the birch grove.

With some other kids I was a witness to an unexpected conversation between Dybakov and one "shkeleton."

Dybakov was the party first secretary in our district, a tall man in a semi-military jacket who had straight-hewn shoulders and wore a pince-nez on his thin, hooked nose. He walked around with his hands behind his back, his back arched, and his chest—decorated with patch pockets—puffed out.

Some kind of district conference was taking place in the railway workers' club. The whole leadership of the district with Dybakov at the head was making its way to the club along a path strewn with crushed brick. We, the kids, with nothing exciting to look at, also followed Dybakov.

Suddenly he stopped. Across the path, right in front of his feet in box calf boots, lay a man in rags—all bones with worn-out skin that was terribly loose. He was lying on the crushed brick, his brown skull resting on the pathetic, dirty bones of his hands, and he was looking up as all those dying of hunger look—with timid sorrow in his unnaturally big eyes.

Dybakov took step after step, making a crunching sound on the brick-gravel path, and was about to skirt the living skeleton he had chanced to encounter when suddenly the skeleton opened his leathery lips, flashed his large teeth, and said hoarsely but distinctly, "Let's talk, chief."

Silence descended; far beyond the vacant lot by the barracks you could hear someone singing in a tenor voice from nothing to do, to the accompaniment of a balalaika:

> He who has one leg
> Is well off.
> A lot of boots aren't needed,
> Just one foot cloth.

"Or are you afraid of me, chief?"

District committee worker Comrade Gubanov, with an unlocked briefcase under his arm as always, emerged from behind Dybakov. "Silence! Si-lence!"

The man lying there looked up at him timidly and grinned in a terrible way. Dybakov waved Comrade Gubanov to the side with a motion of his hand.

"Let's talk. You ask—I'll answer."

"Tell me before I die . . . what . . . what did I do . . . ? Can it seriously be because I had two horses?" the murmuring voice asked.

"Because of that," Dybakov answered quietly and coldly.

"And you admit it! Lord, you're a beast . . ."

"Si-lence!" Comrade Gubanov ran up to him again.

And again Dybakov waved him off to the side nonchalantly.

"Would you have given bread to the worker for his cast iron?"

"What do I need your cast iron for? To eat it with my gruel?"

"That's exactly it. The collective farm needs the iron, and the collective farm is ready to feed the workers for it. Did you want to join a collective farm? Only be honest!"

"I didn't want to."

"Why?"

"Everybody wants his bit of freedom."

"It's not your bit of freedom that's the reason but horses. You didn't want to part with your horses. You fed them, tended to them—and suddenly you're told to give them up. You didn't want to part with your property! Isn't that so?"

The goner said nothing, blinked sorrowfully, and seemed even ready to agree.

"Take away the horses, chief, and stop. Why take my life as well?" he asked.

"And you'll forgive us if we take them away? You won't start taking up arms behind our backs? Be honest!"

"Who knows . . ."

"And we don't know either. What would you have done with us if you had felt we were taking up arms against you . . . ? You're silent . . . ? Nothing to say . . . ? Then good-bye."

Dybakov stepped over the thin, stick-like legs of the man he had been talking to and moved on, his hands behind his back, his chest with the patch pockets puffed out. Others started moving too and followed him, skirting the goner with disgust.

He lay there in front of us small boys, a flattened skeleton in rags, his skull on the crumbled brick—a skull preserving a human expression of submissiveness, weariness, and perhaps pensiveness. He lay there and we kept scrutinizing him with condemning looks. He had two horses, the bloodsucker! For the sake of those horses he would've taken up arms against us. "If the enemy does not surrender . . ." Dybakov got rid of him splendidly.

And nonetheless I felt sorry for the evil enemy. And probably I wasn't the only one. No kid started to dance in joy over him or to tease:

> Enemy-big enemy,
> *Kurluk* big kulak,
> He gorges on tree bark,
> He kills lice,
> Strolls with his *kurkulikha*,
> And sways in the wind nice.

I would sit down at the table at home, reach for some bread, and memories of those images would unfold in my mind: somewhat crazed eyes directed into the distance, white teeth gnawing bark, a cold hulk with gurgling insides, a gaping black mouth, a rattle, and foam . . . And I'd feel nausea rising in my throat.

Before all this, when talking about me, my mother would say, "I can't complain about that one. No matter what you put before him, he puts it away, wolfs it down." Now she'd start shouting, "You've become so choosy! You don't know when you're well off . . . !"

I was the only one who "didn't know how well off" I was, but if my mother began scolding, she always scolded the two of us right away—me and my brother. My brother was three years younger; in his seven years he knew only how to worry about himself, and for this reason ate "wolfing things down."

"You've become so choosy! We don't want soup, we don't want potatoes. All around us people are happy, so very happy to get a stale crust of bread. But I might as well serve you hazel-grouse!"

I had read only some verse about hazel-grouse: "Eat pineapples, chew hazel-grouse, your last day is coming, you bourgeois louse!"[5] I couldn't announce a hunger strike, and I couldn't refuse food altogether. First of all, my mother wouldn't have permitted it. Secondly, nausea is nausea, images are images, but I still wanted to eat, though hardly bourgeois hazel grouse. I was made to swallow the first spoonful, and the rest followed without being forced on me. I'd finish my dinner quickly and get up from the table heavier.

And here is where it all began . . .

It seems to me that it is more natural for conscience to awaken in the bodies of people who are full rather than hungry. A hungry man is forced to think more about himself, about getting daily bread *for himself*; the very burden of hunger forces him to be selfish. A full man has more of a chance to look around, to think about others. For the most part ideological fighters emerged from the ranks of the full with the satiety of a certain caste—the Gracchi[6] in all times.

I'd get up from the table. Isn't that the reason why people in the park by the station are gnawing bark? Isn't it because I ate too much?

But those are *kurkuls* gnawing bark! Why are you pitying them . . . ? "If the enemy doesn't surrender, he's annihilated!" And they are "annihilated" probably like this, that's probably how it's supposed to look—skulls with eyes, elephant legs, and foam around a black mouth. You're simply afraid to face up to the truth.

My father happened to relate at one point that there were villages in other places where the inhabitants had all died to the last soul—the adults, old people, and children. Even nursing infants . . . There's no way you can say about them, "If the enemy doesn't surrender . . ."

I'm full, very full—totally satiated. I just ate so much that there probably would've been enough for five people to save themselves from a hungry death. I didn't save five, I ate their lives. But whose? The lives of enemies or non-enemies . . . ?

And who's an enemy . . . ? Is the one gnawing bark an enemy? He was—yes!—but now animosity is far from his mind, there's no flesh on his bones, and there's no strength left even in his voice . . .

I ate my whole dinner and didn't share it with anyone.

I have to eat three times a day.

Once toward morning I suddenly woke up. I hadn't dreamt of anything; I simply went and opened my eyes and saw my room in the twilight that was mysteriously ashy—there was a nice, cozy, grey dawn outside my window.

Far off on the station tracks a "goat"[7] whistled. Early, blue titmice were chirping in an old linden tree. A father starling was clearing his throat, trying to sing like a nightingale and doing a bad job of it! A cuckoo began cuckooing softly, with conviction, in the back part of the swamp. "Cuckoo bird! Cuckoo bird! How many years will I live?"[8] And it lets out its "cu-ckoos" like silver eggs.

And all this takes place during twilight, surprisingly peaceful and grey, an intimate, cozy world. In a minute unexpectedly stolen from sleep, I suddenly quietly rejoice at an obvious fact: a certain Volodka Tenkov, a human being about ten years old, exists in the wide world. He exists—how wonderful! "Cuckoo! Cuckoo! How many years will I . . . ? "Cu-ckoo! Cu- ckoo. Cu- ckoo . . . !" It's unceasingly generous.

At that point there was a thundering sound far off, at the very end of our street. Ripping open the silence of the sleepy small town, a rickety cart was drawing near, replacing the silver voice of the cuckoo, the chirping of the blue titmice, and the vain attempts of the untalented starling. Who is this, and where is he so angrily rushing so early in the morning . . . ?

And suddenly it strikes me: who? It's clear who! The whole small town is talking about these early trips. The komkhoz[9] stableman, Abram, is going "to collect carrion." Every morning he drives his cart straight into the birch grove and shakes the people lying there—alive or not? He doesn't bother with the living, and he piles the dead into the cart like blocks of wood.

The rickety cart thunders, waking up the sleeping town. It thunders and grows quiet.

After its appearance, you can't hear the birds. For about a minute you can't hear anyone or anything. Anything . . . But what's strange—there's no silence either. "Cu-ckoo! Cu-ckoo . . . !" Oh, don't! Does it really matter how many years I will live in this world? And do I really want to live that long . . . ?

But just like heavy rain pouring off a roof, sparrows that have awakened come swooping down. Buckets start ringing, women's voices resound, and the well crank begins squeaking.

"Roofs fixed! Wood cut! Garbage cans cleaned! Any work at all!" a strong baritone shouts, calling out to people.

"Roofs fixed! Wood cut! Garbage cans cleaned!" a boyish alto repeats.

These are exiled *kurkuls* as well—father and son. The father is a tall man with broad bony shoulders, bearded, sternly important; the son is sinewy thin, freckled, very serious, and two or three years older than me.

Every day begins with their two voices offering loudly, almost haughtily, to clean the town's garbage cans.

I mustn't eat my dinner alone.

I'm obligated to share it with someone.

With whom . . . ?

Probably with the most, the most hungry person there is, even if he's an enemy.

Who's the most hungry . . . ? How to find out?

It's not difficult. I should go to the park with all the birches and extend my hand with a piece of bread to the first person who comes along. It's impossible to make a mistake; everyone there is the most, most hungry, there are no others. Extend my hand to one and not notice the others . . . ? Make one happy and hurt ten others by denying them food? That would truly be a mortal wrong. The ones to whom my hand won't be extended will be taken away by the stableman Abram.

Can the ones who are passed over agree with you . . . ? Isn't it dangerous to extend a helping hand openly?

Of course, I didn't think like that then and use the words with which

I now write, thirty-six years later. Most likely I didn't think at all at the time but had a keen feeling, like an animal that senses intuitively the complications to come. At that time I realized not with my rational mind but with my intuition that the noble intention—break your daily bread in half and share it with your neighbor—could be carried out only secretly from others, only thievishly!

Furtively, thievishly, I saved a part of what my mother had placed in front of me on the table. I thievishly packed my pockets with three pieces of bread saved honestly, a lump of millet porridge wrapped in paper and the size of a fist, and a clean, crystal-perfect lump of sugar. In broad daylight I walked out to do my thievish deed—to hunt secretly for the most, the most hungry person.

I met Pashka Bykov, who was in my class and lived on the same street as me, with whom I wasn't really friendly, but with whom I was careful not to quarrel either. I knew that Pashka was always hungry—day and night, before and after dinner. The Bykov family—seven people in all—lived on the ration cards of the father who worked as a coupler on the railroad. But I didn't share my bread with Pashka—he was not the most . . .

I met the old woman Obnoskova, bent with age, who lived on what she gathered—grasses and roots on the sides of the road, in fields, and at the edges of the forest—and dried, cooked, and steamed what she found . . . Other old women like that who lived alone had all died. I didn't share with the old woman—still not the most . . .

Boris Isaakovich Zilberbruner, in galoshes tied with string to dirty anklebones, trotted past me. If I had met this Zilberbruner earlier, then who knows, I might have decided he was the one. Not long ago he had been one of the "shkeletons" who hung around a cafeteria, but he adapted and made fish hooks out of wire, and was paid for them even in chicken eggs.

Finally I ran into one of the "elephants" staggering through the town. He was very broad like a wardrobe, and wore a roomy, unbelted peasant caftan the color of plowed land; he had a rook's nest in his Zaporozhye Cossack hat. His swollen, pale-blue legs that shook with each step like oat flour pudding, would have fit in a bathhouse wash-tub only one at a time.

Perhaps even he wasn't the most . . . Had I continued my hunt, I probably would've run into a more unfortunate person, but the remains of my dinner in my pockets were burning me, demanding that I share immediately . . . !

"Uncle . . ."

He stopped, breathing heavily, and from his towering height directed his eyes that looked like narrow slits straight at me.

Standing near him, I was struck by his pale, swollen face with its unnatural, gigantic size—cheeks that moved and floated like flabby buttocks, a chin crashing down to his chest, eyes which had totally disappeared under his eyelids, and the broad bridge of his nose stretched to a corpse's blueness. You can't read anything in a face like this—neither fear nor hope, neither emotionalism nor suspicion—it was a pillow.

Rummaging in my pocket, I began to free the first piece of bread awkwardly.

The flattened face twitched, the thickly swollen hand with the short, dirty, unbending fingers reached out and took the piece gently, insistently, and impatiently. A calf with a warm nose and soft mouth takes bread from a hand that way.

"Thank you, my boy," the elephant said in a falsetto, using the Ukrainian word for "boy."

I laid out everything for him that I had.

"Tomorrow . . . In the vacant lot . . . Near the piles . . . Something more," I promised and ran away from there with lighter pockets and a lighter conscience.

I was happy the whole day. It was cool and quiet inside, under my ribs, where my soul lived.

In the vacant lot, near the piles . . . This time I was carrying eight pieces of bread, two pieces of fatback, and an old jar filled with fried potatoes. I was supposed to eat all this myself and didn't. I saved it all when my mother wasn't looking.

I ran, skipping along to the vacant lot, with both hands holding my shirt which bulged out in the front. Someone's shadow appeared under my feet.

"Young man! Young man! I beg you! Spare me a moment . . . !"

Are people addressing me so respectfully . . . ?

Me.

A woman in a dusty hat, known to all by her nickname, Otryzhka,[10] stood blocking my way. She was neither an "elephant" nor a "shkeleton" but simply an invalid disfigured by some kind of strange illness. Her whole dried-up body was unnaturally crumpled up, bent, and deformed—her small shoulders were twisted, she was leaning backward, and on her small bird-like head there was a greasy cloth hat with a dingy feather sticking out somewhere in the back of her body. From time to time this head shook despairingly as if its mistress were preparing to exclaim quickly, "And now I'll do a dance for you!" But Otryzhka didn't dance and would usually start winking really, really hard, scrunching up her whole cheek.

Now she was winking at me and saying in a passionate, teary voice: "Young man, take a look at me! Don't be shy, don't be shy, take a careful look . . . ! Have you ever seen a being wronged by God . . . ?" She kept winking and coming towards me, and I kept backing away from her. "I'm sick, I'm feeble, but I have a son at home. . . I'm a mother, I love him with all my heart, I'm ready to do anything to feed him . . . We've both forgotten how bread tastes, young man! A little piece, I beg you . . . !"

The dreadful, cheerful winking with her whole cheek, the dark hand holding a dirty bit of rag for dabbing her eyes . . . How did she find out that I had bread under my shirt? The "elephant" who was waiting for me in the vacant lot wouldn't have told her. It was to the "elephant's" advantage to keep quiet.

"I'm prepared to get on my knees before you. You have such a good . . . . You have an angel's face . . . !"

How did she find out about the bread? From the smell? Sorcery . . . ? I didn't understand then that I wasn't the only one trying to give some food to the exiled *kurkuls*, and that all simple-hearted rescuers had an eloquently thievish, guilty facial expression.

I was unable to resist Otryzhka's fervor, her gleeful winking, and her crumpled, dirty bit of rag. I gave her all the bread and the pieces of fatback, keeping only one piece and the jar of fried potatoes.

"I promised that . . ."

But Otryzhka was devouring the jar with her crow's eyes, shaking her dusty hat with the feather and moaning, "We're dying! We're dying! Me and my son—we're dying . . . !"

I let her have the potatoes as well. She shoved the jar under her knitted jacket, flashed her greedy eyes at the last piece of bread left in my hand, jerked her head—"I'll do a dance!"—winked once more with her cheek and walked away, listing to the side like a sinking boat.

I stood and scrutinized the bread in my hand. The piece was small, dirty and squashed from being in my pocket, but I had called him myself—come to the vacant lot—I had forced the hungry man to wait a whole day, and now I was going to treat him to such a small piece. No, better not shame myself . . . !

And from vexation—and hunger as well—without leaving the spot, I ate the bread. It was unexpectedly very tasty and . . . toxic. The whole day after eating it I felt poisoned: how could I have done that—I had torn it out of the mouth of a hungry man! How could I . . . !"

And in the morning when I looked out the window, I grew cold. The familiar "elephant" was hanging around our gate, under a window. He stood wrapped in his immense caftan the color of a newly plowed field, his toad's hands folded on his huge stomach, and a breeze ruffling the dirty fur on his Cossack hat—he was immovable and tower-like.

I immediately felt like a miserable fox cub, driven into a burrow by a dog. The "elephant" can stand until tomorrow, he can stand like that tomorrow and after tomorrow; he has nowhere to rush to, and standing promises bread.

I waited till my mother left the house, got into the kitchen, broke off a thick end piece of a loaf of bread, which was of considerable weight, got ten large, raw potatoes from the sack and ran out . . .

The caftan the color of plowed earth had bottomless pockets into which all our family supplies of bread could have probably disappeared.

"Son. Don't believe that vile old woman. She doesn't have anyone. No son, no daughter," he said in Ukrainian.

I had guessed even without his saying so. Otryzhka was deceiving me, but try and refuse her when she's standing before you all broken, winking with her cheek and holding a dirty bit of rag in her hand to dab her eyes with.

"Oh, what misery, my son, what misery. Death, and she's robbing people . . . Oh, what misery, what misery," he continued in Ukrainian. Sighing huskily, he pushed off slowly, dragging his swollen feet with difficulty on the town sidewalk along boards full of splinters. He was wide like a haystack and majestic like a dilapidated windmill. "Oh, woe is me, woe . . . !"

I turned to go into the house and winced: my father was standing before me, a patch of sunlight playing on his smoothly shaven head. He was somewhat stout and solidly built, dressed in a canvas soldier's blouse tied with a thin belt from the Caucasus with metal decorations on it. His face wasn't sullen and his eyes weren't covered over by his eyebrows—it was a peaceful, tired face.

He stepped up to me, put his heavy hand on my shoulder, stared for a long time somewhere to the side, and finally asked, "You gave him some bread?"

"Yes."

And he again peered into the distance.

I love my father and I'm proud of him.

People now sing songs and write tales about the great revolution, about the civil war. It's my father they're singing about, it's him they write tales about!

He's one of those soldiers who were the first to refuse to fight for the tsar, who arrested their officers.

He heard Lenin at Finland Station. He saw him standing on an armored car in person, not as a statue.

He was a commissar of the Four-Hundred Sixteenth Revolutionary Regiment during the civil war.

He has a scar on his neck from a Kolchak[11] shell splinter.

He was awarded a silver watch with his name engraved on it. It was stolen later, but I held it in my hands myself and saw the engraving on the cover: "For demonstrated courage in battles with the counter-revolution . . ."

I love my father and I'm proud of him. And I'm always afraid of his silence. Right now he'll stay silent for a while and then say, "I fight our enemies my whole life, and you're feeding them. Are you a traitor, Volodka?"

But he asked quietly, "Why this one? Why not another one?"

"That one turned up . . ."

"Another turns up—you'll give?"

"I d-don't know. I probably will."

"And will we have enough bread to feed all of them?"

I kept silent and looked at the ground.

"The country doesn't have enough for all. You can't scoop out the sea with a teaspoon, my son." My father poked me lightly in the shoulder. "Go play."

The familiar "elephant" began to wage a silent duel with me. He'd come under our window and stand and stand—motionless, slovenly, and faceless. I'd try not to look at him, I'd put up with him, and . . . the "elephant" would win. I'd run out to him with a piece of bread or a cold potato pancake. He'd receive the tribute and slowly go away.

Once running out to him with bread and a cod tail fished out of yesterday's soup, I suddenly discovered that one more "elephant" was lying around near our fence on the dusty grass, covered with a wet, dirty railway worker's overcoat that had once been black. As I was walking toward him, he only raised his head of uncombed, matted hair covered in scabs, and said hoarsely, 'Boy-y, I'm dy-i-ing . . . !'"

And I saw it was true and gave him a piece of cooked cod. The next morning three more "shkeletons" were lying near our fence. I was now under total siege, now I couldn't take anything out to buy them off. You can't feed five with your dinners and breakfasts, and my mother wouldn't have had enough supplies for all.

My brother would run out to look at the guests and return excited and happy. "One more 'shkeleton' has come crawling to Volodka!"

My mother would swear. "Made a place for themselves to lie around in, as if we're richer than the rest. Found parasites to feed, those tyrants of mine!"

As always, she was scolding the two of us right away, although my brother had nothing to do with it whatsoever. My mother would swear, but she couldn't bring herself to walk out and chase away the hungry kurkuls. My father, too, walked past the ground where they lay. He didn't say a word to me in reproach.

My mother issued an order. "Here's a pitcher—run to the cafeteria and get some kvass. And be quick!" There was nothing to be done; I took the glass pitcher from her.

I darted through the gate to freedom without difficulty; it wasn't for the sluggish "elephants" and barely crawling "shkeletons" to stop me.

I spent a long time jostling people in the small cafeteria-café as I tried to buy the kvass. The kvass was the real thing, made of bread—it was by no means fruit water with vitamins added to it—because it was not sold to anyone who wanted it, but only to those on a list. But you can hang around all you want; you still have to return home.

They were waiting for me. All those who had been lying down were now standing solemnly. Cascades of patches, the copper color of skin showing through holes in their rags, ingratiating smiles with sinister bared teeth, burning red eyes, faces without eyes, hands stretching towards me that were thin like bird claws and round like balls, and cracked, raspy voices saying, "Little boy, some bread . . ."[12]

"A crumb for each . . ."

"I'm dying, b-boy-y. A bite before death . . ."

"Want me to, I'll eat my hand? Want me to? Want me to . . . ?"

I stood before them and pressed the cold pitcher with the cloudy kvass to my chest.

"A bit of brea-ea-d-d . . ."

"A crust . . ."

"Want me to . . . my hand . . . ?"

And suddenly Otryzhka swooped down from the side, the feather on her hat shaking energetically.

"Young man! I beg you! On my knees I beg you!"

She actually fell to her knees in front of me, wringing not only her hands but twisting her neck and back as well and winking at some point above, at the blue sky, at God . . .

And this was now too much. Everything went dark before my eyes. Someone else's wild cry escaped from me at a wailing gallop. "Go a-way! Go a-way! Bastards! Sons of bitches! Bloodsuckers! Go away!"

Otryzhka got up matter-of-factly and shook the dirt off her skirt. The rest all grew feeble at the same time, dropped their hands, turned their backs to me and moved off slowly—unhurriedly, sluggishly.

But I couldn't stop and I kept screaming in a wailing tone, "Go a-way!"

The hard workers—the staid, bearded father with the freckled, very serious son who was only two years older than me—approached with tools on their shoulders. The son casually motioned with his chin in the direction of the *kurkuls* wandering off and said, "Jackals."

The father nodded in agreement with an air of importance, and they both looked with open contempt at me—disheveled, red-eyed, gently pressing the pitcher with the kvass to my chest. I wasn't a victim for them with whom one had to sympathize but one of the participants in the jackals' game.

They walked by. The father carried a saw on his straight shoulder, and it was bending in the sun like a wide cut of cloth, sending out soundless flashes of lightning; one step—a flash, another step—a flash.

My hysterics were probably perceived by the goners as my being completely cured of my boyish pity. No one stood near our gate any more.

Was I cured . . . ? Perhaps. Now I wouldn't have taken out a piece of bread to the "elephant," had he stood in front of my window right up until winter.

My mother kept moaning and groaning that I wasn't eating anything and getting thin, that there were big, dark shadows under my eyes . . . Three times a day she'd torture me. "Again you're staring at your plate? Again I haven't pleased you? Eat! Eat! It's cooked in milk and I've added butter. Just you dare turn away!"

She baked pies for me with cabbage and chopped egg, using the flour set aside for the holidays. I liked those pies very much. I ate them. I ate them and suffered.

Now I always awoke before dawn and never missed the sound of the cart going by which the stableman Abram was driving to the station public park.

The morning cart was thundering . . .

> Don't sleep, arise, my curly-headed one,
> Its workshops filled with ringing . . .

The cart thundered—a sign of the times! The cart was rushing to collect the corpses of the enemies of the revolutionary fatherland.

I listened for it and realized I was a stupid, incorrigible boy. I couldn't do anything with myself—I felt sorry for my enemies!

Somehow one evening I was sitting with my father on the porch at home.

Recently my father's face had turned somehow dark, his eyelids red; in some way he reminded me of the station master who would stroll along the station public park in his red cap.

Suddenly below, near the porch, a dog appeared as if from out of the ground. It had lifelessly dull, somewhat dirty-yellow eyes, and its abnormally rumpled fur lay in clumps on its sides and back. It stared at us for a minute or two with its lifeless eyes and disappeared just as instantly as it had appeared.

"Why is its fur growing like that?" I asked.

My father kept quiet, then explained reluctantly: "It's falling out . . . From hunger. Its owner is probably growing bald himself from starvation."

And suddenly it hit me. It seemed I had found the most, the most unfortunate being in our small town. Someone will take pity on the "elephants" and "shkeletons" once in a while, be it even in secret and feeling ashamed of himself; once in a while a fool like me will be found who will slip them some bread . . . But a dog . . . Even my father felt pity not for the dog but for its unknown master—"growing bald from starvation." The dog will die and even an Abram won't be found who'll take it away.

The next day, from morning on, I sat on the porch with pockets full of pieces of bread. I sat and patiently waited—would that same dog appear . . . ?

The dog appeared just like yesterday—suddenly, noiselessly—and stared at me with its lifeless, unwashed eyes. I made a motion to get out my bread and it dashed aside . . . Out of the corner of its eye it had time to see the bread I'd taken out, stood frozen to the spot, and stared at my hands from afar—lifelessly, without any expression.

"Come . . . Come on! Don't be afraid."

The dog looked and didn't move, ready to disappear at any moment. It didn't believe either my affectionate voice or my ingratiating smiles, or the bread in my hand. No matter how much I entreated it—it didn't approach, but it didn't disappear either.

After a half-hour struggle I finally threw it the bread. Without taking its lifeless, impenetrable eyes off the bread, it drew close to it, moving sideways, always sideways. One jump—and . . . no piece of bread and no dog.

The next morning—a new encounter, with the same exchange of lifeless glances, the same unyielding distrust of any affection in my voice and the bread I was offering out of kindness. The piece was grabbed only when it was thrown to the ground. There was no chance to give it a second piece.

The same thing the third morning, and the fourth . . . We didn't let a single day go by without meeting, but we didn't get any closer to one another. I never could teach it to take the piece of bread from my hand. Not once did I see any kind of expression in its yellow, dull, and lifeless eyes—not even a dog's fear, not to mention a dog's sweetness and friendly disposition.

It seems that even here I had encountered a victim of the times. I knew that some of those people who had been exiled fed on dogs—

enticing them, killing and cutting them up. My acquaintance had probably fallen into their hands too. They couldn't kill it, but on the other hand they killed its trust in people forever. And it seems it didn't trust me in particular. Raised on a hungry street, it couldn't imagine a fool who was ready to give it food simply like that, without demanding anything in return . . . even gratitude.

Yes, even gratitude. That's a kind of payment as well, but it was quite enough for me that I was feeding it and supporting a life. It meant that I too had the right to eat and live myself.

With those pieces of bread I was feeding not a dog that had lost his fur from starvation but my own conscience.

I can't say that my conscience really liked this suspicious food. I continued to have pangs of conscience from time to time, but not such strong ones and not so dangerous to life.

Written in 1969-1970; published posthumously in 1988. This version was prepared by N. Asmolova-Tendryakov and published in 1995.

NOTES

1. that is to say, without a formal court hearing.
2. Collectivization: Stalin's First Five-Year Plan (1928-32) called for combining individually owned farms into large state collective farms. Peasants were forced to give up their land and cattle, and those who resisted were killed or exiled. This policy of forced collectivization devastated agriculture and led to the horrific famine of 1932-33, during which millions of people starved to death.
3. *kurkul*: Ukrainian word (equivalent to the Russian "kulak") for a comparatively well-to-do peasant who had cattle, or could hire laborers, etc., the kind who in the late 1920s and early 1930s were dispossessed of their property and forcibly collectivized or exiled, or even killed. Historical studies indicate that the term "kulak" was also applied indiscriminately when the city or regional authorities wanted to fulfill the quota of people being shipped to the Gulag.
4. Gorky, Maksim (pseud. of Aleksei Peshkov; 1868-1936): short story writer, novelist and playwright, who came to prominence at the end of the 19th century with his stories about the downtrodden and worked in support of major social

change. He is recognized as "the father of socialist realism" because of his novel *Mother* (1905). He guided and influenced many young writers.

5. A famous couplet by the poet Vladimir Mayakovsky (1893-1930), written in 1917.

6. Gracchi: one of the very rich and politically important families of Rome in the 2nd century BC.

7. "goat": railroad term for locomotives used in yard switching operations.

8. Russians believe that the number of times you hear the cuckoo bird go "cuckoo" is the number of years you are fated to live.

9. *komkhoz*: acronym for *kommunal'noe khozyaistvo*, communal services.

10. Otryzhka: literally, "Burp."

11. Admiral Aleksandr V. Kolchak (1874-1920): in 1917 supported Kerensky's Provisional Government. Appointed Minister of War and Navy in the anti-Bolshevik government established in Omsk, Siberia; led the White forces against the Red in Siberia during the civil war. Executed by the Bolsheviks in 1920.

12. This line and the dialogue that follows contain a mixture of Russian and Ukrainian.

YOU CRIED BITTERLY IN YOUR SLEEP

Yury Kazakov

It was one of those warm summer days . . .

My friend and I were standing and talking near our house. And you would be walking near us in grass and flowers that came up to your shoulders, or else you'd be crouching down and examining a pine needle or blade of grass for a long time, and a vague half-smile, which I tried to fathom and couldn't, never left your face.

Having gotten his fill of running among the hazelnut trees, our spaniel, Chief, would sometimes come up to us. He'd stop with his side somewhat turned toward you and, thrusting a shoulder forward like a wolf and slowly turning his neck, he'd look in your direction with his coffee-colored eyes and beg, waiting for you to give him an affectionate glance. Had you done so, he'd have instantly fallen on his front paws, wagged his short tail, and begun to bark furiously and conspiratorially. But for some reason you were afraid of Chief and would walk warily around him and hug my knee; and with your head thrown back, you'd look me in the face with your blue eyes in which the sky was reflected and say cheerfully and tenderly, as if you'd come back from far away, "Daddy!"

And the touch of your little hands brought me even a kind of painful pleasure.

Your random embraces must have touched my friend, too, because he'd suddenly grow quiet, tousle your fluffy hair, and gaze at you pensively for a long time.

Now he'll never look at you again with tenderness or talk to you, because he's no longer in this world and, of course, you won't be able to remember him, just as you won't be able to remember many other things as well . . .

He[1] shot himself in late fall, when the first snow fell. But did he see the snow? Did he look through the windows of the veranda at the surrounding area wrapped in silence? Or did he shoot himself at night?

And had the snow already been falling since evening, or was the ground still black when he arrived on the commuter train and walked to his house as if to Golgotha?

After all, the first snow is so calming, so melancholic, that it forces us to immerse ourselves in leisurely, peaceful thoughts . . . .

And when, at what moment, did that relentless idea, frightening like a poisonous fang, enter his head? Probably a long time ago . . . He told me more than once what bouts of depression he'd experience in early spring or late fall when he lived at the dacha by himself, and how he wanted at those times to end it all at one go—to shoot himself. But it must be said—who among us in moments of depression hasn't had such words suddenly escape from his lips?

And he had terrible nights when he couldn't sleep and kept imagining that someone with cold breath was trying to get into the house and cast a spell on him. That was death, you know, trying to get in!

"Listen, give me some cartridges, for God's sake!" he asked me one day. "I'm all out. I keep imagining at night that someone's walking around the house! But everywhere it's quiet—like in the grave . . . Will you give me some?"

And I gave him six cartridges or so.

"That should be enough for you," I said in jest, "to defend yourself."

And what a worker he was, what a reproach his whole life always was for me—a life that was constantly up-beat and active. Anytime you'd visit him—say, in the summer—and if in the summer you'd come from the veranda side, raise your eyes to the open window upstairs in the mezzanine and shout quietly "Mitya!", a "Hel-lo!" would immediately resound in response, and his face would appear in the window and look at you for a whole minute with a befogged, vacant expression. Then, a weak smile, a wave of his slender hand.

"I'll be right there!"

And here he is already downstairs, on the veranda, in his coarse-wool sweater, and he seems to be breathing particularly deeply and regularly after working, and you look at him with pleasure, with envy, as you'd look at an energetic young horse constantly straining at the bit, constantly speeding up from a walking pace to a trot.

"Why do you let yourself go like that?" he'd say to me whenever I'd get sick or be down in the dumps. "Follow my example! I swim in the Yasnushka well into the fall! Why do you always sit or lie around? Get up, get some exercise . . ."

The last time I saw him was in the middle of October. He came to see me on a wonderful sunny day, nicely dressed as always, wearing a fluffy cap. His face was sad, but our conversation started off lively—about Buddhism for some reason, about how it was time, time to tackle great novels, about how one's sole joy was to be found only in daily work, and you could work every day only when you were writing some big book.

I went with him as he left. He suddenly started crying and turned away.

"When I was like your Alyosha," he began to speak, after calming down a bit, "the sky seemed so high, so blue to me! Then it faded for me, but that comes with age, doesn't it? The sky's the same, isn't it? You know, I'm afraid of Abramtsevo.[2] I'm afraid, afraid . . . The longer I live here, the more I feel drawn here. But it's sinful, isn't it, to give your heart to one place? Did you carry Alyosha on your shoulders? You know, at first I'd carry mine, and later we'd all ride our bikes to a spot in the woods, and I'd talk to them, tell them about Abramtsevo, about this land of Radonezh.[3] I so wanted them to love it, to really love it, because it's their native land. Ah, quick, take a look! What a maple tree!"

Then he began to talk about his plans for the winter. The sky was so blue, and the maple was thick with leaves that gleamed golden in the sun. And our parting was especially friendly, especially tender . . . And three weeks later, in Gagra[4]—it was as if a thunderbolt had struck me! As if the shot in the night that resounded in Abramtsevo flew and flew across all of Russia until it reached me at the seashore. And Gagra was exactly the same way as it is now, as I write this. The sea was crashing against the shore and violently spewing out its deep-sea smell in the darkness; far to the right, a pearly strand of street lights was glowing, lining the bay like an arched bow.

You had already turned five! You and I sat on the dark shore, near the breakers that were invisible in the darkness, listening to their roar, listening to the wet clicking sound of the pebbles as they rolled back after each retreating wave. I don't know what you were thinking about because you were quiet, but I imagined I was walking to Abramtsevo, home from the station, only taking a different road from the one I usually took. And the sea disappeared for me, the nighttime mountains disappeared, and the houses presumably spread out on them here and there, judging by the glowing lights. I walked along a cobble-stone road covered with the first snow, and when I'd glance back, I'd see my clear, dark footprints in the ash-grey snow. I turned left, went past a dark pond whose shoreline I could still make out, entered the fir-filled darkness and turned right . . . I looked straight ahead and at the end of the street saw his dacha, under a canopy of fir trees, with the windows all ablaze.

Still, when did it happen? In the evening? At night?

For some reason, even in early November, I waited for the hesitant dawn of winter to come, that time of year when you sense the approaching day by the way the snow has grown brighter and by the way the trees have become visible and stand out in the darkness all around.

Now I approach his house, open the wicket-gate, climb the steps of the veranda and see . . .

"Listen," he asked me once, "a load of small-shot—is that a powerful charge? If you shoot at close range?" "You bet!" I answered. "If you shoot at an aspen tree, say as thick as your arm, from a half-meter away, that little aspen tree will be cut down like with a razor blade!"

To this day I am tormented by the thought: What would I have done, had I seen him sitting on the veranda with a cocked shotgun and one foot bare? Would I have pulled on the door, smashed the glass, and shouted for everyone in the vicinity to hear? Or would I have averted my eyes in fear and held my breath, hoping that if he weren't disturbed, he'd change his mind, put down the shotgun, carefully release the trigger he was holding with his big toe, sigh deeply and, as if waking up from a bad dream, put on his shoe?

And what would he have done if I had smashed the glass and yelled? Would he have thrown the shotgun aside and thrown himself joyfully at me or just the opposite? After glancing at me hatefully with his already dead eyes, would he have rushed to pull the trigger with his foot? To this day my soul flies to that house and him on that night; it tries to merge with him, follows his every movement, strives to guess his thoughts, and can't—it gives up.

I know that he got to the dacha late at night. What did he do in those last few hours of his? First of all, he changed his clothes and hung up his city suit in the closet carefully, as was his habit. Then he brought in some firewood to heat the stove. He ate some apples. I don't think the fateful decision took hold of him right away—what person contemplating suicide eats apples and prepares to heat a stove!

Then he suddenly changed his mind about heating the stove and lay down. It was then, most likely, that *it* occurred to him. What did he recall, if he did, in his last minutes? Or did he just get ready? Did he cry . . . ?

Then he washed up and put on clean underwear.

The shotgun was hanging on the wall. He took it down, felt its cold weight, the coolness of its steel barrels. The fore-end came to rest obediently in his left hand. The bolt catch released stiffly to the right with a pull of his thumb. The shotgun opened at the bolt, revealing a cross-section of the back of its two tunnel-like barrels. And the cartridge went easily, smoothly into one of the barrels. *My* cartridge!

The lights were on everywhere in the house. He had turned on the lights on the veranda as well. He sat down in a chair, took off his right boot. In the deathly silence, he cocked the trigger with a loud click. He put the gun in his mouth and gripped the barrels with his teeth, tasting the cold, oily metal . . . the barrels.

Yes! But did he sit down right away and take off his shoe? Or did he stand the whole night, pressing his forehead against a window pane, his tears fogging up the glass? Or did he walk around his plot of land, bidding farewell to the trees, the Yasnushka, the sky, and his beloved bathhouse? And did his toe find the right trigger immediately or, because of his constant ineptness and naiveté, did he pull the wrong trigger and try to catch his breath for a long time, wiping away cold sweat and trying to summon up new courage? And did he shut his eyes before firing the shot, or did he look at something with his eyes wide open until the last viperous spark?

No, not weakness—great staying power and resolve are needed for cutting your life short the way he did.

But why, why? I search for an answer and can't find one. Or was there secret suffering in his life, so upbeat, so active? But we see plenty of suffering people around us! No, it's not that, not that, which brings you to the barrel of a shotgun. So does it mean that he was marked with a fateful sign from birth? And can it be that every one of us bears an invisible stamp that predetermines the whole course of our lives?

My soul wanders in darkness . . .

But back then we were all alive and, as I've said before, it was the height of a long, long day, one of those summer days, which when we remember them years later, seem endless to us.

After saying goodbye to me and tousling your hair once more and tenderly touching your forehead with his lips—framed by his moustache and beard which tickled you and made you laugh happily, Mitya went home, and you and I took a large apple and went on the hike that we had been looking forward to since morning. When Chief saw that we had set out, he immediately followed us, overtook us right away and, almost knocking you off your feet and flapping his ears like a butterfly flutters its wings, he bounded off and disappeared into the woods.

Oh, what a long way we had to go—almost a whole kilometer! And what a variety of things awaited us on the way—true, already partly familiar to you since you had walked this way more than once. But can one time resemble another, can even one hour resemble another? It would be overcast as we walked, then sunny or dewy; now the sky would be completely covered by storm clouds, and thunder would rumble and roll, and then it would drizzle; beaded drops would stud the dry, lower branches of the fir trees, and your little red boots would glisten endearingly, the path would grow dark and shiny; then the wind would blow, and the aspens would murmur, and the tops of the birch and fir trees would rustle; first it would be morning, then noon, now cold, then hot—not one day was like another, not one hour, not one bush, not one tree—nothing!

This time there wasn't a cloud in the sky; it was a tranquil pale-blue color without that piercing blueness that pours like a river into our eyes in early spring or strikes our soul in late fall as it breaks through low storm clouds. And on that day you were wearing brown sandals, yellow socks, red shorts, and a lemon-yellow T-shirt. Your knees were scratched up; your legs, shoulders, and arms were pale white, and your big eyes—grey with pistachio-colored flecks in them—for some reason had turned a dark and deep blue color . . .

At first we walked in the opposite direction from the front gate toward the back garden gate, along a path mottled with splashes of sunlight as we stepped over large roots of fir trees whose needles felt soft and springy under our feet. Then you stopped in your tracks and looked around. I realized at once that you needed a stick without which, for some reason, you couldn't imagine taking a walk; I found a hazelnut switch, cleaned it off, and gave you your stick.

You looked down, happy that I had guessed your wish. You took the stick and again ran ahead quickly, using it to touch the trunks of trees that grew close to the path and the tall fiddlehead ferns, still wet in the shade.

Looking down at your little feet flashing by, at your sweet little neck with a silvery pigtail and the small fluffy tuft of hair on the top of your head, I tried to imagine myself as a little boy, too, and was immediately surrounded by my memories. But no matter what part of my early childhood I'd remember, I would always be older than you, until suddenly into a forest clearing on the left, into the forest scent that was all around us, the summertime smell of meadows warmed by the sun came rushing from the other side of the valley, at the bottom of which flowed the Yasnushka.

"A-lyo-sha's lit-tle fee-t . . . " I said mechanically in a sing-song voice.

"Awe wun-ning down the woad . . . ," you obediently responded at once, and from the slight twitch of your transparent little ears, I could tell you had smiled.

Yes, and I ran like that once, ages ago, and it was summer, the sun was blazing hot, and a sweet-smelling wind carried the same kind of scent of the meadows . . .

Somewhere near Moscow I saw a large field on which the people gathered there had been divided and separated. In one group, standing at the edge of a sparse grove of birches, there were only women and children for some reason. Many of the women were crying, wiping their eyes with red kerchiefs. And on the other side of the field stood the men, lined up in columns. Behind the columns towered a raised embankment, on which brownish-red, heated box cars stood, with a steam locomotive panting far out in front and releasing black smoke high in the air. And people in soldiers' blouses paced in front of the columns.

And my nearsighted mother was crying as well and constantly wiping away the tears that welled up in her eyes. She kept squinting and asking, "Can you see Dad, son, can you? Where is he, at least show me which side he's on?" "I see him!" I answered, and I really could see my father standing on the right side. And father saw us too; he smiled and waved from time to time, but I didn't understand why he couldn't come to us, or we to him.

Suddenly a current swept through our crowd and several boys and girls with bundles in their hands ran out timidly into the open space in the meadow. After hurriedly thrusting a heavy bundle with clothes and tin cans into my hands, my mother nudged me forward and shouted,

"Run to daddy, son, give it to him, kiss him, tell him that we're waiting for him!" And I, tired from the heat and from having to stand for a long time, was overcome with joy and started to run.

I ran across the field along with the others, my bare, suntanned knees flashing, and my heart pounded from excitement at the thought that my father would finally hug me, pick me up, and kiss me, and I'd hear his voice again and smell the comforting aroma of his tobacco. I hadn't seen him for such a long time that my brief memories of him seemed to be covered with ashes and had now turned into self-pity because I was lonesome and missed his rough, calloused hands, the sound of his voice, the way he looked at me. I ran, looking now at my feet, now at my father, whose birthmark I could already make out on his temple, and suddenly I saw that his face had become unhappy, and the closer I drew to him, the more restless the column grew where my father was standing.

After walking out through the garden gate into the woods, we turned right towards the rotunda our neighbor had begun to build at some point but didn't finish, and now its concrete dome and columns looked absurdly grey amidst the greenery of the fir and alder grove that you delighted in looking at for long periods of time.

To our left the tiny brook, Yasnushka, sent streams of water rolling over the pebbles. For the time being we couldn't see it behind the thick hazelnut and raspberry bushes, but we knew that the path would lead us to the steep slope below the rotunda, at the bottom of which pine needles and occasional leaves whirled slowly in a small, dark pool of water.

The sun broke through to us in almost vertical columns; wavy patches of resin glowed a honey color in the sunlight; wild strawberries suddenly appeared here and there like drops of blood; weightless, small clouds of gnats swarmed all around; birds which were invisible in the foliage called to one another, and a squirrel, leaping from one tree to another, appeared for a moment in a beam of sunlight, and the branch it left behind a moment before began to sway; the world was fragrant . . .

"Look, Alyosha, a squirrel! Do you see it? There it is, looking at you . . ."

You looked up, saw the squirrel, and dropped your stick. You always dropped it if suddenly something else caught your attention. Following the squirrel with your eyes until it disappeared, you remembered the stick, picked it up, and again went on your way.

Chief leapt out onto the path in front of us and jumped so high that it seemed he wanted to fly. After stopping, he observed us for a while with his eyes, deep and big like a gazelle's, asking if he should keep running ahead, or were we going to turn back, or go off to the side? I pointed silently to the path we were taking; he understood and rushed on.

A minute later we heard his excited barking that, judging by the sound, indicated that he wasn't moving but standing still. That meant he wasn't chasing anything but found something and was calling us to come quickly.

"Do you hear that?" I said to you. "Our Chief has found something and is calling us!"

I picked you up so that you wouldn't prick yourself on the fir trees and so that we'd get there faster. The barking sounded closer and closer and soon, under a beautiful birch tree standing somewhat by itself in a vividly green, lilac and yellow mossy glade, we saw Chief and heard not only his barking but also his impassioned panting and whimpering.

He had found a hedgehog. The birch tree was about thirty yards from the path, and once again I was surprised at his sense of smell. All the moss around the hedgehog was trampled. Catching sight of us, Chief began barking even louder. I put you down on the ground, pulled Chief away by his collar, and we squatted in front of the hedgehog.

"It's a hedgehog," I said. "Repeat after me: hedgehog."

"Hedgehog . . . ," you said and touched it with your stick.

The hedgehog made a grunting sound and jumped slightly. You drew your stick away quickly, lost your balance, and plopped down into a sitting position on the moss.

"Don't be afraid," I said, "only you mustn't touch it. Now he's all curled up in a ball, only the spines are sticking out. And when we leave, he'll stick out his little nose and go about his business. He's also out for a walk, just like you . . . He needs to walk a lot because he sleeps the whole winter. He gets covered with snow and he sleeps. Do you remember the winter? Remember how we pulled you on your sled?"

You flashed an enigmatic smile. Lord, what I wouldn't have given just to know what you were smiling about in such an indefinable way either just to yourself or while listening to me! Perhaps you knew something that was much more important than all my knowledge and experience?

And I recalled the day when I came to get you at the maternity hospital. Then you were a tightly, firmly wrapped bundle, rather heavy, or so it seemed to me, that for some reason the nurse handed to me. I hadn't even gotten you to the car when I felt something warm and alive inside the bundle, even though your face was covered and I couldn't feel you breathing.

At home we unswaddled you right away. I was expecting to see something red and all wrinkled, the way newborns are usually described in writing, but there was no redness or wrinkles. You were all shining whiteness, you wiggled your strikingly thin little hands and feet and looked at us seriously with your big, vaguely greyish-blue eyes. All of you was a miracle, and only one thing spoiled your appearance—the bandage applied to your belly button.

Soon you were all swaddled again, fed and put to sleep, and we all went into the kitchen. Over tea a conversation began that captivated the women: about diapers, expressing the milk before feedings, bathing, and other equally important topics. I kept getting up, sitting down beside you and examining your face for a long time. And when I came to see you for the third or fourth time, I suddenly saw you were smiling in your sleep and your face was quivering.

What did your smile mean? Were you dreaming? But what kind of dreams could you have? What could you have been dreaming? What could you have known? Where did your thoughts wander? And did you have any thoughts at all then? But not only your smile, your face acquired an expression that suggested higher knowledge of things to come; some small clouds ran across it, your face would be different at any given moment, but it didn't lose its basic harmony, it didn't change. Never in your waking hours—whether you were crying or laughing or looking silently at the colorful rattles hanging over your crib—did you have an expression such as the one that so amazed me when you were sleeping, and I held my breath and wondered what was happening to you. "When babies smile like that," my mother told me later, "it means the angels are playing with them."

And so now, bending over the hedgehog, you replied to my question with an enigmatic smile and said nothing, and so I still didn't know if you remembered the winter. And your first winter in Abramtsevo was wonderful! There'd be such a heavy snowfall at night, and during the day the sun would cast such a rosy glow that even the sky and the birches covered with fuzzy frost would turn a rosy color . . . You'd go outside,

into the snow, in your felt boots and in a coat so heavy that your arms—
with thick mittens on your hands—would be spread away from your
body. You'd get on a sled, invariably take a stick in your hand—several
sticks of different lengths were always leaning against the porch, and
each time you'd choose a different one—and we'd pull you through the
gate, and an intoxicating ride would begin. Drawing a line in the snow,
you'd begin talking to yourself, to the sky, the woods, the birds, and the
crunching of the snow under our feet and under the runners of the sled.
Everything listened and understood you—we alone didn't understand
because you couldn't talk yet. And different sounds came pouring out
of you—you gurgled and cooed, and all of your va-va-va and lya-lya-lya
and yoo-yoo-yoo and weep-teep-weep meant for us only that you were
happy.

Then you'd grow quiet and, after looking around, we'd see that your
stick was lying far back on the road and you—with your arms flung
apart—would be sleeping and your firm cheeks would be burning red.
We'd pull you around for an hour or two and you'd keep sleeping; you'd
sleep so soundly that later, when we'd bring you into the house, take off
your shoes, undress you, unfasten and untie various pieces of clothing
and put you to bed—you wouldn't wake up.

Having looked our fill at the hedgehog, we came back onto the path
and soon reached the rotunda. You saw it first, stopped and, like always,
said with pleasure, "What-ta warge, bea-u-tifuw tawah!"

You looked at it for a while from a distance, repeating in astonishment,
as if seeing it for the first time, "What-ta to-wer!" Then we went up to it
and you began to touch its columns with your stick, one after another.
And then you shifted your gaze downward, to the small transparent
pool, and I immediately gave you my hand. In this way, hand in hand, we
carefully descended the steep slope to the water. A bit lower there was a
sand bar with babbling water; the small pool seemed still, but you could
find the direction of the current if for a long time you followed a floating
leaf moving towards the sandbar with the slowness of a minute hand.
I sat down on a fallen fir tree and lit a cigarette because I knew that I'd
have to keep sitting here until you had fully enjoyed all the wonders of
the small pool.

After dropping your stick, you went up to a tree root that was conveniently located for you at the very edge of the water, lay face down on it, and began to look into the water. Strange, but that summer you didn't like to play with ordinary toys but liked to amuse yourself with the tiniest of things. You could take a grain of sand, a pine needle, or a tiny blade of grass and move it around in the palm of your hand endlessly. A piece of paint only a millimeter wide that you had picked off the house wall would bring you hours of contemplative pleasure. The life and existence of bees, flies, butterflies, and gnats would amuse you incomparably more than the existence of cats, dogs, cows, squirrels, magpies, and other birds. And what an endless, what a boundless world opened up for you at the bottom of this small pool when, lying on the root, with your face brought almost right down to the water, you examined that bottom! There were so many large and small grains of sand, so many pebbles of every possible shade of color, and such a delicate, green fuzz covered the large stones. There were so many transparent fry— one moment motionless and the next quickly scattering together to one side—and, in general, so many microscopic objects that could be seen with your eyes only!

"Wittle fishies ah s'imming . . . ," you told me a minute later.

"A-ah," I said, coming closer and sitting down near you, "that means they haven't yet left for the big river. These are little fish called fry . . ."

"Fwy . . . ," you agreed cheerfully.

The water in the little pool was so clear that only the blueness of the sky and the treetops reflected in it made it visible. Hanging over the root, you scooped up a handful of small pebbles from the bottom. A small cloud of the tiniest grains of sand formed near the bottom, lingered a while, and then dissipated. You threw the pebbles into the water, the reflection of the trees began to waver, and by the hurried way you began to get up, I knew you'd remembered your favorite pastime. It was time for you to throw rocks.

I sat down on the fallen tree again, and you chose one of the larger rocks, examined it lovingly from all sides, walked right to the edge of the water and threw it into the middle of the small pool. Water went splashing up in the air and the rock, surrounded by undulating streams of air, hit the bottom with a dull thud, and circles formed on the water. After enjoying the rippling water, the splashes, the thud of the rock, and the lapping of the water, you waited until everything was still, took another rock and, after looking it over as you did with the first rock, threw again.

And so you kept throwing and throwing, enjoying the splashes and waves. The world around us was quiet and beautiful—the noise of the commuter train didn't reach us, not one airplane flew by, no one walked past us, no one saw us. Only Chief would show up occasionally, coming now from one side, now from the other, with his tongue hanging out; he would run into the brook and splash, lap up some water noisily and, after looking at us inquiringly, he'd disappear again.

A mosquito landed on your shoulder; you didn't notice it for a long time, then you drove it away, frowned, and came up to me.

"Moswito bit me . . . ," you said, frowning.

I scratched your shoulder, blew on it, and patted it.

"Well? What are we going to do now? Are you going to throw some more rocks, or are we going to walk farther?"

"Let's go faw-ther," you decided.

I picked you up and crossed the Yasnushka. We had to walk across a small, wet gully, along which great masses of lungwort stretched like white foam. Its white, bonnet-shaped flowers seemed to blend together in the sun and to flow, full of the happy buzzing of bees.

The path began to climb up—at first through fir and hazel trees, then through oaks and birches until it brought us out onto a large meadow, framed by a forest on the right and changing into a rippling field on the left. We were now going up across the meadow, higher and higher, until we reached the top and could see way into the distance; the horizon opened up with barely visible aerial wires in the distance and a thin haze over invisible Zagorsk.[5] Haymaking had already begun in the meadow and, even though the hay was still in windrows on the ground, the barely noticeable breeze was already carrying the scent of drying grass over the land. You and I sat down in the flowers and the grass that hadn't been cut yet; I sank in them up to my shoulders, but you became submerged in them completely, with only the sky above you. I remembered the apple, took it out of my pocket, wiped it on the grass till it shone, and gave it to you. You took it in your hands and immediately took a bite, and the bite mark looked like a squirrel's.

All around us stretched one of the most ancient Russian lands—the land of Radonezh, a quiet, feudal principality of Moscow. Two black kites were flying in smooth, slow circles high above the edge of the field. Nothing from the past was left for us; the land itself had changed, and the villages and the woods, and Radonezh itself had disappeared as if it had never existed, only the memory of it remained; and way over there those two kites flew in circles the way they did a thousand years ago, and maybe the Yasnushka still flowed in the same river bed . . . You were finishing your apple, but I saw that your thoughts were far away. You also noticed the kites and tracked them with your eyes for a long time; butterflies were flying above you; some, attracted to the red color of your pants, tried to land on them, but then they would immediately fly away, and you would follow their delightful flight with your eyes. You talked little and used few words, but it was obvious from your face and eyes that you were constantly thinking. Oh, how I wanted to become you even for a moment to learn your thoughts! You see, you had already become a person!

Yes, our world was blessed and beautiful! Bombs weren't blowing up, cities and villages weren't burning, corpse-seeking flies weren't hovering over children lying in the streets, people weren't freezing from the cold, they weren't walking in rags seething with all kinds of parasites, and they weren't living in ruins and all kinds of burrows like wild animals. Children's tears flowed now too, they flowed, but for a completely, completely different reason . . . Is this not bliss? Is this not happiness?

I looked around again and thought that this day, these clouds that at the moment perhaps no one around here except you and I were watching, this brook in the woods below us and the pebbles on its bottom that your hand had thrown, the clear streams of water flowing around them, this meadow air, this white trodden path in the field between walls of oats already tinged with silvery-blue hoarfrost and, as always, the beautiful village in the distance and the shimmering horizon behind it—this day, like certain other, utterly beautiful days of my life, would stay with me forever. But would you remember this day? Would you some day direct your gaze far and deep into the past? Would you feel as if the years lived had never even existed and that you were again a little boy, running through flowers up to your shoulders, startling the butterflies? Can it really be, can it really be that you won't remember yourself and me and the sun, baking hot on your shoulders, this taste, this sound of an unbelievably long summer day?

Where will all this disappear to? By what strange law will it be cut off and become covered with the mists of oblivion? Where will it disappear to, this most blindingly happy time of the beginning of life, the time of the most tender infancy?

I even clasped my hands in despair at the thought that the greatest time, the time when a person is born, is hidden from us by a kind of veil. And here you are! You already knew so much, had already acquired a personality, your own habits, had learned to talk, and to understand what people said even better; you already had likes and dislikes . . .

But no matter whom you ask—all remember themselves from five or six years of age. And before that? Or is it that not everything is forgotten after all but sometimes returns to us in a flashback from our earliest childhood, from the beginning of our days? Hasn't almost everyone, upon seeing something even completely dull and ordinary— for example, a puddle on a road in the fall, or upon hearing some sound or perceiving some smell—been suddenly struck with the strong feeling that this has already happened to me, I've seen this, lived through it! When, where? And in this life, or in a completely different life? And you try to remember for a long time, to grasp a moment from the past—and can't.

It was time for your daily nap and we went home. Chief had come back a long time ago; he had trampled a little place for himself in the thick grass, stretched out, and was sleeping, his paws twitching from time to time.

The house was quiet. Bright squares of sunlight lay on the floor. While I was undressing you in your room and pulling on your pajamas, you remembered everything you saw that day and told us. At the end of our conversation you yawned openly a couple of times. After putting you to bed, I went to my room. I think you fell asleep before I even walked out the door. I sat down by the open window, lit a cigarette, and began to think about you. I tried to imagine your future life, but strange to say, I didn't want to picture you all grown up—shaving, dating girls, smoking cigarettes . . . I wanted to picture you as a small boy for as long as possible—not the way you were then, that summer, but say, as a ten-year-old. What journeys we embarked on! What things captivated our interest!

Then from the future I returned to the present and again thought with sadness that you were wiser than I was, that you knew a certain something that I once knew, but now have forgotten, forgotten . . . That everything in the world was created only to be looked at by the eyes of a child! That God's kingdom belongs to you! These words were said long ago, so does it mean that people felt the mysterious superiority of children even thousands of years ago? But what elevated them above us? Their innocence or some higher knowledge that disappears with age?

More than an hour passed in this way, and the sun had noticeably shifted its position and the shadows lengthened when you began to cry.

I crushed my cigarette in the ashtray and went to your room, thinking that you had awakened and needed something.

But you were asleep, with your knees tucked up. Tears were pouring down so profusely that the pillow was quickly becoming wet. You were sobbing bitterly, with despairing hopelessness. You weren't crying at all the way you'd cry when you had hurt yourself or were fussing. Then you'd just wail. But now it was as if you were lamenting something that was gone forever. You were choking from your sobs and your voice sounded different!

Are dreams—are they merely a chaotic reflection of reality? But if that's so, what reality were you dreaming of? What did you see except our caring, affection-filled eyes, except our smiles, except your toys and the sun, the moon, and the stars? What did you hear except the sounds of water, the rustling of woods, the singing of birds, the calming sound of rain hitting the roof, and your mother's lullaby? What did you have time to discover in the world, except the quiet happiness of living, to cry so bitterly in your sleep? You hadn't suffered, had no regrets, and the fear of death was unknown to you! What were you dreaming of? Or does the soul already grieve in its infancy, afraid of the suffering in store for it?

I began to gently wake you up, patting your shoulder and stroking your hair.

"Son, wake up, my sweet," I said, lightly shaking your arm. "Get up, get up, Alyosha! Alyosha! Get up . . ."

You woke up, sat up quickly, and held your arms out to me. I picked you up, pressed you close to me, and said in an intentionally upbeat voice, "There, there now! It was a dream. Take a look at the sun!" And I began to draw the curtains apart and fold them back.

The room filled with sunlight, but you kept crying, burying your face in my shoulder, filling your chest with air and gasping, and gripping my neck with your fingers so tightly that it hurt.

"We're going to have dinner now . . . Look what a bird has just flown by . . . And where's our fluffy, white Vaska? Alyosha! Come on, Alyosha, my sweet, don't be afraid of anything, it's all over . . . Who's that coming, is that mom?" I said anything that came into my head, trying to distract you.

Gradually you began to calm down. Your mouth still had a grimace of suffering, but a smile was already forming on your face. Finally you beamed and glowed when you saw your tiny, glazed pitcher hanging on the window, and said tenderly "Pitch-cha," delighting in that one word.

You didn't reach for it, didn't try to grab it the way children usually grab a favorite toy. No, you looked at it with your eyes washed by tears and therefore especially clear, and you reveled in its form and colored enamel.

After washing you, tying a napkin around your neck, and sitting you down at the table, I suddenly realized that something had happened to you. You weren't banging your spoon on the table, you weren't laughing or saying, "Hurry up!" You were looking at me seriously, intently, and not saying anything! I felt you were leaving me, that your soul, which up to now had been fused with mine, was now far away, and that it would move farther and farther away with each passing year; that you were no longer me, no longer an extension of me, and that my soul would never catch up with you—that you would leave forever. In your deep, un-childlike look I saw your soul leaving me; it looked at me with compassion, and it was saying goodbye to me forever!

I tried to keep up with you, hurried, in order to just be near you; I saw that I was falling behind, that my life was carrying me in the same old direction, whereas you from this day forward were now going your own way.

Such desperation overcame me, such grief! But hope sounded within me in a hoarse, weak voice—that our souls once more would become one someday, never to part again. Yes! But where and when will that be?

It was time for me to cry too, my boy . . .

And that summer you were one and half years old.

1977

NOTES

1. Kazakov is referring to the death of a close friend, the writer Dmitry Golubkov (1931-1972).
2. Abramtsevo: an estate not far from the Trinity Monastery at Sergiev Posad (about thirty-six miles north of Moscow) which became an artists' colony in the 19th century and played a significant role in the development of Russian culture.
3. Radonezh: a historical village in Moscow Oblast, located about 9 miles from Sergiev Posad. It is associated with St. Sergius, who founded the Trinity Monastery in the 14th century.
4. Gagra: a town in Abkhazia, on the northeast coast of the Black Sea, at the foot of the Caucasus Mountains. A popular health resort in Imperial Russia, in Soviet times it was one of the favorite destinations for writers.
5. Zagorsk: the name of Sergiev Posad in Soviet times.

LITTLE ARM, LEG, CUCUMBER . . .

Yury Dombrovsky

On a very stuffy June evening he was lying on the couch, perhaps sleeping or simply dozing fitfully, and through his delirium it seemed that they were talking to him on the phone again. The conversation was rough, along the lines of blackmail; they were threatening him, promising to break his bones, or do something even worse than that—to lie in wait for him somewhere in an entryway and bash his head with a hammer. Such a thing had actually happened not long ago, except that the killer didn't use a hammer but a heavy bottle. He struck the man on the back of the head from behind. The man was in the hospital for a week without regaining consciousness and died. And he hadn't even turned thirty yet, and he had just published his first book of poetry.[1]

These thoughts woke him up and he heard someone really calling him.

He went to the phone and glanced out the window. It was dark already. "Once again I'll arrive at night," he thought and picked up the receiver.

"Hello," he said.

A young, ringing, slightly brazen voice responded, "And who's this?"

"That's another one already," he realized. "What is this, has a whole bunch of them gathered over there?" He asked, "Well, and who do you want?"

"Who's this?"

"Who is it you want?"

"Maybe I got the wrong number. Who . . ."

"The right number, the right number, absolutely the right number. Four of you guys have called me today already. So go ahead."

"So it's you, damned son-of-a-bitch, shitty writer. Just keep in mind: we're warning you for the last time. If you, bastard, don't stop your hateful . . ."

"Wait. I'll get a chair. Listen, do they hand out cue cards to you over there or something? Why do you all rattle off the same thing? I don't see any free creativity or flights of fancy from you. Have at least a few words of your own instead of everything from "uncle.""

"From what uncle?"

"From Uncle Zick.[2] No, seriously. Don't you have minds of your own? Only 'damned son-of-a-bitch,' only 'we'll bash your head,' only 'vile activities.' By the way, one of your freaking guys simply says 'activities.' Hey, men! Tell him I said hi!"

"Fine, cut the smooth talk—there's no need to put a spell on my teeth. They're healthy."[3]

"Oh! And all the better to knock them out!"

"Hey, you!" the voice in the receiver was totally taken aback for a second. "I'll chew you up alive."

"And are you far from here?"

"No matter where I am, we'll get you. So we're warning you, and for the last time . . ."

"Hang on! Someone's at the door. Just don't hang up."

He went to the door, looked through the peep-hole and saw her standing there, the one for whom he had been waiting for three days now, the one he had desperately needed this morning. She was supposed to play a role in his movie, and the whole country knew and loved her. Her portrait—young, beautiful, smiling—hung in the lobby of almost every movie theater, and the newspaper stands were full of her photographs. She was always recognized when she appeared on the street with him. He had been really, really waiting for her these three damned days, but now she was simply of no use to him.

"Here's something else for me to worry about," he thought. "Why has everything started crashing down on me at the same time?"

He opened the door. She didn't so much walk in as she flew in, and immediately rushed toward him. Actually more at him than toward him. She had such an expression on her face and was breathing so hard and gasping for air that for several seconds she couldn't get a single word out.

"What's the matter with you?" he asked a bit roughly. "Has something happened, God forbid! Just look at you! Look at you!" He shook her lightly by the shoulders. "Well?"

She licked her dry lips. "Oh, I'm so happy to see you're all right. Your phone is always busy."

"Well, yes. I was taking a nap and took the phone off the hook. All kinds of riff-raff keep calling."

"And they called my brother too, asking for you and threatening to lie in wait for you in the entryway. I just got back from the set and he told me about it. I rushed here right away. As you can see, I haven't even changed."

True, she was wearing her work outfit—a blouse, slacks, and big sunglasses.

"Well, sit down and catch your breath. I'll finish my phone conversation. Are you listening, buddy?" he asked the receiver. "Good boy. So, are you far from here?"

"And why do you need to know that?" he could suddenly hear real confusion in the voice. He seemed to hear other voices in the background as well. "You want to track us down, you son-of-a-bitch, is that it?"

"No, I want to propose a business deal. You've been to my neighborhood many times and know it well. How can it be otherwise? If you're planning to kill me, then you know everything over here. So look, there's an empty lot diagonally from my place. There used to be a shack there before, but it's been torn down. And drunks guzzle vodka there until eleven. You know it?"

"And just what are you leading up to, you dumb ass?"

"Well, here's a proposition. There's no one there now. The drunks are all at home. In fifteen minutes I'll head there and wait for you. Do come. Be it with a hammer, a bottle, alone or with a gang—I'll be waiting for you. That's the deal . . ."

"What do you mean, you son-of-a-bitch? I'll . . . you . . ."

"Stop, no swearing! I'm sick of all this, you blockhead." He lightly pushed away the actress, who had rushed to him and was squeezing his fingers.

"For God's sake," she said "you know it's . . ." He waved her away.

"So, do come. We'll have a talk. But remember, come prepared. If you miss, they'll take you away in an ambulance, that I can guarantee you. I know how to do it. You know where I've been, and what I've seen, and what crap I've been through."[4]

"Don't try scaring me, you son-of-bitch. We'll lie in wait for you and get you even in an empty lot. Just you wait!"

"Why do you need to lie in wait for me? I'm going on my own. I'm sick to death of you—you blockheads, mindless babblers, well-fed bastards."

"One of your nice guys, a crappy painter—has already been shot. A drive-by . . ."

"See how they treat you over there, you ignorant bastard. They didn't even tell you who was killed, and how and why. It wasn't a crappy painter or a doctor, but a real artist. And he was shot accidentally by some piece of trash—a money collector. He got scared to death and fired from a car. But the poet was killed in an entryway."

"Like I was saying . . ."

"And it wasn't you who killed him but someone more powerful. You only bark like sons-of-bitches from phone booths for two kopecks. You're morons and nothing else. When someone really wants to kill somebody, they don't call. So then, be there in fifteen minutes on the dot. Got it?"

"Are you going to get some police volunteers?"

"Don't shit in your pants just yet. I'll come alone. You can see everything from a distance. Everything. I'm hanging up."

The actress was sitting on the couch and looking at him. Her face wasn't even the color of chalk but of cocaine, which has that deathly crystalline sparkle.

"What's all this about?" she asked quietly.

"What do you mean, 'what'? A very business-like conversation."

"And you're going to go?"

"Absolutely . . ."

He went over to the table, opened the drawer, rummaged through the papers, and took out a hunting knife. A year or so ago a dark figure had jumped him on the stairs with it. It happened on the ninth floor around eleven at night, and the light bulbs had been unscrewed. He had wrenched open the dark figure's hand and the knife fell out. In parting he gave him a couple more blows across his whitish, grayish-red face and said calmly, "Leave, you idiot." If nothing else, they had taught him how to fight properly over there. The knife was homemade, beautiful, with inlaid work and all, and he prized it. He grasped it in his fist, took a swing, and admired his fighting arm. It really looked great. The knife was shiny and had a blood-red, coral handle.

"Just like this, madam," he said.

The actress stood there and stared at him, looking wild-eyed.

"I won't let you go anywhere. It's suicide. Right in front of me . . . No, no!" she shouted.

He frowned and tossed the knife on the table.

"Just like in my stupid screenplay! Listen here, silly," he said affectionately, "they can't do a damn thing to me. I swear to you on my honor. On my honor and yours. They're bull-shitters, hoodlums, drunks, ordinary wretches up to no good. They used to steal rations from us in the North[5] and we dunked them in the latrines for that. Not to kill, but just so they'd swallow some. And I'll teach them a lesson today, I will."

"There'll be at least a dozen of them. They won't even let you turn around. There's nothing but bushes over there."

"But I'm not blind either. I'll see them. And with that type of crowd it's like this: you punch one in the mug, knock another off his feet, and they'll all run away. But look how they've terrified you. How can I not teach those dimwits a lesson after that?"

He spoke easily, confidently, convincingly, and she gradually calmed down. He could always make her believe whatever he wanted. So now, too, she looked at him—calm, collected, and composed, as he was not in his personal life—and she almost believed that nothing terrible would happen. They'd just have a talk man to man, and that would be it. He, too, realized that she had calmed down, and so he laughed and patted her on the shoulder.

"C'mon. Be a good girl. Sit here and wait . . . Then you can take me to the train station. I'll go to the dacha. I've been stuck around here for three days, drinking with all sorts of riff-raff, but my work is waiting for me. Take your cosmetics bag, powder your nose, and wipe your eyes. Right now they're redder than a grouper's, and your mascara is running. Take a look in the mirror. Isn't Masha a beauty?"

"And there's no other way?" she asked, taking out her cosmetics bag.

"No. Don't you understand, no other way! They're getting more brazen. And if they realize that I've lost my nerve, then they might really sneak up on me from behind a corner and clobber me with something, or lie in wait for me in an entryway like they did to that poor guy. But here—it's all out in the open!"

"Oh!" And she jumped up again.

"Sit tight! I'll be right back. You can look out the kitchen window— you can see everything from there."

"Then I'll go with you too . . ."

"That'll do me a real favor! Are we putting on a show for them or something? A four-part film by Yulian Semyonov?[6] Just sit tight."

And he took her by the shoulders again and nudged her towards the couch.

However, less than five minutes had passed since the phone conversation. And it was only a couple of steps to the empty lot, just a matter of crossing the street. So what was there to do—hang out in plain sight?

He sat down at the table again, propped up his head with his hand, and fell into thought. The phone rang. He picked up the receiver reluctantly, listened, became animated and said, "Yes, hello. But of course I recognized your voice." He listened some more and responded, "I'll be there the whole day. Please. No, it's not too early. I get up at six. So I'll be expecting you." He hung up the receiver and grinned. "This meeting on the empty lot—that's nothing! Tomorrow morning the editor is coming to see me, out of the blue . . ."

She understood at once whom he was talking about and sympathized. "You dislike him that much?" He frowned.

"No, it's not that I dislike him, it's just . . ."

She got up from the couch, went over to the mirror, then got a chair and sat down at the table next to him.

". . . It's just that you don't like him." And suddenly, on green paper, her finger began to trace something elongated, rounded, curling, with lots of flourishes and indentations going here and there, in and out.

"What's that? A snake?"

"Close. A French curve—a ruler for drawing curved lines. That's him. And here's you!" And quickly—one-two-three—she traced an oval, and on the oval two lines on the bottom, two lines on the top, and a small circle above them, and on the circle lots and lots of little lines sticking out above, below and to the sides—a head, messy hair, arms and legs.

He laughed. "I learned that as a child too. Little arm, leg, cucumber—and you've got a little man . . . "

"Yes, you've got a little man," she smiled right into his eyes.

"Hmm! So that's what I look like—little arm, leg, tufts of hair—not very flattering, you know."

"Not very, of course, but the French curve is much worse."

"Worse? Even though it's so elegant?"

"I hate it. It's sly, winds around everything, hugs everything, and slithers up to everything. It doesn't have any straight lines—it's all curves, twists, and turns."

"And do you know many like that?"

"They're all like that where I work. And I take first place."

"Terrific! And here's what I'm like . . ." He pointed at the spot where she had done the invisible drawing.

"Yes, you're like that." She used the informal form of "you" to him for the first time.[7]

He thought a bit and got up.

"Well, I think it's time. I'm going. Stay put. I'll be quick."

But he was gone a long time. She was now sitting calmly because she saw that no one had approached him or stopped at the empty lot. He just sat around for half an hour for no reason on an empty crate that used to hold Moroccan oranges.

"Damned sons-of-bitches, bullshit artists," he said forcefully. "Oh, just try messing with me again!" And he slammed a cut-glass tumbler—a drunkard's salvation—on the table. He had a whole cupboard full of them; someone had told him that they brought good luck to a home. "Here, I made a dandelion wreath for you while I was sitting there. Look, it's like the sun. Smell it. And there are so many bumblebees over there that all you hear is buzzing. Is your car here? Your hands aren't shaking? Show me. Excellent. Can you drop me off at the train station?"

"Today I can drive you wherever you're going."

"No, there's no need today to drive me all the way. It's the weekend. There'll be traffic checkpoints everywhere. It'll be faster by train."

"Maybe you'll stay here? Couldn't you go tomorrow?"

"I can't. My wife has lost all track of me. The cats are yowling. They love me. Let's go!"

There was a good half hour left until the last commuter train for the dachas, and there weren't many people. It was now completely dark. The streetlights were lit. After an oppressive, sultry day, the air was still and somewhat stagnant. The dusty poplars looked weary in the purplish light from the street lamps. A man came up and sat down next to him.

"Would you happen to know what time it is?" he asked the man.

"The train will be here in five minutes," the man replied. "But don't you recognize me, my friend?" And the man addressed him by his first name and patronymic.

"Good Lord!" he exclaimed. "Fancy meeting you here! Do you live on this line now?"

"No, I don't live here, I'm just staying with a friend. You know him." And he named a rather prominent essayist. "I set him up in a dacha out there and so sometimes I come to spend the weekend with him. In the morning we hike, swim, and drink vodka. It's great."

"I bet!" he said with a smile, looking closely at his neighbor.

This was a former employee of the district newspaper and these days the chairman of the regional bibliophile society. Once, a couple of years ago, he had called and asked him to speak at one of their evening events. Just to give a talk or read an excerpt. The evening was a great success. There was lots of applause, and people picked a bunch of gorgeous carnations and presented them to him, walked him back in a big group, and begged him to come again. From then on, he and the bibliophile became not quite close friends but certainly good acquaintances. The bibliophile had an attractive appearance: such a robust fellow, with a round face, brown eyes with little specks in them, and a funny turned-up nose. A real tractor driver or foreman. The bibliophile would often invite him here and there—to read a story or give a speech on the occasion of some anniversary, or just talk about writers and the writer's craft. He was very courteous, direct, and always paid well, which the writer also appreciated. The writer was always short of money. His work wasn't published much and never republished. A year ago he had finished his big novel and it began to make the rounds. That was when all kinds of unpleasantness began to rain down upon him, beginning with the phone calls and ending with rejections by editors. But he had anticipated it all and was not too upset.

"And where do you get off now?" he asked the bibliophile.

He named a station, one not very close but not terribly far either, about a half hour away from where the writer lived now.

"Well, that means we'll have plenty of time to talk. You know, I was starting to miss you already."

The train pulled in. The cars were practically empty. The electricity was working at half-power.

"By the way, how's it going with the novel? Any prospects?"

"Fat chance. It's a real dead season for me, my friend!"

"They say you've been writing it for eleven years?"

"And even a bit more."

"Ahh!" the bibliophile sighed again and even shook his head. "And now, they say, you're starting to have some unpleasantness? Some thugs are threatening you . . ."

"Exactly, thugs. But no, it's nothing serious. You know, the usual nonsense."

"Don't worry. If something happens, we won't let them hurt you. See?" And he held up his small, not strong-looking fist.

"Oh, I'm not afraid," the writer smiled, "but thanks anyway."

"Listen!" the bibliophile suddenly grabbed him by the sleeve. "Why don't you get off with me? We still have a bottle left of the stuff that will put hair on your chest. How about it?"

"It's tempting!" the writer smiled. "You're a serpent! A green serpent[8] from paradise, that's what you are!"

"No, seriously! And tomorrow morning you could head on home. Why drag yourself all the way there in such darkness? Your wife has probably been sound asleep for hours by now. And I could introduce you to one of your ardent readers. He lives there too. A young guy. He's writing a historical novel. He'd be so happy! Let's get off together. How about it?"

"It's very, very tempting. Half a liter, you say? And what sort of novel is that guy writing?"

"You know, I haven't read it. But I know it's historical."

"Our history or some foreign country's?"

"Foreign."

"Which country?"

"Denmark."

"Wow! So he knows Danish history that well? That's pretty rare. And what's his name?"

"Name? Damn! I forgot it too. I usually call him, you know, by his first name—Sasha, Sasha. I used to know his last name too, of course. Damned if I know what's going on with my memory."

"That's exactly it. Who in the hell knows what's going on in the world," the writer thought. "Everyone's going crazy for some reason. Everyone's memory is going."

"So, maybe you'll make up your mind and we'll get off!" the bibliophile said again. "It's a ten-minute walk from the station. We'd have such a good time."

"You see, I'm afraid my wife will run off. Why in the blazes does she need a husband like that? He drinks, disappears hell knows where and with whom. But otherwise it would have been such a pleasure . . ."

"You have a wonderful woman," the bibliophile said with heartfelt emotion. "The only thing is, she doesn't really like me very much."

"Where did you get that idea?" The writer was very surprised and remembered that his wife had seen the bibliophile only once and that, indeed, she had disliked him from the start. To be precise, something about him made her wary.

"For some reason she thought I was . . ." And he tapped the bench with his finger.[9]

The writer said nothing because that was in fact true. They had discussed it—where did he come from so to say, such a nice guy, and in these uneasy times no less—but she shared her doubts with only one male acquaintance. His name had been mentioned both by the bibliophile and the woman he had brought with him that time. So it turned out that they had mutual acquaintances. And it was this mutual acquaintance his wife had called, but she didn't find out anything specific. "No, that woman is very nice," the mutual acquaintance said. "Only she doesn't act very prudently. She has some undesirable acquaintances. She reads all sorts of literature and passes it around. She has a bit of a loose tongue. Maybe she's involved in something even more serious, so it's possible he's keeping an eye on her. Though it's unlikely, or I'd know about it."

And that was their entire conversation. So how had the bibliophile found out about it? There was no way the mutual acquaintance could have let something slip, and suddenly it came to him in a flash! They had been talking on the phone. So . . .

The train began to slow down. Station buildings and brick towers began to flash by.

"Well, I'm here!" the bibliophile said and got up. "So then, shall we get off?"

"No, I'll go home to my wife!" the writer cut him off firmly. "I'm beginning to get the chills."

"Well then, I guess it's bye-bye!" the bibliophile said, throwing up his hands.

"All the best," the writer said, nodding and thinking to himself, "No,

I'm clearly sick. All kinds of crazy ideas are creeping into my head. I should run and see a psychiatrist!"

His eyes followed the bibliophile absent-mindedly. He was walking along the platform and suddenly stopped and waved to someone outside the writer's field of vision. And then the writer saw that it was not at all the station that the bibliophile had mentioned earlier. That one was still a few stops away. "It's the oddest thing!" And he did not even have time to think when the bibliophile came back quickly, almost at a run, and plopped down in the seat he had occupied earlier.

"Got it mixed up!" he said. "What a head! By the way, I remembered that writer's last name. Virmashev. And the book is from Hamlet's time, the seventeenth century."

"It's Shakespeare who wrote his *Hamlet* in the seventeenth century, but Hamlet lived much earlier, in the eleventh century! At least that's what Saxo Grammaticus[10] says. There are no other sources, so maybe there wasn't even any Hamlet at all!"

"You know everything," the bibliophile said with some emotion and took out a notepad.

"So Varmishev?" the writer said and interchanged two letters on purpose. The bibliophile nodded. "You say he has half a liter?"

"Yes, maybe even more. They made some moonshine for a wedding over there."

"Hey, I'll get off," the writer decided quickly to himself, "it's the only way to get well, otherwise you can really lose your mind. And what have I got to be scared of? The novel's written and in a week I'll be sixty-eight! That's enough! And he's a swell guy. I'm the blockhead—damned if I know what I'm inventing. I'm scaring myself."

"All right," the writer said. "Let's get off."

"That's just great!" The bibliophile was happy and even rubbed his hands.

The writer automatically stuck his hand in his pocket. But the knife was not there. "To hell with it," he thought, "you don't cure fear with fear, you cure it by being fearless . . ."

. . . They got off two stops later. It was a way station in the woods, not even a way station—just a platform. It had gotten quite dark. A lone, yellow light illuminated the cool semi-darkness. There was probably a pond somewhere nearby, because the smell of scum and stagnant water was coming from somewhere, and frogs were out in full force. There were large, warm, still puddles on the pavement and in the potholes. Tiny, brown baby frogs were jumping around. The writer bent down and ran his hand affectionately along the tall grass.

"There was a nice rain here," he said, inhaling and filling his chest with the resinous smell of pine trees.

The bibliophile gently took the writer's arm, and the writer could feel the bibliophile's pocket against his hip, that is, the flat, smooth and massive thing that was in his pocket. "A Browning, not too big, probably Belgian," the writer realized and asked, "What's that you've got there?"

"A Browning," the bibliophile smiled. "Look!" He pulled out the Browning in a flash and aimed it at the writer. "Now then," he said and, putting the revolver to his own temple, clicked something. A tall, blue, transparent flame popped out.

They both laughed.

"I got it from some drunk for a fiver," the bibliophile said and put away the lighter. "Made in Germany. Burnished steel. Could scare someone if need be. Well, like the guys who call you."

"To hell with them! Will we be there soon?"

They went into the woods and right away the smell of resin and pine needles intensified. The bibliophile was still holding the writer by his arm, lightly pressing him to his side, and the writer felt his strong, hard muscles that seemed to have been cast from a mold.

"We're almost there. And you, are you really tired?"

"I am tired," the writer sighed. "I'm very tired, my dear friend. Things have been so difficult lately."

"You've been writing for eleven years . . . Well, it's all right, now you'll have a break from all your work," the bibliophile seemed to be smirking about something.

"A deadly grip," the thought pierced the writer's mind. "More like pistons than muscles. Like the ones in a locomotive. Can't break loose from someone like that. The woods, and in the woods a little hut on chicken legs . . ."[11]

Suddenly the bibliophile turned on a flashlight. Why hadn't he taken it out earlier? It illuminated a door. This was apparently a forest ranger's hut. It was in a remote place, and only a very brave or well-armed man could live in it. The bibliophile touched the door and it sprung back as if it were automatic. They entered and the door shut behind them with a wolfish, steely clank.

"That's it," the writer thought growing cold, but also relieved in a way. "And no one will know where my grave is to be found. Simply got on a train and never got off. Vanished into thin air. No one to blame. No traces. Complete annihilation."

A second door opened. Two strapping fellows were sitting at a table covered with oilcloth, and there was also oilcloth on the floor. White, slippery, and spine-chilling. A lamp with a green glass lampshade was turned on. "Father had one like that in his study," he thought. One of the guys was somewhat round, with a neatly trimmed head of hair, ruddy like a winter apple, and tanned. The other resembled a horse with a white mane. They looked at him silently. The ruddy one was smiling. The white-maned one just kept silent. The bibliophile stood in the back. No one said anything. There was simply no point in talking anymore.

"So, in the empty lot on the crate?" the white-maned one asked. "And just look at where we invited you—to a nice dacha, with a breeze." And he smiled, revealing flat and horsey teeth. He didn't move at all, but was somehow frighteningly, deathly tense, and this tension of his seemed to create an invisible but oppressive force field in the room with things covered with white oilcloth.

"Yes, that one will crush your bones instantly," the writer thought.

"Now he'll get a small box with a lid," the ruddy one smiled. "He's about to kick the bucket. Enough—he's caused trouble, slandered, sucked our blood, the slime-bucket."

The writer wanted to move away but couldn't; even though his legs were still holding him up, they didn't move, as if in a force field. At that moment something iron and unyielding squeezed his neck and crushed his throat. He didn't even have time to let out a scream; he only choked on his own blood. Evidently the bibliophile was a distinguished master of his craft. A blinding, hot, crimson light, a whole sheet of it, remained before him for a fraction of a second not in his eyes but in his brain; his body, which over the long years had gotten used to everything, even to death, was still alive and answered evil with evil. The bibliophile doubled over from a powerful kick in the groin area. His grip loosened. "Well," the body said, instantly jumping away and pressing against the wall. It was a terrifying sight—all bloody, covered in something sticky and vile, crimson, with eyes hanging out of their sockets. All this had happened in mere seconds. The ruddy one jumped up, grabbed at his pocket, but sat back down right away. And then the horsey one, screaming "you lie, you bastard!" hurled himself at the man pressed against the wall who was still frightening and ready to fight to the death. He hurled a flat paperweight at him, and its sharp corner struck him right in the temple. The body collapsed to its knees. But when the horsey one ran up to strike again, it—the body—grabbed him by a leg and brought him down. They rolled on the floor. The horsey one immediately ended up on the bottom. And then the ruddy one came up and, with a precise, well-calculated motion, struck the one on top with a lancet. The blow landed right in the hollow at the back of the head. The body's hands unclenched. The two lumped together came apart. The ruddy one struck the same spot again. The horsey one got up. He was dripping. He went into a fit of coughing. And the ruddy one bent down and felt the man's pulse like a professional—the medical pin he was wearing suddenly flashed crimson as he turned—and then glanced into the quickly fading eyes.

"It's all over," he determined.

"Thanks boys, you really hammered him," the bibliophile said in a hoarse voice, straightening himself up and catching his breath. "Just step back, step back! As you can see, everything's spattered here! Oh, hell! That's what it means not to be prepared. He could've easily killed me, the bastard! The car will be here any moment. It wasn't far behind us. I went out and signaled them."

The horsey one stood and watched. He had taken a good beating. His breathing made a kind of whistling, sobbing sound.

"Whew!" the bibliophile said with hatred and kicked the corpse in the temple with the tip of his shoe. "Whew, the bastard!" He struck again and again, but the head just rolled gently on the oilcloth.

The horsey one continued standing; his mouth was half-open and his teeth gleamed.

"A strong one!" he said. "I never would've thought he'd go with you. 'Come on over, guy.'" It was hard to tell what in particular there was in the tone of his voice and in those words. But it was definitely there. That's why the bibliophile looked at him.

"And you, sit down, sit down, you're shaking all over," he said. "Where did he get you? Too bad we couldn't shoot him."

"He talked to me on the phone, swore, called me a muzhik. That woman came running to him, tried to convince him not to go, cried—I heard everything—but no, he went. He even picked a bouquet for her—dandelions. How can you convince someone like that?"

"What's this? You feel sorry for him?" the bibliophile became angry right away. "He didn't punch you hard enough? Here, have some water."

The one with the white mane was shaking; right away his face became wet and not because he was crying, but because all of him began to turn inside out.

"Do it, go ahead, all over him," the bibliophile yelled mockingly. "What a cry-baby I have . . . If you start crying over every bastard . . ."

The car horn sounded.

"Coming, coming," the bibliophile said and walked out.

"Now there's someone I'd do in," said the white-haired one, "right away . . ."

"What's he got to do with it?" the ruddy one with the medical pin responded in surprise. "He got an order, and he gave us an order. That's all."

The white-haired one sat on the table, opened a box, took out a bottle, bit off the metal cap, poured a full glass, and gulped it down all at once. Then he sat for a while, gnashed his teeth, and suddenly hit the pedestal of the table with his foot. The table made a groaning, vibrating sound—it was made of plywood. Everything here was fake—made of plywood and oilcloth, except for the locks; those, it's true, were steel and automatic.

"I'd just crush his bones," the horsey one said. "I heard that order. When I radioed him that he was coming to see me, he said 'Oh, no, that's no good. Go and wait in the guardroom. Since he's not afraid, no more warnings—just get on with the job.'"

"So what? That was right," the ruddy one said. "And we did our job."

"And then after a while he radios me, 'Go to the guardhouse in the woods. You're not needed. He went to the dacha.'"

"He sent a car with three guys to the dacha too. He would've met his end one way or another," the ruddy one said, "so don't take it so hard."

"And that doll couldn't stop him. She even gave him a ride, that brainless broad."

"Quiet! They're coming. Stop carrying on."

"So Varmishev?" the writer asked and interchanged two letters on purpose, "And you say he's got half a liter?"

"Even more, probably. They made some moonshine over there. So maybe we'll get off?"

"No," the writer smiled. "Looks like I'll be going home, to my abode." But suddenly, when the bibliophile was already in the exit area of the train car, the writer shouted: "Just a second! A counter invitation. Let's go to my place. So what if they're asleep? We'll sit in the hallway. I've got a nice secret stash there. For God's sake, just don't say no! Because I'm going out of my mind! Here I am, just sitting with you, fully awake, but I keep seeing all kinds of crazy things."

And then the bibliophile returned obediently and sat down in his seat.

"With you, anywhere."

And he, an old man, an engineer of human souls, as someone put it once,[12] sadly and with deep self-deprecation thought to himself: "What cowardly creatures we are after all! Let them call us like that a couple more times and we'll be running away from everyone. Those snakes know perfectly well what they're doing. Here I got all brave, went to meet them and came back all proud, not scared of anything, I said, and then I was dying of fear the whole way home." He felt so awful that he didn't even know what to say or do. A normal, ordinary guy who was sincerely fond of him was now sitting beside him, and he came to regard even that affection as hypocrisy or some kind of set-up. So then did he ever deserve real love? He thought about it while they were on the train, and then walking, and for that reason jabbered about something insignificant and nonsensical the whole time just to stifle the shame he was feeling. No, he wasn't even ashamed anymore; he was simply hurting and feverish like an open, inflamed wound. Those babblers! Worthless nothings! Those shitheads, as they say in the North. Nothing's done directly, everything's done in a roundabout way. Nothing for others, everything for themselves. Coiled up like vipers in a swamp, at each other's throats like dogs in a cage at the dog pound. Little arm, leg, cucumber . . . If it were at least like that, but it's not like that at all.

"A French curve," he said loudly and stopped, "damn French curve."

"Why such a negative attitude?" the bibliophile became upset. "I was a draftsman myself. You can't get along without a French curve."

"Yes, but I'm not a drawing!" he shouted in despair. "No matter what, I'm still a man. I'm a little arm, leg, cucumber! Not some French curve."

Someone laughed in the dark, and a woman's voice said in explanation, "It's always people like that who come back on commuter trains from

Moscow. They get plastered back there . . ."

They walked another half a block or so, and at this point the bibliophile said, "Well, it looks like we're here. There's the 'House of Creativity' sign. Goodbye. And I, excuse me . . ." He started to run back. "Or else I won't be able to leave. And I have to be there without fail. Today."

"So you won't stop by?" the writer shouted after him with disappointment.

"Sorry. I can't! Another time! I was only seeing you home. I saw that you weren't quite yourself. I don't have a minute left. Bye!"

"And what about the pint?"

"But I don't drink," the bibliophile laughed. "Did you forget or something? Yes?"

Yes, yes, he had forgotten everything, everything.[13]

1977

NOTES

1. Reference to what happened to the poet and translator Konstantin Bogatyryov (1925-1976).
2. In Russian the name is *Zuy*, which rhymes with the word for the male organ, *khuy*. We've rendered the name as "Zick" (to rhyme with "dick").
3. The phrase the speaker uses (*zuby zagovarivat'*) carries two meanings. The first is idiomatic, "meaning to engage in smooth talk." But when the speaker goes on to say, "they're healthy," it quickly becomes clear that he is simultaneously referring to the literal meaning of the phrase, "to cast a spell on teeth." Such spells, believed to cure tooth pain, were part of Russian folk belief.
4. Dombrovsky himself spent seventeen years in labor camps.
5. The North: reference to the camps of the Gulag.
6. Julian Semyonov (1931-1993): writer of popular spy and detective novels, some of which were turned into movie serials.
7. Russian has "thou" (*ty*) and "you" (*vy*).
8. The idiom *do zelyonogo zmiya* literally means to get drunk to the point of having hallucinations, seeing a "green snake," being dead drunk.
9. Tapping a finger or knocking on a surface signaled that an informer was present.

10. Saxo Grammaticus (c. 1150-1220): Danish historian who wrote the first important history of Denmark.
11. "Hut on chicken legs" immediately brings to mind Baba Yaga, a witch who lives deep in the woods in such a hut. Descriptions of her appearance and powers vary, but she is often portrayed as an old crone who eats children who stray into her domain.
12. In 1932 Stalin called writers "engineers of human souls."
13. Dombrovsky's novel, *The Faculty of Useless Knowledge*, set in the years of the Great Terror and based on his own experiences in the Gulag, was published in Paris in 1978. He was killed a few months later by thugs who attacked him outside the Writers' Club in Moscow.

MY OLDER COUSIN

Sergei Dovlatov

Life turned my first cousin into a criminal. I think he was lucky. Otherwise he would have inevitably become a party functionary.

For the latter there was a multitude of the most diverse prerequisites. However, let's not get ahead of ourselves . . .

My aunt was a well-known literary editor. Her husband—Aaron—was in charge of a military hospital. In addition, he gave lectures and collected stamps. This was a good, friendly family . . .

My older cousin was born under rather mysterious circumstances. Before she married, my aunt had an affair. She fell in love with Sergei Mironovich Kirov's[1] deputy. His name was Aleksander Ugarov. Old Leningraders remember this prominent regional committee figure.

He had a family. And although he was married, he loved my aunt.

And my aunt found herself in a family way.

Finally it was time to give birth. They took her to the hospital.

My mother went to Smolny.[2] She managed to get an appointment. Reminded Kirov's deputy about her sister and her problems.

Ugarov sullenly gave a few orders. Carrying fruit and flowers, the menials of the regional committee headed in formation to the maternity hospital. And a miniature inlaid card table was delivered to my aunt's living quarters. Apparently it was requisitioned from alien class elements.

My aunt gave birth to a nice, healthy baby boy—Borya. My mother decided to go to the regional committee again. She couldn't get an appointment. And not because Ugarov put on airs. Rather, the opposite. During those days the happy daddy had been arrested as an enemy of the people.

It was 1938[3] . . . My aunt was left with the infant.

It's a good thing that Ugarov wasn't her husband. Otherwise my aunt would've have been exiled. The way it turned out—they exiled his wife and children. Which, of course, is also unpleasant.

Apparently my aunt was aware of what she was getting into. She was a beautiful, energetic and independent woman. If ever she was afraid of anything, it was only party criticism.

Besides, Aaron appeared. Apparently he loved my aunt. He proposed marriage to her.

Aaron was the son of a hat-shop owner. Furthermore, he didn't look like a typical nearsighted, sickly, pensive Jew. He was a tall, strong, masculine man. A former student revolutionary, Red Army man, and nepman.* Later on, an administrator. And finally, in his declining years—a revisionist and dissident . . .

Aaron adored my aunt. The child called him "daddy."

The war began. We found ourselves in Novosibirsk. Borya turned three. He attended kindergarten. I was an infant.

Borya would bring me pieces of lump sugar. He'd carry it in his cheek. And at home he'd take it out and put it in a saucer.

I was capricious and didn't want to eat the sugar. Borya would say anxiously to our parents, "Sugar, you know, melts . . ."

Then the war ended. And we no longer went hungry . . .

My cousin was turning into a handsome teenager of the Western European type. He had light eyes and dark, curly hair. He looked like the youthful heroes in progressive Italian movies. All our relatives thought so . . .

He was a model Soviet boy. A Pioneer,* high achiever, football player, and collector of scrap metal.[4] He kept a diary in which he wrote down aphorisms. He planted a birch tree in his courtyard. In the drama club he would invariably be given the role of a Young Guard[5] . . .

I was younger, but not as good as him. And he was invariably held up to me as an example.

He was truthful, shy, and well read. They would say to me—Borya is a good student, helps his parents, is involved in sports . . . Borya won a regional contest . . . Borya nursed a baby bird back to health . . . Borya built a crystal radio receiver. (To this day I don't know what that is.)

And suddenly something fantastic happened . . . that doesn't lend itself to description . . . I actually can't find the words . . .

In short, my cousin urinated on the school principal.

This happened after classes. Borya was putting out a wall newspaper* for Athlete's Day. His classmates clustered around him.

Looking out the window, someone said, "There goes the Informer."

(They called the school principal, Chebotaryov, "the Informer").

To continue the story, my cousin climbed up on the windowsill. He asked the girls to look away. He had calculated the trajectory expertly. And doused Chebotaryov from head to foot . . .

This was unbelievable and crazy. It was hard to believe. A month later some of those present doubted this had really happened. Such a scene seemed totally outrageous.

The reaction of Chebotaryov, the principal, was also quite unexpected. He totally lost face. And suddenly he began shouting loudly in rapid, vulgar speech: "I used to give it to the likes of you back in camp . . . ! You'll be eating shit for me . . . ! You son-of-a-bitch . . . !"

The old prison camp work-assigner awoke in Principal Chebotaryov. Who would have thought it . . . ? A green felt hat, a Chinese cloak, a tightly packed briefcase . . .

My cousin did this deed a week before the end of school. Thereby depriving himself of a gold medal. His parents had a difficult time persuading the principal to grant Borya his high school diploma . . . .

At that time I asked my cousin, "Why did you do it?"

My cousin answered, "I did what every schoolboy dreams about in secret. When I saw the Informer, I understood—it's now or never . . . ! I'm going to do it . . . ! Or stop respecting myself . . ."

At that time I was already a rather angry teenager. I said to my cousin, "A hundred years from now they'll hang a memorial plaque on the facade of your school: Boris Dovlatov studied here . . . with unexpected consequences ensuing from here . . ."

My cousin's unbelievable behavior was discussed for several months. Then Boris enrolled in a theater institute. He decided to become an art historian. People began to forget about his crime. Especially since he was an outstanding student. He was the secretary of the Komsomol.* And also a blood donor, and an editor of a wall newspaper,* and a goalkeeper. . .

As he grew into manhood, he became even more handsome. He resembled an Italian movie actor. Young women followed him with unabashed enthusiasm.

All this notwithstanding, he was a chaste and shy youth. Female flirtation sickened him. I remember his entries in his student diary: "The most important thing both in a book and in a woman is not form but content . . ."

Even now, after a countless number of life's disappointments, this guideline seems somewhat boring to me. And, as before, I like only beautiful women.

Moreover, I am endowed with a superstitious cast of mind. It seems to me, for example, that all fat women are liars. In particular if fullness comes with a small bust . . .

However, we're not talking about me . . .

My cousin finished the theater institute. Graduated with honors. He had an irreproachable Komsomol file that would follow him.

He went to the virgin lands[6] and was a construction team leader. Took an active part in a voluntary police force that assisted the police. A terror to petty bourgeois sentiments and vestiges of capitalism in people's consciousness.

He had the most honest eyes in the whole neighborhood . . .

He became the head of a literature section. Got a job in the Lenin Komsomol Theater. This was almost unbelievable. A young boy, a recent student, and suddenly such a position!"

He was demanding and business-like in his position as the person in charge of the literary section. He fought for progressive art. And tactfully, in a restrained manner, and carefully at that. Skillfully pushing through Vampilov, Borshchagovsky, Mrozek[7]. . .

Celebrated Soviet dramatists were somewhat afraid of him. The rebellious, young theater crowd was enraptured with him.

He was sent on important trips. He took part in several meetings in the Kremlin. It was recommended to him delicately that he become a Party member. He vacillated. He thought he was—unworthy . . .

And suddenly my dear cousin distinguished himself again. I don't even know how to put it . . . In short, Borya committed twelve robberies.

He had a pal named Tsapin at the institute. And so he and Tsapin looted twelve foreign tourist buses. They carried off suitcases, radio sets, tape recorders, umbrellas, raincoats, and hats. And incidentally, a spare tire.

Twenty-four hours later they were arrested. We were in shock. My aunt ran to her friend Yury German.[8] He called his friends—police generals.

The best lawyer in the city, Kiselyov, defended my cousin at his trial.

Some details and particulars emerged during the course of the trial. It turned out that the victims of the robberies were representatives of developing countries. And also—members of progressive socialist organizations.

Kiselyov decided to take advantage of this. He asked my cousin, "Defendant Dovlatov, did you know that these people were citizens of developing countries? And also, representatives of socialist organizations?"

"Unfortunately not, "Boris answered wisely.

"But if you had known . . . ? Would you have dared to encroach on their personal property?"

My cousin's face took on an expression of extreme hurt. The lawyer's question seemed to be absolutely tactless to him. He raised his eyebrows in vexation. Which meant, "And you're even asking . . . ? How could you think that?!"

Kiselyov became noticeably animated.

"So," he said, "and finally, the last question. Didn't you think that these upper class people were representatives of the reactionary strata of society?"

At that moment the judge interrupted him. "Comrade Kiselyov, don't make out the accused to be a fighter for world revolution . . . !"

But my cousin managed to nod his head. Such an assumption, so to say, had flashed through his mind . . . .

The judge raised his voice. "Let's stick to the facts which the investigation has at its disposal."

My cousin was given three years.

At the trial he behaved courageously and simply. He smiled and teased the judge.

When the verdict was announced, my cousin didn't flinch. He was escorted under guard from the courtroom.

After that there followed an appeal . . . Some efforts were made, negotiations and telephone calls. And everything was in vain.

My cousin found himself in Tyumen.[9] In an intensive regime camp. We corresponded with him. All his letters began with the words, "Everything's fine in my life . . ."

Further on, there were numerous but restrained and sober requests: "Two pairs of wool socks . . . Teach yourself English book . . . Leggings . . . Ordinary notebooks . . . Teach yourself German book . . . Garlic . . . Lemons . . . Fountain pens . . . Teach yourself French book . . . And also— teach yourself to play the guitar. . ."

The news reaching us from camp was quite optimistic . . . Senior teacher Bukin wrote my aunt: "Boris Dovlatov follows all camp regime rules faithfully . . . Enjoys popularity among the inmates . . . Systematically over-fulfills work assignments . . . Takes an active part in amateur theatricals . . ."

My cousin wrote that he had been appointed barracks orderly. Then team leader. Then chairman of the Council of Team Leaders. And finally, bathhouse manager.

This was an astounding career. And it's extremely difficult to make a career like that in a labor camp. Such efforts in freedom lead to a sinecure of leadership in a bureaucracy. To retail establishments closed to the general public, dachas, and trips abroad . . .

My cousin was swiftly becoming reformed. He was a camp beacon. He was envied, he was admired.

In a year he was transferred to "chemistry."[10] That is, to a settlement where he would be free. With obligatory job placement at a local chemical complex.

That's where he got married. His selfless classmate Liza came to visit him. She acted like the wife of a Decembrist.* They became man and wife . . .

And in the meantime I had been thrown out of the university. Then I was conscripted into the army. And found myself in the security forces. I turned into a camp guard.

So I was a guard. And Borya—a prisoner.

It so happened that I even guarded my own cousin. True, not for very long. I don't feel like talking about it. Otherwise everything will be too literary. Like in Sholokhov's *Tales of the Don*.[11]

It's enough to say that I was a guard. And my cousin—an inmate . . .

We returned at almost the same time. My cousin was given his freedom, and I was demobilized.

Our relatives arranged a grand banquet in the Metropol Hotel. The celebration was mainly in my cousin's honor. But they also said a few nice words about me.

Uncle Roman expressed himself as follows: "There are people who bring to mind reptiles. They live in swamps . . . And there are people who bring to mind mountain eagles. They soar higher than the sun, their wings spread wide . . . Let's drink to Borya, our mountain eagle . . . ! Let's drink to clouds being left behind . . . !"

"Bravo!" the relatives shouted. "Great fellow, eagle, skilled horseman . . . !"

I caught motifs from Gorky's "Song of the Falcon"[12] in my uncle's speech.

Roman lowered his voice slightly and added, "Let's also drink to Seryozha, our eaglet! It's true he's still young. His wings haven't grown strong yet. But vast expanses await him too . . . !"

"God forbid!" my mother said rather loudly.

My uncle glanced reproachfully in her direction . . .

Again my aunt made calls to various people. And my cousin got a job at the Leningrad Film Studio. They made him something like a lighting technician.

And I went to work for a major journal. And in addition began to write short stories . . .

My cousin's career grew with increasing speed. Soon he became a laboratory assistant. Then a dispatcher. Then a senior dispatcher. And finally, assistant producer of a movie. That is, a financially responsible person.

It was not in vain that my cousin strived to reform himself so quickly. Now, apparently, he couldn't stop . . .

In a month his photograph was hanging in their hall of fame. Directors, cameramen, and the head of "Lenfilm" himself, Zvonaryov, all fell in love with him. What's more, even the cleaning women fell in love with him . . .

He was promised his own movie in the future.

Sixteen old communists from "Lenfilm" were ready to recommend him for party membership. But my cousin vacillated.

He brought to mind Levin from *Anna Karenina*.[13] On the eve of his wedding Levin was troubled by the virginity he had lost in his youth. My cousin was tormented by an analogous problem. Namely, can one with a criminal past be a communist?

Old communists assured him that one can . . .

My cousin stood in sharp relief against my dismal background. He was cheerful, dynamic, and verbose. He was sent on important trips. Everyone expected him to make a brilliant career in administration. It was impossible to believe that he had been in prison. Many of my not very close friends thought I was the one who had been in prison . . . .

And then something happened again. Although not right away, but gradually . . . Some strange irregularities began. As if the grand sound of the "Appassionata"[14] was being violated by the sharp cries of a saxophone.

My cousin was making his career as before. He made speeches at meetings. Went on trips. But at the same time he began to drink. And court women. And with unexpected enthusiasm at that.

He began to be noticed in questionable company. He was surrounded by drunkards, black marketeers, and some shady veterans of Khalkin-Gol.[15]

When he'd sober up, he'd run to meetings. After successfully addressing a meeting, he'd hurry to see his friends.

At first these itineraries didn't intersect. My cousin was making his career and at the same time—destroying it.

He wouldn't come home for three days in a row. He'd disappear with some whores.

Totally unattractive women predominated among them. One of these women, I remember, was named Greta. She had a goiter.

I said to my cousin, "You certainly could do better than that."

"You barbarian," my cousin became indignant, "do you know that she gets grain alcohol at work? And in unlimited quantities at that . . ."

Apparently my cousin was still led by his youthful doctrine: "In a woman and in a book the important thing is not form but content!"

Then Boris beat up a waiter in the restaurant "Narva." My cousin demanded that the waiter perform "Suliko"[16] . . .

He began to wind up in police stations. Each time the party office of "Lenfilm" would get him out. But each time with less willingness.

We waited to see how all this would end . . .

In the summer he went to the shooting of the film "Dauria"[17] in Chita.[18] And suddenly we learned that my cousin ran over a person with a government car. And an officer in the Soviet army to boot. Killed him . . .

This was a terrible time of suppositions and conjectures. We received the most contradictory information. People said Borya was driving drunk. It's also true that people said the officer, too, wasn't sober. Although it didn't matter, since he was dead . . .

All this was hidden from my aunt. My uncles collected around four hundred roubles. I was supposed to fly to Chita—to find out the details and take some judicious steps. To come to an agreement about some money transfers, to hire a lawyer . . .

"And if possible, to bribe the investigator," Uncle Roman reminded me . . .

I began to get ready.

Late at night the telephone rang. I picked up the receiver. Out of the silence came my cousin's calm voice, "Were you sleeping?"

"Borya!" I shouted. "You're alive? You're not going to be shot? Were you drunk?!"

"I'm alive," my cousin answered, "they won't shoot me . . . And remember—this was an accident. I was driving sober. I'll get four years, no more. Did you get the cigarettes?"

"What cigarettes?"

"Japanese. You see, Chita has a separate trade agreement with Japan. And excellent cigarettes, 'Highlight,' are sold here. I sent you a carton for your birthday. Did you get them?"

"No. That's unimportant . . ."

"What do you mean it's unimportant? They're top-grade cigarettes, manufactured in accordance with an American license."

But I interrupted him, "Are you under guard?"

"No," he said, "why? I'm living in a hotel. The investigator comes to me. Her name is Larisa. Such a plump woman . . . By the way, she sends you her regards . . ."

A strange woman's voice resounded in the receiver, "Hi there, cutie!"

Then my cousin started to speak again. "There's absolutely no reason for you to fly to Chita. The trial, I think, will be in Leningrad . . . Does mom know?"

"No," I said.

"Good . . ."

"Borya!" I yelled. "What should we send you? You're probably in an awful state of mind?! After all, you've killed a man. Killed a man . . . !"

"Don't shout. Officers are made to perish . . . And I repeat once more—this was an accident . . . But the main thing is—where did the cigarettes disappear to . . . ?"

Soon two direct participants in the events arrived from Chita. In this way the details of the matter became known. Here's what seems to have happened.

It was someone's birthday. They were having a celebration out in the open air. Borya arrived only in the evening, in a government car. As always, there wasn't enough liquor. The guests became a bit gloomy. The stores were closed.

Borya announced, "I'm going for some moonshine. Who'll go with me?"

He was tipsy. They tried to dissuade him. In the end, three people went with him. This included the driver, who was dozing in the back seat.

Half an hour later they struck the motorcyclist. He died without regaining consciousness.

The trip participants were hysterical. But my cousin, on the other hand, sobered up. He acted clearly and decisively. Namely, he still went for the moonshine. This took fifteen minutes. Then he dispensed generous amounts of the moonshine to all the trip participants. Including even the slightly sobered-up driver. The latter dozed off again.

Only then did my cousin call the police. Shortly thereafter, a police car drove up. They found a corpse, a smashed up motorcycle, and four drunken people. And my cousin turned out to be the most sober at that.

Lieutenant Dudko asked, "Who's the driver?"

My cousin pointed to the sleeping driver. He was put in the police car. The rest were driven home, once their addresses had been taken down.

My cousin hid for three days. Until all traces of alcohol had disappeared. Then he appeared at the police station and turned himself in.

By that time the driver, naturally, had sobered up. He was being held in a jail cell until the trial. He was convinced that he had run over the man while drunk.

At that point my cousin appeared and said that he had been driving the car.

"Why did you point to Yury Petrovich Krakhmalnikov?" the lieutenant got angry.

"You asked who the driver was and I answered . . ."

"Where have you been for three days?"

"I got scared . . . I was in shock . . ."

The affected grimace on my cousin's face conveyed his fragile psychological state.

"Oh yeah, as if someone like you would get scared!" The lieutenant didn't believe him.

Then he asked, "Were you drunk?"

"Not at all," my cousin answered.

"I doubt it . . ."

However, it was now impossible to prove anything. The other people in the car swore that Borya hadn't had anything to drink. The driver got off with a reprimand at his place of employment.

My dear cousin acted wisely. Now they had to try him not as a drunken man behind the wheel of a car. But as the person responsible for the accident.

Larisa, the investigator, would say to him, "Even in bed you continue to fool the investigation."

Within a week he appeared in Leningrad.

My aunt knew everything already. She didn't cry. She called writers who had dealings with the police. Always the same ones—Yuri German, Metter, Saparov.[19]

As a result, they didn't touch my cousin. They left him in peace until the trial. Only took a signed statement from him that he wouldn't leave.

My cousin dropped in on one of his first days back. He asked, "You served near Leningrad, right? Do you know the local system of camps?"

"In general, yes. I was in Obukhovo, Gorelovo, Piskaryovka . . ."

"Where would it be best for me to do my time?"

"The regime is milder in Obukhovo, I think."

"In short, I have to go and familiarize myself . . ."

We went to Obukhovo. Went into the barracks. Talked with the barracks orderly. Found which career soldiers I knew were still there. In a minute Sergeants Goderidze and Osipenko came running into the barracks.

We embraced. I introduced them to my cousin. Then I found out who was left from the old camp administration.

"Captain Deryabin," the career soldiers answered.

I remembered Captain Deryabin well. He was a comparatively good-natured, wild alcoholic. Prisoners swiped his cigarettes. When I was in the service there, Deryabin was a lieutenant.

We called over to the guarded compound of the prison camp. Within a minute Deryabin appeared in the guard shack.

"Ah!" he shouted. "Seryoga's come!! Let me see what you look like. Did I hear you've turned into a writer? Here, take and write up an incident from life. I had a *zek*[20] who was catapulted out of a camp sub-section. I took a sanitary engineering team to the camp sub-section. Placed a guard. Went to take a leak. I came back—one *zek* was missing. Flew away . . . They bent a pine tree, you see. Tied the *zek* to the top with a safety belt—and let him go. And the *zek* became unbuckled in flight and that's the last that was seen of him. He flew almost beyond the highway crossing. However, he miscalculated a bit. He hoped to land in the snow near the timber yard. But it turned out that he fell into the *raivoyenkomat*[21] . . . And then—such a purely literary detail. When they were taking him, he bit the *voyenkom*[22] on the nose . . ."

I introduced Deryabin to my cousin.

"Lyokha," said the captain, offering his hand.

"Bob."

"So," I say, "wouldn't it be good to have some of that . . . ?"

We decided to leave the barracks and go to the nearest woods. Invited Goderidze and Osipenko. Took four bottles of "Zveroboi"[23] out of the briefcase. Sat down on a fallen spruce.

"Well, to all things good!" the jailers said.

Five minutes later my cousin was hugging Deryabin. And in-between, asking him questions: "How's the heating? Are there a lot of guard dogs at the block stations? Do they observe the practice of keeping people in their cells?"

"You won't die," the career soldiers assured him.

"A good compound," Goderidze repeated, "you'll gain weight, get some rest, become a *bogatyr*[24] . . ."

"And the store is very close," Osipenko chimed in, "beyond the highway crossing. . . White wine, red, beer . . ."

In half an hour Deryabin was saying: "Get put in prison while I'm still alive, guys. Because when Lyokha Deryabin is discharged, it'll be the end of you . . . Different bosses will come who haven't completed higher education . . . Then you'll remember Lyokha Deryabin . . ."

Borya wrote down Lyokha's home telephone number.

"And I'll write down yours," Deryabin said.

"No point," my cousin answered. "I'll be here in a month . . ."

In the commuter train heading home, he said, "For the time being things aren't so bad."

But I was almost crying. Apparently the "Zveroboi" affected me.

Soon the trial began. The same lawyer, Kiselyov, defended my cousin. Those present applauded him every now and then.

It was curious that he depicted my cousin as the victim of the events and not the deceased Korobchenko.

In conclusion he said, "Human life brings to mind a mountain road with a great many dangerous turns. One of them became fateful for my client . . ."

My cousin was again given three years. This time—a strict regime camp.

On the day of the trial I received a package from Chita. It turned out to contain ten packs of Japanese "Highlight"cigarettes . . .

Borya was sent to Obukhovo. He wrote me that the camp was good and the camp guards—quite humane.

Captain Deryabin turned out to be a man of his word. He appointed Borya as a bread slicer. This was an enviable, privileged position.

During this time my cousin's wife managed to give birth to a daughter, Natasha. One day she called me and said, "We're being granted a family meeting. If you're free, let's go together. It's hard for me to go alone with the baby."

The four of us went together—my aunt, Liza, two-month old Natasha, and me.

It was a hot August day. Natasha cried the whole way. Liza was nervous. My aunt got a headache . . .

We drove up to the guard shack. Then we found ourselves in the visitation room. Besides us there were six other visitors. A glass barrier separated the prisoners from the visitors.

Liza undid the swaddling clothes her daughter was wrapped in. My cousin still hadn't appeared. I went up to the career soldier on duty.

"Where's Dovlatov?" I asked.

He answered somewhat rudely, "Just wait."

I said, "Call the barracks supervisor on the phone and send for my cousin. And tell Lyokha Deryabin I asked you to hurry them up."

The man on duty softened his tone somewhat.

"I don't answer to Deryabin. I answer to the security officer . . ."

"Go on," I say, "call . . ."

At that point my cousin appeared. He was in gray prison overalls. His hair, which had been cleanly shaven off, had grown back a bit. He was tanned and seemed to have grown taller.

My aunt handed him some apples, sausage, and chocolate through the opening.

Liza was saying to her daughter, "Tatusia,[25] that's daddy. See—that's daddy . . ."

But my cousin kept looking at me. Then he said, "You have awful trousers. And the color is sort of shit-like. If you like, I'll put you in contact with a certain Jew. Here in camp there's a Jew who sews terrific trousers. By the way, his family name is Portnov.[26] Such coincidences happen . . ."

I started shouting. "What are you talking about?! Of what importance is that?!"

"Don't think," he continued, "that it's free. I'll hand you some money, you'll buy the material, and he'll make the trousers for you . . . The Jew says, 'The behind is a man's face!' And now take a look at yours . . . Some kind of creases . . ."

It seemed to me that for a repeat offender, he was being much too exacting . . .

"Money?" My aunt was put on her guard. "From where? I know one isn't supposed to have money in camp."

"Money is like germs," Boris said, "it's everywhere. We'll build communism, then everything will be different . . ."

"Take a look at your daughter," Liza implored him.

"I did," my cousin said, "A lovely girl . . ."

"How's the food here? How do they feed you?" I asked.

"Not too good. True, I don't go to the mess hall. We send one of the career soldiers to the grocery store . . . There are times when there's even nothing to buy. After one o'clock you can't get any sausage or eggs anymore . . . Yes, Nikita[27] has ruined agriculture . . . And there was a time we fed Europe . . . There's one hope—the private sector. The restoration of NEP* . . ."

"Don't talk so loud," my aunt said.

My cousin called the career soldier on duty. Said something to him under his breath. The latter began to justify himself. Only fragments of phrases reached us.

"But I asked," my cousin said.

"I remember," the career soldier answered, "don't get upset. Tolik will be back in ten minutes."

"But I asked by twelve thirty."

"There wasn't an opportunity."

"Dima, I'm going to get offended."

"Borya, you know me. I'm the kind of a man who if I promised, I'll get it done . . . Tolik will come back in exactly ten minutes . . ."

"But we want to have a drink right now!"

I asked, "What's going on? What's the problem?"

My cousin answered, "I've sent some character for vodka, and he's disappeared . . . This is a madhouse, not a military sub-unit . . ."

"They'll put you in the cooler," Liza said.

"And those in the cooler, those aren't people?!"

The child began to cry again. Liza felt hurt. My cousin seemed to her inattentive and indifferent. My aunt took one medication after another.

The time for our visit was running out. One of the *zeks* was being led away practically by force. He kept trying to break free and shouted: "Nadka, if you whore around, I'll kill you! I'll find you and cripple you, like a monkey . . . That I can guarantee you . . . And remember, you bitch, Vovik loves you . . . !"

"It's time to go," I said, "time."

My aunt turned away. Liza was rocking the little one to sleep.

"And the vodka?" my cousin asked.

"Drink it yourself," I said.

"I wanted to . . . with you."

"Not worth it, cousin. What fun is it to drink here . . . ?"

"As you like . . . But I'll still kill that career soldier. For me the most important thing in a man is taking responsibility seriously . . ."

Suddenly Tolik appeared with a bottle. It was obvious he had been rushing.

"Here," he says, "a ruble thirty in change."

"Do it so I don't see it, guys," the man on duty said, handing Borya an enamel mug.

My cousin filled it quickly. And everyone took a swallow. Including the *zeks*, their kinfolk, the supervisors, and the career soldiers. And the man on duty himself . . .

One unshaven *zek* with tattoos, raising the mug, said, "To our great country! To Comrade Stalin personally! To victory over fascist Germany! From all the weapons on earth—boom . . . !"

"Long live the double-dyed reactionary clique of Imre Nad!"[28] a second person said in support . . .

The man on duty touched my cousin's shoulder. "Bob, sorry, it's time for you . . ."

We said our goodbyes. I shook my cousin's hand through the opening. My aunt looked at her son in silence. Liza suddenly started to cry and woke up Natasha who'd fallen asleep. Natasha began to wail.

We walked out and began trying to catch a taxi . . .

About a year went by. My cousin wrote that everything was going fine. He was working as a bread cutter and, when Deryabin retired, he became an electrician.

Then a *UVD*[29] agent found my cousin. It had been decided to make a documentary film about prison camps. About Soviet camps being the most humane in the world. The film was earmarked for domestic use. It had a rather dry title, "Methods of Guarding Strict Regime Labor Colonies."

My cousin traveled to various remote camp locations. He was given a "GAZ-61" government car. He was issued the appropriate equipment. Two escorts invariably accompanied him—Goderidze and Osipenko.

My cousin managed to visit home frequently. Several times he spent some time at my place.

By summer the film was ready. My cousin performed the duties of cameraman, director, and announcer all at the same time.

The screening took place in June. Generals and colonels sat in the hall. At the discussion about the film General Shurepov said, "A good, much-needed picture . . . Watching it is just like watching 'A Thousand and One Nights'. . ."[30]

Borya was praised. He was supposed to be released by September.

I finally detected my cousin's most important characteristic. He was an unconscious, spontaneous existentialist. He could act only in borderline situations. Build his career—only in prison. Fight for his life—only on the edge of an abyss . . .

Finally he was released.

To go on with my story, I have to repeat myself. My aunt called Yury German. My cousin was hired as an unskilled worker in a documentary film studio. Two months later, he was working as a sound operator. And half a year later—as the manager of the procurement department.

Roughly during the same time, I was let go at work once and for all. I wrote stories and lived on my mother's pension . . .

When my aunt got sick and died, they found a portrait of a charming grey-eyed man among her papers. This was Kirov's deputy—Aleksandr Ivanovich Ugarov. He reminded me of my cousin. Although he did look significantly younger.

Borya knew even before that who his father was. Now people began to talk about it openly.

My cousin could have made an attempt to find his relatives. However, he didn't want to. He said, "I have you, and no one else . . ."

Then he became pensive and added, "How strange! I'm half-Russian. You're half-Jewish. But both of us love vodka with beer . . ."

In '79 I decided to emigrate. My cousin said he wouldn't go.

He began to drink again and fight in restaurants. He was in danger of losing his job.

I think he could live only in captivity. In freedom he would become undisciplined and even fall ill.

I said to him for the last time, "Let's leave."

He reacted lethargically and with sadness. "All that isn't for me. You have to go through the channels. Convince everyone that you're a Jew . . . I'm uncomfortable with that . . . If only you could wake up from a hangover and zap!—you're on Capitol Hill . . ."

At the airport my cousin began to cry. Evidently, he had aged. Moreover, it's always easier to leave than stay . . .

It's my fourth year of living in New York. It's my fourth year of sending packages to Leningrad. And suddenly a package comes—from there.

I opened it at the post office. It contained a light-blue tricot jersey with the Olympic Games emblem. And also a heavy metal corkscrew of an improved design.

I fell into thought. What were the dearest things in my life? And I realized: four pieces of lump sugar, Japanese "Highlight" cigarettes, a light-blue jersey, and this corkscrew here . . .

1983

(Ann Arbor, Michigan.)

NOTES

1. Sergei Kirov (1886-1934): a rising star in the Communist Party when assassinated in 1934. His murder was used by Stalin as a reason to initiate purges and show trials.
2. The Smolny Institute for Noble Maidens: Established in St. Petersburg in 1806-08; it became Lenin's Bolshevik headquarters during the October revolution. When Lenin moved to Moscow, the Smolny became the headquarters of the local Communist Party.
3. 1938: one of the peak years of the purges or Great Terror, when millions of people were executed or sent to prison camps.
4. To help rebuild the Soviet steel industry after World War II, children were encouraged to collect scrap metal and bring it to a collection point.
5. The Young Guard was said to be an underground, anti-fascist Komsomol organization in the Nazi-occupied city of Krasnodon with about one hundred members; they were betrayed to the Nazis, tortured and killed. Alexander Fadeev wrote a novel based on the activities of the Young Guard which he entitled *The Young Guard* (1946).
6. virgin lands: in 1954 Nikita Khrushchev decided to open up to agriculture vast tracts of land in the steppes of the northern Kazakh Soviet Socialist Republic and the Altay region of Soviet Russia. More than 300,000 people joined in the effort to plow land that had never been cultivated ("virgin" land). For a few years Khrushchev's initiative was a great success.
7. Aleksandr Vampilov (1937-72): a major Russian playwright; Aleksandr Borshchagovsky (1913-2006), author of historical novels in Ukrainian and Russian, who caused a sensation in 1980 by writing a play about the 1941 Nazi massacre of Kievan citizens, mostly Jews, at Babi Yar; Slawomir Mrozek (1930-), gifted Polish playwright.
8. Yury German (1910-1967): a Soviet prose writer whose first major work, *Our Friends* (1936), depicted the everyday life of ordinary people. Also famous for his works about Dzerzhinsky, Chekists,* and the militia.
9. Tyumen: a region in northwestern Siberia which is rich in oil and gas.
10. "chemistry": This is a reference to a labor camp with a mild regime: the prisoners live in dorms, have permission to go into the town or city, and are assigned to work at a plant with dangerous or hazardous materials.
11. Mikhail Sholokhov (1905-1984): His *Tales of the Don*, which included "Family Man," appeared in 1926 and depicted Cossack life, which he knew well from spending some of his formative years in the Don area in the south of Russia.
12. Maksim Gorky's "Song of the Falcon" (1895), a short, neo-romantic work about a falcon who would rather soar high and perish than live like a snake hiding at the bottom of a ravine, was written in praise of the idea of the revolutionary hero.

13. *Anna Karenina*, one of Leo Tolstoy's great novels.
14. "Appassionata," or more properly "Piano Sonata No. 23 in F minor, opus 57," is one of the great piano sonatas by Ludwig van Beethoven. According to the memoirs of Maksim Gorky, this was Lenin's favorite music.
15. The Battle of Khalkin-Gol was the decisive engagement of the undeclared Soviet-Japanese Border War, a battle fought on the border between Mongolia and Manchuria in 1939. It ended with the defeat of the Japanese forces.
16. Suliko: Stalin's favorite Georgian song.
17. Dauria: one of several names for the mountainous region to the east of or "beyond" Lake Baikal in Russia.
18. Chita: an oblast in southeast Siberia.
19. Yury German (see #10 above); Izrael M. Metter (1909-1996), short story writer; A.V. Saparov (1912-1973), a children's writer, famous for his books about the siege of Leningrad during World War II.
20. *zek:* inmate of a Gulag prison camp.
21. *raivoyenkomat*: a good example of the Soviet love of acronyms; it stands for "district military registration and enlistment office."
22. *voyenkom*: military commissar.
23. "Zveroboi": a vodka flavored with the herb St. John's wort.
24. *bogatyr*: an epic hero in Russian folklore.
25. Tatusia: an endearing form of the diminutive form (Tasha) of Natasha.
26. Portnov: an appropriate name for a tailor, since *portnoi* means "tailor."
27. Nikita: i.e., Nikita Krushchev
28. Imre Nad: the Russian version of the name Imre Nagy (1896-1958), twice the Prime Minister of Hungary, who was executed two years after the Hungarian Revolution of 1956 against Soviet rule.
29. *UVD: Upravleniye vnutrennikh del*, Administration of Internal Affairs.
30. *The Book of Thousand and One Nights* (also known under different titles, such as *Arabian Nights)*: a collection of stories compiled over thousands of years by various authors, translators, and scholars whose roots can be traced to ancient Arabia and Ancient Persia.

GIRL OF MY DREAMS

Bulat Okudzhava

I remember how I went to meet my mother in 1947.

We had been separated for ten years. She had parted with a twelve-year old boy and here was a young man who was already twenty-two, a university student, someone who had already fought in a war, been wounded and been through a lot in his life although, as I recall now, was perhaps rather shallow and thoughtless. Strange as it may seem, there was a noticeable lack of seriousness in me.

We had been separated for ten years. Well, the circumstances at that time, the reasons for the grievous losses and long separations—now all this is well known, now we understand it well; we offer explanations and view it as historical fact, even forgetting sometimes that we stewed in all this ourselves, forgetting that we were participants in those events, that it affected, and even struck and wounded us.

Back then ten years was a huge period of time for me, not like now, when the years flash by just like the clicking sounds on a pay phone, so that by evening you look and several more years have gone by without a trace. But back then, almost my whole life fit into this stretch of time and seemed endless, and I thought that if I had already managed to live through so much and reach adulthood, then my mother must be a wizened, little old woman, completely grey . . . And I'd become frightened.

The circumstances of my life back then were as follows. I returned from the front, enrolled at the University of Tbilisi, and lived in a first-floor room my aunt had left me after moving to another city. I studied in the language and literature department, wrote unoriginal poetry, and lived the way a single student could in those post-war years—without worrying about the future, without any money, without any feelings of despair. I kept falling in love and getting burned, and this helped me forget about hunger; and trying to keep my spirits up, I'd think that I'm alive and well, what more do I need? But the dark, black secret, the bitter secret of being separated from my mother, I kept deep in my heart as I thought of her.

There were several photographs in which she was young, with large dark-brown eyes, her hair combed smooth and pulled back in a bun at the back of her head, in a dark dress with a white collar, a serious look on her face, but with lips that were ready to break into a smile. Well, there were also the memories of her intonation, the way she laughed, some words of affection that now eluded me, all kinds of little things. I loved that fading image and suffered from being separated from her, but that image was nothing more than a symbol for me, dear and ghostly, grandiloquent and vague.

In the room next to mine lived my neighbor Meladze—elderly, corpulent, with ears that stuck out and had grey hair coming out of them—a slovenly, scowling man, a man of few words, particularly with me, as if he were afraid that I'd ask him for a loan. He'd return from work by some unknown way—no one ever saw him come in through the door. Now it seems to me that he'd fly in through the ventilation windowpane and fly out with his worn, brown briefcase. Who he was, what he did— now I don't remember, but even back then I probably didn't know. He stayed in his room and almost never left it. What did he do there?

We were lonely—both he and I.

I think it was hard for him to live next door to me. Sometimes groups of young people just like me would flock into my room—hungry, always in a rush, and excited. Girls would come too, and we'd bake dry flat cakes out of corn flour in a frying pan, open bottles of cheap wine, and then shouts and laughter, the sound of glasses, whispers, and kisses would travel through the thin wall into Meladze's room. And he, judging by everything, would tolerate our noise with disgust and despise me.

Back then I wasn't able to appreciate the extent of his patience and his highly noble behavior; not a word of reproach ever left his lips. He simply paid no heed to me, didn't speak to me, and if I asked him sometimes for some salt or matches or a needle and thread in a neighborly way, he wouldn't refuse me but hand them to me in silence and look away.

That portentous day I returned home late. I don't even remember where I'd been hanging out. He met me in the kitchen that was also the entrance hall and held out his hand to me with a folded piece of paper.

"A telegram," he said in a whisper.

The telegram was from Karaganda.[1] It burned my hands. "Meet arriving on the 501 kisses mother." Meladze shuffled by my side, breathing heavily and noisily and watching me. Without rhyme or reason I lit the small kerosene stove, then put it out, and placed the teakettle on it. Next I began sweeping around my kitchen table, but I didn't finish and started to scrape the oilcloth.

And so the most unlikely thing had happened and so suddenly! The symbol I was accustomed to now assumed a clear shape. What I had been dreaming of without any hope, what I had bemoaned in secret alone at night, had become almost tangible.

"Karaganda?" Meladze murmured.[2]

"Yes," I said sorrowfully.

He clicked his tongue sadly and sighed loudly.

"Some train 501," I said, "a mistake, probably. Do trains really have such numbers?"

"No," he whispered, "no mistake. Five-o-one means five-hundred happy."

"Why happy?" I didn't understand.

"Freight cars, katso.[i] Travels long time—everyone happy," and again clicked his tongue.

I couldn't fall asleep that night. Meladze coughed from time to time behind the wall. In the morning I set out for the train station.

The terrible thought that I wouldn't be able to recognize my mother haunted me as I quickly made my way down Veriysky Slope and rushed down Zhores Street toward the station. I tried to imagine how I'd be standing in the midst of train cars and crowds of people and, there, in the tumultuous vortex, I'd catch glimpses of a small, grey old woman, and we'd rush to meet each other. Then I imagined we'd head home on streetcar #10, have supper, and I'd see how nice she finds civilization and peace, and the new times, and her new surroundings. And I imagined everything that I'd tell her, and everything that I'd show her that she'd forgotten, managed to forget, and feel estranged from as she wept over my infrequent letters.

The train with the strange number really existed. It wasn't listed on any schedule, and the exact time of its arrival was a mystery even for the railroad dispatchers. But people were waiting for it nevertheless and even hoping it would arrive in Tbilisi by evening. I went back home. I

---

i   "boy" in Georgian. —Trans.

scrubbed the floors, washed the one tablecloth and the one towel that I owned, and tried all the while to imagine that moment, that is, how my mother and I would meet, and if I'd be able to recognize her right away—the way she was today, much older, stooped, and grey-haired; and if I didn't recognize her, let's say I didn't recognize her and ran past, but she was searching me out anxiously in the station crowd and feeling distressed, or if she saw in my eyes that I didn't recognize her, how that would aggravate her wounds . . . .

By four o'clock I was back at the train station again, but the happy five-hundred was lost somewhere out there. Now they were expecting it at midnight. I went back home and, in order to get rid of some of the fever of anticipation that had taken hold of me, I ironed the tablecloth and towel, swept the room, shook out the small rug, and swept the room again . . . Outside it was May. And I rushed again to the train station on streetcar #10, surrounded by other people's mothers and their sons who didn't have an inkling of what a festive occasion it was for me, and I again burned with the hope that now I wouldn't return alone, but embracing her thin shoulders . . . I knew that when the endless line of cars arrived at the platform, I'd have to run up and down more than once, and that I'd have to find my mother in the crowd of thousands, to recognize and embrace her and press myself close to her, to recognize her among thousands of other passengers and the people who had come to meet them—a small, grey, fragile, emaciated old woman.

And so I'd meet her. We'd have supper at home. The two of us. She'd tell me about her life, and I about mine. We wouldn't go deeply into things, searching for explanations and those who were to blame. Well, it happened, so it took place; and now we're together again.

. . . And then I'd take her to the movies and let her regain her peace of mind. And I had already chosen the film. That is to say, I didn't choose it, but it was the one and only film in Tbilisi that everybody was crazy about. This was a "war trophy film,"[3] "The Girl of My Dreams," with the sensational, irresistible Marika Rökk in the leading role.[4] Normal life in the city came to a halt; everybody was talking about the film, people ran to see it every free moment they could, they whistled melodies from the film in the streets, and the sound of pianos playing the same tunes that had captivated the ears of the inhabitants of Tbilisi resounded from open windows. This film was in color, with dancing and singing, romantic adventures, and comic situations—a striking, lively show that astounded the viewers in the difficult post-war years. I personally managed to see it about fifteen times and was secretly in love with the magnificent Marika and her blinding smile and, although I knew this film by heart, each time I saw it, it was as if I were seeing it for the first time, and I'd identify with the characters. And so it was not without reason that I thought back then that with my help my mother would be able to pick up her life after ten years in the desert of suffering and hopelessness. She'd see all this, I thought, and at least for a time she'd forget her sorrowful thoughts and enjoy contemplating the beautiful, and her heart would fill with peace and tranquility, well-being and music, and all this would return her to life, to love, and to me . . . And the heroine? A young woman, exuding happiness. Nature was generous and endowed her with a supple and healthy body, golden skin, long irreproachable legs, and an enchanting bust. She'd open her laughing blue eyes wide, in which the sensuous inhabitants of Tbilisi would drown with pleasure; and she'd smile, displaying a perfect mouth, and dance, surrounded by carefree, passionate, and handsome men. She accompanied me everywhere and would even sit on my old cot, legs crossed, gazing at me with her blue eyes, and smelling sweetly of some mysterious fragrance and exuding Austrian health. I didn't dare, of course, even to think of insulting her with my crude way of life, or my post-war sorrows or allusions to the bitter Karaganda desert, criss-crossed by barbed wire. She was also beautiful in that she didn't even suspect the existence of those overpopulated deserts, so incompatible with her wonderful blue Danube on whose shores she danced in blissful ignorance. Injustice and bitterness had nothing to do with her. Let us . . . for us . . . but not her, not for her. I cherished her like a precious jewel, and from time to time I'd take her out of my secret place and admire her for a while, gluing my eyes to the screens of theaters that smelled of carbolic acid.

There was a deafening hubbub in the square next to the train station. The whole area in front of the station was packed with crowds of people. Suitcases and bundles were heaped up on the pavement; there was laughter and crying, and shouts, and sharp words . . . I realized I was late, but apparently not by much, and there was still hope . . . I asked people sitting on their things if they had arrived on the 501. But they turned out to be from Batumi. I felt a sense of relief. I forced my way through the crowd to the information window and shouted something about the damned five-hundred, but the woman at the window, worn out and deafened by the noise, didn't understand a thing for a long time, since she was trying to answer several people all at once, and when she finally understood, she shouted to me callously, as her face became covered with pink splotches, that the 501 had arrived an hour ago, that this insane train had arrived long ago, and now there was no one left, that everyone had gotten off an hour ago, and there hasn't been anyone here for a long time now . . .

On the square next to the station, which looked like a market on Sunday, a stooped old woman was sitting on a pile of suitcases and packages and looking around helplessly. I headed for her. I thought I saw something familiar in her facial features. I slowly moved my stiff legs. She noticed me, looked me over with suspicion, and just put her little hand down on the nearest package.

I headed home on foot, hoping to catch up with my mother along the way. But I reached the door of my building without seeing her. My room was empty and quiet. Meladze coughed once behind the wall. I had to run down the road to the station once more, and I walked out and saw my mother on the nearest corner! She was slowly approaching my building. A small plywood suitcase was in her hand. She looked the same, tall and slender, just as I remembered her, and wore a grey, cotton print dress, wrinkled and odd-looking. Strong, tanned, and young. I remember how happy I was to see her like that, and not stooped and old.

It was early dusk. She embraced me and rubbed her cheek against mine. Her small suitcase sat on the sidewalk. Passers-by paid no attention to us since in Tbilisi, where everybody exchanges kisses upon meeting someone and this happens many times in the course of a day, there was nothing unusual in our embraces.

"Just look at you!" she kept saying. "Just look at you, my little boy, my little boy," and it was like before, like it had been once when . . .

We slowly headed for my building. I put my arms around her shoulders and wanted to ask her as people ask someone who's just arrived: "Well, how are you? What was your life like there?" But I thought better of it and didn't say anything.

We walked into my building. Into my room. I sat her down on my old couch. Meladze coughed once behind the wall. I sat her down and looked into her eyes. Those large, dark-brown, almond-shaped eyes were now right next to me. I looked into them . . . Getting ready to meet her, I thought there would be many tears and bitter lamentations, and I prepared the following phrase to comfort her: "Mom, you see that I'm well, that everything's fine with me, and you're healthy and just as beautiful as before, and now everything will be fine. You're back and we're together again." I repeated these words to myself many times, preparing myself for the first embraces, the first tears, for what happens after ten years of separation . . . And now I looked into her eyes. They were dry and remote; she looked at me but didn't see me; her face had become frozen, it had turned to stone; her lips were slightly parted, and her strong tanned hands lay limply in her lap. She didn't say anything, only "yes" from time to time in response to my chatter intended to console her, my idle talk about anything and everything except what was written on her face . . . "It would be better if she wept," I thought. She lit a cheap cigarette. She stroked my head with her hand . . .

"Now we'll have something to eat," I said cheerfully. "Do you want something to eat?"

"What?" she asked.

"Do you want something to eat? You must have a bite to eat after your trip."

"Me?" she didn't understand.

"You," I laughed, "of course, you . . ."

"Yes," she said submissively, "and you?" And she even seemed to smile but continued to sit like that—with her hands in her lap.

I dashed into the kitchen, lit the kerosene stove, and made some dough out of the remaining corn flour. I sliced a small piece of feta cheese that was miraculously left among my pathetic supplies of food. I put all of this on the table in front of my mother so that she'd be happy for a while and come out of her stupor: here's the kind of son she has, and here's his home, and here's how he manages to get everything done, and we're stronger than our circumstances, and here's how we overcome them with courage and love. I rushed about before her, but she remained apathetic and only smoked cigarette after cigarette . . . Then the tea kettle began to boil and I set it on the table. It was the first time that I was dealing so nimbly, so quickly, so carefully with the dishes, the kerosene stove, and the simple food; let her see that she wouldn't perish with me. Life goes on, it goes on . . . Of course, after all that she'd been through, far from home, far from me . . . you can't restore everything right away, but gradually, with patience . . .

When I was taking the flat cakes off the heat, the door squeaked and I heard Meladze breathing heavily behind my back. He offered me a bowl of *lobio*.[5]

"No need," I said, "we have everything . . ."

"Take it, *katso*," he said sullenly, "I know . . ." I took the bowl from him, but he didn't leave.

"Come on," I said, "I'll introduce you to my mother," and opened the door wide.

My mother was sitting the same way, with her hands in her lap. I thought that when she saw a guest, she'd get up and smile, as is customary, say "It's a pleasure, it's a pleasure" . . . and give her name, but she extended her tanned hand in silence and dropped it in her lap again.

"Please sit down," I said and pulled up a chair for him.

He sat down across from her. He also placed his hands in his lap. Dusk was setting in. They looked like motionless statues against the window, frozen in the same pose, and their profiles seemed similar to me.

What they talked about, and if they talked at all when I ran to the kitchen, I don't know. Not a sound came from the room. When I returned, I noticed that my mother's hands were no longer resting in her lap and that she was leaning a bit forward as if she had cocked her ear towards him.

"Batyq?"[6] Meladze uttered in the silence.

My mother looked at me, then said "Zharyk"[7] and smiled in embarrassment.

While I rushed from the kitchen to the room and back again, they continued to exchange short, incomprehensible words, almost in a whisper at that, just moving their lips. Meladze clicked his tongue and shook his head. I remembered that Zharyk was the station near which my mother had been staying and from where her letters sometimes reached me, letting me know that she was well, in good spirits, and everything was wonderful in her life, "only study, study hard, I beg you, my dear son." And it was there that I sent news of myself, that I was well and in good spirits, and that everything was fine, and that I was working on an article about Pushkin and everybody was praising me, "don't you worry about me," and that I was sure everything would come out all right in the end and we'd meet again.

And so we've met, and now she'll ask about the article and other irresponsible cock-and-bull stories . . .

Meladze declined the tea and disappeared. My mother looked at me with awareness for the first time.

"Was he," I asked in whisper, "was he also there?"

"Who?"she asked.

"Who, who . . . Meladze . . ."

"Meladze?" she responded in surprise and looked out the window. "Who's Meladze?"

"What do you mean who?" I couldn't restrain myself. "Mom, do you hear me? Meladze . . . my neighbor that I just introduced you to . . . Was he also . . . there?"

"Quiet, quiet," she frowned. "Don't talk about it, my sweet son . . ."

O Meladze, breathing heavily and shuffling around in your loneliness! You too were once lean like a branch of a Cornelian cherry tree, and your youthful face, with its hot and burning mustache, was aglow with a million desires. Your lips have turned pale, your mustache now droops, your inspiring cheeks have become sunken. I used to laugh at you and point you out to my friends on the sly; look here, I'd say, children, if you don't eat your cream of wheat, you'll look like that man . . . And we, who still had our full lips and were sharp-eyed, would marvel and go into fits of laughter when we saw you shuffling your feet awkwardly and sticking your neck out the door guardedly. What were you afraid of, Meladze?

We drank tea. I wanted to ask what her life had been like there but got scared. And I quickly began to lie about my life. She seemed to be listening, nodded her head, and her face showed interest; she smiled and chewed slowly. She touched the hot teakettle and looked at her blackened hand . . .

"It's all right," I started comforting her, "I'll wash the tea kettle, it's nothing. It always gets black, you know, from the kerosene stove."

"My poor little boy," she said to no one in particular and suddenly began to cry. I tried to calm and comfort her, saying it was no big thing, just a tea kettle. She wiped away her tears, pushed the empty cup away from her, and smiled in embarrassment.

"That's all, that's all," she said, "pay no attention," and lit a cigarette.

"What was it like for her over there," I wondered, "there, among the salt marshes, separated from me?"

Meladze coughed once behind the wall.

"It's all right," I thought, "things will sort themselves out. We'll finish drinking tea and I'll take her to the movies. She doesn't know yet what she's about to see. Suddenly after everything that's happened in her life, there'll be blue waves, music, joy, sunshine, and Marika Rökk," I thought, my eyes closed tight, "this after everything that's happened . . . Here, take the most vivid, the most delightful thing. The most valuable thing that I have—it's my gift to you," I thought, choking on the weight of my own generosity . . . And at this point I said to her, "You know, I have a surprise for you, but we have to leave the house for it and walk a bit . . ."

"Leave the house?" And she frowned.

"Don't be afraid," I laughed. "Don't be afraid of anything now. You'll see something wondrous, honestly! This is a wondrous thing that can be prescribed instead of medicine . . . Do you hear me? Let's go, let's go, please . . ."

She got up submissively.

We walked through Tbilisi in the evening. I wanted to ask her again what her life had been like there, but I didn't; everything was falling into place so nicely, it was such a gentle, honey-sweet evening, and I was happy to walk beside her and support her by cradling her elbow. She was slender and beautiful, my mother, even in that wrinkled, grey cotton dress so unlike anything worn in Tbilisi, even in those worn-out sandals of an indeterminate shape. "Directly from there," I thought, "to here, into this caressing warmth, the light pouring through the foliage of the plane trees, the noise of the happy crowd . . ." And I also thought, "Of course, I should have made her change her clothes and asked her to make herself look prettier because, well, she's wearing the same things that she wore *there* . . . It's time to forget."

I led her along Rustaveli Boulevard, and she walked submissively alongside me without asking any questions. While I was buying our tickets, she stood motionless by a wall, looking at the floor. I nodded to her from the cashier's—she seemed to give me a smile.

We sat in the stuffy cinema hall, and I said to her, "Now you will see something wondrous. It's so beautiful there are no words for it . . . Listen, did they show you anything there?"

"What?" she asked.

"Well, some movies . . . ," and I realized that I was saying something dumb, "at least occasionally . . ."

"Us?" she asked and laughed quietly.

"Mom," I began to whisper in irritation, "what's wrong with you? Well, I asked . . . There, where you were . . ."

"Well, of course," she said, sounding aloof.

"It's nice we're together again," I said like an experienced peacemaker, anticipating the enjoyment to come.

"Yes, yes," she whispered in response to something she was thinking about.

. . . I looked now at the screen, now at my mother; I shared my riches with my mother, I made her a gift of the best that I had. The hall was beside itself with excitement and laughter—it groaned, applauded, and hummed the songs . . . My mother sat with her head down. Her hands were in her lap.

"Isn't it great?" I whispered to her. "Just you watch, watch, the most interesting part is coming up . . . Just look, mom!"

By the way, who knows how many times the likely thought—that it was impossible to combine *those* circumstances with this blinding Austrian carnival on the shores of the beautiful blue Danube—had already stirred in my slippery and inconstant mind, had stirred and immediately disappeared.

My mother heard me exclaim, raised her head, didn't see anything, and lowered her head again. Beautiful Marika, without any clothes on, was sitting in a barrel filled with soap bubbles. She was washing herself as if this were nothing out of the ordinary. The audience in the hall worshiped her and hooted in delight. I laughed loudly and kept glancing into my mother's eyes with hope. She even tried to give me a polite smile in response, but in the end she couldn't manage it.

"Let's get out of here," she suddenly whispered to me.

"Now's the most interesting part," I said with chagrin.

"Please, let's leave . . ."

We slowly made our way home. We didn't speak. She didn't ask about anything, not even about the university, as a mother from t h a t world should have.

After the luxurious and bright outfits of the incomparable Marika, mother's dress seemed even more grey and embarrassing.

"You're so tanned," I said, "so beautiful. I thought I'd see an old woman, but you're so beautiful . . ."

"Is that so?" she said without showing any interest and stroked my hand. In my room she settled in the chair she had sat in before; she sat staring in front of herself with her hands in her lap while I feverishly made our beds. For myself on the cot, for her, on the only real bed. She tried to resist; she wanted me to sleep on the bed because she liked sleeping on a cot. "Yes, yes . . . no, no, I beg you, you must listen to me" (trying to give her voice a joking intonation). "I'm your mother . . . you must listen to me . . . I'm your mother . . . ," and then she said to no one in particular, staring into space, "your mo-ther . . . your mo-ther . . ."

I went into the kitchen. Meladze, breaking his old habit, was sitting on a stool. He looked at me inquiringly.

"I took her to a movie," I complained to him in a whisper, "but she left in the middle, didn't want to . . ."

"A movie?" he asked in surprise. "What movie, *katso*? She needs to rest."

"She's become totally different," I said. "Maybe I don't understand something. When I ask her a question, she repeats it as if she didn't hear it . . ."

He clicked his tongue.

"When a person doesn't want to say something unnecessary," he said in a whisper, "he speaks slowly, takes his time—he thinks—understand? He thinks . . . He needs time . . . He now has the habit . . ."

"She's afraid to say something unnecessary to me?" I asked.

He got angry. "Not to you, not to you, *genatsvale* . . .[ii] There," he raised his index finger, "you weren't there, there others asked questions: what for, why? Do you understand?"

"I understand," I said.

I place my hopes on tomorrow. Everything will be different tomorrow. She has to discard the heavy burden of the past. Yes, dear mom? Everything will be forgotten, everything will be forgotten, everything will be forgotten . . . We'll head again to the shores of the blue Danube and blend into the crowds of people, becoming indistinguishable from them, and enjoy beauty, youth, and music . . . yes, dear mom? . . . ,

"Buy her some fruit . . . ," Meladze said.

"What kind of fruit?" I didn't understand.

"Buy her some sweet cherries, sweet cherries . . ."

. . . Meanwhile, in her grey dress, without any covers and all curled up, my mom had settled on the cot. When I walked in, she looked at me and smiled slightly in such a familiar way, so simply, as in evenings past.

"Mom, "I said reproachfully, "I'll sleep on the cot."

---

ii   "my dear boy" in Georgian. —Trans.

"No, no," she said with childish stubbornness and laughed.
"Do you like sweet cherries?" I asked.
"What?" She didn't understand.
"Sweet cherries, do you like sweet cherries?" I asked.
"Me?" she asked . . .

December 1985

NOTES

1. Karaganda: both a city and an oblast in Kazakhstan. Labor camp prisoners worked in the coal mines there.
2. Meladze speaks with a Georgian accent (he does not palatalize his consonants, for example) and makes grammatical mistakes in his Russian. It is difficult to capture the quality of his speech in English.
3. When World War II ended, the Soviet Zone included the Berlin suburb of Babelsberg, where there was a very rich archive of films and documents. The archive was sent to Moscow and eventually tens of films made in Germany were shown to the Soviet public. Such films, seized after the war, were referred to as "war trophy" films.
4. In German, "Die Frau meiner Träume." The film, a musical comedy, was made in 1944 in Berlin. Marika Rökk (1913-2004), of Hungarian background, was born in Cairo, Egypt. She appeared in movies in England and Hungary and then moved to Berlin in 1935, where she married a German director. Extremely popular with German audiences, she also socialized with high officials of the Third Reich.
5. *lobio*: a popular Georgian dish made from string or red beans, garlic, walnuts, and other ingredients.
6. Batyq: a city in the Karaganda Oblast, Kazakhstan.
7. Zharyk: a city in the Karaganda Oblast, Kazakhstan.

THE FAKIR

Tatiana Tolstaya

Filin—as always, unexpectedly—was suddenly on the phone, issuing an invitation to take a look at his new passion. The program for the evening was clear: a crisp white tablecloth, lights, warmth, special puff-pastry pirozhki Tmutarakan[1] style, the most pleasant music coming from somewhere in the ceiling, and engaging conversation. Dark blue curtains everywhere, glass cases with his collections, and beads hanging here and there on the walls. His new toys—be it a snuffbox with a portrait of a lady reveling in her rosy, naked powdered self, or a beaded change purse, or perhaps an Easter egg, or something else—useless but valuable.

Filin himself won't offend the eye either—clean, small, in a velvet smoking jacket, his small hand weighed down by a ring. And not a cheap, run-of-the-mill one, "for a ruble fifty with the box"—what in the world for? No, directly from excavations, Venetian, if he's not lying, or else with a coin in the setting—some Antiochus,[2] Lord forgive me, or something even more grand . . . That's Filin. He'll be sitting in his armchair, lightly swinging the slipper on his foot, his fingers on both hands brought together to form a steeple, his eyebrows the color of coal-tar, wonderful Anatolian eyes the color of soot, and a small, dry, silvery beard that rustles and is black only around his mouth, as if he had been eating coal.

There's certainly enough to look at.

Filin's ladies are not just ordinary ones either—they're the rare, vintage kind. Either a circus performer hovers on a pole to a drum roll, her scales glittering, or simply a young girl, a pampered little thing, paints in watercolor—no brains to speak of, but on the other hand her skin is unusually white, so that Filin, in issuing an invitation to the viewing, even warns: be sure to come in dark glasses, he says, to avoid snow blindness.

Some people, without saying a word, didn't approve of Filin with all those rings of his, the pirozhki and snuff-boxes; they would snicker at his raspberry robe with the tassels and his supposedly silver Janissary[3] slippers with the turned-up tips; and it was amusing that in his bathroom he had a special brush for his beard and cream for his hands—he, a bachelor...

And nevertheless, if he called, people would come running and secretly always grow numb with worry: would he invite them again, allow them to sit in the warmth and light and be cared for in comfort—although, generally speaking, what does he see in us, ordinary people, what does he need us for...?

"...If you're not doing anything today, please come at eight o'clock. You'll meet Alisa[4]—a cha-ar-ming creature."

"Thank, thank you. Of course."

Well, like always, at the last minute! Yura reached for his razor, and Galia, wriggling into her pantyhose like a snake, instructed her daughter: the kasha's in the pan, don't open the door to anyone, do your homework, and off to sleep! And don't cling to me, don't, we're late as it is! Galia stuffed some plastic bags in her purse. Filin lives in a high rise and there's a grocery store on the first floor; perhaps they'll be selling herring spread, or something else will come her way.

Behind their building the beltway lay like a hoop of gloom where it was freezing cold and the wind whistled from time to time, where the cold of uninhabited plains penetrated your clothing, and where for an instant the world seemed terrifying, like a cemetery. They didn't want to wait for a bus and travel in a crowded metro, so they caught a taxi and, collapsing in comfort, they gently criticized Filin for his velvet jacket, for his passion for collecting, and for the Alisa they had not met yet. But where is Ninotchka, the one from before? Gone with the wind. They wondered if Matvei Matveich would be a guest, too, and made critical comments about him in a friendly way.

They had met him at Filin's and were greatly taken with the old man because of those stories of his about the rule of Anna Ioannovna,[5] and then there were the pirozhki, and the steam from English tea, and dark-blue collector's cups trimmed in gold, and Mozart murmuring from somewhere up above, and Filin, caressing his guests with his Mephistophelian eyes—goodness, they lost their heads and wangled an invitation to visit Matvei Matveich. They acted too rashly! He received them in the kitchen, its floor made of planks and the walls brown and bare, and in general it was a nightmarish neighborhood, just fences and holes; he was in his sweat pants, now completely an off-white color, the tea was weak, the preserves had crystallized into sugar, and he put them down on the table with a thud, right in the jar they came in, and stuck a spoon in: dig them out, so to speak, dear guests. As for smoking— only on the staircase landing: asthma, please don't judge me too harshly. And Anna Ioannovna never even came up. They made themselves comfortable—never mind the tea—to listen to the murmuring talk about the hanky-panky at court and all kinds of revolts there, but the old man kept undoing the string around some awful folders, poking at something with his finger, shouting about some plots of land and saying that Kuzin, a man lacking in talent, a bureaucrat and intriguer, kept him from being published and was setting the whole department against him, but here they were, right here: very valuable documents, he had collected them his whole life! Galia and Yura wanted to hear again about villains, torture, the ice house[6] and the wedding of the dwarfs,[7] but there was no Filin next to them and no one to direct the conversation to something interesting, and the whole evening it was only Ku-u-zin! Ku-u-zin!—and poking at the folders, and valerian drops. After they put the old man to bed, they left early, and Galia tore her pantyhose on the old man's stool.

"And Vlasov the bard?" Yura recalled.

"Oh, be quiet!"

With Vlasov, everything seemed to turn out just the opposite, but the shame was terrible; they also hooked up with him at Filin's, invited him to their place, called a lot of friends to hear him, and stood in line for two hours to buy a "log" cake.[8] They locked their daughter in the nursery, the dog in the kitchen. Vlasov the bard[9] arrived—gloomy, sullen, with his guitar—and he wouldn't even try the cake because the cream would soften his voice, and he wanted it to be hoarse. He sang a couple of songs: "Auntie Motya, your shoulders, your *persi*[10] and cheeks, are developed through exercise like Nadia Comaneci's[11] . . ." Yura disgraced himself, went out of his way to show his ignorance and whispered loudly in the middle of the singing: "I forgot, *persi*—what part of the body are they?" Galia fretted and asked him not to forget to sing "Friends" as she pressed her hands to her breast: it's such a song, such a song! He had sung it at Filin's—softly, sadly, mournfully; here, so to say, old friends—bald, failures—"have gathered over bottles of beer at a table covered with oilcloth." And everyone has something not right, everyone has his own sadness: "one doesn't have the ability to love, another doesn't care for even a prince"—and no one can help anyone, alas!—but here they are together, they're friends, they need one another, and isn't that the most important thing in the world? You listen—and it seems that—yes, yes, yes, you have something roughly like that in your life, yes, indeed! "What a song—the best one!" even Yura whispered. Vlasov the bard became even gloomier and adopted a far-off look—there, to that imaginary room where the bald guys who loved one another were opening some beer far away. He ran his fingers over the strings and began sadly, "at a table covered with oilcloth . . ." Dzhulka, who had been locked in the kitchen, started scratching the floor and howling. "Gathered over bottles of beer," Vlasov the bard pressed on. "A-woo, a-woo," the dog howled, upset. Someone grunted; feeling insulted, the bard stopped playing and lit a cigarette. Yura went to reprimand Dzhulka. "Is it autobiographical?" some fool asked politely. "What? Everything's autobiographical at some point with me." Yura returned, the bard threw away his cigarette butt, and concentrated. "Around a table, co-o-ver-ed with an oilcloth . . ." An agonizing howl came from the kitchen. "A musical dog," the bard said angrily. Galia dragged the resisting sheep dog to some neighbors, the bard finished singing in a hurry—the howl was penetrating faintly through the walls of the cooperative apartment building—raced through the program; and in the entrance, as he zipped up his jacket, he announced with disgust that generally he received two rubles per person, but since they didn't know how to produce a creative atmosphere, then a ruble apiece would do too. And Galia ran again to the neighbors—a nightmare, lend me a ten-ruble note—and they, who were also waiting for their payday, collected small change for a long time and even emptied their children's piggy bank to the bawling of the robbed children and the barking of Dzhulka straining to get out.

Yes, Filin is good at dealing with people, but we, for some reason, are not. Well, perhaps the next time it'll turn out well.

There was still time before it turned eight, just enough time to stand in line for pate in the grocery on the bottom floor of Filin's building— why, you can also see cows roaming in our outskirts in broad daylight, but for some reason there's no pate to be seen. Three minutes to eight, get in the elevator and Galia, as always, will look around and say, "You wouldn't mind living in an elevator like this," then the waxed parquet floor of the immense landing, the copper plate: "I. I. Filin," the bell—and finally he'll appear on the threshold—his black eyes beaming, head tilted to one side. "Punctuality is the politeness of kings . . ." And how terribly pleasant it is to hear this, these words, as if he, Filin, is a sultan and they really are kings—Galia in her inexpensive coat and Yura in his jacket and a knitted hat.

And they will float in, the royal couple, chosen for one evening to come for the warmth and light, for sweet piano roulades, and they will move to the table, where languid roses haven't the faintest idea of the frost, wind, and darkness that surround Filin's inaccessible tower, powerless to get inside.

There's something elusively new in the apartment . . . oh, it's clear: the glass case with the beaded nick-knacks has been moved, the sconce has been shifted to another wall, the arch leading to the back room has been curtained off and, pushing aside this curtain, Alisa, the seemingly charming being, comes out and offers her hand.

"Allochka."

"Yes, she is, as a matter of fact, Allochka, but you and I will call her Alisa, isn't that right? Please come to the table," Filin said. "Well! I recommend the pate. It's special. Such pates, you know . . ."

"You got it downstairs, I see," Yura was overjoyed. "We-e go down there too. From c-conquered h-heights. In the past even the gods would come down to earth, wouldn't they? Isn't that right?"

Filin smiled slightly and raised his eyebrows—to say, perhaps, yes, I did buy it downstairs, and perhaps not. You have to know everything, don't you? In her mind's eye Galia kicked her husband for his lack of tact.

"See what you think about the tartlets," Filin tried a new approach. "I fear you're the last people on this sinful earth to try them."

Today for some reason he called the pirozhki "tartlets"—it must have been because of Alisa.

"What's happened—is flour being taken off the market? On a global scale?" Yura was enjoying himself, rubbing his hands; his bony nose had turned red in the warmth. Tea began making gurgling sounds.

"Not at all. What's flour!" Filin's beard fluttered. "Galochka, some sugar . . . What's flour! The secret has been lost, my friends. The last owner of the ancient recipe is dying—I just got a call. Ninety-eight years old, a stroke. Do try them. Alisa, may I pour you some tea in my favorite cup?"

Filin became misty-eyed, as if hinting at the possibility of special closeness which could arise from such intimate contact with his beloved dishes. The delightful Alisa smiled. What's so delightful about her? Her black hair shines as if it's been greased, and she has a hooked nose and a little mustache. Her dress is simple, knit, the color of pickles. Big deal! There were better ones here before her—where are they now?

". . . And just think," Filin was saying, "only two days ago I placed an order for tartlets with Ignaty Kirillych. He was still baking them yesterday. I was still able to get them this morning—each one wrapped in wafer-thin paper. And now—a stroke. I was informed by people in Sklifosovsky."[12] Filin took a bite of his puff-pastry bombe, raised his beautiful eyebrows and sighed. "When Ignaty was still a boy and worked in "Yar," the old pastry chef Kuzma, as he lay dying, passed on the secret of these baked creations to him. Go on, try it." Filin wiped his beard. "And this Kuzma worked in his time in Petersburg for Wolf and Berange[13]—the famous confectioners. It is said that before his fateful duel, Pushkin dropped by Wolf's and asked for some tartlets. But Kuzma lay drunk that day and hadn't baked any. Well, the manager comes out and gestures helplessly. 'There aren't any, Aleksandr Sergeich. That's the kind of people we have. Would you like a bouchée? A h-horn with whipped cream?' Pushkin became upset, waved his hat, and walked out. Well, we know what happened afterwards. Kuzma slept off his drunkenness, and Pushkin was in his grave."

"Oh Lord . . . ," Galia became frightened.

"Oh, yes. And you know, this affected everyone so much. Wolf shot himself, Berange converted to Orthodoxy, the manager donated thirty thousand to charitable institutions, and Kuzma—he simply went mad. People say he kept repeating, "E-ekh, Leksan Serge-i-ich . . . You didn't have any of my tartlets . . . Should have waited a little bit . . ." Filin tossed another pirozhok in his mouth and began making crunching sounds. "That Kuzma, however, survived until the beginning of the 20th century. With his old, infirm hands he passed on his recipe to his students. The dough to Ignaty, the filling to someone else. Well, afterwards, the revolution came and the civil war. The one who knew the filling joined the Socialists-Revolutionaries.* My Ignaty Kirillych lost sight of him. A few years passed—and Ignaty was still with the restaurant—something suddenly possessed him and he walked out of the kitchen into the dining room, and that fellow was there, with a lady. A monocle, he'd grown a mustache—unrecognizable. Just the way he was, covered in flour, Ignaty went up to the table. 'Come with me, comrade.' The man began to rush about, but what could he do? Pale, he goes to the kitchen. 'Give me the meat filling, you bastard.' Where could he run—he had a tarnished past. He gave him the recipe. 'Tell me the cabbage one.' He shakes all over, but reveals it. 'Now the sago.'[14] But his sago filling was absolu-u-utly secret. He says nothing. Ignaty: 'Sago!' And picks up a rolling pin. The man remains silent. Then suddenly a-a-a-a-a!—and he runs away. That one, the SR. They dash after him, tie him up, and take a look at him—and he's not all there, his eyes are rolling, and there's foam coming out of his mouth. And so the sago secret was not discovered. Yes . . . and this Ignaty Kirillych was an interesting old man, fastidious. What feeling he had for cream puffs, Lord, what feeling! . . . He baked them at home. He'd close the curtains and double-bolt the door. I'd say to him, 'Igna-a-ty Kirrilych, my dear man, share your secret with me, what's it to you?' No way. He kept waiting for a worthy successor. Now, there's the stroke . . . Go on, try some."

"Oh, what a pity . . . ," the charming Alisa became upset. "How can one eat them now? I'm always so sorry for the last of anything . . . My mother had a brooch before the war . . ."

"The last one, here by chance!" Filin sighed and took another pirozhok.

"The last cloud of a dissipated storm," Galia kept the conversation going.

"The last of the Mohicans," Yura remembered.

"No, my mother had a pearl brooch before the war . . ."

"Everything's transitory, dear Alisa," the pleased Filin chewed. "Everything gets old— dogs, women, and pearls. Let's give a sigh for the fleeting nature of existence and render our thanks to the Creator for allowing us to partake of this and that in the feast of life. Eat and wipe away your tears."

"Perhaps he'll still regain his senses, that Ignat?"

"He can't," the host assured them. "Forget about it."

They chewed. Music sang above their heads. It was nice.

"What new thing will you indulge us with?" Yura inquired.

"Ah . . . By the way, you've reminded me. Wedgwood—cups, saucers. A creamer. See them? The dark blue ones on the shelf. I'll just . . . Here . . ."

"Oh," Galia carefully touched the cup with her finger, "white, carefree figures dancing in a dark blue, foggy meadow."

"Do you like the dishes, Alisa?"

"They're nice . . . Now before the war my mother . . ."

"Do you know who I bought them from? Guess . . . From a partisan."

"In what sense?"

"Just listen. It's an interesting story." Filin brought his hands together to form a steeple and looked lovingly at the shelf where the captive service sat carefully, afraid of falling. "In the fall I was wandering through some villages with a rifle. I walk into a hut. The peasant brings me milk straight from the cow. In a cup. I look—real Wedgwood! What's this? Well, we got to talking, his name was Uncle Sasha, I have his address here somewhere . . . well, it's not important. Here's what became clear. During the war he was a partisan in the forest. Early morning. A German plane was flying overhead. Zh-zh-zh," Filin imitates the sound. "Uncle Sasha raised his head and the pilot spat—and the spit landed directly on him. By chance, of course. Uncle Sasha's temper went wild, he let out a bang from his gun—and killed the German outright. Also by chance. The plane came crashing down, they took a good look—and there, if you please, were five crates of cocoa, the sixth—these dishes. Evidently the German was taking it all to a breakfast. I bought them from him. The creamer has a crack in it, but that's nothing. Given the circumstances."

"Your partisan is lying!" Yura said with delight, looking around and hitting his knee with his fist. "Boy, how he lies! It's fantastic!"

"Nothing of the kind," Filin was displeased. "Of course, I do not exclude the possibility that he was no partisan but simply a vulgar little thief, but you know . . . somehow I prefer to believe."

He frowned and took away the cup.

"Of course you have to believe people," Galia pressed Yura's foot a few times under the table. "I, too, had an unusual thing happen to me. Yura, do you remember? I bought a change purse, brought it home, and there were three rubles in it. No one believes me!"

"Why not, I believe you. It happens," Alisa broke in. "Now my mother . . ."

They talked a while about things out of the ordinary, premonitions, and prophetic dreams. Alisa had a girlfriend who had predicted her whole life ahead of time—marriage, two children, divorce, and division of their apartment and belongings. Yura told in a thorough, detailed way how a friend's car was stolen and the police cleverly figured out who the thief was and caught him, but what the point was—he couldn't remember exactly now. Felin told a story about a dog he knew that would open the door with a key and warm the dinner as it waited for its owners.

"No! How did it do that?" the women gasped.

"What do you mean how? They have a French electric stove, with an operating mechanism. You press a button—everything turns on. The dog looks at the clock: it's time—it goes to the kitchen and takes care of things. Well, at the same time it heats up something for itself as well. The owners come from work, and the cabbage soup is already boiling, the bread has been sliced, and the knives and forks have been laid out. Nice."

Filin talked, smiled, shook his head, and glanced from time to time at the pleased Alisa; the music died down and the city seemed to appear in the windows. Steam rose from the dark tea in the cups, sweet cigarette smoke curled upward, there was the scent of roses and, outside the window, the Garden Ring Road screeched quietly under the wheels of cars; happy people poured down the street, the city shone with bundles of golden streetlights, frosty rainbow rings, and multi-colored crunching snow, and the sky of the capital was scattering a wonderful new snow—freshly made. And just think, this whole feast, all these evening wonders are spread out for the sake of this Allochka, pompously renamed Alisa, who's not special in any way. There she sits in her vegetable dress, her mouth with its mustache open, and she's looking with rapture at the all-powerful gentleman who's transforming the world beyond recognition with a wave of his hand and a motion of his eyebrows.

Soon Galia and Yura will leave, crawl away to their suburb, but she will stay, she can . . . Melancholy overcame Galia. For what, oh, for what?

Filin's palace, nestled in the middle of the capital, was a pink hill, decorated here and there in the most diverse way—with all kinds of architectural whatnots, thingamabobs, and decorative touches: there are towers on the plinths, crenels on the towers, ribbons and wreaths between the crenels, and a book—the source of knowledge—protrudes out of laurel leaves or a compass sticks out a pedagogical leg; or you look and in the middle is a protruding obelisk, and on it solidly stands a solidly-built plaster wife, embracing a sheaf of wheat with a super radiant look that rejects snowstorms and night, and with chaste braids and an innocent chin. . . One even imagines that right now some kind of trumpets will sound, cymbals will be struck somewhere, and drums will play something stately and heroic.

And the evening sky above Filin, above his overly ornate palace, is playing with the light—the color of brick, lilac—a real Moscow theater-concert sky. But where they live, on the beltway—good God, what a dense, oil-coated, frosty darkness there is now, how empty it is in the cold spaces between the buildings, and even the buildings themselves aren't visible. They have merged with the night sky weighed down by snow clouds, only the windows are illuminated here and there in an uneven pattern: small gold, green, and red squares are trying to dispel the polar gloom . . . It's late, the stores have been locked and bolted, the last old woman has cleared out, taking a package of margarine and cracked eggs with her; no one simply goes out for a walk on these streets, no one looks at anything or looks around, everyone has burst through his door, closed the curtains, and is now reaching for the TV. You look out the window—the beltway, an abyss of darkness marked by double scarlet lights, the yellow beetles of someone's headlights . . . Over there something large has driven by and nodded its lights as it hit a pothole . . . There comes a bright stick—the lights in the bus's forehead, a shaking center of yellow light with living grains of people inside . . . And beyond the beltway, beyond the last weak strip of life, on the other side of a snow-covered ditch, the invisible sky has come down and is pressing the beet fields with its heavy edge—right there, just beyond the ditch. It's impossible, inconceivable to think that this god-forsaken darkness extends even farther—over fields that merge into a white roar, over wattle fences built in haphazard fashion, over villages pressed into the cold earth where a doomed, melancholy light quivers as if held tight in an indifferent fist . . . and farther on again—dark-white cold, the edge of the forest like a heel of a loaf of bread, where the darkness is even thicker, where perhaps an unhappy wolf is forced to live. He walks out on the hill in his stiff wool coat, smells of juniper and blood, wildness and trouble, looks gloomily, with disgust, at the indistinct, windy, distant places, pellets of snow packed between his yellow, cracked nails, his teeth clenched in sadness, and a frozen tear hangs on his furry cheek like an ill-smelling bead—and everyone is his enemy, and everyone is a killer . . .

The last thing they ate was pineapple. And then they had to get out of there. And to get home—Oh Lord, how many . . . Boulevards, boulevards, boulevards, snowstorms and dark squares, vacant lots, bridges and woods, and more vacant lots, and suddenly factories wide-awake, light blue inside, and more woods and snow flying in front of headlights. And at home—the cheerless green wallpaper, the cut-glass light fixture in the entryway, the dingy crowded conditions and familiar smell, and the cover in color of a woman's magazine thumb-tacked to the wall as a decoration. A rosy-cheeked, disgusting married couple on skis. She's grinning, he's warming her hands. It's called "You're freezing?" It would be good to rip off the damned thing, but Yura won't allow it—he loves everything to do with sports, everything optimistic . . . So let him try and catch a taxi!

It was now the dead of night, all the gates were closed, off-duty trucks shook as they drove past, the starry roof had petrified from the cold, and the raw air was turning into a thick, tangled mass of snowflakes. "Driver, to the beltway . . ?" Yura rushed about. Galia whined, lifted one foot, then the other, jumping around on the side of the road and, behind her back, in the palace, the last window was growing dim, and the roses were sinking into slumber, Alisa was babbling about her mother's brooch, and Filin, in his robe with the tassels, was tickling her with his silver beard. "Oo-oo, my dear! More pineapple?"

That winter they were invited one more time, and Allochka now rushed about the apartment quite at home, boldly grabbing the expensive dishes, smelling of lily-of-the-valley, and yawning from time to time.

Filin showed off Valtasarov to his guests—a crude, bearded man, remarkable for his talent for ventriloquism. Valtasarov imitated a knock on a door, a cow being milked, the rumbling of a wagon, the distant howling of wolves, and a woman killing cockroaches. He couldn't do industrial sounds. Yura begged and begged him to make an extra effort and imitate at least a street car, but he wouldn't agree for anything: "I'm afraid of rupturing myself." Galia didn't feel quite herself; she seemed to see in Valtasarov that same degree of the uncivilized that was a stone's throw away from her and Yura—across the beltway, beyond the ditch, on the other side.

Maybe she'd grown tired recently . . . Even half a year before she would have rushed to get Valtasarov to come to their place, invited a lot of friends and, let's say, served lump sugar, rye flat cakes, and radishes—what is that peasant wonder used to eating over there?— and that peasant would have rattled a cow bell or clanked a chain from a well to everyone's general amazement and noisy excitement. But now it somehow suddenly became clear that nothing would come of it. If you invite him—well, the guests would have a laugh and leave, but Valtasarov would stay, perhaps ask to stay. Free up a room, but it's a room you go through to get to another; he would drop off around nine, there'd be the smell of sheep, cheap tobacco, and the hayloft; at night he would feel his way to the kitchen for some water, bump into a chair in the dark . . . Quiet cursing. Dzhulka would start barking, their daughter would wake up . . . And maybe he's a lunatic—he'd walk into their bedroom in the dark—in a white shirt and felt boots . . . He'd rummage about . . . And in the morning, when you actually don't want to see anyone, when you're rushing to get to work and your hair is disheveled and it's cold—the old man would be sitting in the kitchen, drinking his tea a for long time, and then he'd pull out scraps of paper he couldn't read from his homespun coat. "Daughter, look, they gave me some medicine . . . Cures everything . . . How can I get it . . . ?"

No, no, there's no point even in thinking of getting involved with him!

It's only Filin, the tireless one, who's capable of picking up, feeding, and entertaining no matter who—and us, us, too, of course! Oh, Filin! Generous owner of the golden fruit, he passes it out left and right, gives food to the hungry and drink to the thirsty; if he waves his hand, gardens bloom, women grow prettier, bores become inspired, and crows sing like nightingales.

That's what he's like! That's what he is!

And what remarkable friends he has . . . Ignaty Kirillych, the dough expert. Or that ballerina he visits—Doltseva-Yelanskaya . . .

"It's a stage name, of course," Filin swings his foot, admiring the ceiling. "When she was a girl—Sobakina, Olga Iyeronimovna. With her first husband's name—Koshkina, with the second—Myshkina. A game of demotion,[15] so to say. Her name resounded, resounded in her time. Great princes stood in line, brought her sacks of topazes. She had a weakness for smoky topaz. But a very simple, amiable, and progressive woman. After the revolution she made up her mind to give her precious stones to the people. No sooner said than done. She takes off her beads, breaks the string, and scatters them on the table. At this moment the door bell rings: they've come to seal the apartment.[16] Well, she did this and that, and when she returned—her parrot had pecked the table clean. Birds, you know, need stones for their digestion. It ate about five million rubles worth—and off it flew through the ventilation windowpane. She went after it: "Kokosha, where are you going? What about the people?!" It headed south. She followed it. Made her way to Odessa, how—don't even ask. And here a steamship is casting off, the smokestacks are smoking, shouts, suitcases—people are escaping to Constantinople. The parrot lands on a smokestack and sits there. It's warm there. So this Olechka Sobakina, what do you think, hooked her trained foot on the gangplank and stopped the ship! And she wouldn't let go until they caught her parrot. She shook everything out of it to the last kopeck and donated the beads to the Red Cross. True, her foot had to be amputated, but she didn't lose heart—she danced on crutches in hospitals. Now she's piled up a heap of years, lies flat on her back, and has put on weight. So I go and visit her, read Sterne[17] to her. Yes, Olechka Sobakina, from a family of merchants . . . How much strength there is in our people! How much unspent strength . . ."

Galia looked at Filin with adoration. Somehow, he had suddenly revealed his true self—attractive, unselfish, hospitable . . . Ah, that mustached Alka is lucky! But she doesn't appreciate him, looks with the indifferent, shining eyes of a lemur at her guests, Filin, and the flowers and pastries as if all this is in the natural order of things, as if that's the way it's supposed to be! As if far away, on the edge of the world, Galia's daughter, dog, and "You're freezing" aren't pining away—hostages in the darkness on the threshold of an aspen forest shaking with rage.

For dessert they ate grapefruit stuffed with shrimp, and the magical old man drank tea from his saucer.

And the heart was heavy.

At home, as she lay in the dark, listening to the glassy ringing of the aspens in the wind, the droning of the sleepless beltway, the rustling of the wolf's fur in the distant forest, and the stirring of the frozen beet leaves under the snow cover, she thought: we'll never make it out of here. Someone nameless, indifferent, like fate, gave the orders: let this one, this one, and this one live in a palace. Let them feel good. But those over there, and those, and those too, and Galia and Yura—live there. No, not there, but wa-a-ay o-over there, yes, yes, that's right.

By the ditch, beyond the vacant lots. And don't try to push your way in, there's no point. The conversation is over. But why?! Allow me to ask?! But fate has already turned her back and is laughing with the others, and her iron back is strong—you won't get any response. If you want to—go into hysterics, roll on the floor, and kick your legs; if you want to—keep your head down and quietly go berserk, accumulating doses of cold poison in your teeth.

They tried to get out, tried to exchange apartments; they put up ads, cut out apartment notices and eviscerated apartment exchange bulletins until the paper was all lacy holes, made phone calls and humiliated themselves: "We have a forest here . . . wonderful air . . . it's great for a child, don't even need a dacha . . . you're like that! I'm hearing it from a lunatic . . . !" They filled notebooks with jottings: "Zinaida Samoilovna will think about it . . . Ksana will call again . . . Peter Ivanych wants one only if it has a balcony . . ." Miraculously, Yura found some old woman; she lived alone in a three-room apartment on a first floor on Patriarch's Pond[18] and was capricious. Fifteen families began spinning on the exchange chain, each one with its own demands, heart attacks, crazy women neighbors, broken hearts, and lost birth certificates. They took the capricious old woman here and there in a taxi, got her expensive medicine, warm shoes, ham, and promised her money. Any minute now everything was to come true, thirty-eight people trembled and snarled at each other, weddings were called off, summer vacations fell through, some Simakov in the chain dropped out—a perforated ulcer, not important, out of the way!—the ranks closed, more effort, the old woman fusses, resists, signs the documents under awful pressure, and at the moment when a rosy angel was filling in the orders with an air pen somewhere there in the spheres beyond the clouds, whammo!—she changed her mind. Just like that—she went and changed her mind. And all of you—leave her alone.

The howl of fifteen families shook the earth, the axis of the equator deviated from its position, volcanoes erupted, typhoon "Anna" washed away a young, poorly developed country, the Himalayas rose even higher, and the Mariana Trench descended even deeper, but Galia and Yura stayed just where they were. And the wolves roared with laughter in the forest. For it is said: if you've been told to chirp, don't purr. If you've been told to purr, don't try to chirp.

"Should we write a denunciation of the old woman?" Galia wondered. "Yes, but to whom?" Looking drawn, Yura didn't give a damn; it was sad to look at him. They considered this and that—no place to write to. Perhaps to the Apostle Peter, so that he wouldn't admit that toadstool into paradise. Yura picked up some rocks in a quarry and went at night to Patriarch's Pond to break the windows on the first floor, but he returned with the news that the glass was already broken—they weren't the only ones who were that clever.

Then, of course, they cooled off.

Now she was lying and thinking about Filin: how he brings his hands together to form a steeple, smiles, swings his leg, raises his eyes to the ceiling, and talks . . . She would have so much to say to him . . . Bright light, bright flowers, his bright silver beard with the black area around his mouth. Of course, Alisa is no match for him, and she can't appreciate his wonderland. And she doesn't deserve it. There should be someone understanding . . .

"Bla-bla-bla," Yura began making smacking sounds in his sleep.

. . . Yes, someone sensitive . . . To steam his raspberry-colored robe . . . Draw his bath . . . Slippers . . .

Divide their things this way: let Yura take the apartment, the dog, and the furniture. Galia will take their daughter, some bedding, the iron, the clothes washer. The toaster. The mirror in the hallway. Mother's good forks. The pot with the violet. And that's probably all.

No, that's foolishness. Can he really understand Galia's life, Galia's third-rate existence, the humiliations, the jabs at her soul? Can you really tell him what it's like? Can you really tell him—take, for example, how Galia got—through cunning, bribery, and the required phone calls—a ticket to the Bolshoi Theater, in the orchestra section!!!—just one single ticket (true, Yura was not interested in the arts); how she washed, put her hair in steam rollers and curled it, preparing for the big event; how she tip-toed out of the house, anticipating and cherishing the golden feeling of the sublime in herself, but it was autumn, rain came pouring down, and a taxi couldn't be found, and Galia rushed around in the mud, cursing the heavens, fate, and the city builders, and when she finally made her way to the theater, she discovered that she'd forgotten her dress shoes at home, and her feet—oh, my . . . The tops of her boots were stained, there were yellow-red pancakes of mud on her soles, with grass sticking out of them in clumps—vulgar wheatgrass, crabgrass from the outskirts, omnipresent vile stuff. And even her hem was dirty.

And Galia—so what did she do? She simply slipped quietly into the ladies room and cleaned her boots with her handkerchief and rinsed off the disgraceful hem. And at this point a toad came in—not one of the staff, but also a lover of the beautiful—all of her like violet jelly. She began shaking her cameos: how da-a-a-re you! In the Bolshoi The-a-ter! Scraping your filthy feet! You're not in a ba-a-th-house! And she went on and on, and people began to turn around, whisper to each other and look at her sternly without knowing what was the matter.

And now everything was spoiled, destroyed and lost, and Galia no longer was in the mood for lofty emotions, and the small swans pounded out their famous dance briskly to no purpose; with angry tears welling up in her eyes and feeling unavenged hurt, Galia gave the dancers crushing looks without taking any delight in it and made out through her opera glasses their yellowish laborers' faces and workers' neck veins; and she repeated to herself over and over, sullenly and without pity, that they weren't swans but members of a trade union, that they had the same things as the common people—both ingrown nails and unfaithful husbands, that now they'd do their dancing as much as ordered, put on warm leggings, and head for their homes: to icy Zyuzino,[19] to muddy Korovino,[20] and even to that awful beltway, where Galia howls quietly at night, to that insurmountable horror where only predatory sub-humans should be prowling and cawing like crows. And let a white, secure, fluttering woman like that one, for example, make Galia's daily trek. Let her fall into torturous clay up to her stomach, into the sticky Precambrian of the outskirts, and let her try to move around and clamber out—that will be a fouetté!

But can you really tell this to him!

In March he didn't invite them, and in April he didn't invite them, and the summer passed with no word from him, and Galia became all nervous: what happened? Did he get tired of them? Were they not worthy? She got tired of dreaming, tired of waiting for the phone to ring, and began to forget his dear features. Now she saw him as a giant, an afreet,[21] with a frightening dark gaze, huge hands sparkling with rings, and with the metallic rustling of his dry, oriental beard.

And she didn't recognize him right away when he walked past her in the metro—small, in a hurry, preoccupied—he passed by and didn't notice her, just walked on, and now you couldn't call out to him!

He's walking like an ordinary person; his small feet, used to waxed parquet floors, spoiled by velvet slippers, step on the bathhouse tiles of the underpass—dirty with footprints— and run up the worn-down steps; his little fists fumble in his pockets, find a handkerchief, swipe at his nose—swish, swish—and back in his pocket. He's just shaken himself like a dog, adjusted his scarf, and moved onward, under the arch with the shabby gold mosaics, past the statue of the partisan patriarch who has spread his bronze hand wide in bewilderment, with a troubling mistake in the arrangement of his fingers.

He's walking through the crowd, and the crowd—now thicker, now thinner—moves and pushes along as it comes toward him: a cheerful, stout lady, an amber Hindu in snow-white Moslem pants, a soldier with boils, and old women from the mountains in galoshes, overwhelmed by the din and bustle.

He walks on without looking back; he has no interest in Galia, her greedy eyes, her craned neck—he just jumps like a schoolboy, slips onto the escalator, and off he goes—vanished, gone. There's only the warm, gusty wind from the train that has just come rushing in, the hissing and thumping of the doors, and the sound of voices in the crowd, like the sound of many waters.

And that very evening Allochka called and with indignation said that she and Filin had gone to the registry office to file a marriage application and there, while filling out the papers, she discovered that he was an imposter, that he was renting the apartment in the high rise from some polar explorer, and that all the little things were probably not his but the polar explorer's, and that his legal residence was in Domodedovo![22] And that she proudly flung the papers at him and left. Not because of Domodedovo, of course, but because her pride wouldn't allow her to marry a man who had told her so many lies. And so that they, too, should know who they were dealing with.

So that's how things are . . . And they associated with him! Why, he's in no way better than they are, he's the same as them, mimicking, pretending; he's simply a pathetic dwarf, a clown in the robe of a padishah! She and Yura are a thousand times more honest! But does he at least now understand that he's guilty, that he's been found out, that he's been caught?

Even from the landing you could tell that someone had been cooking fish. Galia rang. Filin opened the door and was clearly surprised. He was alone and looked bad, worse than Dzhulka. Let him have it! Why stand on ceremony? He was alone and brazenly eating cod to the music of Brahms, and he had placed a vase with white carnations in front of him.

"Galochka, what a surprise! Didn't forget me . . . Come in—pike-perch Orly, fresh." Filin moved the cod toward her.

"I know everything," Galia said and sat down just as she was—in her coat. "Alisa told me everything."

"Yes, Alisa, Alisa, that treacherous woman! Well, how about some fish?"

"No, thank you! And I know about Domodedovo. And about the polar explorer."

"Yes, it's an awful story," Filin became upset. "Three years the man spent in Antarctica, and he would have stayed there longer—it's romantic—and suddenly such misfortune. But Ilizarov[23] will help, I have faith. They make them in our country."

"Make what?" Galia was taken aback.

"Ears. You don't know? My explorer's ears got frostbitten. A Siberian who does things in a big way, they were celebrating March 8[24] there with the Norwegians, and one Norwegian liked his hat with the ear flaps, so he went ahead and traded hats with him. For a cap. But outside it was 80 degrees below and in the living quarters, twenty above. A hundred degree difference in temperature—is it conceivable? They called him from the outside: "Lyokha!" He poked his head out, and before you could count to two, his ears fell off. Well, of course, there was panic, they reprimanded him, and the ears—into a box and now they're heading on a plane to Kurgan,[25] to Ilizarov. So . . . I'm leaving."

Galia tried in vain to find something to say. Something more painful.

"And in general," Filin sighed, "it's fall. Sad. Everyone has abandoned me. Alisa has left . . . Matvei Matveich doesn't show his nose. . . Perhaps he's died? Only you, Galochka . . . Only you could, if you wished to. Well, now I'll be closer to you. Now closer. Have a bite of the pike-perch. 'Einmal in der Woche—Fisch!' which means: once a week—fish! Who said it? Well, who of the great ones said it?"

"Goethe?" Galia mumbled, softening involuntarily.

"Close. Close, but not entirely." Filin became animated and looked younger. "We're forgetting the history of literature, my oh my . . . Let me remind you: when Goethe—here you're right—as a really old man fell in love with the young, cha-a-r-ming Ulrike and had the imprudence to ask her hand in marriage, he was rudely rejected. From the threshold. More precisely—from a window. The charmer stuck her head out of the ventilation windowpane and berated the Olympian—now, you already know that, you can't but know. You're old, she said, and no better than the others. One more Faust. You have to eat more fish—it has phosphorus—so that your head works better. *Einmal in der Woche— Fisch!* And the ventilation windowpane slammed."

"Oh, no!" said Galia. "Why ... I've read ..."

"We've all read something, my dear," Filin blossomed. "But I'm giving you the bare facts." He made himself more comfortable in the chair and raised his eyes to the ceiling. "Well, the old man drags himself home, completely broken. As the saying goes, farewell, Antonina Petrovna, my unsung song ... ! He hunched over, the star on his neck—jingle-jingle-jingle-jingle. And here it's evening, supper time. He was served wild game with peas. He had great respect for wild game, you won't disagree with that, I hope? Candles are burning, there's silver on the table, of course, the German kind—you know, with a pine cone design—the aroma ... So, the children are sitting, and so are the grandchildren. His secretary, Ekkerman, has perched himself in a corner and is scribbling. Goethe picked at a wing—and gave up. He doesn't feel like eating it. And the peas even more so. His grandchildren say to him, 'Granddad, what's wrong?' He got up, moved his chair roughly, and said bitterly: once a week, he said, fish! He burst into tears and left. The Germans, they're sentimental. Ekkerman, of course, immediately recorded all this in his dairy. Do read it if you haven't had the time yet: *Conversations with Goethe.* An instructive book. By the way, that piece of game—now absolutely petrified—was shown in a museum in Weimar until 'thirty two."

"And what did they do with the peas?" Galia asked, growing furious.

"Gave them to the cat."

"Since when does a cat eat vegetables?"

"Just try not eating them in Germany. They have discipline!"

"You mean Ekkerman also writes about the cat?"

"Yes, in the footnotes. Depending, of course, on what edition."

Galia got up, walked out, went down the stairs and out into the street. Farewell, pink palace, farewell, my dream! Go where you damn well please, Filin! We stood begging—before whom? What did you present us with? Your tree with the golden fruit has dried up, and your stories are only fireworks in the night, the momentary rush of a colored wind, and the hysterics of fiery roses in the darkness over our heads.

It was getting dark. The fall wind was playing with pieces of paper, pulling them out of trash cans. In the end she dropped into the store that had undermined the foot of the palace like a transparent worm. She stood a bit at the depressing counters—beef bones, mashed potatoes "Dawn." Well, let's wipe our tears with our fingers, spread them on our cheeks, and spit at the icon lamps: our god is dead and his church is empty. Farewell!

And now—home. It's not a short way. Before us—a new winter, new hopes, and new songs. Well, let us sing of the outskirts, rains, buildings turned grey, and long evenings on the threshold of darkness. Let us sing of vacant lots, brown grasses, and the cold of the earth layers under our timid feet. Let us sing to the slow dawns in autumn, the barking of dogs amidst aspen trunks, fragile golden webs, and the first ice, the first bluish ice in the deep imprint of somebody's footstep.

1987

NOTES

1. Tmutarakan: ancient city in Russia that controlled the passage from the Black Sea to the Sea of Azov. In colloquial Russian speech used to refer to something very distant or remote.
2. Antiochus: the name of several generations of Greek rulers of the Seleucid Empire in the second and third centuries BC.
3. Janissary: infantry units that formed the Ottoman sultan's household troops and bodyguard. Originated in the 14th century, abolished in 1826.
4. Alisa: Russification of Alice, a name that sounds unique and exotic because of its association with "Alice in Wonderland."
5. Anna Ioannovna: daughter of Ivan V, niece of Peter the Great; ruler of Russia from 1730 to 1740.
6. During the reign of Anna Ioannovna, who kept finding new ways of entertaining herself, a palace was constructed out of ice on the Neva River, elaborately decorated with ice statues, etc. In February, 1740 Mikhail A. Golitsyn, a member of one of the noblest houses in Russia, married a Kalmyk woman (The Kalmyks are closely related to Mongolians of Mongolia and Buryats of Russia.) and was forced to spend his wedding night in the ice palace on a bed made of ice.
7. In Peter the Great's time it was fashionable to have dwarfs; they furnished

entertainment in the court and in nobles' houses. In 1710 two dwarfs were married in court with all the rites and pomp of a duke's wedding.

8. "log" cake: a cake formed of dough rolled into small cones or "logs" which—layered with nuts, cream, cocoa, and sometimes jam—are piled on top of each other to resemble a log.

9. The bard movement which developed in Russia during the 1960s-1980s centered around people (poets, professional writers, and amateurs) who wrote and performed their own songs in clubs and homes and festivals. The two outstanding representatives of this movement were Vladimir Vysotsky and Bulat Okudzhava.

10. *persi*: obsolete word for "breasts."

11. A reference to Nadia Comaneci, a Rumanian gymnast who captured the world's attention by winning three gold medals at the 1976 Summer Olympics and becoming the first gymnast ever to be awarded a perfect score of 10 in an Olympic gymnastic event.

12. Sklifosovsky Hospital: named for Nikolai Sklifosovsky (1836-1904), a surgeon and professor of medicine in St. Petersburg and Kiev.

13. Wolf and Berange, founded in the first years of the 19th century, was a famous confectioner's shop in St. Petersburg where in 1837 Pushkin met with his second before the duel.

14. sago: a starchy foodstuff derived from the soft interior of the trunk of palm trees. It is used in making puddings.

15. Sobakina, "dog's"; Koshkina, "cat's"; and Myshkina, "mouse's."

16. After the revolution large apartments were taken away from their owners. The invariably big rooms were divided and partitioned to house many more families.

17. Sterne, Laurence (1713-1768): Irish born English novelist, perhaps best remembered for his novel *Tristram Shandy*.

18. Patriarch's Pond: a tranquil corner in the center of Moscow. In the opening pages of Mikhail Bulgakov's masterpiece, *Master and Margarita*, the devil appears here in disguise to wreak havoc on Moscow society.

19. Zyuzino: a district in southwest Moscow, at some distance from city center.

20. Korovino: a village about ten miles from Moscow.

21. afreet: a powerful evil spirit or gigantic and monstrous demon in Arabic mythology.

22. Domodedovo: a region an hour's drive from the center of Moscow, where Domodedovo International airport is located.

23. Gavriil A. Ilizarov (1921-1992) was an orthopedic surgeon who invented a device and technique for lengthening and reshaping limbs.

24. March 8: International Women's Day.

25. Kurgan: a city in Western Siberia.

GALOSHES

Victor Erofeyev

The holidays were over. A little boy was frantically clinging to the fire escape ladder. It was scary to climb higher, but he was too afraid of the rocks to climb down. A third grader was standing below and throwing rocks at him. One of the rocks hit his back, another his shoulder, and finally a third struck the back of his head. He let out a weak scream and fell backwards.

The school principal, like an experienced captain, was guiding the school through the new problems brought on by coeducation. Izya Moiseyevich, the literature teacher, was sharing his views on a recently published book by Ilya Ehrenburg[1] with a grade school teacher, Zoya Nikolayevna. She was young and shy about everything.

One day the principal came right up to her and pinched her stomach through her dress. The principal was dark-haired but still had a young-looking face. Zoya Nikolayevna didn't know how to react. He pinched her not in an obscene but rather in a playful way. He made a fist and said, "You're right here, in my fist." She lowered her eyes. Then the principal said, "Zoya Nikolayevna! I'm asking you not as the principal but as a man. Don't wear that long lilac underwear of yours. It doesn't go well with your face."

Zoya Nikolayevna blushed. She wanted to disappear off the face of the earth from embarrassment.

She was lying on an ottoman and reading Ehrenburg, but it was slow going. She was picturing the principal—side-swept hair on his forehead, skinny. Zoya Nikolayevna tried to sort out her feelings. She took off the lilac underwear once and for all. She found a use for it when doing housework.

A worker came in the morning. He came so early that it was as if he were part of some dream. With a white rope in his hands. He crossed the room and threw open the balcony door, letting in the damp air and wind. After reaching to see if he could get hold of it, he struggled on the balcony with a five-pointed star as big as a human being, all covered with light bulbs like eyes. Unable to get hold of it right away, and with blood rushing to his face, he began to tie it up. The janitor strained his voice shouting something to him from the street. The worker came back into the room wet from the foul weather—sweaty and weak from the battle—and in a muffled voice asked for something to drink.

"And what do you like in the field of cinema?" Izya Moiseyevich tried to ingratiate himself with her by asking a question. "I like the film *Alexander Nevsky*,"[2] Zoya Nikolayevna said sadly, after giving it some thought. The principal had been finding fault with her lately. You're not filling out your grade book correctly, and why don't you take part in the wall newspaper?* Once during a lesson she opened the door to the hallway. He was standing there, eavesdropping. He looked her straight in the face and left without saying anything. "He hates me and wants to get rid of me," Zoya Nikolayevna thought and let out a sob as she lay curled up in a ball on the ottoman. At the time Zoya Nikolayevna's younger brother, who lived with her in the same room, was getting the stove going. A petty hooligan, the terror of their back street. He heard her sob and turned around. Walking past her, he slapped his sister's heavy leg and, breaking into loud, horse-like laughter, said, "You've fallen head over heels in love!"

"Moron!" Zoya Nikolayevna yelled with the pitiful cry of a wounded bird.

They gave the worker some water from the tap. He had time to look around: an expensive television that came with a magnifying glass[3] and was not widely available, and on it a musketeer of some sort with a sword and in short trousers, and in a gilded frame a painting that depicted a bouquet of mimosas, a knife, and a lemon.

With his head resting on his small fist, a sleepy little boy in pajamas was observing the worker closely with his black eyes. Above his ottoman, stuck into holes left by nails that had been used at one time to hang an old, dusty carpet, were thin sticks with small red flags. Every holiday, imitating the way the street looked, the boy would hang up decorations—stars, slogans and portraits of leaders—and on the ottoman he'd conduct a parade of tin soldiers and chess pieces with peeling paint. The horses' faces were completely torn off.

"Left his footprints, damn him!" his grandmother flew into a rage as she wiped the floor after the worker who had already left.

Fumbling with his fingers, the boy buttoned up his uniform pants. Right before he left, there was an unpleasant scene: his grandmother told him to wear his new galoshes over his shoes. She had weak nerves and was proud of it. She had lived through the Leningrad Blockade.[4] In her rage the grandmother pushed the boy out the door in his galoshes without saying goodbye. Swallowing his tears, the boy banged his foot against the metal door of the elevator, summoning the elevator operator. While the elevator operator was on his way up, his grandmother stuck her head out the door, cheerful and young once more. The boy wanted to stab her with a knife.

"Petrovich," the grandmother said to the old elevator operator in a faded uniform of who knows what army. "Here, take some cabbage soup. There's no reason to throw it out. Just bring the pot back." "Work hard," the grandmother said affectionately to the boy.

The elevator operator smiled with his toothless mouth and bowed. As he was going down with the boy, he lifted the lid and sniffed the cabbage flavored liquid with pleasure for a long time. In his youth Petrovich worked as a cook for a number of princes of the Yusupov family. He had gone to study the art of cooking at the "Hunters Club" in Warsaw, and then even farther away, in Paris. Members of the upper crust also lived in that part of the building; clean, black automobiles would come and pick them up. Petrovich would stand at attention and salute. A chocolate-colored "Pobeda"[5] would be sent to pick up Papa. The elevator operator's eyes watered. The boy sniffed: Petrovich smelled bad, but a bit different from the worker.

Outside it was still dark. It was sleeting. The boy could have travelled one stop in a packed trolley bus, but he never did that. People were taking down decorations along the whole street. It seemed for forever. The boy became very upset. Even the forty kopeks he had saved today didn't make him happy. The cap with the letter "S"[6] on the cockade slid down over his eyes. It was too big, the cap, because they didn't get the right size. His grandmother had lined it on the inside with tufts of cotton, but the cotton was now matted down. The boy walked with his heavy school bag through the rain and snow. He turned off the street and went under an archway badly damaged by a German bomb, walked for about a minute more through an alley, and saw his brick school building.

The principal's window was brightly lit. The principal often spent the night in his office because he didn't want to go home. The principal had a damp room of thirteen square meters that had been converted from the bathroom of the apartment in which the actor Kachalov lived before the revolution. There were pipes sticking out. The principal was unhappy with himself. He, a Soviet officer who had served at the front, was putting off the decision from one day to the next. He had executed Germans without a moment's hesitation.

The boy entered the coatroom. There was a swarm of pupils. The boy hung up his coat on the coat rack, his cap was knocked off, and he rushed to pick it up. They started to chase it around like a ball. They kicked it into a corner. He bent down and got a kick in the behind. He turned around. A third grader spat in his face good-naturedly. He didn't say anything, turned away, and wiped it off; someone kicked his heavy school bag, the school bag flew out of his hands, came open, and textbooks, notebooks and a pencil case fell out of it. He began to pick everything up. Someone's footprint was left on one of the notebooks, and pages with rows of pen strokes got folded over.

Zoya Nikolayevna strongly disliked slovenly pupils. She would show sloppy notebooks to the whole class, holding them by the corner with two fingers like a dead mouse by its tail. In the end she did finish reading Ehrenburg. Nothing special. It was about some painters. They argued among themselves. It was boring.

When he had gathered up his notebooks, there was no one left in the coatroom. He stood feeling lost and didn't know what to do. Where should he put the galoshes? Leave them under the coat rack? But would the kids really leave them alone? The boy saw the screaming throat of his grandmother, a survivor of the Leningrad Blockade. The bell rang. Zoya Nikolayevna strongly disliked pupils who were late. She'd make them stand in a corner and send them to the assistant principal, who was nicknamed "Caspian Roach."[7] The boy's cheeks became flushed. He opened his school bag, hoping to put his galoshes there, but there was no room. Suddenly it dawned on him. He stuck one of the galoshes in the right pocket of his pants, and the other in the left one. The galosh didn't fit as well in the left pocket because his handkerchief was in the way. He took the handkerchief out and put it in the chest pocket of his shirt; the galoshes went in, only the heels stuck out a bit. He pulled the bottom of his shirt over the pockets, tightened his belt with the letter "S", made sure he looked all right, and ran out of the coatroom.

The principal was standing by the entrance to the stairs. The principal himself. It was impossible to slip past him. The principal's face was frightening. The principal saw the boy and took a step towards him. Children made the principal sick. As someone who had served at the front, his appointment to the school was painful for him. He had aimed higher. Well-off little boys smelling of children's soap were especially repulsive to him. The principal got distracted: the perpetually late Izya Moiseyevich was flying like a bullet towards him. The principal blocked the way to the stairs with his body. The principal said, "Look here, you . . . stop spreading your Ehrenburg around here!" The literature teacher lost his temper. "But everyone is reading him!" "'Everyone!' Oh, come on, stop it! 'Everyone!'"

The literature teacher's face grew dark and he muttered through his teeth, "Treacherous woman!"

The principal squeezed a bunch of keys in his fist and said, "I have you right here, in my fist!", and left, jingling his keys.

The boy slipped past the angry men. He ran up to the second floor, ran halfway down the deadly silent hallway, pulled on the doorknob, and closed his eyes tight. In the classroom, the electric light burned cold and bright. Zoya Nikolayevna was standing next to her desk and speaking loudly and distinctly. She finished her sentence and shifted her gaze to the boy. He was standing by the door: buzz haircut, black eyes, his ears red. Disheveled. Dirty school bag. She took a closer look at him.

"What do you have in your pockets?" the teacher asked in surprise.

All forty pairs of children's eyes became glued to the boy. The boy kept silent. He could feel the water dripping from his wet galoshes, soaking through the fabric of his pocket and through his brown stockings, and making his legs unpleasantly cold.

"I'm asking, what do you have in your pockets?" the teacher pronounced each word clearly and distinctly.

"Nothing . . . ," the boy barely murmured.

"Come here."

He approached her hunched over to one side from shyness. Zoya Nikolayevna lifted up the bottom of his shirt, tugged, and pulled out a black galosh with pinkish lining. She picked up the galosh with two fingers, held it up, showed it to the class, and said two words, "A galosh."

The class roared with laughter, squealed, and yelped. The children— many of them with rickets and sickly faces—threw themselves down on their desks and grabbed their tummies. The following laughed: Adrianov,

Baranov, and Bekkenin, who later turned out to be a Tatar, and the not fully formed wunderkind Berman. Dorofeyev and Zhulev laughed, hugging each other like Herzen and Ogaryov.[8] The chubby, bug-eyed girl Vasilyeva, who suffered from Basedow's disease,[9] had a prematurely adult, chesty laugh; the magnificent Kira Kaplina blew saliva bubbles; the little monkey Naryshkina squealed (Five years later Izya would ask her, "Are you one of those Naryshkins?[10] Why don't you answer? There's nothing to be afraid of anymore." And she just didn't understand. Which Naryshkins was he talking about? She was one of the Naryshkins from Uzhinsky Street). The following laughed: Goryainova, who went on a two-year business trip with her husband, and the fidgety Artsybashev— he would later become a rather famous literary figure and join the Writers' Union; Trunina, who graduated with a gold medal; Zolotaryova and Guseva, a doctor with a medical epidemiological unit, and also Gadova who went gray at thirty—she learned to play the guitar. Sokina laughed, the one with the skinny legs who would die young from blood poisoning; and the curly-haired Nyushkina who fell down an empty elevator shaft; but on the other hand, the red-haired fool Trunina got lucky—her husband is a member of the Central Committee, granted, probably in the *VLKSM*.[11] Nelly Petrosian also got lucky—she married a Hungarian, and would be speaking Hungarian for the rest of her life— yegish-megish—an incomprehensible language! The frail Bogdanov is laughing; in two years he'll get a powerful kick from Ilya Tretyakov— there he is, laughing at his desk in the back row!—that will break his tail bone; Los, who has a sweet tooth, is laughing—she's a tattletale; Yakimenko will throw herself out of a window in a state of drunkenness, become a cripple, and give birth to twins; Yudina will outlive everyone— on the day of her ninetieth birthday she will walk into the communal kitchen in a colorful, little bathing suit. The astounded neighbors will break out in applause. Only Khokhlov was not laughing, because he never laughs. The following laughed: Sukach the mathematician, who'll move to Vorkuta,[12] and the murderer Kolya Maximov—he'll cut the throat of a dovecote owner; Sasha Kheraskov and the black marketeer Verchenko, who from a young age had been going to the Peking Hotel area to beg for chewing gum from foreigners, shook with laughter. Zaitsev, four-eyed Shub, and Stella Dickens, a Romanian girl from an anti-fascist family, joined in. Ensign Shchapov, who got a concussion during the colonial campaign, karate expert Chemodanov, and Wagner, the flat-chested

Wagner, crowed with all their might. Baklazhanova, Mukhanov and Klyshko fell out of their seats into the aisle from laughing so much, like some kind of fruit.

And Zoya Nikolayevna was also consumed with laughter. She was infected by the children. Zoya Nikolayevna couldn't contain herself and let out a delicate, silvery laugh. "Ha-ha-ha-ha-ha," Zoya Nikolayevna laughed, powerless to control herself, "ha-ha-ha-ha-ha . . ."

The one guilty of all this excitement, everyone's laughingstock, was standing next to her desk with his dirty pants pockets turned inside out. Burning tears ran down his long face from his eyes black as coal and, suddenly, through her non-pedagogical laughter and through the children's laughter, Zoya Nikolayevna heard the boy whispering in desperation and with abandon.

"Lord," the boy whispered, "forgive them. Lord, forgive and have mercy on them! They're innocent and kind, they're good, Lord!"

Zoya Nikolayevna stopped laughing and, continuing to hold the galoshes in her hand, stared wide-eyed at the boy. And at this point she noticed that above the head of the sloppy first-grader, above his closely cropped little head of hair, glowed a thin, round halo, like a crust of ice. "I love them, O Lord!" the boy whispered. "A saint!" the teacher exclaimed, feeling faint, and her face took on a terribly stupid look.

"What's going on here?!" the principal all of a sudden loomed in the doorway. "A madhouse! Stop it!"

Everything died down. Zoya Nikolayevna stood with the child's galoshes in her hand and looked vacantly at the principal.

"You're disrupting the classes in my school!" the principal hissed at her, shaking the side-swept hair on his forehead. "Come out into the hallway!"

Without understanding anything, as if in a dream, Zoya Nikolayevna went out into the hallway with the galoshes. The principal shut the classroom door, and the abandoned children immediately resumed making a racket.

"And so, what are these galoshes?" the principal asked with a savage look on his face.

"They belong to one of the boys . . . ," Zoya Nikolayevna babbled. "You see," she opened her eyes wide, "he turned out to be a saint . . ."

The principal took the small galoshes out of Zoya Nikolayevna's hands, put them in his big hand, and thoughtfully examined their pinkish lining.

"Zoya Nikolayevna!" he said, the sharp, bad smell from a man's mouth hitting her in the face. "Really, this can't go on any longer. I have a room of thirteen square meters. Right in the center. Move in with me. Be my wife."

Zoya Nikolayevna let out a weak scream and fell backwards from the fire escape.

1988

NOTES

1. Ilya Ehrenburg (1891-1967): a prolific writer and journalist. The reference is to his novel, *The Thaw*, published in 1954.
2. Alexander Nevsky: a famous 1938 film by Sergei Eisenstein chronicling the story of the 13th century Russian price who led an army against the Teutonic Knights.
3. Early Soviet TV sets had such small screens that a magnifying glass was mounted in front of the screen in order to enlarge the picture.
4. Leningrad Blockade (or the Siege of Leningrad): German forces encircled Leningrad in September 1941, intent on capturing the city. The Russians would not surrender and suffered through a blockade that continued until January 1944, when it was completely lifted. Hundreds of thousands of people perished from German bombings and lack of food and fuel.
5. "Pobeda": a passenger car produced in 1946-1958, named in honor of the victory (*pobeda*) over Germany in World War II. It came to symbolize post war life because it was the first car to have a heater, radio, electric wipers, etc.
6. The "S" (Ш in Russian) on his cap (and on his belt) stands for schoolboy (*shkol'nik*).
7. Caspian roach: a species of fish commonly found in the Caspian Sea. It was the cheapest fish available and was widely eaten by the masses.
8. Alexander Herzen and Nikolai Ogaryov were 19th century Russian writers and lifelong friends.
9. Basedow's disease: also known as Graves' disease, a condition usually caused by excessive production of the thyroid hormone and characterized by an enlarged thyroid gland, protrusion of the eyeballs, a rapid heartbeat, and nervous excitability.
10. Naryshkins: Russian boyars of Tatar origin. Natalia Naryshkina was the second

wife of Tsar Alexis I and gave birth to Tsar Peter the Great.

11. VLKSM: acronym for *Vsesoyuznyi Leninskii Kommunisticheskii Soyuz Molodyozhi*—All-Union Leninist Young Communist League, or the Komsomol.

12. Vorkuta: a city in the tundra territory above the Arctic circle about 1400 miles northeast of St. Petersburg, the site of one of the infamous labor camps of the Gulag.

SURREALISM IN A PROLETARIAN DISTRICT

Vladimir Makanin

A huge hand was trying to catch a man. This man, metal worker Kolya Shuvayev, worked in the plant workshop; he was a modest metal worker, ordinary, one who didn't drink often. Returning home from the plant, the workers would travel for a rather long time in a crowded trolleybus, and then at the trolleybus stop they would go their separate ways. Kolya would turn and head for the dormitory and there, where he entered his dorm—entrance No 3—he'd be alone for a moment or so. At that moment, a huge hand (so big that all of Kolya could fit in its palm) would suddenly grab him. Kolya would break free, dart into the entrance and, breaking into a run with his heart pounding, he'd rush up to his room on the second floor.

In the entryway to the dorm behind the front door there was a kind of anteroom, an unoccupied patch of space, and then past it, a second entrance door led right into the dorm. As a result, there was an empty corner on the left in the anteroom which, naturally, was put to use. There were shovels and a broom there and, since a demonstration a few days before, flags had been added that some guys put there in a hurry just for a couple of days; after that, the flags were supposed to go back to the local trade union committee. The shovels, broom, and now the rolled-up flags as well, kept falling because the entry door banged so often; they'd be on the floor in people's way, and each time he was rushing out, Kolya was afraid he'd trip on them. Jumping over the fallen shovels, he'd wrench the front door open, and the hand would be in pursuit right behind him. Although it wasn't able to grab Kolya, the hand would manage to hit Kolya's behind or back with its enormous finger that felt like a log; after such a blow, the metal worker would run up the stairs as if he'd been shot out of a cannon. But once at home, he was safe.

However, recently it had gotten so that even in his room he had to be cautious. Kolya's girlfriend, Klava, had the healthy habit of sleeping with the window wide open. (A stocky young woman, a cook by profession who spent many hours behind a hot stove, she thought the room was stuffy even at night. Kolya, on the other hand, froze at night.) That night Klava felt parched from thirst; she apparently woke up, got some water, and opened the window again. Or maybe he had just forgotten to close it himself. In the middle of the night Kolya felt like he was being crushed. He thought that Klava must have turned in her sleep and clumsily pressed her shoulder against him, but no, Klava had rolled away from him—she was sleeping a bit to the side of him (stretched out from the heat). And at this point Kolya felt two huge fingers crushing him. The hand couldn't fit through the window, but it was able to push through two fingers (each like a small, moving log) and, searching for Kolya, they'd grope around the bed. Jumping up, Kolya grabbed the first available thing (Klava's umbrella, which she had brought with her) and hit and then jabbed one of the huge fingers with it. An umbrella isn't a needle, but it's still sharp enough, and in his fury Kolya used it with great force. The groping fingers drew back. One huge finger bent in pain and began to creep away through the open window, and the second one did as well. The hand cleared off. Kolya stood at the window. He was still trembling. He smoked a cigarette, exhaling the smoke out of the window into the night, and finally lay down again on the bed next to Klava, whose large body looked white in the darkness. The metal worker moved closer to her and, unable to calm down any other way, began to embrace her, squeeze her a bit, one of his hands playing with her breasts, the other moving below. "Come on, Kolka! Give me some peace," she grumbled, then she let him have his way while she went on sleeping. He fell asleep only toward morning. He lay on his side with his eyes open and wondering—what to do . . . ?

The hand lay in wait for him during the lunch break (he had dashed out of the workshop to run to the grocery store; there were lots of people in front of the store). After doing his shopping, Kolya decided that he'd first run with the food to his dorm and throw it in the refrigerator. But out on the street he found himself alone. A sunny day, lunchtime, but there wasn't a soul in sight. And that instant and transformation (there never was a particular instant or transformation) was perplexing, when suddenly the hand came down from above and, seizing Kolya with its huge fingertips, began to choke him, crushing his chest and then moving along his shoulders to his throat. Letting out a squeal, the metal worker broke free; the thickness of the fingers and, to some extent, their clumsiness, gave him a chance to get away in the middle of the empty street. Kolya quickened his running pace, flew into the dormitory and, taking several steps at a time, made it to his floor—to his room. The ten eggs[1] he had bought were almost all crushed. The loaf of fresh bread was now flat like a pancake, and the butter (a scarce commodity in those years) got all squashed and stained both his bag and the left side of his shirt through the broken wrapper. (Evening is one thing. But the hand had never attacked him so openly before, in broad daylight.) For the next ten minutes or so, Kolya couldn't calm his nerves. But he had to go to the workshop. Kolya hung about at the exit door, waited and smoked, and it was only when three or four guys came out of the dormitory all at once and headed for work after having had their lunch that he walked out with them. It was a non-eventful day at work. The pieceworkers worked non-stop. In the workshop Kolya picked up a metal dowel pin that was just lying there. The dowel pin was half a meter long, rather thin, but at the end of the day Kolya sharpened it some more, just in case. He took it with him. It was all right. You never know where and why a metal worker is going with a metal dowel pin.

After work he dropped in on Klava at the cafeteria; their cafeteria had been allocated a heart[2] and some blood for supper. But the meat apparently had walked off somewhere to be disposed of on the side (where the profit was). "Just look how observant he is—wanted some fresh meat! Freshly killed, eh?" the cooks began to laugh. But Kolya didn't want anything. He simply said what was on his mind. He sat down at a distance from them and waited for Klava.

The cooks took over two large stoves, that is to say eight burners, all at once; they poured blood into the eight frying pans over the flames (into six dark, cast-iron frying pans used for about a hundred years, and two light, white ones—totally modern). Klava ladled out the blood from a bucket with a large wooden spoon, and carefully, without spilling any, she filled each frying pan approximately a third of the way. A second cook chopped onions. As everyone knows, it's best to fry blood with onions, then the smell of blood doesn't assault the nose as much. "But why take away the taste? Suppose someone likes it with that taste?" the second cook said. "It's better with onions," Klava answered, continuing to ladle out the blood and pour it. The blood poured into the iron frying pans imperceptibly, as if into darkness, but as for the other two pans, it poured in covering the white bottom; when a white frying pan was shaken, the blood would flow from side to side in waves, showing again how white the bottom was. "Why does your metal worker look so uninterested? Why does he look bored?!" the talkative cooks asked Klava after which they, of course, pawned off on Kolya—who was sitting with nothing to do—the task of chopping up the heart meat for all eight frying pans. Using the same wooden spoon, Klava took out the heart—unwieldy, slippery and dripping blood. It was easy to chop it into four parts, but you had to exert real effort to cut each quarter in half. The knife wasn't terribly sharp and the pieces kept slipping away, but in the end Kolya chopped it into pieces that were small enough, and the second cook picked up the pieces and scattered them in the pans. After being plopped into the frying pan, the pieces immediately released small waves of blood which flowed from one side of the pan to the other. The heat was turned up and it began to smell. There was a light haze. And as soon as the door to the kitchen opened, the haze around all eight frying pans would drift in the same direction. They would close the door and the blood would smoke evenly again. Like eight lakes, peaceful and motionless, the metal worker thought with some interest. They turned up the flame and the blood curled up. Bubbles formed and popped and the blood burned. Eight lakes, like eight battle fields, began to smoke and became enveloped in the smell of burning, and it seemed that after gun fire, cannons had finally entered the battle.

Kolya sat for an hour, if not more, waiting around, but when the chief cook came, it became clear that the work in the cafeteria wasn't finished; the girls had to stay, including Klava. Department representatives had arrived and had to be fed. Nowadays money isn't handed out easily. Yes, yes, they have to cook vermicelli again and rice without fail; they love rice. The chief cook brought out two enormous pieces of beef—there was some meat after all. "Girls, make them some steaks, but don't overdo it when you're cutting the portions!"

And the chief cook began to laugh. "So that we have some meat left over for ourselves too. Clear?"

It was clear.

They started to cook all over again; it was going to take a long time

(Klava told Kolya not to wait; she'd be late but, of course, back by midnight). Kolya left. He rode a trolleybus for a long time.

It was already dark near the building and only one solitary light was burning above the entrance to the dormitory. Kolya had already crossed the dark area; everything was quiet. He decided that he had left the danger behind him. He had already begun to whistle when he heard a rush of air, a gust of wind.

Immediately the hand was there. It had probably lost Kolya in the semi-darkness, but now overtaking him, it swiftly pushed itself through the open door of the dormitory and began to grope around there with its three huge fingers (usually it was able to force only two of them inside). Kolya got the dowel pin ready and wondered if he should jab the hand. But he hesitated—pain would make the hand even more angry and active. It was simpler to dash between the groping fingers (searching blindly, the hand would stick them inside and then slowly withdraw them again), and Kolya, of course, would have succeeded, if he had jumped with a bit more daring. The third finger, although it got in the way of the other two fingers groping around in the anteroom, nevertheless was also moving about and blocking his way. And when Kolya jumped, the dowel pin in his hand somehow got in the way of the fingers in the limited space; Kolya stumbled, managed to throw down the dowel pin and even run past to the entrance, but he fell. Immediately huge fingers grabbed him by the foot and dragged him outside, and an enormous fingernail—a lusterless oval mirror—came right up to his face. Then these fingers began to press Kolya's face into the mirror. His nose, eyebrows, and lips—everything became flattened. The metal worker began to twitch, but his face was being pressed ever more firmly against the giant, lusterless fingernail. The size of the fingers got in their own way, and Kolya struggled with all his might, wriggled, thrashed his feet in the air, and in the end managed to break free. He rushed to the entrance steps on all fours while the hand, with its sizable fingers searching for what it had lost, moved along the pavement right next to him. In that instant Kolya saw his cap which had fallen off his head during the first minute of the attack; enraged, he suddenly dashed for the cap, saying "it's my cap," picked it up and, along with it, he also grabbed the dowel pin lying next to it and now, armed, he jabbed and hit and again jabbed the big, light-grey flesh. Blood streamed from the blue wounds. The hand grew still, the fingers drew back in pain, and Kolya jabbed it again as hard as he could. The hand moved away from the dormitory entrance—this time it spurted away—and Kolya, in a surge of daring, jumped out in pursuit, brandishing the dowel pin like a sword. Immediately he was hit and fell down in a puddle near the entrance; his cap flew off again.

But now it was over; the hand was totally gone. Kolya got up. He went up to his room and there, at the sink, washed the dirt off his face and his knees, skinned from the fall. "It's a good thing I shoved the pin under its nail," Kolya thought, washing himself and still shaking.

To have a talk and drink some beer with Valera Tutov—that's what Kolya felt like doing. (Valera Tutov was bold, women loved him, he mixed easily with his educated neighbors and, in general, he knew all kinds of things about life, or at least had heard about them; moreover, they were buddies, no matter what. A friend is a friend.) But Valera Tutov was far away, on vacation. So there was nothing left for Kolya the metal worker to do on this free evening but wait for Klava. Kolya sighed. Klavka was also a good person—he and Klava were going to get married.

Downcast, Kolya went to the dormitory living room, a long common room on the first floor where there was a TV and where the men who had returned from work were already seating themselves and arguing excitedly; they were waiting for soccer. But for the time being there were only images of a desert on the screen: a line of camels was trudging along and yellow sands extended to the very horizon. Kolya said hello to some of the men, sat with them for a while, looked at the white grains of sand rolling along in the desert in the wind (little by little, one grain of sand moved toward another—that's how whole sand dunes moved and covered cities!), but then he just couldn't stay put. He began to feel bored and, even before the football began, went back to his room where he lay face down on the bed and waited for Klava. Klava wouldn't be back anytime soon. (The administration likes to eat well, without rushing.) Kolya fell into thought about something else. He didn't know how he was to act and live with that hand pursuing him. He certainly couldn't go to a doctor. The doctor would force him to provide details. The doctor would write things down. Kolya was a simple metal worker, but he understood, of course, that to speak about a huge hand was embarrassing. The devil knows what that was. How would you say anything, even to Klava?

He began to recall how it all started. It seems that during lunch in the cafeteria (in their plant cafeteria), he had focused on a man's big right hand. When you look closely, every man's right hand is stronger.

Yes, the man was eating cabbage soup . . . And later (the same day) Kolya saw a poster. A huge poster done in bright colors: a mighty worker's hand was placing now high buildings, now kindergartens and schools, and even beautiful cafes, around our whole country, and at the bottom were the words BUILD WELL! LIVE WELL! The poster exhorted the builders in such a clear, understandable way. Next to this poster there was a building crane, a real working crane (or perhaps behind this poster hung one more large poster with a crane drawn on it?) Kolya had his doubts; he no longer remembered), and under the crane's boom some riggers were working on the scaffolding of an almost finished high-rise building. There, high up (that detail he remembered), two riggers had a disagreement; putting aside their blow torches, they shouted and waved their hands, and one of them suddenly stumbled. (Either he had forgotten to fasten his safety belt or the belt fastener simply didn't hold.) The man, falling from the height of the building under construction, plummeted down screaming, his falling speed increased and his screaming stopped, so that the man was now falling to the ground with his breathing cut off, and undoubtedly he would have been killed when suddenly a hand—that one, the huge one that had been placing high rises, schools and even cafes in a green field—grabbed the falling construction worker and carefully lowered him onto a mound of sand near the cement mixer. Such a strong hand . . . Kolya fell asleep and did not finish his thought.

"Why are you in bed so early?!" Klava came perhaps an hour later. She shook him out of his slumber and got him up. And no matter how exhausted she was from her smoky cafeteria, she said that she wanted to go the movies today. "Let's go, let's go, Kolka, hurry up . . ."

Pulling on his cap and yawning, Kolya said, "I see a movie every day without even going."

Kolya was getting used to it: for example, if he walked out in the morning and noticed that at that moment he was alone in the middle of the street, he would cover the empty stretch with a quick step and rush to the trolleybus. (Where, at the bus stop, there were always people and it was safe.) He learned to cross quickly, to run to the other side of the alley closer to the school since the school fence was made of iron pales with sharp ends, and the hand (and the hand always came down from above) was forced to conduct itself with restraint. The hand would make itself known in an instant; it seemed to hang above, at the height of the neighboring building with the sixteen floors, and it would come down swiftly, spreading out its fingers and trying to find and catch Kolya with those fingers while still in motion, but Kolya would run and jump (he dodged and jumped adroitly like a little man trying to get away). He made deceptive movements and used simple ruses in the alley that was now coming to an end, calculating that the hand would fly into the light pole, jab itself on the sharp ends of the school fence, and withdraw. (And in the meantime he would be already dashing to the noisy street, to the trolleybus stop, where people were standing or walking.)

At night Kolya generally slept peacefully, but only after putting his dowel pin under the bed. If in the middle of the night the window would turn out to be open and Kolya heard the maneuvering of the groping hand in his sleep, he'd wake up (he didn't try to awaken Klava, he didn't say a word), lower his hand from the bed to the floor, take the dowel pin and, sleepy—with his eyes barely open, he'd hit one of the fingers, aiming under the lusterless oval fingernail. The hand would clear off and head wherever it had come from, after which Kolya would turn toward the wall and continue his disrupted sleep. Life is life, and if it's impossible to solve some question, then a man lives side by side with that question. He lives with that question and that's about it. Night continued. Kolya slept. Klava, who hadn't heard the noise, slept soundly too, like always.

They poured themselves half a glass more—Kolya and the compressor operator Valera Tutov, who had finally returned from his vacation.

"I'm beginning to see all kinds of crazy things. My head's filled up with so much nonsense I could go nuts," Kolya began carefully. (He was determined to tell his friend Valera about the hand pursuing him. If the conversation didn't come out right, then he'd explain to Valera later that he'd been drunk and talking nonsense. It would be chalked up to drunken babble.)

Valera Tutov, back from his vacation, answered, "It's the crazy weather. I can't work either. I sit by the compressors and constantly see women, women, women . . . It's enough to drive you mad!"

Kolya: "Ha-ha, women . . . ! I seem to see a hand instead of women. A hand. It pursues me. I might as well head to the loony bin!"

In practice the hand was totally real, but circumspect Kolya said it like that for appearance's sake and as a way of beginning his story—"I seem to see."

The compressor operator Valera Tutov answered sternly. He assumed a certain air. "You know, that's good. Every man should imagine now that he sees a big hand. There would be more order . . ."

But unable to bear the sternness of his own tone, he guffawed, "Ha-ha-ha, it's called surrealism."

"What?"

"Surrealism."

Valera told him that when he had a knee problem and was in an exclusive hospital the year before where he had his meniscus cut out, he heard the doctors discussing among themselves all kinds of cases and psychological displacements.[3] No, they didn't talk about a hand. But be thankful a leg is not after you. A hand tries to catch you, but a leg crushes—surrealism . . . ! (Valera loved to trot out an unfamiliar word. Kolya was put on guard for another reason—he didn't like the talk of psychological displacements. The word "psychological" carried with it the unpleasant word "sick.") "You have to give it some thought," Valera continued. "Take a good look at yourself."

Kolya poured still another half glass; the port went down easily.

"All right, Valera. What else did the doctors say?"

"They said everybody has a moment in his life when something shakes him up. One such moment and the man becomes a schizo."

They drank up.

They were approached by young women from their dormitory, who began to tease them. "How long can you keep blabbing?!" "Just look, how comfy they look sitting on the bench. They drink and chatter all by themselves—oh, that Valera!" "Valerochka! Didn't you have enough to drink on your vacation?" They blabbered like that, their faces bright, and music could now be heard coming from the dormitory. The young women had organized a disco party that evening. (There was dancing. The women textile workers lived on the other side of the dorm; there was a separate entrance). It was either Sunday, or else they were celebrating some event—it wasn't clear. But it was clear that they would definitely get in the way of the conversation. The women wanted to dance.

"We're talking about doctors," Kolya answered somewhat somberly, trying to get rid of them.

"About doctors?!" The young women began to giggle.

One of them, right then and there, led off Valera Tutov. Kolya sat alone on the bench for a while and thought about Klava—should he go and see her at the cafeteria . . . ? No, he still had to spend some time with Valera. (A friend is a friend. After all, Kolya had been waiting for him. How nice it was to get together with another man and make him worry a little by unloading some of your life's problems on him; now you carry that load, so to speak . . .) Kolya decided that their conversation wasn't finished yet. He went to his room, grabbed another bottle of port (from some that he had stashed away. Cheap liquor, but it went down pretty easily today!), and also headed for the dancing.

He asked some young thing to dance, fondled her a bit as they danced, and kept mulling over what Valera had said. They had a really good conversation. It turns out that you can talk about that kind of thing too. And a non-frightening word had been found: surrealism.

It was convenient to stand by the windowsill; you could sip some wine and lean on the windowsill and look out the window at the trees too—nice! Everybody who had gathered in the hall (this was really a movie hall) was dancing, making noise, bustling and walking back and forth, but the two of you are a bit apart from them—you're drinking a nice little port and looking out the window. The glasses and bottles had been carefully placed behind the rubber plant. The drinking was good. And the talk was good too—free and easy.

" . . . I'm a vertical man. I think a lot about the point of life. (I love women.) I see every film there is. That is, spiritually I'm rich, and that's why from above, that is when it comes to spirituality, I'm protected. But when it comes to people—so along the horizontal—I have to fear all kinds of blows and dirty tricks," is the way the compressor operator Valera Tutov developed his train of thought.

"And me?" Kolya the metal worker asked.

"And you're precisely the ordinary kind of man, horizontal. You love to eat, you get along with your Klava, you take home the liver she steals and carry bags of potatoes—everything is good along the horizontal, and everything turns out fine of its own accord. You live like the grass. An ordinary fellow. Everything is wonderful in your life. But in return for all this, be good enough to pay for the trip! And that means wait for a blow along the vertical . . ."

"This way?" The metal worker Kolya made a slow motion with his hand, tracing a line perpendicular to the ground.

"Something like that. From above. For you, since you've made a great life for yourself on earth, the danger is from the sky, got it? Not from the side but from above."

They had a bit more to drink.

"The port goes down great, don't you think?"

"Yeah. It tastes good. But soon it'll be all gone . . . Note there's no vodka in the whole district."

"What a me-e-ss!"

"I don't like this danger from above," Kolya sighed, having in mind the hand that kept coming at him from somewhere among the rooftops of high-rises.

"And me?" Valera Tutov whined sarcastically. "I don't have it any better either: just wait for a blow from people."

Music thundered; now dance followed dance non-stop. Valera Tutov would periodically go off to dance (Valera also danced the long-forgotten twist superbly), so that the conversation continued, but it continued fitted around the fun, in snatches. Kolya became pensive. As always, there was an unfamiliar newness to Valera's words. No, Kolya didn't become frightened. On the whole, he had gotten used to the huge hand; he had gotten used to it and even adapted to its pursuit. He could survive by himself too, without any explanations, but still it's better when there are such words (when these words place your cares in known or understandable places).

"Come on, Kolya, cheer up!" Valera picked up the conversation when they each had half a glass more to drink. "Do you know what that hand could mean? Whatever you want . . . ! One lecturer told me that love always comes to him in the form of an old woman. That's the sign. You're standing in line, let's say, and suddenly someone behind you touches you on the shoulder ever so gently. You turn around and an old woman is standing there. With a string bag. Or with some other bag, an ordinary old woman. That means love will come to you soon."

Kolya answered, "But I already have Klavka."

"Kla-aavka. Do you know how many Klavkas there are?"

Kolya became somewhat annoyed, but then he agreed. That was exactly it: Klavka is one thing, and love, perhaps, is something else entirely . . .

Kolya suddenly became animated. "Listen! Perhaps it's really an old woman . . . ? She's trying to catch me with one hand! One! Her two hands would have caught me right away. But the hand is just one of her hands, and that means in the other hand she has a string bag. Or some other bag. Such a huge old woman. It's mind boggling!" His imagination went to work and Kolya the metal worker got all red.

He imagined a huge old woman, but somehow she's able to walk on her huge legs. Her legs must be like columns . . . ! Kolya (overcome by the port) liked to think about it: such a ridiculous, enormous old scarecrow, like in a movie!

But Valera was no longer listening to him.

"Who's that?" Valera Tutov asked.

He asked and then signaled with his eyes to a young woman with a voluptuous body; she came with a new group of people who had just piled into the dormitory. It got crowded in the movie hall where people were dancing. All the chairs were taken out. That group, as it turned out, had brought liquor with it. The dorm began to hum and buzz again. The voluptuous young woman with a somewhat unusual name, Vassa, who had made such an impression on Valera Tutov with the way she looked, turned out to be new—one of those who had moved into the dormitory quite recently. Valera asked her to dance and now wouldn't let her go. He pressed her skillfully to himself as they danced, and he moaned, but she held back and didn't say anything; when he tried to kiss her, she'd turn her face away and, along with her face, her lips. Valera tried to catch the right moment, but Vassa would turn away from him again (at that very moment). The lights in the hall were almost totally out. The music was turned up full blast.

In the group of people who had come in and made themselves comfortable on the chairs, there turned out to be a big, strapping construction worker; he apparently had come directly from the construction site (he hadn't even had time to take off his work clothes). The hard worker was sitting near Kolya and, after having some vodka, was eating in a business-like fashion what the women textile workers were able to bring out of their rooms in a hurry. Skillfully, he cut a package of processed cheese in half, then moved a can of fish closer and, dabbing the can with some bread, ate it clean.

Kolya got bored watching Valera and his new young woman in the dancing crowd, and now this energetically eating construction worker came into his field of vision, more precisely, his hand did. (It seemed larger than the usual hand; it was strong, all covered in lumps. His right hand.) But could it be an optical illusion? Kolya began looking at his own hand for comparison and also at the hands of the guys who were dancing so sweetly with their girls in the semi-darkness. The construction worker continued to sit in his chair and chew, this time stuffing down a salad; true, the hard worker was sitting close to him, and the other guys were farther away, so that even here it could be a matter of optics and self-deception. That's what you call a hand! Kolya wanted to go up to the guy, get acquainted and ask, for example, how things stood, say, with living space for construction workers, and so on, but the most important thing was to shake this hand as they got acquainted. At precisely that point the construction worker finished eating the salad, got up from the table, and headed for the floor where the women textile workers lived.

But he was passing right by Kolya, who grabbed him by the sleeve of his work uniform.

"What d'you want?" the construction worker jerked away.

Kolya didn't let him go. On the contrary, he grabbed his hand and began to twist it lightly.

"Wha-at d'you want?" the builder flew into a rage.

"Oh, nothing."

The construction worker moved to the side and hit Kolya with his left hand (Kolya had already let him go), but Kolya managed to dodge the blow; it just grazed him. The guy left. Kolya smiled; the construction worker's hand turned out to be ordinary, a hand just like any other.

As he entered the dormitory, Kolya didn't even have enough time to open the second entrance door, so swiftly did he have to jump into the corner with the shovels. (He was almost brought down by a blow.) But the hand couldn't slip inside any farther. Kolya stood huddling in the corner, and the huge fingers kept coming closer, almost touching him. (But nevertheless without reaching him. "That's some surrealism," Kolya thought.) He pressed against the wall and the hand maneuvered with great flexibility as it tried to somehow make its way farther and farther into the entrance; the entrance door made cracking sounds from the pressure. The fingers pressed together so that they could get through a little bit farther, but the metal worker, who had guessed subconsciously that any second now the frightening moment was coming, managed to pull open the second entrance door. At the moment when he thought the fingers would be regrouping, he rushed between them inside the entryway, and even bumped one of the fingers that looked like a huge, white sack of flour. And then he was on the staircase, out of reach.

* * *

At that point Valera Tutov, unusually excited, was accompanying Vassa back to her room The young woman said to him that it was time for her to go, it was already late, and a chance to see her back to her room seemed to Valera already like a bit of success (Vassa shared a room with a girlfriend and she, also new, had left for somewhere just today). Valera tried to seduce her. He spoke in an ingratiating way. Valera spoke boldly and impudently, and then openly yearned to get into Vassa's room and worked on persuading her as he stood in the doorway so that, given the smallest positive sign, he would be able to squeeze inside. A well-known dormitory rule—keep your eyes open—has behind it an unwritten law: if you really like a young woman very much, it means that others like her too (if she's new and hasn't been in the dormitory long, each hour is precious).

But Vassa didn't let him in. In the end she hit Valera Tutov in the face. He was forced to leave. The image of the beautiful and voluptuous woman just wouldn't leave his anxious heart; one remarkable part of her body in particular stayed in his excited mind. This part of Vassa's body was disproportionally large (but not monstrously large, not at all!). "What strength! What mounds!" Valera thought and smiled. He chuckled. But he couldn't forget. Even at work, by the humming compressors, he thought of Vassa. The part of her voluptuous body that had captivated him stayed in his mind all the time.

In the evening Valera Tutov invited her to the movies—it didn't work out. She refused him. From that moment on Valera pined away. He suddenly felt too excited and pure in heart which, to tell the truth, oppressed him. He valued the noble (vertical) impulses of his soul, he valued them very much, but when it came to relations with a woman, he didn't trust those impulses because, after giving in to those impulses, he'd become timid. And because of that, he wouldn't respect himself. "An angel," he said through clenched teeth, "an angel, soon I'll grow wings . . ." Vodka was needed—one had to get good and drunk, which is exactly what Valera did, dropping in on one of the guys he knew (he simply peeked in the room behind whose door he heard voices—there was drinking there).

He quarreled with one person, swore friendship with another. But even drunk, an hour later Valera Tutov continued to wander aimlessly through the dormitory, pining away and still feeling that he was an angel in flight. (It was time to come down to earth. Yes, yes, he had to ground himself and become coarse; his soul yearned too strongly to soar upward.) Valera didn't know what he should do, but it seems his stumbling feet knew. His feet led him. Wandering aimlessly through the dormitory, Valera found himself exactly at the turn in the hallway where the much older women textile workers lived. You could go to them even totally drunk. You could be foul-mouthed, even fight.

That's where he went. His eyes could barely make out a faceless, grey woman in the room (But at least she lived alone. And the room was clean. And there was always something to eat). And looking at Valera Tutov, she shook her head and said, " Oh, you're really something . . ." But it was late and, although Valera Tutov was terribly drunk, the faceless and grey woman of around forty was now wondering what to do. She vacillated: send him out of the room immediately with a good kick, or perhaps do exactly the opposite—give him some strong tea, sober him up, show him some affection, and have him share her bed till morning? She had noticed him in the dormitory hallways even before. Young. But not a bad-looking guy, strong. He'd do.

She pondered and Valera Tutov, silent as well, sat nodding off, and any second now he was going to fall off the chair. However, sensing the situation too, he didn't leave; he wanted affection. He waited. "Ti-li-ti." "What?" "Ti-li-ti, Valera said and finally, choking on the sounds, uttered with great effort, "Tililiv'sion," trying to say, "Turn on the television. I'll watch. I feel like it." He was assuming the role of her future cohabitant somewhat ahead of himself.

"You sure wouldn't go drunk to the young ones."

She upbraided him. Valera Tutov nodded his heavy head and agreed—after all, it was true. He'd never go to Vassa or any other young woman that drunk. He had visited them a bit drunk, he had visited them quite drunk, but never falling down drunk. And now he was falling down drunk.

"Do you have money to get home?" the woman asked.

He nodded.

"Want me to call you a taxi . . . ?"

He shook his head. He had no strength to explain to her that he, Valera Tutov, lived here, in the same dormitory, only his entrance was from the other side; he had no strength left.

"Tea," he said.

And this essentially trifling request (he was barely able to get out "tea") turned out to be a happy accident, sent from above. Valera Tutov drank three cups of hot tea one after another, sobered up, and his heavy lips began to smile. He seemed to become a different man. He smiled (his facial muscles were still working poorly, but they were already beginning to relax). He straightened out his shirt collar and, thanking her for the tea, suddenly left. And his awkward smile hadn't yet left his face when right there, around the turn in the hallway, he ran into Vassa—very calm, domestic-looking, in a robe. The young woman was carrying a bottle of milk from the refrigerator everyone shared in the kitchen.

At this point Valera immediately rushed after her, made it into her room, and hugs and kisses followed. Valera closed the door, slammed it shut, but they didn't turn on the light overhead because Vassa didn't even have time to reach for the switch—so quickly did the young fellow embrace her. The bottle of milk fell and spilled in the darkness, but Valera kept squeezing Vassa, kissing her, even gnashing his teeth and moaning. But this time she didn't hide her lips; she kissed and hugged him too and allowed him to touch and squeeze everything he wanted to, with the exception perhaps of that part of her body which excited him and was rather big. (Vassa was probably instinctively leaving at least something for herself so that she could feel that she hadn't given herself fully and right away. Unintentionally, of course, and partly because she sensed a heightened interest in her voluptuous body.) Her unintentional self-defense, usual for any young woman, in this case became her triumph and her victory and . . . the end of a free life for Valera Tutov. Now Valera couldn't live without this plump, beautiful woman; he had to have her. The next day he and Vassa filed a marriage application at the registry office.

They drank tea with sweet-smelling wild strawberry jam Vassa's Tambov[4] relatives had sent her. And then again and again, joyfully and trembling with anticipation, they would rush into bed. But now, even relatively calmly caressing Vassa during the minutes of passion that overtook them or during short pauses, Valera Tutov was still trying to get close to his cherished desire. Vassa Tutov didn't fully understand her husband. (Now and then she would become afraid of his bursts of passion precisely from a lack of understanding.) Finally during one of the last nights of their honeymoon, already after two o'clock on that crazy night, tired and resigned, she let him. He began to fondle, squeeze her, press himself against her, bite and groan, and seemingly even bellow, "Sur. . . Sur. . . Surrealism . . . !"—with his voice swelling and also sounding more and more triumphant and victorious, but suddenly it all ended badly. His heart began to beat harder and harder and skipped a beat, and then there was one more, strong, disrupting beat, and Valera stiffened as he lay in the bed, his mouth half-open, feeling as if a heavy old tank had rolled on his chest.

Vassa let out an "oh," jumped up, and for a long time and with great effort tried, as best as she could, to pull Valera's trousers on his naked body because she didn't understand how she could summon people here otherwise. Calling for help, crying out, at first only in her slip, then in a robe she had thrown on, Vassa rushed about the corridor the way all young women do in similar situations—confused and howling. And something even worse would've happened if in her rushing from dorm room to dorm room she hadn't dashed into the room near the turn in the corridor where the plain-looking female textile worker lived, about forty years old. The woman realized right away that the fellow had drunk a lot and allowed himself a lot and that, of course, it was his heart. She dissolved a crushed nitroglycerin pill in water and poured the liquid into his mouth, opened the window wide, threw all the staring and gasping people out of the room, and urged Vassa to call an ambulance.

Valera Tutov, his eyes wide open and his mouth gaping, was carefully moved to the floor, and the bearded men in white coats who arrived began trying to save him. By morning Valera regained consciousness and was taken to a hospital. Only after three or four weeks did he, fortunate man that he was, return to Vassa.

In the meantime the hand continued pursuing the metal worker without changing its attacks in any way. And Kolya continued to live in a state of heightened perception. (Only the scurrying noises and rustling sounds gave away the movements of the large, lithe being which would come down and seemingly fall on Kolya from the high roofs of sixteen-story towers near their dormitory.)

During the lunch break, the hand pursuing him somehow lingered by the entrance and, making its way inside, got its fingers awkwardly stuck in the doorway. Kolya made it through easily. Now standing on the staircase, he thought that nevertheless he mustn't anger it today, inept as it was, but at the same time, thinking sensibly yet mischievously, Kolya walked down the steps where he felt safe, kicked the huge index finger with his shoe and jumped back again. (A bit of mischief! A slanting black line appeared across the finger. The tip of the shoe was covered with mud black with oil from the construction.) It was not painful for the hand; after all, Kolya's shoe was not a sharpened dowel pin. But the hand cleared off. It cleared off somewhat languidly and strangely, with a suppressed threat that lingered on. "Scram, scram!" the metal worker shouted courageously.

When they were returning from work together, Klava, ahead of him as always, entered the dormitory, as simple fate would have it, but Kolya was at the entrance, at the door, and he lingered for just an instant; he wondered if he had bought cigarettes for the night. Kolya became alarmed right away and already even heard the characteristic rustling, but he vacillated—and here the flying hand seized him as it came down. The hand moved Kolya's shoulders to its very fingertips and began to choke him (Kolya tried vigorously to free himself, to wiggle out); afraid of losing its grip on him, the hand threw him back into its palm, took hold of him and squeezed him, not too hard at first and then, with all its might. Brains came splattering out of poor Kolya, and all his warm liquid in general, whatever form it took: blood, brains, lymph nodes, urine, and sweat—all of it together, in such a colorful mass, squirted out of him upwards, toward the clouds, and a minute later his skin and bones were thrown over the buildings to the edge of the railroad station, to a dead-end. (Where reeking railroad ties lay scattered and old train cars rusted. Thrown almost under their wheels.)

This is the 2004 edition of the story, which was originally published in 1991.

NOTES

1. Russians buy eggs not by the dozen but in cartons of ten, in keeping with the decimal system of measurement.
2. It is a beef heart, judging by what is written later about "enormous pieces of beef" being prepared for the some important visitors. A beef heart is large and weighs 4-5 pounds.
3. psychological displacement: an unconscious defense mechanism. Ideas, emotions, and wishes are transferred from an object felt to be dangerous or unacceptable to one felt to be safe and acceptable.
4. Tambov: a city 480 kilometers south-east of Moscow, a large industrial and cultural center.

PASSING THROUGH

Vladimir Sorokin

"Well, on the whole, comrades, your district has been working well this year." Georgy Ivanovich smiled and leaned back slightly. "That's what I've been instructed to tell you."

Those sitting at a long table began smiling in return and exchanging glances.

Georgy Ivanovich shook his head and threw up his hands.

"When things are fine, comrades, then they're truly fine, and when they're bad, why take offense? Last year you were late with the sowing, and your complex let down the plan, and there were screw-ups, if you remember, with the sports facility. Eh? Do you remember?"

Stepanov, who was sitting on the left, nodded his head. "Yes, Georgy Ivanovich, we admit it—we've only ourselves to blame."

"Yes, yourselves. You're the directing body, and here you thought that the builders could do without you and be able to meet their deadlines. But they only carry out orders, why should they hurry? But the complex is yours, it's famous throughout the whole Soviet Union and, by golly, plastics are really needed, but last year 78% . . . What's that? Is that a business dialogue? Panteleyev came to see me, 78%—well, what can you say? Can you really say—thank you, Comrade Panteleyev, for your good organization of the district industry, eh?"

Those gathered there began smiling; Georgy Ivanovich took a sip of his tea which had grown cold in the glass and licked his lips.

"But along that line, a real treat. Your new secretary—it's too bad he's not here now—came when it was just spring. Panteleyev, he came toward fall at best, but Gorokhov came in the spring. And he reported business-like, you know, and he related all the reasons, everything, truly in a business-like way. Cement for the builders was brought from another district. Well now, that's just too much. Panteleyev couldn't get into the Kirov district for six years. A plant for drywall is close by, just some 160 kilometers away, and next to it is the cement plant. Well, that's just too much."

"Georgy Ivanovich, we did go there, generally speaking," Vorobyov leaned forward, "but they immediately turned us down. They were linked with the Burkovsky plant, with the construction, but now they've gotten rid of it and are free, that's why it worked out."

"If not for pressure from above, they wouldn't give us anything even now," Deviatov interrupted him. "Everybody needs cement."

"Georgy Ivanovich, of course Panteleyev was at fault. He should've put pressure on them at that point—perhaps there were some reserves."

"Of course there were, it can't be that there weren't any. There were, there certainly were." Georgy Ivanovich finished drinking his tea. "In general, comrades, let's not make guesses, but henceforth you must be more professional. If you haven't figured it out yourselves, shake up the deputies, consult with the executive managers, with the workers. And henceforth let's uphold our reputation like this year. Once we've begun, let's keep it up . . . Agreed?"

"Agreed."

"Agreed, of course."

"Agreed, Georgy Ivanovich."

"We'll try."

"We'll give it a try."

"Well, that's good," Georgy Ivanovich got up. "And we'll get to see your secretary. Don't let him get upset that I didn't warn him—I'm just passing through, you know. Let him get better. And that it's tonsillitis in August, that's not a good thing."

Those gathered there also started getting up.

"He's strong, Georgy Ivanovich, he'll get better. It's just a coincidence, since he rarely gets sick. It's a pity that it's exactly when you've come."

Georgy Ivanovich looked at them, smiling.

"It's all right, all right, now I'll come see you when you don't expect me. Otherwise, as it would happen, as soon as Panteleyev would walk into my office, everything would be clear: he had come to repent his sins."

Everybody burst out laughing. Georgy Ivanovich continued: "But I've just looked in here while passing through—everything's fine. So, the secretary's new. Well, fine, comrades." He looked at his watch. "It's after two, we've stayed too long . . . So here's what—please go now to your various places, and I'll walk around for half an hour and see how things are here in your complex."

"Georgy Ivanovich, maybe we'll go and have dinner?" Yakushev approached him. "Close by, we've already made the arrangements . . ."

"No, no, I don't want to, thank you. I don't want to, but you go on— have dinner, work, in sum, do your work. And please don't follow me around. I'll walk through the floors myself. In sum, to your work places, comrades."

Smiling, he walked through the reception room into the hallway. The workers of the *raikom** walked out after him and, looking around, began to leave. Yakushev was about to follow him, but Georgy Ivanovich shook his finger at him, and he smiled and stayed behind. Georgy Ivanovich went down the hallway. The hallway echoed and was cool. The floor was laid with light stone slabs and the walls were a calm, pale light-blue color. The large square-shaped light fixtures on the ceiling had been turned on. Georgy Ivanovich walked to the end and went up a wide staircase to the third floor. The two employees he encountered greeted him loudly and amiably. He greeted them in return.

The walls on the third floor were pale green. Georgy Ivanovich stood a bit in front of the information stand. He picked up a tack that had fallen out and stuck it into the corner of a sheet of paper. A woman walked out of the adjacent door.

"How do you do, Georgy Ivanovich."

"Good day."

The woman went down the hall; Georgy Ivanovich looked at the adjacent door. There was a metal sign on light-brown padding: "Fomin, V. I., Director of the Propaganda Department."

Georgy Ivanovich cracked the door open.

"May I?"

Fomin, who had been sitting at his desk, raised his head and jumped up. "Please, please, Georgy Ivanovich, come on in."

Georgy Ivanovich came in and took a look around. A portrait of Lenin hung above the desk, and two massive safes stood in a corner.

"And here I sit, Georgy Ivanovich," Fomin walked up to him smiling. "For some reason a lot of work piles up in the summer."

"But it's a sleepy time in the winter," Georgy Ivanovich smiled. "You have a nice office, cozy."

"Do you like it?"

"Yes, small but cozy. What's your name?"

"Vladimir Ivanovich."

"Well, there you are, two Ivanoviches."

"Yes," Fomin burst out laughing, tugging at his jacket, "and two department heads."

Georgy Ivanovich smirked and went up to the desk.

"And so, is there really a lot of work, Vladimir Ivanovich?"

"Yes, enough," Fomin became a bit more serious, "soon now there'll be a conference of press workers. And the press fraternity isn't very active, and there are problems with the plant's anniversary album. Can't seem to solve them . . . Various difficulties . . . And the party secretary is sick."

"And what's the problem? What kind of an album?"

"Anniversary. Our plant is 50 years old this year."

"That's a big number. I didn't even know."

"Well, and we're planning an anniversary album. That is, it's already made. I'll show it to you right now." Fomin pulled out a desk drawer, took out a sample of the album and handed it to him.

"Here's what the sample looks like. Two fellows from Kaluga made it for us. Good artists. Our complex is on the front cover, and our lake and pine woods, on the back."

Georgy Ivanovich leafed through the sample. "Aha . . . yes . . . a beautiful thing. And so what's the problem?"

"The first deputy doesn't like it. Boring, he says."

"What did he find boring in this beauty? It's a wonderful view."

"And I say that too, but he won't have it for anything."

"Is that Stepanov?"

"Yes. The secretary is sick. We haven't been able to get his approval for two weeks. We're holding up both the artists and the printers."

"Well, let me have it, I'll sign it for you."

"I would be very grateful to you, Georgy Ivanovich. You'd lift a heavy load from my shoulders."

Georgy Ivanovich reached for a pen and wrote on the back cover: "I approve of the lake view" and signed with a flourish.

"Thank you, oh thank you," Fomin took the booklet from his hands, looked at it, and put it away in the desk drawer. "Now I'll kill them all with this booklet. I'll tell them the *obkom** *zav** approved the lake. Let them stop dragging their feet."

"Say it just like that," Georgy Ivanovich smiled and, squinting, looked at the papers lying near the blotter. "And what is this neat little thing?"

"That's the June directive from the *obkom*."

"Aha, about carrying out the harvest?"

"Yes. You probably know it better than us."

Georgy Ivanovich smiled.

"Ye-e-s, I had to spend some time and effort on it. Your secretary came twice and we sat and racked our brains."

Fomin nodded seriously. "Of course."

"Yes," Georgy Ivanovich sighed, "Vladimir Ivanovich, we only dream of peace. We'll have peace when they carry us out feet first."

Fomin nodded his head in sympathy and smiled. Georgy Ivanovich took the directive, looked at the neat typing, leafed through it and lightly shook the pages, which made them flutter.

"Well, and what do you think of it, Vladimir Ivanovich?"

"The directive?"

"Yes."

"Very business-like, in my opinion. Everything is clear, precise. I read it with interest."

"Well, then it means it was worth the time and effort that went into it."

"It's a document we need, no question about it. Not just a formal piece of paper but an honest document in party style."

"I'm glad you like it. These directives usually collect dust in a safe. Vladimir Ivanovich, here's what you . . . take this directive and put it on the safe."

"On top?"

"Yes."

Fomin took the packets of sheets from him and carefully put them on top of the safe. In the meantime Georgy Ivanovich walked up to the desk, pulled out the drawer, and took the sample album.

"It's a good thing I remembered." He began leafing through the sample. "Vladimir Ivanovich, you know what we'll do . . . that's it . . . perhaps here's what. So there won't be any . . . that's it."

He put the open sample on the desk, quickly took off his jacket and threw it on the chair. Then he slowly climbed up on the desk, stood up, and drew himself straight. Fomin looked at him, smiling in amazement. Georgy Ivanovich unbelted his trousers, dropped them, dropped his underpants and, after looking back at the sample, squatted down. He clasped his dry and scrawny hands in front of him. Fomin looked at him with his mouth open. Georgy Ivanovich glanced back again and, with his legs bent, took a step awkwardly and stood still, and then began groaning, looking intently past Fomin. Pale, Fomin was about to stagger to the door, but Georgy Ivanovich said in a constrained voice, "You . . . yourself . . ." Fomin cautiously approached the desk and raised his hands in bewilderment.

"Georgy Ivanovich, what is this . . . why . . . I don't understand."

Georgy Ivanovich groaned loudly, his pale lips stretched tight, his eyes slightly open. Avoiding his knees, Fomin walked around the desk. Georgy Ivanovich's flat behind hung over the open sample album. Fomin reached for the neatly done book, but Georgy Ivanovich turned his angry face toward him: "Don't touch, don't touch, you smart aleck." Fomin moved back toward the wall. Georgy Ivanovich let out some gas. His hairless behind rocked. Between his buttocks something brown appeared, growing quickly and getting longer. Fomin gulped convulsively, turned away from the wall, and reached with his hands for the sample album, shielding it from the brown sausage. A small piece of the sausage broke off and fell into his hands. A second came out after it, a bit thinner, lighter. Fomin caught it the same way. Georgy Ivanovich's white, short organ swayed, a wide yellow stream spurted out of it and moved over the desk in a broken stream. Georgy Ivanovich again let out some gas. Groaning, he forced out a third portion. Fomin caught it. Urine began dripping from the table onto the floor. Georgy Ivanovich reached and grabbed several satiny sheets of note paper from a small box on the desk, wiped his behind with them, threw them on the floor and straightened up, grabbing his dropped pants with his hands. Fomin stood behind him, holding the warm excrement in his hands. Georgy Ivanovich pulled up his trousers and looked back vacantly at Fomin.

"Well, there . . . but why are you . . ."

He tucked in his shirt, clumsily jumped off the table, took his jacket and, holding it under his arm, picked up the receiver of the phone lightly sprinkled with his urine.

"Listen, how do I call that man of yours . . . now, what's his . . . "

"Yakushev?" Fomin murmured, opening his lips with difficulty.

"Yes."

"327."

Georgy Ivanovich dialed.

"It's me. Well, comrade Yakushev, it's time for me to go. Probably. Yes, yes. No, no, I'm with a comrade. With Vladimir Ivanovich. Yes, with him. Yes, better in two, yes, you can immediately, right now, I'm already walking out. Fine, yes, yes."

He put down the receiver, put on his jacket, looked back once more at Fomin and walked out, closing the door behind him. Steady drops fell from the edge of the table onto the floor; a puddle of urine gleamed motionlessly on the polished wood. The notebook, cigarette holder, glasses, and the edge of the album sample were in it. The door opened slightly and Konkova's head appeared.

"Volod, was that him who was just with you? Why didn't you, funny man, call me?"

Fomin quickly turned his back to her, hiding his hands with the excrement.

"I'm busy, can't right now, can't . . ."

"Wait a minute. Tell me what you talked about. It's kind of stuffy in your office . . . there's a smell . . ."

"Don't come in, don't! You can't, I'm busy!" Fomin yelled, turning red, and hunched his shoulders and pulled his head in.

"Fine, fine, I'm gone, just don't shout."

Konkova disappeared. Fomin glanced at the closed door, then quickly bent down and was about to thrust both hands with the excrement under his desk, but a car horn sounded a long beep. Fomin straightened up and ran to the window. A black "Chaika" and two black "Volgas" were parked by the *raikom* committee entrance. Georgy Ivanovich was going down some granite steps toward them, surrounded by the *raikom* workers. Yakushev was saying something, gesticulating happily. Georgy Ivanovich was nodding, smiling. The "Chaika" turned around and driving up, stopped opposite the staircase. Fomin watched with his forehead pressed against the cool glass. His hands holding the excrement separated a bit, and one of the brown sausages fell off and plopped on the tip of his shoe.

1992

THE YOUNG

Aleksandr Solzhenitsyn

An exam in *sopromat*[1] was in progress. Anatoly Pavlovich Vozdvizhensky, an engineer and assistant professor in the bridge-construction department, saw that the student Konoplyov had turned an intense ashen-brown color, was breathing heavily through his nose, and passing up his turn to go up to the examiner's table.[2] Then he walked up with a heavy step and asked quietly to be given different questions. Anatoly Pavlovich looked at his face—the lower part of his forehead all sweaty, the helpless, imploring look in his bright eyes—and he gave him different ones.

But approximately half an hour more passed, several more gave their answers, the last four who took the course were already sitting and preparing and Konoplyov was among them—looking even more ashen-brown—but he still didn't go up.

And he sat like that until the last student left. The two of them were left in the classroom.

"Well, now, Konoplyov, I can't wait any longer," Vozdvizhensky said without anger but firmly. It was already clear that he didn't know a damn thing. On his sheet were some kind of scribbles that bore little resemblance to formulas and drawings, little resemblance to engineering ones.

Broad-shouldered Konoplyov got up, his face sweaty. He didn't go up to the board to give his answer but, moving with difficulty to the nearest table, he sat down at it and said in a simple-hearted, simple-hearted way, "Anatoly Palych, my brain will fall apart from such a weight."

"You should have studied regularly."

"Anatoly Palych, how regularly? After all, in each subject they tell you an awful lot of things in a day, and it's every day. Believe me, I don't go having a good time, and I sit nights studying—it just doesn't go into my head. If they gave us a bit less, in lighter doses, but this way, my head can't take it in."[3]

His eyes had an honest look and his voice was sincere—he wasn't lying; he didn't look like a fellow who lived it up.

"You've come from the *rabfak*?"[4]

"Yeah."

"And how long did you study at the *rabfak*?"

"Two years, accelerated."

"And from where to the *rabfak*?"

"From Krasnyi Aksai.[5] I was a tinsmith."

A large, broad nose, and the whole face big-boned, with thick lips.

It was not the first time that Vozdvizhensky pondered: why do they torture ones like that? And he could have continued tin-coating dishes in Aksai.

"I sympathize with you, but I can't do anything. Have to put down 'unsatis.'"

But Konoplyov didn't accept this reasoning and didn't hand over the record-book[6] in his pocket. Instead he placed both hands, like paws, to his chest. "Anatoly Palych, that's not possible for me, no way! For one thing—they'll lower my scholarship. And give me tongue lashings in the Komsomol.* There's no way I can pass *sopromat*, not in a million years. I'm already on my way out anyway, it's not the thing for me—and where do I go now?"

Yes, that was clear.

But then, the life of many *rabfak* students is also "on the way out." What were the authorities thinking when they pulled them into the *vuzes*?* Even such a case as this was probably anticipated. The administration actually specifies openly: lighten the demands on the *rabfak* students. Their policy of educating the masses.

Lighten—but certainly not to such a degree? Even *rabfak* students passed today. Vozdvizhensky was actually lenient with him. But not to an absurd degree! How do you put down "sat.," if he, generally speaking, doesn't know anything? What is left then of all your teaching, of the whole point of education? If he starts doing engineering work—it will be quickly discovered that he doesn't know beans about *sopromat*.

He said once, "There's no way I can." He said it twice.

But Konoplyov begged, almost with tears in his eyes, which didn't come easily for such an unpolished guy.

And Anatoly Pavlovich thought: if that's what the policy of the authorities demands, and they understand what they're doing, what an absurd thing, why should I be the one to worry more?

He lectured Konoplyov. He advised him how to change his classes; how to read out loud for better mastery; how to go about renewing his brain power.

He took his record-book. Sighed heavily. Slowly wrote "sat." and signed his name.

Konoplyov lit up and leaped to his feet. "I'll never forget what you did, Anatoly Palych! Perhaps I'll even survive the other courses, but *sopromat*—they give too much in it."

The institute of communications was located beyond the outskirts of Rostov; Anatoly Pavlovich still had to travel a long time to get home.

In the trolley car it was quite noticeable how the appearance of the city public had become more simple and ordinary than it used to be. Anatoly Pavlovich's suit was modest, and far from new, but still, he was a white-collar worker, in a necktie. In their institute there were also some professors who intentionally wore a simple shirt outside their pants, with a belt. And one, as soon as it was spring, even wore sandals on his bare feet. And this no longer surprised anyone but was exactly in keeping with the time. Time passed like that and, nowadays, when NEP* ladies got all decked out, it irritated everybody.

Anatoly Pavlovich made it home exactly at dinner time. His tireless wife, his darling Nadya, was at the moment in Vladikavkaz,[7] visiting her older son who had just married and was also a railway engineer. A cook came to Vozdvizhensky three times a week; today was not her day. But Lyolka bustled about so that she could feed her father. And she had already set their square oak table, with a small branch of lilac in the middle. And she brought a decanter of vodka from the ice box to go in his daily, indispensible, silver shot glass. And she had heated up and was pouring soup with spoon-size dumplings.

In school, in the 8th grade, she was an excellent student in physics, chemistry, and mathematics, did her drafting wonderfully, and was perfect for the institute where her father worked. But four years ago, with the decree of 1922, they were required to check on the candidates— to strictly limit the acceptance of individuals of a non-proletarian background, and the entrants without a Party or Komsomol assignment had to show evidence of their political trustworthiness. (His son had managed to enter a year earlier.)

Today's stretching of the truth in the record-book was not forgotten—it lay in his heart like sediment.

He asked Lyolia about school. Their whole nine-year school ("named for Zinoviev,"[8] but his name had been eliminated from the sign) was still shaken by a recent suicide: several months before school ended, a 9th grade student, Misha Derevyanko, hanged himself. They raced through the funeral, and immediately meetings, *talks*, began in all the grades, saying that this was the fruit of bourgeois individualism and the decadence of daily life. Derevyanko—this was rust which everyone had to clean off from himself. But Lyolia and her two girlfriends were sure that the school Komsomol unit had made his life miserable.

Today she added with alarm that it was no longer a rumor but a certainty: the school principal, Malevich, adored by everyone, the old teacher of the gymnasium who had managed somehow to hold on all these years and keep a tight rein on the whole school and lead it with his inspiring strictness—Malevich was to be *removed*.

Lyolia ran to the Primus stove for the beef-stroganoff and then they had tea and pastries.

The father looked at his daughter with tenderness. She tossed her head so proudly with its curly, chestnut-colored hair that had escaped the fashion of being cut short; she had such a wise way of looking and, wrinkling her forehead, expressed her opinions clearly.

As is often true with girls, her face held a wonderful mystery about the future. But for a parent gazing at it, the mystery was even more painful: to envision in that future, not known to anyone, the crowning success or waste of so many years of her growing up, getting an education, and his worries about her.

"But still, still, Lyolenka, you can't avoid joining the Komsomol. One year left, you can't take risks. Because, you know, if you're not accepted—even I won't be able to help you at my institute."

"I don't want to!" she shook her head, and her hair got all tangled up. "The Komsomol—it's a vile thing."

Anatoly Pavlovich sighed again.

"You know," he tried to convince her gently, and yes, in fact he fully believed it himself, "the new young people have some kind of truth that is beyond our comprehension. It has to exist."

Three generations of the intelligentsia were not wrong about how we'd give the common people access to culture, release the people's energy. Of course, not everyone is up for this uplifting, this leap. Here they are, wearing out their brains, unsure in their hearts—it's difficult to develop outside the tradition of whole generations. But we must, we must help them rise and meet the challenge, and we must bear their awkward, negative actions with patience.

"But you must agree, their optimism is remarkable, and the power of their faith is enviable. And inevitably you have to swim in this current, not fall behind ... Because otherwise, my dear daughter, it's true, you can miss a whole epoch, as people say. You see, be it ridiculously, awkwardly, or not right away, something grand is being created. The whole world is watching, holding its breath, the entire Western intelligentsia. They're not fools in Europe, you know."

Having successfully gotten rid of *sopromat*, Lyoshka Konoplyov eagerly joined up with friends who were going that evening to the *Lenraisovet*[9] house of culture. Not only Komsomol members but also non-party young people who wanted to go were being assembled: someone from Moscow was coming to read a lecture, "On the Tasks of Youth."

The hall was for about six hundred people and was full to overflowing, with some, in fact, standing. There was a lot of red: at the back of the stage two flowing banners—slanting toward each other—embroidered in gold; in front of them on a stand—a large bust of Lenin, bronze in color. And red scarves around the necks of young girls, some of whom had red calico head-bands as well, and red Pioneer ties on the Young Pioneer leaders, some of whom had also brought small groups of older Pioneers with them, who sat near their Pioneer leaders.

Here's how it looks: we, the young people, are solid friends, although we don't really know each other. This is *we*, here are all *our own*, all of us are as one. As they say, builders of the New World. And because of this, everyone has triple strength.

Then three buglers came out and stood in front of the rostrum, their bugles also decorated with red material. They assumed their positions and sounded the beginning of the meeting.

They whipped up even more excitement with their bugles. There was something engrossing about such a grand confluence: the red banners in corners, the bronze Ilich, silver-plated bugles, piercing sounds, and the proud bearing of the buglers. All those present became fired up by the strong rallying cry and the solemn oath.

The buglers left with the same parade step, and a lecturer walked out on stage—a short, fat little man, with restless hands. And from behind the podium he began to speak not from notes but off the top of his head—quickly, confidently, and insistently.

At first about how the great period of the Revolution and the Civil War gave young people a turbulent content, but it also weaned them of the humdrum.

"This transition has been difficult for the young. The emotions of the specific material of the revolution hit the transitional age particularly painfully. For some, it seems, it would be actually more fun if a real revolution began again; it would be immediately clear what to do and where to go. Quick—press on, blow up, shake up, otherwise it was not worth making the October Revolution either. Well—if only there would be a revolution in China real soon; why doesn't it break out? It's good to live and fight for World Revolution, but they make us study nonsense, geometry theorems. What do they have to do with anything . . . ?"

Or *sopromat* theories? True, how much easier it would be to stretch your legs, hands, and back from standing too long.

But—no, the lecturer tried to persuade them, and he would step from behind the podium, and scurry across the stage, very much carried away by his own speech.

"You have to understand the contemporary moment correctly and make it your own. Our youth is the most fortunate in the whole history of mankind. It occupies a militant, effective position in life. Its characteristics are, first of all, godlessness, a feeling of total freedom from everything outside science. This liberates a tremendous fund of courage and zeal for life by those who had been made prisoners by some god. Second, its characteristic is avant-guardism and planetarism, to outstrip the epoch, both friends and enemies are watching us."

And he looked around with his round little head as if looking over those friends and particularly the enemies from all the distant, foreign places.

"This is death of the psychology 'of looking at things solely from your own point of view'—every detail is examined by our young people unfailingly from a world point of view. Third—an irreproachable class system, indispensable, although temporary, the renunciation of 'human feeling in general.' Next—optimism!"

He walked up to the front edge of the stage and, not afraid of falling off, he bent down as much as he could toward the hall of people. "Try to understand! You are the happiest youth in the world! What steadfastness, what joyous energy you have!"

He ran across the stage again, but poured out his speech without stopping: "And then you have—a thirst for knowledge. And a scientific organization of labor. And a craving for rationalizing your biological processes as well. And a militant impulse—what an impulse! And then—a craving for leadership. But from your organic class brotherhood—you have the collective spirit, and it's so much a part of you that the collective intervenes even in the intimate lives of its fellow members. And this is appropriate!"

Although the lecturer behaved rather strangely, no one thought of laughing either. And they didn't whisper to one another but hung on every word he said. The lecturer was helping the young people to understand themselves—this was a useful thing. And he got excited, and one minute he would raise one short arm, and another minute, even both—calling on them, trying to persuade them even more.

"Look, even among young women, in recognition of the power of socialism being created . . . In a short period of time woman has acquired personal and intimate freedom, sexual freedom. And she demands of the man a reexamination of his attitudes, or else she overcomes the male slave owner's inertia and brings revolutionary freshness into sexual morality as well. Thus even in the sphere of love a revolutionary resultant is sought and found: to switch bioenergetic reserves onto socially-creative tracks."

He finished. And didn't get tired—apparently he was used to it. He went behind the rostrum.

"What questions are there?"

Listeners began asking questions directly from their seats, or by written notes which were handed to him.

The questions started—more about sexual emancipation. One, who could be Konoplyov's brother, commented that it was easy to say, "grow ten years in two," but from this tempo the brain would burst apart.

And then even the Pioneers got bold and asked questions.

"Can a Pioneer girl wear a ribbon?"

"And what about using powder?"

"And who should listen to whom: the good Pioneer to his bad father—or the bad father to his good Pioneer . . . ?"

2

Already in '28 the "The Miners' Case,"[10] so close to Rostov, frightened the Rostov engineers greatly. And they started to *disappear* even here.

People didn't get used to this right away. Up to the revolution an arrested person continued to live behind bars or in exile, he was in touch with his family, his friends—but now? Descent into non-existence . . .

And in the previous year, in '30, in September, news of the sentencing of 48 men to be shot—"saboteurs in food supplies"—passed through threateningly. "Reactions from workers" were published: "The saboteurs should be wiped off the face of the earth!" On the front page of *Izvestiya*: "squash the snake" (with your boot), and the proletariat demanded that the OGPU* be awarded the Order of Lenin.[11]

And in November a guilty verdict was printed "in the case of the Industrial Party"[12]—and this now had the whole engineering community by the throat. And chilling words again began appearing in the newspapers: "agents of the French interventionists and White emigres," and "We'll rid ourselves of the traitors with an iron broom!"

One's heart would contract helplessly. But it was not possible for everyone to express his fear, only if people knew each other well, like Anatoly Pavlovich knew—well, about ten years—Fridrikh Albertovich.

On the day of the opening of the trial of the Industrial Party there was in fact a four-hour demonstration in Rostov: people demanded that they all be shot! It was unbearably ugly. (Vozdvizhensky found a way to avoid it, didn't go.)

Day after day—a tightness, a heavy feeling in one's chest, and a growing feeling of doom. Although: *for what* . . . ? The whole Soviet time they had been working with inspiration, resourcefully, faithfully—and only the stupidity and blundering of the party directors got in the way at each step.

And not even two months had passed since the trial when *they came* at night for Vozdvizhensky.

Then some kind of nightmarish delirium that made no sense dragged on for many days and nights—from making him strip naked, cutting off all buttons from his clothing, and puncturing his shoes with an awl to taking him to some basement facility without any ventilation, with stale air that many had been breathing, without a single window, but with opaque glass pieces, the color of green bottles, in the ceiling; it was never day, in a cell without beds, they slept on the floor, on boards spread out on the cement without being nailed together, all at their wits' end because of the lack of sleep and interrogations at night; some beaten blue, some with hands that bore cigarette burns, some silent, others telling half-insane stories. Vozdvizhensky had not been summoned anywhere even once, was not touched by anyone even once, but he already had an unbalanced mind not capable of understanding what was going on, or of connecting it at least somehow with his former—oh, so irretrievable!—life. Because of ill health, he wasn't in the war with Germany, they didn't bother him during the civil war either, which passed like a storm through Rostov-Novocherkassk,[13] a quarter of a century of unhurried mental work, and now to flinch every time the door opened, day and night—what if they send for him? He wasn't, he wasn't ready to endure torture!

However, they didn't send for him. And everybody was surprised in the cell—in this basement storage facility, as it became clear; and the bottle-green spaces in the ceiling—they were part of the sidewalk of the main city street above, where unconcerned people walked and walked who were not doomed, for the time being, to finding themselves here; and the rumbling produced by passing streetcars reached them through the ground.

They didn't send for him. Everyone was surprised: the new arrivals—they kept dragging them for questioning from the moment they were brought in.

So perhaps it's really a mistake? They'll let him go?

But for a few days they mixed up their counting; he was sent for, "hands behind your back!", and a guard with hair the color of coal led him led him up some steps—to the ground level—and to some higher and higher floors, all the while clicking his tongue like some exotic bird.

An investigator wearing the uniform of the GPU[i] was sitting at a table in a dark corner, you couldn't see his face well—only that he was young and had a big, fat mug. He pointed silently to a tiny table in another corner, diagonally opposite. And Vozdvizhensky found himself on a narrow chair, facing a distant, clouded window; the lamp wasn't burning.

---

i   The author means OGPU*, which he uses in the beginning of this chapter.

He waited with a sinking feeling. The investigator was silent as he wrote.

Then in a severe tone, "Tell me about your sabotage activities."

Vozdvizhensky was more astonished than afraid.

"There was nothing of the kind, I assure you!" He would have liked to add something clever: how can an *engineer* ruin anything?

But after the Industrial Party . . . ?

"No, tell me."

"There was nothing and there could not be!"

The investigator continued writing, still not lighting the lamp. Then, without getting up, in a firm voice: "Did you get your eyeful in the cell? You haven't seen everything yet. You can be on cement even without boards. Or in a damp hole. Or under a lamp with thousand-watt-power bulb—you'll go blind."

Vozdvizhensky was barely able to prop up his head with his hands. And, you know, they'll do everything. And—how do you endure it?

At this point the investigator lit his table lamp, got up, put on the light above as well, and stood in the middle of the room, looking at the man under investigation.

In spite of his secret police uniform, his face was very, very ordinary. Large bones, a fat, short nose, big lips.

And in a new tone: "Anatoly Palych, I understand perfectly well that you didn't sabotage anything. But you must understand as well: no one leaves *here* cleared. Either a bullet at the back of the head or a sentence."

It was not these cruel words that astonished Vozdvizhensky— it was the kind voice. He stared at the investigator's face—there was something, something familiar about it. Artless. When did he see it?

But the investigator stood like that, in the light, in the middle of the room. And he didn't say anything.

He had seen him, had seen him. But he couldn't recall where.

"Don't you remember Konoplyov?" the investigator asked.

Ah, Konoplyov! Yes, yes! The one who didn't know *sopromat*. And then disappeared somewhere from the department.

"Yes, I couldn't get through my courses. I was accepted into the GPU on orders from the Komsomol. I've been here three years already."

And—what now . . . ?

They talked a bit. Completely freely, like human beings. Like in *that* life, before the nightmare. And Konoplyov: "Anatoly Palych, the GPU doesn't make mistakes. No one leaves here that easily. And although I want to help you, I don't know how. You do some thinking as well. Something's got to be made up."

Vozdvizhensky returned to the basement with new hope.

But with gloom filling his head. He couldn't *make up anything*.

But then go to a labor camp? To Solovki?[14]

Konoplyov's sympathy amazed him, warmed him. Within *these* walls? In such a place?

He fell into thought about those *rabfak* candidates from the ranks of the masses. So far, something else was evident. A conceited, crude man had been Vozdvizhensky's superior in his engineering work. And in the school Lyolka finished, in the place of the gifted Malevich who had been removed at that time, a dull ignoramus had been appointed.

And you know, long before the revolution poets had a foreboding— of those future *Huns* . . .

Three more days in the basement under the street, under the feet of ignorant passers-by—and Konoplyov sent for him again.

Only Vozdvizhensky hadn't thought of anything yet to make up.

"But—you have to!" Konoplyov tried to impress upon him. "You've no place to go. Don't force me, Anatoly Palych, to use *measures*. Or for the investigator to be changed. Then you're lost."

For the time being he transferred him to a better cell—not so damp, and bed boards for sleeping. He gave him some tobacco and allowed packages from home.

The joy in getting the packages—it was not even in the food and not in the clean underwear—the joy was that the people at home knew: he's *here*! And alive. (His signature on the package list was given to his wife.)

And Konoplyov sent for him again, and again tried to persuade him.

But how do you spit on your twenty-years of work that you performed diligently and enthusiastically? Simply spit on yourself, on your own soul?

And Konoplyov: "Without a *result,* the investigation will be given over any minute to another."

And one day he also said, "I've thought of something. And I've received approval. There is a way to freedom: you must sign a commitment to provide us with information that's needed."

Vozdvizhensky leaned back in his chair.

"How can . . . ? How . . . such a thing? And—what information can I give you?"

"Oh, about the mood in the engineering area. About some of your acquaintances, for example, Fridrikh Verner. And there are more things on the list."

Vozdvizhensky clutched his head.

"I can't do this—I cannot!"

Konoplyov shook his head. He simply couldn't believe it.

"So—to the camps? Bear in mind: your daughter will be dismissed from her last year as a class enemy. And perhaps the confiscation of your property, your apartment. I'm proposing a good thing for you."

Anatoly Pavlovich sat without feeling the chair under him and as if he had gone blind and couldn't even see Konoplyov.

He fell on his hands on the table—and started to cry.

In a week he was freed.

1993

NOTES

1. *sopromat*: acronym for *soprotivleniye materialov*, meaning "the study of the strength of materials."
2. In Soviet times oral exams were the rule. Students would pick up written questions lying on the professor's desk, take some time to prepare in the classroom, and then approach the professor and answer the questions.
3. His speech shows the influence of Ukrainian.
4. *rabfak*: acronym for *rabochii fakul'tet*, "workers' faculty," a division of courses for peasants and workers set up to prepare them for entrance to institutions of higher learning.
5. Krasnyi Aksai: a plant founded to produce soil-cultivating machinery; located in Rostov-na-Donu (Rostov-on-Don) in the southwestern part of Russia.
6. In the Russian system, the student brings a small booklet in which his grades are recorded.
7. Vladikavkaz: capital of North Ossetia, located at the northern foot of the

Caucasus Mountains.

8. Zinoviev, Grigory (1883-1936): Bolshevik revolutionary who, with Trotsky and others, opposed Stalin in 1926-1927, was forced to capitulate, and paid the price for his opposition by being executed after the first Moscow show trial of the Great Purge.

9. *Lenraisovet*: acronym for *Leningradskii raionnyi sovet* (Leningrad Regional Council).

10. Trial of the Mining Engineers: in 1928 fifty-three engineers who worked in coal mining in the North Caucasus and in the nearby Donbas in Ukraine were accused of a "foreign-based criminal conspiracy to wreck the Soviet coal industry . . . by deliberate mismanagement." Stalin fabricated the circumstances as evidence of continued "imperialist enmity" toward the USSR (Robert C. Tucker, *Stalin in Power*).

11. Order of Lenin: one of the highest national awards in the Soviet Union.

12. Prompartiya: "Industrial Party." At the end of 1930 a trial was held concerning this allegedly underground counter-revolutionary organization made up of the technical intelligentsia.

13. Novocherkassk: a city in the Rostov Oblast of Russia, in the southwestern part of the country.

14. Solovki: The Solovetsky Islands in the Onega Bay of the White Sea, including the Solovetsky Monastery, became one of the notorious camps of the GULAG. The Cheka began sending prisoners to the islands in 1922.

BUTTERFLY. 1987

Leonid Yuzefovich

Four people got together: Rogov, Rogov's wife, Galkevich and Paul
Dreyden, a man the same age as the others, but already a professor at one
of the Ivy League universities. In the morning they took him to the New
Jerusalem Monastery and quickly went through the museum there; then
Paul Dreyden and Rogov's wife took a walk along the fortress wall while
Rogov and Galkevich stayed down below, walked here and there along
the arcades with embrasures for cannons—embrasures grown over with
dry, September grass and from which no one had ever fired a shot—and
continued trying to establish who felt what about Patriarch Nikon, who
had built this monastery. The Jew Galkevich had recently been baptized
and now maintained that Nikon had torn the church from its deep roots
in national life.[1] Unbaptized Rogov defended the patriarch. They had
started arguing while they were on the commuter train on their way
here. Each wanted to map out his attitude toward society before Paul
Dreyden without stooping to a banal argument about politics. They had
a rule in their group that the first one who pronounced the name of
Yeltsin in any discussion had to pay a ruble. Stalin and Trotsky cost fifty
kopecks.

Finally Paul Dreyden and Rogov's wife came down from the wall,
and Galkevich took them all to a small stream that flowed behind the
monastery, which Nikon renamed the Jordan when he was erecting
his new Jerusalem here. Two old women wearing slips that had faded
beyond all hope from too many washings sat on the shore. It was early
September, warm, but too cold for swimming, and they had evidently
washed only their feet and filled their jars with water from the Jordan.

Rogov did not want to take off his clothes, but Galkevich felt it his
duty to go in the holy river. Now in his bathing suit and facing the
cupola of the church which was being restored and was covered with
scaffolding, he crossed himself, bravely got into the water, and started
swimming close to the shore and diving down into the water. The old

women looked at him approvingly; one asked him to scoop some water into a jar in the middle of the river where it was cleaner. Galkevich threw himself happily into fulfilling her request. He was happy to share with these women their naive, ancient belief in the healing power of the water here. The current was carrying thin stems of water plants; he had to scoop up some water several times and throw it back as he tried to get the cleanest water possible.

Rogov's wife also took off her clothes, but the sight of her in a bathing suit did not give him the same pleasure as before, when he would call his friends to the beach so that they could appreciate what a fine figure his wife had. She felt the water with her foot like a cat and sat down next to her husband on his jacket, doubling up her part of the jacket so that she would not catch a cold sitting on the ground in the fall. Paul Dreyden asked her if the water was very cold. She said languorously that she could not swim today, although Rogov was positive that she could because her period was supposed to start at the earliest on Tuesday. He had no desire to figure out why she had said that, but there was probably some kind of a challenge in it directed at him, Rogov. In the past his wife had tried to take him in hand, but now he held her in his fist like a butterfly, and with each year he squeezed her harder so that she would not flutter in vain and lose the pollen on her little wings.

Paul Dreyden felt that he liked this Jordan no less than the real one, which he had seen in the real Jerusalem, but no more either. He took a dip, changed in the bushes, shoved his wet trunks into a bag, and pulled his jeans over his naked body like a hippie. Combing his hair, he looked peacefully at the trees that were just barely changing color and at the white monastery walls and towers drowning in the pale northern sky of early fall. Galkevich was jumping on one foot next to him, shaking out the water in his ears, and sluggishly trying to finish arguing about Nikon. Paul Dreyden could have cared less about their attitude toward society; the subject of the argument interested him as long as it could lead to a discussion about the heroes of his own novel—Peter the Great, Charles XII and, most important, Tsarevich Aleksei.[2] He felt that a new look at the unfortunate tsarevich who had died under torture and was hated by his contemporaries and descendants was long overdue. Two summer months spent in the Vienna archives gave him serious cause for criticizing the old, outdated, and superficial concepts.

After their swim, they headed to the station, boarded a commuter train again, and went to the Rogovs. Rogov's mother-in-law, who had stayed back at the house to watch her four-year old grandson, said goodbye right then and there and left, not wishing to argue yet another time with her son-in-law and upset her daughter, but Rogov, it goes without saying, did not appreciate her tact. He noisily rejoiced at the departure of his mother-in-law, who referred to having some supposedly pressing matters to attend to. His wife was forced to explain to him that in fact there were no pressing matters, just her innate tactfulness.

While the men were smoking on the balcony, she cut up tomatoes for salad in the kitchen and chatted with her son about a subject of vital importance: they talked about the kindergarten that he was soon to attend. Today he and his grandmother had been there to reconnoiter; they had looked over the cafeteria, the room for naps, the bathroom, and the playground with swings. Rogov's wife asked her son if he understood everything about his future life. Her son answered dolefully that he did. And did he see that the children there got dressed and undressed by themselves? Yes, he did. And that they did their buttons by themselves, did he understand?

"There's only one thing I can't understand," her son said and fell silent, because Paul Dreyden had walked into the kitchen and asked to hang his swim trunks somewhere so that they could dry.

Rogov's wife threw them over a line and asked, "What didn't you understand?"

"When there's stewed fruit for dessert," the son said, "where do the children throw the pits?"

His face was serious; the rest he had understood. She felt tears welling up in her eyes and choked with hatred for Rogov who insisted that the child attend kindergarten. He, you see, disturbed his work at home! She got on her knees before her son and said, "Forgive me, my little one!"

He was surprised. Didn't she know where those pits went either?

"Ask your father," she advised him. "Your father knows everything."

The son, dumbfounded, got down from the stool and slowly went to the room where Paul Dreyden, trying to steer the conversation to Tsarevich Aleksei, had already diverted it to Charles XII.

Dreyden was married to an American of Swedish origin, of Finnish-Swedish origin, to be precise; therefore, besides the basic European languages, including Russian of course, he had learned Swedish so that he could communicate with his wife's relatives and a bit of Finnish so that he could talk with the relatives' neighbors if the occasion called for it, whereas Rogov and Galkevich could barely read English with a dictionary. Both had never been abroad, but Paul Dreyden had studied in Stockholm the reports of Swedish ambassadors to Charles XII and had come to the following conclusion: as he began the war with Peter, the king had no other goal in mind than the Europeanization of Russia.

Galkevich said, "Europeanization, read colonization."

Rogov, as always, began arguing with him and opportunely remembered a historical anecdote which actually refuted the very idea he was about to illustrate. Once, Rogov related, Charles and his army were pursuing the enemy either in Poland or Ukraine or perhaps Livonia[3]— it's not important where—and the Swedes had no food supplies left; they were forced to stop the pursuit. Then within sight of everyone the king fell from his horse to the ground and began to tear at the grass madly, shoving wisps of grass into his mouth and chewing. The generals also dismounted and ran up to him. Well, let's say those people Pushkin writes about. How does it go? "Rozen leaves through the gorge, ardent Shlippenbakh surrenders . . ."[4] So this Rozen and ardent Shlippenbakh run up and ask, "What's wrong, Your Highness?" But he only bellows. Finally he spits with disgust and begins to cry. "Oh, "he says, "if only I could teach my soldiers to live on grass, I would be the ruler of the world!"

Galkevich burst out laughing with gloating delight.

"Do you see? A Viking, berserk—what Europeanization can there be? With ideas like that, what could he have taught us?"

Paul Dreyden was forced to agree with Galkevich, and Rogov finally understood that he had related something that really did not serve his purpose. He took a bit of salad from his plate, put it in his mouth and started choking and puffing out his cheeks as he depicted the mad king, and his wife, who had walked into the room behind her son, thought with hatred, "Oh you clown, clown, clown!"

"Your son," she announced, "wants to ask you something."

The son now felt that he had accidentally hit some important mark. He stepped forward and in a ringing voice stated his question concerning the pits in the stewed fruit. Rogov pulled him tenderly toward himself and began to explain that children collect those pits in a large box and plant them in the ground in the spring. When the son will be all grown up, there'll be a rustling orchard full of apricot, peach, sour cherry, and sweet cherry trees.

"Stop playing the fool," his wife said to him.

Galkevich smirked. Why was she actually surprised? This was fully in the spirit of her husband. He's justifying those who, watering the ground with blood, wanted to grow a garden paradise from the pits of stewed fruit.

She said to Galkevich, "Stop it!"

Paul Dreyden was silent; he was trying to pull out the dog, Zyuzia, hiding under the couch. She was in heat and Rogov's mother-in-law had put her grandson's old underpants on her so that she would not dirty the rug. Zyuzia apparently imagined that she looked obscene in them. Paul Dreyden was pulling her out by her front paws; she was resisting and whimpering.

"Let her be," Rogov's wife said.

She brought salad and something else. They sat down at the table where a bottle of vodka, bought by Paul Dreyden for hard currency, was already on the table. Rogov poured, Galkevich offered toasts: to the guest, to the woman of the house, to learning. Then they got down to talking. Rogov remembered another American historian from a different university, which did not belong to the Ivy League. They had met at an international conference five years ago and, although they talked chiefly about the *Chelobitennyi prikaz*[5] in Ivan the Terrible's time, he, Rogov, was then invited to a certain establishment for a chat. Paul Dreyden said that they did the right thing; that colleague of theirs—he was acquainted with him—was interested in the *Chelobitennyi prikaz* least of all since he was a paid agent of an establishment analogous to the one Rogov had been asked to visit. Not long ago, for example, he had published a collection of anecdotes about the Soviet army.

Rogov, smiling in anticipation, asked, "Is there an anecdote here?"

He did not get a chance to tell it. Paul Dreyden said that he himself was not involved in such things; he had spent the whole summer in the Vienna archives, studying documents about Tsarevich Aleksei's escape to Vienna in 1716, and came to the conclusion that the tsarevich was not a conservative at all, and most certainly not an Orthodox fundamentalist, as he was generally regarded, but a liberal and a secret Catholic. He understood the need for change as well as Peter, except that in his plans for reform he intended to rely not only on Western technology, as his father did, but on the spirit of the West itself. Unfortunately, here in

Russia, they do not want to see this. Last week, he, Paul Dreyden, had read a paper at an institute and a certain professor, who had written three monographs about Peter's era, declared, "Excuse me, but your tsarevich drank like a fish." Paul answered, "You, my respected colleague, perhaps don't know this, but during the war Churchill drank a bottle of cognac every day, and the English did not complain that they were badly ruled."

The vodka in the bottle was finished. Galkevich went out into the hallway, searched in his bag, and returned with a half-pint bottle.

"Take that away immediately!" Rogov's wife commanded.

Galkevich reminded her that during the war Churchill drank a bottle of cognac daily, and now it was peacetime. Paul Dreyden silently took the half pint and poured it in three glasses. Looking doomed, Rogov's wife went to the kitchen to fry some potatoes. As she was leaving, Rogov said, "Rozen leaves through the gorge."

It began to get dark. A wind was blowing; the autumn foliage on the poplars which was turning dry rustled uneasily outside the windows.

Paul Dreyden wanted to continue the conversation about Tsarevich Aleksei, but Rogov, pensively tapping his nail now on the half pint, now on the regular vodka bottle, and comparing the timbre of the sounds like a piano tuner, said he had just remembered a story about something that happened to him in his youth. At that point he had already finished the university and gone on to graduate school, but in general this could have happened to any drinking Russian intellectual, including Tsarevich Aleksei, so Paul Dreyden would benefit from hearing it.

It began when Rogov went home to bury his village grandmother on his mother's side. The grandmother lived in one village and his mother in another, about fifteen kilometers away, and at that time she was very sick and so he had to go to the funeral without her. The rest of the relatives gathered, buried the grandmother, prayed for her, and after the funeral feast, when they began dividing her property, Rogov somehow got his grandmother's goat. He wanted to get rid of it right away, but the relatives, sorting through the belongings of the deceased, said that they were taking everything to remember her by. He was too ashamed to get rid of the goat. Rogov tied a rope to its horns and the two of them started back, to his mother's. They left toward evening; it was already getting dark. It was winter and suddenly a snowstorm started; they were walking across a field and snow covered the road. Rogov decided to spend the night in a snowdrift. He had not yet fully sobered up after the funeral feast; he made a place for himself by the goat's side, wound the rope around his hand, piled up some snow, and fell asleep. It wasn't exactly hot, but it was quite bearable; he got very cold only toward morning, and the goat was getting cold too. In the morning they crawled out of the snowdrift and slowly went on their way. Soon they reached a large village located approximately halfway between the village where his mother lived and the grandmother's village. They did not have far to go, the weather took a turn for the better, but at this point Rogov desperately wanted to have a drink. But he didn't have even a kopeck on him; his first wife had cleaned him out before he left without leaving him money even for the ticket back. There, back home, she said, they wouldn't let him die. Then Rogov turned again to the seditious thought of selling the goat. He began stopping passers-by, knocked on doors of farmsteads, but no takers were found. Finally one local money-grubber agreed to buy his grandmother's worthless animal for three rubles. He would not give more, the swine, saying that even that was too much. He said he was taking a sin upon himself, because it looked like the goat had been stolen. Rogov spit, gave him the goat, took the three-ruble bill, and went to the store. He had looked in there even earlier and noted that they had quarter-liters, so it meant he could do all right with just a three-ruble bill. There was a line in the store; the peasants were taking two and three bottles each, like epic heroes. Rogov felt awkward buying one pathetic quarter-liter bottle. He looked like an intellectual. Although no one asked him anything, he began justifying himself in advance to his neighbors in line and explaining that he was going to take a quarter-liter bottle not to drink it but for a compress for his daughter who had caught a cold. Such a version seemed preferable to him. The common folk respect those who abstain, but not those who are small drinkers. He was already approaching the counter when an old woman standing nearby beckoned to him with her finger and whispered to give her the three rubles—he wouldn't regret it. Rogov decided that she would bring home-distilled vodka for the money and agreed. The old woman left and returned in ten minutes, but not with a bottle and not with a jar but with a little mayonnaise jar filled with a thick, yellow ointment, or perhaps fat. She said to rub the daughter's back and chest with it and disappeared, melting away in the air like a fairy. Numb with grief, Rogov was left with the glass jar. In his rage he wanted to throw it against the wall, but changed his mind, however, put it in his pocket and, as it turned out, not in vain.

If up to this point the story still preserved the appearance of plausibility, then further on everything became jumbled in a mystical fog. After that Rogov was walking or riding a bus, came upon someone's house where the family's only child was sick and failing—no medications were helping. The doctors had already admitted their powerlessness, but Rogov rubbed the child with the ointment, after which she fell asleep peacefully for the first time in many days and in a few hours woke up and asked for food. The happy parents made a feast for Rogov. He drank, ate, had a good time, then suddenly dropped his head on the table and started crying, because he was ashamed both before his grandmother for selling her favorite goat and before the goat which had kept him warm in the snowdrift, but which he sold for three rubles. The hosts became alarmed: what's wrong with him? Rogov told them; then the man of the house stood up, put on his fur coat and said, "Let's go!" They went, found the money-grubbing guy, and demanded that he return the goat. The clever money-grubber wanted the exorbitant sum of two hundred rubles for it and wouldn't take a kopeck less. Rogov was ready to give him his watch, hat, and mohair scarf, but the girl's father said, "Don't!" In his joy he did not begrudge the money. The goat was bought back for two hundred, and it lived for many more years at his mother's and was milked like a cow until it died.

Rogov fell silent and Galkevich felt another bout of familiar envy to which he was painfully accustomed. That one could sell a goat for three rubles and buy it back for two hundred, but Galkevich would not have been able to do it even for a million in that situation. He saw a hidden meaning in the story, a portent of a spiritual crisis which Rogov himself was not yet aware of. The goat was a symbol of truth, entrusted to him by his forefathers but forgotten, sold, betrayed and returned through repentance and penitence.

Paul Dreyden knew that a Moscow conversation over a bottle was similar to a circle in the universe whose center was everywhere but whose circumference was nowhere, and yet he could not but be surprised at how easily and naturally they jumped from Tsarevitch Aleksei to the goat. However, he believed in vain that they could return with the same ease to the topic they had begun with. The name of the poor tsarevich had barely been mentioned when Galkevich said that Peter was a revolutionary, and the children of revolutionaries were something else; here we were unintentionally plunging into the abyss of abnormal psychology. In a moment some Zhanna, the daughter of a certain prominent Bolshevik, a famous fighter against religion, surfaced from this abyss. A neighbor, an old landscape artist, had told Galkevich about her. She and the neighbor had been friends in their youth; they had gone to school together. Her father had spent his whole life struggling with religious obscurantism, and he named his daughter in honor of the Maiden of Orleans.[6] She was unusually attractive in appearance—tall, good figure, lithe, with bulging, green, Jewish eyes so prominent and limpid that, were you to look from the side in front of a lamp, you would see how luminous her eyeballs were. But for all that, she was a terrible slob. Once at an evening get-together she asked the landscape painter to get her handkerchief from her handbag. He opened it. My God! Apple cores, crumbs, dirty cotton, and a very greasy comb. And shish kebabs were grilled in her house her whole life. She loved meat. One husband, then a second, a third who was a hammer thrower, a fourth, Khrushchev was deposed, grandsons were born, but the shish kebabs were grilled and grilled. But she was an amazing beauty, one of those over whom time has no power. She was already more than fifty, but it made no difference— she was in the bloom of life and young people fell in love with her. About ten years ago, Galkevich, as happens in one's youth, found himself at a masquerade party at the home of some famous pianist who gave such parties for the chosen. Zhanna was also there—in tight-fitting clothes, in something terribly clingy, red and black, her heels clicking like hooves. Ye-es . . . Galkevich fell silent because that very minute he again caught himself double-thinking. Patriarch Nikon, Peter, Zhanna's father, and she herself—all those people with their Western style demonism— seemed understandable, kindred spirits, almost related to him; he felt a criminal sympathy for them which he would not admit to anyone, even his own wife if one were ever to appear in his life, which he had begun to doubt. The elderly woman in her devilish tricot, with the girlish figure, smiled invitingly and blew him a kiss.

Paul Dryden asked politely, "And your point?"

"The point," Rogov said, "is that you can judge the parents by the kind of children they have. All revolutionaries possess colossal life energy, but in the older generation biological instincts were suppressed by ideology. Hence the conclusion: oh how strong that idea must have been if it was able to crush such instincts in such people!"

Galkevich squinted ironically: did it really suppress them? Examples from the life of different, minor leaders connected with his native city in the Urals were brought as evidence to the contrary. He did not miss an opportunity to underscore his provincial background and to emphasize in a low-key way that he had nothing to do with those Jews who established themselves in Moscow after the revolution and scattered poison arrows over Russia from there.

Rogov's wife said to her husband that there was no reason to cloud the truth. Zhanna grew up like that because she was well fed in her childhood. In the spring she had taken her son to a neurologist and he advised, "If you want your son to grow up to be a bright and happy man, give him black caviar to eat."

She hushed her son, who had crawled under the couch to hug Zyuzia, and went to the kitchen. Taking advantage of her absence, Paul Dreyden lit one more cigarette. He had reason to believe that Rogov and Galkevich, by taking care of him in Moscow, were secretly hoping to receive an invitation to read a lecture or a series of lectures at his Ivy League university, but he did not understand why, in that case, these almost forty-year old men were acting like two students who were flirting with a mature matron, calculating on touching her with their artlessness.

"O-o!" he said with respect, because Rogov's wife walked into the room with a frying pan in hand.

Shoveling the nicely sizzling potatoes onto plates, she said that one can judge revolutionaries not only by the kind of children they have but by their wives as well. When she was in a maternity hospital, one of the female doctors there had worked in the gynecological unit of the Fourth Medical Administration and told the following story. A granny, a frail old woman, came to see her on an appointment. It turned out she was a party veteran, the widow of a *narkom* or a *kraskom* man.[7] He was shot in '37,[6] but she served her years in prison and lived to receive treatment in the Kremlin hospital. She came and complained about some gynecological problems: she had pains there and there. The doctor explained to her: at your age nothing can hurt anymore in that place; you probably feel pain somewhere else and it carries there. The granny would not accept that explanation: no, it hurts there. All right, if there, then it must be there, you can't argue with such people. They sent her for an X-ray, took one, and indeed, there was a tumor. It looked like a cyst, but it was very strange-looking. She says: cut me open, don't be afraid, I'm tenacious of life. They had her sign a form, cut her open, and removed the tumor . . . Rogov's wife paused artistically and finally announced, "A gold ring! A really thin ring made of old gold. Who can guess how it got there?"

Paul Dreyden said, "She hid it too deeply when searched."

The others kept silent. She had to explain to them, those stupid people, that at the beginning of the twentieth century such rings were used as contraceptives by women. Well, like the coil today. It goes without saying that decent women didn't do that; there was a different morality then. It was mostly young women in houses of prostitution for the rich who resorted to this method. So, the granny had that biography. The ring was put in, then flesh grew over it like over a splinter, and she simply forgot about it. Usually those who toward the end of their life are notable for their tenacity for life are flippant when they're young.

Galkevich asked if they didn't have the custom of using this ring as an engagement ring when getting married, that is, as they turned to an honest life. In the tradition, so to say, of the Decembrists* who had cast-iron rings made from their own chains as a remembrance. They didn't?

Rogov got angry. "You understand everything perfectly well, don't play the fool!"

"What exactly?"

"Everything! This man married a fallen woman because he was an idealist and believed in the possibility of remaking the world, changing human nature."

"Idealists like bitchy women with big tits," Galkevich noted. "Or is it your opinion that it was a sacrifice on his part, that he married a prostitute?"

Rogov answered hesitantly that yes, to some degree—yes, sacrifice kept the world going round.

Rogov's wife said, "Please, cut me up for silage if that's a way to restore our agriculture." She saw that her son, frantically pushing Zyuzia away, was struggling to get out from under the couch, and she crouched down to help him. He crawled out of there in dirty leggings, excited, his eyes shining. An old paper ruble, worn with age and furry with dust, found under the couch, triumphantly quivered in his little hand.

"M-mom," he said, stuttering from the excitement, "look,what I found! N-now you don't have to go to work anymore and earn money. Here . . . !"

She realized that her son was happy for both of them, because he too, of course, wouldn't have to go to kindergarten if his mother stayed at home. She had an urge to hit Rogov, who understood nothing and had let out a loud, horse-like laugh, the idiot. Tightly pressing the boy to herself, she said in a colorless voice, "We have one room. It's time for the child to go to sleep."

In ten minutes Rogov with Zyuzia on a leash, Galkevich, and Paul Dreyden walked out of the building entrance into the courtyard. The moon was already high and shadows of trees lay on the ground—thick, black and bottomless, like in the south. The air was also southern—warm and unsettling. Somewhere beyond the houses an invisible street car scattered some blue sparks. With a sound reminiscent of the hissing of beer foam as it subsides in mugs, cars rushed by on a neighboring street. The Rogovs lived on the outskirts of the city, but beyond their outlying area stretched another, even more dreary. There, among the trash-covered copses, construction pits, vacant lots, cemeteries, dumps, and cement fences guarding the billeting of military units, the bus routes ended under a canopy of sickly pines with crushed roots; farther on began a no man's land, planted with potatoes, in the eternal war between Moscow and the rest of Russia.

Rogov undid the leash; now Zyuzia was running alongside him. From time to time she would stop in her tracks and smell the ground. Her panties had been taken off back home.

He felt in his jacket for cigarettes and without any particular surprise came upon a small glass in his pocket. Every day as he was getting dressed, and sometimes even later, on the street or at the institute, he would discover in one of his pockets either a plastic soldier or some other cute little thing, or a teaspoon with traces of the morning's soft-boiled egg, or something else just as small, endearing, and domestic. His son would furtively thrust these little things into his jacket to remind his father about himself in that life for which he left home daily. It was nice to feel the small thin glass. He lost his desire to smoke.

They walked to the bus stop. A somewhat frightening night life swirled around the building entrances and in the gazebo behind the wire enclosure of the kindergarten. Someone swearing hard could be heard there, and the excited woman's laughter that accompanied it sounded like the promise of a reward for those who would come out of the shadows today to have their way. A silent shadow slipped along the wall, and around the corner two Asian men stealthily carried something long, wrapped in a sheet that resembled a corpse. Rogov was sorry that he had offered to accompany his guests to the bus stop. The road back alone seemed frighteningly long, and recently he tried not to return home late. He would even take Zyuzia for a walk earlier, before it got dark. His former tranquil life had disappeared; Galkevich envied him needlessly.

He ran into a man with the face of a murderer. Somewhere in the bushes cats were crying in the voices of his future victims. Rogov thought that Moscow was becoming like that town they had read about with his son in the fairy tale about Sinbad the Sailor. In sunlight people had control of the city, but with the coming of darkness their power would end. They would run in droves to the sea and cast off in boats to spend the night in them, and hordes of monkeys would descend from the neighboring hills and sit in the coffee houses, trade in the market, and stroll the streets and kill those who had remained in town, only to leave at dawn for the hills and return again the following evening.

It was September, with each week the small amount of daylight growing ever smaller, ever more imperceptible in the ocean of darkness. Rogov carefully touched the glass treasure in his pocket. He did not wear a cross, but this small glass could keep him safe from all dangers on the way home from the bus stop.

The courtyard was sunk in gloom; trees rustled. Soon the foliage would turn yellow and fall off, then you would be able to see through the bare branches the two windows of his one-room third-floor apartment lit up in the evenings.

There Rogov's wife had put their son to bed, but he just would not fall asleep: a drink of water, have to pee, then sing me a song. Finally she got angry and went to wash the dishes. The son began to cry. She wanted to stand firm, but of course could not, and so returned. He said, "Mommy, sit with me a little bit, I'm scared."

"What are you afraid of?" she asked.

The son in a prepared way referred to ghosts and some folklore characters, but she sensed that it was not really about them. They were merely imaginary tokens of something else, something inexpressible, formless, and nameless. The left curtain was moving unpleasantly from a draft as if someone were behind it. In order to make it stop, Rogov's wife shut the little ventilation windowpane, turned on the table lamp, and promised to turn on the light in the hallway and come the minute he called, after which her son, letting out a suffering sigh, agreed to fall asleep alone. Her kiss remained on his forehead like a seal of safe passage.

On the way from the room to the kitchen, she mechanically checked to see if the entrance door was closed and just as mechanically looked in the door peephole. This had become her habit ever since the time that her neighbor, forbidden by his wife to smoke in the house, got in the habit of smoking on the landing before going to bed. She was forced to chase him away because all the smoke was drawn through an air vent into the Rogovs' apartment, which was being carefully aired for the night. Now there was no smell of smoke, but there was someone on the landing: the peephole was covered over by something alive, dark, and moving. She thought that Rogov had returned and wanted to open the door for him before he used his key, but suddenly realized that she didn't hear either the leash jingling, or Zyuzia's usual yelping. There was a dead silence behind the door.

She leaned against the wall, waiting for the bell to ring. A minute passed, no one rang. She pressed her eye against the peephole and felt her legs growing weak. The man was also leaning heavily against the door on the other side; now she could clearly hear his breathing, his almost heavy breathing, as if he were out of breath after running, or drunk. What was he doing here? Lying in wait for Rogov?

Gathering her strength, she asked hoarsely, "Who's there?"

Silence. She asked once more and ran to the phone, feverishly trying to think whom she could call for help. All her friends were too far away; the closest one could be here no sooner than forty minutes from now. There were the neighbors. On their landing there were four apartments, including their own. In one lived a very old woman who never left home; once a week her daughter would come and bring her supplies of food. In another apartment there was no phone. In the third there was, but she did not know its number just as she did not know the name of its inhabitants, which she needed to get the number from information. She and Rogov did not maintain any contact with the other neighbors who shared the same building entrance. She could call the police, but what would she say? Lie that they're breaking down the door? That way they'd come. She picked up the receiver but hesitated, holding down the telephone hook which suddenly jingled and vibrated under her fingers. She jerked her hand away and an unfamiliar male voice asked for Rogov.

"Who's calling?"

Something incomprehensible was given in answer. She said, "Wait a minute!"

With the phone in her hand and dragging the cord along the floor, she walked from the room to the hallway and loudly, taking into consideration the man standing behind the door, said, "My husband has gone out with his friends. They're going to return any minute now—all three of them—and the friends are going to spend the night with us. I've borrowed a folding bed from the neighbors."

The other end hung up. Only then did the suspicion arise in her mind that this call and the man on the landing were somehow connected with one another. The voice on the phone was strangely close, good volume, as if the call was from the phone booth around the corner. So, there are two of them here? Perhaps all because of Paul Dreyden? What if in America he also works in the establishment just like the one that had summoned Rogov? It's not so frightening, given the times today. Calming down a bit, she took the phone back to the room. Her son was already sleeping. He always fell asleep and woke up in an instant. For her the two worlds in which they all dwelled—sleep and reality, play and life, the past and the future—had separated long ago, but they were very close for him. It would not take the least bit of effort for him to step from one into the other.

When she was putting the phone on the table, she seemed to hear the man behind the door fiddling with the lock. Her heart sank and her legs grew weak as she rushed into the hallway. No, everything was quiet. She put her ear to the door, peered again into the peep hole, and suddenly realized that the man on the landing was doing the same. Two eyes, separated by a tiny piece of glass which bulged on the outside, were looking at each other; she could even make out his blinking, the weak and intense blinking of an eyelid pressed to the glass. Someone was scrutinizing her point blank and, although she knew that nothing in the room could be seen through the peephole, she felt the blood turning cold in her veins and a loathsome coldness passing through the roots of her hair. Rational explanations didn't work now. It was hard to believe that the lens of the peephole was capable of defending one from that look. The very senseless horror of life had fixed its savage pupil on her.

Lights were going out in the buildings, only the windows of the entryways were like oversized, dark-blue wells in the darkness. They turned the corner and Paul Dreyden said guiltily to Rogov, "I forgot my swim trunks at your place. They're hanging on the line in the kitchen."

"So, are we going to go back?" Galkevich asked.

Paul Dreyden said nothing. It was awkward for him to insist and for Rogov to show how happy he was at the unexpected opportunity to make the return trip as a threesome. He would not go to see them off again, of course.

"Let's go home," Rogov announced.

At these words clever Zyuzia ran off a little way, realizing that any moment now they would put the leash back on her, take her to the apartment, and put those hateful underpants on her. The wind was blowing harder and harder, wash flapped on the balconies. Rogov shouted, "Zyuzia, Zyuzia, come here!"

She pretended that she didn't hear. He said, "Let's go on, she'll come running by herself."

At that moment Rogov's wife saw the man behind the door winking at her. His eyelid twitched, closed, then opened, and his eyelashes brushed the glass of the peep hole. She jumped back toward the wall; the small of her back broke out in a sweat. He was winking at her as if he knew that today she had hated her husband all evening and now was letting her know that the signal had been received; now he'd act. In her faint-hearted way she wanted to wake up her son, walk out on the landing with her son in her arms, and shield herself with him from this nightmare, and then she became even more frightened because such thoughts had occurred to her. She stood and let out a thin howl from a feeling of hopelessness. It was not that late, but for some reason none of the neighbors could be heard on the landing. No footsteps, no voices, no one to call out to. Not one door slamming. She looked at the time: ten forty-five. It was half past when Rogov went to see the guests off, which means that he would return in about five minutes, well in ten or fifteen, if there was no bus for a long time. He was the kind, you know, who would not leave for anything until he saw that they had boarded and he had waved good-bye. She was afraid for her husband, afraid that someone was lying in wait for him here, but it seemed no less frightening to see the face of the man behind the door. Some dreams are like that: you notice someone next to you, you try to understand who it is, what he wants, but you can't understand; your soul languishes on the verge of recognition and yet is unable to cross that line with a final effort because there is fear, darkness, a variant of death in the puzzle itself, and the horror of continuing your life with what you could find out about yourself.

Her thoughts began to scatter and get confused, like in a fever. She said to herself: stay calm, you fool, don't panic, and turned off the light in the hallway and in the kitchen so that her eyes would get used to the darkness. Then she would have the upper hand if that man still tried to break in and burst into the dark room from the landing. Their door could be kicked in—it barely stayed on. She had been telling Rogov for a long time that it should be reinforced, or else replaced with a steel door, but he just laughed. And when he did give it some thought, this pleasure was too expensive for him.

Trees were rustling and swaying to and fro outside. The street light, its glass globe hidden in a bluish fog, was shining at the entrance to the building, at times showing through the trees' raging crowns. Shadows ran along the walls and pressed into corners. She had to do something. Deliberately taking loud steps, she went into the kitchen, got a hammer from a drawer, and then she tip-toed back quietly to the hallway. If that man was trying to eavesdrop, let him think that she's not here. The plan was as follows: the second Rogov's footsteps were heard on the landing, open the lock instantly and run out to help him.

She turned on the light again in the hallway so that she would not have to screw up her eyes when she was running out on the landing. Huddling near the door, she thought about which end of the hammer she should use—the flat side of the head or the sharp claw—when she suddenly remembered that their windows faced the courtyard. She could warn Rogov beforehand, as soon as he was approaching the building. Fool, fool, what a fool, Lord! She rushed into the room and opened the door to the balcony. The overgrown poplar trees which needed care blocked everything around; the foliage had not yet fallen off. She hung over the railing without taking her eyes off the small lighted area in front of the building entrance and began waiting.

Galkevich noticed her first. She shouted, "Hey, stop!"

Rogov recognized his wife's voice, but at first it seemed to him as if he had mentally said those words himself. There was a time when he constantly talked to himself in her voice, but then he lost the habit. He stopped near the building, calling Zyuzia who, as before, was keeping her distance, and Galkevich craned his neck and saw Rogov's wife. She was smiling from relief, from her husband being not alone, from all three coming; for this reason Rogov, on seeing her on the balcony, was not at all alarmed. He said, "Paul forgot his swimming trunks. We've returned for the trunks."

She was smiling in a strange way and said in a whisper, as if she had become hoarse in the wind, "Stop, stop!"

"Perhaps you'll throw them from the balcony so that they don't have to come up for nothing?" Rogov proposed.

"Wait," she said, "someone's standing there."

"Where?"

"On the landing behind the door."

"Who?"

"I don't know who."

"And what's he doing?"

She was at a loss for words and said, "Nothing."

"Fine, I'll come up right away."

Rogov headed for the entrance. She shouted, "Stop!"

Something made a rustling sound in the foliage and tumbled heavily down to the sidewalk. Paul Dreyden bent down; a hammer was lying in front of him. He picked it up and looked at Rogov and Galkevich. They did not have time to form any ideas, but he already understood everything, grasped the wooden handle firmly in his hand, and headed for the entrance. They were about to move after him, but Rogov's wife shouted again from above, "Stop! Take something too!"

"What?" Rogov asked.

"Well, a rock, a stick, something!"

Galkevich began to rush around under the windows, looking for something to arm himself with. Rogov waved his hand in irritation and took a step. His wife screamed, "For God's sake, take something!"

He stopped in his tracks.

"There really is someone there," she said quietly. "I'm afraid."

The moon became hidden; the branches of the poplars in front of the street lamp were being lashed by the wind. The light fell on his wife's face—tired, grey, no longer young. Only now did he finally believe her, only now did he feel that they had lived all these years together not in vain—they had produced a son. It was her fear that had produced that tight feeling around his heart ten minutes ago when he was walking past the kindergarten and feeling the small glass in his pocket. His blood curdled and he turned to Paul Dreyden.

"Give it here!"

He shook his head and did not give him the hammer. Zyuzia was jumping around at his feet, begging forgiveness. Rogov pushed her away and took a look around. In a neighboring building major repairs had been dragging on since spring, and behind a sandbox some rusty water pipes lay in a heap. He ran up and grabbed one of the shorter pieces. In that instant Galkevich emerged from the bushes under the windows and dashed to the building entrance. While he was rummaging about there in the bushes, frantically grabbing some light dry branches, it suddenly occurred to him that this was not the way, not the way a man with his genealogy should conduct himself in a moment of danger. Unarmed, his hands empty, he spurted to the entrance, but Paul Dreyden managed to slow him down somewhat as he ran; they went in together. Zyuzia squeezed through adroitly behind them.

A five-story building, no elevator; there was a wall security device with a mechanism which released the lock on the entrance door if you played the three-number code correctly on the ten-button accordion, but it did not work. They walked in, the wind began to howl, resounding in the mail boxes; the fringe on the rug fluttered before they even stepped on it. Paul Dreyden stepped on the rug with the feeling that farther on began that chaos in which the poor tsarevich could be found. The hammer grew heavy in his hand in a calming way, and with his other hand he tightly pressed Galkevich's elbow, who was trembling from the excitement. The door slammed, everything died down. Up above there was an unnatural silence as well. Paul Dreyden wanted to wait for Rogov so that they could go up together, but Zyuzia grew seriously frightened on the staircase. Breaking away, Galkevich ran after her, taking half a flight of stairs at one time with his long legs and flying toward the wall on the turns, and darted out on the third-floor landing. Empty. There was no one in front of the Rogovs' apartment. He listened carefully. The lock clanged. Rogov's wife, unable to bring herself to open the door right away, was slowly pulling it toward herself and asking in a loud whisper from the widening crack, "You're here? You're here?"

Galkevich did not hear the quiet echo of her words and her breathing but sensed it with his skin. He heard someone above him stealing upstairs, noiselessly climbing the cement stairs. Cautious, retreating steps could be heard there, at the curve of the staircase; an icy cold wafted from there which penetrated into one's very heart.

In the meantime at the bottom of the building entrance a hollow sound resonated: Boo-m-m! Rogov had caught his piece of pipe on a heat register. This sound stirred one's soul like the peal of a bell. Now no longer hesitating, Galkevich rushed to the fourth floor, then the fifth, and stopped in his tracks before an iron ladder which led to an attic hatch in the ceiling. There was no lock on the hatch. He wanted to crawl into the attic and grabbed a crosspiece at a run, but at that moment Paul Dreyden reached the Rogovs' apartment and saw a butterfly sitting on the peep hole.

He immediately understood everything and shouted to Galkevich, "It's a butterfly, a butterfly! Come here!"

At this point Rogov arrived with his pipe. Paul Dreyden said to him, "It's a butterfly!"

Rogov's wife finally opened the door, but the butterfly did not fly away. It just kept rubbing against the glass and moving its little wings— now pale, autumn-like, with a faint design and pollen that had lost its brightness.

Galkevich came down. Paul Dreyden explained once more, "It's a butterfly!"

All four looked at it in silence; no one was smiling. Galkevich's legs were trembling. Suddenly Rogov guffawed wildly. He embraced his wife; she pushed him away, squatted down, pressed the back of her head against the door frame, and began to cry.

Rogov threw the pipe away; it rolled down the staircase, making a lot of noise. On the second floor someone's door latch clanked, someone said something, Galkevich answered, something was said back to him, and then Rogov said loudly, "Lord! What are we all afraid of? Can you tell me?"

No one answered him. He put his hand in his pocket and the non-smoker Galkevich asked, "Shall we have a smoke?"

Instead of cigarettes Rogov got a small cognac glass and showed it to them as he held it in his flat palm. Paul Dreyden became animated. He decided that after the glass there would also appear the stuff you could pour into the glass, but Rogov suddenly squeezed it tight in his fist and crushed it like an egg.

His wife became alarmed. "What have you done? Why? What do you want to prove to me? You madman! Show me, did you cut yourself?" Her eyes were glistening.

Rogov opened his hand with pieces of glass sticking to his skin, shook off the pieces, cleaned the palm of his hand against his trousers, and brought it up to the light. There was no blood.

He smiled triumphantly.

"You see? Not a scratch. That means I'm right."

"About what?" she asked.

"There's no need to be afraid. Understand?"

She nodded.

"Give me another one," Galkevich shouted, "I'm going to try too!"

Rogov's wife said with pride, "You won't be able to do it."

Rogov carefully removed the butterfly from the peep hole, walked out on the balcony, and let it go. It was immediately swept away by the wind.

"Babochka. 1989" (Butterfly. 1989) was published in Znamia, No 5, 1994. We have translated the version sent to us by the author, in which the year in the title is changed from 1989 to 1987.

NOTES

1. Patriarch Nikon forcibly introduced reforms in the 17th century which called for the correction of divine service books and certain rituals of the Russian Orthodox church so that they would be in accord with the Greek Orthodox Church. The reforms were passionately resisted by those faithful to the old rites and books, a conflict that resulted in the Raskol or Great Schism in the Russian Church.

2. Tsarevich Aleksei Petrovich of Russia (1690-1718) was the son of Peter the Great. Relations between the father and son were strained; reactionary circles opposed to Peter's reforms viewed Aleksei as being sympathetic to their resistance to Peter's changes. Aleksei eventually fled Russia and took refuge with the Hapsburg emperor. Lured back by his father to Russia, he was accused of treason, tortured, and died before his scheduled execution.

3. Livonia: once the land of Finnic Livonians, it came to designate an area ruled by the Livonian Order on the eastern coast of the Baltic Sea (present-day Latvia and Estonia).

4. "Rozen leaves through the gorge, ardent Shlippenbakh surrenders" is from Aleksander Pushkin's poem, "Poltava" (1829).

5. The *Chelobitennyi Prikaz:* Instituted by Ivan the Terrible in the middle of the 16th century, it was a kind of department of justice which handled civil grievances in the name of the Tsar.

6. Jeanne d'Arc or Joan of Arc (1412-1431), as she is known in the English-speaking world, lifted the siege at Orleans.

7. *narkom: narodnyi komitet* or "people's committee"; *kraskom: krasnyi komitet* or "Red committee."

8. 1937: the height of the purges in the USSR.

THE LAST WAR STORY

Oleg Ermakov

The door slammed. Meshcheriakov stopped. Dirty cars were rushing past on the road. It was fall and the street was covered with puddles. Near a factory gloomy men and women who had finished the first shift crowded together waiting for a bus. Cathedral Hill, with its dark gardens, private single-story houses, and a massive cathedral with many cupolas, towered almost directly opposite the publishing house. One could ascend by walking up a small side street paved with cobblestones. He didn't feel like either suffocating in a bus or walking on the street covered with puddles, which cars sent splashing every now and then.

Meshcheriakov crossed the road and went along the small paved street, past some rather gloomy old houses on which rusted street signs were mounted. Red Brook—that's what this street was called. Somewhere nearby there was one more Brook—Green. Green Brook was one of the oldest names in this town. Meshcheriakov ascended the Red. On the left there were houses and bare gardens, and on the right, a hillside overgrown with bushes. Farther on began an old, red-brick wall, already half in ruins, its brick crumbling and falling onto the street's cobblestones. And one could think that it was precisely this brick wall that gave the small street a name with such resonance. No. It was renamed by the Reds in honor of the revolution and their comrades who had spilled blood in the town, both their own and that of others. In earlier times the street was called Egoriyevskaya or Georgiyevskaya, taking its name from the Church of St. George the Victorious which had been built with donations from the townspeople and the Streltsy.[1] It may be the most picturesque street in the whole town. Particularly in the spring. Although it smells worse here in the spring. And certainly not of the gardens in bloom. Although the gardens are blooming.

A woman was coming down the hill. She was stepping carefully, afraid of spraining an ankle on the cobblestones. When she saw

Meshcheriakov, the woman put her purse under her arm. Yes, it's a quiet side street, although it's in the center of town. But she was afraid for nothing. The man in the light black coat had money. He had just received an honorarium from his publisher. This was an honorarium for a book. Holding her purse tightly, the woman walked past. She was wearing a spicy perfume.

Meshcheriakov knew ten years before that his book would come out, although no one believed him. He knew it even there, on the roads of mysterious Asia; he kept diaries. True, his notebooks had disappeared; he had to bury them in the sand right at the airport, taking the good advice of an officer of the special department who had warned him that this cargo would be confiscated in Kabul anyway and, what's more, he would have to send Meshcheriakov and his diaries back to the regiment so that they could read, research, and carefully investigate everything. At this point the officer of the special department left for a time and, when he returned, he noted the empty briefcase with satisfaction. Well, not totally empty. The toilet articles remained, and beads and a rock. A small rock of a reddish color that looked like a clay figurine. A rock tempered by the Afghan sun. At Kabul customs Meshcheriakov was not detained, they let him get on the plane. He flew away, abandoning his diaries. But he remembered everything. He remembered people's names, the names of towns, mountains, *kishlaks*,[i] the color of the steppes in the spring, and the smell of the dust—that last phrase is what he even wanted to call his book. The roads there are covered with dust, everything is impregnated with dust: the clothing, the tents, the trees, and after a brief sprinkling of sudden rain, an inexpressibly delicate scent hangs in the air. The smell of dust. The smell of wormwood. And the smell of diesel fuel. Those are the smells of the road. And all it takes is for a bus to pass by, releasing clouds of burned diesel fuel, for you to recall instantly the road in the hills and the yellow-grey steppes and the walls of the *kishlaks* illuminated by the sun. This connection is ineradicable. Just like a lot of other things.

For example, if you turn now toward the cathedral, walk out on the square behind it and see the valley, you'll remember the Valley for sure.

---

i   *kishlak*: the particular kind of village found in Central Asia which the author describes in his story. Ermakov uses some non-Russian words to evoke the exotic nature of this land. Footnotes that follow are supplied by the translators.

He had already remembered it. Although these valleys aren't even alike. But looking at a Russian river valley evokes the same feelings in his soul that he happened to experience in the Valley of Central Afghanistan. However, the Afghan feeling was deeper. Here, at the base of the cathedral, you could catch only the weak echoes of that feeling.

Meshcheriakov didn't turn toward the cathedral and didn't walk over to the observation point, but the whole history of the Valley had already passed through his mind—the whole story, from beginning to end.

Walking out on Great Soviet Street, Meshcheriakov headed even higher, to the center of town. And immediately he caught the smell of burning diesel fuel.

Strange, but he liked it.

I simply love the road, he thought, now sitting in a restaurant and waiting for the vodka and appetizers he had ordered.

All the road expeditions involved firing weapons. And someone inevitably lost his legs.

And yet that's the way it was; he wanted to be on the road. To see the steppes, the mountain ranges, the *kishlaks* illuminated by the sun . . . In some German town a grey German, a soldier of the third Reich, sits now and, sipping his beer, thinks roughly the same thing. That he had liked the roads in Russia. Oh, dis is zo goot: the churches, the Bryansk[2] forests, the villages illuminated . . . Or an American, recalling the exoticism of Vietnam.

It's simply because you didn't have your legs blown off on the road. And you've forgotten where those roads took you.

He had forgotten nothing.

A waiter with a tray: vodka in a small decanter, a glass, bread, some appetizers. Thank you.

He had forgotten nothing, although he had left a pile of notebooks with his notes in the Afghan sand. He remembers enough for one more book.

Yes, there's enough thundering noise, dust, yelling, crude jokes, longing, shell splinters whistling by, sun, the smell of wormwood, and shadows for one more book.

How many books like that have already been written.

And how many more will be . . . !

It's a good thing that there weren't any musicians with guitars hanging about on the stage. It was rather quiet in the restaurant. Forks clinked from time to time and quiet voices could be heard. There were five or six customers—six to be precise: a group of three, an elderly pair, and a single lady on the wrong side of thirty.

And so he wrote that book. Wrote about what he knew. He had experienced the weariness of living in military tents in the steppe drooping from the heat, the fear of catching a bullet, the infectious cruelty. And he had written about it. He wrote it the way he had experienced it all.

. . . But he was dreaming about another book.

What book was he dreaming about?

A book that would satiate his heart.

He had gotten that wonderful book from the library. In a library with the usual shelves and a table for magazines, heaped with the usual Soviet newspapers full of lies. The only unusual thing was that Meshcheriakov got a library card and checked the book out secretly. This wasn't permitted to a soldier of the lowest caste: young, a "son,"[3] green—in a word, a Shudra.[4] The unwritten regulations—which were stronger than the army regulations, isn't that so?—strictly forbade this. But he, a Shudra, used to reading in his free life, dared to. Two or three months earlier, they had arrived in the regiment and settled in a small tent city; at some distance there were outposts that guarded the regiment, and several days in a row Meshcheriakov went with a sergeant to one such sub-unit to work on "the Lenin room"[5]: to draw and paint posters. Meshcheriakov had wonderful penmanship. That day he had gone alone; the sergeant had been in a bad mood and started smoking pot in the morning to raise his spirits, and now was lying on his cot. It was on the way to the outpost that Meshcheriakov checked the book out of the library. After arriving at the outpost, he escaped into the Lenin room, a tarpaulin-covered shed with a few tables and chairs, and immediately took the book out from under his shirt.

He started with the first page. And the first phrases penetrated him instantly: "In the Meshchersky region[6] there is no particular beauty of nature . . . What can you see in the Meshchersky region? Meadows in bloom or already mowed . . ." He wasn't reading this for the first time. He had read this in his school years and knew about the consonance of his family name with the land described by this man with a leisurely manner of writing. And it was not the consonance that struck him. The half-forgotten lines resonated so melodiously and clearly in him, so fervently and affectionately that, overcome with emotion, he couldn't continue and closed the book. This was incredible. Meshcheriakov had already forgotten this simple, utterly sincere language which originated in the heart itself—and instantly touched your heart.

He didn't touch the book for a while and unexpectedly for himself thought about the correctness of the ban on books. But nothing could stop him now and, of course, he picked up the book again and opened it. Did he read it? He satiated himself with it. He digested the lines as if eating a honeycomb. "The haystack retains its warmth all winter long." He resembled a bear after hibernation that came across a log full of honey. "What can you hear in the Meshchersky region except the hum of pine forests? The cries of quails and hawks . . ." This honey was perpetually fresh, sweet-scented, and clear. "The dry breath of the forests and the smell of the junipers . . ." Every line was liberating. And Meshcheriakov's head was spinning as if he were flying over those eternal pine forests alongside a plane, with the dry breath of the forests and the smell of junipers reaching him. Every line sang like a bird. Every line grew into a branch which showered his heart with its fall leaves, or blinded him like the sun with its young, rain-covered greenery, and overripe apples fell onto his solar plexus in the garden, where there was a bathhouse that had become a home for the wandering writer. A lazy silver fish was moving somewhere to the side, leaving circles in the mist-covered water. And a star was beginning to shine at his left temple, and at his right, the wick of a kerosene lamp. And the smoke of aspen wood tickled his nostrils.

"You're not doing anything here!"

Meshcheriakov looked back. The window was open and a warrant officer was standing outside—bare-headed, with a broad, flat forehead, blue-eyed, a classic straight nose, broad-shouldered, his reddish-blond hair slightly curly. Meshcheriakov unconsciously thought that's how Odysseus had probably looked, but finally came back to reality and shoved the book under some posters.

"Come on, work, draw, otherwise what is this?" the warrant officer said. After keeping silent for a few minutes, he added, "And now go to dinner."

Meshcheriakov didn't go to dinner. He felt sick from the thought that now he would get up and go into the shed, where steam was rising from a vat of borscht with old yellow pork, where the Shudra were darting about timidly, and the old-timers[7] were screaming their lungs out.

Would the warrant officer tell the sergeant tomorrow that he wasn't doing anything, that he was reading? Meshcheriakov looked at the posters with texts of regulations and quotations from multi-wise, multi-volume works—did he really have to write this? And he felt the same revulsion as when he thought of the borscht with the yellow pork.

But he had to get a hold of himself and write. And for some time he wrote without understanding what the words meant . . . No, this was impossible. Meshcheriakov took out the book, moved into a corner, hid himself from the window with a poster, laid another poster on the floor in front of him, took a quill in his right hand, and placed India ink next to him—and continued reading and listening to the man with the webby[8] and grassy, pensive and expansive last name like wasteland: Paustovsky.[9]

In the evening he walked out of the Lenin room and saw the steppe, and the deserted, clay toy village—the *kishlak*. The pale, hot sun. He headed for the regimental camp. He walked not on the road which was covered with a thick layer of hot dust, but along the steppe, avoiding the stiff, faded bushes of camel burr. At times a beetle with a pellet of soldiers' shit would run backwards, maneuvering nimbly along the dry ground cracked from the heat.

The steppe—it stretched everywhere—old, infertile, monotonous and endless, like death. In the middle of the deathly steppe stood rubberized tents. Soldiers lived in them. They lived suffering from the heat, lice, dysentery, typhus, jaundice, fear of being killed or taken prisoner—and they tortured each other and, during operations, their enemies, if they got hold of them.

Meshcheriakov walked on the rustling ancient land, and his mind clouded over from the thought that he too would live here for a very long time. If, of course, he was lucky.

But if he were lucky, if he were lucky, he'd return to the country of grasses and big, dazzling clouds, the country of dews and the people of Rus.[10]

He was lucky. He returned. He was sitting behind the fortress walls of heroic times of yore; he was sitting in a restaurant and saying something to himself, something about roads: he seemed to love them, those roads. And he wasn't even drunk yet.

How, in general, can all these things exist side by side: explosions, executions, longing for the Meshchorsky region, the absurdity of the caste system, and simply the absurdity of army service, the appeal of roads along mountain slopes, the appeal of snow-covered mountain peaks, empty steppes, and fortified, clay farmsteads in the valleys, the appeal of the diversity of colors in the towns and the evening calls to prayer being carried from a minaret slightly illuminated by the stars . . . Yes, that's exactly how everything was. It was not an illusion evoked by time. In the beginning the longing for the Meshchorsky region ate away at him, but already by the first spring something suddenly penetrated inside him and dissolved in his blood. What to call that "something"? The voice of the steppe? Its soul?

Yes, after the fall rain at night everything changed. The rain washed, cleansed the air, and suddenly it became clear that all around there was an enormous amount of open space. And in this vast, open space smoky clouds floated. The wind rang monotonously in the rigid, metal-like bushes of camel's burr, and the hard earth emitted the somewhat bitter smell of wormwood. And when the sun broke through and lit half of the land area, a file of dark people and reddish-brown camels appeared in the distance. They were bravely making their way somewhere through the huge masses of sunny-yellow and blue-grey air. This landscape seemed to be an illustration for some epic poem yet to be written: it was simple and majestic.

And later, on more than one occasion, he had to travel with a caravan —a line of armored vehicles—through the expanse of the steppe. And he saw the steppe covered with hoarfrost, turning rosy from the rising sun, and he saw smoke from clay *kishlaks* lost in the peaceful expanse.

In the summer dust storms would arise in the steppe. But in early spring the steppe was sleepy, wet and foggy; a clay tower, a tree, or a turbid, cackling river would suddenly come into sight in the fog. And high up cranes would be making their cries, or geese that had wintered in the warm swamps and lakes of nearby India and now were flying to distant northern regions would honk enchantingly. The steppe would dry out, it would bloom brightly and fade quickly, but the gardens would keep blooming, and the *kishlaks* would stand like clay vases in which people and birds sang at dawn: *dzen! chen! fyu-fyu! al-mulk li-l-llakh!* And bullets would sometimes sing: *fyu!* and *vzhik!* They would make a popping sound against the armor and bounce back, or pierce the rubber tires. Death lay hidden in the expanse of the steppe. It was difficult to predict its lightning-quick lunges, at times impossible. Death was everywhere. But, strangely enough, everyone got used to it. At least its presence didn't prevent him from being aware of the uniqueness, the majestic beauty of the Afghan steppe.

Time was perceived completely differently there than in any other place. It felt drawn-out. And not only in the steppe and the mountains, but even in the towns, and even in noisy and bustling Kabul.

Perhaps the whole problem was that he, like all the soldiers of the Doomed Contingent, was rushing time, was impatient? Of course he was rushing it; of course he was impatient, especially the first year. But during the second year he no longer got so worked up about time, about returning home. And at times he didn't think about returning altogether. Moreover, he would sometimes get a strange feeling . . . a longing for the land where he was living.

All the pilgrims who went to the East would write about time slowing down, so a soldier's feelings have nothing to do with it. It goes without saying that this was only an imaginary slowing down . . . Incidentally, the same thing happens with a city dweller who goes to the country: he feels first and foremost that time is different there. But he feels this not in the same measure as it's felt in the East. It's simply that the signs of a Russian landscape are too young and haven't been recorded yet in the proto-memory of humanity. There, in the proto-memory, you have steppe, desert, mountain, resinous cedar, sea, garden, rock. Pre-flood dwellings of clay with a flat roof. Camels, donkeys. Nomadic tribes . . . The waiter: "Do you need anything . . . ?" "Not for the time being, thank you." And when a traveler sees all this and understands that he's looking at the past, he senses that he has drawn close to the origin of human time, to the beginning of history. There, at the origin of time, is also the origin of all religions that interpret not only the origin of time but also the origin of everything that exists under people's feet and above their heads—the whole universe, cosmos. And it seems that the imprint of the beginning lies in the East. And in the beginning there was no time. And time distorts the imprint. A trip to the East is a trip in the direction of eternity.

Meshcheriakov once happened to experience a strange, inexplicable something—perhaps this was in fact time slowing down and his drawing closer to something that could be called timelessness. This happened in the Valley.

2

Meshcheriakov saw the cliffs of the Valley in the fall when the poplar trees and gardens were losing their leaves, and when it was cold at night and the fields had been fully harvested.

The cliffs extended for two or three kilometers—violet-grey, with hundreds of caves, tunnels, and rock staircases—and in one of the caves a deserter was hiding.

From time to time someone would disappear from the regiment: he would be taken prisoner or desert. It was the young soldiers who deserted. The kind who couldn't bring themselves to set off a grenade fuse in their hand and be left with no fingers. The kind who didn't dare to fire a whole magazine of bullets at their older fighting comrades, their tormentors. When they kick you like a dog, force you to answer to a nickname and carry out idiotic actions, when they read your letters, take away your money, crush you every day, every hour—it's difficult . . . Yes, it's difficult to suddenly find yourself in the wild mountains of Asia in the skin of a Shudra. And to wait for half a year for initiation into the next caste and fight the temptation to take vengeance or to desert. To take vengeance or to desert—who of the soldiers of the Doomed Contingent had not thought about it during the first year of service?

But this time an officer deserted.

They had to comb all the holes and passageways in the cliffs that extended like a wall from east to west for two or three kilometers because the Afghan peasants had seen him there.

Tanks and armored personnel carriers occupied more or less convenient positions and aimed their muzzles at the groves and cliffs and at the pisé[11] walls of the fortified farmsteads. Here was a dangerous area, almost fully controlled by the mujahideen. During the two-week raid the convoy was fired upon twice. It's true a few times mines went off, but the soldiers suffered only light injuries and scratches. But nevertheless the last explosion turned out be disastrous—the driver and his partner, full of shrapnel, were thrown through the windshield onto the road. Then and there a suspicious character was seized. He had been walking along a *duval*[ii] and didn't react to the shouts and shots. They caught up with him finally in a grove. This was a young man in white wide trousers and a long white shirt and a woolen sleeveless jacket. They searched him and found nothing except prayer beads. Smiling, he straightened his astrakhan fur hat; a gold ring flashed on his finger. Sergeant Nuraliyev asked him why he didn't stop, why he was running away. "And what's he so happy about?" asked senior lieutenant Kozhevnikov—pockmarked, healthy, dark, puffy from the mountain sun, cold nocturnal winds, and the soot from engines and campfires. "Well?" the senior lieutenant shouted. The fine-featured, swarthy face of the Afghan continued to radiate a strange smile as if all that was happening had nothing to do with him, and at that instant Kozhevnikov's massive fist made an arc and landed a crushing blow on his face. Nuraliyev, for his part, hit him and his astrakhan hat flew off; the rest of the soldiers ran up, hiding the Afghan, as well as Kozhevnikov and Nuraliyev, from view. Meshcheriakov didn't see that Afghan again. But he remembered that face forever, with that strange, radiant smile.

But he couldn't remember the face of the lieutenant who had deserted. A few days later word spread that a lieutenant from the Third Company had disappeared, and Meshcheriakov, who served in the Seventh Company, tried to recall him but couldn't.

What happened?

No one knew. Only one thing was known: the lieutenant left late in the evening after telling his sentry that he was going to the artillerymen for tea, that he had been invited, although, as it later became clear, no one had invited him anywhere.

Or had the sentry and those peasants confused everything?

Well, you can't trust the peasants; they could have killed him with their spades and covered him with rocks. And how do they know that it was actually a Soviet man who was hiding in the caves and not some

---

ii   *duval*: a clay wall around a village or a home in Central Asia.

solitary Buddhist monk? After all, there are still Buddhist monks in the world. This Valley in the highlands in the center of Afghanistan was once famous throughout the Buddhist world. Pilgrims came here from China and India; they lived in the caves and built new rooms for prayer; later hippies from the West came here to meditate. And so, perhaps the peasants saw a solitary Parisian or a man from Chicago? A wild hippie?

Like pygmies, soldiers would come and crane their necks at the foot of the colossus cut into the cliff, a fifty-meter statue of Buddha. The upper part of his face was carefully cut away to the lips—it was said that this was the handiwork of Muslim iconoclasts or some ancient monks who would hoist a gold mask over the face during the holidays, and that the mask was hidden in one of the caves. The idol had a thick neck, a round chest, and a deeply set navel. His pillar-like legs were badly damaged to the knees. Between his feet, more precisely stumps—the stumps seemed to have been made by an explosion from an antipersonnel mine—a wide opening into the cliff was visible. The soldiers closed and locked the bolts of their rifles and crawled into the darkness.

From the outside it seemed that pitch darkness reigned in the caves, but in fact it wasn't that dark in there, and in some tunnels that had fissures in them it was even light—the sun, raging over the mountains, penetrated even here. The vaults of the caves were black from soot. Here and there a stone ornament protruded. The caves connected to stone stairways and passageways. The soldiers wandered through the caves and called out to each other, and their voices boomed and echoed deep in the caves.

On one of the walls Meshcheriakov saw the remains of frescoes, and in the half-faded lines and spots he could make out a floating, half-naked figure. "A woman?" Sergeant Khodortsev asked, stopping beside it. Other soldiers drew near. They began to make out the curve of a hip like a woman's, but the hands were big and strong like a man's. Khodortsev lit a match, and immediately everyone let out a sigh: the reddish flame highlighted marvelous circular lines and large nipples. "And they say monks lived here, Buddhists!" Khodortsev lit a second match. "And what's this?" Below, under the left foot of the heavenly woman, an outline of a head became visible. But when three matches were lit at the same time, it became clear that this was the bud of some large flower.

At noon the sun stopped opposite the cliffs and soon it got noticeably warmer in the caves. Squinting, the soldiers walked out on a small ledge and climbed still higher, to the top layer of the cliffs. From here there was a good view of the Valley, the pisé walls and flat roofs of the box-like houses, the fading gardens, the poplars losing their leaves, the brownish, dove-grey patches of harvested fields, and the brown, steep slopes on the opposite side of the Valley and the peaks of the Hindu Kush Mountains.

On the right an area with cliffs and caves sloped down and then turned into an area of ravines, but farther on, more cliffs towered above with walls full of holes. Down below there were poplars and pisé fortresses—and above these cliffs, poplars and dwellings, a dark bird glided, its wings broad and round, and it seemed small although this was probably a bird of prey—an eagle or a vulture—a large bird.

The sun became warmer. There was no desire to go anywhere. The soldiers smoked, their submachine guns resting on their knees.

Someone speculated that the lieutenant received a letter from his wife or girl: forgive me and goodbye—and lost it. But objections were raised, the argument being that there had been no mail for almost a month, plus for the two weeks of the raid—a total of one-and-a-half months. Perhaps he had gotten it long ago and seethed and seethed and then it all came to a head and erupted.

The company commander shouted from below that he would come up right now and drive out everyone—enough smoking! Everybody started to move. Kukharenkov, the guitarist from Petersburg—tall and awkward—picked up his gun and aimed it at the bird. "Too bad, but I don't want to raise an alarm." Everyone looked at the eagle or vulture which was still soaring.

The searching continued until five in the evening without any dinner and the soldiers were angry. But it was the officers who were particularly angry. And the regimental commander was darker than a storm cloud, and his gold teeth flashed like lightning when he issued orders.

They spent the night, as always, in the vehicles on the protective shields without getting undressed, covered with their greatcoats and jackets. They lay with the armor protecting them. Their weapons were next to them. They lay tightly packed together, shoulder to shoulder, tired but full; crude, sometimes cruel to each other but not strangers, they were linked by one language, their memories, and hope for the future. Surely they wouldn't be traveling forever on these exploding roads, they wouldn't forever . . . eat barley and canned fish.

Outside, the poplars were rustling, the weather had gotten worse in the evening, the sun was setting behind the clouds, and now at night a wind was rising. Before going to sleep, they listened to "Mayak."[12]

No, you can't carry a submachine gun, cartridge pouches, and a mortar on you forever. The day will come, and they . . . What will they? . . . They will climb the boarding ramp, traveling light, and go where everything around them speaks, looks, and breathes differently, where every tree rustles differently. And where clouds float along in a different way. No matter where you look there are roads and towns, villages, rivers, the land is soft, out of the ground grow white trees with black spots—birches, right now they're yellow—and you can drive fast on a motorcycle or in a car down a road without being afraid of anything. The color blue and sunlight flash in the puddles, the white walls of churches, faces, girls with grey eyes, old women in kerchiefs, workers, policemen, retirees, and children. The land flooded with fall sunlight, the noise and gleam of trains, the droning of the current in high-voltage lines in heavy sheathing which hang above dense forests where mushrooms abound and fields that are covered with cob-webs. Pipes and faucets in towns, squares, stadiums, libraries, sunny windows of high-rises, and two windows on the eighth floor, in the kitchen and the bedroom, and a third window that faces west. In the evening, when the sun is setting, everything in the room becomes covered with a dark-red gilt: the floors, the sideboard with the crystal glasses, the TV, the chairs, and the photographs in wooden frames. Photographs of grey-eyed girls, old women in kerchiefs, village boys, a pavilion on the shore of the Black Sea, a dashing man with a big mustache and a St. George Cross on his chest, a tank crew member by some ruins in Berlin . . .

But the lieutenant is now sneaking around at night—lonely, hungry, and alien to the whole world.

It was a cold morning. The sky was covered with clouds. Glum cooks were preparing breakfast. Fires burned red in the iron field kitchens that looked like country stoves. There was a smell of diesel fuel. The soldiers who had gotten up went to wash in an irrigation ditch lined with willows. Smoke was rising above the flat roofs of the Afghan houses.

The water in the irrigation ditch was icy and transparent . . . The soldiers washed and wiped their faces and necks hard with waffle-cloth towels that were no longer clean. Soon breakfast was ready. The soldiers took their rations in mess-tins, climbed on their tanks, tractor-trailers and armored personnel carriers, found a more comfortable sitting position, took the stale bread and a spoon, and spooned up the steaming kasha. While they were having breakfast, it began to rain; there was a light drizzle. All the mountain ridges and peaks on both sides of the Valley were hidden in clouds. Clouds hung right over the cliffs. The caves in the grey cliffs loomed black in a disturbing way. It kept drizzling and they had to get their tarpaulin coats.

Pouches with magazines of cartridges and grenades on their belts, an individual first aid kit with bandages and gauze on their sleeves, submachine guns on their shoulders. Forward! Search for the lieutenant, keep your eyes open, and don't miss the slightest opening!

The rocks were damp and slippery for the soles of the kersey boots and shoes. The soldiers clambered up the cliffs, looked into the caves, and moved along the ravines.

Where was the lieutenant hiding? What was he thinking? Why did he run away? Did he turn coward? A warrant officer-artilleryman had said during a smoke break that he apparently turned coward. But here was a soldier from the lieutenant's platoon, a gloomy man with a wrinkled forehead whose nickname was Rooster, and Rooster said that he and the lieutenant had run into trouble a number of times. In what kind of trouble? "How about the time we went down into a *kiariz*,"[iii] Rooster answered reluctantly. "And . . . ?" "He went down first and got out last," Rooster said, flicking his cigarette butt away. "He kept returning fire. So first the three of us crawled out, and then we pulled him out." "Well, maybe he had it in him for one time. But zilch for anything more!" Rooster glanced at the warrant officer and said it was best not to say such things to anyone. "So why in the hell did he desert, this hero?!" Rooster didn't say anything. "And now we're looking for him and getting wet." "Maybe he smoked too much pot?" Sergeant Khodortsev asked. Petukh tutted and shook his head. "So, it did get to him," concluded the tall and gangly Petersburg guitarist Kukharenkov.

---

iii   *kiariz*: an underground irrigation canal or an underground gallery for collecting surface water to be used for irrigation purposes.

Someone immediately remembered a former old-timer, Dzhambul, how it got to him too, and in broad daylight, without hiding from anyone, he went straight into the steppe and headed wherever his legs would carry him. He was ordered to stop, but he didn't. The captain got in an armored personnel carrier and fired a burst of machine-gun fire, not at Dzhambul, of course, but close to him—only a column of dust rose. But in response Dzhambul ripped off his cartridge belt and flung it away and grabbed his Panama hat and threw it to the ground—and went on. The captain fired another burst of machine-gun fire. He didn't stop. The captain yelled: take him! No one moved. Then he started the armored carrier, caught up with Dzhambul, jumped down, and hit him in the ear. Dzhambul hit him back. They grappled with each other, fell down in the dust, rolled around wheezing. Later on, in the brig, lice ate away at his balls. And the question arises: what was his problem? It had gotten to him. You bet. They discharged everyone, but they wouldn't release him, instead dragged him off on a mission. It's now his third year of service.

But the lieutenant had served only nine months.

"All the same, he's a son of a bitch," Khodortsev said at the end of the second day of searching.

It drizzled the whole day but stopped toward evening. The waterproof tents were damp. The barrels of their submachine guns shone dully. With dark pebbles crunching under their feet, the soldiers returned to their vehicles. Khodortsev never did get an answer. Only gangly Petersburg Kukharenkov sang under his breath, "The sky is blue over Canada, and the rains come down there at a slant . . ."

They were walking at the foot of the darkened cliffs, resting their arms on their submachine guns, watching where they were stepping and listening to Kukharenkov. Meshcheriakov stopped to take out a tiny piece of stone that had been rolling around in his boot for a long time and now was between his toes. He undid the footcloth, wiggled his toes, and the tiny piece fell out; he put on his boot, straightened up, and saw his comrades.

They were walking at the foot of the cliffs, drawing near the place where the faceless stone colossus towered above. The voice of the gangly soldier, which was barely audible but actually quickly recognizable, combined with the sound of their steps, and this made it sound like an impressive tune. And everything seemed strange: the gloomy, long-anticipated cliffs, the dull sky, the trees looming on the right, and the figures wrapped in cloaks.

Suddenly a small bang resounded, and a red flare flew up from behind the trees and lit up dimly. A tank was moving and clanging behind a line of dark trees.

Late at night, lying on a tank shield and covered with his jacket and greatcoat, Meshcheriakov recalled those moments, and they seemed strange to him all over again as if they had doubled in number, and he again had an inexplicable feeling of excitement and longing.

The next day the search continued. In the morning helicopters were able to circle over the mountains and roofs of the small clay town in the Valley, but soon visibility grew worse. It was cold and damp. At times there would be gusts of wind, snatching handfuls of blackened leaves off the branches. And finally it started to snow. A fine, wet snow, it came down at a slant and stuck to the cliffs and soldiers' jackets.

Kharchenko slipped and hurt his knee. "Hey you, be more careful!" the officers shouted. The snow flew into their faces and piled up on their eyelashes. Now everyone was really angry at the deserter. If yesterday and the day before it was actually interesting to do some searching in the caves, today no one wanted to crawl into the cold holes again and wander in the darkness. It was time to return to the regiment. But they were forced to dart in and out like bloodhounds, to sniff out the lieutenant who got it in his head to desert. Why did he desert? Perhaps he had quarreled with someone? With the brass? But no, people said that he hadn't quarreled with anyone, not that day, not before. What, never at all? Well there were times, of course. Right after a mission his soldiers were being sent to unload a convoy, so what else could he do? He had to go to the brass and scream his lungs out. Or they were taking a building near Herat—Moscow generals were observing—and a model assault was needed, but the lieutenant made a mess of all the orders, saying let the choppers use their rockets to assault the house with the machine-guns, and so all his soldiers just lay in an irrigation ditch until the choppers actually came flying in. And then, of course, there was a hearing. But the brass didn't cover things up, just when he would have received his next rank. An ordinary officer. Only through conscription, not because of any inner calling. He found himself in the army after finishing the institute, just like Meshcheriakov. After the institute one had the right to choose either serving a year-and-a-half as a soldier or two as an officer. He decided to be an officer, and Meshcheriakov, a soldier.

Of course, an officer's life is not like a common soldier's—it is cleaner, there's more food, more freedom. Here the officers sleep in real houses, not in tents like the soldiers. They are well fed; the "officer's" bread alone is worth something—it's white, wheat—not like the rye "soldier's" loaves, which are underbaked and black like coffee and give you heartburn. And then, the food rations—evaporated milk, cheese, butter, sugar, filter cigarettes. Leather boots, a jacket with a fur collar. More free time than a soldier has, and you can spend it in various ways: watch TV, read, or go visiting without asking anyone's permission. An officer doesn't have to steal gas, diesel fuel, or flour that he can sell to the Afghans; he has decent pay, double pay—he's paid both in the Soviet Union and here, so he can allow himself to buy some vodka or the affections of one of the regiment's women. He can go on missions carrying little equipment, and he doesn't have to stick his neck out first as the bullets fly but, of course, it will be noticed right away, and then don't expect the soldiers to at least respect you, if not to have that special, sincere, crudely filial feeling toward you which is called a soldier's love. To be the leader among young men isn't that simple. Yes, it's not that simple to subject each one to your will. And decide who will go where and when and do what. And decide who will die today. After all, you can run into the kind of trouble when you can't lie low in an irrigation ditch and you can't expect help from anywhere—not from the sky and not from under the earth. You have to do something, move, and sacrifice one or two so that the others stay alive. But how do you choose? Whom? Why this one and not another one? Does he really want to live less? Or is his mother not waiting for him? Who are you to decide that? In what way are you different from them—with your epaulettes, your knowledge?

"We're looking here, but he's already somewhere far away," Kukharenkov noted. "Walking to Europe." "He'll get his fill of Europe pretty fast!" senior lieutenant Kozhevnikov responded, angrily brushing the snow off his mustache. "What's there for him? Are they waiting for him?" someone said. "He'll arrange for a press conference," Kukharenkov answered. "He'll tell them how intelligence agents finished off some boogymen.[iv] But the boogymen were peaceful." "Is it written on their foreheads?" Kozhevnikov protested. "Enough babbling! Let's move on."

What Kukharenko was talking about took place a month before. Intelligence agents and some infantrymen executed a group of Afghans, first robbing them and then beating them up; some were injected with air from a syringe by the medic. They dragged the corpses into a *kiariz*, set off several grenades from above, and covered everything with rocks. But the *kiariz* was not dry—there was a stream under the rocks that fed into the river—and the inhabitants of the *kishlak* that was located further downstream of the underground river saw blood in their water jugs, set out to do some searching, and found the well with the corpses. The matter received publicity, and an investigation was started; it was being conducted even now, as the regimental units hung around the Valley, searching for the lieutenant who had deserted.

It was really dangerous to crawl along the slippery, dusty cliffs. And in fact one of the soldiers fell from a height of ten meters and hurt himself so badly that he couldn't even get up. When they tried to pick him up, he cried out so loudly and wildly that everyone convulsed with pain.

The medic came running, took out a syringe, found a vein in his arm, and injected some narcotics into his bloodstream. The moaning soldier soon quieted down.

Meshcheriakov saw it all from above, from a cave.

The snow kept falling. But now straight down, slowly, and in big flakes. The flakes were big, like the leaves of some tree. Of some unknown huge tree beyond the clouds, a spreading and lavish tree. The white leaves flew and swayed, came down on the rocks, and covered the cliffs absolutely silently. Meshcheriakov looked at the snow, at the poplar branches below, the grey-red clay walls, and yesterday's strange feeling awakened in his heart again . . . That inexplicable feeling connected somehow with time and with these caves and the roads leading to this valley through passes, deserts, and colorful towns. Now this feeling was so deep that it's doubtful he could have answered a simple question: What are you doing here? What time is it?

Time didn't exist. More precisely, it existed, but it didn't affect him. It flew and, like snow, it streamed and fell silently somewhere nearby.

---

iv   Boogymen (*babay*, sing., *babai*, pl., in Russian) is how the Russian soldiers called the mujahideen they were fighting.

And somewhere nearby people were carrying a man on a stretcher. Where and why? And what are they searching for here? What are they searching for in general?

Nothing.

They move forward and turn back, turn left and right, crawl on the cliffs and descend, get in vehicles and drive, stop and jump to the ground—and get nowhere. They eat canned food and kasha, they sleep, shoot, wait, and talk—about nothing in particular. They beat each other, write letters, poison lice, and lie around on dusty mattresses as if everything's clear to them and there's nothing more to understand. They run, jump, and shout, and if an opportunity arises, they readily shed the blood of those who look and think differently. Unformed, they wear a uniform and the uniform dictates their actions, thoughts, and words: Yes, sir! No, sir! Yes, sir, fire! They act without a moment's hesitation, like gods. And like gods, they can fly in the air and speed along the ground, belching fire and smoke. And so they move about, fly, burn the earth, its gardens, its women and children—and seek nothing. And one of them is you.

Someone entered the cave; he looked at the man who had walked in and didn't realize right away that it was Sergeant Khodortsev. It was Sergeant Khodortsev. He was sniffling; he had caught a cold.

"I've got a cold," Khodortsev said.

Meshcheriakov kept quiet.

"Some tea would be nice."

"With honey," Khodortsev added.

Khodortsev sighed.

. . . The last day was bright; a weak frost wouldn't let the newly fallen snow melt. In the morning the vehicles formed a column, the driver-mechanics waited for the order to move, and everyone else waited. They were tired of life on the move. They wanted to rejoin the regiment.

They didn't find the lieutenant. And so they didn't find out what happened to him. Did he perish in a rock crevice or die of hunger? Did he fall into an abyss? Or did the spade of an enraged peasant catch him? A mujahideen bullet? Did they take him prisoner and throw him into a grotto to rot? Was he forced to fight, but now for the other side? Perhaps they took him across to Pakistan and from there—with the assistance of the Red Cross or the intelligence service—to Europe or America?

Finally the command was given and the column set out with a

deafening roar; it moved slowly along the Valley, past the fall groves and gardens, past the pisé houses; it moved slowly, emitting small black clouds. But there was not even the smallest cloud in the sky; only a solitary bird was soaring, its huge, unflapping wings spread wide in the blue expanse of the sunny morning and the splendor of the alien, deathly beautiful, snow-covered mountains. Meshcheriakov saw it when he turned around to cast a last glance at the Valley's cliffs.

3

New customers appeared in the restaurant: an elderly, fat, and flabby man in a uniform and a second one—young, tow-haired, wearing the uniform of a military pilot. A major, approximately the same age as Meshcheriakov. Or a bit older . . . In the army the majors were like respected uncles. And captains. But how old were they? Twenty-five, thirty . . . The senior lieutenants and lieutenants were even younger. How were they in command of us? How did their tongues move to give us orders? Here he is, Meshsheriakov, past thirty, but could he have given orders even to a platoon? Without pausing to think for a second? Perhaps they're a different breed? Perhaps in military school they're initiated into some secret and with this sacred knowledge they're capable of doing whatever they like wherever they like, and of having a couple dozen or even a hundred lives follow them?

But it's time to have another glass. Of this evil vodka. This stupid vodka, as a matter of fact.

Taking a few bites of food, he glanced again at the pilot; he and his companion had already taken seats nearby, and Meshcheriakov now saw that the pilot was not his peer at all. His forehead was wrinkled, there was a deep wrinkle on each cheek, and he had a double chin. His eyes were bright, cold. Could he fly in the Afghan sky? Bombing the *kishlaks*?

In Afghanistan flying was not such a simple matter.

There happened to be children in those *kishlaks*. And in the caravans. As in the caravan—whatever was left of it—which they reached immediately after a raid by an attack plane. A small child from the caravan who was still alive—a small, half-naked, dirty being—was crawling among the pile of camels and bodies of people. The caravan was carrying arms, crates of grenades, mines, and medicines. The caravan men were dead. And two women. They knew what cargo they were carrying. They were the mujahideen. And their wives knew. The half-naked being with the disheveled, coarse black hair and black eyes knew nothing.

We stopped and stood over him. The child seemed to be fine and unhurt. Pozdniak bent down, touched him, and said *"bacha."*ᵛ The small child winced but kept quiet. He sat bent over like an old man and stubbornly looked at the ground.

We stood over him and tried to decide what to do. We stood in the blinding sun among the rags, bales, and the camels and people struck down, and tried to decide his fate.

On the way here we had noticed the black tents and flocks of some nomads in the steppe, at the foot of hills bare like skulls—and so we decided to take him there. Pozdniak picked up the child, the child kept turning his head away but remained in his arms all curled up. But when warrant officer Seliunin fired a shot to finish off a camel, the child began to cling to Pozdniak, grabbed his *khebe*ᵛⁱ with his curled up fingers and didn't open them either on the way to the armored vehicle, or in the armored vehicle on the way to the nomads.

While we were going to the nomads, the remaining solders collected some trophies and poured fuel on what was left and set fire to it. Thick clouds of smoke rose to the sky . . .

The pilot picked up his glass and clinked with his friend, downed it, wincing a bit, and began to eat some food. His friend also downed his glass and said something. The pilot nodded, smiled. Perhaps he'd never been there. And he hadn't attacked caravans and *kishlaks* in which there were women and children. He had flown only in the Russian sky and hit only the training targets. And he hadn't become entrapped—he was a free bird. And his face won't become distorted with pain and hatred, and memories of war won't pierce his soul with the simple question: What did I do that for? Just me, it doesn't concern the others. Justifications will always be found for the people and the country. The people were poorly informed. The country had certain interests, certain geopolitical reasons. The leadership? Where is it? And the country is no longer the same. Everything has changed. Only lone soldiers are left . . .

Meshcheriakov looked at the window covered with a lace curtain. Snow was already falling outside. A sober snow for a beastly fall. And

---

ᵛ   *bacha*: "child" or "boy."
ᵛⁱ   *khebe*: a cotton jacket that is part of the summer uniform.

he's sitting as if in a cave, and he's trying again to break loose of time, its chains, so that he can see everything from a detached point of view, from some firm and high vantage point. To see everything as something that has already gone by, to see all the wars and times of peace as something that has passed, all the desires and thoughts as cold, all the novels and stories as finished—to see in order to understand why all this happened. Why did they put on uniforms, salute each other (to exchange a salute—what does that mean?), learn to shoot and throw grenades, fire weapons, conduct hand-to-hand combat and, obeying commands, move from place to place on the face of the earth and attack people, using all their training, all their available energy, all their daring? Trained doctors kept saving them, sewing up the holes in their young bodies, taking shrapnel out of their eye sockets and even bullets out of their hearts, cutting off shattered legs and bones, bones that were so well adapted to many tasks, bones which had created and were creating everything—from a nail to a sputnik sent into space. In what lies the real reason for this incomprehensible behavior? They loved life and kept ending it. They kept repeating words about peace and organized bloody slaughter. They repented and immediately committed new slaughter. They burned each other in ovens, drowned each other in water, poisoned each other with gas, and sprinkled their heads with ashes. Dumbfounded, horrified at what they had done, they took up arms once again. How can one understand this?

Meshcheriakov was no longer sober and felt that nothing would come of his attempts to understand, to see everything from some inconceivable vantage point . . . But could he at least conclude peace for all time? Right now. Right here, in the restaurant, sitting at the table. How much can you write about it? Again and again, to speed along on a rumbling piece of iron in the heat and dust, with fear and death: where to? And then to return, return eternally, like Odysseus. To return now under one name, then under another; now with one color of eyes, now with another; first a sergeant, then a common soldier or a lieutenant. Or a warrant officer. Will he be able to conclude that peace, or is he doomed to an endless war? He's filled with war themes—they move around in him like shrapnel.

Perhaps he should write the kind of story that would take everything that he remembers, thinks, and knows about war and pull it all in like a magnet? Write about a prisoner abandoned by his army, by his generals in the mountains of Asia; about the fate of the lieutenant who deserted in the Valley. Tell about a goddess, a party whore, the whole newspaper fraternity who sang in the war years about revolutionary fury, about heroism and rubber boots—the generals gave the boots free to the peasants, boots and land. And about how a Kremlin Areopagus[13] decided to defend the honor of the revolution which was endangered in a foreign country, and how armies of glistening helmets crossed the river and the land shook under their wheels; how a nomad placed his rifle on a rock, took aim at a figure in a vehicle, and clicked, "*Allahu akbar!*"[vii] A plane with paratroopers flew into a mountain at night before reaching Kabul. And the last war of the great empire began, the war of the Doomed Contingent with the mountains and nomads of Asia. And after that war, which lasted almost as long as the Trojan War, a warrant officer who looked like Odysseus was returning home. He had arrived from Afghanistan to Soviet Asia, was ordered about, was unable to get a ticket either for a plane or a train and took off in a car that showed up, and went to the seashore since it was nearby—he had not seen the sea even once. Of course, he wasn't able to get a hotel room in the seaside town, but he didn't get depressed, didn't become despondent . . .

No, it's too much for one story. Moreover, even this isn't all. No. Have to write about the main thing. Here's what: a story about the last war story. A certain former soldier has a book coming out and he heads to a restaurant, drinks vodka, eats some bread, thinks that he won't ever be able to free himself, that he'll break the peace agreement he had concluded with himself because just barely after concluding it, he's already wondering if he shouldn't write one more war story, a story which would take in everything. And even more than everything. More than he knows himself. Everything that everyone knows who waged war at any time: about the past, present and future. A story that like a magnet would pull out all the shrapnel from all the wounds. A story that would turn out to be magical and would arrest all eyes, all wills, like the rising moon—the old, worn-out prophetess—which arrests all eyes as it rises and warns: don't be lunatics, and the earth won't become like me tomorrow. That's what that magnetic moon is saying. This magical old woman. This medal on the belly of dead space. And medals from all wars and nations jingle in safes and sideboards. The hearts of generals

---

vii   *Allahu akbar*: "God is great."

stick to their collarbones. And in all rocket silos, in all warehouses, there is movement, and a menacing crash resounds. And an invisible force squeezes the rook bills of the fighter bombers with seemingly powerful fingers and starts pulling them up. That's the kind of story he was thinking about, this soldier, a story about a rising magnetic moon. And outside the restaurant window, after a snowfall, a fall moon really did rise above the rooftops.

And in fact, this story would be his last, because death was already sitting next to the soldier.

No, not the pilot, and not the woman on the wrong side of thirty. Death was making clinking sounds with forks—it was chewing, drinking, carrying on a conversation in the image of three friends. And when he was paying the waiter, one of them—a round-faced, blond, pimply guy—evaluated his wallet with a glance, and the soldier's fate was decided.

After paying his bill, he walked out of the large room and put on his black fall coat. The moon was shining brightly on the old Russian town lightly covered with snow. The air felt good. The soldier walked, breathing in the cool air. He walked past houses and trees, a veteran. And death followed him.

The street led him downhill. Cars were whizzing by on the road. The river valley loomed below and glowed. The sounds of a railroad and working factories could be heard in the distance. The soldier was thinking about his daughter; he was planning to buy her something in the department store on the other side of the river if it hadn't closed yet. He looked at his watch. The moon was shining generously, and he had no difficulty in making out what time it was. The department store was still open. He again turned his eyes to the valley and instantly remembered another valley, the Valley in the highlands of Central Afghanistan; he remembered the cliffs and the snow, and the stone lips of the colossus, and the last day, more precisely, the last morning—bright, sunny, and frosty, when the column of vehicles stretched way back and the driver mechanics waited for the command . . .

The soldier was now below. He walked past a stop and he knew there was no streetcar—there was no rumbling of wheels behind him, only the sound of someone's steps. He passed a stop where no people were waiting and approached the bridge, and the steps suddenly caught up with him; somebody passing by suddenly grabbed him under the arm and pulled him into the shadows. The soldier looked to the left: from the left appeared one more man—tall, broad-shouldered, wearing a cap, with a red scarf around his neck—and in that instant the soldier's head shook from a blow and he lost his balance and fell. He tried to get up, and someone's hands seemed to help him up, holding him or feeling under his shirt, but one more blow landed on him, and he dropped halfway down to the ground and leaned on one knee. He tried to get up again and rip off something heavy which was sticking to his head, but he couldn't cope with the monstrous weight and fell down the slope, trying to cling to the cold earth, clawing slimy, rotting foliage and dirt and realizing that now he would fall into the water, the black water in the patches of light of the magnetic moon.

Meshcheriakov tore his glance away from the invisible vantage point, which was located somewhere between the clay vase with a sprig of juniper and the plate of spongy, grey-looking bread, and looked around vacantly. Faces of some people—male and female. Now there were a lot of people; fans of restaurant smells and adventures tended to come here in the evening. It was already noisy in the restaurant . . . But here's a familiar face, familiar blue eyes, eyes full of some cold weariness. The pilot. It's the pilot. At this point Meshcheriakov glanced to the left: the three were still sitting there. The round-faced one was telling them something, twisting his pale lips, moving his eyebrows. The other two were listening to him—one grinning, and the other one who'd be wearing the red scarf, who would land the first and most terrible blow, was listening sullenly, with his fists lying relaxed on the white tablecloth. Sensing someone's gaze, he was about to turn toward Meshcheriakov, but at that point the round-faced one said something particularly funny and all of them started to laugh. Hearing their laughter and seeing their simple smiling faces, Meshcheriakov had his doubts about everything that he had daydreamed. And is this really the main thing? Even if everything would happen precisely like that.

And what is the main thing? What would he write the story about?

No, not about the fate of the lieutenant who deserted in the Valley. And not about the warrant officer who was returning home from the war. And not about the prisoner who was abandoned in the mountains of Asia.

He would like to tell about the pilot and his child, how the two of them lay together in the world at night. A child and a father, who was short, dressed in an old summer leather jacket. They found themselves outside the town, got lost, and spent the night in a haystack, yes, precisely that haystack that keeps its warmth all winter; but it was not winter yet, it was still a remarkable time, Indian summer, and the weather stayed dry and sunny the whole week, and on Saturday they decided to go mushroom hunting. That's what he would like to describe. How Saturday finally came and the pilot and child got on a train, and the train left, and cement fences, pipes, brick buildings, warehouses, summer homes, fields, maples, and villages went past the windows, and all around people talked of prices for piglets and wood, cows and spare parts . . . And this would be his last war story . . . The train suddenly sped over a river, banging loudly with its wheels. Light-yellow, greenish water, the shore overgrown with willows. Above the river the train found itself in sunlight—the sun had just come out—and his little daughter's hair, the color of dark honey, began to shine. The old man opposite them half-opened his mouth in admiration but didn't say anything, just nodded his head and looked at him, her father.

They got off at a whistle stop. Two women in brightly colored kerchiefs and a man in a grey cap who immediately lit a cigarette headed along a path in the direction of dogs barking and roosters crowing; a wall of fir trees hid the village from view. But he and his daughter went straight through a field with piles of golden straw, breaking the threads of a spider web. The barking of dogs and all the village sounds gradually died down, but the birds sang even louder. They turned toward the woods. Unruly red oaks, fragrant pines, and birches with delicate pink bark grew on its edge. And farther in, the tops of spruce trees. They walked along the edge of the woods, parting the yellow feathers of the grass and searching for mushrooms. For dinner they stopped near a juniper bush crowned with tiny, bluish berries. His daughter tried one and spit it out. But the birds like them. She took a cluster of grapes from a package and compared the grapes to the size of the juniper berries. Isn't that wonderful? It's a pity that grapes don't grow in our region.

The sun was pouring its light on the bushes, the grasses, and the little girl with the dark red hair. She was eating large grapes, saying something . . . He was sitting, his back against a pine tree, and looking and listening. There weren't many mushrooms and after dinner they went deep into the woods, hoping to find milk mushrooms, but they didn't find any milk mushrooms either and got lost. They wandered a long time along the twilight galleries of the fir and birch woods, finally found their way to an open area, walked past a thicket of small aspens and saw a commuter train—the color of bricks—in the distance. It had braked at the whistle stop, then took off and floated triumphantly past the setting sun, and disappeared from view. The sun was already touching the tops of the distant trees. The little girl was happy that they were late for the train and clapped her hands. But when they headed back toward the woods, to the meadow where there was a haystack and he hollowed out a grotto and brought some dead wood, and the sun went down and it became dark in the woods, the little girl grew quiet, pricked up her ears, and remembered her mother. "Mommy will probably get scared," she half whispered. He laughed. "Don't be afraid! And Mommy . . . We'll be at Mommy's on the very first commuter train."

The little girl looked at him distrustfully. He made a fire and only then did she stop looking around and listening. The tiny stack of dry branches turned into a large house of fire. And perhaps the fire reminded her of some creature, some young wild animal. The animal bristled its hair, crackled, curled, and attempted to bite her hand or knee. She kept setting fire to one end of a branch and raising it like a torch. Her face got all red and her eyes shone. There was a bit of bread left, but he decided that it would be better to finish it in the morning.

In the haystack that was their cave they lay down with their heads facing the opening. The hay pricked them, but it was exceptionally warm in there. His daughter, covered with his old leather jacket, quickly fell asleep. He didn't sleep. He lay there and looked. He could see limpid constellations above the woods. The constellations were shifting, moving slowly somewhere . . .

Something fell with a crack in the forest; the little girl shuddered, but she didn't wake up. Probably an old tree. The old tree was not able to bear the weight of its years. Well, nothing can fall on them. Even if the tall fir tree at the edge of the woods were to come down, it would not cause any harm. The helmet of grass was safely protecting them.

Meteors sometimes glittered in the black sky.

But from a red-hot spark in the sky their refuge could burst into flames too. Like the straw in the sheds which would burst into flames from their tracer bullets.

Who will direct the spark here, what night pilot in the heavens?

There was a crackling sound in the forest at times as if someone were making his way through the fir trees. At times he thought he heard sighs.

He couldn't stand it and, trying not wake up the little girl, he carefully made his way out of the haystack and walked around it, peering into the darkness and listening. Animals were probably wandering in the woods, following their night-time paths. Elk. Roebucks. Or wild boars. Yes, better to have elk and wild boar than a man stealing up.

He walked up to the campfire. A few coals were still smoldering. He got a pack, took out a cigarette, stuck a sharp twig into the violet-crimson coals, and lit his cigarette with it. It was surprisingly warm. He sat down on a piece of wood from a tree trunk. The haystack was clearly outlined in the middle of the meadow.

The choking smoke of the cigarette was unpleasant, but he continued to smoke. He smoked and frowned, sensing how everything had changed in him. Just before, in the evening, he had been in a wonderful mood because luck had forced them to stay in the forest and see a very delicate, soft sunset and hear the hoots of an owl flying over the meadow with the solitary birches and juniper bushes. The boughs of spruce trees. The smell of the small juniper cones which his daughter had crushed, his nice daughter with moles on her hands like the ones he had—her father, a loyal dog who was ready to fight the whole world to defend her. Never before had he been so clearly aware of being a father. More precisely, he had known he was a father, but had not felt it. Either his army service got in the way, or their meetings were infrequent, or something else. But now he's been discharged, now he's been brought to earth and is stunned to discover that he's a father, the one who gave her life—her voice, her eyes, and her laughter—and is obligated to protect her. These thoughts were good and heart-warming, and he smiled involuntarily.

But now everything has already changed. And now he no longer wants to smile. He senses uneasiness, as if something is drawing near, is imminent and unavoidable.

It can't be—not a soul around. Who would take it in his head to come here? And set fire to the haystack? People are asleep in the villages and towns. And it's possible that he alone isn't sleeping and is looking at the stars, at the bright-blue dot of a quickly moving sputnik. Who would take it into his head . . . What madman . . . And in the final analysis, he's free not to sleep and instead guard his daughter. And to think the whole night about what he has no strength to think about, what is already rising in his throat.

Those thoughts were always there, but he wouldn't allow them to develop fully. He would drown them out with some strange and stupid noise, with some idle, empty talk. And now they've become fully developed.

He passed his hand over his face as if he were trying to take off something, something unpleasant and sticky, but this unpleasant thing was simply his face. And suddenly he felt an overwhelming disgust for this face, a face on which everything was registered that had lain on the path covered by him to the bitter end with loyalty to an oath and an officer's honor—all the crudeness and dirt of the barracks, all his longing, all his vain aspirations and the complexities of building a career, all his awards and medals and documents in bloody frames, all the smoke and fumes of the military fraternity, all the faces of people twisted in pain and the faces of animals with bared teeth running in different directions on the ground, trying to get away from his terrible winged shadow. Why did he chase them down? Where did they all disappear to, those who needed this? Who gave the orders and seemingly took everything on themselves, all the planned and accidental deaths of all the camel drivers and all the old men. The ones who gave orders only pretended that they were taking everything on themselves, but everything stayed with him, on his face, on his face soft like clay and covered with scabies—heavy, red all over, impossibly old. And would he really be able to shake it off, throw it off like a cover, like an alien mask? And never more plunge into the sky of war, never more chase down camel drivers and their dark-eyed children in hopes of obtaining awards, money, and stars on his epaulettes?

Awards and stars on his epaulettes . . . !

Now the stars in the sky would be enough for him.

1995

NOTES

1. Streltsy: units of Russian guardsmen established in the middle of the 16th century. They carried firearms, formed the bulk of the Russian army and provided the tsar's bodyguard for about one hundred years.
2. Bryansk Oblast is in western Russia.
3. "son": a soldier in the first months of army service.
4. Shudra: the lowest of the four castes in India.
5. Lenin room: A room decorated as a memorial to Lenin, with reading materials, posters, etc. Also referred to as "Lenin's corner."
6. Meshchersky region: in the Ryazan Oblast, western Russia.
7. old timer: someone who has served at least a year and half in the Soviet Army.
8. The adjective Ermakov applies to the writer's last name is *pautinnyi* or "webby" (as a spider web), thus drawing attention to the first two syllables of the writer's name, *Paustovsky*.
9. Paustovsky, Konstanin: Russian prose writer (1892-1968) whose style has been described as "lyrical and contemplative." He never gave in fully to the pressure to follow the socialist realist method of depicting reality. The story character is reading Paustovsky's book, *Meshcherskaya storona* (Meshchera Region, 1939), written during the years of the Great Terror.
10. Ermakov writes "the country of *ros i rossov*," a play on words in Russian. The word "ros" is the genitive plural form of *rosa*, "dew." *Ross* is the genitive plural form of *rossy*, and *rossy* is a variant of *rusy*, the name given to people inhabiting Rus, the area around Kiev in the IX-X centuries.
11. pisé: a mixture of sand, loam, clay, and other ingredients, similar to adobe.
12. Mayak: a popular station of Soviet State Radio.
13. Areopagus: the highest judicial and legislative council in ancient Athens.

A BRIEF HISTORY OF PAINTBALL IN MOSCOW

Viktor Pelevin

One has Jean Paul Sartre in his pocket
And proudly knows it,
Another sometimes plays his *bayan*[1] . . .

B. G[2]

There is no higher or more noble goal in art than to arouse mercy and indulgent gentleness toward others. And they, as each of us knows, aren't always worthy of this, far from it. It's for a good reason that Jean Paul Sartre said, "Hell—it's the others." These are truly surprising words—it's rare for such an amount of truth to be squeezed into a single sentence. However, for all its depth, this maxim is insufficiently developed. To acquire definitive completeness, "Jean Paul Sartre—that's hell, too" must be added to it.

I'm really not saying this so that I can once again reprimand the French leftist philosopher in the dusty pocket of my intellect. I have enough to be proud of as it is. I simply have to find some smooth way of changing the topic to people who "play on the bayan" or, to translate this expression utilizing the criminal jargon found in police dictionaries from the TransSib and Magnitka[3] days, use firearms to shoot each other.

And so we've changed the topic—I hope that the reader occupied with thoughts of Sartre didn't experience any discomfort as this took place.

Yakov Kabarzin, nicknamed "Kobzar,"[4] the leader of the Kamennomostovsky criminal group and the eminent ideological Soskovets[5] of the criminal world, without a doubt had the right to put himself in the category of "shooters." It's true he hadn't taken a gun in his own hands for a long time now, but it was precisely his will, which passed through the nerves and muscles of various thugs, "boys," and other mechanisms of the simplest kind, that was the cause of the great number of sensational deaths described in detail on the front pages of Moscow tabloids. Not one of these killings was engendered by his cruelty or rancor; only the inexorable laws of the market economy impelled Kobzar to take extreme measures. In terms of his character he was indulgently gentle, sentimental within reasonable limits, and inclined to forgive his enemies. This came through even in his nickname, somewhat unusual for a thieves' culture which, in choosing a totem, prefers inanimate, hard objects like clothes iron, nail, or globe.

He was given that nickname still in school. The point is that Kobzar wrote poetry from childhood and, like many famous historical figures, considered the important thing in his life to be precisely poetry, not the administrative operations for which his contemporaries valued him. Moreover, as a poet he enjoyed a certain recognition; his short poems and longer narrative ones, full of moderate patriotism, Nekrasov's[6] social pathos (with a not fully clear addressee or sender), and love of the simple and unpretentious nature of the north appeared still in Soviet times in various almanacs and collections. The *Literary Gazette*, in its section "Congratulations to those celebrating a jubilee," several times printed comments about Kobzar, decorated with what looked like a sketch of his passport photo (because of the peculiarities of his work, Kobzar didn't like to be photographed very much). In a word, among the morose criminal bosses on the eve of the third millennium, Kobzar occupied approximately the same place as that of Denis Davydov[7] among the partisans of 1812.

Therefore, it's not surprising that such a man would want to change the bloody confrontations with firearms—which in Moscow alone provided a living for no less than a thousand journalists and photographers—to a more civilized form of settling mutual claims.

This thought occurred to Kobzar in the casino "Yeah, Bunin!"[8] that had just opened when, half-listening to the famous smash hit "Gang Members, Don't Shoot Each Other,"[9] he was thinking about Russian history and weighing whether to place his next bet on black or red.

It so happened that at that very moment the TV, secured directly over the gambling table to distract the players, was showing some American movie in which the characters, vacationing in a natural setting, were shooting each other with a colorful paint from paintball guns. Unexpectedly, the program changed and famous scenes of a bank robbery from the film *Heat* began to flicker on the screen.

Kobzar thought with sadness that the "action" genre, which in the civilized world relieves the littered sub-conscious of millions of fat old ladies consuming pizza in front of the TV as they wait for death, for some reason in gullible Russia becomes a direct guide to action for the flower of youth and, no one, absolutely no one, understands that the large-caliber rifles in the hands of elderly movie heroes are simply a metaphor and a sedative for menopause. At that moment a waiter who was passing by tripped and a yellow stream of egg liqueur splashed out of the tipped glass onto Kobzar's white jacket.

The waiter turned pale. White fire flared in Kobzar's eyes. He examined the yellow stains on his chest carefully, raised his eyes to the TV screen, then lowered them at the waiter, and stuck his hand in his pocket. The waiter dropped his tray and staggered back. Kobzar took out his hand— in it was a crumpled wad of hundred-dollar bills and several large chips. Cramming all this into the breast pocket of the waiter's jacket, he turned around and quickly headed for the exit, dialing a number on his tiny "Motorola" as he walked.

The next day on one of the highways near Moscow seven black limousines with tinted windows and a gold Rolls-Royce with two flashing lights on the roof went by, spaced far apart. Each car was followed by jeeps with guards in them. The police cordoning off the area kept an arrogantly important silence; wild rumors circulated that somewhere near Moscow a secret summit of the big eight was taking place or, as one critically thinking newspaper delicately put it, the "group of seven and a half." But people in the know understood everything after they recognized the gold Rolls-Royce as Kobzar's car.

Using his authority as the spiritual Soskovets, in just one evening Kobzar placed calls to the leaders of the seven largest criminal groups and set a general meeting in a suburban restaurant, "The Russian Idea," well-known for similar meetings.

"Brothers," he said, looking round with the burning eyes of a prophet at the leaders sitting at the round table. "I'm not a very young man any more. And to tell the truth, not young at all. And I no longer need anything for myself. At least because I've had everything a long time already. If someone wants to say it's not true, let him spit it out and say so right now. Let's take you, Varyag.[10] Maybe you think I still want something I don't have?"

"No, Kobzar," Kostia Varyag the thief from Kaliningrad answered, who was called that not because of his Nordic looks, as many mistakenly thought, but because the Ukrainian mob invited him several times to Kiev as an observer, as Riurik[11] had been at one time. "Indeed, you do have everything. And if you don't have something, I can't imagine what such a thing could be."

"You speak, Aurora," Kobzar turned to the leader from Petersburg.

"What else could you want, Kobzar?" pensively responded Slavic Aurora, who was famous in criminal circles for his legendary shot from an artillery gun aimed at the dacha of the intractable Sobchak.[12] "You have everything except perhaps your own space station. And it's because you don't need it. And if you needed a space station, Kobzar, I'm confident you'd get one. You have a gold Royce with two flashing lights on the roof, but those flashing lights don't impress me. Any piece of trash can put those on for himself. I'm impressed by something else— you're the only one in the world who—it's just amazing!—has all zeroes for numbers on his license plate. That can't be so, but it is. So you've understood something about life that we don't know. And we respect you for it like an older brother. So spit it out—your mates in this life also want respect for themselves."

Slavic Aurora loved to express himself metaphorically and in a multi-layered way. He was feared because of this.

"Fine," Kobzar said, realizing that the ritual of praising him could be considered completed. "Everybody believes I have everything. The important thing is I believe it myself. Therefore you won't think that I have to make a deal just for me personally. I'm thinking about our whole big family, and this time you can consider my mind with all its thoughts as our communal fund. Listen up. Here's the thing . . ."

And Kobzar expounded his idea. It was simple to a primitive level. Kobzar reminded them that the brotherhood had tried many times to divide spheres of influence once and for all, and each time a new war proved that it was impossible. "And this is impossible," he said, "for the very same reason it's impossible to build communism. Our most important father doesn't want this, the one who added an awful lot of the human factor to the clay from which he molded us . . ." And he motioned expressively upwards.

His comrades-in-arms began to hoot in approval—everybody liked

Kobzar's words. Because at the table sat people for whom that stupid anecdote about a gymnast[13] whom someone supposedly wanted to remove from the cross was insulting. In fact the gymnast did not bother anyone.

"But every time," Kobzar continued, "one of our boys is being buried and everybody follows his coffin—both his friends and yesterday's enemies—it doesn't feel quite right because of the bitter absurdity of such a death."

He looked round at the gathering with an expressive look. All were nodding in agreement.

"Life can't be stopped," Kobzar said after pausing theatrically. "No matter what we decide right now, all the same we'll be dividing up this world again tomorrow. So that new blood enters the veins, the old blood has to flow out of them. The question consists of something else: why should we really die doing this? Why should we help the trash fulfill their rotten plan for their struggle with us?" No one could give a clear answer to this. Only the Kazakh boss Vasia Chuiskaya Shupa took a deep drag on his cigarette and asked, "And how do you propose we die? Fake it?"

Instead of answering him, Kobzar took out a box from under the table, opened it, and showed the tense brotherhood some kind of strange instrument. On the outside it resembled the fashionable Czech automatic "Skorpion," but it was more crudely made and gave the impression of being a toy. Over the barrel it had a tube like an optical gun sight, only thicker. Kobzar aimed this strange weapon at the wall and pulled the trigger. The quiet chatter of the weapon resounded ("like a whip with a silencer," Slavic Aurora muttered) and red spots appeared on the wall—as if behind the wallpaper there was some dystrophic informer with whom retribution had finally caught up. In Kobzar's hands was a paintball gun that shoots balls filled with gelatin and dye.

His idea was brilliant and simple. In order "to resolve problems," there really was no need to actually kill each other. In any shooting, a paintball cartridge could replace live cartridges, if all the shooters striving to remake the world would voluntarily assume the responsibility of giving up the business in the event of their conditional death, leave Russia within forty-eight hours, and not undertake any retaliatory actions. In a word, pretend that they really had died.

"I think, brothers, we all have a place we can go to," Kobzar said, looking dreamily into the squinting eyes of his companions-in-arms.

"You, Slavik, have your chateau in the Pyrenees. You, Kostik, have so many islands in the Maldives Archipelago that it's all but impossible to understand why people still call them the Maldives. I have a few places as well . . ."

"We know, Kobzar, that you do."

"So let's drink to our peaceful old age. And let's prove to those louts that we're not a gang of pickpockets from Kursk Station but truly organized crime. In the sense that if we embark on something in an organized way, we'll get what we want done."

In a few hours the agreement was concluded. The problem of control seriously worried the participants, and they agreed that any one of them who tried to violate the agreement would have to deal with all the rest.

The first result of the agreement was that the cost of paintball equipment rose sharply. The owners of two small stores where the weapons and paint were sold made a fortune in two weeks. All the TV channels showed their faces drunk with happiness, and in this context the newspaper "Izvestiya" made a cautious prediction about the beginning of the long awaited economic boom. True, the merchants soon went bankrupt because with all the money they had made they bought a huge amount of equipment used in paintball—masks, coveralls, and visors—for which no demand arose. But the newspapers didn't write about it.

Not without some tension in Moscow criminal circles, guesses were made as to who would become the first victim of the new method of resolving problems. That turned out to be Suleiman, the representative of the Chechen crew. He was shot from three paintball guns right at the Karo Club as he was walking from the door to his Jeep to get a fresh supply of coke. Since this was the first shooting that followed the new rules, all of Moscow awaited the event, and what took place was recorded with cameras from four or five angles. The film was then shown several times on TV. It looked like this. Suleiman, holding a cell phone in one hand, approached his car. Three black figures appeared out of nowhere behind his back. Suleiman turned around and at that very moment gelatin-filled balls began to drum on his green velvet jacket.

It became immediately clear that the guys had blown it—all the guns were shooting green paint without leaving any visible traces on the velvet of the same color. Suleiman looked at his jacket, then at his killers and, gesticulating, began to explain something to them. He was answered with a new hailstorm of green paint. Suleiman turned away, bent over the door, and tried to open it (he was getting a hangover, and he was a bit nervous, and so he couldn't get the key into the hole). The delay led to his ruin. The phone he had been holding suddenly rang. Shielding his face with his free hand, he brought it up to his ear, listened for a few seconds, was about to argue, but then apparently heard something very convincing. Nodding unwillingly, he selected a clean spot and fell to the sidewalk. This was just the right time to do this—the attackers were coming to the end of their supply of balls.

A control shot followed which made Suleiman look like Ronald McDonald with a green mouth. Throwing their weapons on the sidewalk next to the conditional corpse, the gunmen took off in a hurry. To leave the paintball guns at the place of execution subsequently became chic in its way and was considered very stylish, but it wasn't always done—the equipment cost a bundle of money.

People in the know said that some especially powerful people had called Suleiman from Grozny,[14] where the execution procedure was being watched live by satellite (naturally, the Chechen group took part in the convention; without it, any agreement would have lost its significance). The incompetence of the Moscow mafia sent the Chechen TV viewers into shock. Nothing of this kind had ever been shown on Grozny TV. "How can there be talk of a joint destiny with such a people?" the Chechen newspapers asked the next day.

Suleiman was loaded into an ambulance that had driven up, and a day later he was already nibbling sunflower seeds on the Azure Coast. After this first try, which had almost turned out to be a flop, the rules for a paintball shooting were quickly worked out and became a part of the corporate criminal code of honor. The weapons began to be loaded with paintballs in a red-blue-green sequence so that the result was guaranteed whatever the color of the clothing. A small camera was mounted on one of the barrels (because of the close range, there were usually several killers) so that the whole shooting process could be documented. Not all agreed right away to consider themselves dead. No one, of course, dared speak out against the criminal bosses who had approved the new ritual, but many maintained that, had these been real bullets, they would have been only wounded and within a week or two would have recovered and "brought down the bastards" themselves. Therefore, there arose the absolute necessity of third-party judges and, naturally, the role fell to the chief criminal bosses.

Examining the jackets and coats, at times brought from thousands of kilometers away for checking, they would decide who had been knocked off, and who could still live and be able to return to the capital scene after a period of time. They approached this work responsibly: they consulted with a whole synod of surgeons and, as a rule, didn't stretch the truth because they knew that for any uproar they would have to answer with the viscose, flannel, or silk on their own chests.

But nevertheless the criminal bosses were not always believed. With an obtuse insistence the Moscow brotherhood tried many times to invite Chuck Norris as a chief expert—someone who was a big specialist in beating people's brains out, or getting rid of his business neighbor. Norris respectfully declined, claiming that he was very busy with a process which in his faxes showed up as "shooting." And although in English it simply meant "shooting a film," the brothers-in-crime, more familiar with the first meaning of the term, nodded their small heads with respect. Evidently in their minds reality didn't fully divide into the cinematic and everyday kind. No one knows if Norris was truly that busy or, from an American way of looking at things, he simply didn't want to count the spots on Kenzo and Cardin jackets permeated with "bull's"[15] sweat, although this would have promised his Moscow business[16] stunning prospects at that.

Noticeable progress in the cultural paradigm was taking place parallel to all this. Shufutinsky[17] finally found himself on the spiritual rubbish heap—even the hastily prepared pop tune "Colors from Small Spasskaya" didn't help. In Moscow and Petersburg the nostalgic hit "Painter Man"[18] by the "Boney-M" group and a song about an artist who paints rain became all the rage—the latter affected the imagination with its significance and dreadful ambiguity. Aesthetes, just as ten years ago, preferred "Red Is a Mean, Mean Color"[19] by Steve Harley and "Ruby Tuesday" in the Marianne Faithfull rendition.

"The path Russia has taken these past few years," a critic of one of the Moscow papers wrote with satisfaction, "can be judged if only by the fact that now no one will start searching (and find! And people did find, you know!) for political allusions in these songs." In general, in any bar any mention of coloring substances in combination with a simple melody produced streams of tears of repentance and generous tips to the musicians, which pop culture parasitized in the most vulgar way.

The new fashion led at times to unpleasant consequences. Mick Jagger almost lost his eye at a concert in "Russia Hall" when, performing "Paint It Black,"[20] he happened to put the sounding board of his guitar to his shoulder like the butt of a firearm. To the excited roar of the audience, kilos of gold chains were taken off and thrown onto the stage, one of which scratched his cheek.

Things couldn't go on, of course, without some monstrous misunderstandings. In an editorial, the erotic weekly *MK-Sutra*[21] described something called "a popular variety of virtual-colophonic exhibitransvestism" under the name "Painted Balls." This almost caused a scandal with the patriarchate, where they were reading the *MK-Sutra* in order to know what the life of contemporary young people was based on. At the last minute they managed to convince the hierarchs that entirely different colored balls were meant and nothing was threatening the country's spiritual flowering.

But it must nevertheless be acknowledged that the high point of influence on the cultural life of the two capitals was the opening of several offices for psychoanalysis where the spots left by the paint were interpreted as Rorschach inkblots,[22] based on which the conditionally surviving victims received a scientifically grounded explanation of the subconscious motives of the murderer and even of the person who had ordered the action. However, the offices existed for a short time only. The private power structure of "Chain Mail" (later "Palette"), the same one that had the brilliant advertising slogan, "We'll dispose of your problems with a flick of the finger," saw a competitor in them.

The eight leaders who at one point had gotten together in "The Russian Idea" for concluding the convention were becoming victims themselves, one after the other, of the smoldering reworking of the peace. In that sense their fate was no different from the fate of the other criminal bosses.

Slavik Aurora was forced to leave for his chateau in the Pyrenees after an egg (seemingly Faberge) filled with compressed paint, which Kostia Varyag had given him for his birthday, broke in his hands. Soon after that, Chechen goons, avenging Suleiman, covered Kostia Varyag himself with bunches of zeroes with the sadism of the Middle Ages, and his whole first week in the Maldives was spent with a pumice stone rubbing off the zigzags of indelible red acrylic covering his whole body. And Kobzar's leaving the business was full of tragic symbolism.

The reason turned out to be his passion for literature, which we already spoke of in the beginning of our story. Kobzar not only wrote poems, but he published them, and then attentively watched for the reaction which, to be honest, as a rule simply didn't exist. And suddenly an article, "Ifkobcroaked," written by a certain Bisinsky[23] who worked for the *Literary Bazaar*, descended on him.

Notwithstanding the fact that Bisinsky worked for a publication whose title placed such high expectations on him, he not only couldn't rise to the level of *Bazaar* but in general didn't know how to choose his words carefully for this bazaar. He understood nothing about poetry and was a specialist basically in Moldavian port wine and Russian gestalt. Moreover, he didn't even have any notion as to who Yakov Kabarzin was; the poems published in the almanac "Day of Poetry" were the first that had turned up in his hand trembling from a hangover.

There's some sad irony in all this. Had Bisinsky written a good review of Kobzar's poems, he would have perhaps become a frequent customer in "The Russian Idea" and would've gotten some idea of the real nature of Russian gestalt, not the one sucked out of Spengler[24] whom he never did understand. But he dashed off one of his usual stinking, hack denunciations to a non-existent channel of authority, as a result of which, people said, food products wrapped in *Bazaar* spoiled twice as quickly as usual. Kobzar was particularly incited by the following turn of speech: "if that ass and homo feels offended by my grumbling article . . ."

"Who's an ass? Who's a homo?" Kobzar got boiling mad, grabbed the phone, and scheduled a meeting—naturally not with Bisinsky, but with the owner of the bank who had received all publications from "I" to "U" according to an interbank agreement about the division of newspapers. It was so unclear where to look for Bisinsky and what to grab him for that he seemed elusive and invisible.

"You have a certain columnist," he said to the pale banker at the meeting, who isn't a columnist but an insolent hack. And he's become so insolent that someone will pay for it."

It became clear that the banker simply didn't know about the existence of the *Literary Bazaar*, but was ready to hand over the whole editorial staff to appease Kobzar.

"I hadn't wanted to take the letter L," he complained. "It was Borka who dumped and forced the letters up to 'M' on me. And there's no arguing with him, is there? If you want to know, I can't stand the word *literatura* (literature; trans.) at all. It's such a natural monopoly. If done with one's head, it should be written with a 'd' in it, then privatized and broken into two new ones—*litera* (letter, as in an alphabet; trans.) and *dura* (female fool; trans.). No, I won't give them any money, don't be afraid. Think about it yourself—they have a photo rubric, "Dialogues, dialogues." In each issue, thirty years in a row. All kinds of Mezhduliazhkises, Lupoyanovs of some kind . . . Who they are, no one knows. And all the time—dialogues, dialogues . . . The question is— what did they write their bullshit about for so many years? And they're still writing their fucking bullshit—dialogues, dialogues . . ."

Kobzar listened gloomily, holding his hands in the pockets of his heavy coat and frowning at the banker's generous stream of foul language. It finally began to dawn on him that the unfortunate columnist could hardly have been able to insult him personally, because he wasn't acquainted with him and had only dealt with his poems—so that the "ass" and "homo" were apparently aimed at those minor working demons of which there are many, according to Blok,[25] at the disposal of every artist.

"Well, all right," Kobzar growled unexpectedly to the banker trying to justify himself, "let the demons figure it out then."

The banker was taken aback, but Kobzar turned and, accompanied by his retinue, went to his gold Royce. No orders with respect to the columnist were given, but the cautious banker saw to it personally that the columnist was given a good beating and sacked. He was afraid to kill him because he couldn't predict how Kobzar's mood would be affected.

Two years passed. One morning Kobzar's car stopped on Nikolskaya Street by an establishment bearing the name "Salon-Image-Maker Lada-Benz," where his young girlfriend worked. Kobzar stepped from the car onto the sidewalk and suddenly a small, ragged homeless man rushed up to him with a bicycle pump in his hands. Before anyone could understand anything, he pressed the plunger and Kobzar was spattered from head to toe with a thick solution of yellow gouache. The homeless man turned out to be that same columnist, who decided to take vengeance for his lost career.

Kobzar swayed nobly, wiped the paint off his face (its color reminded him of the glass of egg liqueur which had started all this), and looked at the building of the Slaviansky Bazaar.[26] For the first time he sensed just how much this rumbling nothing into which he strode every morning with his voracious horde of Komsomol members, thieves, shooters, and economists wearied him. And here a miracle took place—a huge sports hall, white with gold, unlike any on earth, with gold rings hanging from the ceiling, suddenly opened in his mind's eye for a second—and there, in the emptiness between the rings, was some kind of invisible presence in comparison with which the Slaviansky Bazaar and others not quite of that caliber had no value, no goal, and no point. And although his guards, kicking the weak-willed body of the columnist, were shouting "Doesn't count!" and "It's no good!", he closed his eyes and collapsed energetically, with enjoyment, to the ground.

All of Moscow came to Kobzar's funeral. For days and nights his open coffin stood on the stage of the Hall of Columns[27] overflowing with flowers. Only once, during a break, did he crawl out of it for a few minutes to have something to eat and drink a glass of tea. The people in the hall stood and applauded and, barely noticeably, Kobzar smiled from his coffin in response, recalling what he had lived through on Nikolskaya Street. Then people with whom he used to have dealings filed past; stopping, they would say a few simple words and move on. According to the conditions of the convention, Kobzar couldn't respond, but sometimes he would nevertheless close his eyes for a second, and the companion-in-arms walking past realized that he had been understood and heard. Several times Kobzar's eyes would become moist and shine from particularly warm words, and all TV cameras would turn toward his coffin. And when the mayor, who that evening had put on a simple shirt with large blue-red-green polka dots, recited from memory one of the best poems of the deceased to the gathering, for the first time in many years a teardrop quickly ran down Kobzar's cheek. He and the mayor exchanged a faint smile which the others didn't see, and Kobzar understood that the mayor had undoubtedly also seen the Gymnast. And tears no longer stopped but poured down his cheeks right onto the white brocade.

In a word, this was a solemn occasion which was imprinted on everyone's memory. The only thing that clouded it was the news that the columnist Bisinsky had been drowned in a barrel of brown nitro paint by unknown people. Kobzar didn't want this and was sincerely upset.

The morning of the next day found him at Vnukovo airport. He was flying without luggage through Ukraine. After stopping at the entrance for the last time, he looked over the cars, the pigeons, the taxi drivers and the trash that was called police, and strode into the airport building. At the end of the general hall a short young man bumped him lightly, who had an anchor with a snake entwined around it and the word "acid" tattooed on his hand. He was holding a large black bag in which some kind of heavy metal clanked when they collided. Instead of excusing himself, the young man raised his eyes at Kobzar and asked (mixing Russian and Ukrainian; trs.), "Tough guy, eh?"

In Kobzar's pocket there now was a real Glock-27 with hollow point bullets which could send (and more precisely, immediately lay flat) the brazen fellow to a rather distant place—somewhere to the opposite wall of the hall. But in recent days something had changed in Kobzar's soul. He looked the young man up and down, smiled and sighed.

"Tough guy?" Kobzar repeated the question. "Sort of."

And he pushed the transparent door with the "Business Class" sign.

What went on in Moscow for the rest of the summer, fall, and the first half of winter was best expressed by the title of one article about the jubilee of the artist Saryan[28]—"an orgy of colors." By the end of December this orgy began to die down and gradually the outline of a truce to come took shape. The rules of paint-ball, established in Kobzar's time, were adhered to with reverence, and many outstanding figures had to leave Russian life for quiet island paradises, far from the wet and dreary Moscow boulevards, high above which twirl green funnels of financial tornadoes visible only to the third eye of a banker.

The final meeting for dividing everything and anything anew was earmarked for the same restaurant, "The Russian Idea," where at one time the historic meeting of the great eight took place with Kobzar at the head.

The meeting coincided with the New Year and music was thundering in the restaurant. Rolls of streamers flew above the heads of the gathering, confetti poured from the ceiling, and one had to speak loudly in order to outshout the orchestra. But the meeting, in essence, was purely a formality, and all five of the chief criminal bosses felt calm. Only one man aspired to the role of the ideological Soskovets of the criminal world—the mighty, law-abiding Pasha Mercedes, who was called that, naturally, not because of his car—he rode only in a made-for-order Ferrari. According to his passport, his full name was Pavel Garsiyevich Mercedes; he was the son of a pregnant communist woman who ran away from Franco,[29] received his first name at birth in honor of Korchagin,[30] and grew up in an orphanage in Odessa, as a result of which he brought to mind Babel's [31] heroes in his habits.

"Kobzar is no longer among us," he said to the gathering, casting a sidelong glance at Father Frost,[32] who was walking through the hall and offering gifts from a large, red sack to the people sitting at the tables.

"But I promise you that the bastard who ordered it will drown in a sea of paint. You know I can do that."

"Yes, Pasha, you can do a lot of things," people at the table responded deferentially.

"You know," Pasha continued, glancing at the gathering coldly, "Kobzar had a gold Royce which no one else had. So I say to you that I don't feel envious. Have you heard of the space station 'Mir'? Well, it's hanging in the sky only because I give that black hole half of everything I get from the Moskvoretsky market."

"Yes, Pasha. We have yachts and helicopters, some even have planes, but no one has such a showy thing like yours," said Lyonia of Arabia, expressing the general opinion, who had big dealings with Saddam himself and was just passing through Moscow.

"And for the dough that comes to me from Kotelnicheskaya Embankment," Pasha continued, "I support three thick journals which Zhora Soros[33] abandoned when he realized that it wasn't him that was important to them, but a couple of local Dostoevskys. I don't have a single kopeck from this, but on the other hand we're becoming many times over more influential because of these lads."

"Right on!" the Sukhumi criminal boss Babuin agreed.

"But that's not all. Everybody knows that when one half-wit from the Ministry of Defense got in the habit of calling himself part of my clique in the newspapers, Aslan and I saw to it that that half-wit was removed from his position. And this wasn't easy, because papa Boria, for whom he answered at the rendezvous, liked him . . ."

"We respect you, Pasha . . . You'll have no argument from us," swept over the table.

"And therefore I say to you—I will now take Kobzar's place. And if anyone wants to say he disagrees, let him say it right now."

Grabbing two small atomizers with red and blue dye from his jacket, Pasha squeezed them menacingly in his hands, wet with perspiration from nervousness, and fixed his eyes on the faces of his partners.

"Does anyone have anything to say against?" he repeated his question.

"No one has anything against," Babuin said. "Why have you taken out that crap? Put it away and don't frighten us. We're not children."

"So no one wants to say anything?" Pasha Mercedes repeated his question, lowering his paint containers.

"I want to say something," a voice resounded unexpectedly behind his back. All turned their heads.

At the table stood Father Frost in a hat tilted to the side. He had already ripped off the beard he no longer needed, and everybody noticed that he was very young, excited, and, it seemed, not totally sure of himself, but in his hands was an old PPSh[34] which he had taken out of the sack, one that had clearly lain the last half century in some dugout in the middle of the Bryansk[35] swamp. On one of his hands there was a strange tattoo—an anchor, with a snake entwined around it, under which the word "acid" was visible in blue. But the most important thing, of course, were his eyes.

The thought-form twinkling in them could be expressed most precisely with visual-linguistic means as follows:

GIVE BACK THE MONEY

And in his eyes there was still such a mad desire to make his way into the world—where life was easy and without cares, where the sea and sky were blue, the air clear, the sand clean and hot, the cars reliable and quick, the conscience obedient, and the women compliant and beautiful—that those gathered around the table almost believed it themselves that such a world truly existed somewhere. But this continued for only a second.

"I want to say something," he repeated shyly, raised the barrel of his machine gun and released the breech lock.

And here we will leave our heroes, reader. I think that now is just the right time to do so, because their situation is serious, their problems deep, and I don't really have a clear idea as to who they are in order for our imaginations to follow these dark bogeymen to their last maneuver. Do you want to follow them, reader? I don't. As far as I'm concerned, it's like in war—there's no air and they shoot real bullets.

So to hell with them.

Let us drink, have a good time—Happy New Year, friends! Happy New Year, which I'm absolutely sure, will be bright, happy and lucky and—what we especially wish all the shooters—unusually colorful.

1997

NOTES

1. *bayan*: a type of accordion.
2. B.G.—Boris Grebenshchikov (1959-), a popular rock musician and songwriter, the lead singer of the band Aquarium. The epigraph cites his song to "tractor drivers."
3. TransSib (Trans Siberian Railroad) and Magnitka (Magnitogorsk Iron and Metal Works): There were various organized crime contenders for control of these two giants in the 1990s.
4. Kobzar: *Kobzar* is the name of the first book of poetry of the Ukrainian poet Taras Shevchenko, published in 1840. The name Kobzar also brings to mind Iosef Kobzon, the Russian "Frank Sinatra," who is widely reputed to have ties with organized crime.
5. Soskovets, Oleg N.: First Deputy Chairman of the Russian Federation, 1993-1996. In 1991, Minister of Metallurgy of the USSR.
6. Nekrasov, Nikolai (1821-78): Russian critic, poet, editor and publisher. His civic-minded verses and satirical stories appealed to the radical and reform-minded intelligentsia.
7. Denis Davydov (1784-1839): a Russian soldier-poet of the Napoleonic Wars who gained fame as an indefatigable fighter.
8. Bunin, Ivan (1870-1953): a major prose writer who emigrated to Paris after the Bolshevik revolution. Awarded the Nobel Prize for Literature in 1933. He was rediscovered by the reading Russian public in the 1960s, and again in the 1990s.
9. A song performed by Evgeny Kemerovsky on his 1995 album *Moi brat* (My Brother), which became a big hit, especially after a video became available. A stanza that is repeated three times (in prose translation): "Gang members don't shoot each other, You've nothing to divide in life. Forget your grudges, sit at a round table, Because it's hard for everyone to bury his friends."
10. Varyag: His name brings to mind the Varyags or Varangians, who were Vikings, Norsemen. Among the Slavs, by the 9th-10th centuries they had a reputation as pirates, skilled tradesmen and soldiers. The Varangians established the great trade route from Kiev to Byzantium, often referred to in history books as "the trade route from the Varangians to the Greeks."
11. Riurik: according to legend, a Viking prince who was invited to come and rule over quarreling east Slav and Finn tribes in approximately 860 A.D.
12. Sobchak, Anatoly: Chairman or Mayor of the Leningrad City Soviet in 1990; he organized opposition to the coup of 1991 and played the same crucial role as Boris Yeltsin did in Moscow. There is some question as to what extent he tried to wage a struggle with the growing crime rate in St. Petersburg.
13. One version of this anecdote: A "New Russian" found out that it was a great thing to be religious in the 1990s. He decided to buy a cross for his new office,

the biggest he could find. He went to a church and began selecting a cross, but all of them were too small for him. Finally he bought a cross that was about two meters long. "Fine, I'll take it, wrap it up," he said, "but take off the gymnast."

14. Grozny: the capital of Chechnya, a republic in Northern Caucasus. When the Soviet Union collapsed in 1991, Chechnya declared its independence from Russia. This has led to years of fighting and political maneuvering, since Moscow has not been willing to relinquish its control of this area.

15. "bull": someone who is in the lowest caste of the mafia hierarchy. He is the one sent to "teach someone a lesson" by beating him or breaking some bones. Equivalent to "soldier" in the American mafia.

16. A casino in Moscow in the 1990s bore the Chuck Norris name.

17. Shufutinsky, Mikhail (1948 -): a performer of ballads, cabaret and prison songs.

18. "Painter Man": "Painter man, painter man, / Who wanna be a painter man?" is the catchy refrain.

19. The chorus to this song: "He's just a body, a beat-up body / He gets his kicks on a fatal crash / And he carries a sign that screams / "Red is a mean, mean color!"

20. "Paint It Black": One of the best songs of the Rolling Stones, it begins, "I see a red door and I want it painted black."

21. MK-Sutra: MK can be read as a reference to Moskovsky Komsomolets, a newspaper founded in 1919, whose popularity in the 1990s grew in part because of its entertaining and sensational stories. The Sutra brings to mind the Kama Sutra, an ancient India text from the 4th century A.D., which is widely considered as the standard work on love in Sanskrit literature. Pelevin is making fun of MK-Sutra, a pulp tabloid which caters to low tastes.

22. The Rorschach inkblot test: a method of psychological evaluation created by Hermann Rorschach in 1921; it was further developed by other researchers and is still used today.

23. Bisinsky is a caricature of the critic Pavel Basinsky, Pelevin's longtime enemy. Literary Bazaar is a parodic reference to the Literary Gazette, which in the 1990s began to lose its importance as the main organ of the intelligentsia, a position the periodical enjoyed in the 1970s and 1980s and during perestroika.

24. Spengler, Oswald (1880-1936): German historian and philosopher. His major work, The Decline of the West, brought him world fame.

25. Blok, Aleksandr (1880-1921): the principal representative of Russian Symbolism, whose poetry is imbued with mystical elements.

26. Slaviansky (Slavic) Bazaar: a famous, expensive restaurant in Moscow in the 1990s.

27. The Hall of Columns in Moscow's House of Unions is where many political leaders have lain in state before their funerals.

28. Saryan, Martiros (1880-1972): an Armenian artist whose paintings are famous for their brilliant, joyous colors.

29. Franco, Francisco (1892-1975): the military leader whose name is most closely associated with the army's victory in the Spanish civil war. Appointed generalissimo of nationalist Spain in 1936 and head of state of all of Spain from 1939 until his death in 1975.
30. Korchagin, Pavel: the hero of Nikolai Ostrovsky's autobiographical novel, *How the Steel Was Tempered*, serialized in 1932-1934. The novel was printed in millions of copies and Korchagin was touted as the model of utterly selfless devotion to the Communist Party.
31. Babel, Isaac (1894-1940): a short story writer whose works include a cycle of stories about Benya Krik, a flamboyant Jewish gangster in Odessa in the 1920s.
32. *Ded Moroz*, which translates as Grandfather Frost, but is usually referred to as Father Frost by English speakers, brings presents to children on New Year's Eve.
33. Soros, George (1930-): born in Hungary; a global financier and philanthropist whose foundations support the development of democratic societies.
34. Pelevin must be referring to the PPSh41 produced after the German invasion of 1941 in response to the urgent need for a light and simple weapon capable of a high volume of fire.
35. Bryansk: a city and oblast southwest of Moscow in western Russia.

THE QUEEN OF SPADES

Lyudmila Ulitskaya

For Natasha

The difference in age between Mur and Anna Fyodorovna formed a rapidly diminishing quantity. No one knows why—either the little wheels in the world's time mechanism had become worn out, or the cogs got ground down—it's just that time began to roll by at a quickened pace, now and then falling into cardiac fibrillation, and so it turned out that the speed of motion of this waning period of time, thirty years—if they are placed between sixty and ninety—hardly meant a thing. Anna Fyodorovna only noticed that things that were normally done quickly were done more and more slowly but, on the other hand, now less time went for sleep.

She woke up early, if one doesn't call it the middle of the night—it wasn't even four—from a bad dream. A grown man, reduced in size to a large doll, was lying in a desk drawer and complaining, "Mommy, I feel so bad here . . ."

It was her son and her heart constricted from grief; there was no way she could help him . . .

In fact there was no son at all; there was a daughter, and Anna Fyodorovna woke up terrified because the dream was more powerful than reality and, for the first few moments after waking up, she was sure that she had a son, but that she had completely forgotten about him. Then she turned on the light, and in the light the delusion dissipated, and she remembered that the evening before she had had to rummage through the desk drawers for a long time, searching for a certain lost document, and because of this search, this stupid dream had started.

Anna Fyodorovna lay in bed awhile and then decided to get up, particularly since she never found the document the day before.

Now the document turned up right away. It was her review of a dissertation ten years ago, and now it was suddenly needed.

The whole house was sleeping and this was bliss, be it a gift or stolen. No one demanded anything from her, all of a sudden two hours of personal time were created, and now she was weighing in her mind what to use them for: to read a book which a patient from long ago, a famous philosopher or philologist, had given her, or to write a letter to a close woman friend in Israel.

She fixed her hair, the color of sparrow feathers, and threw an old sweater over her robe. Her house clothing was never becoming on her; in a robe, she always looked like a housewife from the suburbs at her dacha. People thought that the suits which she had started to wear in her student years looked good on her. Now, whether in a grey or blue suit, she looked like a professor, which fully corresponded to reality.

Anna Fyodorovna made herself coffee, opened the book on literature by her famous patient, got a piece of paper ready for the letter and put a blue dish of candy, which she usually did not allow herself, right next to her. She inhaled the smell of coffee with pleasure, but did not have time to take a swallow: Mur, with her back straight as a ruler, appeared in the kitchen, the wheels of her walking apparatus squeaking now and then.

Anna Fyodorovna checked the buttons of her sweater nervously to see if they were done up right. In any case, she could never predict what in particular she had not done right. If her sweater was buttoned correctly, then it meant that she had put on dreadful stockings or combed her hair wrong. And why wrong, if her whole life she had kept the same look, a braid twisted into a bun at the back of her head. However, the morning remark could be about anything: the curtains, for example, were dirty, or the kind of coffee she had made was revolting and smelled of cooked cabbage . . . The only surprising thing was the freshness with which Anna Fyodorovna reacted—she would apologize and try to justify herself. Sometimes she even tried to refute the comment, but later she always reproached herself. This did not lead to anything good; Mur would only raise her penciled-in eyebrows even higher so that they would become hidden under her strawberry-blond bangs, flutter her long eyelashes slowly and, with eyes the color of an empty mirror, look at Anna Fyodorovna with disapproval.

This time, after rolling out to the middle of the kitchen, Mur was silent. Her black kimono hung in empty folds as if there were no body under it. Only yellowish, bony hands covered in rings that were never taken off and a long neck with a small head stuck out like those of a marionette.

Her whole life, as far back as she could remember, Anna Fyodorovna would prepare herself ahead of time for communicating with her mother. In childhood, she would stand still in front of her door like a swimmer before diving into the water. When she became an adult, she would get ready not for victory but a respectable defeat, like a boxer before a bout with a very strong opponent. At this pre-morning time, her mother caught her by surprise and, since she had not prepared herself in advance, for the first time she saw her with detachment, as if through someone else's eyes: an angel stood before her, without gender or age, and almost without any flesh. Alive only in spirit. But Anna Fyodorovna knew very well what this spirit was like. Clutching a new book in her hand, the spirit uttered:

"What a lot of rubbish there is in these memoirs! Who palmed them off on me . . . ? In 1916 my father and I were still living in Paris. I was a little girl. Kaspari made me a gift of a tiara in '22; I was married to him then and I gambled it away in '24 in Tiflis.[1] By that time there was no Kaspari any more, I was already with Mikhail. He was a great musician," she giggled delicately and meaningfully, and Anna Fyodorovna shuddered because from that point on followed the usual vulgar lexicon, and it was specifically this shuddering that brought her mother enjoyment. "But he couldn't give anyone a good f . . k," Mur laughed gently. "When it came to using his prick, he was incredibly bad. There, in Tiflis, I lost the tiara in a game of cards, and in the portrait Bakst drew, there the tiara is completely different, a piece of junk, a theatrical prop . . ."

This was the best page in her recollections—her famous lovers. Their names were legion. A great deal of paper had been covered by the best pens in honor of her pale locks and unspoken secrets of the heart, and one could study the artistic movements at the beginning of the century through her portraits kept in museums and private collections.

There must have been some mystery to her; it was not only her lovers who would grow weak before her. Anna Fyodorovna, Mur's only daughter, the child of a rare, virtuous caprice, wrestled her whole life with this riddle. Why was Mur given power over her father, her younger sisters, men and women, and even over those undefined creatures found in the narrow and agonizing gap between the sexes? Besides ordinary men with the most simple-minded intentions, effeminate homosexuals and confirmed lesbians who had strayed from the boring female path fell in love with her constantly. Anna Fyodorovna could not find an answer to this question, but submitting to some unknown power, she rushed to fulfill the next whim of her mother. But Mur, like a pregnant woman, constantly wanted something new, something indefinable—in a word, go I know not whither, bring back I know not what.

People who showed even the least bit of resistance to her superhuman charms simply disappeared from view: Anna Fyodorovna's husband was forgotten by all long ago, and the husband of Mur's granddaughter Katia and all the relatives of Mur's last husband as well . . . It was as if they had never existed.

"You've made coffee." Mur placed the mendacious volume before Anna Fyodorovna and wrinkled her delicate nose.

It smelled good, but she always wanted something else.

"I would like a cup of hot chocolate."

"Cocoa?" Anna Fyodorovna got up readily from the table without even having a chance to lament the small, would-be holiday.

"Why cocoa? It's something disgusting, your cocoa. Can't I simply have a cup of hot chocolate?"

"I don't think there's any chocolate."

There wasn't any chocolate in the house. That is to say, there were, of course, mountains of chocolate candies in huge boxes given by patients. But there was no chocolate either in powder form or in bars.

"Send Katia or Lenochka. How can it be that there's no chocolate in the house?!" Mur became indignant.

"Right now it's four in the morning," Anna Fyodorovna tried to defend herself. But right away she clapped her hands and exclaimed, "There is, Lord, there is!"

She took an unopened box from the sideboard, quickly ripped the crackly cellophane, poured out a handful of candy, and with a kitchen knife separated the fat bottoms of the candies from their worthless fillings. Mur, who had gotten ready for a fight, immediately lost all her fire at the sight of such ingenuity.

"Why don't you bring it to my room . . ."

Carefully protecting her hand with a thick oven mitt, Anna Fyodorovna heated the milk in a small briki.[2] She took care of her hands like a singer takes care of her throat. And she did have something to protect: a slender hand with long plump fingers and short, oval-shaped, iodine-edged nails. Every day, armed with a manipulator, she would reach into the very center of some eye, carefully avoiding the fibers of the stretching muscles, the tiny vessels, the tendon of Zinn, and the dangerous Schlemm's canal, maneuver through the many membranes to the ten-layered retina, and with these crude fingers patch, darn, and glue the most delicate of the world's wonders . . .

With her mother's gilded teaspoon she was skimming the thin milk foam from the thick chocolate when the ringing of a little bell resounded; Mur was calling her to her room. After placing a pink cup on a tray, Anna Fyodorovna entered her mother's room. She was already sitting at the card table in a pose characteristic of a lover of absinthe. The bronze bell, its petal side pressed against the faded cloth, was before her.

"Please give me just milk, without any of that chocolate of yours."

"One, two, three, four . . . ten," Anna Fyodorovna counted as always.

"You know, Mur, the last bit of milk went for this chocolate . . ."

"Send Katia or Lenochka for some more."

"One, two, three, four . . . ten."

"It's half past four in the morning. The store is still closed."

Mur sighed with satisfaction. She arched her narrow eyebrows. Anna Fyodorovna got ready to catch the cup. Her dried out lip, with a deep crease in it and radiating a multitude of tiny wrinkles, stretched out in a derisive smile.

"Can I get a glass of plain water in this house?"

"Of course, of course," Anna Fyodorovna rushed to comply.

The morning scandal, it seems, did not take place. Or was put off.

"Getting old, poor little thing," Anna Fyodorovna noted to herself.

It was Wednesday. Appointments at the clinic from twelve. Katia can get her fill of sleep today. The grandchildren are left to fend for themselves on Wednesdays. Seventeen-year old Lenochka takes little Grisha to grammar school before going to the institute. Katia will pick him up, but they must return home no later than half past five. Katia works from six, teaches English in night school. There's food for dinner. Before leaving, have to buy some milk. The sound of the bell.

"One, two, three, four . . . ten."

"Yes, Mur."

A thin hand is holding dainty metal eyeglasses gracefully in the air like a lorgnette.

"I remember on TV, there was the company Oreal.[3] A very beautiful girl was recommending a cream for dry skin. Oreal. I think it's an old company. Yes, yes, Lilechka ordered that perfume in Paris. She wanted a liter bottle, but her poor lover sent a tiny bottle; he couldn't manage a big one. But the scandal was big. But Maetsky brought me a liter-size one . . . Ah, what am I saying, that was L'Origan Coty[4] and not at all Oreal . . ."

This was a new disaster. Mur turned out to be exceptionally prone to succumbing to advertising. She needed everything, be it a new cream, a new toothbrush, or a new super-duper pot.

"Sit down, sit down for a minute," Mur said in good humor, pointing to a round piano stool.

Anna Fyodorovna took a seat. She knew all the circles, figure eights and loops, like the ones in Grisha's railroad, along which locomotives of old thoughts glided, making stops and transfers in places of the great biography that Anna Fyodorovna knew ahead of time. Now the thoughts of perfume got her going. Then it was about her friend and rival Lilechka. Maetsky, whom she took away from Lilechka. A famous director. Her being in a movie, which made her famous. Divorce. Skydiving—no one could even imagine that she could do that. Then an aviator—a test pilot and handsome man. He crashed half a year later, leaving her with the best memories. Then an architect, very famous; they made a trip to Berlin, she created a furor. No, neither in the Cheka,* nor in the NKVD,* that's silly; she never served anywhere, slept around—yes. And with pleasure! She had a lot of men there. "But you and Katka are fur stockings . . . bristly asses . . ."

Forty years ago, Anna Fyodorovna felt like hitting her with a chair. Thirty years ago—grabbing her by the hair. And now, sick at heart and with revulsion, she let the boastful monologues go right past her and thought with sadness about how the morning, which held such promise, was now being lost.

The telephone rang. Probably from the department. Something must have happened, otherwise they wouldn't be calling so early. She quickly picked up the receiver.

"Yes, yes! It's me! I don't understand . . . From Johannesburg?"

How could she not have recognized that voice right away, rather high but not at all a woman's, with the throaty "r" and with long pauses between words, as often happens with stutterers who have been cured. He's choosing his words carefully. Thirty years . . .

At first everything came rushing into her head; she became hot and, a second later, it all receded, and she broke out in a sweat and terrible weakness followed . . .

"Yes, yes, I recognized your voice."

"How are you?" is an awkward question after so many years.

"Yes, you can. Yes, I've no objection. Goodbye."

She hung up. The blood left even her hands, and the tips of her fingers became smaller and puckered up, like after a big wash.

"Who called?"

"Marek."

She should have gotten up and left, but she had no strength.

"Who?"

"My husband."

"Unbelievable, he's still alive! How old can he be?"

"He's five years younger than me," Anna Fyodorovna answered drily.

"So what does he need from us?"

"Nothing. Wants to see me and Katia."

"That worthless man, totally worthless. I don't understand how you could . . . with him . . ."

"He has a clinic in Johannesburg," Anna Fyodorovna tried to change the topic and succeeded.

Mur livened up. "A surgeon? That's amusing! Your father was a surgeon. I was in an automobile accident in the Caucasus. If not for him, I would've lost my leg. He operated brilliantly," Mur giggled. "I seduced him while still in a cast . . ."

The most surprising thing was that the details were endless. Anna Fyodorovna had known for a long time about Mur marrying on a bet and winning a diamond broach from a famous friend. Hearing about the cast for the first time, she was suddenly overtaken by unkind feelings towards her long-deceased father whom she had loved passionately in her childhood. He was twenty years older than her mother, the last representative, if you did not count Anna Fyodorovna herself, of a German medical family, who devoted himself to his profession to a degree not compatible with life. But a chance occurrence protected him. At one point in his youth, when he was a doctor in a district town, he performed trephination of the skull of a young worker who was dying from a suppurative inflamation of the middle ear. Under the new regime the worker rose to the most unbelievable heights, but Dr. Shtork, who had completely forgotten about him, was not effaced from the memory of the grateful patient, and the latter gave him something like a permit for safe passage. At any rate, his service as a military doctor in the tsarist and, subsequently, the Volunteer Army did not prevent him from succumbing to an honorable and difficult death from cancer in his own bed.

"Please tell me, this Johannesburg, is it in Germany?"

Someone might think that the old woman's thoughts were leaping like hungry fleas, but Anna Fyodorovna knew about her mother's striking peculiarity: she always thought about several things simultaneously, as if she were spinning yarn out of several strands.

"No. It's in Africa. The South African Republic."

"Just think, the Boer War, I remember, I remember . . . amusing. So don't forget to buy me face cream," and she passed her weak fingers over her skin, loose and wrinkly like an old apricot.

In times past Mur was interested in events and people as a decoration for her own life and as extras in her play, but with the years everything that was of secondary importance was fading away and, in the center of an empty stage, she alone and her various wishes remained.

"And what's for breakfast?" Her left eyebrow went up slightly.

Breakfast, dinner, and supper did not belong among secondary things. Food was to be served on a strict schedule. The full silver service, with a knife rest and a napkin in a ring. But more and more often now, she would take her fork in her hand and immediately drop it next to her plate.

"I don't feel like it," she would utter with irritation and resentment. "Maybe I'll have a grated apple or ice-cream . . ."

Her whole life she enjoyed wanting and getting what she wanted, and the real misfortune was that her wanting had ended, and death was terrifying precisely because it signified the end of desires.

The evening before Marek's arrival Katia cleaned the apartment till very late. The apartment was run-down. No repairs had been done for such a long time that the cleaning made little difference: ceilings with yellowed corners and crumbling molding, old furniture that needed restoration, dusty books in bookcases with cracked finishes. An intellectual's mixture of luxury and poverty. Late in the evening, Katia and Anna Fyodorovna, both in old, warm robes and looking like worn-out plush toys, sat down on the Gobelin sofa, which was as worn out as they were.

Anna Fyodorovna was leaning against one of the arms and Katia, with her thin legs tucked beneath her, was nestling under her mother's arm like a chick under the wing of a flabby hen. There was truly something chick-like about Katia, although she was almost forty: round eyes on a small, blond, feathery head, a thin neck, and a long nose shaped like a beak. A bird-like charm, a bird-like incorporeality. Mother and daughter had boundless love for each other, but that love kept them from becoming really close; most of all they were afraid of hurting each other. But since life consisted mainly of different types of grief, their constant reticence took the place of quiet complaints and sweet moments comforting each other, and of thoughts they both harbored and could have voiced, and for this reason they talked most of all about Grisha's head cold, or Lenochka's exams, or sleeping medications for Mur. When something significant happened in their life, they only cuddled closer and longer than usual and sat in silence in the kitchen with empty cups in front of them.

"Before leaving, he gave me a microscope, small, copper. It's unbelievable how pretty it was," Katia smiled, "and I immediately took it to Tanya Zavidonova. Do you remember, she studied in the second grade with me?"

"You've never told me about the microscope." Anna Fyodorovna, without raising her eyes, wrapped herself up even more snugly in her robe.

"I thought you would get upset if I brought it home . . . And Zavidonova never did return it to me. Maybe her father drank it away . . . You know, I loved him so terribly much . . . But why did you still get divorced?"

It was a difficult question and there were too many answers, like going down steps into a cellar: the deeper you go, the darker it gets.

"We got married and rented a room in Ostankino from a woman who made communion bread. Her kitchen range was always busy, but her house was filled with communion bread. And that's where you were born. Your first food was this communion bread. We lived there for four years. Mur lived with her sisters. Eva in the city, Beata at the dacha. Aunt Eva served Mur her whole life, starched her blouses. An old maid, a secret Catholic, she was unusually strict, never forgave anyone anything, and adored Mur. She died suddenly, wasn't even sixty. And my mother immediately asked for me. Couldn't stand strangers serving her."

"Why didn't you say no?" Katia shot back brusquely.

"Well, she was almost seventy and she got that diagnosis . . . I couldn't abandon a dying human being."

"But she didn't die, did she . . ?"

"Marek said at that time that she was immortal, like the theory of Marxism-Leninism."

Katia snorted. "Witty."

"Oh yes. But as you can see, he was wrong. Mother, thank God, survived even Marxism. And the tumor was localized. It ate away part of a lung and went into remission. I looked after her, Aunt Beata after you. Mur couldn't stand children—you were immediately moved to Pakhra[5] and taken back only as school approached."

"Why didn't father move with you here?"

"We didn't even talk about it. She despised him. And so he lived at Ostankino until the moment of his departure."

"Did they really let people out then?"

"A special case. Through Poland. His mother, a communist, escaped from Poland to Russia with him and his older brother; his father stayed in Poland and perished. It was a big family; many were saved—some left for Holland, some for America. I don't remember any more. Marek used to talk about them. You have a whole lot of relatives throughout the world. And, as you can see, he himself went to the RSA," Anna Fyodorovna said, sighing.

"And what about Mur?" Katia continued her delayed investigation.

Anna Fyodorovna began to laugh quietly. "She's ordered a manicurist for tomorrow and has given orders for her striped blouse to be ironed."

"No, I mean back then . . ."

"Mur forbade me to correspond with him. One time an Israeli of Polish origin arrived, brought several hundred dollars and toys and clothing for you. She found out and made such a scene that I didn't know where to hide. I don't know what I was afraid of more. In those times people were put in prison simply for having dollars. I returned everything to the Pole and asked him to tell Marek not to send us anything so that nothing would happen to us."

"How stupid all this is . . . ," Katia whispered condescendingly and stroked her mother's temple.

"No, this is life," Anna Fyodorovna sighed.

But the conversation left a bad aftertaste. Katia, it seems, gave her to understand that she didn't have the right approach to life . . .

She had not noticed that before.

After many days of freezing weather, it let up a bit—snow began to fall, and Zamoskvorechie[6] was being covered with snow right before one's eyes. From the inhumanly tall entrance of a Stalinist building with a somber granite foundation an elderly man stepped out in a thick sheepskin coat and a fur cap with two ear flaps and a back flap which must have used up two whole fox skins. Walking up towards him on the wide staircase was some madman in a beige jacket, a red scarf thrown over his shoulder, no hat, and grey curls covered with snow.

The door had not yet slammed shut when the grey-haired man agilely skirted the man that was all bundled up and plunged into the entrance.

The man who had entered rang the door bell he was looking for and heard the sound of someone's steps some distance from the door, then a clear woman's voice shouting, "Grishka, give back the modeling clay!" Then he heard the light ringing sound of glass and an irritated cry, "Go on, open the door!" Finally the door opened.

Behind the door stood a large elderly woman with a familiar, small seed protruding from deep within her face. It is possible that this seed was a small purplish-blue bean on her cheek that, in years long past, looked like a nice, light mole. The woman was holding the broken-off neck of a glass jar and looking at him with fright.

At the end of the corridor, there where it turned toward a small room, was a puddle, and in it, with a rag in her hands, stood an unknown girl, not the daughter but the granddaughter of the man who had entered. She was very tall, awkward-looking, with narrow shoulders and round eyes. Shouting resounded once more from a room in the back: "Grishka, give back the modeling clay!"

The guest pulled his suitcase with wheels behind him and stopped. Anna Fyodorovna, sucking the blood on her cut finger, said to him dully, "Hello, Marek!"

He gave her a hug. "Anelia, one could go insane! The whole world has changed, everything is different, only this building is the same."

Katia with the resisting Grisha walked out from a back room.

"Katushka!" exclaimed the man who had entered.

This was Katia's long forgotten name from childhood, given to her in those distant times when she was a plump little infant.

Katia, looking at his youthful sun-tanned face, much more handsome than she had seemed to remember, recalled how much she loved him, how ashamed she was of this love and hid it from her mother because she was afraid of causing her pain. And now it suddenly turned out that in the depths of her heart this love had not been forgotten, and Katia felt embarrassed and turned red.

"Here are my children, Grisha and Lenochka."

And at this point he noticed that Katia's face was wrinkled and no longer young, and that her small hands clenched under her chin were also no longer young looking. And he did not even have time to take a good look at his newly acquired grandchildren when a door in the back of the apartment opened slowly and Mur appeared in the doorway, delicately jingling the metal bars of her walker.

"The Queen of Spades!" the guest whispered in great surprise. "One could go insane!"

For some reason he began to laugh happily, dashed to kiss her hand and she, extending her dry hand with an old world flourish, stood before him—fragile and majestic—as if it were precisely her that the well-dressed gentleman, this hot number from abroad, had come to visit. With her manicured hand, the high-society old woman dispelled the awkwardness everyone felt, and it became clear to all the members of the family how one should behave in this extraordinary situation.

"You look marvelous, Marek," she noted amiably. "The years have been kind to you."

Marek, without letting go of the hand that had saved them, began to rattle on in Polish.

... It so happened that this was the language of their childhood—the language of Miss (nee) Charnetskaya, who had been born in one of the narrow, semi-Gothic houses of the Old City, and of the grandson of a pharmacist from Krokhmalnaya, known to the whole world for a variety of reasons as a Jewish street in Warsaw.

Katia exchanged glances with her mother; even now Mur captured his attention first, before his daughter, before his grandchildren.

"You may come to my room," she invited Marek graciously, as if she had forgotten how strongly she had disliked him thirty years ago. But at this point something unexpected happened.

"I thank you, Madam. I have only an hour and a half today and I want to spend it with the children. I'll come by tomorrow to see you, but now, permit me to see you to your room."

She did not have time to object when he resolutely and cheerfully turned the carriage carrying her around and pushed her into the boudoir.

"Your place is as elegant as before. May I help you to that chair?" he proposed in a tone that did not contain even a suggestion that it could be otherwise.

Anna Fyodorovna, Katia, and Lenochka stood in the doorway like a living tableaux, waiting for the screeching, screaming, and breaking of cups. But none of this happened: Mur sank meekly into the chair. He bent down, touched her slender foot, slipped it into a dried-out, blue leather slipper, and said in a rather severe tone, "Now, you absolutely must not wear such shoes. I'll send you shoes which will be perfect for you. A special company. Just let the girls measure your foot."

He left her alone, shut the door softly behind him, and Anna Fyodorovna, totally dumbfounded, asked him, "How can you talk to her like that?"

He gave a wave of his hand with an air of nonchalance.

"Experience. In my clinic eighty per cent of the patients are over eighty, all rich and capricious. I studied for five years how to get along with them. And your mother is a real Queen of Spades. Pushkin created his in her image. All right. Let's go, Grisha, and take a look at what's in the suitcase."

And Grisha, immediately forgetting about the modeling clay with which he had just so nimbly blocked up the drain in the sink, started to pull behind him the small, well-made suitcase with the promising exterior.

Anna Fyodorovna stood by the table which was set for dinner. Everything that was taking place seemed to have nothing to do with her. Even loyal Katia did not take her eyes off Marek's tanned face, and her smile seemed lame and stupid to Anna Fyodorovna.

"What a good thing," she thought, "that I didn't color my hair with that stuff in the dark bottle I bought yesterday. He would've imagined that I was making myself younger for him. But still, it isn't good that I've neglected myself so much. When he leaves, I'll color it."

He turned and glanced in her direction, made a familiar gesture with his hand as if he were playing ping-pong, and Anna Fyodorovna recalled how adroitly he had played ping-pong, which was just becoming fashionable during their courtship.

He talked with the children easily and freely. He held Katia by the shoulder and did not let her go, and she relaxed under his hand like a cow.

"Exactly like a cow," Anna Fyodorovna thought.

The gifts were perfect: a cordless phone, a camera, and some high-tech things. He produced a photo album from the inside pocket of his fleece jacket. He showed his house in Johannesburg, the clinic, and one more beautiful, two-storied house at the seashore, which he called his dacha.

Then he looked at his watch, patted the back of Grisha's head, and asked when he could come tomorrow. He had actually spent only an hour and a half in their house.

"I'd like to come earlier. May I?" He turned to Anna Fyodorovna and it seemed to her that he was a bit afraid of her.

"You don't have a coat?" Grisha was enraptured.

"As a matter of fact, I do have a jacket at the hotel, but why do I need it? I have a car waiting for me downstairs."

The children were looking at him with such admiration that Anna Fyodorovna became a bit upset and immediately was ashamed of herself; everything, in the final analysis, was understandable. He had always been charming, and in his old age had even become handsome . . . But she was sick at heart from a vague bitterness and bewilderment.

* * *

As is often the case, the family tradition of an absent father intensified with each new generation. As a matter of fact, the last man of the house—the last father in their family—was old Charnetsky, the descendant of a fierce Polish provincial governor, the gentlest parent of three beauties: Maria, Evelyn, and Beata.

In the beginning Anna Fyodorovna herself was left without a mother when Mur suddenly left Dr. Shtorkh on a moment's whim and walked out of the house, seemingly forgetting to return. After a few days she sent for her most essential things; her year-and-a-half daughter was not among them. Mur's new marriage was not her last, but already in the right direction. Her intuition told her that the time of decadent poets and uncontrollable heroes was over. Mur's first test in the field of new literature was not the most successful but, on the other hand, the rest that followed were crowned with success in the end. A real Soviet classical writer came into her life, a genius at hypocrisy, an ascetic to outward appearances, and with the utmost nouveau-riche passions in his heart. Showing a porcelain collection, a newly acquired Borisov-Musatov[7] or a Vrubel[8] sketch, he would throw up his hands in a charming way and say, "These are all Murka's caprices. I took a woman of noble birth and now have to answer for it . . ."

The last marriage was perfect and little Anna stayed with her father— and for a while was forgotten. Mur became part of great literature again; she had an affair with a major playwright and with a prominent director, and then several other casual affairs against the backdrop of first-class health resorts in the south which were quite conducive to such alliances. Finally a large building was built in Zamoskvorechie, where apartments were issued not on the basis of plebeian calculations of so many meters per person but in accordance with the true scope of a writer's soul. But even here, there were some bureaucratic limitations; they had to register both sisters in the apartment, and it was decided to go and collect the little girl. Moreover, Mur discovered that the classical writer who belonged to her was looking with a non-platonic eye at buxom servers and young chambermaids, and she decided that the time had come for consolidating the family by giving the classical writer an opportunity to prove himself as the parent of a little girl who was no longer a child.

Mur took her seven-year old daughter away from the old surgeon. The little girl who adored her father was moved from sweetly lazy Odessa to a newly received, elegant and proper Moscow apartment and gradually forgot her father, with whom she was now forbidden to communicate. At Mur's insistence the girl's bird-like German family name[9] was changed to one known throughout the USSR, she was ordered to call the bald fat man her "daddy," and the second aunt—who lived year round at the writer's dacha—was left in charge of her. In a few years came war time and evacuation to Kuibyshev,[10] which left them with the unforgettable horror of hunger for the rest of their lives, the return to Moscow in a hot, official government train car, and the happy reunion with Moscow which, precisely in those first months after their return, became Anna's native city. She never did see her own father again and only dimly guessed at her deep-seated resemblance to him.

Anna Fyodorovna's daughter, Katia, preserved even dimmer memories of her own father. They were somewhat fragmentary, but captured in enlarged photos: here she is, ill, with her ears all wrapped up for warmth, and her father bringing her a puppy right into bed . . . Here she is standing on the porch and watching him trying to catch a lost bucket in a well with a long stick with a hook on the end . . . Here they are walking out of a wooden house smelling of bitter smoke, heading along a snow-covered road to a huge tsarist palace where there are large windows from floor to ceiling, stoves covered in ornamental tile, paintings on the walls, and the smell of summer and the forest . . .

For some reason Katia had almost no memory of her father's visits to Pakhra, where she, just as her mother had in her time, lived before attending school. Only one vivid memory remained: she, Katia, in a dappled cat-fur coat and fur hat, is walking along a narrow path toward the bus stop, holding Aunt Beata by one hand and her father by the other . . . The bus is already at the bus stop, and she is terribly afraid that he will be late and won't have time to get on and, pulling her hand away, she shouts to him, "Run, run quickly!"

In the same year he actually carried out Katia's recommendation.

It is really surprising how deeply the child's love had been buried; for many years Katia neither thought of him nor of the honest German thing good for studying the cells of an onion skin or the legs of a flea . . .

Katia's daughter Lenochka, born early in the marriage, had no memories of her father whatsoever. Katia divorced her husband a year after Lenochka's birth. She never received any alimony from him and only heard through mutual friends that he was alive.

Until Grisha's birth, the family consisted of four women, but the total absence of men did not trouble anyone but Mur. Mur, accustomed to regarding her daughter Anna as a sexless, colorless being good only for the hurried care of the household, was at a loss to understand why her granddaughter Katia lived such a boring life. The surprising thing for Mur was where the children had come from, given such a total lack of talent in these women. Just like animals, they f . . k exclusively for propagation . . .

Mur was deeply wrong when it came to Katia. She had an extremely successful, unfortunate love affair for the sake of which she had even left her incomprehensible first husband and had a fairly hard time with the object of her great love, bore him Grishka and now, for thirteen years running, met on rare occasions with her contrite lover and put off, from one year to the next, the moment of her son's real acquaintance with his secret father—who knew about Grisha's existence but whom Grisha had never met. Family is holy, he would maintain, and Katia could not disagree with him.

In this way, the absence of fathers became a deeply inherited phenomenon in their family, since it asserted itself in three generations. It would have never occurred to either Anna Fyodorovna or Katia or even Lenochka, who was becoming a grown-up, to bring even the most modest, the most insignificant of men into this house which totally belonged to Mur. Such a right Mur—full of magnificent scorn for her female descendants—did not grant them. Anna Fyodorovna and Katia became fully resigned both to the fatherless atmosphere and to their female loneliness, and Lenochka, a girl infantile precisely in the area where her great-grandmother's gifts were manifest in all their glory, gave men no thought whatsoever.

Thus Anna Fyodorovna felt all the more keenly the whole house going mad after Marek's first visit. At the sound of Marek ringing the doorbell, not only eight-year-old Grishka but also that beanpole Lenochka, who grew to almost 1.8 meters that winter, and even Katia herself, ran out with such excited quickness that it seemed at the very least that Grandfather Frost[11] was standing behind the door. And Marek even kept that tasteless, red-white motif: his bright white, wavy hair rose like smoke above his African tan and, instead of a banal red robe with white cotton trim, there was a scarf around his neck of a deep blood-red color and of that very high quality which almost transforms material values into spiritual. As was expected of Grandfather Frost, he was cheerful, red-cheeked, and incredibly generous with all kinds of treats and gifts, and still more generous with promises. Even Mur showed an excessive interest in him.

Anna Fyodorovna was tortured by feelings of personal humiliation which she had not experienced for a long time. Marek, who three days ago did not know about the existence of Grisha and Lenochka, was playing such a role in their lives today: Lenochka only talked of where she could go for her schooling— England or America, and Grisha was hallucinating about some Greek island where Marek had a dacha—a two-storied villa backing onto a pink cliff and facing a small bay with a white yacht secured in the middle of the gulf like a bone broach on blue silk . . . Grisha gutted an album with Marek's photographs, and the color impressions of someone's unreal life lay scattered throughout the apartment, even in Mur's room. But the most painful thing was that Katia walked around with a stupid, little smile and even hummed a bit, exactly like her grandmother . . . In addition to everything else, Anna was also tortured by the fact that she was harboring such base feelings herself and could not cope with them.

At work Anna Fyodorvna had an unpleasant incident as well. One of the most difficult patients lately, a young policeman who had come in not for scheduled treatment but because of a trauma, was operated on exceptionally successfully, and it could be said with certainty that at least one eye had been saved. And the other day he moved the television in the hall from one corner to another, and all the intricate work came to nothing; new ruptures appeared in the retina, and now it was totally unclear whether she would be able to save the eye again for this fool . . .

Marek had come to Moscow on business. His total work came to one, single meeting with medical officials, and it was scheduled precisely for the first evening of his arrival. The talk was of some special equipment for post-operative care of the sick whose production involved him in some way. As he himself said later, the negotiations were an excuse for him to see his daughter. All those years he had not renewed that first attempt at establishing relations with his former family; he had too much experience dealing with Soviet power, both in its Russian and Polish variants.

He expected anything and everything from this trip, but in no way had he counted on meeting such open-hearted and touching children, his family in fact, who were managing wonderfully without him and knew nothing about him.

Even the old shrew evoked in him a tinge of gentleness and interest. He spent several hours with her that day. It so happened that Grisha had gone to a classmate's home to jump around this year's Christmas tree, and Lenochka had gone to fail her scheduled exam.

Marek, the cunning devil, asked Mur a very good question—about the Stalin Prize which her classical writer had received at some point. And Mur plunged into pleasant recollections. Her husband's last success coincided with Mur's new flights of fantasy—a whole string of bright successes in a closely related field: a stormy affair with a secret general who held the whole literary process in his hairy fist, an amorous relationship with her husband's secretary, and with the husband of a dear female friend, and with some biologist academician, and with many others, and the witness to all this was her frowning daughter, Anna, with Puritan melancholy and deep despair in her heart which she felt because of the impossibility of loving, and yet her inability not to love, this thin, inhumanly beautiful, theatrically dressed woman who happened to be her mother.

Mur told her story in a disjointed way, selectively, sprinkling it with names and details, but the picture Marek got was drawn with total clarity. In addition he knew a lot from Anna . . .

After surviving the glorified leader for a very brief time and demonstrating his brilliant farsightedness for yet another and last time to his envious friends, the classical writer died a timely death. He was put under a heavy grey stone in Novodevichy Cemetery,[12] and for a time Mur's life became somewhat more somber. There was lots of money, however, and it came flowing in rivers—author's compensation, payment for theater productions and royalties. Another woman would have lived quietly, but Mur began to fret, she became bored with her affairs, they became dull, her desires lost their former flexibility, and the years between fifty and sixty turned out to be a bore. Later she would explain this as menopause. But her menopause ended nicely. Mur had two small operations, rare in those times; her friend Verochka, a famous actress, gave Mur her own doctor—and a certain freshening of her life began. An affair, it goes without saying. Blinding, unforeseen, with a young actor. Forty years difference. All records were broken, all sheets rumpled. Her friends were in poorhouses and hospitals, some were whiling away their last years in exile, but she—vibrant, with perky breasts, a small behind and the loose skin on her neck tightened—was entertaining a handsome Gypsy boy whose young wife was raging at the front door. Moscow rumbles, life goes on . . .

And at this point it all came to an end. Unbelievably quickly, the boy actor became a drunk, her female friends fell away one after another, her daughter Anna left home and married a skinny student, Jewish—the type Mur had never liked since childhood. That is, let them live, of course, don't put them in gas chambers, but don't marry them either . . .

"Interesting, very interesting, who does she take me for?" Marek thought, but he did not ask any questions. He listened attentively.

. . . Her former lovers died one after another, both the generals and the civilians. And the most annoying thing—her sister Eva died, ten years younger, loyal, devoted . . . She was forced to take Anna back into the house, and soon Katia was settled there too. She did not have time to turn around and the house was full of children, a worthless life without any fun, without any interests . . .

Entering her mother's room to remove the teacups, Anna Fyodorovna noted to herself that Mur had a happy look just like the children and, moreover, was in a state of full battle readiness: her voice was an octave lower than usual, purring, her eyes seemed to have doubled in size, and her back was even more straight, if that is possible. A tigress on the hunt—that's how Anna Fyodorovna called her mother in those moments.

Marek was sitting with a befogged smile.

The last evening of family bliss was taking place, one in which Anna Fyodorovna tried to participate as little as possible. Grisha was hanging onto Marek and from time to time would let go of him, but only so that he could take a run and jump on him even higher and hold him even more tightly. Lenochka was on her way full speed to failing her exams, but she neglected her studies in these decisive days, as she followed her new grandfather like a shadow. Since the tempting thought of England made her lose her appetite for studying in her own country, she experienced not the least bit of worry about the next day's exam. Anna Fyodorovna tried not to look at Katia: Katia's facial expression was unbearable.

Shortly after eleven, after saying goodbye to everyone, Marek went into Mur's room. Holding a warm hot-water bottle with her feet, she was watching television and eating chocolate. This was one of her basic principles: one pleasure must not get in the way of another. As for the hot-water bottle, which Anna Fyodorovna had refused to use for the last thirty years, Mur got accustomed from an early age to getting into a warm bed even on those occasions when the warm hot-water bag was not her sole night companion.

To Marek, who respectfully bowed down before her, she proffered a narrow piece of paper condescendingly, half-covered with letters written by an unsteady hand.

"That's for you, my dear friend. I need a few things."

Without looking, Marek stuck the piece of paper in his pocket.

"With great pleasure. . ."

He knew how to deal with old ladies. He walked out; Anna Fyodorovna lingered on, fluffing up the pillows behind Mur's back.

Mur, licking her finger covered with chocolate, smiled mysteriously and asked provocatively, "Well, do you see now?"

"What?" Anna Fyodorovna said in surprise. "See what?"

"How my lovers treat me!" Mur smirked.

"First signs of the dimming of the mind," Anna Fyodorovna decided.

The children wanted to accompany him to the hotel. He was staying not far away, in the former "Balchug," which in recent years had become transformed into something magnificent, like the crystal bridge which in one night moves from one shore to another through the magic of words.

"No, let's say that we've said our farewells already," he announced unexpectedly firmly, and Grisha, who was used to complaining on every occasion and getting his way, submitted immediately.

Marek wound the insufferably red scarf around his neck and once more for the last time kissed the children as naturally as if he had not gotten acquainted with them just five days ago. Then he took Anna Fyodorovna's fur coat off the hanger, which had lost a lot of its fur in the front, and said in a peremptory tone, "Let's go for one last walk."

Anna Fyodorovna submitted for some reason, although a minute before she had not even thought of going outside with him. Without saying a word, she stared at the fur coat and threw on the Orenburg scarf she had received as a gift. She took gifts if they brought them to her—boxes of chocolates, books, envelopes with money. She took them and thanked the people with restraint. But she never named the prices for her operations, that is, in this respect she behaved exactly like her deceased father. Which she never suspected.

Once outside, he took her under his arm. From Lavrushinsky Lane they walked out onto Ordynka. It was clean, white, and empty. The rare passers-by would turn and look at the lean foreigner, wearing only a light-colored jacket and strolling slowly with a not-so-young woman bundled up in a thick fur coat who could not be related to him in any way: too intelligent looking to be his housekeeper, and too old and badly dressed to be his wife.

"What a wonderful city. For some reason I remember it as being gloomy and dirty . . ."

"It's different at different times," Anna Fyodorovna responded politely.

"Why did you come?" she thought. "You've turned everything upside down, upset everybody." But she did not say this.

"Let's go somewhere and sit a while," he suggested.

"Where? At night?" she said in surprise.

"There are lots of night establishments. There's a marvelous restaurant nearby—we ate there with the children yesterday . . ."

"You have to get up tomorrow at the crack of dawn," Anna Fyodorovna evaded the suggestion.

Marek was leaving on an early flight; she herself got up at half past six. The reference to tomorrow calmed her. He'll leave, everything will return to normal, and the unsettled state in the house will come to an end.

"I want to invite the children to Greece for the summer. You've no objection?"

"No objection . . ."

"You're an angel, Anelia . . . And my greatest loss . . . "

Anna Fyodorovna kept silent. Why did she come out here with him? From a long-time habit of submitting in domestic matters . . . She should have refused.

He sensed her inner irritation and grabbed her fluffy mittens with his hand in a thin glove.

"Anna, do you think I don't see anything and don't understand? The emigration experience is very difficult, very. And I had three of them. From Polish to Russian, from Russian to Hebrew, the last fifteen years English . . . And each time you live through everything all over again, starting with the alphabet . . . There were lots of things, all kinds of things. And I was in the war, and went hungry, and even spent time in prison . . ."

What a sweet boy he was once, a third-year student who in no way resembled the strong bucks who performed the energetic ritual of a dog's wedding near her mother. Because of her duties as a graduate student, she was then in charge of a student club and their love affair began among the lab flasks and bacilli. For a long time and with great care she hid their relationship from everyone. She was ashamed that he was so young. But it was exactly his youth, the absence of aggressive flesh in him, which unconsciously drew her to him. He had a white hairless chest and on the left, near one nipple, there was a constellation of moles—the Big Dipper. And he remained the only man in her life, but she never regretted that he was her only one, nor the fact that it was precisely him . . . But she always knew that marriage was incidental for her. At around sixteen she had decided that she would never marry; there was nothing more repelling for her than the purring voice, excited laughter, and drawn-out groans from her mother's bedroom . . . the eternal pursuit, being in heat, being in heat . . . For a moment she plunged into a very strong child-like feeling that sex was dirty and could never be washed off, when it was awkward to look at a married couple because a picture would come to mind of how they, sweating and groaning, were occupied with this abomination . . . How wonderful to be a nun, in clean white clothing, without all this . . . But still, what happiness that she had Katia . . .

Marek was talking and talking, but it flew past her like snow. Suddenly his faltering words broke in on her reverie: ". . . a real miracle that damnation is turning into a blessing. This monster, with a genius for egoism, the Queen of Spades, destroyed everyone, buried everyone . . . And how do you put up with it? You're simply a saint . . ."

"Me? A saint?" Anna Fyodorovna stopped in her tracks as if she had run up against a post. "I'm afraid of her. And there is duty. And pity . . ."

He brought his face closer to hers and it was apparent that he was not that young at all, that his skin was that of an old person, covered in small, sharply outlined wrinkles and dark age spots under a year-round tan.

"How, how can I help you?"

She waved her grey mitten. "See me home . . ."

* * *

Marek called from his Johannesburg more often than her female friends called from Sviblov. Grisha waited eagerly for his calls; he would throw himself at the phone like a kite[i] and shout to everyone indiscriminately, "Marek! Is that you?" Lenochka was studying only English, intent on leaving. A business-like approach suddenly awakened in her which had not been part of her character before; she was selecting the place of her future studies in a sensible, exacting way. Even Katia,

---

i   kite: small bird of the hawk family. —Trans.

always calm and a bit sleepy, was waiting for some vague changes in one way or another connected with her father's appearance and, it seems, she had cooled somewhat toward her secret friend who, on the other hand, had begun lukewarm talk about him possibly leaving his family.

Marek began fulfilling his parental promises with enthusiasm. The first heralds were shoes for Mur that had a completely orthopedic look. They were extremely ugly and probably just as extremely comfortable. They were brought directly to the house by practically the Secretary of the Israeli Embassy, an old friend of Marek's. Mur did not even try them on; she just went "hmm." The shoes had low heels and the kind of rubber soles that old folks like, but for the last seventy years Mur wore only open toe pumps with elegant heels which varied and depended on the latest fashion.

The pair of shoes was followed by a pair of two small computers whose price, at that, was in reverse proportion to their size. He had also taken the trouble to find computer games for Grisha. Lenochka had not yet recovered from the amateur movie camera he had left her before leaving, had not yet gotten her fill of that special perspective on the world which opens up through the viewfinder, and the new gift was already goading her on, demanding she learn as quickly as possible everything that could be done with its magical power.

Finally, six weeks after Marek's departure, an invitation came from Thessalonica, signed by a certain Evangelia Daula, who was a close friend of Marek's wife, about whom the only information was that she had a Greek friend who would send the invitation . . .

The invitation was worded in such a way that they could go at any time, from June through September.

Grisha, so excited that he was on cloud nine just from the look of the envelope with the rectangular window, flew around the apartment with it until he ran against Mur who was heading for the kitchen in her metallic apparatus. He thrust the envelope in her face.

"Look, Mur, we're going to Greece, to the island of Serifos. Marek has invited us!"

"What foolishness!" Mur snorted, who never made any allowances for age. "You're not going anywhere."

"But we will go, we will!" Grisha shouted, jumping up and down from the excitement.

And then Mur tore her hand away from the handle of her walker and brought a magnificent "fig"* right under the nose of her eight-year-old grandson, with her thumb and its bright-red nail prominently visible. With her other hand she adroitly grabbed the invitation from the boy who had not expected such a brazen attack and was taken aback. Leaning her elbows against the side bars for support, she crumpled the envelope and threw a large ball, the size of a good snowball, right toward the entrance door. . .

"You reptile! Reptile!" Grisha howled and rushed to the door.

Katia ran out of her room and grabbed her son without understanding what had happened between her son and her grandmother. Grisha was straightening out some piece of paper and continuing to scream out words one did not expect from him.

"You vile snake! You freaking bitch!"

Lowering her sad eyelids, Mur turned to her granddaughter with a gentle reproach. "Take your little bastard, my dear. Children must be taught manners, my dear." And with her wheels squeaking, she headed into the kitchen.

Katia, without understanding yet what the paper ball was that the sobbing Grisha was fiddling with, dragged him to his room, where his sobs resounded for a long time.

That day Anna Fyodorovna came home more tired than usual—there are things that wear a person out more than work itself. A girl who had been seriously injured was brought in. There was no doctor in the children's section with the required training and qualifications. The girl was Grisha's age, with a wound caused by a fragment of broken glass. The operation was very difficult.

Putting the instrument for measuring blood pressure in its case, Anna Fyodorovna reflected: where does Mur get her energy? Given her blood pressure, she should feel sleepy, weak . . . Instead there is aggressiveness, sharp reactions. Probably some other kind of mechanisms come into play. Yes, gerontology . . .

"You're not listening to me! What are you thinking about? I'm against it, do you hear me? I haven't been to Greece! They won't go anywhere!" Mur pulled at Anna Fyodorovna's sleeve.

"Yes, yes, of course. Of course, mom."

"What—of course? What's this 'mom' stuff?" Mur screamed.

"Everything will be as you want," Anna Fyodorovna said, trying to appease her.

"No, my dear, this time—no," Anna Fyodorovna firmly decided. For the first time in her life. The word no had not yet been said out loud, but it already existed, it had already broken through like a weak shoot. She decided simply to confront her mother with the fact of family insubordination and not conduct any preliminary discussions about it. One could only imagine what a storm this transparent insect would raise when it became clear that the children had left.

Toward the beginning of June the foreign passports were ready, the visas obtained. The tickets were ordered for Athens for the twelfth of June. That day, in accordance with Anna Fyodorovna's shrewd strategy, was earmarked for the move to the dacha. Everything was thought through to the smallest detail. In the morning Katia would leave with the children for Sheremetyevo Airport, which should not evoke any suspicions since Katia always headed for the dacha earlier in order to prepare the house for Mur's arrival. A car was ordered for twelve to take Mur and Anna Fyodorovna to the dacha. With the turmoil of the move, Anna Fyodorovna hoped to soften the blow, especially as the dacha preparations would happily mask their criminal flight. Grisha and Lenochka were flying high as they waited, especially Grisha. The half-Greek grandfather had turned up at the perfect time. All of Grisha's classmates had already spent some time abroad; he was almost the only one who had not been farther than Krasnaya Pakhra. And his grandfather himself, grey and curly-haired, standing on board a white yacht, was shown to the whole class and successfully compensated for the absence of a father.

The night before they were to leave, Anna Fyodorovna and Katia had a hard time sleeping. Toward morning Marek called and told them not to take any extra belongings; Greece had everything, as everyone knows. He was waiting with anticipation and would meet them at the airport.

At half past seven Mur demanded coffee. The morning coffee was served with milk, and the after-dinner coffee had to be black. Anna Fyodorovna helped Mur get dressed and made the coffee. After which she discovered that the milk carton in the refrigerator was empty. This was Lenochka's negligence; she constantly put empty cartons back in the refrigerator. It was getting towards eight. The taxi to Sheremetyevo had been ordered for half past eight.

Anna Fyodorovna, in a blue house dress, in slippers over bare feet, slipped out of the house and ran to Ordynka Street for the milk. This never took more than ten minutes. At first she hurried at a light run, but then she suddenly slowed down—the morning was unusual: a smoky, barely light-blue light, the sky iridescent like the iris of the bluest big eye, and the purest greenery on the cleaned up square near the round Church of the All Sorrowful, where Anna Fyodorovna would drop by from time to time. She walked on slowly and freely as if she were not hurrying anywhere. Galia the saleswoman, a local Tatar woman on Ordynka who had worked her whole life in the local stores, greeted her affectionately. About fifteen years ago Anna Fyodorovna had operated on her mother-in-law.

"How's Sofia Akhmetovna?"

It is surprising, given the number of gold teeth, how a smile can appear timid and childish . . .

"She's gone totally deaf, doesn't hear a thing. But her eyes see!"

Anna Fyodorovna took a cool carton of milk in her hands. In fifteen minutes the children would leave, and in two more hours Mur would find out that they had left. Most probably this would be when she was already in Pakhra. She imagined Mur's pale eyes, her usually quiet, rather hoarse voice rising to a piercing, crystal clear scream. Pieces of broken dishes. The most foul, the most intolerable swearing—that of a woman . . . And suddenly she saw it as if everything had already taken place: she, Anna, swinging her limp hand and landing a sweet blow on the rouged old cheek . . . And she did not care what happened after that . . .

A feeling of wonderful freedom, victory and triumph was in the air, and the air was so intensely bright, so incandescently bright. But there and then it went out. Anna Fyodorovna did not have time to realize what was happening. She fell forward without letting go of the cool carton, and her light slippers slipped off her strong and heavy German feet.

Mur at that time was already raising a storm.

"The house is full of good-for-nothings! Is it that hard to buy a bottle of milk?"

Her clear, resonant voice was full of rage.

Katia looked at her watch: fifteen minutes remained before the taxi was due. "Where has mother gone to?" she puzzled. But there was nothing to be done and she ran for the milk.

Galia, a saleswoman she knew, was rushing about on the sidewalk.

A thin crowd had gathered in front of the store entrance. There, on the sidewalk, lay a woman in a blue dress with stars on it. An ambulance came in about twenty minutes, but nothing could be done for her.

Katia, pressing the still cool carton of milk to her chest, said over and over to herself, "milk, milk, milk . . ." until they sent her to get her mother's passport. And when she was already approaching the house, she repeated, "passport, passport, passport . . ."

At home Katia found a noisy argument. The taxi driver, who had been waiting for them downstairs for about twenty minutes as per agreement, went up to the apartment to find out why the people who had to get to Sheremetyevo were not coming down.

Grisha, shaking from impatience like a puppy before its morning walk, began to yell in a happy voice, "Mur! We're going to Sheremetyevo Airport!"

Mur, rolling from side to side in her metal cage, walked out into the hallway and guessed that they had wanted to fool her. She forgot about both the coffee and the milk. Using expressions which even the driver did not hear every day in his life, she announced that no one was going anywhere and that the driver could get the hell out of there, which brought the driver, a young fellow with a diploma from a theatrical institute, into a state of purely professional excitement; he leaned against the wall, enjoying the unexpected drama.

"Where is that fucking chicken? Whom did she want to fool?" She raised her boney hand and the sleeve of her precious old kimono fell back, revealing a dry bone which, if one is to believe Ezekiel,[13] was supposed to become covered with new flesh with the passing of time.

Katia walked up to Mur and, swinging her limp hand wide, landed a sweet blow on her yet-to-be-rouged old cheek. Mur staggered in her small cage, then grew still, clinging to the railing of her captain's bridge from which she directed life in general for the last ten years after breaking the neck of the femur in her thigh, and said distinctly and quietly, "What? What?" Everything will be the way I want it anyway . . ."

Katia walked past her, opened the carton, and splashed some milk into the coffee which had already grown cold.

1998

NOTES

1. Tiflis: the old, non-native name of Tbilisi, the capital of Georgia in the Caucasus.
2. briki: Greek term for the traditional Turkish coffee pot. This term is perhaps more familiar to the American reader than the Turkish term, ibrik, because of the large Greek population in the USA.
3. Oreal: i.e., L'Oreal (Fr.), well-known manufacturer of cosmetics.
4. L'Origan, a scent developed by François Coty in 1905.
5. Krasnaya Pakhra: a dacha colony in the suburbs of Moscow for the elite—Communist Party and government officials, prominent writers, artists, and scientists.
6. Zamoskvorechie: meaning "on the other side of the Moscow River," this is probably the biggest residential area in the center of Moscow.
7. Borisov-Musatov, Viktor (1870-1905): Russian painter.
8. Vrubel, Mikhail (1856-1910): Russian Symbolist painter.
9. Shtork in German means "stork."
10. Kuibyshev: from 1935 to 1991 the name given to Samara, a city on the Volga River.
11. Grandfather Frost: In the Soviet Union it was Grandfather Frost, not St. Nicholas, who brought children gifts on New Year's Eve.
12. Novodevichy Cemetery: the most famous cemetery in Moscow, where well-known writers and political figures are buried.
13. Ezekiel: a reference to "The Book of Ezekiel" in the Old Testament, which contains many prophecies.

MORE AND MORE ANGELS

Yury Buida

After the death of her son, a widower, old woman Stefania was left
at home with her grandson Ivan, a stout young man and slow on the
uptake. Soon he married, started a home of his own—a cow, pigs,
chickens, turkeys and rabbits—and had a son, Vitya. After which his
wife said loudly, looking at the calendar pinned to the wall, that there
was barely enough room in the house for three to turn around and that
the fourth—the old woman—"was nothing" to them.

The old woman Stefania immediately gathered her belongings in a
bundle and packed herself off to a small woodshed that adjoined the
brick wall of the pigsty. Ivan brought her a cot and, wrinkling his large,
white forehead, said hesitantly, "How are you going to spend the winter
here?"

Stefania smiled, showing her two front teeth.

"I'll manage somehow, Vanya. Just don't eat your heart out because
of me."

And so she lived in that wooden shed for several years, going out into
the yard very rarely so as not to anger Ivan's wife, who would say, "Granny
Stefa, you should sit quietly in the shed, otherwise our neighbors will
say we don't respect you."

For whole days on end the old woman, perched on a small block
of wood, would observe through a crack in the door the life in the
courtyard—the chickens and the ducks, the dog that scratched its
forehead with its paw, and the doves and sparrows . . .

Her great-grandson Vitya, who was bigger now, one day saw an eye
in a chink, opened the door, and met the old woman. He liked to sit
secretly in the half-dark shed that smelled of rotting wood and chat in a
low voice with his great-grandma.

"And did you live well in the past?" Vitya questioned.

"Badly. I thought only about food all the time, but God told me to
think about eating just enough to exist." The old woman suddenly smiled

at the boy with her two teeth. "But there were good dreams, I won't start lying. They were sweet dreams, a man's sweet dreams . . ."

"And what's good now?" her great-grandson, who looked like his father because he was plump and had a large, white forehead, continued asking questions.

"Over there—there's a hole . . ." Stefania motioned to her great-grandson to go to a blind wall, where there was a hole from a knot that fell out of a pine board. "I look in it and admire the angels. You have to look for a long, long time—only then will you see them. At first a pair of them will appear for a fleeting moment, then a whole brigade will go flying past, and then more and more of them, and all are beautiful, with wings . . ."

Vitya pressed close to the opening, but no matter how much he stared, he could not make out anything except light clouds in the summer sky.

"You're still young, Viktor Ivanych," the old woman said cheerfully. "If you live to be my age, you'll see angels. And when nothing remains in the sky except them—it means it's time to die . . ."

The little boy frowned and asked, "Do angels go poo-poo?"

The old woman went into fits of quiet laughter.

"When your times comes—you can ask them yourself."

Soon she died.

Twenty-five years went by.

Viktor and his wife and two daughters, and his father who was paralyzed after a stroke, lived in the same house, kept pigs in the same pigsty, and wood in the same shed where there was a hole in the wall. Viktor's mother had left them long ago and lived with her new husband somewhere on the Volga. At twenty-seven Viktor was found to have an ulcer. The younger daughter had cerebral palsy, and Viktor's wife Marina devoted almost all of her time to the care of the poor girl and the immobile father-in-law. Viktor worked for the road-building department—turning the steering wheel of a heavy dump truck from morning till night. In order to somehow make ends meet, he had a lot of farm animals—a cow, pigs, chickens, turkeys and rabbits. At times he would reach a state of complete stupor and smoke cigarette after cigarette in the kitchen, massaging his stomach and listening to the stifled sobs of his wife who lay in the next room with her back to the television. He loved Marina and felt sorry for her until his heart ached, but he had no strength left to comfort her. At such moments he was afraid to think about the future.

Putting out his cigarette in the ashtray, he would go to the woodshed, latch the door and, perched on a log, press close to the hole in the wall shown to him sometime in the past by the old woman Stefania, who had departed for an eternity of a man's sweet dreams. He would look in the hole for a long, long time until his eyes hurt and filled with tears, until angels—tiny and transparent like butterflies—appeared fleetingly among the clouds, and the pain would leave his worn-out heart, and his soul would become lighter and seemingly even bigger the more angels there were in the sky . . .

1998

THE SAMURAI'S DREAM

Yury Buida

Yukio Tsurukava was a Japanese-Russian from Sakhalin.[1] After he finished the wood pulp and paper vocational school, he came to our small town and became a foreman at the paper plant. In his passport he was listed as Yukio Toyamovich, but the townspeople called him Yury Tolyanovich. When she first saw him, the old woman Grammofonikha inquired suspiciously, "My son, you aren't Jewish, are you?" He was given the nickname "Samurai," although Yukio himself would always try to disassociate himself from it: "My father is an accountant, my mother a teacher. What kind of a samurai am I?" His Japanese background was suggested perhaps by the *ofuda* that hung next to a mirror—a folded, diamond-shaped sheet of paper with hieroglyphics representing the name of the sovereign of the heavens—the goddess Amaterasu-o-mikami.

It was at the paper plant that he met Lida Kortunova, a beautiful and spirited girl. They soon married and received an apartment on Seventh Street. Lida's stomach barely began to show when Yukio put up a swing in the yard for their future child. In the spring he would take his wife out of the house every day to admire the cherry tree in bloom, and on autumn evenings, after carefully seating her in the motorcycle sidecar, he would take her out to Detdomovsky Lakes, where they would sit in silence for an hour or two, looking at the moon's reflection in the water. "What for?" Lida was puzzled. "My rear end is freezing." "So that the child will be handsome and bright," Yukio would answer. And he recited poetry to her:

> Oh, how bright,
> Oh, how bright, bright,
> Oh, how bright, bright, bright,
> Oh, how bright is the moon.

"That's the Japanese moon," Lida said pensively. You can't say that about ours . . ."

Lida suffered a miscarriage. She cried day and night, and Yukio sat on the swing in the falling snow and smoked cigarette after cigarette.

"Our blood is different," Lida said. "Mine is Orthodox, and yours is foreign."

"If you want me to, I'll get baptized. It doesn't hurt."

Lida shook her head dubiously. "You even have foreign dreams."

"How do you know?" Yukio asked.

"You can't fool God."

After a second miscarriage, Lida started drinking and carrying on with other men.

Yukio went to Kabartai and got baptized.

When he returned, he found Lida in the kitchen with a crazy alcoholic, Vanatya, nicknamed Stink.

"Beat it!" Lida screamed when Yukio had barely crossed the threshold. "I fuck whoever I want! But at least we have the same blood!"

Yukio went out in the yard and sat down on the swing.

Snow was falling quietly, like in a dream.

"All who are asleep are of one blood," Yukio thought.

In the morning, when the long-singing bird, the rooster, had finished his song, Lida walked out into the yard and found her husband dead—his heart had stopped beating.

The swing was being swung by two hands—on one side Jesus Christ was most likely pushing it, on the other, Amaterasu-o-mikami, the sovereign of the Japanese sky.

The moon was shining, it was snowing, it was Russia.

Squeak, squeak, squeak . . .

1998

NOTES

1. Sakhalin Island: a 600-mile-long narrow island in Russia's Far East, located between Japan and the Russian mainland.

CURRENCY[1]

Yury Mamleyev

It was 1994. Salaries in the small but noisy establishment were being paid in coffins.[2]

"Whoever wants to, take them," the higher ups said, throwing up their hands in bewilderment. "We don't have any money, they don't give us any. We're, as you know, in the budget. It's good if at least coffins start turning up, because a coffin is better than nothing."

"That's for sure," said the subordinates, confused. "You can make a table out of a coffin. Or sell it at the market."

"I'm not going to take any coffins," Katia Tupikova, the cleaning woman, announced. "I'd rather die of hunger, but I refuse to take any coffins."

But the majority didn't agree with her and a long line formed for the coffins. They were issued according to the person's salary and, of course, people had to sign for them.

"We have democracy here!" the higher ups shouted. "We won't cheat anyone."

"The coffins are all but worthless," Boris Porfiryevich Suchkov, an old worker in this office said, knitting his brow. "They look defective. If anything happened, it would be a disgrace to get into such a coffin."

"And where would you go?" asked a nimble, energetic young girl who was dumpy looking. "I've already put away two coffins for that salary of mine. If I die, I'll have coffins readily available."

"That's right!" people in line shouted. "We'll take what's ours, we won't miss out on it."

Boris Porfirich nodded his head pensively. He was a forty-five-year-old man who looked like a hard worker but had a surprised look in his eyes.

The line became packed with relatives of the workers as well, because a coffin, as everybody knows, isn't a light object, and some people had to carry it five or six kilometers to get it home, and all around were the living, you know, who could beat you up . . . anything could happen.

Boris Porfirich came alone, without his wife and son, but with his wheelbarrow. He could have moved a whole cemetery with that wheelbarrow. In his youth he sowed his wild oats by getting drunk and then, quite often, his father would come to take his son Borya from the pub in the wheelbarrow. The wheelbarrow in fact was left from that time, although fierce dogs almost chewed it up once. But they didn't touch Borya. Now he used the wheelbarrow for carrying coffins. The wheelbarrow also brought to mind a coffin, but from some fantastic place.

After loading up (the coffins were cheap, which also roused suspicion in the working people), Boris Porfirich headed home. On the way he dropped in at the pub, knocked back a bit of brew, and continued on his way.

At home they were having tea and discussing coffins. Even Mustygin, a neighbor and an observant, elderly man who was an expert at his job, came dragging in.

"We're getting teapots!" he shouted.

Moved upon hearing this, Sonia, Boris Porfirich's wife, plump and soft like down, said: "It's better to get paid in teapots. It's somehow less worry. After all, it's a teapot. But it's just a bit depressing here. Look how many have piled up over there and are crowded together by the wall like penguins."

"What's there to be scared of, Mom?" their son, twenty-year-old Igor, answered cheerfully. "A log is just a log. Why are you splitting hairs all the time?"

"Shoo, Igor," Boris Porfirich interrupted him sternly, "you're a puppy, but already yapping at your own mother!"

In the meantime Mustygin was examining the coffins.

"The coffins are second-hand!" he suddenly shouted in a voice that didn't sound like his.

"What do you mean second-hand?!" Sonia screeched.

"Just that! Used." Mustygin threw up his hands. "No good, in a word. They've been already used for dead people. What, think I can't see? And I have an extremely keen sense of smell. I can tell their smell, of corpses that is, right away . . ."

"Impossible!" a frightened Suchkov ran up to the coffins. "That's terrible!"

"A disaster, what a disaster!" Sonia began to sob in a heartrending way.

"Be quiet, Sonka! I'll see the mayor himself if I have to!" And in his nearsighted way Suchkov bent over the coffins.

Mustygin kept quacking, saying yes, yes, and pointing with his worker's hand at some dark spots, supposedly bedsores, and in one place he even pointed to what he said were traces of barf.

"It's the first time I'm hearing that the deceased barf," Sonia lost her temper. Her son, Igor, agreed with her. But Suchkov, the father, thought otherwise.

"Simply defective coffins," he concluded. "How is it I didn't notice?"

"And if it's barf?" Igor asked.

"The living, you know, could've barfed," Suchkov said, offering a plausible explanation. "More than that happens from a hangover. So they wandered off, so they fell . . . No big deal."

"But why the barf?" Sonia got angry. "Did it drop from the sky or something?"

"Quiet, quiet," Mustygin got scared. "Don't be disrespectful."

"Kostya Kryuchkin is to blame for everything," Boris Porfirich said angrily. "He gave out the salaries. And slipped me some soiled ones. And he calls himself a friend! He betrayed me!"

"He always envied you," Sonia broke in. "And so out of envy he slipped you those coffins."

"I'm offended!" Mustygin shook his head. "Coffins must be in the right condition . . . It's currency," and he stuck out his lip. "If it's instead of a salary. And international currency at that! After all people die everywhere in the whole wide world."

"I'll never forgive Koska for this," Boris Porfirich declared firmly and sullenly. "And I'll smash that mug of his with this here barf-covered coffin."

"Why don't you trade it? In a friendly way," Sonia cut in tearfully. "Why make an enemy? He won't forget what you did to him."

"Of course, pop," Igor added strongly.

"Tell him, you, Kostya, made a mistake," Sonia said, becoming uneasy and starting to worry. "It happens to everyone. And say, let's settle it in a friendly way. Change the coffins and that's it. You won't be able to sell them, even to the poorest folk . . . Only don't shove the coffin in his ugly mug, hear me, Borya?"

"Well, what can you do! It's too late today, and tomorrow is Saturday," Suchkov said downcast. "How upsetting! We always have some kind of trouble. And I'll tell them in the trade union not to give out salaries in used coffins. Our patience is not endless."

Everyone sat down at the table again.

"Perhaps you can get rid of that coffin, the defective one?" Sonia began daydreaming, holding up her little cheek with her plump hand. "And why not? I heard Mrachkovs' grandfather just died. They're poor, how can they buy a normal coffin? Pawn it off on them. And it's better not to get involved with Kryuchkin—don't you see the kind of man he is? He'll eat you alive the first chance he gets . . ."

"All the same I'll get even," Suchkov snarled.

And the next day he went to sell the coffin, the used one, and possibly even with barf on it. He quickly went to see the Mrachkovs—not went, but ran . . .

"Granpa's died, Anisia!" Boris Porfirich cried out from the threshold.

"Everybody knows he's died."

"And so I've come here to help. I'll let you have a good coffin real cheap! Otherwise we won't have anything to eat. We're getting our salaries in coffins."

"I heard."

"Well, if you've heard, take it, don't wait."

Suchkov was so abrupt, so pushy, that Anisia Fyodorovna finally gave in.

"I'll take it, I'll take it," she grunted, "except there's no money. Maybe you'll take it in teapots?"

"I'll smack you, woman, for words like that," Suchkov flew into a rage.

"Why hit me? Anisia defended herself. "There's still no money. Whether you hit me or not."

Suchkov ran home.

"Take them, Borya, take them!" Sonia urged him. "Don't be an ass. A teapot is still better than a coffin. It's less worry. More cosy. Even better—take it in samovars."

"What samovars are you talking about . . . ?"

"Never mind, take them."

Suchkov called his son. Together, the two of them managed to get the coffin to its destination, making their way across streetcar tracks and through people swearing and using foul language. They didn't use the wheelbarrow—they carried it under their own power.

The Mrachkovs reacted to the coffin somewhat rationally.

"Not much of a coffin, but still, it's a coffin," Anisia's sister said. "Coffins don't lie around on the street. Phew, it's a load off my shoulders."

Suchkov filled a sack with teapots, but all of them were kind of old. True, there were some half-new ones too. Coldly saying goodby to Anisia, Suchkov (his son had actually run off earlier) headed for his house with the sack on his back. On the way there he had something to drink, and half of the teapots got broken. The Mrachkovs were happy with the coffin.

"A good deal," they decided.

But Boris Porfirich had to endure a scene.

"Almost all the teapots are broken," Sonia screeched "What is this, did they get their salaries in broken teapots? Don't lie!!"

Suchkov frowned.

"Anisia said they got new ones, but they smashed them out of anger themselves. I also broke about two of them while drinking from grief. Just don't bug me, Sonia, don't!"

Sonia grew quiet.

"All right, sit down, have some nice oatmeal. There's nothing more in the house. You look all worn out."

Suchkov obediently started to eat the oatmeal. Sonia kept staring at him. Suchkov finished the oatmeal and licked his spoon.

"Borya," Sonia said ingratiatingly, "I think Mustygin exaggerated. I climbed all over our coffins. Well, yes, the one you pawned off was really barf-covered. But the others—not at all. Clean coffins, sparkling like glass. Only one—well, yes, it does smell a bit of a dead person and in general is questionable."

"Which one?"

Sonia indicated with a glance the coffin which stood near the dining table.

"It would be good to pawn it off on someone as quickly as possible," Sonia continued, drinking her tea. "It's upsetting, really. Maybe the dead person was a cancer or cholera victim. Tomorrow is a non-working day—take it to the market on the sly, without being noticed. Trade it at least for a piece of meat."

"What am I gonna lug it to the market for?" Suchkov got angry and even hit the plate with his fist. "What am I, a New Russian or something, to be trading all the time and speculating?"

"Oh, don't shout, Borya! Think, what are we going to eat tomorrow? There's even no bread."

Suchkov thought about it.

"Here's what," he said decisively. "I gotta go to the Solntsevs. Right away."

"But they've got a lot of coffins!" Sonia opened her mouth wide in amazement.

"A lot of coffins!" Suchkov mimicked her. "I know it without your help. But they've adapted them. The whole apartment is covered in coffins, and all of them have been put to a specific use. At times they even bathe the little one in a coffin instead of a washtub, saying that it's good for the child. Maybe they'll adapt ours for some use too. One of their coffins serves as a table for magazines, another is for dirty clothes, and a third has been suspended from the ceiling for some reason—they say it's nice."

"Well, all right, go see them."

Suchkov sprang up from his seat like a madman, picked up the coffin that was by the dinner table, put it on his back, and ran out.

Sonia was left alone. Igor had disappeared somewhere long ago. "He'll probably come home only at night," she thought. "Even the cat has disappeared somewhere."

Her heart was uneasy not because there was nothing left to eat tomorrow but from some global anxiety.

"Might as well not live," she decided.

But then and there she decided she did want to live.

Boris Porfirich came back half an hour later. With the coffin. Barely made it through the door.

"So, what happened?!" Sonia shrieked.

"They wanted to beat me up. Their fourteen-year-old daughter yelled so much she alarmed all the neighbors. She said she was already sleeping in a coffin instead of a bed and she'd had enough of it! What are we now to make out of the coffin, a toilet bowl, is that it, she shouted, although her dad was a jack-of-all-trades, but enough already! And her mother agreed with her. Bellowed like a female bear."

Sonia sighed. "Thank God you got away."

"It looks all right, but there's something bad about the coffin. It would be good to get rid of it. The others I'll exchange for potatoes during the week. I know where," Boris Porfirich said, as he sat down at the table. "Puzanov. He has stolen potatoes—he'll exchange them for whatever you want. He never begrudged something stolen."

"We'll survive somehow. Igor now earns his own daily bread. And what can you do, otherwise you'd die. Now's not the time for school. But this coffin is sort of foul . . ."

"Why are you harping on it? It's a coffin like any other coffin. Yes, it's lousy. Yes, it's defective. But it's still a coffin. There aren't any coffins lying around in the pub. It's still a valuable thing."

Sonia looked deep within herself.

"Smell it one more time, Borya. What's it smell like?"

"All right. Out of love for you I'll smell it, so be it."

Suchkov walked up to the coffin and began to sniff and check it out. Even to tap it.

"Don't tap, the devil will come," Sonia became frightened.

"Sonia, the smell of the dead person, you know, can't last that long. Well, let's say they sold this coffin on the side," Suchkov said finally, "but they must've cleaned it after the previous corpse, and the smell is bound to go away by itself because they couldn't have taken the dead person out of it and used it right away as wages. The smell is bound to go away."

"Bound to. But this one doesn't go away," Sonia began to get stubborn. "That's what's suspicious. Why does the smell of the corpse last so long? Can't you really smell it?"

"It seems just the least little bit," Suchkov said dumbfounded.

"It doesn't 'seem' and not 'just the least little bit,'" Sonia the plump one answered firmly, approaching the coffin. "I'll tell you bluntly, Borya, no matter how supernatural it might seem to you, this coffin really reeks of a male corpse. That's how it is. I'm a woman and I can always tell the difference between a man's smell and ours, a woman's."

"Stop trying to make a fool out of me!" Borya Porfirich screamed. "Don't be ridiculous, Sonia. The coffin, I'll say it right out, is not a coffin but a piece of shit, but there's almost no corpse smell. Why are you breaking the laws of chemistry?"

"Let's each of us keep our own opinion, Borya," Sonia answered calmly. "Let Igor come and sniff. He's a sober man."

"He may have a sober mind, but he'll come home drunk. What will he be able to figure out? Why don't we play a game of cards?" Suchkov suggested.

And they played a game of cards.

It was already getting dark; Sonia put on the samovar and got their supply of dried bread crusts from under the bed. The cat still hadn't come back. About eight o'clock there was a knock on the door. Boris Porfirich opened it. Mustygin's face poked in.

"You have a guest, Sonia, from your uncle."

"From Artemy Nikolayevich! From Penza!" Sonia exclaimed.

A plain old man—tattered, disheveled, all worn-out somehow, threadbare, and all covered with spots—appeared from behind Mustygin's back.

"Come on in!" Sonia responded.

Suchkov gave his wife a questioning look.

"Yes, my uncle was always strange," Sonia burst out laughing. "And people around him were strange. Come right in, my dear old man!"

The old man looked around and blew his nose. Mustygin disappeared behind the door and went back home.

"Where are you from, looking like that, old man?" Boris Porfirich asked a bit rudely.

The old man suddenly cast a glance at him from under his grey beetle brows—damp, distant, and rather frightening. And suddenly there was something mysterious about the old man himself.

Sonia got scared.

"I'm from that coffin," the old man said sternly, pointing to the smelly coffin.

The husband and wife were struck dumb with astonishment.

"That's my coffin. I'll take it with me."

And with a heavy gait the old man headed to the coffin.

"Don't touch other people's coffins!" he said harshly and, glancing at the husband and wife, waved a large black finger.

The finger was more alive than his head.

Then he turned around and again surveyed the pair with the same damp but penetrating gaze.

"My children, why have you become so gloomy?" he whispered suddenly like a hundred-year old man. "Come, come here . . . Sit down at the table. I have such things to tell you . . ."

The Suchkovs sat down.

In the morning Igor, sober, came home. Neither his parents nor the coffins were to be found anywhere in the house. Everything else was there, safe and sound. Then the police appeared.

The Suchkovs, husband and wife, disappeared forever.

1999

NOTES

1. The name of the story in Russian is "Valyuta" (Currency). It is interesting to note that in Soviet times "valyuta" usually referred to foreign or hard currency which was traded on the international market, as opposed to the ruble (some Russians quietly referred to the ruble as "wooden"). In the story one character refers to coffins as potentially international or "hard" currency.
2. In 1992-1993 the value of the ruble declined drastically and many Russians stopped receiving salaries. Sometimes they were paid in goods.

SNOW FALLS EVER SO QUIETLY

Irina Polyanskaya

If Boris Danilovich had not realized himself what was happening to him, there would have been people who would have given him to understand that from this day on he was a stranger in this world, a guest who had been standing in the entrance too long. The mistress of the apartment, crowding him with her chest as she held a package of pirozhki in one hand and opened the door with the other, was pushing him out into the darkness of the hallway, and the man of the house, with his tail between his legs, was rushing to hand him his coat guiltily and limply, which ultimately turned in Boris' soul into the same firm gesture of pushing him away, out into the *corridor* of street lights and under the sleepy snow covering him—a guest, a beggar, a passer-by with a good head on his shoulders—until it dawned on him to close his eyes. And now he had to show to the world pushing him away, if not his last shred of pride, then at least his obedience. There was no point in extending his hands in entreaty to them, because they would not give him anything except a handful of snow. People had respectfully stepped away from him, as if clearing a space for him for some last thoughts and matters. And he was supposed to slip off the winter path completely alone, as if he were carrying a shameful secret in him, like a leper. They stopped looking straight at him; even his neighbor, with whom he had played chess a whole eternity, turned into someone who was always busy.

What had happened demanded deep, pure and undisturbed solitude, and not that oppressive semi-slumber, not that anxiety of a gladiator who sees flashes of restless people around the arena. This rotten solitude could not right his thinking and send it to its source, to his heart, and from there scatter its rays—like morning does around the world— through the jungles of other human feelings, opinions, and self-esteem. But Boris Danilovich nevertheless made one discovery: he realized that he had considered himself and his friends to be intelligent, educated people in vain. As he faced the oncoming snow, his bravado left him, and his usual talkativeness and sweet absentmindedness disappeared. There was no reason to feel uncomfortable about death, as there was no reason to be uncomfortable in front of a doctor, whom he had been in the past, but which was not important now. Intelligence was what was important—knowing how to die, but he did not know how to die and was ashamed much too soon of his body, which afterwards was supposed to participate in the vile ritual and spectacle of being put away in the ground and wait there for the repelling process of decomposition in the ground that would follow. And in order to cope with this thought, intelligence was needed, simplicity, a vision of the truth, and not its flickering on some pages, not its shadow in some person's eyes.

When his son came and asked him, "What can I give you, dad, for your birthday next spring?", he did not have enough presence of mind and said to his son in a hollow voice, "Don't worry about it." After all, it was clear to the both of them that he would not make it to spring. The son turned away and the father said more gently, "Give me some flowers." At this point he realized what he had said in wanting to comfort his son, and a haunted look appeared in his eyes. The son began taking packages of food out of his briefcase. "What is that you have there?" "I've bought myself a notebook, a beautiful thing," the son said, turning the notebook absent-mindedly in his hands. "Make me a present of it," the father said. "I want to write down some thoughts." "Take it," the son said, and on that note they parted. Incidentally, the son did not want to leave; the father pushed him into the depths of the hallway—as he held his son's briefcase in one hand and already groped for the door lock with the other—pushed his little boy out into the cold, under the icy stars. The son walked and thought that his father was a lucky man in the sense that before dying he had a chance to think about a few things and gain some insights about himself, to breathe the freezing cold air to the last moment and recall his childhood. Whereas he, his son, was living all the time as if he were drowning and gasping for breath, grabbing with his weakening hand now this bush, now that one, now this woman, now that one, first one job, then another, so that he would have enough money for alimony payments to this woman and for living with that one. And he would finally drown like that when the last bubble of air burst on the surface of the river, whereas his father had lived his life like a man and was dying like a man, even getting ready to give his death a certain festive air, like that of a family holiday . . .

The father died at the end of February. In the hospital where they went to claim his body and later at the funeral, people respectfully moved back from the son, making way for his sorrow, which was nevertheless cramped by the people all around him with their serious eyes and mouths with swirling, steamy breath. Life with its daily minutia had retreated from him for three days, frozen like a cobra[1] with its mouth open before a reed pipe but with warm breath swirling from its mouth. He knew what thoughts were running through the heads of those bidding farewell to his father: thoughts of a warm corner in a restaurant and a long table filled with all kinds of food at one end of which, propped against a column, stood a portrait of his smiling father, waving smoke away from his face. What else could they be thinking of, after doing their duty which, by the way, was not so easy to fulfill because the bus from the undertaker's lost its way in the snowstorm and came in at a crawl two hours later, when people had gotten their fill of standing around in the freezing weather. The son threw a handful of icy soil, more precisely snow, into the hole, those bidding his father farewell did the same, and the power shovel roared as it pushed in the rest of the soil. The people around the son moved back, trying not to exhaust their expressions of sympathy until the end of the funeral feast, and the son was left all alone with the fresh mound which the snow had covered softly with the gentleness inherent in all truly living things. Invisible stars hung above the falling snow, and not one of them could now reach his heart with its light and fill him with it for even an instant; but then—now there, now here—a faint light would flicker in people's eyes, and the son would look around as if he were being harassed by them. Muffled voices could be heard, like the coughing in the orchestra section of a theater. And snow fell ever so quietly. It fell, but ever so quietly, without any goal before it, without any memory behind it. Why should it have to make any noise, where did it have to rush to . . . ?

A few days later, going through his father's things with his wife, he came upon the notebook he had given his father two months before. To be more exact, his wife took it out of a desk drawer, held it respectfully and carefully opened it, but the son grabbed the notebook out of her hands and put it in one of his jacket pockets. They took certain things and books right away; packed dishes stood at his feet. He had his hand on the notebook and at that moment could feel it seemingly radiating warmth on his skin, and he wondered, "What did you understand?

What?" It was radiating warmth like something old permeated with something good; he heard the quiet rustle of its pages, and he pictured his father's tiny, energetic handwriting.

At home the son locked himself in the bathroom, took out the notebook, and opened it in the middle. It was empty. He opened it closer to the beginning and for some reason became frightened: those pages turned out to be clean too. He leafed through a few more pages—empty.

And he got an eerie feeling as if he were floating in emptiness, in oblivion more absolute than the one that encompassed his father. He brushed off several more pages covered with snow and found himself at the very beginning of the notebook where at the top of the first page one solitary phrase had been written: "Snow falls ever so quietly."

2001

NOTES

1. In the Russian text, the author mistakenly refers to a boa constrictor (*udav*); snake charmers generally use cobras.

Two Stories from *Language Cases* by Lev Rubinshtein

TEACHERS WITHOUT PUPILS,
or FROM UNDER THE RUBBLE

In the middle of a platform in the Berlin metro station "Güntselstrasse" and in broad daylight stood a man who was not young but not old either, well-dressed, as it were, and peeing intently on the floor. Sick? Drunk? Who knows. At least he didn't give any signs of being one or the other. He simply stood in his suit, tie, and hat and wet the German tile floor. *No one said anything* to him. People simply walked around him, phlegmatically trying to evade the spray. The process of the rather intensive urine-letting was so unusually long that I didn't even have enough patience to wait for the outcome of this engaging *mise-en-scène*, i.e., the inevitable appearance of the police.

The Germans, just like other people in the West, don't tell each other what to do as a rule. For all this there's the police.

Some German mores have the effect of completely shocking our people.

If a German sees out of his window that another German has parked his car where he shouldn't have, instead of shouting through the window's small ventilation pane, "Hey, man, isn't that sign for you too?", he calls the police, regarding this as his responsibility as a citizen.

If in the neighbor's apartment above him there's singing and dancing till half past two, the German will absolutely never go to have it out with him. Again, he will call the police.

Such behavior in our country usually falls in the category of informing on others which, in general, is true. Our people either put up with it or cause a row. But they don't inform on others. Especially since it's even foolish to do so.

Our communications field is unusually powerfully loaded with didactic energy. All are tirelessly educating each other. ("Hey, man, do you throw paper on the floor at home too?") This permanent educational process which has drawn in everyone—from the auntie in the line to the writer on television—doesn't have, in essence, a real goal. It's directed neither at enlightenment nor, moreover, at correcting mores. Most likely, even the opposite. It's fully an end in itself; there are no students, there are only teachers.

A friend of mine who is Estonian admitted to me how struck she was, when she first came to Moscow, by the Muscovites' habit of peering into other people's baby carriages and even strongly reprimanding the poor mother, "Why have you wrapped him up like that? Should you have done that?"

General didacticism is nothing else but a seemingly civilized form of aggression and violence which thickly impregnates the atmosphere of public and private life.

But the stronger the manner in which the total aggression is executed, the greater the emotion and hope with which we look at small local "happy endings," timidly breaking through here and there.

On finding himself in a small town on the order of Torzhok,[1] one of my friends, out for a stroll, went into a phone booth to call his local acquaintances. Dialing the number that was busy for a long time, he suddenly noticed that the telephone booth was surrounded by a group of young people of an unambiguously certain type, in sweat suits and with cigarettes in their mouths. They were looking at him with a curiosity that was difficult to interpret as simply friendly. Remembering from his childhood that in situations like this it is appropriate to take things in hand and initiate the conversation, he—trying to show a carefree good-will both with his facial expression and tone of voice—looked out of the booth and, for the sake of asking something, inquired, "Boys, can you tell me the time?"

"Do you need the exact or approximate?" with a politeness that chilled the soul asked the one who appeared to be their leader.

"Approximate is fine." The circumstances disposed my friend toward acting complaisant.

"It's growing dark," the "chief" said even somewhat in a sing-song voice. And suddenly he smiled totally in a child-like way. In short, everything worked out fine.

Or there's the suburban commuter train. Almost half the car is occupied in a forceful, resolute way by a group of guys with a clearly criminal look. Naturally, swearing back and forth and all the rest. The public is keeping silent which, in principal, is also natural. Suddenly out of somewhere appears a very old woman who is uncompromising.

"Young people," she shouts in an unexpectedly ringing Pioneer* voice, "there are children here! How can you use such foul language?" And even such a phrase, "*use foul language* " . . . The car literally stopped breathing and almost closed its eyes so as not to see what would be left in a minute or two of the irrationally brave, old woman-kamikaze. But something entirely different happened. One of the gang members turned his disapproving mug to her and in a most sincere way, with a criminal "tear," said, "Mom, don't be angry with us, all right? The brothers, you see, are all nerves. We're going from being locked up in prison to Vysotsky's[2] grave."

One could just simply start crying.

And one more happy incident. From long ago, but also connected with a suburban commuter train. I was returning home from somewhere, on the last train as usual. That time I was sitting in the car all alone. At one of the stops a huge, drunken and frightening man built like a tank, in a shirt torn to his navel and with a badly beaten face, burst into the car. After turning in all directions, he plopped down next to me, gave me a semi-hug and asked in a trusting way, "Lis'n, friend! What do you think, *who should I kill here*?" A question, it must be noted, rather interesting under the present circumstances.

I really don't remember what I said to him. And perhaps I didn't say anything to him. Perhaps I even sang. It is fully possible that it was a lullaby, for my infernal fellow traveler rather quickly began to snore like a giant in a cartoon. And I walked out on the platform and, without appreciating what I had just avoided, walked along the empty streets and tried to understand what it is that art really engages in: does it wage a battle with evil in an open duel, or does it enchant it, lull it, force it to snore heavily but powerlessly on the fragile shoulder of the artist?

Also, by the way, an interesting question.

NOTES

1. Torzhok: a town in the Tver Oblast, Russia, with a population of around 49,000 people.
2. Vysotsky, Vladimir(1938-1980): Russian actor and singer. He was an immensely popular figure who wrote his own songs that satirized Soviet living conditions, official hypocrisy, ridiculous bureaucracy, prison life, and the like. Few of them were recorded during his lifetime, since recording studios were owned and controlled by the government. People listened to his songs on homemade, illegal tapes.

INTO THE MAUSOLEUM OF THINE

The discussion about the Mausoleum and the further fate of its ill-starred inhabitant has reached a new and, most likely, final phase.

This discussion, born with the construction of the Mausoleum itself, was never broken off, even in those times when just one suggestion of its existence threatened with you know what.

The attitude to the master of the Mausoleum during its existence drifted from Pioneer-like* respect in the 1950s to the sharply allegorical in the 1970s. But an elemental, unconscious iconoclasm always manifested itself and, at times, in unexpected and fantastical ways. I remember how my older brother, who finished school in 1955,[1] didn't receive a gold medal simply because in his final paper he had omitted the soft sign (ь) in the word "Il'ichom" (Ильичом)—I remembered it that way, in the instrumental case—as a result of which it read "Ilichom" (Иличом)[2] At home, almost crying, he shouted, "Because of some shitty Il'ich!" But then and there, becoming terribly frightened, he added hastily, "Just don't say anything to anyone. I was just joking." I—a seventeen-year-old—understood this already and, of course, I didn't repeat it to anyone. But I didn't forget "the joke."

Just as there were two cultures in our country—the official and the other—so, accordingly, there were two Leninianas.[3] There were

Krzhizhanovsky,[4] Bonch-Bruevich[5] and Zoya Voskresenskaya,[6] but there was also the *chastushka*:[7] "Lenin's sitting on a fence, hammer - sickle in his hand, and before him stands a worker without shirt or pants."

Chastushkas, anecdotes, incredible speculations, and legends from different times (and peoples, by the way), taken together, constitute an immense field for folklore research.

The culmination of national Leniniana occurred in the year 1970, the hundredth anniversary of Lenin's birth. The barrage of agitation and propaganda during the anniversary reached such overwhelming proportions that it gave rise to an irrepressible stream of jokes from the population intoxicated almost to the point of death by the rhetoric.

It was precisely in that year that people became aware of jokes about a triple bed called "Lenin is With Us,"[8] a toilet-soap "Around Lenin's Places,"[9] a cheap wine "Bottled Lenin,"[10] a condom "Nadenka" (with the stress on the second syllable)[11] and the big word "ANNIVERSARYBENUMBED."[12]

It is precisely in that year, it seems, that the icon began to show a noticeable crack along its whole surface.

And precisely in that year a friend and elementary-school teacher told me how, after showing the children an educational film about, let's say, the vegetable kingdom around Moscow, she asked, "What's the film about, boys and girls?" A long, strained silence. "Well, boys and girls? What did we just see in the film? Well? Seryozha!" Bewildered Seryozha stood up and in a semi-questioning way, as if taken by surprise and making a guess, uttered, "About Lenin . . ." I don't think that it's something that couldn't have happened. It could have, of course. They got to the children.

"Lenin and Children" forms a special part of folklore Leniniana.

A legend serves as testimony that they stopped taking children in pre-school establishments to visit "granddad," because after one of the visits the children were reported to be playing a quiet but dangerous game: a boy would lie on two chairs without moving, two would stand at his side with toy weapons, and the rest, with glum faces and in solemn silence, would file past. The children were playing the game of "Mausoleum."

One little boy from an educated Jewish family, in his non-stop chatter to which, the adults got accustomed to turning a deaf ear out of feelings of self-preservation, began from some point in time to constantly and persistently mention a Lerner. "Who's this Lerner?" the father couldn't contain himself. "We have no such friends. What Lerner are you talking about!" "Why do you say that?" the boy said astounded. "You really don't know? Lerner, remember? The one near the Kremlin who lies in a *sandbox*." Lerner, sandbox . . . Not bad at all.

Another boy, but a bit younger, came from kindergarten all in tears. "What's the matter?" his mother demanded to know. "Did someone hurt you? Or did something else happen?" "I'm afraid of Lenin," the boy said in a trembling voice. "Meaning what?" his dear mom became frightened no less than him. "Galina Nikolayevna said that Lenin died, but that he's still alive and loves children very much."

The third boy was totally irrational about his relationship with the object in question. Once, after putting on an African mask, he crawled on all fours into the room where a group of guests were sitting and drinking and, in a frightening voice from beyond the grave, began to wail, "I'm V. I. Lenin!" Precisely like that: "V. I."

And so, the discussions about "where to put" . . .

There is already experience with moving, as we know. During the days of the XXII Congress, which became the apogee of Krushchev's de-Stalinization campaign, the additional "settler" was dragged out of the Mausoleum under the cover of night and buried nearby. In terms of the mischievous haste and dangerous secrecy of what was taking place, this brought to mind the subject of a cheap popular print, "How the Mice Buried the Cat."

Now times are different and the matter has begun to smell of a nationwide referendum.

The range of opinions, in this respect, is indeed huge, extending from the uncompromising idea of using an "aspen stake"[13]—to the "centrist" idea of burial in Volkov Cemetery[14]—to the restoration of Post No. 1 in all its former magnificence and with the traditional Line.

The cult associations connected with the line are so obvious that it's strange even to make any note of them. But this was not simply "bowing to relics." This was also a specifically Soviet ritual. This was "The Line." The most important of all Soviet lines, line number one.

The line for the Mausoleum was an original test for "Soviet essence." A Soviet man, recognizing himself as such, simply felt obligated to stand in this line at least once, to become a part of it and "receive communion."

For some people, particularly visitors and children when they got to Moscow, Lenin seemed to appear everywhere. One of my friends happened to be sitting one summer day on a bench in the Aleksander Garden.[15] He sat and sat and dozed off. The rapturous, heart-rending cry of a child awakened him: "Mommy! Look! Lenin!" "That's not Lenin. It's just a man," the mother said a bit embarrassed. For some time this "just a man" planned to write a story, "How I Was Mistaken for Lenin," but he never got around to it.

With the coming of perestroika, the Line began to lose its monolithic character, to thin out and fall away. New reference points began to loom up. There was a perceptible smell of the West in the air and the Line, which had disintegrated near the Mausoleum, materialized for a while at the eerily glowing walls of the newly opened MacDonald's. This was the same Line, but no longer formed to go down into the area draped in bright red cloth but into "heavenly" America, glowing like a Christmas tree. Then even it somehow dissipated imperceptibly, and the MacDonald's restaurants which multiplied in great numbers ceased being "America" and simply became part of everyday Moscow. Then even the lines for the "common people" disappeared here and there and a totally different story began.

The Mausoleum, as we know, was thought up as a temporary shelter for the "eternally living one." Our country, so to say, is big, and there must be time for everyone to bid farewell to our beloved leader. The country turned out to be not simply big, but so big that the farewell dragged on for more than 70 years. And the crypt, which at first was made of wood, turned to stone like in a fairy tale and, it seems, continued to harden evermore.

And if the population of our Homeland has not been able up to now, so it would seem, to bid farewell to the dear deceased, then what can be said about the unfortunate nations of the world?

The idea of a farewell engagement, an ambitious world tour, has been in the air for a long time, occurring now to one person, now to another.

And truly, shouldn't we take our "Lerner" to all the world museums? Like Tutankhamun?[16] Or Shliemann's[17] gold? Or "The Mona Lisa"? Or Kobzon,[18] for that matter? There's no reason to doubt the success of this super undertaking, including its commercial aspect. One can boldly assume—in the words of Gogol[19]—that "this merchandise will bring no harm to the further prospects of Russia." Let him finally go like a man for a spin around the whole wide world. And then he can even be buried.

Or perhaps try our luck with Sotheby's? No, this is probably going too far. Bury him.

In the middle of the 70s, one of my philologist friends, while he was doing research in the archives, discovered a whole pile of popular creative work sent at one time or another to the editorial staff of the journal "Literary Studies," either for the first or second anniversary of Ilich's death. There was more than enough material of interest there, as one can easily guess. One small chef-d'oeuvre imprinted itself on my mind. In the editor's response attached to it, there was written something like, "Dear comrade so and so. Your poem is undoubtedly sincere and imbued with this and that. At the same time its literary level is, unfortunately, not that high. *Some* (italics mine, L. R.) lack of originality and a somewhat weak control of the poetic form is noticeable . . . Keep writing . . . Keep trying . . . Read the classics . . . Avoid imitation . . . Seek your own voice." Well, and so on—everything that was required. And, "Greetings, lit. worker Panyushkin." And the poem went like this:

> Sleep, my Lenin, beauty of mine,
> Lullaby and goodnight.
> Into the Mausoleum of thine
> The quiet moon shines ever bright.

This "innocent like childhood" motif, dear to us all, this fantastic transformation of a *grandfather* into a *child*, and a *coffin* into a *crib* in a non-violent but radical way—by arbitrarily changing the masculine form of the word "Mausoleum" to the feminine[20]—changed the tone of the whole theme from an aggressively heroic to an intimately homey one.

Let this touching lullaby not only illustrate for us the post-modernist principle of intertextuality in an obvious, blatant way, but let it also serve, if not for "the cause of national reconciliation," then at least for "smoothing out the rough edges" and "softening the mores."

Let us be, as has been said, like children. And let the dead bury their own dead.

NOTES

1. With Stalin's death in March 1953, a more liberal atmosphere had started to develop.
2. Patronymic of Vladimir Lenin. We have inserted the original Russian in parentheses to aid the reader and placed an apostrophe in the linguistically correct transliteration to indicate the place of the soft sign. It should be noted that Lenin's patronymic is usually spelled as "Ilich" in texts written in English.
3. Leniniana: everything and anything connected with Lenin.
4. Krzhizhanovsky, Gleb (1872-1959): Soviet economist and state figure. In 1920 appointed chief of Russian Electrification Commission. He was also Chief of the State Planning Committee (Gosplan) in 1921-1923 and 1925-1930.
5. Bonch-Bruevich, Vladimir D.(1873-1955): historian, journalist, and a state and party official. Lenin had high regard for him and put him in charge of transferring governmental operations from Petrograd to Moscow. One of his last posts was as the director of the Museum of Religion and Atheism (1944-1955) in Leningrad.
6. Zoya Voskresenskaya (1907-1992): involved for many years in intelligence gathering in China and various European countries. Also wrote about Lenin and authored children's books.
7. *chastushka*: a two-line or four-line rhymed verse on some topical or humorous theme.
8. *Lenin s nami*, "Lenin is with us," was a popular phrase, paralleling in form *Bog s nami* or "God is with us."
9. This particular phrase (*Po leninskim mestam*) was the name of an excursion always made available to foreign tourists as well Soviet citizens, a trip to places connected with Lenin's life. Applied to soap, it conjures up Lenin's body.
10. *Razliv* (bottling) rhymes with *zaliv* or "gulf." Part of Lenin's revolutionary life is connected with the Finnish Gulf.
11. The humor lies in wordplay: Nadenka, with the stress on the first syllable, brings to mind Lenin's wife, Nadezhda (Nadenka is the diminutive form). Nadenka, with the stress on the second syllable, is a combination of the imperative form plus the particle *ka*; thus Nadenka, as a condom, translates as "go ahead and put it on."
12. The Russian word here, *ostoyubileinelo,* is a clever linguistic concoction of the verb "to grow stiff, numb" (*ostolbenet'*) and the noun "anniversary" (*yubilei*).
13. aspen stake: in Russian folk belief an aspen stake driven through the heart of a werewolf or vampire will kill him.
14. In the mid 1990s it was reported that Yeltsin would order Lenin's body to be moved from the mausoleum to Volkov Cemetery, where his mother and one of his younger sisters are buried. It did not happen.
15. The Aleksander Garden: a park by the western wall of the Kremlin.

16. King Tutankhamun's tomb was discovered in 1922 by Howard Carter; it was the first time that archeologists found a tomb in the Valley of the Kings, Egypt, that had not been robbed. There were over 3,000 treasures in the tomb. Tutankhamun's mummy rested in a coffin (inside several others) of solid gold, and an exquisite gold mask covered the face.

17. Heinrich Schliemann (1822-1896): a German archeologist who excavated in Turkey and Greece and found many ancient treasures. A collection of gold objects from ancient Troy was seized by Soviet troops in Berlin in 1945. Germany has pressed for the return of these objects.

18. Kobzon, Joseph (1937-): An iconic Soviet singer who performed at countless official concerts, was awarded prestigious prizes, performed in many foreign countries when others were not allowed, and in 1987 was made "People's Artist of the USSR." He is now more involved in politics.

19. Gogol, Nikolai (1822-1896): great novelist, playwright, and satirist, best known for his novel "Dead Souls," the play "Inspector General," and such stories as "The Overcoat" and "The Nose."

20. *Mavzolei* in Russian is a masculine noun and calls for the masculine form of the possessive adjective (*tvoi*). The writer uses the feminine form (*tvoyu*) because he wants it to rhyme with the second line of his poem, which ends in *bayu*. In fact, he has basically taken a familiar lullaby, made some changes, and replaced the child with Lenin and the crib with the mausoleum.

THE LORD OF THE STEPPES

Vladimir Tuchkov

Dmitry was the product of great Russian literature. It was this literature that fostered his development in childhood and adolescence and guided him through life in his mature years. However, his character formed not as the sum of spiritual instructions with which our country's 19th century novels are saturated, but in opposition to them. The writers tried to awaken in the reader, for whom they were morally responsible, such qualities as contrition, the primacy of feeling over reason, goodness, kindness toward the fallen, contempt for riches and an aversion to a lust for power, integrity, liberal spirituality, and a generous nature.

Dmitry's favorite reading was the works of Fyodor Dostoevsky and Leo Tolstoy, which he all but memorized; he would read and laugh with derision at the lofty scenes and enjoy the base ones in which evil triumphed over good. So he was a man exceptionally unscrupulous, calculating, evil, and cruel when it came to those lower on the social ladder than him, selfish and power hungry, dishonest, spiritually impoverished and miserly.

These characteristics of his personality contributed to the swift rise of Dmitry's career in the financial sphere. However, his business pursuits basically indulged only two of his passions—his self-interest and his lust for power. All the other feelings and experiences that were so keenly necessary to Dmitry's energetic nature had to be gleaned from everyday life.

And so, as soon as an opportunity arose, he immediately bought land one hundred fifty kilometers from Moscow. Precisely *land*, and not some insignificant parcel, because this land came to some three hundred hectares. He enclosed his extensive property with an extra high fence and began building. First of all a manor house was erected with wings for the servants. Soon kennels, a granary, and stables were added to it. And after that, instead of busying himself with planning a park with pavilions, a pond and a bathing hut, Dmitry issued an order that twenty-five ramshackle huts be built in a distant corner near a swamp. Precisely ramshackle, in view of which the builders made walls with chinks in them and stoves that were crooked, and covered the windows with sheets of mica which blocked out most of the light.

When everything had been built, Dmitry began to hire serfs in the local villages with the help of his head of security. An agreement, printed on a laser printer in two copies, was entered into with those who expressed a desire to work. The essence of the agreement boiled down to the following. The peasant serf receives the temporary use of a hut, a plot of arable land, cattle, agricultural equipment, and essential clothing: Russian shirts,[1] sarafans,[2] homespun coats, coats of heavy cloth, etc. And he lives in the village without going away for an instant, feeding himself on the fruits of his labor and paying the lord half of his harvest. For this the serf receives two thousand dollars every year for every member of his family, including himself.

The lord, in turn, is granted the right to call on the serfs, at his discretion, to perform work connected with the beautification and upkeep of the estate; to physically punish them for any carelessness and instances of negligence; to permit, forbid or arrange marriages among the serfs; and to pass judgment single-handedly in the case of any conflicts arising among them . . . The last point indicated that the serf had the right to break the agreement only on St. George's Day.[3]

Finally the small village was fully staffed. And life behind the high fence took on shocking, anti-evolutionary dimensions.

The lord, burning with an unquenchable passion for outrageous behavior, immediately, on the second day of the new era, arranged a blood bath for the recruits. After gathering all the peasant men, including foolish children and feeble old men, he ordered them to dig a pond. But suddenly voices were heard, appealing to the lord's wisdom, saying, "There's enough digging here for about two weeks, but we haven't had time to arrange our households yet, and there's the haymaking now. If we let the right time go by, we'll have to go hungry in the winter."

Dmitry ingratiatingly and seemingly with an understanding of vital peasant needs asked, "Who else thinks so?" Everybody thought so. And then, arming himself with a long hunting whip, the lord gave everybody a whipping with the support of four strapping guards. Initially this business got him so excited that he overestimated his strength and could not give a good whipping to the last few but rather only tapped their bare backs.

As he acquired experience in his life as a lord with unlimited powers, Dmitry realized more and more that beatings with his own hand were not the most entrancing. So he often turned the floggings over to the guards, who were more professional in this respect.

In many ways, Dmitry's barbaric amusements were in keeping with the historical traditions he had read about in great Russian literature, which exerted a baneful influence on his unconventional psychology. He and his fifteen-year-old son, Gregory, rode their horses hard, hunting rabbits bought in the necessary quantity from the local gamekeepers. And as they filled the surrounding area with their whooping which, combined with the intermittent barking of the greyhounds, terrorized all things living and capable of thinking at all, they tried to chase the hares into the peasant plots of land so that they could trample the crops and vegetable gardens to their heart's content and in the excitement bring down someone's scraggly cow with their two guns.

So that later, sitting in his study in a grease-stained bathrobe and scratching his hairy chest with all five fingers of his hand, he could question his poor little people—who were trembling like aspen leaves— about their arrears, slowly check the notes in his stores' ledger, confusing names, and listen to their plaintive babble interspersed with the words "lord, lord, lord . . ." And finally to assign a just punishment, that is, in keeping with the table he had thought up himself that correlated missing poods* with strokes of the whip.

Sometimes he would go into the yard to hold court and, to increase the pedagogical effect, he would turn to the people without beating around the bush. "What do you say, you dirty thieves, have you gathered for a just trial?!" He would choose someone more sinewy so that he could put him on the rack and slowly question him in sight of all his souls[4] about the depth to which he had ploughed, what he had fertilized with, how much rye he had sown, how much wheat, how many times rain had fallen, and whether he had kept the crows off the ripe fields.

No less lamentable was the women's lot. And although the peasant women were whipped less frequently and not as harshly, the husbands— embittered by their debasement—repaid the poor Russian women a hundredfold for everything that fell short in the lord's view. It was even worse for those who found themselves as house serfs—the cooks, maids, housekeepers, and the nannies to the five-year-old Vasily and three-year-old Natalia. Sexual violence was the least heavy burden in physical terms. However, this shortcoming was more than compensated for with moral degradation, because the mistress of the manor, Liudmila Sergeyevna, corrupted by her husband to the extreme, would be present at this event. As the lord was satisfying his lust, she would sensually whip the house maid lying on top.

Dmitry's favorite intellectual pastime in the whole world was organizing domestic theater, where the audience was he, his wife, his older son, and the head of his security guards. And all those same household servants, stark naked, played the roles. There was only one play in the repertoire—Griboyedov's "Woe from Wit."[5] Moreover, the men were played by the women, with mustaches and beards drawn with soot from the stove. A special feature of the production consisted of actresses having to clobber each other wholeheartedly as they delivered their lines. Pretending to was not allowed; the lord watched for it with a special passion. The final scene showed all the women fighting in the most repelling way—with faces being scratched until they bled, hair being pulled out, and incredible yelling and foul language. The curtain came down at the tinkling of a bell by the lord when he had had his fill. The lord's love, without a whipping, and a very cheap ring with a stone of colored glass awaited the actress who had been the best.

The most puzzling thing in this story is the fact that, notwithstanding the progressing disintegration of his personality, Dmitry held his ground in his business affairs. The bank, which he visited three times a week, was making successful financial transactions, the number of depositors was growing, loans were bringing excellent interest, and playing the stock market invariably led to gains. Dmitry was growing rich in spite of everything.

In the remaining four days of the week he did the unimaginable. Matters reached such a point that once in late fall, in a mad drunken rage, he set fire to the hut of a peasant who had not taken off his hat to him. And this was not just any peasant, but a half-blind old man. And the hut was not his, but the first one Dmitry happened to come across when he was steaming mad. It was a windy day and so the whole village burned down. And the peasants had to spend the winter in hastily made dugouts. However, not only did they all survive, but they rebuilt their huts by spring.

Apparently severe trials harden a Russian man to such a degree that he is able to bear even worse kinds of adversity, truly inhuman ones. It was always thus: during the Tatar rule, in Ivan the Terrible's time, in Peter the Great's time, and in Stalin's time. Dmitry completely re-affirmed this rule.

Dmitry waited with great curiosity for St. George's Day, which for some reason was set for the middle of summer. And finally it arrived. Long tables of unplaned boards were slapped together in a meadow. Three buckets of cheap peasant vodka—"white brew," as it is called by the folk—was placed on them. And two buckets of port wine for the women—"red brew."

The lord, in a stylish frock-coat, called out the peasants' names from his stores' ledger and paid each peasant for every member of his family. After this, each person in that family respectfully kissed the lord's and mistress's hands and took his place at the table with the refreshments. As the buckets grew empty, the folk grew happy and flushed. A colorful round dance formed and obscene *chastushkas*[6] rang out. The vigilant guards stopped squabbles which arose not so much because of the drinking as because of envy, with someone saying, "I was whipped more times than you, but you and I received the same amount." The drunk ones were placed on straw that had been prepared ahead of time. The lord was kind and cheerful that day and he did not introduce any additional, outrageous behavior to the folk festivities.

The next morning all the serfs extended their agreements for another year. They were guided by the fact that although the lord often behaved eccentrically, one could live quite well. And five years later, before you know it, you'd even be able to retire because you would have earned exactly enough money to live on for the rest of your life.

However, as for leaving, it was not as simple as the downtrodden peasants imagined. In about three years Dmitry, conducting his business with a firm and merciless hand, instilled a new self-consciousness, a new morality, and new principles in his serfs. They began to relate to the lord not as an eccentric rich man but as their father, strict but fair, continually caring for their well-being. All of them deep in their hearts recognized that without their lord they would not have started either ploughing the land or going to church, and that they would have killed each other off. By the way, Dmitry even built a church for them and found a priest who, completely justifiably, had grown disenchanted with contemporary civilization.

Finally it reached the point that the peasants understood, justified and accepted as inevitable two murders—one by accident during a hunt, the other as punishment for fighting with the young lord. And so the serfs, whose psychology was so seriously reshaped, counted on the possibility of returning to contemporary society completely in vain. They could not have lived in it; its laws would have seemed barbaric and inhuman.

With time Dmitry settled down a bit—either he had begun to feel his years, or he had gotten his fill of the play of unbridled passions. He even began to give some thought to reform. For example, about lessening the *obrok*[7] from fifty percent to thirty. However, by that time his older son, Gregory, who took a liking to his father's games, began to gain power. Life in the small village took root so well that the serfs began to give birth to children who had a perfect resemblance to portraits of Gregory.

1998

NOTES

1. Russian shirt: a shirt with a collar that fastens on one side.
2. *sarafan*: a peasant woman's sleeveless dress or jumper that buttons in front.
3. St. George's Day: 26 November (Julian calender), associated with the right of peasants to move from one landowner to another.
4. The phrase "in sight of all his *souls*" brings to mind Nikolai Gogol's satirical novel, *Dead Souls* (1942). In Russia prior to 1861 serfs were considered the property of the landowner and as such, could be bought, sold, or mortgaged as any other property. The word "soul" was commonly used to count serfs.
5. Griboedov, Aleksandr: (1795-1829): Moscow playwright, whose *Woe from Wit* (first staged in 1831) poked fun at the baseness, banality, and hypocrisy of Moscow society.
6. *chastushka*: a type of traditional folk poetry, consisting of two- or four-line stanzas, that is humorous, satirical, or ironic in nature and often set to music and sung.
7. *obrok*: land rent paid by a peasant to his lord in kind or money.

NEVER

Lyudmila Petrushevskaya

A certain woman, still young and not bad-looking (notwithstanding life's difficulties), like all city inhabitants—i.e., still blonde with the help of drugstore hydrogen peroxide and still with a good figure—this woman came face to face with country life. That is to say, after sending her child to a pre-school camp in the country for the summer and staying to take care of her sick father in their burning hot apartment, she began to miss her five-year-old son and decided to visit him for a day. Like many city women, she could overcome any obstacle. She arranged for a neighbor to feed the old man once on Saturday and twice on Sunday and intended to return no later than Sunday evening. And she would have returned as planned, had it not been for the circumstances.

The first difficulty was finding a place to spend the night in the country. The reason she had to spend the night was that the trip took two hours one way, and the last bus to Moscow in the evening left at five. The old man had his dinner at three. That is to say, she would just get there and have to leave right away.

But fortunately the world is not without good people, and there was a village in the vicinity of the pre-school camp and, by asking around in the village, the woman found Granny Lyuba, an old woman who had a free sofa in her other room.[1] The woman (her name was Lena) covered the whole village trying to find a place to spend the night. It was Saturday, and the country folk were sitting on boards and logs by their gates and on their porches and benches. They wore clean, holiday clothes and were a bit tipsy. Here and there stovepipes on bathhouses sent out smoke, a sweet-smelling smoke wafted from them, and the women in particular readily advised Lena whom to ask, and all the people made the best and nicest impression on her.

She herself wore a light *sarafan*[2] with a jacket, summer style; it was June.

After finding night lodging for herself, Lena, with a relieved heart, ran through the woods to her child in the pre-school camp and spent time with him until supper and a bit more after supper.

Happy, in the full light of the setting sun, Lena returned to the village walking through the woods along a pleasant road with puddles; wild strawberries, with their modest star-shaped flowers, were in bloom everywhere. The smell in the woods and in the fields was delicate and sweet, still spring-like, and the sky was bottomless.

Once again she walked down the wide, sandy village street to her temporary home, but now completely crazy with happiness.

When she got to Granny Lyuba's place, Lena hurried to lay out her modest treats—gingerbread cookies and sandwiches with smoked cheese. The old woman was very pleased, they had some tea, and then Lena got ready to go to the bathroom.

And here it came to light that Granny Lyuba did not have such a facility.

"Go out in the yard," the old woman said artlessly.

"What do you mean—out in the yard?"

"Just out in the yard. We all go there—over by the sheep and chickens. When you finish your business, use the shovel to cover it over—it's in the corner."

Lena went to the entrance hall and, after turning left, opened the plank door. Some rickety stairs led down and there, in a covered space, the chickens were already asleep on their roosts, and four brown and black sheep lay huddled together on the earthen floor sprinkled with hay.

Lena stopped and hesitated.

In the meantime a voice resounded behind the thin wall, which sounded just like a thunderbolt from a clear sky.

"Drink your covcoa [sic], there's still a can left," said a woman's gruff voice. "Eat that bread there."

Something started to bubble. Then someone, clearly wheezing, with a stuffed-up nose, began to chew noisily—right above Lena's head.

Yet another woman's voice said hoarsely, "I'll go outside."

"Sit still! Who did I make the covcoa for?"

"So what?"

"Eat, sit and eat. You'll still have time to get into a fight."

"But gran!" yelled the voice with a full mouth and swore.

"And you'll get a few more whacks if you wriggle around," the "gran" said and also let out a stream of obscenities.

The chomping and loud wheezing, like in a pigsty, continued.

Lena was in an idiotic position. She wanted to wait it out until the "gran" and the granddaughter left. However, the waiting dragged on. Lena, a city woman, a translator from English (technical texts), stood like a post and could not force herself to give in to the circumstances. She didn't dare move a muscle.

After standing for about ten minutes (while there was chomping behind the wall, wheezing, swearing, slapping on the neck, and the sound of "covcoa" bubbling), Lena left without taking anything, ran out of the hut quickly and, with a quick step headed across the field to the familiar woods, which upon a closer look also turned to be sort of sparse, but at least there were some bushes.

Then Lena shuffled off slowly toward her night lodging and sat down for a little while by a pond, catching the rays of the setting sun. It was quiet and warm; the grass had a pungent smell, a marshy smell wafted from the water, mosquitoes started buzzing, the sun stayed and stayed above the horizon, and then Lena, sighing from the feelings that came over her, headed under the wing of Granny Lyuba.

For the past two years Lena had not had any time to relax; her sick father could hardly do anything for himself and she had old parents. Then her mother died in a fire in a hospital—she was smoking on the sly in bed during her first night of hospitalization, somehow found a way to hide her cigarettes from Lena, and evidently got matches from someone in the ward. Her mother had not been able to walk for a year before that, and Lena managed to get her into the hospital because of her bronchitis. Her father could walk, but he was close to eighty, and he understood almost nothing when his beloved wife disappeared forever, just kept mumbling inquiringly as he went into her room: "Lyolia? Lyolia?"

And in fact Lena was called Lyolia for short.

Lena tried not to recall her mother's name; it was painful—mom and mom.

Her father, fortunately, kept all the habits of an adult man; he automatically repeated all movements taught to him since childhood, although now he could not feed himself. On the other hand, sitting in his armchair, he would regularly "read" the newspaper, sometimes upside down, and on request from little Pasha, he could pronounce the word "Izvestiya"[3] when Pasha would point with his little finger and say,

"What is this word?"

Lena did not want to think about the future; she only kept practicing her sorcery with sleeping pills, selecting them so that her father would at least sleep but not sink into animal-like apathy for the entire day. But it was also essential to eliminate any extra agitation that would start after taking haloperidol.[4] The next stage of her father's illness was immobility.

But the closer her father drew to that threshold, the more Lena moved about and the more desperately she tried to enjoy herself, saying to herself, "We're alive for one more day."

Today her neighbor will feed her dad, he'll lie down, as always carefully feeling the whole sheet and smoothing it out with his large withered hands, say his prayer "Lyolia-Lyolia" and fall asleep. All the medications in powder form have been diluted and put in the mashed potatoes, and a separate small bowl for each meal is in the refrigerator. Lena is also a very precise person, just like her parents.

Lena lived like a nurse's aide without any relief, and the only bright spot were the quiet evenings that sometimes came along for her and her dad and Pashka, when her father was not fretting or shouting and would even hum something like "The River is Flowing," an old Cossack song.

Pashka was very fair, his hair was like a straw roof, his eyes lively and small, and he was already beginning to read a bit at his five years of age, especially the credits on the TV screen. The boy would gladly stay by his grandfather's side and not cry when his mother would run once a week to turn in her translations and get new ones, and the grandfather clearly loved the boy, too, and would keep trying to get some point across in his own language.

"He had five terms of service," the grandfather would say to his grandson. "That's what it's all about."

Or he would say, "Leave my silence in peace."

The little grandson, not understanding what he meant, nevertheless felt secure in his grandfather's presence, and the whole crew—the old man, the small boy, and the cat Fomochka—would joyfully meet Lena coming back from work, although during her absence a great many things would be left on the floor like after a search. Books, pillows, newspapers, plates, and turned over chairs would be strewn about.

Lena would throw herself into cleaning up, Pasha would busily help her—get in the way, and granddad would be happy and mumble his nonsense, although there was a lot of mystical meaning in it, if you pondered.

And so now Pasha was in a pre-school camp in the country for the whole summer, and Lena got a free evening at sunset on the banks of a pond, in silence.

Lena, happy, all red from the sun (today she and Pasha had sat on the banks of the Pakhra River), was on her way back to Granny Lyuba's place, thinking that she could try to come the following Saturday and Sunday as well. What luck that there was a neighbor, a simple woman, the wife of a deaf-mute painter, who loved grandad in her own way and felt sorry for Lena after that misfortune.

The village folk were still sitting by their gates like before—the old men in caps, the younger men in T-shirts after going to the bathhouse, and the old women in scarves.

Two fellows were tinkering with a motorcycle which made one terrible roar and immediately died.

All the village folk, however, seemed to become dumbfounded when Lena appeared; they looked at her wide-eyed. The fellows drew themselves up by their motorcycle and, smiling somehow not in a nice way, looked at her too.

"Delirium," Lena thought and went into the hut.

In the entrance hall Lena was met by a new person—a strongly built woman of pension age, red-haired, barefoot, with a wet rag in her hands. The woman was standing by her plank door, and a nice-looking, chubby boy of about eight, also red-haired, was peeking out from under her elbow. He was chewing a piece of sausage.

"Went for a walk?" the woman asked.

"Yes, it's nice here," Lena answered.

"Did you get everything done?" the woman also asked.

Lena nodded awkwardly and was about to go to her corner in the hut, but the woman began asking something again, suddenly started loudly praising her grandson, Yurka ("he beats up all the older kids 'round here"), and saying that Yurka drinks a whole pot of "covcoa" at one sitting.

"His father says he'll grow up to be a fighter," the woman said with a kind of frightening intonation.

The woman (her name was Raisa) quickly found out everything she wanted from the totally flustered Lena and finally let her go, all the while holding a dirty, wet floor rag in her hand.

Lena finally lay down on her small sofa, and at this point Grandma Lyuba started to speak to her timidly.

"There you were taking a walk, but we called the police."

"Oh? What happened?"

"Nothing, we looked at your passport in your purse . . . Sorry . . ."

"What for?"

"Well . . . Raisa said that you came here for an abortion."

"Me? An abortion? Why an abortion?"

"Well . . . Raisa said that you aborted in the yard, buried the baby . . ."

"Baby?" Lena exclaimed, laughing. "What baby are you talking about? What nonsense!"

Here it occurred to her that while she was standing still "in the yard," Raisa, as she fed her grandson, was listening to the sounds behind the wall, just as Lena was, and through the chomping, wheezing and the bubbling of the "covcoa" she made out some kind of indistinct sounds that followed logically one after another, perhaps, blood gurgling? What else?"

"What a wild fantasy," Lena said.

"They didn't find anything, dug up my whole yard," the old woman said, blinking guiltily.

In the meantime Lena looked in her purse and began straightening it out.

"We didn't touch your stuff," Granny Lyuba said. "The police promised to come tomorrow. They had an explosion at the forty-five kilometer mark and left on their motorcycle."

In the meantime the teakettle began making sounds, Lena again called Granny Lyuba to come and have some sandwiches and gingerbread cookies, and during supper the grandma said that it was already the third year now that Raisa had been renting her storage room and that she wanted her to sign the house over to her. "But I have a niece in Vladimir," the old woman muttered, blinking often. "I've signed the house over to her. And that there Vasilyevna signed a gift deed to her son, but her son died, and his wife settled in and is trying to drive Vasilyevna out, saying, this isn't your house, it's my house."

"Go 'way from here," the grandma whispered, "the boys are threatening to beat you up."

"What boys, for heaven's sake?" Lena asked briskly.

"From the neighborhood," Granny Lyuba said, giving Lena a strange look, her eyes open wide either from fear or perhaps from burning curiosity.

"It's like she's taking me to be burned at the stake," Lena suddenly thought. "To be executed. Well, you won't do a damn thing to me!"

"Where do you keep your axe, Granny Lyuba?"

"In the entrance hall, behind the bench," the old woman answered, choking slightly. Lena ran to the entrance hall, found the axe right across from Raisa's closed door (something stirred there, behind the door), and put it on the couch beside her.

It took a long time to get dark and finally a relative darkness ensued. Granny groaned behind the stove, repeating, "Thy will be done."

"One dawn hastens to succeed another . . . ,"[5] Lena repeated to herself mechanically, listening carefully to what was going on outside. Her heart was pounding.

Outside there was the hum of voices; some young people were evidently standing together in a group. Then the drone of voices became more distinct and finally someone came up to the windows and said, "Let her come out, Auntie Lyuba!"

"Yes," another one picked up, "we need to talk."

They laughed weakly. They made a loud noise with something on the window frame, perhaps with a stick.

Granny, almost crying, said, "They'll break my window! Go on out to them. Nothing will happen to you. They'll break my window."

Lena, in her nightgown, walked up to the window, pushed aside the curtain and looked down.

The shady bunch gathered even more tightly together.

"Come on out," someone said, bending down.

The flame of a cigarette lighter flashed and someone quickly lit up a cigarette. A face with closed eyes and with protruding lips like those of a monkey became illuminated.

"I've got an axe!" Lena shouted, raising the axe closer to the glass pane. "An a-axe!"

Stepping away from the window, Lena said to granny, "I'll kill the first one who pokes his nose in."

They hit the window frame hard once more.

Raisa's voice resounded from the entrance hall, "Open the door, Auntie Lyuba!"

And she began pounding her fist on the canvas-covered door.

Granny shouted, "Why did I ever take you in! They'll break my window to pieces! Get out of here! She's got an axe! She's got an axe! Look under the bench!"

"Grandma, don't open the door, for God's sake," Lena said. "Tomorrow I'll make a statement to the police about her."

"Leave, for Christ's sake, you forced yourself on me," the old woman muttered to God knows whom.

Only toward morning did these shouts and banging on the door and window stop.

Exhausted Lena fell asleep and immediately woke up: granny had slammed the hall door and walked out. It was already daylight.

Lena packed her bag, left some money for the granny on the table, thought a bit and left her the sandwiches as well. She felt sorry for the old woman who was between a rock and a hard place—her heiress, the niece in Vladimir, and the combative Raisa.

It was difficult to walk yet again through the village on a Sunday morning. For some reason people were standing by all the houses and exchanging remarks, like during the arrest of a big criminal, Lena thought. She tried to walk with her usual step, but people were looking at her the same wide-eyed way and, as Lena passed by, a woman said, "She waves an axe! Wanted to hack our children to death!"

Lena walked on, her head held high, and suddenly caught herself smiling like a criminal—but she couldn't do anything with herself—her face stretched like that of a plastic doll.

The road though the woods lay ahead.

"Why did I tell Raisa where Pashka's pre-school camp was!" Lena thought with despair.

Crossing a field, Lena noticed two women with their things.

She caught up with them. The women were heading not at all in the direction Lena needed, not toward the pre-school camp but to the bus, but Lena kept following them for two kilometers straight to the bus stop and, trembling all over, got on the packed bus that had arrived.

After going one stop, Lena, like an experienced spy covering her tracks, got off (the women stared at her openly), waited until a bus going in the opposite direction came, and returned to the pre-school camp in an hour and a half.

As if nothing had happened, Lena took Pashka to the river, sat there with him the whole rest period until afternoon snack time and then, with her knees still trembling, went to the same bus stop.

There were so many people there (Sunday evening) that Lena, after managing to get on almost last, stood the whole way with her weight on one leg, squeezed from all sides by people, but now not at all people who were frightening and somewhat drunk and strange, and she happily rode the subway to her father's to clean, wash and feed him, do his laundry and put him to bed, her sweet old child, and she imagined her life as pure and bright, only she had to forget the horror of the village on the outskirts of Moscow, the horror of Raisa and the crowd at night.

But she was never able to forget—never.

2000

NOTES

1. A typical peasant hut (izba) usually consists of an entrance hall (where people leave their coats, hats, boots, etc.) and two main rooms: the living quarters, i.e., one large room for cooking, sleeping and eating and a second room for company as well as sleeping (*gornitsa*). There is also a small storage room.
2. *sarafan*: a loose, sleeveless dress (like a jumper) intended to be worn over a blouse or sweater.
3. *Izvestiya*: one of the leading newspapers in the Soviet Union.
4. Halopiderol: a tranquilizer, used especially in the treatment of psychotic disorders.
5. "One dawn hastens to succeed another" is taken from Aleksandr Pushkin's narrative poem, "The Bronze Horseman" (1833).

EXPERIENCE IN DEMONSTRATING MOURNING

Marina Vishnevetskaya

When my second husband died, in the morgue I wore a straight, mid-calf black skirt, a black fitted jacket, and his favorite blouse of artificial silk, also black, but with white polka dots in the front, because we had been divorced for several years already. I was lucky because it was already the end of August and it was rather cool, so I could allow myself to wear my mother's old black hat dating to prewar times—a hat with a flat crown and a raised brim in the front, a reddish-brown feather, and a small veil. I chose this hat precisely because of the veil. After all, I didn't know what effect the general atmosphere of the funeral hall—which had been opened at our central morgue approximately a month before—would have on me, if I'd cry or not, and how the relatives from his last marriage would look at me if I cried. Just look, they'd say, at how she's sobbing as if she had loved him more than we did! Or on the other hand, his colleagues, whom I knew inside out, and who knew me and knew how he cheated on me, would still say: she's lived so many years without him, but she hasn't gotten all the tears out of her. So the veil fit the general situation absolutely perfectly. And I was glad that I had ignored my mother's advice and put on her hat. On the veil there were little black velvet dots that could be taken for a mole or even a tear that had been wiped near an eye. It's a pity that our industry doesn't make such useful things any more.

As for jewelry, I decided to allow myself only two wedding rings: the first in memory of the deceased, and the second as a ring affirming the continuation of my life, which now no longer had anything to do with the deceased. I put on old shoes, first of all because they were worn and second, in case it rained and there was mud at the cemetery which, by the way, later proved to be so. Into one jacket pocket I placed a white handkerchief embroidered in white silk at the corners—nowadays practically no one knows how to starch and add just a little bluing to linens so that it doesn't show—this handkerchief had the crunch of first snow and the sheen which snow can have from the blueness of the sky. In the other jacket pocket I had my third husband's large handkerchief, a very dark one with a barely noticeable double stripe along the edges. In the morgue and at the cemetery I crumpled the large, dark handkerchief in my hands and dabbed my eyes with it, which was fitting for the grief of the moment, and then later, at the funeral feast, in a long communal apartment where his new family had two adjoining small rooms, nine by twelve square meters, I took out my small one, the white handkerchief which now no one starches and adds bluing to, so that the guests could have visual proof of what conditions he had walked away from and what mire he had settled in. I allowed myself to put on lipstick only during the second half of the funeral feast, when the atmosphere became more relaxed and people began to remember funny things—at first about the deceased, and then even other ridiculous incidents. And about that time I took off my jacket, after which it became apparent that my black blouse with the white polka dots was made of different pieces of material, so for example, the back was all black, but the collar, which had been hidden up to now under the jacket, was bright white. I also had an attachable white ruffle for this blouse that stayed on by being fastened to buttons that extended from the neck opening down to the waist, but I left it at home because a ruffle was clearly not suitable for the funeral feast. I can't give all the reasons for this, but I feel fine distinctions like that very strongly.

By the way, the funeral of the eight-month-old granddaughter of our neighbors at the dacha can serve as proof of this, to which I came wearing precisely that white ruffle, fastened to the same blouse of different materials which, first of all, very fittingly made my face pale, and second, noticeably changed the blouse, since I had already worn it that summer to their anniversary celebration. As for jewelry, I only wore artificial pearl earrings, two wedding rings, and a gold chain. I wore delicate black stockings and new, blue, high heel sandals which, given my venous legs, was almost a heroic deed on my part. But since our neighbors were at that time rather high-placed people and I understood what kind of a circle would gather and how badly they would react if someone tarnished their reputation, it wouldn't have been nice, on my part, not to accommodate them, and on such a day as that. Because how much easier it is to show how cultured you are in places where you can relax: at a name-day party, a concert, a ceremony where commendations are presented to front-rank workers, at the seashore in the Crimea, or a park of rest and culture[1]—oh,

I always knew how to do that too. To be totally in keeping with the tone of a particular funeral—only this shows an intelligent person, because only culturally sophisticated natures are capable of it. For example, when my mother finally died—she lay in bed for three and a half years, soiling herself so that no one could even enter the house and I, on the other hand, couldn't leave it—and so there she lay, small, washed for the last and final time, in her old, blue dress which seemed to have been made to grow into, and a white kerchief with a tiny flower design on it, which I immediately tied under her chin. And I stand and don't know, for the first time in my life I don't know what I should wear now. Mom's ordeal has come to an end, and my ordeal with her has come to an end. Should I cover myself like the mirror,[2] I wonder, from head to toe? People will come and say: what's all this, don't we know how she wore herself out taking care of her? Why put on a show in tragic tones for us? But on the other hand, if you don't dress exactly right, my mother's sisters will nag you to death. And I have a first cousin, such a crude woman, her son was in the army and was brought home in a zinc coffin—they never opened it and no one knew what he looked like lying in there. It would seem that the thing to do is just stand there, if your legs still support you, and think about what you will live on from now on, but oh no, she walked right up to his girlfriend at the cemetery—moreover, specifically not to his bride-to-be but to his girlfriend with whom, before going into the army, he went for a while—so then my cousin spat in her face and even began wiping off the girl's blush and lipstick with her handkerchief.

And so I stand near my mother, weighing all this inside me. It's one thing to go to someone else's funeral, but it's an entirely different matter to receive people in your own home. And in my home I received them only once: when my first husband drowned and left me with two small children, got soused, as they say, for the last and final time. He was taking reinforced concrete blocks to the worsted cloth factory, so that later they had to get a five-ton crane from the district to pull him out of the lake. And if he hadn't drowned, he would have been shot and executed—he first ran into a "Pobeda"[3] and smashed it to smithereens at a crossing. It would have been fine if it had been just the "Pobeda," but some important managers were riding in it. After that for about a month I was visited by people from various government organs, asking if anyone provoked him to do it. And I said to them: Where were you, my dear people, when he was chasing me around the house with an ax, a scythe, a pitchfork, and once even with an artillery shell left over from the war—it was in our attic, as it turned out. Perhaps someone did provoke him besides the demon drink? We lived in the countryside then, and the funeral was there—oh, that absolute culmination of life—and then nine days,[4] and then forty days[5]—you show your respect to everyone, feed them, and give them drink. On the ninth day I wasn't myself yet—his mother dressed me in appropriate clothes, but at the fortieth-day funeral feast I showed them *what a guy we had lost and how we would all miss him*—and, true to her type, the mother of that woman time-keeper at the trucking company who, as everyone knew, he had gotten mixed up with, howled the loudest of all. And so my mother-in-law and I made a lot of pancakes and, when it was time to receive the guests, I went to my room and took the same dress in which we had recorded our marriage at the registry office and put it on. Pink, satiny, with twenty-two buttons in the back— wooden on the inside but covered with the same satin on the outside, the kind they don't make any more—in the front an inset of white lace, the skirt bell-shaped, the bottom ruffled, ruches in the shoulder area and around the neck opening, and a belt with felt inside to give it shape, thick and wide, which gave my figure a tiny waist. I just threw on a small black shawl so that his friends would not try to press their advances on me when they became drunk. And their interpretation was that I, so to say, considered myself his eternal bride—that's how my father-in-law presented it to them. But he himself caught me in the dark when I went back into the cellar to get some homebrew, dragged me to the hayloft, and began ripping off my dress; it's a good thing he didn't rape me in his drunken state. I can't say anything; he was a contrite man, subscribed to two newspapers, *Pravda* and *Soviet Sport*, and two journals as well, *Small Flame* and *Soviet Beekeeping*, and *The Woman Worker* for me.

And so here I stand next to my mother, recalling my life, but I can't make up my mind. Although I'm not an old woman, the color black is far from becoming on me. And my husband is almost young—the last husband I've taken is five years younger than me. Why should my mother be offended by me? For three and a half years she lay like a doll—clean, her hair combed, taken care of. And my husband would become disgusted with me in black, he'd turn around and leave. A woman must never forget about that. Because, while you're still alive, your life goes on. Only before, when I'd attend funerals, I never thought about myself, you know, but only how not to hurt people's feelings and show them my cultured side.

And now it has become particularly difficult, when my pension is very modest and my clothing—given my circumstances—far from what I could have permitted myself earlier. But it doesn't matter. When last year an old woman and mother of my neighbor on our landing threw herself out of a window—she had asthma, she would gasp for breath because of the cats, take and put a chair beside the elevator and sit there, breathing the air or sprinkling herself with scent from a perfume bottle. And her daughter bred cats, fleecy, special ones, with flat faces—she made her living from breeding them, those cats, and although the old woman who threw herself out of the window had an apartment to which she was registered, a separate one, her very own—she told me herself that the bedroom, hallway, and kitchen were eight square meters—her daughter started renting the apartment to some blacks[6] and used this money to pay for her son's studies at an institute. But her mother, the old woman, kept sitting by our elevator and then evidently she finally had enough. Many women who lived in our section of the building actually refused to go to her burial, saying that it was because she was a great sinner. The coffin, as is customary, was placed on stools in the courtyard, only it was closed, of course—after all, the person fell from the ninth floor. So those self-righteous women of ours stood at all the windows like flies when winter is approaching, but didn't walk out into the courtyard. It wasn't nice. Only her grandson stood and wept, the one who was a student at the institute because of the money that came from the apartment rent. And her daughter evidently also had hurt feelings toward her mother; she stood in a green jacket and sulked and pouted.

And for this occasion I went to some trouble, darned the elbows in the sleeves of my black knitted jacket, mended the holes moths had made in my straight, black skirt which came to mid-calf, put on a brown sweater with a "noodle" weave under the jacket, and on my feet new black pumps which didn't fit my daughter-in-law, so she gave them to me at half-price, and I covered my head with a dark kerchief that had tiny, tiny flowers, although I don't wear scarves on principle because they make you look like you're from some village.

If someone doesn't understand this, you won't be able to explain it to him, but personally I feel such small nuances. And in spite of the sadness of what's taking place, in my own way I always get satisfaction from them. And this satisfaction gradually balances the sorrow.

I can offer another example, when there was an ammonia explosion in our workshop and three people died where they stood, and one woman died on the way to the hospital. And since the management forbade them to be buried on the same day in order not to attract unnecessary attention to the incident, the funerals continued for three days in a row. And at all four funerals I was dressed differently as befitted each occasion. But right now I want to say something else. This woman, who died on the way to the hospital, had asked me to change shifts with her, and this wasn't even very convenient for me, but nevertheless I gave in to her out of respect, and now here she was lying in a coffin, with seventy percent of her body burned, and I stood by the coffin, with a black gauze scarf over my chignon (such high hairdos with hair combed back or in a chignon were the fashion back then). I also wore a black, light nylon coat, high patent leather boots with spike heels, and carried a black purse over my shoulder—at that time shoulder purses were just beginning to come into fashion. Because the dead woman was twice my age, and no matter how sorry I was for her orphaned children and grandchildren and especially for her husband, who had to be supported under his arms all the time, otherwise he'd start toppling over, I may have dressed in mourning clothes, but I was mindful of the fact that I was a beautiful, young woman, so that they would realize with their own eyes that I hadn't lived that long yet and still had two children to bring up as well, and if I were lying there in place of their very old mother, that would have been a much greater injustice. And you know, I had dressed like that for their sake, to make them understand and thereby bring them at least some comfort, but they interpreted it their way, saying that there was no gratitude on my part, and they said many other things about me later—only why repeat their nonsense?

All in all, I want to say that you can't please everyone. And the most important thing in life is not to lose the level of development you've reached inside yourself, and let other people try to come up to that level if, of course, they can. This thought, by the way, also encouraged me somewhat after my mother's death. And then I remembered how my mother loved me, how she respected my mind and my ideas about what is proper, and what a difficult life she had led—she was bloated from hunger in childhood, Germans killed her father during the First World War, her husband and older brother were killed during the Second, and the only happy things in her life were that once she received a free trip from her trade union to Postal and Telecommunications Worker, its vacation hotel near Berdyansk, and that her children lived better than her and could allow themselves a lot of things. And I then remembered that more than anything she loved my crimplene dress—dark-green, raglan style, trimmed with a black herringbone design on the sleeve bottoms and around the neck opening. I'm wearing it in a photo, eighteen by twenty-four, when we, the front-rank workers, were being photographed for the Bulletin Board Honor Roll.[7] I was only afraid that it wouldn't fit me, which later proved to be so, but since things were made well earlier and there were generous seams, I let out the side seams and did an excellent job of making it bigger.

And I sensed later, noting people's looks, that this was more or less correctly understood. And even my second cousin who can spit in someone's face asked, once the funeral feast was over: you made it, so to say, for the occasion? I said: let's suppose for the occasion, what of it? And she said: attagirl, you showed your respect for your mother, your mother was the best of all the sisters, and compared to my mother—what's there to say? But I didn't continue this conversation.

Now I've already given enough examples. Other examples won't show you anything new now. Only I don't want you to be left with the conclusion that I take all this too much to heart, that I don't know my place in life. That would be a mistake. When our dear General Secretary Leonid Ilich[8] died, I alone came specifically to work, and not to the memorial gathering later as some did after me, in a black kerchief, although you already know my feelings about kerchiefs, and in a dark-grey, mid-calf skirt, a flannel blouse of a purely black color, and black wool stockings. And still later, when our leaders would die before their time, I always knew how to show in a timely fashion how I felt about the sorrow which would befall our government.

I've recalled all this so that in our troubled times, when people have gone crazy because of money and have confused one thing with another and have now accepted the fashion of burying their dead cats and dogs in a cemetery, I can tell you how cultured people behaved earlier and how much I would like to pass this on to my two children, five grandchildren and great-grandchildren, and not only to them.

2001

NOTES

1. park of rest and culture: a public park that usually contains statues, monuments, fountains, amusement rides, cafes and restaurants, play areas for the children, etc., like the well-known Gorky Park in Moscow.
2. All the mirrors in a house are covered after the death of someone in that house in the belief that if anyone were to look in a mirror, the deceased could pull his soul in, leading to a second death.
3. "Pobeda": See Victor Erofeyev's "Galoshes," note 5.
4. On the 9th day (as well as on the 3rd, 40th, and the first anniversary of the person's death) funeral masses are celebrated in church, and family and close friends are invited to partake of a memorial meal. Explanations differ, but one belief holds that on the 9th day the soul is carried heavenward to join the host of angels.
5. On the 40th day the soul finishes its wanderings and is assigned the place it will stay until the Final Judgment.
6. blacks: derogatory term for dark-skinned people in Russia from the Caucasus and Central Asia.
7. In Soviet times institutions would periodically place the names and photos of outstanding or especially meritorious workers on bulletin boards at the work site for all to see.
8. The reference is to Leonid Brezhnev, General Secretary of the Communist Party of the Soviet Union, who died in 1982.

THE DUMP

Andrei Levkin

For N. Gudanets

Of course A. knew that there was a dump in town. Naturally, a big city has this and that, a dump as well as a maternity hospital, and a freight yard, a sobering-up station, a meat processing plant, jails, and a morgue. A. knew this perfectly well; he even knew that not far from town, about thirty kilometers away, there was a sort of cemetery on a side track, a siding where locomotives glistening with oil stood idle. And all this was there somewhere, but actually he had never even been in the sobering-up station, and he had no idea, for example, where the milk plant was, although it was possible that it was nice there, with a heavy damp smell in the wet areas of the plant. As a mammal, he would have felt the vague attraction of fresh-drawn milk with his lymph glands or spinal column, and a feeling of ancestral participation would have brought him some comfort in the middle of the hot summer. So, "in general," he knew that there was a dump too.

A dump, as it was explained to him by someone he met by chance while visiting some friends, is a remarkable thing. First, from a cognitive point of view (you have to see the dump at some point—see the first paragraph); second, in terms of everyday life, at a dump you can find a lot of useful things for your home, your hobby, as well as some other things of minor personal interest; third, it's a way to spend a free day when you're fighting boredom and trying to vary your diet of feelings.

As a diversion, almost an adventure, this was a real find (B., the man talking about the dump, sat half-stretched out in an armchair—looking imposing, his chest stuck out like a traveler in a TV program—and began speaking more slowly, pausing now and then, and stroking his beard). Probably stretching the truth somewhat, B. reported that this was no simple undertaking and there was no way you'd make it there without a guide. The dump occupied an area of two by three kilometers, reached by a single road reserved for garbage trucks, and in front of the entrance to the dump area there was a checkpoint where they scared off the general public. There was, of course, no fence around the dump, that is to say, there was no fence with barbed wire, but the dump had a ditch along its perimeter, and it was impossible to cross it because the ditch was wide, with not water flowing in it but some kind of foul smelling fluid. But B. did offer some encouragement—the ditch didn't surround the dump completely. Where there was no ditch, there was a swamp through which people were able to find their way into the dump. The swamp was a serious matter: here's where a guide was needed, but even the guide wore boots and carried a long walking stick, otherwise you'd simply get bogged down in the quagmire—well, you wouldn't drown, of course, but you'd lose a day. By the way, you should go there in the morning, because bulldozers level the treasures brought by garbage trucks.

B. had a tendency to exaggerate, not to mention the fact that the degree of the complexity of the undertaking had to be divided by some coefficient. B. was a graphic artist (he announced at this point that he had found several subjects for his etchings there) and believed that the quality of any work was directly proportional to the suffering endured during the process—like it or not, you were in effect always giving up a part of your life. Because he fibbed a bit, he could therefore convince himself that the initial loss of life had already taken place in the hardships of the excursion and thus there were no more external impediments to his work.

People got to the dump by commuter train. The sixth stop from town. According to what people said, after walking out on the platform you had to go left, past the station master's small house, then across a narrow strip of meadow toward the highway. It was right here that the highway divided, and a wide road, almost strategically placed, went off to the side, into the forest—leading, apparently, to the dump. Up ahead you could already see the checkpoint, which in fact looked very much like a military one. Swaying heavily, brightly painted garbage trucks and ordinary trucks loaded with junk went past the checkpoint. A.'s dream of somehow making his way to the dump through the gate didn't pan out: in front of the checkpoint there was a vast empty space where, of course, they would have noticed him, and to try to slip some money to the guards or steal past quietly didn't suit A., who didn't like dealing with people on duty.

Actually, there was a fence only in the vicinity of the checkpoint, and it was about a hundred meters in length. Go around it from the left? A swampy forest began there—small aspens, bushes, ditches, and spongy soil—everything fully passable. The plateau of the dump dominated the surrounding area; there, on top, it was quiet and no smoke hung above it (the smoke which A. seemed to imagine in his thoughts the day before)—it was as though it was a day off at the dump. After forcing his way through a sparse, low-growing thicket, making a fairly good detour and finding himself, according to his calculations, a good distance now from the dump entrance, A. began making his way back in the direction of the dump, but soon a trench blocked his way. And the small trench was—boy, oh boy . . . The day before he had thought it was about three or four meters wide and he would jump across it (whereas the artist was lazy and rather plump, most likely not on good terms with physical exercise), but the width of the trench was about seven meters and down in it there was not some dry, black stuff sticking to its sides, but quite a full-fledged river with a revolting smell.

A. didn't get upset; he got going and walked along the trench, where hints of a path were visible in the high grass but made, it would seem, by the same kind of dilettante as he was: the vegetation was thick and it barely parted over the path. Obviously, this route did not have an industrial function. He had begun his trip from the wrong end.

The vegetation came to above his waist and was wet—as ill luck would have it, it had poured all night. Soon the wanderer's pants got thoroughly soaked, and now there couldn't even be the thought of giving up the undertaking. Onward, and that's all there was to it! Several times A. came to the edge of the trench—suddenly the trench would either get narrower or a ford would turn up. No, there were no changes. For lack of anything to do, A. began thinking about what the jobs of the dump workers would be called: junior destroyer, senior leveler, strategist and distributor; about how things stood with the plan there and how bonuses were calculated; what it was that inspection commissions checked and where abuses were possible. Nothing was clear except, perhaps, the source of extra earnings. The walk grew boring, and he began to think that it would be wiser to stop a vehicle and come to an agreement with the driver to take him inside for a ruble, or just walk past the checkpoint, pretending to be a piece of trash or something. Walking out once more to the edge of the trench, he saw that in front of him, about twenty meters away, some kind of crossing had been thrown together: between the two sides of the trench cut-down aspens, boards and crates formed a floating island in the middle.

On the bank, opposite the small island, there weren't many footprints, that is to say, this wasn't the sought-after entrance to the dump, but nevertheless a way across existed. A., however, probably in his joy, took a step right then and there and half-missed the board; to be more precise, the board sank into the water and slipped off to the side and his foot fell into the quagmire. Falling down on his side, he pulled his leg out with a smacking sound, but not before water got into his boots. Now he would get there even if he had to swim . . . Taught by this experience, he carefully made his way to the floating island, where he discovered he could go no farther: either because of the underwater current or the carelessness of the last person who had crossed there, the crate that was supposed to stay between the island and the other side had drifted away. He was forced to turn back.

With his right boot squishing, A. continued on his way. There were no crossings; to be more exact, there were two, but in much the same shape— broken up. Farther on the swamp began, but the trench still continued, and he was forced to walk away from the trench to the left. In general, the complexity of the undertaking was in keeping with B.'s stories.

The small swamp ended and again there was a small forest—marshy, with lush, water-loving grass; then the forest was cut short by a meadow, and a man was walking there who evidently was that sought-after guide, because who else would be here? Nevertheless, B. had exaggerated when it came to complications, because a guide wasn't even terribly needed: a path led through the meadow and farther on, into the forest, and then turned left, bypassing the swamp.

This was, without any doubt, the basic route—well-traveled, running deep into the soft, saturated ground, with boards and stumps thrown across potholes and small streams; junk which evidently had been taken from the dump lay strewn about on both sides—some had either fallen out or turned out not to be worth lugging such a distance. The man was in no rush; he wasn't wearing any boots and he didn't have a walking stick. He was walking slowly so that A. stopped in indecision: he probably shouldn't pass the fellow because who knows what there was farther on, but he didn't want to drag behind either. As it was, it turned out that he caught up with him and followed right behind him. Sensing someone walking behind him, the man stepped aside, allowing A. to get ahead, but A. didn't try to pass and admitted that he was walking here for the first time and didn't know the road.

The man snorted quite loudly and nodded his head in the affirmative, in agreement, confirming with this nod not that he understood his interlocutor, and not even that it was difficult to make it to the dump without an escort, but that he understood the apparent necessity of making it there.

"What interests you?" he asked a bit later.

"Oh, nothing in particular," mumbled A., who was taken by surprise, since he felt, if not exactly like a spy, then at least like a tagalong. "Nothing in particular . . . we'll see."

"This isn't a place for browsing. Whatever you need—that's what you go for."

The fellow was of retirement age, but about ten or fifteen or twenty years before had belonged, it seemed, to the type of hero of our time as depicted on wall posters and in the magazine "The Crocodile"[1]: a cadre worker born at dawn with big, prominent cheekbones, strong arms with shirt sleeves rolled up to the elbows, his eyes staring intently ahead, his mustache thick and grey—more likely not even grey but whitened by wisdom. On posters he was usually accompanied by two younger generations: a youth wearing a Komsomol* pin and a tiny "Octobrist"[2]—one of the many trinities of those years. Besides the latter, there was a black, yellow, and white child; a worker, a collective farm woman, and someone feeble in glasses; a soldier, sailor, and pilot; the founding father, comrade-in-arms, and successor and founder;[3] father, mother and—in hands symbolizing society—a child using a crayon to trace in the sky, "May There Always Be Sunshine."[4] The former god and father had gotten old and heavy, and he kept looking at the ground—after all, you were dealing with a swamp, you mustn't step off the path. After starting up the conversation, he gave a full description of the dump rather enthusiastically and breathlessly, talking about it as if it belonged to him personally, as though it were his own property. From time to time he'd squint ironically and glance at the man walking with him—checking to see if he was worthy of being guided by him. A. pretended, even if a bit awkwardly, that he was interested and believed his cock-and-bull stories, which would have you believing that maybe even the plant that made jewelry brought its rejects here.

"And what are you going for?" A. inquired, after feeling that approving silence on his part was now not enough.

There began the story of the activities of the mustached man in retirement who, in addition to gardening and fishing, spent his time making frames for all kinds of pictures. "What kind of pictures?" A. asked, after hearing a word to some extent dear to his own heart. It turned out for photographs—a dacha neighbor was buying his frames. A. wanted to find out why the neighbor needed them, but C. began talking about how difficult it was to get ornamental molding because they weren't making many new ones, and you could still find something decent only at the dump—well, or in a deserted house, but that would have to be in a village area . . . He ripped the molding off old furniture (a chisel stuck out of the breast pocket of his jacket—you could see it under his open cloak); countless pieces of furniture were brought here. "If you get involved with a secondhand goods store, it'll be more expensive for you, so people send it to the dump," where they brought, judging by what he said, almost suites from the time of Paul the Second (sic),[5] which D., an antique dealer, restored and didn't do badly selling.

"And your neighbor, is he a photographer?" A. returned to what they had been discussing. "What does he need frames for? People put photos in albums."

"No," C. answered, "he's retired. He was an important big-wig, but two years ago he was forced to retire, and so he began printing his pictures."

"Printing? Making photos?"

"Oh, no. Shooting pictures—he'd been shooting pictures his whole life. He'd take as many shots as he wanted, then give them to the people at work and they'd develop the negatives and hang them up to dry for him. He'd stack them up—had no time to spend on them. Too busy. But now he's bought all the photo equipment and sits in the dark."

A. became horrified picturing the neighbor: at first, apparently, he searches through all the corners and drawers of dusty boxes tied with string or colored, faded twine taken from his wife's supplies; the twine, once untied, won't straighten out and surrender its curls, and the boxes contain dry rolls of negatives rolled up as tightly as possible. Gradually getting excited, losing the calmness and imperturbability cultivated through years of being in command, flying into a rage and no longer looking at the unreliable list on the reverse side of the box cover (in indelible violet ink or in pencil, half erased, there is almost a code there, some key words that would seemingly preserve the circumstances of the shoot), he squints at the red-gleaming fluid in the developer bath and, like a popular version of a psychic, stares at a blank sheet that looks white and opaque like leucoma of the eye on which not fully developed shapes, dark spots, and silhouettes appear slowly and lazily, as if fading again, blurred somewhat by the shaking of the water (his hand, hurrying the image, presses the paper flat). Who are they? Who are these people, what's the city? But even developed—who are they? Who is that standing there, leaning against a door post? Who is that holding a wine glass? Who is that raising a glass? What is he toasting? What is this view, this house, and who are these people looking into the lens? He rarely, very rarely, remembers those who float up from the bottom of the developing tray and winces when he recognizes himself—as if he's had too much to drink in a restaurant and suddenly sees his distorted face in the restroom mirror. He prints them, frames them. He hangs them on the walls. A second life, forever. All you have to do is keep up with the dusting.

In the meantime his fellow walker grew silent and started to walk more cautiously: they were nearing their goal. Countless little streams had boards thrown over them, and the streams widened and merged. The companions were cutting across some delta—one branch, and another, here's the last one, it seems and, indeed, the ditch disappeared here and turned into a swamp where boards, stumps, and all kinds of junk had been thrown between the tussocks. They made their way across the swamp without any particular difficulty and, grabbing at the black earth and a broken-off piece of a cement slab, they climbed out onto the plateau.

The first thing that struck A. here was the light. It turned out to be very bright here. The flat area sloping slightly upward in the distance was white, glistening from countless pieces of glass; it shimmered and its glare irritated your eyes. Here and there bits of smoke curled upwards— as if from out of the ground—also light and milky. His fellow walker got a cigarette, sat down on a crate and, taking a breath, lit up.

"Well, now," he said, "try your luck. If truth be told, everything's mixed up here; they don't know what to unload where, but if it's furniture, then your way is with me. If you want pieces from the furniture factory, then they're lying over there," he waved his hand, "and the junk from the motorcycle factory seems to be over in that direction. And where there's smoke, that's from the garbage and discarded food. If someone has thrown out something good, those guys will grab it themselves. They don't like outsiders."

"How about books?" A. asked hesitantly. "Do you ever come across them?"

"Books? All kinds of paper? There's not much of it now. But there are times when you find it under your feet. It seems it's here somewhere. Go and look. So it turns out you're one of those . . . intellectuals," he said emphasizing the first "e." "Well, well," he shook his head as if in disapproval, "go look. All the best."

It smelled disgusting; there was a stench—sour, nauseating. The whole appearance of the dump flabbergasted A. because after yesterday's encounter and after getting an earful of the artist's cock-and-bull stories, he imagined the dump as a version of a special store for the poor, a huge distribution area for second-hand goods, where almost clean, normal things—with perhaps just a small crack—were laid out: walk around, choose. Things that weren't so much worn out by use or broken as simply items the owners had gotten tired of, things no longer in fashion—an echo of something he had read about the shops of Parisian junk dealers. The flea market, the homeless, the *bateau-lavoir*,[6] Apollinaire,[7] the smell of roasted chestnuts, St. Germain,[8] smokey fog, autumn, yellow leaves . . . So, now it was drizzling. His feet stepped on broken glass, scraps of paper, just plain mud, pipes that were crushed and twisted together, rusted trash cans, batteries, wire, rags, and dry bits of old paint; all of these things had been pressed down and now clasped one another and stuck together.

There weren't many people; now one, now another bent-over figure like in mushroom-picking loomed in the distance. In the section set aside and scheduled to be filled in, garbage trucks were grouped together— standing very close to one another and slowly disgorging the stuff they had accumulated on their run. Garbage men turned the garbage over carefully with sticks, now and then pulling something out and putting it in a pile, sorting the bottles, boards, and some other things according to where they belonged. Here bulldozers moved to and fro; they bellowed and leveled the things that had been brought here and piled up the garbage at a slant—widening the plateau.

The bustling, it goes without saying, was reminiscent of flies crawling about on manure. The dump, though, was made up of its own kind of manure—it was the city's cesspool: everything that in one way or another had entered the city's organism inevitably turned up here— everything that had been left undigested, all the fruit skins and pits.

Flocks of birds moved about the dump—now they would take wing from under the blade of a bulldozer, now they would alight; the gulls, by the way, would line up in an orderly fashion, bringing to mind a military cemetery. And the landscape itself forced one to think about war, a city destroyed to rubble, whose flat surface was marred by refrigerators standing by themselves and gas stoves looking morose with hands pressed to their chests, frightened at not finding walls around them and a housewife with a frying pan next to them.

Mountains of grey, broken foam plastic and pieces of board were gathered into small islands on which red flags had been placed, like on the ice of polar explorers—maybe for recycling? The accumulation of bread vans, more precisely, bodies of vans that had been removed, was a surprise; it turned out that they served as houses, huts for the homeless. Their civilian clothes hung there and their bags and bundles with treasures put aside that day were there. One's gaze grew weary of the monotony of small trash, always the same every square meter, and one's eyes would try to pick out something really big: a huge skiff for about twenty people, still in one piece; pieces of a wall, whole sections of brick masonry; a springy rubber mound, like a huge udder; wonderful saffron-yellow cones of sawdust piled up among the trash; a display stand from some school or *vuz** corner with "for to work with book," the text written on plywood in gouache: "and r understanding of the read material you have to learn to pick out the essentially basic, ess will force you to concentrate and understand the content; orks one's ow thought and thereby the reader rives at sults."

The dump as an object of nature created its own organization: some sections, unkneaded by human hands, collapsed, others turned into mounds, and rainwater streamed down channels cut through the plateau. Amidst the garbage, in folds of earth that had no garbage in them, which was unusual, A. unexpectedly discovered big patches of real tomato plants with fruit already turning red. In another place a colony of small glossy, waxy-yellow pumpkins had settled and spread out along the ground.

The stroll, in essence, had nothing more to offer. All right, he had made it here, took a look around, and fine—it was something else if you had an interest in material things. A. tried to follow several prospectors: what were they looking for? They didn't like that. They would turn around disapprovingly and give him sullen, guarded looks and then they'd go back to hunting again as though, with bombs falling, they were really searching among the ruins for something they desperately needed. They carried partly whole pieces of furniture on their backs—how do they get it home? On the commuter train, or do they make a deal with the drivers? They must have made some kind of arrangements. Some boys were sorting through the trash, laughing and trying on crash helmets that had been discarded and were all crushed and banged up—square-looking, plum-colored. They were setting the trash on fire and having a good time.

Inclined by nature not to acquisition but to contemplation, A. now didn't understand why on earth he had come here, but out of inertia he tried to renew his interest in the things that turned up under his feet. A few times he seemed to see something he had discarded. Perhaps that was so, but most likely it was someone else's. And again, broken glass, crushed stone, wood chips, bundles, rags, and gigantic green stems turning brown—flowers ripped out of city flowerbeds, past blooming; a lid from Finnish mayonnaise, something that A. had never seen anywhere else; and a folder with an important official report from a good number of years before—tattered, half-faded: "ur agricultural workers unanimously pport and approve the agricultural policies and the basic positions set f there. All this compels us to scrutinize carefully the state of affairs in agricultural production." Corrections in pencil were visible above the text: "compels" was changed to "obligates," "carefully" to "constantly," and "scrutinize" to "study."

History had slowed down considerably on the plateau: here, in the general present day, lay together the remains of previous times which had only now left the city—though not completely. It was as if the city had paid an income tax for decades past—for each one separately—and it was being kept here in reverse proportion—more from the distant past, less from today. It all lies mixed together and, if you dig around, you can put together a smaller but working model from the parts. Thus a certain E.—the story was told on the way through the swamp—in the space of a couple of years managed to put together a "Singer" sewing machine from various parts dating to different years, a machine that was, nevertheless, the real thing and worked wonderfully.

Gloomy, unhappy people were walking around the dump, trying to scrounge something from the past—old men in worn-out shoes, men moving briskly and efficiently, old women tying up and dragging rags, boys not making any trouble, and way over there yet another oddball sadly looking at the ground, as he tried to spot some silly thing he desperately needed, such as his long-gone childhood. And A.'s past, of course, had also been dumped here. Somewhere behind a pile of broken plumbing fixtures were his memories too: some cast-iron church railings in the orange light of an August evening, concealed by murky, yellow smoke and steam from discarded food. To whom would they matter? Perhaps only to an oddball, to bring him suddenly complete happiness. Like a "Singer" shuttle that's missing some of its parts, for the complete assembly of the machine of his soul a warm evening and those railings would be needed, but it's doubtful that he'd come across them, or that he wouldn't shrink from pulling them out from under kindling and pieces of concrete.

Alas, here you have some pompous philosophizing. Well, he's tired; he reeks of smoke from the garbage and has been left with the sensation of having eaten but not having had his fill. It's like when you come to a big house for dinner, gorge yourself to stupefaction from boredom, return home with physical and spiritual concerns, and then turn to the usual bread and cheese. Sadness doesn't nourish, although it's such delicate decomposition, in seemingly violet tones, a ghostly, naked mortal body, a long, thin cigarette emitting smoke in fingers that are turning blue, and decay, decay—either the tomatoes have become rotten, or you yourself have a hangover and flies—silver ones, with a patina—are buzzing and flying out of your nostrils and ears.

He got lost. The sun was shining through the clouds—if only he could know from what direction it had risen. There were no large reference points here, and he didn't remember the small ones. Vehicles came and went; bulldozers also kept moving around (because of which, by the way, it seemed there was no one inside them). The dump sloped gently up, and he continued his climb. There was a good view of the surrounding area from there: the dump, the forest surrounding it on all sides, the smoking chimneys beyond the forest, the ditch, the path through the meadow, and the crossing through the swamp—you could see people there hauling their finds. Birds of all kinds and types flew energetically above the dump, each flock staying in its own plane, with one flock piercing the plane of another without colliding: white, black, speckled and striped, all different from eating different food. Among them there were probably both foam plastic and metal ones, and all-metal ones with ebonite beaks, and birds with plank wings attached to the body with door hinges that squeaked rustily. Perhaps he should find something for himself as a remembrance, something small with a double meaning— perhaps some key, one that's a bit more unusual, that was fated to return to the dump. To carry the key with him always in order to feel with each passing year almost rubber threads stretching more and more and drawing, pulling it back to the heap from which it had been taken; finally, whistling through the air after ripping through his pocket and breaking the windowpane in his apartment, the key would return here, to the place where oblivion lives—such was the global nature of the thoughts and perspective that came to A. standing on top of the dump.

Noting and remembering more or less the way, he headed down. He was tired and he was already anticipating a shower, or even better, a bath. He didn't watch where he was walking in this world of crushed and broken things as he took everything in, one thing at a time: the next prospector, the accumulation of long shavings curling in the wind, a cash register, and some hardened granules of violet-colored fertilizer; it looked like he had gotten lost again. He didn't feel like climbing up once more and arbitrarily wandered off toward the forest's edge, counting on later simply going along the ditch until he stumbled upon the crossing. Looking yet another time at the ground, he was struck dumb: here, all around him, papers were rustling, rolling along, and briefly flying up in the air. Under his feet there was a thick layer of sheets of paper, torn-out pages and scraps of paper, scattered files, and wrinkled, rust-colored documents.

But the scraps and sheets of paper turned out to be the least interesting in terms of what they were: receipts, prescriptions, tickets, theater programs, forms from a school for senior Young Pioneer organizers, instructions for a floor polisher, and blank application forms—and everything was dirty. Gradually, however, the papers began to be more substantive: pages of newspapers and antediluvian illustrated magazines appeared under his feet, and people appeared here, too, who had settled down on piles of discarded paper and were looking intently at rosy-cheeked, buxom women in their work clothes, and at corn—the tsarina of abstract painters and men in trendy clothes . . .[9] Although there were also visible traces of fires that had been started, all these piles of papers didn't burn—the wetness wouldn't let it.

He spent an hour crawling on all fours, leafing through this and that;

he got all covered with dirt. Alas, it was interesting, but nothing more. A light rain began to come down. A. got up, cleaned himself off, and was about to go on his way when suddenly the ground went out from under him and he went sliding down on his back, his body bouncing up and down, stirring up the discarded paper and sending it flying in the air. Finally he slid out onto a flat place and stopped with a jolt.

"Can't you watch what you're doing?" a man who turned out to be in his way asked him, slightly irritated. "Look what you've done." He showed him a book which had split along the spine.

"Huh? What's the matter? Where am I?"

"Where . . . ? At the dump. You're lucky you bumped into me."

Yes, he could have slid down farther and farther, about . . . No, you can't tell how many meters from above. What was almost a mine shaft extended downward, with steps out of books. On different levels people were rummaging in book stacks.

"Petya," the man introduced himself and, when A. gave his name in reply, asked, "Got anything to eat by chance? No? Well, it's not a problem, we've sent someone out—he should bring something soon. Got anything to smoke?"

A. had cigarettes. They both sat down on a mound of law volumes and lit up. Smelling the smoke, other prospectors came crawling up. They emptied the pack; there weren't many cigarettes—they passed them around.

"Have you been sitting here since spring or something?" A. inquired jokingly. "Why without anything to smoke?"

"Oh, who remembers if it's since spring or not . . . ," Petya answered absentmindedly. "People always bring something to smoke—today there's just a slight absence of coordination. When you go home, you take books, and when you come back, you bring something to smoke. Soon it'll be fall, rain," he sighed, "and next year, they say, they'll bring the road up to here, and all this will be sent to a paper plant."

The people here, it slowly dawned on A., had clearly been here longer than since this morning: they wore shabby, dirty-looking clothing, were unshaven, not a picture of health, and had sunken eyes. After chatting awhile, the folk streamed down to their places, passing cigarettes to some others down there in the depths. Here, about ten meters from the top edge, was a storehouse or something. Within the walls of books, caves had been made with the help of boards taken from the dump, where there were bags, clothing, and stacks of books that had been picked out. A. ran his eyes along the book covers and became weak in the knees. "Lord," he said, his voice trembling, "and all this is just lying here?!"

"Oh, there's lots more here," the man he had been talking to said calmly as he was cleaning a book from a pile in front of him and giving it, little by little, a tolerable appearance. "If you go down, you'll see."

There was no bottom to the well as far as he could see and, as he went down, no bottom came into view. The layers were under more and more pressure, and it was impossible to simply pull out a book that caught your fancy—you had to excavate along the whole row. The well, it seemed, went to the center of the earth, and the books—the farther down they were, the more compressed they became, turning into some other aggregate state; they became charred without a fire and turned hard, almost into minerals with an anthracite gleam to them where the pages had been cut. Descending, he bumped into a fellow whom he had already met somewhere. They nodded to one another. "Vitya," the fellow reminded him, dispelling the awkwardness, "Hello there."

"The technique here," he continued, "is don't pull out too many books one after the other, or else there'll be an avalanche and it'll bury you. We'll pull you out, that's the way it is, but you'll upset the whole order. And," he added, stopping A., who was impatiently looking around, "put the trash aside—we pass it on to the top, to the dump. So that it doesn't get mixed in. If you find some odd volume or other, it doesn't matter—take it, naturally."

It was already getting dark when A., who had buried himself in the books, was called to come to the top. Pressing what he had picked out to his chest and then passing the books to the people above, he clambered up. People were sitting in a circle and getting ready to have supper—food had been brought and, off to the side, water was being boiled for tea. Catching his breath after his climb, A. lit up.

"Yes," Petya sought him out with his eyes, "you'll go home now, is that right? Grab those packages," he pointed to the stacks of packages which had thrown A. into shock during the day, "and when you decide to come here again, grab some food, not much—a loaf of bread, some tea, if it's not too hard. Something to smoke. All right? Whatever your means permit."

"And where should I take these packages?" A. asked, getting to his feet.

"What do you mean where?" the man he was speaking to said in surprise. "Home."

"Whose home?" It was A.'s turn to be surprised.

"Yours . . . ," Petya continued to be puzzled.

"No, fellows," A. said, returning to his place, "that won't do. I just got here today. I'm not going anywhere."

2000

NOTES

1. "The Crocodile": a popular satirical magazine.
2. "Octobrist": any child 6-9 years old. The first of three stages (the other two being Pioneer and Komsomol member) to becoming a member of the Communist Party.
3. founding father, comrade-in-arms, and founding member and successor: i.e., Marx, Lenin, and Stalin.
4. "May There Always be Sunshine": a song created for children in 1962, with words by Arkady Ostrovsky and lyrics by Lev Oshanin. It enjoyed great popularity in Soviet times and can still be heard today.
5. Paul the Second: there was no such tsar.
6. *bateau-lavoir*: a houseboat on a river where people can do their laundry.
7. Apollinaire, Guillaume (1880-1918): French poet, writer, critic.
8. Count of St. Germaine: an 18th century figure who has been described as an adventurer, charlatan and alchemist. He has fascinated people with an interest in things occult.
9. With sarcasm and irony, Levkin combines two references to Nikita Khrushchev. After visiting an Iowa farm in 1959, Khrushchev launched a campaign to grow corn, touting it as "the tsarina of the fields." And in 1962, in an exhibit of modern, abstract art at the Manezh Exhibit Hall, he verbally attacked the painters in crude, vulgar language, saying to one artist that "a donkey could smear better with his tail."

Valentina Brougher is Professor Emerita of Russian Language and Literature in the Department of Slavic Languages at Georgetown University. Her articles on 20th century Russian literature have been published in major academic journals in the USA and abroad, and her translations of 20th century fiction have appeared in several anthologies. She is co-translator of a collection of Vsevolod Ivanov's prose, *Fertility and Other Stories*, and translator of a novel by Aleksandr Kondratiev, *On the Banks of the Yaryn*.

Mark Lipovetsky is Associate Professor of Russian Studies in the Department of Germanic and Slavic Languages and Literatures at the University of Colorado at Boulder. He is the author of eight monographs and numerous articles in major American and Russian journals. His publications include: *Russian Postmodernist Fiction: Dialogue with Chaos*; *Paralogii: Transformatsii (post)modernistskogo diskursa v russkoi kul'ture 1920-2000-kh godov*; *Performing Violence: Literary and Theatrical Experiments of New Russian Drama* (with Birgit Beumers); and *Charms of Cynical Reason: The Trickster's Transformations in Soviet and Post-Soviet Culture*.

Frank Miller is Professor of Slavic Languages in the Department of Slavic Languages at Columbia University and coordinator of the Columbia-Barnard College Russian language program. He is the author of *Folklore for Stalin*; *A Handbook of Russian Verbs*; *A Handbook of Russian Prepositions*; and co-translator of Vsevolod Ivanov's *Fertility and Other Stories*. He is a co-author of the widely used textbook for intermediate Russian, *V puti*, as well as the recently published *Beginner's Russian with Interactive Online Workbook*.

THE RUSSIAN TWENTIETH CENTURY SHORT STORY
A Critical Companion
Edited and with and Introduction by Lyudmila Parts

400 pages
Cloth 978-1-934843-44-4, $49.00 / £40.99
Paper 978-1-934843-69-7, $24.95 / £17.50
A collection of the most informative critical articles on some of the best twentieth-century Russian short stories from Chekhov and Bunin to Tolstaya and Pelevin. While each article focuses on a particular short story, collectively they elucidate the developments in each author's oeuvre and in the subjects, structure, and themes of the twentieth-century Russian short story. American, European and Russian scholars discuss the recurrent themes of language's power and limits, of childhood and old age, of art and sexuality, and of cultural, individual and artistic memory. The book opens with a discussion of the short story genre and its socio-cultural function. This book will be of value to all scholars of Russian literature, the short story, and genre theory.

A COMPANION TO ANDREI PLATONOV'S *THE FOUNDATION PIT*
Thomas Seifrid

204 pages
Cloth 978-1-934843-08-6, $40.00 / £33.50
Paper 978-1-934843-57-4, $21.00 / £17.50
Written at the height of Stalin's fi rst "five-year plan" for the industrialization of Soviet Russia and the parallel campaign to collectivize Soviet agriculture, Andrei Platonov's *The Foundation Pit* registers a dissonant mixture of utopian longings and despair. Furthermore, it provides essential background to Platonov's parody of the mainstream Soviet "production" novel, which is widely recognized as one of the masterpieces of twentieth-century Russian prose. In addition to an overview of the work's key themes,it discusses their place within Platonov's oeuvre as a whole, his troubled relations with literary officialdom, the work's ideological and political background, and key critical responses since the work's first publication in the West in 1973.

A READER'S GUIDE TO NABOKOV'S *LOLITA*
Julian Connolly

208 pages
Cloth 978-1-934843-65-9, $40.00 / £33.50
Paper 978-1-934843-66-6, $21.00 / £17.50
One of the most fascinating and controversial novels of the twentieth century, Vladimir Nabokov's *Lolita* is renowned for its innovative style and notorious for its subject matter and influence on popular culture. *A Reader's Guide to Nabokov's "Lolita"* guides readers through the intricacies of Nabokov's work and helps them achieve a better understanding of his rich artistic design. The book opens with a detailed chronology of Nabokov's life and literary career. Chapters include an analysis of the novel, a discussion of its precursors in Nabokov's work and in world literature, an essay on the character of Dolly Haze (Humbert's "Lolita"), and a commentary on the critical and cultural afterlife of the novel. The volume concludes with an annotated bibliography of selected critical reading. The guide should prove illuminating both for first-time readers of Lolita and for experienced re-readers of Nabokov's text.

CPSIA information can be obtained at www.ICGtesting.com
Printed in the USA
65621BV00005B/1/P

9 781936 235223